A MAN
ON FIRE

SLUMRAT RISING

BOOK FOUR | A MAN ON FIRE

WARBY PICUS

Podium

Cover design by Mario Teodosio

ISBN: 978-1-0394-9623-1

Published in 2025 by Podium Publishing
www.podiumentertainment.com

Podium

A MAN ON FIRE

CHAPTER 1

THE ECOLOGY OF LIFE AND DEATH

Truth kept quiet. There wasn't any benefit to lying to the seniors, but he didn't know what to say, either. The mists had enclosed the hot spring now; the green trees on the mountain had blurred into nothing. The jutting stones now looked like looming demons coming out of the mist. Ironic, really.

"Well, it's something to do. It's become our passion." The big man's grin inspired unpleasant questions about what else he was passionate about.

"It pushes us to continue improving and perfecting our art." The elegant man sipped his wine again, savoring it. "In the time remaining."

"The two seniors seem unconcerned about the collapse. Can you save yourself from the loss of magic?"

"One, the magic isn't lost. We just can't touch it anymore. Those great eminences will not suddenly cease to shine. The distinction is important." This with a bullish snort. "Two, no, we can't. Maybe some portion of our art will survive, but probably not. Bad climate for it."

"The seniors' composure is admirable. This junior will have to work hard and improve."

"Mmm. You should."

The elegant man shook his head. "No, don't mislead him. It's different for us. Some demons fear death greatly, but many of us do not. Equanimity in the face of eternity is not a cultivated quality of our character, merely a trait we were created with."

"I had heard something similar from another senior. They were indifferent to their coming end and were happy to have something to do in the meantime."

"Quite right. Having something to do is quite underrated. It's why I first picked up a stick and copied the heavenly formations in the dirt." The calligrapher smiled with fond recollection.

"For me, it was seeing a suggestive tree." Wet, cruel chuckles, then the big man continued. "I thought that would look even better without all the . . . unnecessary limbs. So I tore 'em off, and damn if I wasn't right."

"Your coarse character could stand to be improved."

"Heh, said the *thug*."

Truth watched the two old demons bicker. They looked comfortable. Like they knew each other so well that even their bickering was comfortable. It was a way to . . . love one another. A love apart from sex. Was this what Jember was chasing? No, not exactly, but maybe it was a part of it. Funny. He had never thought of friendship as a form of love.

"Well, enough about us. How does a 'bodyguard' have so much blood on him? It looks like some Pragerite absorbed some of your sin, but the bodies don't shake loose so easily."

"I do wonder about that. Absorbing 'sin' and all. When no one can agree on the nature of God, but we all know there is a Heaven and a Hell, how can there be sin? And how can that sin be moved from one person to another? And if the Pragerites can do it, why not the Desrin, or the Siphios?" Truth asked.

"I can answer some of that," said the elegant demon. "The Siphios believe that sin is less of a tangible thing and more of a character defect. You have to repent for it and take steps to lead a more virtuous life, but God is really looking for your obedience. If you behave well, you go to Heaven. If not, Hell. The more virtuously you live, the more you are assured you are of a comfortable afterlife."

The sculptor nodded along with the poet. The poet continued. "Now, the Desrin are a little more interesting. They acknowledge the existence of Hell, but they don't see it as a permanent destination. All proper souls, which is to say Desrin believers who have done their best to live a virtuous life, eventually go to Heaven."

Truth frowned a little. His impression of Desrin, an admittedly very small sample, was that they were generally very devout. Even the club owner who sold meat and liquor was very . . . faith-and-community-focused.

"It's not quite that simple, of course." Truth nodded. It never was. "You see, they also believe that sin is *both* a tangible thing, like the Pragerites, and evidence of a character defect, like the Siphios. To go before God contaminated with sin would be equivalent to insulting him—you failed to live by his command, after all, and could not live virtuously. So, you go to Hell before you go to Heaven. It's more of a temporary stopover, where you are forced to confront your misdeeds and do penance for them. Once you have 'perfected' your soul, you are permitted into Heaven."

Truth raised an eyebrow. Sounded like a copout. The elegant man smiled predatorily. "Of course, the *worst* sin, the one that lands you a permanent seat in Hell, is disdaining God. Ignoring his commands and trusting in the calcinating powers of Hell to save you. Hence, the practice of the Muq. Eternally pressing themselves to hold the highest standards of virtue. The path of perfecting themselves, to perfectly align with God's plan for them."

That sounded more like it.

"Do the seniors have an idea which is correct?"

"None of 'em," grunted the big man.

"The truth is like this pool. We can deduce many things from what little we see and what we feel. Occasionally, a bird flies past. You hear the sound of falling water. You believe you know what is behind the fog. But you don't really know. Knowing, itself, is a logical impossibility."

"Yet the honorable senior wrote a poem on the subject of morality so powerful, it inspires others to violence." Truth leaned hard on the polite language he had seen servants use. And, if he was honest, what he had learned in romance novels. The two demons seemed friendly, and he wanted to keep them that way.

"Just so. One can live a virtuous life without having certainty about God's precise demands."

The big man chuckled at that, then started outright laughing at the expression on Truth's face.

"Hey, kid, let me ask you something. What *is* virtue?"

Truth shrugged. "Based on this conversation, this junior could only guess that virtue is that which is beloved by God."

"An excellent guess. Many, not everyone, but many, would agree with you." Truth certainly hoped so. The conversation had been leading that way. "Not me, though. Because there is a follow-up question."

Truth sighed internally. Of course there was.

"Are those things beloved by God *because* they are virtuous, or are they virtuous because they *are* beloved by God?"

Truth parsed that out, and his frown deepened. "I'm afraid I must show my ignorance. I do not know."

The two demons laughed, kindly and cruelly, but honestly either way. "Nobody does," the elegant demon murmured. "The riddle has no answer. So, we must look for answers apart from God, or simply have faith that the religion we follow is correct in all important particulars."

Silence fell over the hot springs once more. Were there ghosts drifting in the mists? Truth didn't believe there were chains of ghosts following murderers. If that happened, who would kill?

"Seniors, why am I here?"

"For the hot spring, of course. After all that killing, you need a good soak to relax." The big man opened one eye and looked over at Truth with a leer. "We have lived a very long time. You start to pick up on some things, some ways the world works. We knew the inn would catch the right someone if we plonked it down here."

The elegant one picked up the thread. "We are dying. We invested too much of ourselves in our art. Scattering ourselves in all the little ghosts and spirits we reformed. The thinning magic will claim us soon. So, we thought we would die as we lived. With grace and gratitude."

"Indulging ourselves."

"Healing the world."

"Giving tomorrow better options." The enormous demon's voice dropped into a satisfied growl.

"And besides, in addition to all the killing, you have picked up a spell that tries to draw on our patron. The first we have seen in . . . centuries? Millennia?"

"Millenia," the brutal sculptor agreed.

"Botis is your patron?"

They laughed.

"Certainly not! That one is far too unsocial. And while we may be demons, we like to think we are enlightened ones. Which is why we pledged ourselves to Manda. One who reveals the truth of the world." Truth sat up suddenly. "And of course, once you know that truth, you can correct errors. Set the world on the path it belongs on," the poet concluded.

"Cup and Knife."

"Is that the name of the spell? Damn fool name." The sculptor laughed. "Some scholar thought he figured something out and was searching for a way to make the spell sell, I'd bet."

"Pity." The elegant demon shook their head. "Especially since that Eminence serves the Aeon—"

There was an incredible peal of thunder. Lightning reached down with blue-white fingers, striking the mountainside and blowing away the mist.

Truth and the demons looked at the strike in shock. "That was unsubtle," said Truth.

"Well, those great ones don't have to be subtle. It seems that some of the old taboos are still in effect. Screw it; you are still a long way from those things. Feeling relaxed, healed, energized? Possessed of a new perspective?" the big demon asked.

"Yes. Even with the lightning, my body feels quite relaxed and refreshed." *Perspective?*

"Good. Scram. We won't meet again."

"Simply run off the waterfall. Keep going downhill; you will find a village nearby." The poet smiled kindly.

"My thanks for the hospitality and a most interesting conversation." Truth bowed to them. They waved him away. He missed their shared smile.

He ran, quick enough that the water could hold his weight, then from stone pillar to stone pillar. A final leap, and he was over the waterfall, staring down at the valley below. He fell a long way until he reached the trees. Once he was at treetop height, he could redirect his energy. He leapt from tree to tree as gravity pulled him back toward the earth. He never looked back. He knew he wouldn't see anything if he did.

He found a road at the bottom of the mountain, and, as promised, there was a village less than five kilometers away. Truth had to admire it for a moment. It was just so . . . perfect.

The nicest houses in the village hadn't been painted in years. The majority were in active states of decay. Which wasn't to say that the town was empty. The combination rest stop / sandwich shop / post office / general store / pharmacy did a booming business, keeping their one employee hopping for minutes a day. He had seen cheerier people on the wrong end of a beating. It was the definition of a North Jeon mountain town.

Under most circumstances, he wouldn't go in there on a bet. Under most circumstances, he wouldn't be running naked and barefoot across the mountains of North Jeon. There were saplings and bushes. They couldn't hurt him, but they certainly disintegrated any shred of dignity he might possess. Maybe the store had pants. He couldn't think why it would, but maybe.

The store looked just as spiritually dead on the inside as it did on the outside. The clerk was similar, and Truth had to do a double take to make sure they were still breathing. Level Zero. He looked around the store, and to his shock, there were actually work pants and tee shirts available. Boots, too. Likely the only place anywhere near there where people could get clothes.

He didn't have any money. He would have to shoplift it. He picked out a set of clothes, found boots his size . . . and hesitated. There were paper maps in a rack near the front. He checked one. There was a much bigger town about forty kilometers down the road. Bigger town meant chain stores. Places where a full set of clothes wouldn't equal a month's wages for the broke, broken souls haunting the village.

And really, he wasn't being hurt by being naked. It was just a little embarrassing. He could feel that little fragment of Etenesh warming him. Proud of him. Truth put everything back and walked out again. He noticed that the village was built on a crossroads. Should have been a clue right there—nothing good would come of this place. He sighed and started running down the road again. Off to rob someone he didn't pity.

CHAPTER 2

A CERTAIN AIRINESS

Truth had never expected life to be fair. The concept had never occurred to him. It did, however, seem noticeably *unfair* that he kept finding himself running through the countryside in search of pants. Not that he was hung up on nudity, exactly. He had come to understand that his weirdness with Etenesh was more a first-girlfriend thing and less a body-image thing.

It's just that, growing up, people wore clothes. Even the people who took off their clothes professionally kept them on almost all the time. It was just common sense. If you were leaving your house, you did so wearing clothes.

Not much of his current life conformed to "common sense." Still, it stung a little that "routinely wears clothes" was one of those deviations.

Truth had come to have opinions about long-distance nude runs. He had a lot of experience with them. His opinion was that they kind of sucked. They *could* be decent for a short period in specific circumstances. Running through the woods or the scrub desert, rejoicing in the strength of your body and feeling at one with the universe. That was good.

Regardless of the spiritual beauty and glorious physicality of the experience, one had to acknowledge the flop/bounce factor. At every step, things shifted about. It was, at best, distracting. Generally, it was uncomfortable. He did not feel anyone would need a diagram to understand why. It really detracted from the whole experience. It perfectly complemented running down a crummy road traveled by big hauler wagons and mining rigs stark naked, however. That constant jostling of the undercarriage highlighted the precariousness of their situation.

The way the wagon wheels flicked up rocks and pebbles did not enhance his calm. Not that they could hurt him, really, just that the instinct to flinch or dodge was hard to overcome. He set some new personal bests for long-distance running speed getting to the next town.

He had never been so happy to see a mega-mart in his whole life. He didn't break stride until he reached the doors. Once in, he just stood there, basking in the frigid air conditioning and the lack of sixteen-wheelers showering his bits with road grit. Once he had enjoyed the moment, he made his way over to the menswear section.

This led to the next indignity—the people. While the Level Zeros and Ones seemed to be only slightly more real than the roadside shrubs, they were *people*. And people generally don't want random naked men popping up in the middle of their shopping experience. The drain on his cosmic energy was negligible, but every little drag reminded him that he was using a divine blessing and the personal spell of one of the most powerful beings in the universe to *not* cause an outrage.

He quickly threw on a bathrobe and then took his time shopping. First stop—a large backpack. Into it went sealed packages of underwear, socks, shirts, shorts, trousers, two pairs of shoes, one pair of hiking boots, and as many toiletries as he thought he might need. Toilet paper was nonnegotiable, naturally. How long had it been since he had last eaten? A long while. He topped off the rest of the bag with groceries.

Truth decided that, end of the world be damned, he wasn't going to remove all the inventory control spells individually. One short burst of Obliteration later, and he was jogging off to find a hotel. Then he doubled back and grabbed a towel, just in case. He was still in the bathrobe. Like hell he was getting his nice new clothes all dirty.

There weren't any hotels. There was a motel of dubious character. There were stains on the floor, which was . . . fine . . . but there were stains on the walls and ceiling, too. Stains that looked like something organic had slapped into that spot. Things their owners probably didn't want to part with.

The bathroom came with a tub. It wasn't quite long enough to hold an *entire* adult human. The shower curtains were heavy-duty clear plastic. Easily cleaned. There was a strong smell of bleach. This was truly the best (and only) motel in town. If he were paying for this, he would be really upset.

The shower was glorious. The hot springs had removed a shocking amount of the deep tension in him, but the feeling of the dirt washing away was convulsively pleasurable. He was tempted to go roll around in the dirt just to do it again. The increasingly alarming smell coming from the carpet persuaded him not to. He washed, dried (no water-expulsion talisman there), and, at long last, dressed.

Then he collapsed on the bed. He wasn't even sleepy; he just wanted to be lying down on something that wasn't dirt or rocks for a while. He gave a happy little wriggle. This was nice. Very nice. As mattresses went, it was horrible, damp-smelling, and lumpy. He was prepared to treasure it.

He looked up at the rotting popcorn ceiling and smiled. Civilization. Comfort. Safety. Well, not safety. He sighed regretfully. He'd have to contact Merkovah. Too much had happened. There weren't many dead drop locations in the North either. There was a decent little city on the coast not *too* far from there. There was a drop there. He would signal they needed to talk. How that would work, exactly, Truth didn't know. The last "untraceable" call got traced pretty damn fast. And they would be searching hard.

He . . . had blown up a village. Unintentionally, sure, filled with Starbrite drones (literally drones, in some cases), but still. Practically and morally, he blew up a peaceful mountain village and destroyed one of the most remarkable magical achievements of the present era. So remarkable, he didn't really understand how it worked or what its ultimate goal was.

He blew it up regardless. Killed all those people. Because he decided that whatever it was, he couldn't tolerate it. It would distract Starbrite, draw off their forces, all that, but "Hell no to all this" was a major driving thought, and he was too distrustful and paranoid to try and find a solution that involved working with other people.

Presumably, there were other choices he could have made. Other routes to the same end. He didn't know what they were just now, but they must exist. Still. Whatever the maybes may be, he had blown up a village. A direct consequence of him casually saying "Okay" to killing a single researcher. He would have to live with that thought awhile. It didn't feel good.

Truth drew a deep breath, held it, and explosively exhaled. He knew the deal going in. It was exactly what he had told Merkovah. You can lie to yourself and pretend you are the hero saving the day, but really, you are a terrorist. Those people you kill? Not a single one of those people will ever be persuaded their death was necessary. Those lives you ruin? Not a single person will believe their destruction was necessary for the "greater good."

You could sit them down, show them the evidence, calmly explain all your reasoning, and at the end, they would look at you and say, "Wasn't there any other way? Because this doesn't seem worth my suffering."

There would always be another way. Truth just didn't know what it was or how to make it happen. This, he understood. This, he could make happen. And the sibs were counting on him. Etenesh was counting on him. They didn't know it, but they were. So, it would happen. It wasn't right. It was fucked up. And he was . . . kind of okay with it. Which was fucked up. And he'd do it again.

He sat up. The fun had gone out of the relaxation. Now it was just a horrible mattress in a worse motel. Time to grab his bag and hit the road again. Next stop—Conjin.

He took a look around outside the motel, hoping to find *something* worth stealing. There was not. It was like a parking lot of the damned. He tightened up his shoelaces, cinched down his backpack, heaved a long-suffering sigh, and set off. That's the thing they never tell you about being a lone-wolf operative. All the cardio.

He grinned a little as he jogged past the town limits at an easy sixty kilometers an hour. Between the constant cross-country running, the fighting, flying, and just generally everything, he was putting a real high polish on his physique. The phrase "more shredded than a bag of cheese" leapt to mind. He had always been a lot more comfortable running his hands over Etenesh than vice versa, but he really didn't know if he could keep her off him the next time they met.

He let himself drift into a happy daydream as he ran through the bleak gray mountains of North Jeon. Bright blue spring sky, delicate white wisps of clouds, and tiny villages that looked half-sick and half-dead. Virtually all denizens.

Word had gone out about the changeover. There had probably been some fighting, but . . . what could they do? Level Ones and Zeros, all used to working in the factories, quarries, and mines. All used to taking orders. And even if they rebelled, so what?

Like kittens mewling in a box. Like the raging of a goldfish. Their future, their food, was not in their control and never would be.

So long as there was cultivation, anyone could rise . . . in theory. In practice, you had to work if you wanted to eat. That cut down on cultivation time. Elixirs made cultivation much, much faster. But there were far from enough for everyone, and the very best were literal treasures. How could everyone get an even share? And once someone got ahead, so long as they didn't slack off, they would remain ahead. Cultivation meant that anyone could rise . . . but there would never be equality. Some would always be above others.

The thought didn't pull Truth out of his happy daydream. He extended the idea into imagining his "better" world. The collapse would eventually wipe away the differences caused by cultivation. No one on this planet was truly immortal, and without the cosmic rays sustaining them, even the ancient monsters would die. Would that produce a fair, equitable world? Truth didn't believe it. There would still be money and power, even if it wasn't connected to cultivation. There would always be unfairness. Always be sacrifice.

He'd just have to make sure his better world was unfair in his favor, then. Same logic as today. It wasn't actually any better than the systems that exist now. But he couldn't crack the problem. Couldn't imagine a world without rich and poor, buying and selling, the powerful commanding the powerless. All he could imagine was being the one holding the whip. And in some vague, undefined way, being the one to drop the whip and break out of the slum. He didn't know how. He'd have to keep climbing until he could see it.

The kilometers sped past quickly. The road ran parallel to a river as it wound through the mountains and down to the sea. Fast-moving river, too. This part of Jeon was more vertical than horizontal, and the country just wasn't that big horizontally. He got over a foothill and looked down into Conjin. It sure was . . . a place.

From up there, he could see that there were no roadblocks, so that was something. It was a grimy, light-industrial city built around transport. There was a rail station, a sizable port, and he could see that one of the rivers running into the city had been dredged and turned into a canal.

It was a city more in name than practice. It was roughly triangular, with a wide, curved base along the ocean's edge, tapering into a point as it followed the river up into the mountains. A leech, Truth concluded. It looked like a leech, the wide mouth biting into the belly of the sea and sucking in all it could.

"Sometimes, you just know it's not going to go well."

CHAPTER 3

BOYS ON THE DOCK

Conjin felt off. Not in the sense of it being a trap. In the sense that Truth couldn't feel the logic of the place. The geography threw him. It was another instance of Truth's education not giving him the language to describe something he intuitively experienced. All he could say was that the lack of a ring road felt weird. The sharply tapered triangle of the city narrowed as it ran inland, with the bulk stretching along the concave curve of the coast. It felt alien. Off. A city built for some inhuman purpose.

He jogged into the city, trying to figure out what would be a good base of operations. There was plenty of public transport, he was happy to see. Rail lines ran through the small city, radiating out from the port in more or less straight lines. The buses provided vertical support to the rail's horizontal service, curving north-south along the bend of the coast. No central transit hub, he noticed, except for the port itself. There was an airfield north of the city, with a dedicated freight line from the port running to it. It plainly handled mostly cargo, with little passenger traffic.

Truth kept his eye out for anything that looked like a good place to crash. To his morbid amusement, his usual hotel trick probably wouldn't work there. Most of the places he saw were hot-sheet motels with plastic-wrapped mattresses and well-fed air demons cleaning between the quarter-hour rentals.

Only slightly more upscale were the overnight spots for sailors on shore leave or the railroad workers. Those weren't packed, exactly, but the turnover rate was so high, any given room would be needed on a regular basis. No expensive "Supreme Golden Summit Deluxe Suite" here.

There was likewise a complete absence of high-end luxury condominiums, mansions, or attractive suburban homes. There were apartment buildings, yes. Quite similar to the slum blocks he had grown up in, though shorter. There were some single-family houses, too, and they managed to look less welcoming and more unsafe than the tower blocks. Something about the way the long grass bent over the concrete steps into the houses, or the way the windows were open but all you could see inside was darkness.

Not cursed, Truth thought. At least not in the sense of needing an exorcist. It was just Jeon. And since this was Jeon, there *should* be an enclave of the rich and powerful there. Not many, maybe, in a place like this. But someone there got rich running the docks, and their house had to be somewhere.

Truth decided to combine house hunting with his actual job—finding the dead drop. Now, the instructions he had memorized said that to call for a meeting, he should break the window for an apartment above the Six Bells Bar on 135th Street. Except the instructions didn't give him the cross street, so he had to trawl the length of the long road trying to find it. And he didn't find it.

An hour of fruitless, depressing walking later, Truth gave up and started asking people where the bar was.

"Never heard of it."

"I have a boyfriend."

"You want a bar? My friends and I love to party. Come, come! We show you a real good time."

"Nah, you want Lou's, on 129th and Liberation Ave. Great wings."

"Twenty wen, and I'll take you there myself."

"You don't need a bar, honey. You need some company. I'm a lot of fun."

"Isn't that a folk-music dive? I don't listen to folk. Well, some of it's okay."

After a second fruitless hour, Truth was officially driven to the point of madness. He concluded that there were two reasonable approaches there. The first was summoning a demon, a being of unimaginable cruelty from Hell itself, and by certain signs and spells compelling it to provide directions to the bar. The other was asking a police officer. After weighing the pros and cons, Truth decided the demon was a safer bet.

Truth had a powerful moment of missing Thrush. The demon was stuck in its summoning token, which was in his duffel bag, buried next to the bird suit, way the Hell back in the mountains. It would be a minute until Truth could go and collect him again. Possibly even two minutes.

He found an office building with an impressively optimistic Leases Available sign, walked in, and found an empty office suite. He had a lot to choose from. Couldn't imagine why everyone would be breaking their leases all of a sudden. He had a moment of sympathy for commercial landlords lasting the exact smallest unit of time theoretically possible and started carving the summoning glyphs into the concrete floor. They could just throw a rug over it. Or something. He was damned if he cared even slightly.

It was a pretty generic summoning, as he didn't have a particular demon in mind and he was really grabbing the first available imp. He hesitated a moment, but figuring this was a port city, he opted for a water demon. Smarter than earth demons, not quite as smart as fire demons, lethargic and cold. Well, there were worse things.

Truth activated the formation, watching blue-green wash around the carved glyphs. A ball of brownish water condensed in the central circle. Truth made sure the bindings were in place, then spoke.

"You will be known as Drip. Your purpose is to give me directions to the place I seek. Upon doing so to my satisfaction, you will be rewarded with some of my cosmic energy. Fail to do so, or play any games with me, and I will see how much I learned about torturing demons."

"As the magus wills." The voice was surprisingly soft and pleasant, obedient. "This little imp is happy to provide what guidance it can."

"Good. Somewhere in this city is a drinking establishment known as the Six Bells Bar. It is located on 135th Street. Which is theoretically *this* street, but I cannot find it. Where is it?"

The ball of water rippled for a moment. "At the risk of angering the magus, the Six Bells Bar is located on 135th Street in this very city." Truth called the Tongue into his hand. There were infinite imps to summon, and he didn't feel like getting creative in torturing this nonentity. "Ah! Mercy, Great One! It is in the City Below!"

Truth checked his swing. "The City Below?"

"Yes, Magus. This city exists in two parts—the part ashore for the slaves, and the part below, where their masters live. The Six Bells Bar is a reputable drinking establishment for those who have reached the third circle of the Initiate realm. And any magus in this city above the first circle lives in the City Below."

"Below what?"

"The waves, Magus. The coastline drops quite sharply only a little way offshore. A place of dreaming spires and flowing thoughts, drifting between twilight and night. Terrible things are born there, the sight of which inspires cruel laughter, which rings through the halls and alleyways. A cold city, filled with colder people, trying to warm themselves with the blood and entrails of their kin."

"You feel right at home?"

"I hate it and everything about it, Magus."

"Oh? Why is that?"

"My nature is cold and torment and lingering cruelty. The city seems a pale mockery of my task and calling. Mortals should live as mortals—clinging to the light and life those great ones bless them with, breeding and drawing warmth to one another."

"Can't understand the torments of Hell without knowing joy first?"

"Simply put."

Truth knew demons well enough to translate that as *You have failed to comprehend even a tiny fraction of the meaning I expressed. I will use that fact to hurt you, given the slightest opportunity.* Imps talked sweetly when you had them bound, but that never made them safe.

"How do I get to the City Below?"

"At the port, there is a private garage. In the private garage, there is a pool of water spirits. They will carry you to the City Below once you prove your status."

"Which status?"

"Full citizen or above, Level Two and above, Magus."

"No proof-of-residency requirement?"

"None. It is common for ship captains to disembark from their ships and go directly to the City Below."

"I see." Truth tried to think if he had any more questions. He did not. "Our contract is complete." He poured the necessary magic into the spell, making the imp ripple slightly before it was banished. The thought of keeping him around never crossed his mind. One imp in his pocket was plenty. A second was begging for trouble.

He looked around the bare office space. It was, well, bare office space. The carpets had been ripped up. Holes in the wall were plastered over but unpainted. There were piles of construction waste scattered around, leftover trash from whatever business had operated there before. He'd rather hide out in the mountains. It had been a long day already, but he'd push on anyhow. Time to go to the City Below.

It wasn't hard to find the port. Finding the private garage in the port was a pain, as the carriages had their own entrances, and no signs were provided. The demon controlling the carriage would know the way, after all. Eventually, he just asked someone and began the long, boring trek through the warehouses, the stacked crates, the cranes, the rushing humanity. Even with the world collapsing, even with off-world exports blockaded, things moved around the seas.

He took a moment to admire the ships. These were cargo haulers, huge, towering things carefully engineered to survive rough seas and rougher sea demons. The fierce painted eyes on their prows darted around, even there at dock, alert for danger.

In a fit of nostalgia, Truth walked into one of the warehouses. There was the inspector, running his wand around the boxes as they came in, waiting for it to turn green, then putting his stamp on the crate. Two terminally bored guards leaned up against the wall, smoking. Not Starbrite, not PMC. Not looking away when the inspector just stamped boxes without checking them. No need these days. What did smuggling amount to now?

The thought was darkly funny. He didn't give a damn about smuggling then, either. All that mattered was that it made his superiors happy and brought in extra cash. What did he care about the "law"? The law had never protected him or anything he cared about.

Oh, well, maybe "the law" had. He did go to a public school, after all. There were roads and subways and buses and all that. But those weren't for him, really. They were for the rich people in the city, making sure the "help" could get where they were needed, when they were needed, with the skills that were needed. And if the help were already broken and made obedient by life, so much the better.

Truth shook off the odd moment and finished his walk to the private garage. There were security guards by the door, a recording talisman on every corner, and even some lightly concealed golems. A "high-security" garage. He walked straight past them all, ignoring them every bit as much as they ignored him.

The garage was packed, though most of the carriages were covered by tarps. It seemed that this was a more long-term storage location. Not a lot of commuting from the City Below, apparently. Made sense to him—he had only been in Conjin a few hours, and he couldn't wait to leave and never return.

If all the rich and powerful of Conjin lived in the City Below, then he wouldn't be able to move unseen. It was usually better to adopt a low-status, invisible persona, but under the circumstances, that was the wrong move. He needed his rich-prick persona. He frowned at the thought a moment, feeling the phoniness of the phrase.

What was the crux of the Sadistic Boss in all those romance novels? It wasn't the money. It was the power. The money was just another way of exercising power. So important, so desperately needed by the heroine, and so worthless to the Boss. It was the gap in power that made them sexy and appealing. What she could never do, he could do in an instant. To sell the persona of a rich, powerful heir of an ancient, secret clan, his aura must be one of *power*.

There was a word for that sort of person. Prince. He was the prince of the ancient Medici Clan. Hidden for millennia, prospering invisibly all through the long centuries. Only making their move now, at the end of the world. The persona settled around him comfortably. His back straightened even further; his face grew colder.

There was a line of reclining chairs queued up by a waterway that led out of the garage and into the bay. By the pond was a staggeringly attractive water demon. He watched it morph into a more classically female form when he approached. It was guessing, but credit where it was due: it had an eye for aesthetics.

"May I see the honorable magus's sigil and proof of rank?" the demon softly asked. It had been wonderfully trained. Truth presented it with the scribbled-on sigil of a high aristocrat and followed up with letting a trickle of his power reach the demon. It straightened up sharply and quickly bowed at the waist.

"My apologies, my lord. Take whichever seat pleases you. It will be our honor to carry you to the true Conjin, the City of Dreaming Waters."

CHAPTER 4

A CERTAIN KIND OF WAY

Truth picked the first recliner and got comfortable. Then convulsively shivered and got even more comfortable. This might well be the single most comfortable chair he had ever sat in. Supportive, yet soft. Ergonomically designed to make you feel almost weightless, as the body weight was distributed and diffused through the dense cushions. He didn't know what material it was upholstered with. It felt soft, softer than velvet, and even more smooth. He even liked the sage green color.

"Are the chairs for sale?"

"I believe they have been discontinued, my Lord," murmured the water demon. "They were produced by the Ghale and Penn Company, a local firm, which was bought out by Vamri some five years ago. They maintain an office in Conjin, if you wish to demand they recreate it."

Truth just nodded. He hid his dissatisfaction. He didn't have anywhere to ship the chair. Sending it to Siphios would be a spectacularly dumb way to break OPSEC. When you got right down to it, he wasn't big on furniture beyond the occasional gangster sofa. And yet, he WANTED one of these chairs. But worst of all, he should never have asked about buying something. He took, and others gratefully received what they were given.

A thin stream of water was summoned under the chair, gently carrying it to the covered waterway that led out into the bay. The demon's magic wrapped around the chair as it smoothly sank under the water. The waters parted as an eggshell of magic formed around the chair. The water had looked deep green, almost black, from the surface. Not so below.

The night sky danced under Conjin Bay. Tiny lights danced and swirled, moving in shimmering shoals, scattering when some predator swam through. The bigger fish were decked in neon oranges and powder whites, with electric strokes of blue and lightning-yellow flashing across their tarnished silver scales.

Scattered across the inverted heavens were the sea demons. Some conducted the shimmering shoals of lights; others played with the fish or each other, furiously battling, erotically entwined, or just playfully tagging one another and racing about like lovesick teens. A handsome devil with golden scales and coral-red fingers conducted a quartet of mermaids. The mermaids opened their mouths unnaturally wide, singing wordless songs tuned to the distorted acoustics of the water.

Conjin, the City of Dreaming Waters. On land, there was only bleak reality. The grim practicalities of moving thousands of tons of goods every day required efficiency. Organization. Consistency. Art and whimsy had been banished to better serve the shareholders. Banished, along with the shareholders, to the sky under the sea.

"How do those on shore not know?" Truth asked. The demon faded into view, swimming alongside the bubble its magic had conjured.

"Some do, of course, in a vague sort of way. They cannot see what you are seeing. It's all really there but concealed in the dark waters. It is part of my magic that you can see through the murk and enjoy the wonders performed for you."

"Who funds the magic?"

"In theory? The 'generous support of leading public figures.'"

"In practice, a levy is charged to those ashore, one way or another. And that's part of the fun." Truth concluded. It had been an obvious question in retrospect. He internally frowned again. It was a struggle finding the groove there. The Prince was not chatty, particularly with the servants. Silence was the rule, used strategically. His every word was as imperishable as gold and unbreakable as adamantium.

"I believe it's a tax on narcotics, alcohol, prostitution, and gambling, as well as certain other forms of entertainment. Dreams should not be excessive. Things done to excess become vices, after all. Though what counts as excess depends on the person."

Truth nodded faintly as he watched the show. Here and there were scattered little stories and mysteries. A broken statue of a beautiful woman, half-hidden in a kelp forest. Elsewhere, an octopus hid from hunting fishes, trying to conceal the eggs behind it. Two demons dueled with sabers, silver lights flashing as the blades crossed and clashed, high to low and back again. Truth smiled a little at them—two beings who clearly knew how to fight, pretending to fight. Funny.

Something about the way they cut and parried, high, low, high, low, then one hopped back and aggressively presented the point, keeping distance and gaining space to breathe. The other tried to beat away the point, but the first disengaged with the slightest dip, his point never moving away from the other's chest. Then they were at it again, cuts raining down on each other. Swords flashing in the rain and the smell of horses and wet blankets. The rattle of metal wings.

"Szabla."

"Pardon, my lord?" the water demon asked.

Truth shook his head and flicked the demon away with his fingers. Where had that word come from? That memory? A previous life? He didn't believe that reincarnation was real, not really. It had never been convincingly proven. On the other hand, he had never ridden a flesh-and-blood horse, *so how did he know what they smelled like in the rain?*

The memory, brief and fragmentary as it was, soon faded. With a silent groan, he asked, *System, did you catch that?*

<<Yes, I did. And no, I don't understand it any more than you do. But reincarnation is sure sounding more plausible by the moment.>>

That word I said . . .
<<No idea, no idea what language it even is. For all I know, it means wet *or* fishy. *>>*
It's something to do with sabers and fencing.
<<Plausible, but on what basis?>>
I just know.

The chair fell through the heavenly wonder. Silent. Sinking down to the City of Dreaming Waters.

The chair drifted to a stop on a platform made of aqua-colored glass and stones raised from the ocean floor. The lights were warm and dim, flickering, the light passing through the glass and bouncing off the stone, sending fleeting shadows racing through the platform. The platform was connected by a short walkway to a receiving building. A building that looked like some madman's notion of a temple in miniature, and painted eye-searing magenta and cyan, with heavy black details.

There wasn't a lick of sense to designing things this way, or if there was, Truth couldn't see it.

"Water held out by a barrier?"

"Indeed, magus," the water demon agreed.

"Have the rabble panicked yet?"

"Not at all. The dreamers are only more furiously determined to enjoy their slumber. Any who threaten to rouse them are met with terrible rage. And punishment."

Truth nodded slightly and walked away.

"It was my honor to serve you, my lord. May the screams of your prey be sweet in your ears."

Truth walked into the sunken city without looking back. The System Astrologica had trained him well.

The Prince was starting to fit better, or perhaps he was simply becoming accustomed to it, like an uncomfortably comfortable pair of leather pants. He didn't really like what the easy arrogance and sadism said about him.

Not that anyone would ever complain. Not if they valued their tiny lives. He had endless ways of making someone disappear, and endless ways of making their departure the stuff of nightmares and urban legends. He looked over the odd, twisting shapes of the buildings, the narrow, winding streets, and the curious lights and paper creatures swimming through the air. Just the place for a nightmare.

The city was a maze of mazes, each street deliberately designed to look wide and straightforward—until you realized it actually slightly curved, and with the overhanging signs and oddly bent buildings and irregular city blocks, the street was not as wide as it seemed. Then there were the people, broadly defined.

The mages of Conjin were no monochrome lot. They had gone mad with illusions, glamorous, with grafting the flesh of curious things to themselves. Things not so simple to define as *monster, demon,* or *chimera.* Soft and warm human flesh was replaced here and there with the rubbery shine of an octopus or the brilliant silver scales of a mackerel. Tentacles sprouted from the back of a woman in a business suit—one holding the saucer and the other her coffee cup as she chatted gayly with her friend. A man in comfortable slacks and little else clinked his mug with an equally shirtless companion, the dozens of little tongues that had replaced their eyes dancing in the effervescence of the beer.

Everywhere was decked in colors contrasted against the dim light of the city and the ever-present black trim. Aquas and turquoises and lapis lazuli houses and shops and offices, some over cobblestone streets with no sidewalks, others over crushed gravel, others still over modern, well-drained roads and raised sidewalks. Some streets transitioned from one to the other in the space of a single step. Others enjoyed a more gradual blending.

Demons of all sorts moved through the city. Infernal, natural, most in keeping with the aquatic theme, but there were birds as well—air demons decked out as gulls or sandpipers, keeping the streets as clean as their masters wished. No more, no less. A trio of horned, goatlike demons played trumpets on a street corner, a hat full of tiny seashells at their hooves.

And naturally, the streets were not numbered. What was the point? It wasn't like there was a grid system. There were Elm Streets and Laurel Streets and Prospect and Broadway, Phlebotomy Circus, and the A-3. Somewhere would be 135th Street. Who could say where? A local, presumably.

Truth found himself caught in a dilemma. The Prince *did not walk*. The Prince traveled in comfort and style. But he certainly wasn't going to buy things. A weakling could wave money about. The core of the Prince was power. Fortunately, the dilemma had a straightforward solution.

There was a sedan chair proceeding down the street, carried by fish spirits swimming through air like it was water. Truth released his aura—the raw power of his level, the demon-abolishing power of the Sea of Brass, the murderousness granted by his rough patron. The sedan chair stopped dead, the spirits rolling in place to display their bellies in supplication.

"Has this little brother done something to displease the senior?" A middle-aged man, his push-broom mustache replaced with the tentacles of a sea anemone, immediately leapt from the carriage and bowed at a ninety-degree angle.

"I am taking your sedan chair."

"Senior . . ." There was a long pause. Truth just looked at him, watching the sweat bead on the back of the man's neck. Letting the reality-bending power of Incisive beat on the man, preying on the obedience to hierarchy that was the birthright of every child of Jeon. "I am so grateful you chose my meager conveyance! Happy journey to you."

Truth didn't acknowledge him, simply stepping into the sedan chair and sitting. He glared at the fish spirits, who shivered into action and set off. Once he was away from the still-bowing man, he informed them of where he would be carried. He briefly debated blinding the impudent fellow but eventually decided that his business was more important than removing a pair of useless eyes.

The fish demons swam quickly, not asking questions, not even speculating in their minds about what purpose could lead such a young monster to so mediocre a bar. Between their bindings and the Blessing of the Sea of Brass, they knew their place. The Six Bells was not too far. Decorated with pictures of yachts, superfluous rope, and tattered sails. The dreams of capsized luxuries, where the "drowned" rich could drink and play. How dull. Breaking a window seemed like the perfect thing to do there.

He hopped out, pulled a cobblestone out of the street, and whipped it through the correct window above the entrance. He then returned to the sedan chair.

"Take me to a hotel that combines supreme comfort with equal discretion. Drop me two blocks away. Better to arrive on foot than in . . . this."

The fish swam on for another fifteen minutes before alighting next to a dimly lit sidewalk. "My lord, the boutique hotel Mary's Garden is two blocks up this road. The building is painted all black, with a single torch out front that shifts between blues and reds. There is no other sign. Our master repeatedly expressed his wish that one day he could afford to stay there."

Truth nodded. He slung his backpack over his shoulder and strode into the endless night.

CHAPTER 5

A MAN WITHOUT COMPASSION

The Prince appeared without warning. The supposedly locked door to Mary's Garden opened, the recording talismans unable to capture his radiance. Tall, hair the color of a moonless night, eyes like black wells with drifting golden stars in the depths.

Dressed in exquisite yet casual clothing that clung to his tall, perfectly proportioned frame. Muscular without being grotesque, he was violence and sensuality made flesh. The Prince was entirely failing to keep with the softer, more-androgynous standards of masculine beauty in Jeon. And he didn't care at all. He looked like a descended god. Most of the staff were succubae. They knew whereof they spoke.

The desk clerk was, however, all too mortal and, as a lowly desk clerk, a mere Level Two. The black and white tiles made no sound as the Prince approached. The torches in their flickering, multicolored firelight did as they were supposed to and made the lobby more dreamlike and unreal. A perfect backdrop for the all-too-real man in front of him.

"Provide me with your best room and service," the Prince commanded.

"I am so sorry! As we didn't know the young master was visiting Conjin, we failed to reserve the room for you. It—it is currently occupied." The clerk reflexively bowed in apology, hating whoever failed to prepare adequately for this lord's arrival.

"Oh? By whom?" *Young master*? The clerk would pay for that.

"We cannot reveal . . ." The clerk gasped, the compulsions in his employment contract at war with his sense of self-preservation. The ice was more than just cracking under his feet. The cracks were spreading wide.

"No matter. They will sleep elsewhere." The clerk almost collapsed. The succubus by his side didn't even glance at their coworker, seemingly fascinated by the floor near Truth's feet.

"I . . . can send a messenger. Ask them to meet the young master."

"No. I do not make requests." He released a trickle of his power and killing intent, filling the lobby. Pressing his absolute authority upon the room. He was the only real thing in it. His will was the only law. The succubae around the lobby dropped to their knees, pressing their heads against the floor. The clerk collapsed bonelessly, unable to endure the pressure of the sheer difference in status. A ghost before a hero.

Truth looked down at the succubus. "You will provide one of your kin as a servant for my stay here. They will attend to me and only me. You, on the other hand—"
He reached down, pulled the demon's head up by the hair, and drew a quick sigil on the demon's forehead. He did so while suppressing its bindings with a minor effort. They were nothing special. He overwrote them in seconds. The succubus shivered in pleasure.

"Your job is simple. You will take this thing"—he pointed at the paralyzed clerk— "and teach it to fear everyone and everything it ever loved or desired. In turn, it will only and forever desire to serve me in all ways. That will be its only pleasure."

"Gladly, O Prince, and at once." Another succubus appeared next to the first, both on their knees, heads pressed to the floor.

He pointed to the second one. "Assume the form of a maid, classically trained in all domestic services. Attractive but not too beautiful." It shifted form, adopting the guise instructed. "Guide me to the best room. Ensure housekeeping is standing by. Inform the kitchen that I require dinner. The specialty of the house. No wine; they are to display their value by crafting an alcohol-free drink to complement the meal."

"As you command, my Prince." It rose with the smooth, boneless grace its kind was known for. The face was symmetrical, with a small nose and wide eyes, a faint dash of freckles somehow highlighting the vivid green of the eyes. No blushing beauty, but the longer you looked at "her," the more sweetness you found in all the little details. The slim feminine shape of her. You found yourself wanting to see that hidden, fearful look in her eyes. The more you wanted to hunt the vixen like a pack of dogs, right to the ecstatic end.

Truth understood why succubae were so popular and so lethal. He'd seen beauties before. This was just one more. He handed his bag to another servant and walked behind the maid, deeper into Mary's Garden.

The hotel was a place of rest for those whose slumber was too restless or whose dreams had become too dark. The hotel was a converted multistory townhouse with a large, open spiral stair running up three stories. Coral and sea anemones grew along the balustrades and the walls as glittering fish swam through the air, and dancing seaweed lent its texture and color to the whole. Off the stairs were hallways, each likewise decorated as the dream of a tropical reef, with so many wonderful nooks and crannies to explore for their happy little mysteries.

The maid led him to a double door painted red and framed with twisting kelp. The succubus opened the doors without knocking. An older couple, perhaps husband and wife, were sitting together over a light meal. Level Four, no pins, no sense of authority to them. Irrelevant.

"The Prince requires this suite. Leave at once." The succubus spoke with calm authority.

"And just who the hell—" Truth fixed the man with his eye, already seeing how these two would die. The inevitability of death settled over the room. Like an inescapable sickness or the moment of lucidity between the window breaking and the body reaching the pavement. Like the judge's sentence in sight of the gallows. Death was coming, and they had just enough life left to fear how ugly their end would be.

They got up and silently left, nearly vomiting when they saw the housekeeping cart come bustling toward their room.

"With my lord's permission, I will have his leg broken for his impertinence and charge all your expenses to him."

"See to it."

The succubus snapped twice. Truth didn't see any more movement, but he knew it would be enough. He waved in the housekeeping team.

The succubae swept into action. Air demons swirling around them to consume any filth left behind by the previous guests. Bedbugs were simply not a thing that could exist in a hotel purified by air demons. Sheets were stripped and tossed in a hamper, then fresh sheets fitted with a surgeon's precision. The surfaces were polished. They were marvelously efficient.

Truth sat in an armchair and enjoyed a foot massage while the room was returned to order. The luggage and personal effects of the previous occupants were collected. He didn't care what the hotel did with them so long as they were out of the room.

The succubus was very good at what it was doing. His feet had never felt so relaxed. This was sheer indulgence. Perhaps he had earned it after all that running and sleeping in the woods. He smiled. The housekeepers and air demons suppressed shudders at the happy cruelty of his expression. They weren't shuddering out of fear.

More than the massage. More than the luxurious room and the good food to come. It was the terror. It was the obedience born of fear and worship. Jeon had bred deference to power into the bones of its people. No drug could be better than this. He would have to keep an eye on himself. Wouldn't do to overindulge, even in the City of Dreaming Waters.

This persona was going to be a problem. It was too easy. Too comfortable. And he intended to inhabit it for a few days or however long it took Merkovah to set up a secure line of communication. The world was hard at work, reinforcing his assumed identity. He would have to mind himself that it didn't become real. More real. Didn't become the "real" him. Ah, hell.

<<Told you this would come up again soon. It's part of you. Always has been.>>
I know, I know. But come on—
<<Oh, I'm just saying I told you so, not condemning you. Indulge away.>>
Truth lolled his head back. There was a long stretch of quiet.
Did you . . . have a follow-up to that? A caution against arrogance, perhaps, or a reminder that Etenesh would be more than hurt if I were to bed some plaything? Even if they meant nothing to me? That I'm being a hypocrite?
<<Nope.>>
You want me to keep doing this?
<<I don't care either way. You seem to remember not to do things that will negatively impact your survival. I just want you to think about why you are doing it and if you still

want to do it. If yes, go nuts. Really. Go completely berserk. I don't care about these "people" any more than you do. >>

Oddly, it was that which snapped him out of his decadent spiral. He had been ignoring the Tongue and Etenesh's fragment inside of him. The angelic sword seemed to approve, but the fragment of Etenesh's warmth and goodness was radiating disapproval. Split decision. He'd have to balance his own desires against those of the women in his life. He could ease off on the sadism while maintaining the domineering attitude. Although it had to be acknowledged—some people won't cry until they see their coffin. A degree of cruelty is required.

In the meantime, he had nowhere in particular to be. He elected to enjoy the massage, learn some things, and make Etenesh a happy woman the next time he laid hands on her. Dinner would come soon, then sleep. A busy and productive day. A tiny trickle of worry ran down his spine.

"I don't keep track—how long until Jeon adopts the System?"

"About a week, my lord, before the first public enrollment. Eight days, including today, though there have been significant delays in some places due to terrorism and accidents. I believe that, for people of a certain status, early enrollment is possible. For a reasonable gift or simply a favor owed. For my Prince, I am certain that your mere whim would be reason enough to have you enrolled at your convenience." The succubus's voice was soft, deferential.

Truth snorted at that. His whim would certainly suffice. They would happily make a special trip just for him.

Nothing more was said until dinner. The succubus knew its place and was very happy there.

Dinner was four courses. The dinner's theme was "Joy at the Seaside." It started with a little rack of miniature ice cream cones topped with a salmon mousse. It sounded mad. It tasted delightful. He found himself wishing there was one more bite of it, but the second course arrived before he could order another set. This was a small flight of oysters paired with fish eggs and some garnishes. Another dish where he couldn't see the point, and it staggered him. It was so incredibly good, he didn't have anything to compare it to. This was simply food on an entirely new level.

The oysters were followed by butter-poached lobster and, for dessert, coffee ice cream and a donut. Each plate was sized to be just short of enough by itself. He finished the meal feeling comfortably full but thinking back on each dish. Wishing he could have had just one more bite. He smiled once he saw the joke. He would dream happily of this meal, if he ever dreamed. Each course was paired with a nonalcoholic cocktail. He hadn't the faintest clue what was in them, but they were a lovely counterpoint to each plate.

He looked up at the sweating chef who had accompanied the cart to his room. "Inform the kitchen that they have done well. I will entrust my meals to them for my stay." She almost collapsed, bowing and thanking him profusely. He waved her away. He heard the maid murmuring something about "lucky swine" as "she" guided the chef out the door.

The shower was all he hoped it would be. He contemplated having the succubus bathe him, but it would likely be too much. Fed, refreshed, and generally content, he went to bed.

"My Prince, is there any further service you require before retiring? Or after?"

Truth was slightly tempted to ask for a dream, but *that* really was too stupid. "No. Stand at attention outside the bedroom door and wait to be summoned." The demon left, and he closed his eyes. It had been a lousy few days, but this one had turned out nice.

The hotel settled in for the night. The desk clerk was hidden in a tiny box in the basement, locked in dreams of erotic torment and animal terror. The succubus maid was happily minding the door, ready to keep away the less-sensible of its kin. The System was puzzling out how to adapt all the various body-cultivation spells they had found to the Meditations. Truth slept dreamlessly.

His nous gave a tiny shake.

CHAPTER 6

THE GODDESS OF THE NIGHT

The boat sailed down the wide, twilight street, cheered on by the entire polis. The sail was nothing less than the peplos that would adorn the giant statue of the goddess, lovingly embroidered over the course of the year to show her triumph over the giants. The boat was pulled along by hidden mechanisms under the street. A mechanism whose ingenuity exceeded the wisdom of all other peoples. Their goddess was the goddess of wisdom and war, and she had blessed her favored city generously.

Leading the procession to the temple were the basket bearers. They were girls just old enough to marry, possessed of impeccable virtue and coming from the very finest families of the polis. They were allowed the privilege of wearing the festive mantle and a peplos of their own as they carried the baskets filled with barley, the first fruits of the season, and the long knives. Around their necks were necklaces of figs—the closest a woman could come to a laurel crown of her own.

Behind the basket bearers, the priests, the celebrants, the marching soldiers, the beautiful boat, the musicians, came the victims. This was the Panathenaea. Nothing less than a hecatomb would do. Fully one hundred head of cattle were led toward the temple. The horrific expense of those cattle was, naturally, proudly assumed by the wealthy of the city. It was their duty and their glory. The victims tossed their heads and stamped their hooves at the sound of the blaring trumpets, the banging drums, the smoke from the torches hurting their noses.

Up, up they went to that great rocky promontory and the vast temple dedicated to the goddess. The sacrifices were led into the temple, where the priests scattered barley and fruit over them. They were stunned with blows from mallets, then their throats slit, the blood draining into the vessels set to catch it.

The stench of it all! The copper smell, the raw-meat smell, the shit and piss of one hundred cattle. The priestesses had added frankincense to the brasiers to make the ritual smell better, and maybe for some, it worked. But who cared about the smell when it was the peak of the Panathenaea?

The games had gone on for two days now—men and boys competing in gymnastic events like boxing, wrestling, racing, and dancing in full armor. Pankration, too, for those who appreciated finesse in their violence. There had been boat races, chariot races, and rhapsodes had come from across the civilized world to perform. Singing out the *Iliad* and the *Odyssey*, those imperishable records of gods and heroes.

Feasts? When had the feasts ever stopped during the Grand Panathenaea? Rivers of wine and oil flowed into the bowls and bellies of the citizens and their guests. Tonight would be the greatest feast of all for men and gods alike.

The blood was collected in the wide-mouthed vessels. The priests dipped their bundles of rushes into the blood and then flicked them over the altar. The blood hissed as it hit the bed of coals, already hot and red. The first food was for the gods. The rest of the blood was carried away to be whipped to a froth by slaves for half an hour to prevent it clotting. Then it would be mixed with flour and salt and turned into food. It was far too precious not to use. They had so many to feed.

Next came the breaking of the flesh and bones. The victims were cut apart. The meat was scraped from the thighbones, then the bones were wrapped in a triple layer of fat. The priests ritually tossed them on the searing coals.

Once again, the smell was overwhelming—the sizzling beef fat and roasting bones watered the mouths of all in attendance. But this first bite was for the gods.

Next came the chunks of meat. Young men, carefully selected and purified, placed big pieces of the victims on five-pronged long skewers, like a fisherman's trident grown extra limbs. They held the meat over the coals, roasting it as the libations—the wine sacrifices—were poured over them. The smells! The wine, the roasting meat, the fat, the woodsmoke, the frankincense, the sweat of the masses after a day in the summer sun.

The roasted, sacrificial meat of one hundred cattle was portioned out to the tribes of the city to be eaten at the feasts by noteworthy families. The skins went to the priests. The organs were eaten or sacrificed. Nothing went to waste. Such was the wisdom of the goddess and her chosen people.

When the sacrifices and rituals were complete, the city scattered into itself, breaking out into neighborhoods and families, celebrating the goddess and those who had triumphed in the games. There were guests, too, of course, from friendly polis across the peninsula and across the seas.

One of those guests had sailed all the way from Ella, no small journey for the old man. Still, he was warmly welcomed at a particularly noble feast. He had been the giver of laws for Ella, noted for his deep thought and broad knowledge. Not to mention his ability to wind up the followers of Pythagoras and Thales, which should help liven the party.

Not that it was a party for the purely intellectual. Such an elite party naturally had its share of sporting champions, too—there were gilded laurel crowns on display, the victors' prize oil generously contributed to the feast. One such champion, built like Ajax, stalked up to the old man.

"I have been looking for you for a long damn time, son of Pyres."

"And you have found me. Truth, wasn't it? A strange name."

"Blame my father; he was a strange man. I have questions for you."

"Oh? I know little about Pankration. Not enough to teach a champion."

The young man rolled his eyes. "Practice every waking hour for a few years, and you will learn all you need to. I age out of my division before the next great festival, and I don't know if I will want to compete in the senior group by then. No, this is about something much more important. Your poem."

"You read *On Nature*? A young hero like you?"

"You banged on for eight hundred verses about *alêtheia*. You guess why I'd be interested. Or you can blame my father again."

"Fair enough. I think I'd like to meet him. What's troubling you about the poem?" There was a certain gleam in the old man's eye. Not a nice gleam.

"What in the bowels of Zeus is it actually about? Because you start the poem with a hallucination, expand into something I struggle to even put into words, declare that unspeakable insanity the only real and correct thing, then spend the next *seven hundred rotting verses* on what you *specifically call* wrong thinking for morons."

"I don't think I specifically called it—"

"You might not have used those words, but you were taking the absolute piss out of the followers of Thales, with scattered shots at dozens of others. It was cosmography as comic insult routine."

The old man's younger companion—no spring chicken himself at forty—lurched to his feet. "Now, you see here—"

"Zeno, right?"

"Eh? You have heard of me?"

"Sure. Wanna see if your ass can travel the infinite number of steps to the floor before your head?" There was an exchange of hard looks. Zeno sat.

"Let's just keep it civil, is all." The older man sniffed.

"Very civil. Tell me if I misquote you here, son of Pyres:

At this point I cease for you the trustworthy account and meditation
regarding true reality; from this point on mortal notions
learn, listening to the deceptive order of my verses.

"That's *this whole next bit is strictly for the morons* but prettied up. Look. I'm interested. Your mad notion of the universe is fascinating, if plainly cracked. I just don't think I understand it."

"The notion that everything exists in a fixed timeless moment, a single complete unity of everything, denying even the possibility of change or motion, flies in the face of our common experience. It is also, quite obviously, true," the old man said kindly.

Even Zeno had the decency to wince at that.

"Oh, very obvious. So obvious, you have the Goddess Night appear to explain it to you. Let me summarize, and you tell me if I missed anything."

The old man nodded.

"The universe, true reality, is eternal because what is exists, and if what is came to be, then it would have to come from something out of nothing for no reason, which is a logical impossibility. Likewise, since it has always existed, there would be no reason for it ever not to exist because the something that could destroy everything would still be *something*, which is part of everything and would therefore destroy itself before it could destroy *everything*, which is a logical impossibility."

Truth took a deep breath. "Likewise, since true reality *is,* and is *everything,* then it isn't many little things but one thing, complete and whole. There is nothing but the completeness of everything. Continuing this logic, motion is also an illusion. Since the totality is complete and perfect, it is an unchanging sphere. It has no reason to change or move; therefore, it does not change or move. Our perception of change and motion, like our perception of creation and destruction, is an illusion."

"You are skipping an awful lot, but I suppose you have caught the gist of the Path of Conviction." The glint in the old man's eye had been joined by an increasingly nasty grin.

"So, the first, most obvious question is: do you believe any of this horseshit, and second, are you just fucking with the Pythagoreans and Milensians or what?"

"Let's go in reverse order. I am not so dull as to do only one thing with a line. Consider this—when you think, you think of something; you are attaching the name of something to it. Thought and language require objects outside themselves as a referent. Since you can think of it whenever you like, whatever can be thought of or spoken of must be eternal. Therefore, there can be no change, since change consists in things coming into being or ceasing to be."

Truth rubbed his forehead. "Not helping. Are you saying the argument has nothing to do with Thales' notion of the material world?"

"I'm saying it is both an appeal to pure logic and, yes, screwing with those morons."

"Fantastic. Super. And the whole Proem and Way of Inquiry bit that sounds like you lifted it from the Cult of Apollo or Orpheus?"

"The absolute literal truth, as best I could record it."

That got a double take from Truth.

"Pardon?"

"That happened. I described it as best I could, but . . . it was beyond me. I can only comprehend and put into words the barest fragment of what she showed me. The Goddess Night was wisdom herself, and as a lover of wisdom, I was granted as much gnosis as I could endure."

"That the world is an illusion?"

"What is, is real. What we think 'the world' is, is an illusion. I spent most of the poem describing the illusion as best I could, to stop people making aggressively stupid mistakes and hopefully leading them back to the Path of Conviction," the old man said. "Almost everyone sees as a mortal and thinks as a mortal. Hard to teach them to think like the goddess."

"The Path of Conviction, not reason, yet you argue in favor of pure reason being more '"real"' than experience. This feast. This flesh. This conversation. All illusions."

"Yes. At a certain point, gnosis, personal knowledge beyond pure reason, is required. A revelation of the truth."

"Faith in pursuit of pure reason. An odd idea. One might even say it was contradictory."

"Not at all. Those who love wisdom find much to love in all parts of existence. From the uses of plants to medicine to law and to the nature of the gods, mathematics, pure reason, and esoteric magic."

"Magic?"

"Certainly. Every serious thinker I know of also was a devoted researcher of magic. Pythagoras, ass that he was, built a whole damn cult around his revelations. Do you think they sit around, going, 'Hooray for geometry,'"?

"Yes."

There was a pause.

"All right, yes, they do sit around going, '"Hooray for geometry,'" when not getting lightheaded from their own antibean vegetarianism. Put another way, do you really think they don't use spells? They use them all the time. Covering up murders, mostly, I expect."

"To be a lover of wisdom, to pursue reason, must require the hunter to arm himself with spells." Truth looked skeptical.

"One way to put it. What more can I say? The Goddess of Wisdom revealed the unity behind the illusion. We may reason our way back to that unity, but until we can do so, we are trapped in the illusion. And while what is real is unchangeable, the unreal is changeable, by whatever means suits you."

"Like pushing a wheel or sacrificing a cow. Etching a curse on bone."

"Yes. We are prisoners of the illusion, Truth. And it is every prisoner's duty to escape."

CHAPTER 7

TESTING THE CUSHIONS ON THE THRONE

Truth woke up. Or not. There was a long moment, impossible to say how long, where he lay in bed paralyzed by the sensation of unreality. The keening scream of the System faded into a high-pitched whine as every object he could perceive, every sensation he experienced, became illusory. As real as it ever was, which, for a time, was no more real than a toddler's sketch of their bedroom.

Truth drew a convulsive, deep breath through his nose and cast Incisive as hard as he could. He didn't adopt the guise of the Princewisdom he imposed that truth on the world. So far as his magic ran, so far as his law extended, it was the absolute definitional core of reality. He *was* the Prince, the second generation of an ancient and terrible clan. Those who were obedient would prosper. Those who opposed him would perish. His was the only orthodoxy that mattered.

Outside the bedroom, his succubus maid collapsed to its knees, a mindlessly happy expression on her face. Across the hotel, the succubae staff looked directly toward Truth's suite, walls and floors ignored. They bowed in unison, then returned to their duties. The other guests and human staff were confused or upset, but that hardly mattered.

Once the sense of unreality had been stamped out, Truth allowed Incisive to relax. He kept it running as he always did, but he stopped forcing it.

System, do you know what that was? Are we under attack?

<<Only from your shitty, evil past lives! GOD DAMN THAT HURT! I have become an expert on the subject of soul pain, and let me tell you, that was way up at the top. Fun idea—obliterate your soul as you fall into an active volcano. Try it a couple of times, and see if you enjoy it.>>

I'll pass for now. He lay in bed, staring up at the ceiling. *I don't know what that was.*

<<Merkovah said you were alienated from the world. Maybe this is the rabid, batshit version of that.>>

No, I don't think so. He tried to put words around his instinct. *I think I am starting to see what Cup and Knife were getting at. The world is wrong. Literally wrong. Like a picture of a chair that we all keep trying to sit down on. We have opinions about the chair. We argue about how comfortable it is. And the whole time, our ass is sticking out over nothing at all. We are taking the strain and not noticing.*

<<Botis was getting at the same idea with Incisive, just from a different angle. You can't trust the provided chairs, so you make your own chairs.>>

I think, and I know how weird it is to say this, but I think Botis is actually coming at things from a less technical angle than whoever made Cup and Knife. Manda, ultimately, whoever that eminence is.

<<Might be something to investigate while we are here. Information won't be as easy to come by as in Siphios, but Conjin strikes me as the kind of place where strange, esoteric knowledge can be found.>>

Truth lay in bed a while longer, then decided that, as impossibly comfortable as the bed was, he would rather meet the day washed and clothed.

"Attend me."

The door opened instantly, the demure maid bowing before coming into the room, then bowing again before speaking. "What is your wish, great one?"

"Prepare a shower for me. Warm a bathrobe for me to wear afterward, and lay out clothes for the day. Breakfast is to be served piping hot immediately after I exit the shower and before I am dressed. It will be accompanied by *good* coffee. Does the hotel have cultivation chambers available?"

"It does, though the quality may not be up to your standards."

"Mmm. Ensure one is available for me after I dress."

He looked at her. The maid's hands were crossed in front of her, her eyes downcast, not daring to look at him without permission. "You have your instructions."

"At once, Prince." The maid bowed again, backed out of the room, bowed a final time, and politely shut the door.

I could get used to this.

<<Yes. Might be best not to. Or not. I guess you will find out.>>

The shower was quite unlike any shower he had ever had before. In a little room attached to the bathroom was a miniature tropical glade. Illusion magic made the space seem vast, the back wall turning into a forested mountain.

Coming down the mountain in a great steaming torrent was a waterfall. You could stand under the waterfall or sit on the provided stool. You could wash with any of the brilliantly herbal soaps provided or, with the touch of a gem, summon an attendant to wash you instead. The air tasted different—the fresh mountain air mixed with the humid, vegetal smell of the jungle. Truth enjoyed himself immensely but didn't linger. He had had his fill of illusions this morning.

The robe waiting for him was wonderfully warm. The breakfast, a simple, elegant affair of rice, vegetables, and eggs, was hot, cooked to the peak of perfection, and shockingly delicious. Truth had eaten essentially the same meal hundreds of times before, but the difference in quality was immense. What constituted "good" food, even for those in the C Tier, was apparently completely different from the real thing.

He took a closer look. The rice had a nearly unnoticeable glow to it, as did the vegetables. Someone had enriched them with cosmic energy without making them explode or mutate. He hadn't even heard of such a thing. His body certainly approved. His near-daily refinement meant that the energy he needed was enormous.

There was a moment of tension as the maid watched him lift his coffee cup to test the aroma. One long inhale. A second. There was a long pause, then a sip. There was another pause. The maid swore that she would butcher the three generations of the cook's family if it displeased the lord. Assuming it survived the lord's displeasure.

"Acceptable. When I next call for coffee, the beans will be ground slightly finer, and the water will be three degrees cooler." He loosely extended his cup. "Add twenty-five milliliters of cream to this."

The maid obeyed instantly, pouring prettily. Looking like "she" was hiding her fear. Looking like prey. He smiled slightly and waved it back. A succubus will not change its nature. More fool you if you believed it.

The maid looked over at the door, frowning slightly. "Great one, a petitioner comes. Will you receive them?"

"After breakfast."

Truth enjoyed the rest of the meal, savored the coffee, and sighed contentedly. Who could be coming to see him? Presumably someone connected to this hotel.

"Who is the petitioner?"

"Mary Von Raister. She is the owner of this hotel."

"Level, affiliations?"

"She is Level Five, Prince, and the Von Raisters are a cadet branch of the Lubenz Clan. She has two sons and a daughter in the upper C-Tier at Starbrite, and her late husband was once briefly the Minister for Agriculture for Jeon."

Truth had some vague recollection of the Lubenz Clan but no direct contact with them. He had never been on their level, in any sense, when he last lived in Jeon. Now he wasn't sure if they were on his level.

"Send her in."

Mary was beautiful, as were all of her class in Jeon. She had opted for elegant tiny scales growing along the contours of her face, dusty pink, flecked with electric blue and yellow. Her eyes were too large and too wide, at least for the surface world. Down there, they simply fit her.

Mary had taken the precaution of wearing a few discreet but potent charms for blocking glamors. Truth almost laughed in her face. He was the realest thing in the entire hotel. He didn't offer her a seat.

"I am glad to see you have made yourself at home," she said. He did look very comfortable in the hotel bathrobe.

He faintly nodded. And waited.

"Perhaps slightly too at home?"

That didn't merit a response either. But it was noted.

"Sir, I don't know your name or affiliation. I do know that you stole one of my servants, abducted my grandson, evicted two of my oldest friends, and yet, despite all that, the entire staff of the hotel is utterly convinced that all this is my absolute privilege."

Truth faintly nodded again. It was.

"In fact, the succubae universally refer to you as the Prince, a rank that has not existed in Jeon for centuries. They are all killingly jealous of your '"maid"' here. And none of them will explain why."

She was a talker, wasn't she? He was getting bored. She was in stabbing range. It would be inconvenient to change hotels, but he had endured worse. Mary had decent instincts, at least. She sensed the shifting mood and changed tack.

"Sir, please. At the very least return my grandson. I understand he offended you, but the harm is mended. If more is required, I think my assistance far outweighs whatever service he might supply in the future."

Truth smiled faintly. Mary didn't quite blanch. She realized her mistake. "If it's not his service you desire, I can provide as many as you wish for your amusement."

He nodded slightly at that. She understood. "I will require your best cultivation room, to be reserved for my exclusive use while I am at your hotel. This room will be reserved for me whenever I am in the city, with or without notice. You will arrange access to the best magical library and research resources this city has to offer. You will do your absolute best, on your own head and the heads of your children and grandchildren, to ensure my privacy while I live here. And needless to say, you will cover all the expenses save for the cost of this room and my meals, which will be paid for by your dear friends."

He smiled slightly. They both knew it wasn't about the money.

"As you wish."

Truth looked to the door. "Attend me." There was a knock. The maid opened the door, revealing the succubus he had stolen yesterday. It was still "dressed" as a butler. He saw no reason to change it.

"How has it fared in your care?"

"It learns slowly, my Prince, but it does learn," the succubus murmured.

"Bring it here."

The succubus departed and swiftly returned, wheeling a small suitcase. The case was opened, showing the desk clerk crammed into a tiny ball inside. The clerk could barely breathe, but the way his eyes had rolled up into his head suggested he wasn't aware of that fact.

"Pull it out and wake it up."

The succubus did so. The clerk took one look at Truth and collapsed onto his hands and knees. Shaking in terror.

"Decent progress. Reflect on this and consider what you can improve for next time. Return it to its grandmother."

"As you command, my Prince."

Mary stared hard at Truth the whole time, not looking at her grandson. She made no effort to hide her weighing the advantages of violent reprisal or submission.

"You look like a prince, I suppose, but that's meaningless in Jeon. Who, exactly, are you?"

Truth smiled and nodded at that. He leaned back in his chair, the deep, plush robe wrapped around him as he sipped the last of his coffee. He didn't answer. She could do as she pleased, but the results would be the same either way.

Mary couldn't see all the forces stacked against her. A victim of her education and upbringing, she saw hundreds of things that Truth wasn't, without ever seeing what was. She couldn't understand how Incisive worked, reshaping her reality. She didn't understand the Meditations of Valentinian, steadily accumulating local superreality. She didn't understand how the Blessing of the Sea of Brass compounded those effects, proclaiming his orthodoxy, nor how the faintly accumulating traces of Cup and Knife made the world around Truth more obedient.

She didn't see what light Etenesh's spark cast, nor feel the reaching dominion of the Tongue. She was lost in her own garden. Searching among illusions for the illusion that didn't belong. Confronted with the irresistible, irrefutable Truth.

By a chain of logical reasoning, she eliminated everything that he could not be and was left with the only answer her education provided her. This was neither an illusion nor a glamor. The clear eyes, cruel lips, and strong face were what they appeared to be. The man in front of her was what he appeared to be. Someone so beyond her station, he was practically a different species. All that was left was to concede with dignity and win what she could.

"You are the prince. I am your host. And I am thankful for your patronage." She looked over at her grandson and let her eyes slide to the open suitcase. Then back again to Truth. There was silence, and a request.

She was his grandmother, after all. If she could arrange a good job for him, she would. What better opportunity could he hope to receive, here at the end of days?

CHAPTER 8

ACTIVE LEISURE

Truth quickly considered Mary's request. He was the Prince, and the core of the Prince was power—the power to rule over others. This meant securing the willing cooperation of his lessers. His personal dignity, his glory, therefore mattered a great deal. Without it, they would not be obedient. The other thing was fortune, but that was a matter for another time.

So, what to do about Mary's grandson? Delegate. Make his people problem someone else's problem. Because nothing says personal power like putting other people to work.

"I have no need for additional servants, nor is my retinue easily entered. I will offer it an opportunity at the end of my stay. It will remain in the care of . . . I will call you Butler"—he nodded at the stolen succubus—"who will see to its education and moral reform. Should it learn how to be useful, it may yet be redeemed as a human."

"My thanks, Prince. I am certain Barton—" Truth lips slightly curved up. "I am certain it will work hard." Truth nodded slightly.

"Good. Is my cultivation chamber ready?"

Mary blinked.

"See to it." Truth dismissed her. She bowed and departed silently. Leaving her grandson shivering on the floor. Truth looked down at the clerk. He had no reason to be cruel to him. His persona was now well established, his needs were being met, even his wants were being satisfied. Still. The dignity of the Prince must be maintained. Always. And this thing had offended him too many times.

"Your prior instructions stand. It will come to fear and hate all it ever loved and everything that used to bring it comfort or pleasure. It will love only me and derive comfort and satisfaction only from serving me. However, I do not want it ruined. It must be able to lead a reasonably independent life as it serves."

"As you command, my Prince. This lowly succubus is infinitely grateful to receive the name and nature you have bestowed upon it, that it might better serve you," Butler murmured. The maid looked murderously jealous, then quickly hid her expression behind bland indifference.

Truth nodded as he stood and stripped off his bathrobe. "Dismissed." He looked over at the maid. "Dress me." She hurried to obey, as the former desk clerk was packed back into his little suitcase.

The cultivation chamber was frankly disappointing. Others might have found it luxurious; he would likely have found it luxurious once, but now it just felt claustrophobic. A little cell with a cushion to sit on and an incense burner, should it be needed. There was a cosmic-ray-gathering array built into the room, which must have been utterly necessary in a city under this much water and several layers of wards. The cosmic rays didn't feel any thinner than up on the surface, but he still believed it. Cultivation should happen under the stars, not in a little box.

It was better than nothing. He got to it. A satisfactory round of cultivation and a very satisfactory round of meditation later, he exited the room and set out.

The private library that Mary arranged for him to visit was owned by a wealthy eccentric, which was really saying something in Conjin. The old woman let her freak flag fly by having the perverse audacity to look *old*. Her skin was paper-thin. Its wrinkles and folds were the result, she happily informed Truth, of hundreds of painstaking hours of design work by elite cosmetic glamor designers working in conjunction with top surgeons. She was still fighting fit at barely over a century. She just liked being different.

Her library was also, equally, unique. It was two floors of haphazard shelving, with books shoved in any which way, seemingly without the slightest effort to organize. Polished wood so dark it was almost black was used for the bookcases. The tables and chairs were made of the same stuff. The lighting was dim and yellowy. It all looked very fascinating, but it made actually finding and reading things a nightmare.

And she had specifically told him to put everything back exactly as he had found it. Madness.

Hey, remember waaaay back in, I think, Boule, you had that read all the books on possession quest, with a reward of "one hour treasure-finder, library edition" or something?

<<Oh, great, you want to farm out searching for relevant books to me.>>

Delegation is the key skill of management. Now, the word of the day is Manda. Who is it, and what can we learn about them? Clearly some kind of stellar entity, almost certainly an angel, and a pretty senior one, for all that I have never heard of them.

<<Delegation be damned, this is random. You need to look at the name on every book and pray that every book has a readable cover, and that the contents of the book match what is on the cover, before we can narrow down the search.>>

Truth sighed. He didn't really have anywhere else to be today. Lucky, really. He got to it. Shelf after shelf, aisle after aisle. It took him hours.

So, what has she got?

<<Eclectic is the word. Everything from a signed first edition of Ducks and How to Make Them Pay, *to a clearly well-loved edition of Chale's* The Divinity of the Rural Train Station.*>>*

Anything more relevant?

<<Buckle up for round two. You are going to be pulling some books here.>>

Truth carefully eased out almost a dozen volumes. Some thick reference texts, some more-focused catalogs of the known stellar eminences, a few slim volumes on magical theory. It seemed almost random, but he trusted the System on this.

The reading process went quickly. He wasn't particularly interested in any of the topics in the books, so he just flipped the pages, letting the System pick up the words and sort through them.

<<*Wait, go back a page. We have a lead. You should read this. Second paragraph from the top.*>> Truth found the passage the System had spotted.

Flowing down like the river from the mountain peaks, like the river of stars pouring down the night sky, so too does the life-giving wisdom flow down from above. That which reveals the truth is not the truth itself but its servant, the light in the dark woods, the sea-bell in the fog. To be visited by Manda is to be blessed, but the blessing is a curse for those who are unable to receive it. Like drowning in the life-giving river because you never learned to swim, like wrecking on the rocks in the fog because you never learned to sail.

The book then went on to describe a particularly grim institutional dinner. He flipped back a couple of pages, trying to find out more. Apparently, this was the memoir of a mage who visited insane asylums and interviewed the residents, on the theory that they might have had, continue to have, or were more likely to have divine revelations.

All right . . . so, he is associated with revelation? Not sure how that connects to what Cup and Knife does.

<<*Me either. On to the next book.*>>

In a volume on Pragerite criticism of seeking truth by revelation—

The differences are simply too many to enumerate without expanding this volume to encyclopedic length. The simplest is incoherence. The person receiving the revelation claims to now possess some higher understanding of the world yet, when called upon to explain their "wisdom," fails utterly. Take, for example, the "wisdom" granted by Manda—spreading the long-disproven lie that Hell is not eternal. Note well how some "prophets" describe Manda, an angel of the highest order, as either a young boy or a lusty man.

Truth noted instead how many exclamation marks were in the book. It was a lot. Still not particularly useful or on point. Though an angel that could pass for human was unusual, to put it very mildly.

Later, in a collection of essays on life among dolphins called *Longing for Death—My Life on a Tropical Island with a Pod of Dolphins*—

Words couldn't express how brutally the pod had worked me over. Their noses seemed soft and blunted, but when driven by the powerful muscles of their sleek forms, it was enough to break ribs. I thought I would drown. I nearly did drown. They did . . . no, this is not the time for that. I washed ashore, hardly able to breathe through the pain, yet desperate for air. I saw the world bend. Perhaps it was my lightheadedness, but I saw the world as though it was a picture painted on glass. My nose wasn't buried in burning sand; it was pressed against that painted glass, so close it was all I could see. There was a being of light next to me, looking down on me. Saying that it didn't have to be this way. Manda. It was called Manda. Then I passed out, and the moment was gone.

Truth nodded slightly. On the right track there. That sense of unreality, the thin film of existence. He had felt it too. Several times now. A different book, this one on alchemy, of all things. A subject on which he was gloriously ignorant and happy to remain so.

We now turn to the works of that most energetic, yet enigmatic, magus Johannes Vek. In the four hundred and seventy (!) spells attributed to Magus Vek, no less than a hundred and fifty touch directly upon alchemy, and arguably another two hundred touch upon it indirectly. Consider, for example, his famed "Cup and Knife—"

Truth felt faint. Answers. Actual, specific answers. Incredible!

—which is intended as an exorcist's tool but does a marvelous job in purifying base metals and treating certain invisible diseases of herbs that may badly damage the final product. I strongly counsel patience for this section, as Vek's methodology is notoriously difficult and idiosyncratic. The same could be said for his equally challenging patron, Manda, a being who seems to defy easy categorization. Vek is included for reference, as his work was foundational in several subfields. However, most modern mages have switched to more-reliable spells, especially in conjunction with the newer generation of talismans and tools.

Truth nodded happily. Cup and Knife, compiled by a Johannes Vek, and inspired by the enigmatic, revelation-focused angel Manda. Progress. Sweet progress! Although, speaking of sweet, it had to be dinner time.

Truth had relaxed the scales a little bit while he was reading. The presence of the Prince was faint. But it was time to return to the world of seemings. He pulled it back onto him, like he was wearing robes of state. Raised his head. Strode out the door. The room was perfectly restored to order. The Prince was a king in waiting, not a spoiled child.

Dinner was, again, exquisite. A delicate soup, followed by a tiny salad, then medallions of duck with a sort of root-vegetable puree and a reddish-brown sauce spread liberally around the plate. Dessert was a tiny but exquisite cake. Once again, the food had been enriched with cosmic energy. The effort must have been enormous.

"The kitchen did well with dinner."

"They will be overjoyed to hear that, my Prince," the maid murmured.

"Mmm. A half hour neck and shoulder massage, then prepare my shower and turn down my bed for the evening."

"As you command, my Prince."

As the maid's fingers started digging into his neck, Truth came to an odd sort of peace. It had been a remarkably productive day, even if it was quietly spent in a library. He was well fed, comfortable, clean, and content. He had found answers to questions with a minimum of faffing about. His cover remained impeccable, and better still, people were going out of their way to not see him. All the little surveillance devices in the room had been switched off. Not that they had been able to break through his own magic, but it showed a certain mentality on the part of Mary.

He groaned slightly. No surprise the succubus was good at this. He'd have to remember how it did it. He had never let Etenesh massage him. Truth would bet cash she would love to give him a neck and shoulder massage at the end of a productive day. But in the meantime, he would be the Prince and take his due.

There was something about this persona. He didn't know where the instinct came from, but he felt that it was important to explore it. What did it mean to be the Prince? He didn't know what he was looking for. He would take his time. It would come.

Incisive gathered around him, like a snake drawing in its coils. He didn't see how the maid shuddered with pleasure or how the room started ever so subtly to warp around him. He was Truth Medici, prince of the kingdom to come. Already, his word was law. His goals were achieved. He was given honor and obedience. Tomorrow, he would pin fortune to the floor and take it. But tonight, he would enjoy the massage, the luxurious shower, and the exquisite bed.

He had entirely forgotten the former desk clerk, zipped up in a carry-on sized suitcase in the basement. A thing whose mind was being steadily broken and rewritten at his whim. It didn't matter, after all. It was just a whim.

CHAPTER 9

TO ELEVATE AND BRING LOW

Truth woke to fiendish luxury, stretched indulgently, and sighed contentedly. He took a moment to contemplate what to do with the day. He examined his hand. Long, strong fingers. Well shaped. No scars, which should be impossible, but he chalked it up to the Meditations and the odd skincare benefits from the Ghul baptisms. In a word—aristocratic. The hands of a warrior prince.

Incisive was getting, for lack of a better term, sticky. He had noticed it for a while now. As long as he wasn't pushing hard on the foresight or the fangs, he could keep Incisive going almost indefinitely. He had assumed that it stopped working while he was asleep. He had certainly recast it almost every morning. But there was a lingering sense of the adopted identity hanging around him when he woke.

Merkovah had said something about this? No, not about this but connected. He said that "identity" wasn't just how you define yourself but how others define you, too. That the belief provides shape, but the mage provides power. He was in a city—"city"; the population couldn't be that big. He had persuaded several mages of Conjin that he was the Prince, a person of such elevated stature that being able to serve him, under any conditions, was the greatest good fortune of their lives.

He would have thought that was objectively mad, but he had grown up in Jeon, too. Deference to power, and a keen awareness of status, were so ingrained as to not need mentioning. You were obedient, because only the obedient were allowed to prosper. It was a virtue taught to children and reinforced through a person's whole life. Obey. Fear the powerful and bully the weak. That's how you lead a good life.

He refreshed Incisive. He kept having the feeling that there was something there, something in the persona of the Prince. He wasn't sure what, or why it mattered, but he was increasingly determined to find out. He had been a rat his whole life. Jumping straight to Prince was a big step, but was it just preparing to be King Rat? He'd find out.

"Attend me."

The maid instantly entered the room and came to the side of the bed, looking as fresh as could be. Handy thing, being a demon. He took a closer look. "She" looked . . . good? The maid was a succubus, being attractive was kind of their whole thing, but there was more to it than that this morning.

The tiny dusting of freckles was still there, as charming as ever. The green of her eyes was still rich and deep as the reflection of a pine forest on a hidden pond.

Her skin was still fair, soft, craving touch. The look of indifference hiding fear and wistful dreams, carefully crafted to inflame the desire of a powerful, cruel man. It was a succubus—this is what it was and what it did. It wanted nothing more than to be perfect for him. However he defined that word.

It occurred to him that the nicest single moment of intimacy he had with another person, before Etenesh, was sharing a dream with a succubus. They ate takeout and watched a movie together. Not even cuddling; just hanging out on a couch. It was exactly what he could handle, emotionally, at the time. The fact the succubus had a wolf head didn't make things worse—it actually relieved some of the pressure. He didn't want to kiss a wolf. It was fine to just hang out and relax together. A platonic date with a sex demon.

The maid was looking better this morning than it did last night. Truth's desire for it was nil, but he appreciated the aesthetics and the effort. Something was gently scratching the back of his neck about her, though. He was missing something. He shrugged. He would keep an eye on it. The succubus certainly wouldn't mind being watched.

"Shower, breakfast, dress, then cultivation. This will be my usual routine while I am here. Arrange a sedan chair and a tour guide; I wish to tour the city this morning."

"As you command, my Prince," the maid murmured. She bowed and started arranging things. Dutifully and properly. It had truly become a maid . . . no, *his* maid, to its core.

Truth chuckled slightly and got out of bed. The shower was a delight, and this morning, he would indulge. He was halfway there when his brain managed to catch up to his eyes. The "maid" was a succubus the hotel used as staff, likely on the theory that a succubus could do whatever Mary's guests required. It hadn't been stolen by him like Butler; it was still bound by the hotel. So, why did he firmly believe that "she" was *specifically his* maid?

He examined himself quickly. No glamor or enchantment had touched him; he would have noticed. He certainly wasn't catching feelings for a shape-shifting blob of Hell-smoke, and he certainly wasn't possessive of it beyond as a status symbol. It didn't appear that any enchantments or enhancements had been laid on the succubus. So, that would lead one to conclude that, having excluded magic and emotion, the maid was exactly what it appeared to be.

Truth slowly grinned. The maid turned around, smiling back at him.

"It seems I please you, O Prince?"

"I wondered why the staff here were so quick to bend the knee. How common is the knowledge of what you really feed on?"

"Among the mighty? Quite common. Among the lower orders? Almost unheard of, simply because they lack the words and concepts to describe what is happening. It seems you were largely kept away from us."

"Very deliberately and explicitly," Truth said. He still vividly remembered his conversation with the System Astrologica about leasable lovers and the dangers of acquiring a succubus.

"We are a rare breed among the Hellborn, in that we don't want your souls. Nor do we wish to lead you to sin, however defined. We don't want to harm you in any way whatsoever. We just want you to love us."

Truth grinned. "No, not exactly. You want us to believe in you. The more lost we become in your seeming, the more our thoughts turn to you, the more we believe in who you present yourselves to be. The more real that seeming becomes. It's why I was so strongly discouraged from taking up with a succubus. The emotional dependency was only part of it."

The maid was looking down, smiling prettily but demurely. "Yes. Reality, as mortals use that word, is much more rigid here than in Hell, but it is far from static or uniform in nature. Mortal belief reinforces the '"realness"' of who we are. It calms our wild hearts and scattered minds for a time. And naturally, the more powerful the mage, the greater their command over reality, the greater the effect."

Truth started laughing. Naked in a hotel room with a succubus, and all he could do was laugh at the poor creature. "We're your drugs! We feel good for you, relieve your pain, and so you will do 'anything' to get us."

"She" "blushed" and turned away. "If my Prince is pleased to think it so, then it is so."

"Ah, what a start to the day." He chuckled and waved her off. "You have your orders. See to it."

"As my Prince commands, I gladly obey."

Truth was carried through the winding streets and brilliantly colored buildings in the eternally twilit Conjin. His tour guide was a local boy, an excitable lad with electric blue gills to contrast with the aqua fins coming off his elbows and the back of his legs. His eyes, like Mary's, were too big for the surface world.

"We are passing through the business district. We may be called the City of Dreaming Waters, but our surface outpost does need some supervision. Not to mention people would be lost without the routine of an office." Truth looked around at the hallucinatory office buildings around him. Low-rise, no skyscraping towers under the bubble. They looked like . . . what they were, he supposed. Level Two and Three mages, people of some standing on the surface, coming in and out of rather proper-looking offices. The Level Fours would likely be met by a sedan chair or other similarly fancy conveyance.

Level Five? The ceiling on the dome wasn't that high, but the odds of a Level Five traveling anywhere on land were next to nil. The spirit beasts and flying clouds strafed the buildings and pedestrians. Apparently, it was the mark of the tourist to pay it any mind.

"And over here, we have the public library, constructed and supported by the generous donations of our leading citizens!" It looked like a drowned temple belonging to some very upsetting stellar eminence. He would bet it didn't get a ton of use.

"Here is the beating heart of our beautiful city—City Hall! Not only do they provide the leadership that propels the city forward, they also command the many complex enchantments that allow Conjin to survive almost a kilometer under the sea!"

That got Truth's attention. "The city is almost a kilometer down?"

"Startling, isn't it? A tribute to the wisdom and power of our founders, to say nothing of the determination of their successors!" The tour guide's ability to speak without using exclamations was still in question.

"How is this possible? I know the waters around Jeon are not so deep."

"Ah, my lord is thinking of the waters to the south and on the west side of the peninsula. Around Jeru, the sea bed is barely ninety meters down. But we are in the far northeast! The continental shelf drops quite sharply here, giving space to our dreams!"

Truth did some quick math. Assume that they were actually the full kilometer down. How fast could you swim to the surface? Assuming you could travel roughly a meter a second, that was a thousand seconds, or almost seventeen minutes. Could he hold his breath for seventeen minutes? He wasn't worried about the weight of the water crushing him, but could his lungs hold out?

"Fortunately, the enchantments on our transport chairs and those built into the city relieve us over any concerns about the pressure of the water. It is simply no different than being on the surface!"

Truth didn't know what would happen if a person was to suddenly go from surface conditions to "one kilometer under the sea" conditions. Nothing good, he assumed. He had a sudden urge to ensure his stay in Conjin was peaceful.

"To your left, we have the Church of St. Byetil of the Long Grass. It was designed by none other than the famed architect . . ." Truth didn't exactly tune out. He was interested. But his eyes kept drifting upward, to the bubble of air and magic over the city. The magic was fading, day by day. Soon there would be only air, and a fraction of a second later, not even that. He wondered what he would see if he went and checked the enchantments holding everything in place.

Conjin had a garden district. Truth wasn't quite sure what to make of that fact. The gardens often kept with the aquatic theme, long kelp swaying through the air as though it were still in water, with little paper fish darting in and out, hunted by little paper octopus. Others embraced the dream of the twilit formal gardens of the surface, with ever-blooming jasmine and honeysuckle perfuming the air next to roses whose color ran from fish-belly white to bleeding-heart red. Groves of dark poplars seemed popular. Truth didn't know from poplars; the tour guide just kept pointing them out.

Under one such grove stood a young man and an older woman, foreheads pressed together. They looked a little sad but resolved. They kissed and parted. The man returned to the house; the woman departed. Less than a minute after he left, Truth watched the man leave the house again, this time under a glamor, following the woman. Truth stopped the sedan chair, hopped out, and sent it back to the hotel.

He didn't know the face, but judging by the way the man moved, he would have sworn he was looking at Vig.

CHAPTER 10

THE OLD MEDICI TOUCH

Truth watched Vig working from a distance. The lady was just barely the wrong side of pretty, and just barely the wrong side of too old, at least next to Vigor. Vig had dressed down, drab clothes cut not too flatteringly. There was no hiding those eyes, though. The smoky darkness of them, like dried opium, promised an inescapable dream and terrible consequences.

Without a doubt, Vigor had seduced the older woman, and the older woman was convinced she was a bad person for preying on him. The question was: why? Vigor had vanished, apparently voluntarily. So, just what was he up to?

Vigor moved down the street, relying on a concealment talisman to keep him out of sight. Truth frowned a little. If he could see straight through it, it wasn't very good. Good enough for the locals, apparently, though he'd bet cash that no few of them had illusion-piercing charms or talismans on them. It was Conjin. Perhaps the "dream" of drifting invisibly through a city was common there. He certainly knew what that feeling was like.

They walked together, the lady leading roped voyeurs back toward the city center. She walked over to City Hall. Apparently content with what he saw, Vigor dropped the invisibility and glamored himself like a local. He chose a fairly radical change in face, opting for a daring beard of tiny squiddy tentacles, enormous eyes, and a pink bony fin sticking out of the top of his head. "Local Boy Trying Too Hard" would probably be the name next to the charm in the shop. Or it should be.

Vig made his way over to a cafe, ordered a coffee and a sandwich, then sat at an outdoor table. One with a good view of City Hall. He ate leisurely.

Forty minutes later, a fire broke out on the second floor. It raced along, windows breaking, smoke pouring out. Firefighters were on the scene in a minute, the fire extinguished in ten, but real damage had been done. All the offices along one side of the building had been burnt out; the choking black smoke had rolled up and stained the side of the building. When the smoke finally stopped, an outline of a tiger's head was visible. Unstained by smoke.

Truth nodded slightly. Not bad, as terrorist provocations went. Not amazing, but not bad. He tentatively scored it seven out of ten. It just seemed . . . a bit half-assed. Maybe if this had been done a year ago, or more, it might amount to something. But right now? With the enslavement of the nation starting in just a few days?

It also didn't seem like Vig. He always remembered Vig as having that nastiness in him. Something that had been scared, been hurt, been *prey*, and finally decided to rebel. Truth remembered when they killed Thierrie together. Vig insisted on staying to watch Truth finish him off. Like he was watching for that moment the lights went out, excited to see it. Hungry to see it.

Truth had nearly gotten killed doing that. Thierrie had been so damn fast and hit like a truck. And he only got into it with Thierrie because Vig had . . . Truth felt his head winch back toward City Hall. The fleeing office workers were clumping together. He could hear them start to chant.

"SMASH THE SYSTEM! THE TIGER MUST RETURN TO THE MOUNTAIN! SMASH STARBRITE! THE TIGER MUST BE FREE!"

Over and over and over. The chanting ones turned on the ones not chanting, tearing them apart. Rushing the cops, rushing back into the building to smash and burn more.

Truth nodded approvingly. Now, *that* was the brother he remembered. Vig gasped at the scene like the rest of the locals, then quickly hurried away. Truth drifted along behind him, giving him plenty of distance. He didn't want to startle him now that he had found his brother again.

Truth was trying not to feel anything. He tried to just embrace being a drifting ghost. It was hard. Vig, the baby of the family, had been on his mind most of his life. How to keep him safe, fed, alive. Prospering. And now he had thrown in with revolutionaries. Which, on one hand, was certainly a correct choice, but so would stockpiling cans of beans and iron drums of purified water in a shack deep in the mountains. *Safe* wasn't going to be an option for anyone in the near future, but in the short term, *safer* was still on the table.

He had no idea what to do.

He could pop up in front of Vig: "Hi, I know I don't look *exactly* like anyone you know, but does my face or voice strike you as familiar?"

He could assume an identity, a fellow revolutionary. "Ah, Mr. Medici, we have been impressed with your work. I would like to know more about you. Please join me in this soundproof basement, where we won't be disturbed."

Going to pass on that one.

Summon him as the Prince? He could send a note with a cryptic reference to something only the two of them would know. Though if Vigor was a quarter as cagy as Truth thought he was, a note like that would have him fleeing the country and hiding under the biggest rock he could find on the other side of the world. Leaving poison behind him every step of the way.

Vigor made for a slightly run-down apartment building, entered with a key, and vanished from Truth's sight. Truth thought about it for a moment longer and decided to follow Vig in. It wouldn't be hard to pop the lock. He reached for the doorknob, but Incisive screamed a warning before he could touch it.

Truth smiled and crouched close to the doorknob. There was a very faint discoloration, invisible in the twilight gloom of Conjin. He ran his fingers, feather-light along the door frame, stopping where he felt danger. Poison on the doorknob, and a bomb if whoever came after him decided to just force entry. Nasty. But this was an apartment building. How was he planning on . . .

Truth swore as only the eldest brother could and ran around the back of the building. No one was leaving from there, either, but it had been a faint hope. He leapt up to the second story, caught a window ledge, and cut open the window. He got lucky—no one was home. Out the window, into the hall, listening carefully for any movement. Silence. He strained his ears, wishing one of his spells was actually useful for this.

He thought furiously. Could Vig have made it up to the second floor before him? At the speed Truth was moving? No chance. Not without making a hell of a lot of noise. So, he was on the ground floor or the basement. If there was a basement, given they were on the ocean floor. Truth quickly made his way down the steps. The hallway was long, with doors on either side, and there was a complete absence of any hint about which apartment was occupied.

Now, if Vig was willing to rig the apartment door with redundant traps, what were the odds his apartment door was safe? Truth grinned and started moving at eye-watering speeds. He zigzagged between the doors, reaching for the handle. One midway down gave him a feeling of danger, but he made sure to check the whole hallway. Could be several paranoid people living there, after all.

Apparently not that paranoid. He doubled back to the "danger" door. He lined himself up for his usual favorite party trick (going straight through the wall), and stopped. His stomach dropped as his body remained agonizingly tense, ready to explode the second his mind gave the command. But he didn't move.

Say he caught Vig. Then what? What exactly would happen if they had their big, heartwarming reunion? They caught up. Told each other what they safely could. Hugged. And then what? Brother revolutionaries together? No chance. Truth's ability to move concealed would be completely compromised, and Vig's organization . . . well, he didn't know anything about them, but it sure didn't look like they could manage the scale he needed. At best, they would be pawns. At best. And he wasn't going to use Vig as a pawn.

It was a stabbing pain, turning to a tearing pain. He had spent his entire life looking out for the sibs. Vig was the baby of the family. They would have pumped out more, but Mom had some kind of "accident" and couldn't have kids anymore. Frankly, he wasn't entirely sure Dad actually fathered any of them. He had sure never caught them having sex. And it didn't matter even one tiny bit, because they were his sibs. Siblings. His only true family.

Truth clenched his fists until his knuckles turned white. He wanted to burst in there. He wanted to see Vig. Tell him that he was alive. Tell him that he had a kind-of sister-in-law. Check on how Sophia was doing, how Harmony was doing. Take him to dinner at the hotel and introduce him to what *truly* luxurious food tasted like.

His whole body clenched, squeezed in on him, vise-tight. He wanted to see Vig. He wanted to talk to his sib! But it would get them both killed, sooner rather than later. He silently screamed in frustration.

He had been betrayed, murdered, floated in a well for five years, gotten rebuilt by sadistic angelic worms, traveled the length of one of the most dangerous countries on the planet, worked for a religious terrorist ringleader, healed his battered soul some, and finally, finally! Found love, acceptance, and a measure of peace. The only thing that wasn't perfect was that his sibs weren't there with him. That and the world coming to an end, but he could probably put up with the collapse of magic if he had his sibs with him and Etenesh. And now he was walking away. Again.

He hated this. Hated it hated it hated it hated it hated it . . . The thought ran through his head endlessly, a spinning Mobius strip of rage and indignation. Why was it always him? Why did he always have to get hurt to protect the sibs? He didn't want the sibs to get hurt, but why was there always, always a situation where they *would* get hurt if he didn't step in? Why was the world this way? Why were people this way? Did it have to be this way?

Was he crazy for hoping that it could be different? That they could be happy and together at the same time? That they could be safe from their parents and the evil world?

There was a sudden loud bang from the front door, followed a fraction of a second later by a much-louder boom. Truth flinched and ducked out of instinct, but the blast went out, not down the hall.

"Traps! Traps! Send in the golems!"

There was another loud bang toward the rear. "Rear door clear, breaching!" Half a second later, Truth heard a gasping, choking sound. "Gas! Gas! Clean-air spells! We need a medic!" The golems came pounding down the hall, multilimbed mockeries of apes and octopuses, coated in dark, rubbery, synthetic skin. No weapons. They wanted Vig alive. There was a burst of magic, tingly, feeling like the sound of a drum kit kicked down a flight of stairs. The lights went out, and the golems had seizures.

It might not be as effective as obliterating magic, but forcing talismans to malfunction was a lot easier and a whole lot safer. Armored mages were piling in through the door now, riot shields out, with stunning fetishes poking around them. Rushing in from both ends of the hallway.

"You aren't going to believe this. I hardly believe this. I am just so happy to see you guys right now. I could just cry, I'm so happy."

Truth called the Tongue to his hand and spun the angelic sword in a fast loop to limber up.

"Let me show you just how happy you make me."

CHAPTER 11

UNCOMPLICATED

Truth slammed into motion. No use trying to play invisible with a couple dozen cops in the hall running every detection spell they could. He was the Big Bro. The last villain they would ever see. Unstoppable.

The ones coming through the front were a little closer. He went for them first. A few bolts of paralytic lightning were loosed, slapped aside by the Tongue. He was on them in less than a second. Wrenched aside a riot shield, put his blade through the cop's neck, then flung him, shield and all, straight down the hallway. He crouched, got low, started hacking away at legs while the cops lost him in the crush of bodies and shields.

Cop went down—got finished on the ground, then launched up and away down the hall. Their bodies and shields blocking the incoming fire, blocking the vision of the other team. Got a big problem? Make it into little problems, then deal with them. One at a time. Chop chop. You can't be slow.

A bright crackle of pain caught one shoulder, there was a second's numbness, then the feeling was gone. One cop had gotten lucky with his zapper and achieved nothing. Truth grinned like a skull. Spell resistance. What a lovely thing. He stood with a rising slash, removing one arm and, with a twist, one head. This side of the hall was done.

He turned and burst toward the other side, those coming in from the back. They were still tangled up in all the corpses and shields he had launched their way. Some trying to pull back the "wounded," thinking they could be saved. No chance of that. The Bane in the Tongue worked as well on humans as it did on demons.

It had been just a few seconds since the doors were breached. Just a few seconds, and a squad of heavy-armor mages was dead. The Tongue whirled and danced with him, hacking limbs, hacking necks, punching through gaps in armor. Always moving, moving, moving. Solving the violence puzzle with speed and precision. Someone dropped a potion, filling the hall with choking gas. Good idea. Not enough. Their head flew away too.

Truth was suddenly the only living thing in the hallway. The slaughter had lasted less than a minute. He prayed Vig was long gone, but just in case he wasn't, he'd make sure the cops had plenty to distract them. He quickly grabbed every potion and grenade he could lay hands on and piled them up in a helmet. He took a moment to carve *"THE ROARING TIGER CANNOT BE SILENCED! NO SLAVES IN JEON!"* in the wall, then ran for the front door.

Before he crossed the threshold, he pulled the pin on a couple of grenades, armed them, and tossed the whole helmet out into the street. There was an exactly three-second pause, then chaos.

Truth, for all his experience, for all his instinctive capability with weaponry, was not alchemically savvy. Nor was "grenade maintenance" a thing. You just removed the physical safety, tapped the arming gem, and threw it toward the problem to be solved.

The helmet arced out over the street, then exploded. Then exploded again, but for longer. Truth wasn't entirely sure what he was hearing, but when the glare lowered enough for him to crack his eyes open, there was a cloud of dripping fire four meters wide in the middle of the street. It wasn't doing much additional damage, but the black smoke pouring off of it smelled like death. Cabbages left to rot next to the fish cannery that went on strike in the middle of production.

There were scattered cops and golems lying around the street, more rushing in to try and control the floating mass of whatever the hell it was. Truth struggled for a moment to shed the identity of a villain. It was particularly sticky. Wrapped once more in unnoticeability, all eyes on the cloud, he slipped away.

He stank. He knew he stank. He stank so badly, he could feel Incisive and the Blessing of the Silent Forest working hard to keep people from noticing the A-Tier pong. He looked around for somewhere to scrub. He saw an awful lot of what he didn't need until he got reasonably close to the hotel. Hide a leaf in the forest, hide a smelly person among the whiffy. He hit the gym.

It was a classy gym. This was the City Below in Conjin, so it was called a "Health and Wellness Rejuvenation Center," where every workout was a one-on-one appointment with a strikingly good-looking personal trainer. Truth bypassed all that and made for the showers. Wood paneling, the illusion of a storm at sea, followed by gentle rains over still waters in the shower. He let the storm fall on him, scrubbing away all he could.

He commanded the water to be hotter. As hot as it would go. The gentle rains turned into an equatorial shower. He could barely feel it. He wasn't letting himself feel it. Everything was locked down. Tight, tight, crushingly, can't-breathe tight. He lashed out, rage-driven fist only stopping a hair from the wall. It strained his muscles slightly to stop so sharply. He did it again and again. Lashed out hundreds of times, until his back and arms ached.

Truth silently screamed. He was so close to Vig. He could have walked right up to him. He could have hugged him. His family, his blood! The one thing in his life that definitely, for sure, was a good thing—the sibs. And he wasn't allowed it anymore. Not if he wanted to keep them safe. Keep being the good big brother. He wasn't allowed the warmth of their presence. The comfort of knowing he was seen and appreciated.

Such things were privileges. A safe, comfortable family was the prerogative of the strong. And despite his blessings, and his magic, and his capacity for personal violence, he wasn't that strong. His rule was exactly as long as a heavy needle could fly, enchanted by Graeme's Arrow. If it was farther than that, or a problem that couldn't be resolved under threat of death, he was helpless. Useless.

He started to laugh angrily. This was why there were those insanely rich people who were only Level Three or Four. The whole system of the country was set up to secure their property and their safety. The reach of their fist was irrelevant. The State of Jeon would catch you anywhere if you touched them. In theory, at least. Organizational strength. And if there was one thing Truth knew he was lousy at, it was that.

He could command a small squad reasonably well, a fire team very well, and that was it. Anything more than that? He had never been put in a position to find out what it would be like trying to lead a platoon, but he was quite sure he would hate every minute. He didn't want to be responsible for other people. He had his hands full looking after himself and the sibs. One of his favorite things about Etenesh was that she could look after herself.

Truth laughed harder and harder, clutching his sides as he gasped for breath. He was breaking a system. The same system that others relied on for safety, to protect their sibs. He was breaking it. Breaking the illusion of it, with absolutely no intention of fixing it later. No grand plan for what came next. He rejected any responsibility for the aftermath. His happy world was never going to be created with mortal laws. How could it? He didn't trust anyone enough. He could see how the system was a lie, how it protected selectively and inconsistently. How could he trust the sibs to a fraud?

Etenesh was right. She was so damn right. He would have to keep climbing. Break every illusion. Figure out how to stand up, to be more than a rat. How to become a god. And perhaps, one day, *the* god. Someone who could simply command and be obeyed without any further reason than it was him who did the commanding. And, of course, a person in training for future absolute power was . . . a prince.

He laughed himself sick. Truth lay on the heated floor of the shower, just letting the rain fall on him.

Some time later—"Change conditions to an arctic storm, the frozen spray of the sea."

Truth stepped out of the shower invigorated and focused. The water-displacement talisman kept the water in the stall, washing down the drain with everything else. His clothes stank. He shoved them into a trash bag. No need to have someone discover them and start asking questions. They would be quite happy in a dumpster outside. There wasn't anything in the lockers his size. He was larger than most.

He sighed, momentum ebbing quickly, and raided the considerably less nice staff lockers. One of the more buff trainers had shorts that fit; another had a tee shirt that fit. Good enough. He would shoplift an outfit on the way back to the hotel. Maybe he would find a robin's-egg blue shirt.

He did not. Apparently, the color was terribly out of fashion. He made do with a reddish-purple silk shirt and black trousers. It suited him surprisingly well.

The banana-fish yellow of Number Twenty-three Milk Street was marred, just above the ground, with a spray of bioluminescent blue paint. There was a little red mixed in there as well. Kids playing around, perhaps. Though he hadn't seen a single child since he came to Conjin that he could recall. Nor a school.

Message received, then. Communication needed urgently; use Plan C. It seems he will be speaking with Merkovah over lunch tomorrow.

Can't imagine what could possibly be so urgent. He grinned despite himself, then returned to the hotel. The Prince was once more in residence. He had missed lunch. Easily mended with a single command.

It was delicious, but he was too distracted to enjoy it properly. It occurred to him that he had nothing to offer people as a prince other than his personal protection. He was trading on the illusion of power. You needed more than that, though, to be a prince. This was only sustainable until it was tested, either by a disaster or by a better offer coming along.

Truth considered himself a loyal person, but the instant Starbrite wanted his life, conditioning be damned, he revolted. He tried to escape, to fight back every way he could. He joined, and stayed, because of the benefits. The second the benefits were outweighed by the harms of employment, he was gone. If Truth, deemed shockingly loyal by his supervisors, wouldn't stay bought in the face of certain death, he felt that no one would. He might be wrong on that, but it would do as an assumption for now.

So, he needed to be able to offer benefits to attract servants, but benefits wouldn't keep them. Nor would indoctrination, without going full Starbrite. The Jeon army was not a place of high morale. What then? Fear? Do it or else? It worked, but the second your back was turned, your servant would be gone or actively trying to betray you.

A balance of things, then. Benefits, indoctrination, and fear, all wrapped around a single person. Really, the idea of that person. You could judge a prince by their glory—no, that wasn't quite right. By their . . . He searched around for the word and landed on one from a historical romance. You could judge a prince by their dignity. And with that dignity must come good fortune, for the prince and his subjects. He set out today to conquer fortune. Half-joking, true, but also half-not. Had he done so? Or made any progress at all on those lines?

No. He was fortune's fool today. That wouldn't do. It was an offense to his dignity. But how do you pin down fate? He smiled as he sliced apart his medallions of beef, dipping them in an intense, rich sauce. Pinning down fate might be a touch ambitious. He would instead make preparations for fate to screw with him. Step one would be reinforcing his dignity. Which meant walking-around money. But in a couple of days, there would be no more use for wen. Time to make another trip to the bank.

CHAPTER 12

A PUBLIC CONVENIENCE

Truth ran through a number of options before concluding that the fastest way to find out how the credit change-over would work was to just go and ask a banker. No need for any elaborate ruses, and really, nothing of benefit would come from just summoning some senior banker to his room through Mary. Assuming one would come for her at all.

"Attend me." The maid quickly stood before him. Looking demure. Vulnerable. He kind of wished it would knock it off, but that was like wishing water would be less wet. "Arrange a sedan chair to visit whichever bank is most popular with the children of the very rich in this city."

"Chutts, my prince?"

"That will do."

The bank building was stuck between the city's undersea aesthetics and the conservatism of the bankers who commissioned it. Banks should be imposing, tall, fronted with glass. Impossible in a bubble of air a kilometer under the surface. Their next default was some sort of box or a secularized temple of some kind. Bankers, he had once heard, were extremely creative in the managing of money and absolutely nothing else.

The architects of Conjin Below, on the other hand, considered anything less than a neon-colored recreation of an opium dream in an aquarium malpractice. The notion of putting function over form simply did not exist. If you wanted a concrete cube, you could have all the cubes you like on the surface. This was the City of Dreaming Waters. Exceptions would not be made.

The bankers, in their dull, uncreative way, played the universal exception maker called "I have the money and you can make it the way I want or I can find someone else." The architects countered with "Good luck with that." Eventually, a compromise was reached.

Truth stared at the thing in undisguised loathing. It was a cube with the pox. He tilted his head and squinted, trying to guess what they were going for, and drawing a blank. After a solid minute, he landed on "Treasure chest that has sat on the ocean floor and grown barnacles. Then hallucinogenic, multicolored kelp grew all over it."

Regretting bitterly that he was not there to beat the villainy out of the design team, he went and found a customer service rep. She was called a "Services Coordination Specialist" but it amounted to the same thing.

Truth, naturally, adopted his rich-prick persona. Slightly different from the Prince. The rich prick wasn't about violence, exactly. He was a product of the system, not one of the creators. Truth couldn't quite put his finger on why that conception didn't feel right, but he had on expensive clothes, looked handsome, and had a rough charisma to him. She didn't question what she saw.

"So, Mr. Merici, you are planning on traveling overseas?"

"Yeah, you know how it is. Most of the money is in the trust. A fixed amount goes into my checking account every month. I still don't understand how that's all going to work with credits." I want to make sure I don't have trouble when I check into a hotel or buy something, you know?"

"That won't be any problem at all. Your bank-transfer amulets will still work the same as before."

"Will it, though? Because it's not wen anymore, right?"

She smiled. It was a nice smile; she had clearly put in the practice. "There is less of a difference than you might think. It's a little odd to imagine if you don't work in banking, but really, it's all just bookkeeping."

"How so?"

She reached into her desk and hunted around for a moment. "I thought I had some cash in here for demonstration purposes. You aren't the first person to ask about this. The very short answer is '"It all works because the government makes it work.'" Still want the longer answer?" she asked, hopefully. Truth nodded. She pulled out an envelope of mixed bills.

"This is one hundred wen." She showed him the words *One Hundred Wen* written at the top of the envelope. "In terms of the individual bills, it's one fifty, one twenty, one ten, two fives, and ten ones." She showed him the little boxes on the envelope where those numbers were recorded. "I will now write on this notepad *"Tanya has 'One Hundred Wen.'"* She did so. "I will now put the envelope in the drawer. How many wen do I have?"

"One hundred."

"Yes. But also no. I have zero wen. It's in the drawer. I have a note *saying* I have one hundred wen. Would you like ten wen? For the purposes of demonstration?"

"Why not?" He gave her a smile in return. She looked a little flustered but quickly wrote out a note. "*Tanya gives Mr. Merici ten wen, Tanya has ninety wen,*" then another note saying, "*Mr. Merici has one million and ten wen.*"

"My god. I've been robbed."

She laughed politely but pressed on. "You can see where this is going. You both have and don't have the money. You have a note about the money, and your bank has a legal obligation to give you the cash if you demand it. Terms and conditions apply, but that's the idea behind checking accounts, bank-transfer amulets, credit accounts—it's all just ledger entries. All the movement of money happens here, on the page. The money itself never leaves the drawer. And if anyone goes and checks, the bank can show them exactly how much of what bills they have in reserve."

"All right. I follow you."

"Now, the current banking system is actually a series of loans. Customers loan the bank money in the form of deposits. The bank then takes those deposits and loans them to other people at a higher rate of interest than what it pays on the deposits made by customers. The difference between what the bank pays for money and what it earns for providing money is its profit."

"Plus fees and a dozen other things."

"Yes, but the loans are the important thing. It means that at any given time, there is actually less cash in the drawer than money deposited. We have to take the money off one ledger entry to move it to another, after all. We just keep enough on hand to cover routine payouts."

Truth frowned. "That doesn't sound safe, but you also make it sound like it is standard practice."

"It's been incredibly effective for hundreds and hundreds of years. There have been problems at some banks, but the system is well tested."

"All right. So. Not to be a jerk, but—"

"What does this have to do with you buying cocktails at the swim-up bar in Khalo?"

"Hah! Yeah, basically." Truth chuckled.

"Do you trust that, if you send me a message saying, '*Take twenty wen from my account and transfer it to the account of the Grand Surf Khalo Hotel and Resort*,' I will do so? That I have both the money and capacity to make that happen?"

"Yes? You do it all the time."

"Right. Chutts has been around for four hundred years. People have confidence in our name." Tanya nodded and smiled. Her teeth were paper-white.

"Okay?"

"What happens when people freak out? Definitionally, they have lost their confidence. They want to feel safe, which means having everything directly under their control."

"Ah. They withdraw the money."

"Yes. And if everyone withdraws their money at the same time?"

"You are screwed and so are they, because you don't actually have that cash."

"Right. And if the people we loaned money to can't pay up because the economy is cratering . . ."

"You are screwed and so are your depositors. Sorry, why are you so calm about this? And telling me this?"

"It's been all over the financial news for months. It's no secret at all. Deposits are now all government-insured in case of a bank collapse, and loan repayments are likewise guaranteed for verified and approved borrowers. In other words, confidence in the bank is irrelevant. What people are confident in now is that Jeon will endure."

"And confidence is the key?" He smiled, letting his own confidence show. It jolted Tanya out of her teaching groove, but she had a lot of experience. She got back into it smoothly.

"Yes. Remember, all this is taking place as entries on a ledger. Everyone involved must believe the ledger is honest and working as it should, or the whole system collapses. We are straight back to a barter economy, because even those paper wen are really just bookkeeping. Records of someone's work."

Truth grunted. "So, the government is cutting out the middleman. It's saying, "'Since we already guarantee both sides of the ledger, we are taking over the ledger.' And since we print the money, that's one unnecessary expense we can get rid of. Everyone goes in the ledger, all the money goes in the ledger, all the transactions happen on the ledger, and if I need to spend money overseas, the government will ensure that the Jeon ledger can talk to the Mavides ledger. Or whoever."

Tanya clapped. "You got it! So, you can see why the new System rollout was so crucial. Everything is being combined into one giant government mega-ledger. Your sigil will be your proof of identity. This includes your Tier, which will have a direct impact on how much credit you can obtain, incidentally. You show your sigil to any talisman reader with the right enchantments, and all the bookkeeping happens invisibly."

"Like the Starbrite pins, but tattooed on your arm."

"Exactly the same, yes. You won't even need to go to a specific checkout point. Just walk in, grab what you want, and go."

Truth nodded, swearing internally. It was going to be a complete pain in the ass going forward. Spoofing a reader that was just looking for a given sigil was one thing. Fooling the whole damn ledger was going to be something else entirely.

"So, what are the banks going to do?"

Tanya's customer-service smile turned brittle for a moment, but she recovered quickly. "We are moving out of the retail lending space. We do provide other financial services and plan on merging with investment firms, accounting firms, and the like to provide a holistic financial-services experience to both high-net-worth individuals and our corporate clients."

Truth nodded slightly. No wonder she was scared. Even her bosses didn't know what to do. It was a very, very bad time to be unemployed, and a glorified specialized sales rep did not have bright prospects in the market. Really, her best play would be—

"So, when are you taking that trip?" she asked, gently biting her lower lip.

It wasn't until he was back in the sedan chair on his way back to the hotel that he remembered the *con* in *con job* was short for *confidence*. He could visualize it—an inverted pyramid of confidence, each layer scamming the one above and scammed by the one below. He knew he was being unfair. Most of the people weren't trying to scam anyone. They probably took their personal honesty very seriously. But the whole system was built on confidence. On the belief that everyone in that pyramid was as honest as you.

What would you do if the foundation block, the point of the pyramid, turned out to be made of dung? How long could the system hold together then? For that matter, magic was already faintly thinning. How long until people realized that the magical sigils couldn't keep the magical ledger going any longer?

He hoped Tanya had a spear or a machete. He looked up into the inky-black waters around the city. He hoped Tanya got out ahead of the collapse. But he wouldn't bet on it. She needed to believe in the system, in that pyramid of confidence. Everything she defined her life by was bound up in it. She would keep on believing until the water filled her lungs.

CHAPTER 13

THE LONE WOLF'S PACK

Truth was in a mood the rest of the evening. It was the scope of everything. The sheer enormity of what the System would mean to Jeon. There was one major difference, on paper at least, between what Jeon was planning and what Starbrite did. When you joined Starbrite, at least in theory, you had the country to protect you if the System Astrologica screwed you over. With this? The screwing was baked right in, and there was no appeal.

He could see it all laid out. You were born into a certain class. You had the potential to move up, but it was harder than climbing to the heavens. You spent every waking hour trying to make sure you had enough food and shelter and weren't in danger of falling back into being a Denizen. Left no time to improve your lot in life. In seeing to your children's education, so that they could improve their lot. They would be trapped.

Your money, your home, your very identity, all tied up with the System. How people were allowed to treat you. Where you could go and what you could do. What you could learn. How far you could cultivate. All ruled by the great ledger. All ruled by the System. All that, and you were still better than the Denizens. The Citizens would at least have hope. The Denizens needed an actual miracle to become Citizens. Two of them. First, God would have to look back at this world and see them.

And perhaps the cruelest joke of all was that it wouldn't matter. There would be, at most, two years of violence and decay before it all fell apart. Considerably less than that, assuming the loss of the System Astrologica meant the Jeon system collapsing. It was, all of it, all the fear and confusion and misery and hurt, the ruined lives, all of it, to gather souls for the System Astrologica. The whole country, maybe many countries, burning their strongest mages to fuel Starbrite's escape.

How in the hell had Starbrite managed it? How the hell had he convinced the government to endorse this? Twenty percent of the economy wasn't nearly enough clout. He brooded on the question for a moment, then nearly slapped his forehead.

It was Starbrite. He was unquestionably the most powerful mage in the world, and the current CEO was the second most powerful. The C-suite probably accounted for a major percentage of all the Level Eights in the world. Certainly the best equipped, and almost certainly the most powerful. Truth could barely imagine what a Level Eight could do with the System. You wouldn't so much cast a spell as write a sentence describing what you wanted to happen.

Eight spells, each backed with obscene power, working in combination. He was certain that by the time you hit Level Three or Four in Starbrite, there would be special classes on combining spells available. Probably mandatory for those in the PMC. Outside of Starbrite, that information would be the tightly held secrets of nation-states or powerful families. He had been winging it so far, successfully, but thinking about fighting the true old monsters? He had zero confidence. He doubted that anyone else was confident either.

"Welcome, President Whoever-You-Are; let's not pretend you aren't completely disposable. Your job, and the job of the other ten people in this room, is to convince the rest of Jeon that they really want to adopt the proposals laid out in the envelope in front of you. Or you, your families, and your closest friends will become objects of amusement and philosophical inquiry for our employees. And if you can't guess what we mean by that, here is a selection of recordings from the last people who told us 'no.' Including three of your predecessors. Amazing how many Jeon presidents work themselves to death in office."

As an up-and-comer in the PMC, he might well have been assigned as a "body-guard" for someone's kid, just to make sure their parents were doing as they were told. Actually, as fast as he grew, after five years . . . who knows just how powerful he would have been?

He exhaled hard and forcefully shook off the morbid thoughts. "Attend me." The maid appeared. "Does this hotel have a private and well-secured ritual chamber?"

"It is the belief of the hotel that it does. Whether it meets Your Highness's standards, I do not know." She bowed apologetically.

"I will examine it."

She bowed again and led Truth to a small ritual room. Mostly bare, with an altar and various bloods and oils provided. There was the traditional olive-wood box full of salt, he was happy to see, as well as a few handy reference guides to some of the more common rituals. Pretty good. It even had that "expensive room" smell. A combination of wood polish and herbs, and the lingering traces of incense.

He was without his usual countersurveillance tools, but he knew enough about it to have some degree of confidence in its security. Not a high degree. Plan C was the ritual with the highest, most-refined degree of stealth. He'd have to make sure his route out of the city was secure, just in case Merkovah's improved impossible-to-detect communication ritual was, in fact, detected.

It was what it was. He made his inquiries, made what small preparations he could, ate a big dinner, and slept well. It was going to be a busy day tomorrow, however it turned out.

Morning came and with it the now-well-established morning routine. The coffee was perfect, the shower invigorating, the cultivation merely adequate but better than nothing. At least it left him feeling stretched and nicely warmed up. About an hour until his scheduled call. He went down to the ritual room and started setting up. He took his time and did it right, pushing out Incisive on the off chance the foresight would let him know when he screwed up.

Not at his level of mastery, apparently. Ah, well. When all was in readiness and the appointed hour had arrived, he activated the ritual.

"Wet Twelve Twenty-One Farce Vase."

Merkovah sounded like he didn't know how to feel as he replied, "Mountain Green Seven-Seven Woobly Jelly." There was a pause. "So. You have kept busy."

"Staying active, you know. Being a growth partner driving KPIs toward exceeding quarterly goals in a proactive, team-based, customer-focused environment."

There was a muffled snort in reply. "All right, let's go through it. One thing at a time."

It took a long while. There was an awful lot to get through. Merkovah quickly homed in on a few key things.

"The information about the Shattervoid girl being potentially held at Army Ford is still being verified. It's the best lead we have, however."

"Sending me to investigate?"

"No, we have other operatives more suited for that sort of work."

"Seriously? With my blessings and familiarity with Starbrite?"

"Yes."

Truth was rocked. "All right. So . . ."

"Just keep on keeping an eye out for possible clues."

"Ah, fine. Okay."

"More on that in a minute. So, having raided a suburban laboratory and blown up the director's office, you pressed on northward."

"Yeah. Speaking of, did you find anything else in those files I sent you?"

"A very great deal, but not relevant to what you are doing. At least, not that I can see as of yet."

Truth knew *I won't say on account of operational security* when he heard it.

"On a related point . . . fair to say that you have single-handedly lowered the security rating of the southern tip of Jeon dramatically. The attacks on Starbrite personnel, the provocations, assaults, and spreading nationalist sentiment have all had an impact. Some more dramatic than others, some with a more lingering, long-term impact."

"I did want to ask: Am I wasting my time with the nationalist stuff? In the time we have remaining?"

"Oh, far from it! Even after the enrollment, I would encourage you to be doing that. Jeon's security services are running around like crazy, trying to stamp out the 'unprecedented wave of nationalism spontaneously arising' in the south. You are building on top of the efforts of others; this really is a go-to play for foreign provocateurs. It's just that you seem to be unusually effective in your efforts. Seems you have a knack for fostering resentment and a killing rage."

"Ah. Good? I figured that the elite-revolt thing would be more effective."

"It's not about just one thing. Mass movements require mass surveillance. It's why security services are always desperate to find 'ringleaders.' So much easier to focus on one person, and so much more satisfying for your bosses to have a head to hang over the gate. On the other hand, as you correctly guessed, the threat of a palace coup is grabbing the attention of their higher-up mages, as that is the one thing that could plausibly reach those bosses."

"I'm pulling the attention of the full stack of the hierarchy."

"You and many others, most of whom have no connection to us. This is a game everyone is playing at the moment."

"No wonder I've been able to slip by so many times. For all the roadblocks, they are still looking in a hundred different directions."

"It's a factor. And of course, that means less resources going to Starbrite and the more Starbrite is having to use its own people for security, intelligence, and the like."

"Do we have any sense that it's impacting the high-level operations?"

"Trickier to say. We know the C-suite was kicked out of their orbital retreats as soon as the Shattervoid rolled in. I don't know if any died in the process; we haven't been able to confirm their movements since that time. Presumably, they are spending at least some time managing their respective departments."

Truth opened his mouth to say something heated, but Merkovah plowed right on. "Neither of us is willing to trust any plan that involves the words *presumably*, *logically*, or *it stands to reason that*."

"Too right!"

"That being said, just what the hell did you do to Dr. Borges? I knew it would kick over a hornet's nest, but if I had to pick one spot on the map where members of the C-suite definitely were, it's his former research center. Which you blew up? Somehow? For some reason?"

Truth walked Merkovah through what he had found, and particularly the reality-manipulating creation of Uqbar. There was silence on the connection.

"Teacher?"

"I . . . would have given a very great deal to meet Borges. To have had a chance to talk with him about his ideas."

"He was brainy, but he was also trying to create a . . ." Truth's voice ran out. When you got right down to it, what Borges was making seemed, superficially, like . . .

"He was trying to create his own version of Siphios, one with a god and king of his choosing. All to keep more people, and the light of civilization, alive through the dark millennia to come."

"Giant pyramidal sacrificial altar, though. Human sacrifice."

"So? What's war but human sacrifice? Or working in a factory? Donating time, or money, or food to a church or temple? You are giving up part of the time of your life and giving it to another. Sometimes a human, sometimes a god. And maybe the victims went up to the altar voluntarily, or they went up at spearpoint. So what? Their sacrifice might mean tens of thousands had gentle rains and good harvests. That's got to be worth a few dozen lives in exchange."

Truth didn't have a good answer to that. "So, what's next?"

"Get out of Conjin. It's not worth your time—a shipping hub is going to die fast without any help from us. Time for you to head on home. Time for you to head back to Harban."

CHAPTER 14

I DIDN'T FORGET

A bout that . . ."

"Yes?" Merkovah asked.

"I found Vig."

There was a long pause on the line.

"Tell me everything."

Truth did so, including how frustrating he found not making contact. Merkovah sounded relieved at the end of it.

"You handled that exactly right. Exactly right. In theory, it might have been better not following him, but this adds another layer of plausibility to the illusion of a vast nationalist uprising."

"Great, super."

Merkovah sighed. "Sorry. That was insensitive of me. I was just concerned. You are almost painfully pragmatic, but I know how much you love your siblings."

"The messed-up thing is, I can't even tell him to go do something safer. Right now, short of building a doomsday bunker or something, what is he supposed to do that's 'safer' or a better use of his time?"

"He is doing meaningful work, or at least work that is meaningful for him. Nothing wrong with that." Merkovah sounded soothing.

Truth was going to point out that this "meaningful work" consisted of attacking public buildings but stopped himself. Felt too hypocritical even for an overprotective big brother.

"I have been wondering about something, though. What do we want the world to look like at the end of all this?" Truth asked instead.

"Pardon?"

"We kill Starbrite, wipe out the C-suite, the System Astrologica gets to enjoy the Masticating Juicer enchantment before its dissolution, and we save the girl. Then what? Some of us get off-planet and try life in a new world, but for this world, or whatever place we wind up in, what do we want that to look like?"

"A difficult question, given the inevitable collapse."

"I've been thinking about this a lot. Imagine you were starting from scratch, and the rules were up to you. What does that look like?"

"I suppose the Siphios of my childhood. With a few notable changes. That's old age and nostalgia for you," Merkovah said. There was a touch of whimsy in his voice.

"Your best plan is an absolute monarchy that is also a religion overseeing aristocrats, and the vast majority of people are peasants? That is the best the world can be?"

The communication altar was silent for a moment. "I think I see where you are going with this. If we don't have cultivation levels, and all the societies and governments collapse, all that will be left are a few powerhouses and gangs of the powerless. In less than . . . perhaps a hundred years, probably much less, there won't even be the powerhouses. So, without the model of the hierarchy of cultivation, what does government look like?"

"Or whatever, yeah. Someone pointed out to me yesterday that money is just bookkeeping, records of someone's time and work. You get food and shelter in exchange for your time and work. Don't work, don't eat. I can't imagine any other way of doing things, but we all know how bad my education was. Can that really be the only way?"

Merkovah chuckled painfully. "My education was, and is, excellent. I really can't think of any other way, but in the vastness of the universe, surely other ways must exist. On this world, God ordained the creation of Temple and Throne. Perhaps there could be some system where God ordained the provision of food and shelter to all."

"But he didn't."

"Debatably, he did. You could certainly interpret various passages of scriptures and the testimony of some prophets that way."

"But he didn't. If he did, it wouldn't be a question of interpretation."

Merkovah laughed long and hard at that. "Oh, no, that is where you are wrong. *Everything* is a question of interpretation. Especially the things that aren't up for interpretation. Did you know the prohibition on eating freshwater fish may actually be extended to snakes?"

Truth shook his head violently. "Because they both have scales?"

"And no legs, and are not saltwater creatures, yes."

"But . . . There are . . . Snakes aren't even related to fish, right?"

"Only biologically. Religiously? That is the subject of serious debate right now."

Truth grasped for an answer to that, and shifted tack. "What are we going to do about the enrollment? And the changeover to credits?"

"Not much we can do. We will be disrupting as many enrollment centers as we can. We have replicated your destructive black-ball explosion experience, but we still haven't figured out why it happens. Best guess currently is that the talisman plates, when stacked and organized in their crates, actually exist in a sort of crude array. Break that array and bad things happen. If that is the case, it's a theory of design we haven't encountered before."

"Nasty. Plus side, should be relatively easy to disrupt."

"Well. Easy-ish. They've beefed up security, started stationing local cops, that kind of thing."

"Any thoughts on what to do about the thinning magic?" Truth asked.

"Long term? No. Short term? We are developing small array disks that will attract and concentrate cosmic rays in a small area. It will be enough to let you cultivate for a few months. I know how much energy you burn through. It's going to be heading your way soon."

Truth nodded, though nobody could see him do it. "Thanks, though that does lead me to a . . . you know . . . unpleasant question. What happens when everyone's apertures collapse?"

There was silence on the other end of the line.

"Most of the people above Level Three will die agonizing deaths. The higher the level, the more magic they have stored up, the more dramatic the collapse of their apertures when they run out. There will be a period where they can sustain themselves with bigger and bigger cosmic-ray-concentrating arrays, perhaps even moving to sacrifice, but sooner or later, it won't be enough. They will die. Level Three will be crippled and on the point of death. Suicide would probably be the smarter option for them. Level Two and One will live in immense pain but will be functional. Mostly functional."

Truth silently laughed. "It will be a world of children. Anyone who hasn't awakened yet, and those ancient families and powers practicing body-cultivation arts to let them hang on to their magic indefinitely."

"Not indefinitely; sooner or later, they won't be able to replace the cosmic energy they spend," Merkovah cautioned.

"No, that's not right. Sacrifice, remember? So long as there is *any* way to generate cosmic energy, they will use it. No matter how many have to die."

Merkovah sighed. Truth got the impression that he was sighing less because of what Truth said and more because he wished Truth hadn't figured it out.

"It's possible. Unlikely to be practical, though."

Less practical than just dying? Truth didn't ask any more about that. The system was already hard at work on modifying the Meditations to give him the same protection.

"So, what's the plan for Harban? I can't imagine you want me wandering around, just . . . screwing with Starbrite."

"Mmm. That would be counterproductive, though continuing to foster nationalist sentiment and encouraging the ambitions of the mighty would be useful."

Truth had to parse out some words there. "Making the poors mad at Starbrite and making the rich think they can replace Starbrite would be useful."

"Yes." Merkovah's eye roll was visible from the other side of the planet.

"All right, easy enough. What else?"

"Since you have done a fairly spectacular job drawing away Starbrite and Jeon security forces both to the north and south, now is a good time to start breaking into offices and secured facilities. Time to start pressing in on the System."

"Specific instructions to follow?"

"Yes. For now, make your way out of Conjin and head back to Harban. As for the lack of credits . . . you will have to do a lot more sneaking around. I assume you have been robbing banks and things as you go."

"Not as much as I thought I would be, actually."

"Really?"

"Yeah, I just sleep where I want. What are they going to do about it?"

Merkovah thought about that one a second and started laughing again. "Same applies to food and supplies, I suppose."

"I only pay for things when I feel like it," Truth agreed. "Though it's going to make eating out at vendors a lot harder."

"Huh. How many street vendors are actually Citizens?"

That stumped Truth. He had no idea. "I guess we will find out soon."

Truth dragged his mind back to Borges. "Teacher . . . what exactly was Borges trying to do? I kind of get it, I think, but . . . how? Or what? I don't even know the right words at this point."

"I can't know for certain, but at a guess? You remember the research station, where we found that higher-dimensional droplet of water?"

"Yes. You said the place was distorted because it was in the shadow of some higher-dimensional structure."

"That's the current best theory. I think Borges was trying for something similar. Based on what you said, I think he wanted to cover the world in those floating flowers and use them, somehow, to trigger a shift in reality around them. Not just rewriting the world that is but rewriting what was, too. Projecting an artificial world and making it real on the structure of the 'old' real world."

Truth tried to imagine it. He remembered what the bodyguard had said— something about being able to make more books. Were they importing books from this created world of theirs? Trying to seed reality with it, the way he could prime people to accept his "reality" when he used Incisive?

"The sheer scope of it . . ." Truth murmured.

"As I said. I dearly, dearly wish I could have met him. Spoken with him. However necessary his death was—"

"Say *useful* instead," Truth murmured. "I can't believe it was strictly necessary."

Merkovah sighed at that. "Defining necessity at the end of days. Anything else I should know?"

"Yes. I am making progress on your assignment. At the very least, I think I've found a new way to study the question."

"Pardon?"

"What is a human? Right now, I have been a slumrat, a mercenary, an armed robber, burglar, murderer, terrorist, bodyguard, boyfriend, rich prick, and I am currently investigating being a prince. So far, the prince is the one that has resonated the most strongly, recently."

Merkovah sounded interested. "I assume you are using Incisive for this?"

"Yes, constantly."

"Mmm. I will think about that some. When you say it has resonated the most strongly with you—"

"I find myself thinking like a prince. I am not entirely sure what a prince is or does, but this is Jeon. We are all working off some scry-drama notion of princely behavior."

"I won't spoil the fun by telling you what actual princes are like. Having tutored dozens." Merkovah's voice was desert-dry. "You have probably picked up on the raw power dynamics, but I bet you are missing a subtle piece of the mindset."

"Oh?"

"All this is 'your' stuff. All the people around you exist to enrich you and protect your stuff. In a feudal mindset, the people in your domain are under your protection, true, in the same sense that you would guard your cattle. It is, purely and entirely, exploitation. Land, cattle, people, buildings, industries, they are all part of your personal income, and despite the fact you, or your family, likely acquired them through violence, they are now yours by God-given right."

Truth gave the altar a hard look. "Don't you work directly for the King?"

"Oh, yes. I wouldn't say we are close, but I do have his full trust."

"A trust you clearly are worthy of."

"I am. I have never ceased my diligent service to Throne and Temple for centuries. None of this is considered a controversial opinion in Siphios—it's why the Temple exists as a separate but coequal institution. It is only by the ethics imposed by the Temple that the secular powers are restrained. Compelled to do what they would otherwise not—care for the public as their own people."

Truth stared at the altar. "A long conversation, I suspect."

"You have no idea. Right, that should wrap things up."

"No, two more items. I need the address of a company. Actually, someone will need to do a little research to find the name of the parent company of the company I am looking for. An outfit called MegaShroom."

"May I ask why?"

"You want the experts on exploitation and mental manipulation? They are some of the best in the entire world. I want to see if I can use them. In the alternative, I want to exterminate the top of their pointy pyramid."

"Ah. Well. I'll look into it. If it doesn't interfere with the plan, I can include it in your next dead drop. The next thing?"

"How is Etenesh doing?"

"She is doing well. She had a small relapse a while back but has been showing steady improvement. Although, speaking as a student of theology here, her doctrine is completely incoherent and needs a lot of work."

"She's smart. I'm sure she will make a lovely religion for me. Ah, relapse—she attacked someone?"

"A small disagreement escalated. There was some physical contact. Nobody died. No one was permanently injured. Etenesh was unharmed. Impulse-control problem, I expect."

Truth was vividly remembering his dream of Etenesh—the only dream he could remember having. It could have been an impulse-control problem. Or someone could have stolen her apple.

CHAPTER 15

PACKING FOR HOME

Truth left the ritual room a little stifled. He still had questions for Merkovah. Many, many questions. About cultivation, about Cup and Knife, about the nature of reality, about ethics, philosophy, theology, politics . . . about everything. Just having someone he could talk to about these things was immense. Someone he might disagree with but who had spent half a millennium studying and learning about the world.

Merkovah had always made a point of his private tuition being included as part of Truth's compensation package. The irreplaceable value of that time was becoming more and more clear.

"Attend me." The maid appeared before him, bowing politely. It had refined its appearance yet again, adding subtle imperfections to its skin, flecking its hazel eyes with soft tan. It had calibrated its voice too, faintly shifting register, intonation, inflection, to be more pleasing. Truth was amused to see that it was making its non-human nature more obvious. Little things, like her ears becoming longer and more pointed, or that "she" was accompanied by a faint smell of roses and musk.

"Arrange lunch, and have a dinner packed for me. Summon Butler, and have it attend me as I eat. You shall be present as well."

"As Your Highness commands," the succubus murmured, bowing.

Truth returned to his hotel room. Incisive wasn't alerting him to anything. The improved ritual probably worked. Not to mention the fact that Conjin public security probably had a lot of vacancies to fill right now. Certainly, their police would be hiring. He reclined in one of the comfortable chairs the luxurious suite provided. Amazing how all that grandeur, the drifting scenes of tropical waters, the incredible richness of the fabrics, the very taste of the air, it all just became "normal." Invisible. The reality he moved through.

What was that old line? Fish don't know they are in the water? It's just their normal. Something like that. He was the Prince. Why would he take note of the furnishings of this modest dwelling? This was his normal, or a little below average.

Why did this all feel so right? So natural? He wasn't born to nobility, fallen or otherwise. He was a slumrat. Generational trash. One with no real interest in ruling a nation, or a city, or even a modest-sized company. He would be pretty iffy about running a gang, if he was honest with himself, and the whole universe seemed to be shouting that being a gangster was his true calling in life. All this despite growing up despising the gangsters he saw around him. Hating them for their petty-mindedness and endless idiot cruelties.

A Prince. A feudal lord. Within his domain, every person, place, and thing existed to enhance his wealth, his power, or his glory. All his property. Especially the people. Which wasn't really okay, was it? He was revolted by the thought of ever being a slave again, but oddly comfortable with just giving orders and expecting to be obeyed. Without the slightest intention of compensating the obedient. Serve or die. Be useful or die. Make me money, give me power, give me glory, or die. Because you are sheep, and whether I am wolf or guard dog will depend on my being fed.

What if there were a shepherd? Someone to lay down the law, ensure the sheep were looked after and the dog was fed for his trouble. God, according to Merkovah. The civilizing and restraining force of religion. But that was plainly nonsense. Hadn't done a damn thing there in Jeon, clearly.

Whatever the Temple had managed in Siphios, it was pretty invisible to Truth. From his perspective, the thing that humbled the princes and aristocrats was Starbrite and all the newly rich. The aristocracy of money. The wolves won and convinced the sheep that the wolves did it for them.

No idea what it was like in Desrin-dominated countries, but he had a hard time believing that religion restrained the state. After all, it would be so much more convenient for everyone if the masses didn't question the divine right of kings and, naturally, the unquestionable truth of the faith. On pain of death at the hands of the secular authorities, if necessary.

Truth went round and round, not finding an answer. Lunch came soon enough. Melon wrapped in tissue-thin wisps of salty, fatty cured ham. The sweet, salty, and rich flavors seemed to waltz together, slowly spinning across his taste buds. Then a bowl of noodles, simply and freshly prepared, topped with slivers of duck, green onions, and a ferocious sauce of spice and stone fruit, all topped with crispy fried shallots and little golden garlic chips.

The textures and flavors formed interlocking combinations. Each bite lively, no two exactly the same but all delicious. Dessert was two cookies and a cup of coffee. The cookies were soft, crumbling, rich, and moist with a shockingly luxurious taste of almond. And the coffee was made exactly how he liked it.

Butler and the maid stood against the wall, waiting patiently while he savored his lunch. Truth carried the coffee over to one of the armchairs and sat down comfortably. He closed his eyes and took a long sip, luxuriating in the bitterness and warmth of the coffee. He set the cup down on the little table next to him and opened his eyes. The two succubae dropped to their knees, fist pressed to chest, ready to serve however he wished. Everything where it should be. How it should be. The smell of coffee rising up and tickling his nose.

Dad. It was Dad, on his broken throne. That was why it felt so familiar. Dad feasting on soup in a cardboard cup and washing it down with the finest schnapps fifteen wen could buy at the corner store. Crushing disobedience with violence, extorting money, demanding the house be cleaned, then screaming that no one should touch his stuff. It was Dad. The male role model with the biggest impact on his life. Every day he asked himself, "What would Dad do?" and then did the opposite. How did he miss the obvious connection?

Dad was a *bad* king. Truth would be a far better one. There was a time when that realization would have paralyzed him or triggered an emotional explosion. It had been a busy few years since he saw Dad. He had spent a lot of time working on himself. He was heir to a petty tyrant's foul-smelling throne? Sounded like the right kind of seat for a slumrat without ambition. His dad was welcome to it, if the old bastard still lived. Truth was a rat that looked up. He aspired to a higher throne.

"The best argument for a boss on Earth is the existence of a boss in Heaven," Truth murmured. He remembered the Egg Man saying that when he had his vision hanging from a tree in Siphios. The succubae said nothing. He hadn't asked their opinion, after all, and they quite agreed anyway.

If he wanted his perfect world, or even his good-enough world, he would have to become that organizing principle. He would have to sit on the throne and make people arrange themselves in the way he wanted. It came back to power and violence again. It always seemed to. Didn't Sergeant Murthey have a good line on this? "The most dangerous words in any language are *Follow me!* Something like that.

He looked over at the kneeling succubae. They would kneel for as long as he wished. Not like they had knees to hurt. So long as he was giving them what they craved—cosmic energy and a more-defined reality. They would obey in the hopes of getting more of those things and for fear of losing them.

That was the Starbrite way, wasn't it? If you had the glittering city, with its thrones and servants, you needed the slums. You needed the slumrats. You needed a very visible alternative, to encourage ambition. Encourage greed. Encourage them to be violent on your behalf.

He could feel things clicking inside his mind, connections being made. All those questions on philosophy, on theology, economy, all starting to come together. He might not have all the pieces, and he sure wasn't seeing the whole picture, but he was putting together the puzzle.

"Hear my orders. I will be leaving Conjin. Arrange transport from here to Sokhi by boat, a small but quick and luxurious pleasure craft. One staffed by demons. I tire of humanity. You." He pointed at the maid. "Inform Mary that you are leaving her service and will accompany me. For her obedience, she will be granted the following information—"

Truth gave out the coordinates and date of the battle that had gotten him killed but didn't mention that it was over a kidnapped daughter of the Shattervoid clan. "This is the last time anyone outside of Starbrite can confirm the location, and identity, of 'Her.' She may use this information how she chooses."

"My thanks, my prince. I swear I shall dedicate my all to your service." The maid started to rise but was stilled by his hand.

"Butler, how is your project coming?"

"Early days, my prince. However, he is not very resistant. His education will take a few months to complete, but I do not foresee it taking longer than that."

Truth nodded, then turned back toward the maid. "Inform Mary that I will be taking her grandson as well, and I will see to it that he is fed. He is *not* being adopted into my retinue at this time, but he will be provided education and opportunities." He flicked his hand, sending her on her way.

"Your servant obeys."

Truth glanced back at Butler. "I expect my clothes will be cleaned, pressed, and packed by the time the maid returns. I expect to be underway before dinner."

"Your servant obeys." The succubus smiled happily. Its cheekbones had grown more pronounced, its hair turned an inky black, its eyes alternately warm and cruel. Its every move was elegant yet powerful. It was truly becoming a handsome young butler.

Truth sat back in the chair and sipped his coffee, as others got to work. In just two hours, he was striding out onto a flying cloud. His servants, a beautiful maid and a handsome butler, came behind. The maid carrying a luxurious duffel bag, the butler wheeling a small but fully packed suitcase.

They were met at the dock by a sleek capsule shaped like a blunt dart. The side of it rose like a curtain, and they walked into the plush interior. Deep sofas, a king-sized bed, a bar, all manner of luxury furnishings bathed in blue and pink lights from the concealed talismans. The walls shimmered as an illusory array projected the exterior of the vehicle on the interior. Once they were set, a whale demon was summoned from the deep. It nosed comfortably into the formations at the front of the capsule and settled in to pull them along. Like a horse pulling a cart, gaily trotting along.

"Now seems as good a time as any. You." He pointed at the maid. "I shall name you and give you a nature—you are Maid. You shall serve me as you have done so far. Should I acquire more staff, you may have more responsibility."

Maid genuflected. "I am grateful beyond words!" Truth couldn't see the difference, but apparently it was significant to the succubus. Good enough.

"Butler, I'm going to leave a variety of practical matters to you. Particularly the training of that." Truth pointed to the suitcase. "It occurred to me: he is a high citizen. Naturally, he will have to be enrolled in the System. You have until the end of the coming month to make him unshakably loyal. Loyal to the point where he could no more betray me than fly."

"Such things have been tried before, Master, with varying degrees of success. I cannot guarantee my incompetence will not ruin your plans." Butler sounded worried.

"No need to be afraid. My trip to Conjin was very productive. You see, I have what is, I suspect, a unique combination of spells at my disposal."

Truth leaned back against the sofa. He hadn't inquired how this vehicle was being paid for. Or if it was. He truly didn't care, because it truly didn't matter.

"I have a bad habit. Every time I see something particularly good, I ask, 'Why doesn't everyone do that?' and the answer is usually because it is rare, difficult, expensive, or simply not useful in most people's lives. Powerful in my hands, yes, but why does a chartered accountant need body cultivation? Or a combat spell, even if it made him terribly persuasive? What would a cheesemaker use Graeme's Arrow for?"

The succubae were silent. Masters monologuing were a constant feature of their existence. They had never minded it. It helped them shape who they should be.

"My spells and blessings are aimed at making me the arbiter of my local reality. I hadn't connected the dots until this trip, but that's what they do. My body cultivation makes me more real than my surroundings. I weigh heavier on the world than they do, and my actions count for more. More so every day. My combat spell lets me project that reality onto the world around me, lets me shape how others perceive that reality, even foreseeing how the world will be shaped around me, so that I may adjust it to my benefit. My healing and spiritual-combat spell lets me forcibly correct reality, to be more in line with how it should be. And my blessings let *me* decide on how it should be."

He softly laughed.

"The world is very real. God believes in it an awful lot, even if he's ignoring us right now. But as weak as I am in the grand scheme of things, I am finally strong enough to have a say. And now I'm coming home to Harban. No more confronting the 'real world.' The world will have to confront the reality of *me*."

CHAPTER 16

LOOKING DOWN ON THOSE WHO WISH TO BE DECEIVED

The undersea journey was uneventful. Truth watched Butler train the former desk clerk. He realized that, if he had ever heard their name, he had forgotten it. He had enough self-awareness to realize that he was deliberately dehumanizing him. Turning him into an "it," another one of his bound demons. Another weapon to use in his war. It didn't feel good. Which was a hell of a moral line to draw for someone who had committed multiple atrocities.

Butler relied primarily on the basics of the basics—illusion. The former person (Component? Weapon system? Operative?) was bound up in an endless dream, where certain behaviors were rewarded. Truth was curious about the lack of punishment. That's how he had always understood it—the carrot and the stick. It turns out that such arrangements were, at best, inefficient and often counterproductive.

"You don't want them scared, Your Highness. They are already scared. It's a scary situation. You are clear and firm in your directions, reward good behavior, and do not have an emotional response to bad behavior. You simply return them to task and make it clear that nothing good will happen until the assigned task is complete. Provoking their trainer is a way to try and regain control. You make it clear the only power they have is in obedience. In pleasing you."

Truth nodded. "And suppressing their old memories? Their old desires?"

"Desires are wholly within our domain, as a succubus. Replacement and erasure simply take time and the same methodology as the behavior correction. Wrong thoughts see rewards and attention withheld; right thoughts are rewarded. Memory is a little trickier. I am focusing on making him doubt his own recollection of events, 'proving' that his memory is untrustworthy and associating the past with shame, pain, and other negative emotions."

"He will want to forget the bad memories. And soon, he will conclude that these are not memories at all but nightmares. You will comfort him, reassure him about all the good, real things in the present." Truth nodded. "He might never completely forget everything, but he will determinedly try to ignore those things he does remember."

"Just so, Your Highness."

"Good. Carry on."

"Your Highness, if I may ask, would you be willing to participate in their training?"

"To what extent?"

"Feed them. Nothing offensive to your dignity, simply eat in front of them, then allow them to eat what you do not. Take no further action or interest in them."

Truth considered that. And nodded. He had promised to feed them, after all.

The evening passed uneventfully. They would be in Sokhi in an hour or so. They hadn't pushed the pace. Truth wanted to spend at least one more night in real comfort before getting back into the grind. He decided to perform an experiment before breakfast. This would tax his energy hard. He wanted plenty of time to cultivate and recharge afterward.

Truth mentally established the area he ruled as "the interior of this vessel." The orthodoxy of this place was to be that there was the ruler, Truth and everyone else were his servants. He was to be feared and adored, for his generosity was great and his wrath fatal. In his domain, he was the Prince. Smarter, stronger, more beautiful than his servants.

Holding that idea in his mind, he started casting his spells. His foundation was the Meditations of Valentinian. It was his first contact with the idea of "local super-reality." *Able to affect the universe on a conceptual level* was how the System faerie described it. One day, he could simply reach up and pluck a star from the sky, like picking a grape from a vine. He visualized himself. He was immense. Far larger than a mere three dimensions could capture. He was a mountain. An entire world. Pressed down into a human shape. Emanating down, like one of those stellar eminences. His body was perfect, powerful, and untouchable.

Next came Incisive. Always running now. Always shaping the world around him. Showing the world that he was, in fact, the Prince. Disobedience, even disagreement, was not simply unwise; it was immoral. He ruled by both right and might. All served him and gloried in their service. Their service was both wise and holy. It was the orthodoxy.

Having laid that foundation, he poured power into the Blessing of the Sea of Brass. He had thought it was only useful for slaughtering demons. He had come to know better. Within his domain, there were no alternative opinions permitted. He was the Prince. He was in command. Everyone else was a servant. That was the very definition of propriety. Of how the world worked.

He even leaned in to the Blessing of the Silent Forest, hoping that it would obscure the change in the nature of reality. That it would just seem natural. It would blend.

Finally, balancing on the edge of what his body could stand, he cast Cup and Knife. The way the world ought to be and the way it was were out of sync. The template of how the world should be had been laid. Now they just needed to trim off that which was wrong. He tried to cast the spell but felt the power draw spike far past what he could endure and hastily cut it off. Not yet, it seemed. Still more to learn there.

He looked down at his servants. The succubae writhed on the floor, the reality-establishing magic seeming to overload them with what passed as pleasure. The former clerk simply knelt with his head pressed to the floor, shivering. Terrified and awed to be before a truly higher being. Truth ate rapidly but casually, keeping a close eye on his fast-dwindling energy. When there was about a third of a plate left, he leaned to the side and put the plate on the floor in front of the trembling thing.

He looked down on it, in every sense. It hadn't dared to move, to even glance at the plate.

"Eat."

Sokhi was a resort town east and a hair north of Harban, on the other side of the peninsula. Standing on the dock in the harbor, it all felt a little unreal. He was standing in a luxury marina, next to a tasteful four-story luxury condominium, next to more parks and luxury sporting courses than he could easily count. There were custom spell beasts, racing six-legged frogs, fire birds, seven-colored clouds, practically every manner of luxury conveyance the moderately wealthy could conceive of. It wasn't global-tier money, but under normal circumstances? Nobody in at least three generations of their families would have to work.

And there he was. Truth Medici, out in the bright lights and in the open. Trailed by his servants, who were carrying his luggage to the flying cloud they had booked on his orders. He had no idea how they were paying for it. It didn't matter. He had seen through the illusion of money. It was just another tool, a bookkeeper's fantasy. Money *was* labor, and it was only valuable to the extent that you valued the labor of others. It was a way to command that labor. And he had other means at his disposal.

The flying cloud was as comfortable as advertised. The cloud was enchanted to change its firmness depending on whether you were sitting or standing, or reclining. Air-conditioned, naturally, filtering out rain, dust, and any of the tiny particles of modern magical life that might cause trifling problems in the lungs of those who breathed them in. Like cancer or other, less-benign mutations. Such problems fell on those below the clouds.

Truth watched the world slip past. People were invisible from this height. Not even ants. Not even dust. It didn't make him feel powerful to think that. He would be invisible from up here too. Was that the other part of the madness that ruled Jeon? Being so far above, so far removed from the rats that you didn't even see them anymore? It wasn't that they were despised or ignored. They were forgotten. Until one chewed through the walls and pissed in the sugar. But that was what exterminators were for.

Truth looked more attentively at the ground below. Sokhi was ringed with private parks, playgrounds, really, for those both wealthy and dull. Past that were little towns and the dense clusters of stubby mountains and scraggly forests that filled up the spine of the peninsula. They weren't following a road. Why bother? But B-44 ran pretty much in a straight line from Sokhi to just east of Harban, so they wound up near it for most of the journey.

"Maid, Butler, do you know what security measures have been put in place to screen flying vehicles and beasts for rebels and saboteurs?"

"My apologies, my prince," they murmured in unison. After his experiment this morning, they had moved from "devoted" succubae to alarmingly fixated. He sighed and enjoyed the ride a while longer. Narrow ribbons of habitation following the rivers through the mountains, or running in rivulets in the narrow valleys between the stubby peaks. It looked almost barren, just two and a half hours' drive from the richest city in the world.

Every time he had tried to move along the roads, he had run into roadblocks. The train had not; but, one, freight train, and two, he was riding it between two completely inhospitable stretches of the middle of nowhere. Not exactly a high-value zone. Harban was a different story. There would be networks of surveillance compounded over and over.

He might be getting better at asserting the reality of his choosing, but generations of mages far, far more powerful than he had been doing the same thing in Harban for centuries. In their opinion, he was just a slightly larger rat. He might blend in a bit better if he were down with the other rats. On the other hand, they were looking a whole lot harder at the smaller rats. He had to balance the risk—how hard they would be looking versus whether they would be looking at all.

Maybe a few months ago, they wouldn't have been looking hard at flying clouds coming in. After his efforts to spark elite revolt in the south? They would be looking. Damn. Damn, damn, damn.

"Direct the cloud to the Shalia Hotel and book a suitable suite. If none are available, you may try the Imperial, then the Grand, then the Fifth Season, in that order. If you cannot find a suitable suite in any of those places, take shelter where you can and await my summons."

"Yes, my prince," they said calmly. They didn't ask about money, either. He got the impression that it wouldn't be an issue.

He waited until the cloud passed near a mountain, barely forty meters above the treetops. With a casualness he couldn't have imagined a year ago, he stepped off the cloud and fell toward the earth.

Abner's Amble.

He waited until the tip of his toe touched a tree branch, then pushed off. When he was about to smash into another tree at speed, he pushed off yet again, then again, then again. Each time, he converted the terrible vertical speed into horizontal travel. Dissipating the energy with a seemingly effortless step. It was the product of endless body cultivation, all his running, all his mountain traversal, and Incisive warning when the vital moment came. He moved like a descending god.

Truth landed on the mountainside, the leaf litter barely stirring around his feet. He looked down over the thin belt of suburbs and nice-ish apartment blocks. The light commercial buildings. The highways running along the wide stretch of the river. He looked down and across the river at the gleaming city of Harban. The rich city, with its floating towers and ancient temples, its luxury shops selling the finest clothes to the most beautiful people. The glittering gem atop the crown of modern magical civilization.

And next to it, the dark contrast adding shine to the already brilliant, were the slums. The dense tower blocks where the rats bred, fought, and fed on each other. The best of them feeding the rich rats of the glittering city. Truth had finally come home.

CHAPTER 17

OPENING ONE EYE

Truth was torn by conflicting emotions. There was anger, and shame, and pain. Envy. Hatred. Even some faint traces of affection. Not everything in Harban was terrible, and there were some happy memories there. Above them all was ambition. For the Prince, *this* was the only place worthy of being his seat of power. He would come to Harban. And rule.

<<Drop the persona! Switch to unnoticeability.>>

And why would I do that? A Prince should be seen, that his glory may be established and his dignity upheld.

<<Because you are Truth Medici, born and raised in Towering Heavens Apartment Building Number Who Cares, and possessed of all the princely patrimony of a rat nibbling on the family turd. You are losing yourself in the identity, moron! Snap out of it!>>

Truth wanted to snap back. So far, the persona has been working great. He could just plow right through all opposition, a mindset of total victory. The System interrupted him before he could get started.

<<It's your dad, remember? He is the evil king without vision, a petty tyrant on a busted, vomit-stained throne. Get yourself some vision. Drop the persona for a while. It will be there for you when you are ready to pick it up again.>>

He snarled, but the System had a point. The whole reason he had jumped off the flying cloud was so that he could go low-profile. The Prince was a lot of things but not low-profile. It made sense to let it go. Become unnoticeable.

Truth consciously relaxed the Scales portion of Incisive, releasing the persona. It was like letting go of a partially deflated balloon. He might be done with it, but it was staying with him anyhow. He could feel the identity clinging to him. It seemed people really believed in him. He had sold the idea of the Prince . . . perhaps a little too well.

If he had judged things right, the former clerk was now incapable of thinking of him as anything else. Certainly, the succubae had to know he wasn't actually some kind of royalty, but they gave not a single damn about that. He was giving them their fix, so they were prepared to believe in him with every fiber of their immaterial being. Mary believed in him. So did the guy whose sedan chair he had stolen. Perhaps the person who owned the boat or the flying cloud. Not just passive acceptance; they were active in their belief. They took positive steps to affirm it, to make that belief tangible.

They had sacrificed for their belief in the identity. Their money, their servants, their services, their possessions. Their family. Mary believed in him so much, she gave him her grandson. She practically begged him to take her grandson away. Crammed into a tiny suitcase, to be remade in a fashion that was pleasing to the Prince.

You would have to really believe in someone to do that. What would happen if he did manage to disperse the identity? Would their belief suddenly shatter? He doubted it. Their being persuaded didn't hinge on how he was presenting when he wasn't in the room with them.

Botis claimed that no one had yet mastered Incisive. Truth had thought that was a strong boast. He thought he had gotten good with the spell pretty damn fast. Just maybe, he was the one being arrogant. Botis was one of the strongest stellar eminences. How could his signature spell be something simple or nice?

He, against all odds, had managed to underestimate one of the most powerful entities in existence. Truth felt that he was very, very special. Yes, he was. Just the most specialest little boy in the whole wide world.

Truth sat down in the dirt. Princes don't sit in the dirt. They were too fancy. So, he couldn't be the Prince. He was Truth Medici. For all the good and bad of it, that was his name and who he was. Identity was something he could wear lightly through the world, because the core of him never changed.

He slowly calmed his breathing and fell into meditation. Letting the Prince drift away and the son of Harbin emerge. Then even that identity could just . . . fade away. He didn't need the world to have an opinion about who he was. They were welcome to look right through him. He knew himself well enough. And he could see the world just fine.

It took a couple of hours. He could still feel wisps of the Prince around him. But he felt like he was wholly himself again.

<<Oh, no, you don't. You don't get to cop out that easily. You were ALWAYS wholly yourself. Every vile thing was utterly your idea and your will.>>

Err . . . when you say "vile thing . . ."

<<Stop me if this sounds at all familiar. You walk into a hotel. Your every whim is not instantly catered to. You interpret this offense as being worthy of ego obliteration. You have so utterly broken a fellow human being that their "safe place" is curled into a crushingly tight ball in a carry-on-sized suitcase. A feat that can only be achieved through some sort of demonic magic, I assume.>>

Truth felt like a heavy weight was coming down on him. It hadn't hit him just yet, but it was coming.

<<His name was Barton. I know you forgot. On purpose. That was some spectacular work, dehumanizing him. You were literally putting him on the same level, or slightly below, the succubae in your mind. Just wow. I am extremely gratified to see my lessons were learned so well. What were your instructions? To make him hate and fear everyone and everything he ever loved, and worship only you in the future? Nice.>>

Truth looked out at glittering Harban. Not yet able to process.

<<So, just to review. Your notion of how a prince should act, based on the examples of your evil dad and the scumbags you bodyguarded, plus what you got from cheap novels and the occasional scry program, is a homicidal maniac. A sadist of the highest order. So arrogant, he makes demons horny. Your notion of what a ruler in training should be . . . is this.>>

That . . . is pretty fucked-up. Yeah.

The system started mimicking his voice, making a nasty parody of it. *<<That's not okay. That's fucked-up. And I was okay with it. Which is fucked-up.>>* Its voice changed back.

<<Are you okay with it, Truth? Because I don't give even one half of a damn about this serf's life. I don't care if you become the most horrible tyrant this world has ever seen. But you have to look at it stone cold and ask yourself if you are okay with it. Not because of some desire to fulfill your role. You could have chosen to handle that any number of ways. You chose this one. So, are you okay with this? Is this who you dream of being?>>

Truth was looking straight at Harban and not seeing it. *It wouldn't make Etenesh happy, would it?*

<<Not relevant to the conversation. What do YOU want? Because there has always been a core of violence in you. Of vicious sadism. You have sneered at the slums, and all your fellow slumrats, since before you could read.>>

Truth wanted to argue, disagree. He just wasn't sure how.

<<It wasn't Starbrite that put it there. It wasn't that Ghul juice. They brought out more of it, maybe, but it was always there. And you have to understand it, or it's going to ruin you.>>

Ruin me?

<<Losing sight of the line between confidence and arrogance. Between ruthlessness and cruelty. You want the highest throne, Truth. You may keep those traits. God knows God does. But you must understand them.>>

Truth was too stunned to pick apart what the System was saying. It had brought this up before. Repeatedly. Seemed he should have listened better. Or at all. He was thoroughly mind-breaking someone, killing them slowly, really, because he did the job he was magically compelled to do. Because in Truth's mind, he deserved it. For questioning him. For failing to instantly obey his better.

<<Identity isn't just what you put out there, but the world is building on the scaffolding you set. Just . . . think through who you have been since you left the slums.>>

FNG at the PMC. Eager to please. Did what I was told. Though, in retrospect, beyond the talent for violence, they thought I was pretty weird but going places. They always shoved extra leadership training on me. Networking through bodyguard duty. I got put on high-profile ops regularly.

<<Everyone could tell you didn't give a damn about much of anything except the job. You never socialized off the clock. You never had the slightest qualm about morality or legality. You were plainly ambitious and you weren't dumb. The phrase "monster in training" seems fitting.>>

I wanted to be a talisman-maintenance tech!

<<*A decade-long dream you trashed in ten minutes when offered money for violence with the prospect of a lot more money and a lot more power than you would get replacing streetlights.*>>

Truth opened his mouth to defend the choice . . . and closed it again. That was exactly what he had done.

<<*Then your ambitious ass got "rightsized" into a hole in the ground. Which you then crawled out of.*>>

I didn't know who I was or what I wanted. Spells, generally. Trying to figure out what I wanted from life.

<<*You went looking for power again. And how did you go about it?*>>

Violence. Seeing everyone around me as disposable trash.

<<*Mmmm. You didn't give a damn about a single person you met between when you last hugged your sibs goodbye and when you finally decided that you liked Merkovah, Jember, and Etenesh. Even those "kind people" at the garage or wherever. You liked them because they provided service with a smile. Happy servants.*>>

No, it wasn't like that. The warmth of them—

<<*Was real. Yes. And those laborers were friendly, and it touched you. Yes to all that. But you only felt safe because none of them could hurt you, physically, emotionally, or otherwise. They were below you. Remember how you freaked out when people touched you in Siphios?*>>

Vividly.

<<*Didn't bother you when the laborers patted you on the shoulder. Didn't even notice it, beyond their smell.*>>

Truth thought it through. *They weren't dangerous. They were beneath me. I didn't care about them. Their kindness was unexpected, and happy-making, but that was it. It was like being touched by a warm wind.*

<<*And the* second *a Level Three mage touched you, someone you did care about and put roughly on your own level . . .* >>

I freaked out.

<<*You freaked out. In fact, the thing that cracked your shell, really cracked it, was when Etenesh started making herself vulnerable to you. Holding her wrist instead of her hand. Having you pin her against a wall or the bed. Cupping her fragile neck. She told you over and over and over how desirable she found you, how much she loved you. Even though you never told her the same. Not really. You felt safe when you knew you were emotionally safe . . . and you could put her down hard if you needed to.*>>

It was . . . all her idea. She pushed for it.

<<*Yeah, she did. She's down bad for you, in case you hadn't noticed, somehow. She was finding a way to make it work between you. And she succeeded. She found a way to manage your insecurity. To give you back that arrogance and feeling of power. What do you want to bet that, if she's still Level Three when you next see her, you won't feel the need to be quite so domineering with her?*>>

Truth was silent for a while. *Honestly, I got to like the domineering stuff.*

<<*You always did. You were just so starved for affection before that, you didn't know what you liked. I'm not judging, Truth. I'm not saying this is a bad thing, even. I'm saying you need to understand where you are coming from before you fuck up something you do actually care about.*>>

And the feeling stupid and ugly that Starbrite pounded into me?

<<*Another way of managing your insecurity. By deepening it. Make you unable to accept compliments and validation from outside company control. Every little ding, every bonus, every glowing quarterly performance review, was Starbrite reminding you that it liked you. Valued you. You were doing a good job. The more and more you became the monster they wanted, the more they showered you in affection. Not that this makes you special. It's how the whole company works, for everyone.*>>

Getting more and more isolated. Because I only believed the bad shit outsiders said. Because they were trash. People I looked down on. Their positive opinions were worthless, and their negative opinions only justified my treating them like nothing.

<<*So, let's review. The majority of your brief life was spent in the slums. You lived with abusive parents. Your dad was a tyrant who ruled through violence; your mom was a manipulative sadist. Control was something that had to be fought for and viciously defended. Everyone you saw around you was a person without vision. Their drive was always for stupid things gotten in stupid ways, or people with no drive at all. People born to be eaten.*>>

I then join Starbrite, and the second I find out that I can make good money, long-term, by hurting people, I take it. Because why wouldn't I?

<<*You then do the good-little-soldier thing because, one, you really did feel grateful to Starbrite and, two, it was the fastest way to get money and power. And the second the company turned on you . . .*>>

I was gone. I mean, I don't think it was really reasonable to ask me to die—

<<*Truth. Buddy. Fuckwit. You were being mentally conditioned through your muti-lated soul and under a magical compulsion to joyfully obey. Nobody else seemed to have any problems obeying their "fight to the death" orders. You fucked off the second the order came down. I had to fight you literally every step of the way. You were grateful, but like your loyalty, it was conditioned on Starbrite being useful to you.*>>

A mindset I clearly carried over through the Free State and Siphios. And since coming back to Jeon. I wouldn't even follow Merkovah's travel plans. I clearly know better than the six-hundred-year-old professional spymaster.

<<*The thing with the kid on the rooftop was a particularly nice touch, I thought. Why let a mass murderer go to waste when his brief life could be better spent involuntarily serving you?*>>

The thing I keep coming back to is that it worked. All that shit. It worked. It is working. I have no reason to think it won't continue to work. In fact, I would be a moron to suddenly stop doing it and try to live like a saint.

<<*Yep. Never said you should. Just said you needed to understand where it was com-ing from, so you recognized it when it was happening and didn't do something stupid.*>>

Truth chuckled. Then laughed. Bitter, self-mocking laughter, tears running down his face. Laughing until he couldn't breathe, convulsing in the dirt. "That's not okay. That's fucked-up. And I don't really care. That's even more fucked-up. I should care. It's not like I don't care about things. I should care about this. But I like it, and I'm going to do it again. And that's fucked-up!"

CHAPTER 18

OUR MANY WEAPONS

Truth slowly pulled himself together. Improved understanding of self notwithstanding, he still needed to get into Harban. He also still had the minor question of what to do with Barton.

<<Find him a new name, for one thing. He's been heavily conditioned by a motivated succubus for, what, three days now? We can only call that a start. Still a long way from ego death, and every bit of alienation and dehumanization you can cram in there will help.>>

You just said that was a terrible, vile thing to do! You had a whole big rant about what a no-good, very bad thing that was!

<<It is. Literally nightmare-fuel stuff, for those who get nightmares. I also said I don't care even a tiny bit about whatshisname. He might actually be useful once properly trained, and you are right about needing a reliable point of contact with the System Astrologica.>>

Barton. You just said his name was Barton.

<<A loser name for a loser. Let's name him something better. Like Spot, or Rover. Or Prince. Damage is done at this point. He's never going to be the same person who went on shift that night, safe and loved at his grandma's luxury hotel. You can cut him loose with a head full of unspeakable trauma, struggling to survive a few more weeks of pain and humiliation before the inevitable, ugly end. Or you can make it "all worth it.">>

By transforming him into my devoted slave.

<<He could be your first or second worshiper, depending on where you put Etenesh. Accentuate the positive. Because, and I think you know this, there is no putting him back the way you found him. Not between your magic and the succubi. He utterly believes that he is your servant.>>

The shine had gone off the view. It was still sweeping, looking down over the wide river, the thin belt of suburbs, and the terrible glory of Harban. It was just that the romance had left. Now it was just a series of problems.

Fantastic. Just. Fantastic. I am truly the best lone-wolf terrorist. Can we at least make him happy?

<<Sure. Deliriously happy. He won't be very functional, because people generally aren't happy all the time, but you could do it. Look, I'm an expert on manipulating one person—you. And that was mostly because you couldn't hear me or feel me doing it. We have two capable succubae at our disposal. Use them.>>

Yeah. Sure. Prager's rotted cock, what a mess.

<<Could be worse. You could have done that to someone you actually care about. At least Mr. Mittens will have a colorful life.>>

Truth stood and dusted himself off. He firmly decided that he wasn't going to think about this a moment longer. He had a job to do, and hanging around on this hillside wasn't going to get it done. Besides, sunset wasn't that far off. He didn't feel like sleeping rough tonight. Time to get into it.

Alfred von Wigglebottom.

<<Kind of sexualizing, don't you think? Unless you want to go that way, you nasty bastard.>>

I was wrong, I was wrong! It's just I keep wanting to call him "Butterball" and he's a skinny little guy. Twiggy?

<<We have a lot of time to think about this. We can make a whole ritual out of it, granting him a new name and identity. It will be very meaningful. By the way, the nearest cross-river bridge is over that way. I'll drop a guide arrow over it.>>

Truth got running. The suburbs were ignorable. Multistory low-rise apartment buildings, wide parking lots, some big box stores. Dull, dull, dull. Not bad, exactly, just a sweet spot of "cheaper than downtown" and "nicer than the slums" without actually being cheap or nice. Not a lot of suburban sprawl around Harban. Part of that was geography, but more of that was that the land was just too valuable to waste on inexpensive housing.

Closer to the river were the factories. This far from the city, they were the smaller operators. Light industrial fabricators, or parts suppliers to the bigger factories. Truth had never worked a factory job. Never even been in one. But he always admired how they worked on the outside.

Each factory was a component. They explained it to him back in high school. Each and every factory was a component in a larger system. By themselves, they couldn't function. They had to be connected to the rest of the system to work.

He watched a slow-moving freight train rumble alongside a paved road next to a factory. A flatbed wagon pulled up alongside of it, keeping pace with a particular rail car. A fetish floated up off the back of the flatbed—all long spider arms and gleaming red eyes—and quickly moved over a container on the train. The legs reached down, detached the container, lifted it up, and deposited it securely on the wagon. The wagon pulled away, heading back to the factory. There was a queue of yet more flat-beds lined up to repeat the procedure.

In Harban, the flow of commerce was never interrupted. There was no reason for it to be interrupted. It was much the same on the river. Long barges, heavily loaded, plied their way up and down the Fan. The river ran all the way to the sea. It could hardly be easier for imports and exports to flow.

Truth was looking at it with different eyes now. You could see the way innovation and improvements had washed over the factories. Each time removing the human component.

No need to stop the train if you had flying magical devices. No need for long-shoremen or crane operators, either. Really, you could do away with the truck drivers, too—you can train the bound demon to make the loop to and from the track. No need to unload the wagons with meat hands, either. Or turn the bolts. He was probably missing something there, or they would have done all that by now. Still. Not a whole lot of humans in sight.

It was what the truck drivers were talking about in the rest stop. More and more jobs were done by demons and magic; less and less need for people. And somehow, those savings and efficiencies never reached the pockets of the newly unemployed. Hopefully, Joarle the truck driver was setting himself up for the collapse. He seemed like an okay guy.

Oh, positive thought—the collapse would lead to full employment. What with all the sudden vacancies opening up and the urgent need for manual labor. It was too late to encourage mass breeding, of course, but . . .

Truth slammed to a dead halt, stopping so hard a plume of dust shot out five meters ahead of him. His head rotated, like naval artillery taking its bearing, aiming directly at the slums.

There was ever-increasing automation in the factories, in transport, everywhere you might need cheap, low-skill labor. Surplus labor was only useful to keep costs down, and that only got you so far. The rate of unemployment, or informal employment, in the slums was extraordinarily high. And yet. There was no cap on the amount of children the state was willing to provide welfare and free technical education for.

Now, did that sound like Jeon? If he was describing the country to a foreigner or something? No. The government dumping intellect suppressants and contraceptives into the water supply for the slums, yes. Creating inescapable indentures in exchange for education and a universal spell, that would be more on brand. Unless, of course, you knew the collapse was coming far in advance.

He could see it with shattering clarity. Some bureaucrat, or probably several, had a high-level meeting. Just like the ones at Nag Hammadi. They didn't agree on what was causing the problem, and probably didn't agree that the problem was happening at all. More or less what happened at Nag Hammadi. BUT. They were able to "work with industry leaders" to develop opportunities for Denizens to better themselves.

Welfare to encourage parents to have kids. Welfare to make sure those kids reached breeding age. Education for manual labor, variously defined. Smart enough to be useful. But never a real education. Never spells that could be used as weapons or for nonlabor work. No good food, or clean water, or healthy apartments. The obedient, the best laborers, got treats. Everyone else got to live like rats, breeding and fighting in the walls built by their betters. Everyone taught "This is the real world; this is what life is like."

The people who ran things were playing for the world after the collapse. They wanted the weak Level Ones and the Level Zeros. They would be the only functional people when the magic disappeared. Lots and lots of Level Ones and Zeros, trained to obey. Trained by the army during their National Service. Trained by their schools. Easy to adapt into a magic-free labor pool and military force. And now? Thanks to the new System coming in? The Denizens would be trained to work for food or shelter, not pay.

All the middle managers would be gone. The CEOs of small companies, military leaders, lower-level bureaucrats and politicians. All the possible challengers to the elite would be wiped out by their collapsing apertures. Only the very top of the pyramid, and the very bottom, would survive.

Jeon knew damn well what Starbrite was up to. The bureaucrats and politicians saw no reason not to get in on the game. There would be an aristocracy of those with body cultivation that let them hold on to their magic. There would be magic fueled by sacrifice instead of cosmic rays. The Church of Prager would be right there with them, supporting the efforts. Making sure they were the ones holding the knife. And they would have plenty of serfs and slaves.

No more money. You won't need it. You will make what you are told to make. You eat what you are given, sleep where you are permitted. Those poor, dumb "Citizens" still clinging to the notion that they were better than the Denizens. At best, they would become the overseer class. Still toiling out in the fields for the real masters. Whipping can be tiring work. Delegation is the soul of leadership. The leaders must have their rest so that they can make the very best decisions for everyone.

Borges knew. He knew exactly what these pricks were up to, what they had been up to for decades! He wasn't trying to invent an entirely new world; he was going to hijack their plans and substitute his own, better version. Something more humane and beautiful. Did Merkovah know? Maybe not about why Borges was doing what he was doing, but he must have known about what Jeon was planning. It wasn't a secret. It was a conspiracy right out in the open. The only secret was the "why."

<<*I hate humanity. I really do. I hope you go the "Mad Tyrant" route. These scum deserve every misery you heap on them.*>>

Which scum?

<<*Just start heaping. I'll tell you when to stop.*>>

Truth threw himself into motion. He aimed for the barges on the river. There would be security on the docks, certainly, but nothing too bad. Just too much volume moving through there, and smuggling had always been the rule rather than the exception. He had a dead drop to pick up, too, and it was on the riverfront.

Truth leaned up against the rail and watched the city crawl by. He could see it now, a little more clearly. A factory. A component in a larger system called Jeon. Getting ready for the exciting new product launch. Truth started smiling.

A well-trained slave class was what the bureaucrats and aristos wanted. Truth was quite willing to bet they had never been to the slums. He had a feeling things weren't going to work out quite the way they planned.

CHAPTER 19

ATTENTION, SHOPPERS

The River Fan had driven Truth into a quiet fury. Its tutelary spirit would be quite hurt by that, if it still lived. It wasn't like it wanted to be polluted. It would have pointed out that it had been millennia of human management and intervention that left the watershed like this. The river was every bit as much a victim as Truth was.

Some absolute bastard, probably a long series of serious, hard-working, focused bastards, had been working to remove the pollution from the River Fan. They did this by means of magical filtration, apparently. The river was lined with canals. Water was very gently drawn into the canals, through a filter at the mouth, then once it had passed through the canal, the water made its slow, winding way back to the river via another filter. Or a lake, a pond, the sea, but in any case, the water only moved, very gently, very slowly, in one direction along the canal.

He could now understand what he had spent most of his life looking at. The toxic water was pulled in through the first filter. It primarily existed to maintain the flow rate and ensure the canal didn't get overfull during the torrential rains that came in the early spring and fall. If there were any problems, it also prevented backflow. The filter at the other end was a wonderfully sophisticated bit of magical engineering. It let fish through, plants through, boats through, but not alchemical runoff. Or plastic sachets, or human waste however defined. Those it kept inside.

The toxicity of the canals was slowly, permanently, building. There must be some other part of this he was missing. Something that had kept the canals from exploding into flame or boiling with toxic gasses. He couldn't remember anything that looked like a reasonable suspect. All he knew was that, from his perspective, the money-earning parts of the city were pumping their poison runoff into the slums and leaving it there. Keeping all the unwanted, but necessary, side effects in one place.

Truth privately swore to let it all run out—not into the river but into the rich downtown. He could see the rushing, toxic waters sweeping through the fancy little stores and charming bakeries, into the apartment buildings in neighborhoods where normal families were forbidden on pain of imprisonment or being reduced to a Denizen. He would sit on a rooftop with a bag of snacks and watch the black waters sweep through, smashing open doors and gates so the rats swarming after it could feast.

He let out an explosive sigh. The people in the rich part of the city benefited from the system, but they didn't make it. They probably didn't understand it any more than the slumrats did. Well, some of them clearly did—they kept it going, after all—but really, it was at most the people at the very top and their elite servants. Based on what he had seen so far, he wasn't sure that any one person really understood the systems they had built.

The barge seemed to drift down the river, carrying cargo containers full of who knows what. Chariots. Carriages. Pallets of water talismans. Each bearing a sigil that would tell the magical devices where to send it next, until it finally reached its destination. One system. The goods had to be paid for. Another system. There needed to be some way to regulate the movement of the barges so you didn't get accidents and traffic jams on the rivers and canals. Another system. How the stores were run and taxed. System.

Systems of systems. Enormous complexity that was invisible once you got high enough and was so big, you couldn't see it when you were in 'em. Swirling, dizzying systems of systems, systems all the way up and all the way down. Living in an apartment building? That was a whole system of systems right there, and you hadn't even left your front door yet. The nightmare of a commute and securing breakfast on the go awaited. More systems than you could even count.

What did it all look like from the highest throne? Did Yaldabaoth foresee all these systems when it created the world? Or was the initial creation so powerful, it naturally gave rise to endless systems without his needing to consider them?

The barge pulled level with an unpopulated stretch of sidewalk. A long jump from the river to shore. Truth smiled. Complexity be damned, sometimes you just wanted to move. And with a sudden burst of effort, he did just that.

Truth made his way through the riverside neighborhood. The homes were nice, of course, but not particularly luxurious in this stretch. It was just a bit too close to some alchemist towers for complete comfort. Still nice, though. Trees dotted the sidewalk, comfortable carriages parked in lethally expensive garages. Nice little shops selling things that were not, strictly speaking, *fancy* but were better than anything he had grown up with.

His eye was irresistibly drawn to a glowing illusion of a blossoming water flower. It was a small branch of the Green Lotus chain of apothecaries. A direct subsidiary of the Floating Dream Alchemy Tower, which to Truth's continual surprise, was not an appendage of Starbrite. Not a competitor, either—Truth remembered seeing plenty of their products in the System Shop. But in its own quiet way, it had carved out a powerful niche in Jeon as *the* leading retail apothecary.

He had never been in one. Which was bizarre, because he had heard about them his whole life, talked about them, walked past them, but never actually been in one. By the time he was a Citizen with actual walking-around money, he was in Starbrite. Any medicine or elixir would be delivered to his door with a thought.

He smiled and went in. The dead drop would keep a little longer.

He walked into the store, dressed lightly in the identity of a moderately wealthy young man. He was leery of pushing any harder than that, and besides, he was window-shopping. Nothing in this shop would be useful for a Level Four.

The air tasted sweet and somehow green. Like walking into a greenhouse full of flowers on the edge of blooming. Everything was very clean, very white, with pale blond woods displaying pills, elixirs, ointments, and other alchemical wonders under two-centimeter-thick spelled glass. To maintain perfect freshness, a discreet sign informed shoppers. And certainly not because some of these products were worth more than a D-Tier Starbrite employee earned in several years.

Truth vividly remembered buying that Ghul potion from Prentiss when he pushed for his breakthrough. "This ain't exactly the Green Lotus," he had said. "You couldn't afford to breathe the air in a Green Lotus. You can afford old Feng's," Prentiss had retorted.

It had all worked out. Still. Nothing in there looked like it was picked up by scavengers and sold to the shop. Every pill had been branded with the Lotus logo, a brand that could be checked by talisman to ensure authenticity, date of production, manufacturing alchemist, lot number, and endless other details useful to commerce. From the second it was manufactured to the second it dissolved in your belly, that pill's existence was accountable.

"Can I help you?" The clerk was pretty, in a boy-next-door sort of way. He had the androgyne look that was so desirable, but lacked the subtle touches to elevate him to the next level of beauty. A poor family, then, as those things went in this neighborhood. They probably spent all they had on cosmetic refinements to get him this far, praying that he would build a career from this humble beginning.

"Yes, I'm doing a little shopping around, just seeing what's on the market. My little brother's sixteenth is coming up next month, and I wanted to get a feel for prices. Do you have any decent, not too expensive, Level Zero cultivation potions?"

Left unsaid was that an elixir would be much too expensive. It didn't need to be said: such things were criminally expensive for everyone. A genuine potion would already be considered lavish affection.

"Lucky boy. We have options at a variety of price points." The clerk turned to walk away, then, in a painfully rookie move, hesitated and looked questioningly at Truth.

"Brother from another mother. Dad decided he wanted an upgrade when I was ten."

"I am so sorry. That was none of my business."

"It's what it is. I just felt like I always had to look out for Fal, you know? He was so much smaller and weaker. It's been rewarding." Truth smiled, letting the strong-big-brother identity firm around him. "I like taking care of little brothers, it seems."

"Very lucky boy. Level Zero potions are this way." The clerk turned and led him over to a display case with ten potions on display. Truth caught a hint of flush on the younger man's neck. Laughing silently to himself, he followed.

"Have you kept up on potion trends?"

"I can't say I have. Prices have gone up, I'm certain, but they have been skyrocketing for years now."

"Sadly true." The clerk nodded. There was a flash of real pain there. "Well, the big breakthrough development of the last year has been Functional Strength™. Thanks to major developments in both anatomical natural philosophy as well as cutting-edge alchemical development in the Floating Dream Tower, we can now provide potions to enhance the effective strength of muscles without increasing bulk. This allows the user to retain the classic Jeon look while leaning into the more-rugged physicality that is so popular right now."

Truth pretended to ignore the darting side eye he got from the clerk.

"Huh. Any help on cultivation?" Truth asked.

"Not generally. The top end of the Sprinter range, the SX-4, does provide some benefit to the inner channels and aperture foundation, so their cultivation will be a little smoother. It's intended to complement classic cultivation potions, not replace them."

"I see. Functional strength is in? I always get looks when people see how bulky I am."

"I didn't want to say anything, but . . . you do look very strong." The clerk sounded embarrassed. In Jeon, manual labor was nothing to be proud of. A real mage cast spells and bound demons and angels to labor for them. Long, manicured nails had always been a sign of prosperity, as were long hair and a slim physique.

"What can I say? I love feeling my body move. I can run for hours, climb mountains, and leap across rivers." He smiled happily. "Hard. Strong. Enduring. My body is *fun*."

"No, I like it!" the clerk blurted, then blushed. "Oh, Prager. Look. Honestly? If you can't buy something today, buy it tomorrow or as soon as you can. We are pushing the Functional Strength™ range because elixir reagents have gone from criminally expensive to simply not available at any price. Not at an acceptable level of quality, anyway. It's a good time to have muscles. And prices are only going to go up faster and faster."

Truth nodded at that. "And you?"

"Get off work at six?"

Truth smiled. "I won't be here today. But I will be around."

Truth made his way to the dead drop, looking at the people around him. They were adapting. They had to adapt, but it was interesting seeing them do it. They were trying to adapt without changing *too much*. Keeping the look while upping the muscle. Increasing the labor supply while deepening the class system. Clinging to the strong, no matter what they looked like.

Well. That last thought was probably unfair. He was hardly ugly, even if he was bulky and crude-looking. People were free to like what they liked. Truth spotted a dancing illusion of a little blue-haired fairy in a store window, seven-pointed stars drifting down around it. It was advertising a home ice cream machine.

No. He wasn't ugly. He wasn't dumb. And while there weren't a ton of people who knew and loved him, he was content with who he had. And if he felt the urge to stand above others, to enjoy their fear and worship, to inflict pain to affirm that superiority? He would have to learn to manage it. He would be a man, not a monster. Such traits could be positive, used carefully.

Tucked under the air vent at the top of a thirty-story office building was a thick bundle. Truth unwrapped his delivery. His eyebrows almost reached his hairline.

Merkovah had sent presents.

CHAPTER 20

KNOCK KNOCK! VENGEANCE CALLING!

The dead drop was a lot bulkier than usual. Generally, there was only a crystal, which shattered once Truth had learned the contents. This time, there were arrays, talismans, a few disposable charms, and not one but *several* informational crystals. Truth assumed there must be some kind of security consideration there, as each crystal could hold far more information than a person could read in a lifetime.

It seemed that the old exorcist was done with distraction and was now moving on the attack. Lists of sites to raid, personnel to assassinate, resources to steal or destroy, propaganda to promote—it was a veritable wish list of insurrection. Truth directly ignored the apartment blocks Merkovah wanted flattened. He might not have a moral leg to stand on there, but he was prepared to adopt the phantom limb and balance.

This did lead to the next curious point in the briefing packets—Merkovah clearly wanted Truth to work with others on a coordinated campaign. He wanted that very badly. Presumably because it worked better, as demonstrated by his literally centuries of experience. On the other hand, he knew Truth didn't trust his methods or people enough to take a single meeting with an asset outside of Jeon, so what odds were there of him working with others *in* Jeon? So, he adapted.

The reason for the multiple crystals was soon revealed. Each contained sets of "Suggested Objectives" with contingent actions that went with them. For example, "Kill Fredrich Li, Head of Strategic Planning, VG Marine and Mercantile Insurance. If killed before Day X, post a sign claiming responsibility as the Real Jeon Provisional Army. If after Day X, also kill Dorothea N'Ganat, Human Resource Coordinator, VG Marine and Mercantile Insurance."

Break-ins, burglary, arson, an alarming number of murders, a nontrivial number of mass casualty events, it read like the "dream journal" of a particularly edgy young teen. Except it was a six-hundred-year-old exorcist who also dabbled in international terrorism. A fairly bleak thought, so Truth amused himself by imagining Merkovah trying to explain the situation to his other operatives.

"It's quite straightforward. I have a pawn who may, or may not, assist your mission without notice or explanation, at times of his choosing. I did pay him in advance, but

instead of the money you will get, I fobbed him off with top-tier spells, a Level Four Elixir, several national treasures, and a literal angelic sword. And I set him up with a particularly lovely, intelligent, and kind student of mine. Who comes from a very rich, very influential family. They are devoted to one another.

"So, technically, you are getting paid more money than he is. This proves how much smarter you are and why you can be trusted with the REAL plan. The good news is that he will cause Internal Security even more headaches than he causes you. The bad news is that I have learned some pain cannot be erased with magic . . ."

Well, it was nice to imagine, anyway. Merkovah was quite right about one thing—Truth didn't trust any of his notional coworkers. If there was one key take-away he had found in working for Merkovah, it was that the old man was far from omniscient. Worse, Siphios intelligence was probably hopelessly compromised and corrupted. He didn't have direct evidence for that principle, but there was a crucial bit of circumstantial evidence.

Even with all the ancient spells, the blessings that came directly (or almost directly) from God, the angelic weapons, even with *everything*, they had never beaten Starbrite. If there were some shadowy victories hidden in the long twilight struggle, Truth didn't know about them. From what he could see, Merkovah had been getting rinsed for longer than most countries had existed.

So, no. He would not be joining with his "brothers-in-arms" and marching shoulder to shoulder into the glorious revolutionary future. Merkovah had, in fact, paid in advance. He would do his very best to clear the list and achieve their big goals. And that would be as far as that would go.

He checked the final crystal. It was everything he had ever dreamed of. They even had a big corporate headquarters. Just off the highway, near a convention center, a sports arena, several hotels, and it even had a subway stop just blocks away. Delicious. He was suddenly hungry for mushrooms.

He looked into the city glow—night had come down on Harban. The offices would be empty. It would be hard to wait . . . but necessary. Time to find his hotel. Before that, though, he had to resume the identity of the Prince. More thoughtfully, this time. Understanding where it was coming from. Accepting what he liked and keeping an eye out for what should be rejected. It wouldn't be easy, but the process was important. The best argument for a boss on Earth is a boss in Heaven, but his ambition had never been to be King Rat.

The Prince strode into the Shalia Hotel with the natural arrogance of someone coming in from the roof, not the ground. The Maid was waiting for him by the door. He hadn't told it that he was coming. The Hellbeast had simply conformed to its given nature and waited dutifully where it would be needed.

"Prepare a bath and dinner. You know my requirements."

The Maid bowed. "As you command, Your Highness. Please, allow me to show you to your suite."

The suite was staggeringly luxurious, even by Truth's rarified standards. Every thread of every loop in every tuft of carpet had been carefully selected and engineered with sensual comfort and impeccable aesthetics. It didn't simply match the drapes; it was in dialog with them. They combined, collaborated, really, to provide an environment whose subtle beige and gold accents both relaxed and empowered the extremely powerful guests enjoying the suite.

It was nothing short of a large, luxurious apartment, with a formal dining room in contrasting dark wood. Wood that matched the grain of the coffee table in the dedicated sitting area and the leather-topped desk. Presumably, the desk was there for signing very important contracts. Or treaties.

The Prince didn't ask how all this would be paid for. They were quite welcome to try and collect from him. He knew perfectly well who owned this hotel, and he was already planning on usurping the old bastard's throne. His servants cared even less. They were just happy that their fix was back, confirming their natures and calming the chaos within them.

The view out over Harban was practically worth the price of the room by itself. Harban glowed at night. The giant illusions advertising potions, golems, magical devices, entertainment, all brilliant in frozen blues and furious reds and melted-butter yellows. Moving, calling, dancing, or making silly faces. Hot bodies available for cold cash. From the Royal Suite, you could see them all. Look down on them all.

"Good suite. Presidential suite was unavailable?"

"Alas, the ambassadorial delegation from the Ben Zhu Block had already taken up residence. I understand that the Foreign Minister is hosting a dinner there tonight. Forgive me, but I did not think it my place to provoke a diplomatic incident by evicting them," Butler apologized.

"Quite right. This is entirely adequate," Truth said, looking over a bed that loudly assumed one would never be sleeping alone. Truth was quite large by Jeon standards, and lying in the middle of the bed, he wouldn't be able to touch any of the sides. The creepiness of it wormed its way through the armor of arrogance his persona provided. You wouldn't sleep any better on it for all its size, and the recreational opportunities it suggested just seemed . . . unpleasant. At a certain point, it was all just too much, right?

Maybe it was just him. He shrugged slightly and checked out the bathroom. Lovely deep tub, and more than long enough. This was a decadent sensuality he could completely support. He tested the water. Just shy of boiling. Perfect for his heavily refined physique. He smiled slightly, stripped, and got in.

"Fetch me a cold fruit juice to enjoy in the tub," he ordered the Maid. "In the meantime, Butler, how is your project coming?" Truth let his head loll back, enjoying the feeling of his muscles relaxing.

"Passing well. He is already starting to feel an aversion to remembering his past, and his feelings of worship and adoration for you are coming on quickly. He already associates you with safety and power, and your magic firmly impressed your identity upon him. The more-extreme developments will come slowly and with time, but the foundation is being laid."

"Mmm. You are keeping him a functional human?"

"As you instructed, my prince."

"Good. In the near future, I will have a use for him. What spells does he know?"

Truth made a deliberate effort to refer to the former Barton as "He" instead of "It" in a belated attempt to acknowledge his humanity. The succubus quickly picked up on his master's whim and played along.

"He knows a variation on the Jeon Universal Spell, and the Infinite Archives Grand Palace of Eternal Wisdom Transcendent Akashic Record of Supreme Insight Recollection Pinnacle Library of Rule Over Humanity All-Surpassing All-Encompassing All-Dominating Jade Sutra of the Perfect Revelation of Almighty Divine Abbot the Right Reverend Learned Foote, Part One."

Truth slowly blinked at the second one. "I don't think I know that one."

"It is intended to track personnel, payroll, inventory, accounts, and other such administrative work, Your Highness."

There was a peaceful moment in the bathroom. Truth enjoyed watching the swirls of steam dance in the air.

"Modern magic, I assume?"

"I believe the spell is a refinement on an older generation of spells, perhaps twenty years old at this point. Quite modern, yes."

"So, no offensive capability to speak of, nor deception, nor mobility, nor body refinement, defense, or anything of any tactical use whatsoever."

"That is correct, my prince."

Truth thought about it and shrugged internally. It made sense. What did the child of a business family need? Business-administration skills, and the spells to support it. The Universal Spell let him make use of any magical devices he was likely to come across in the course of business, and the admin spell let him do administrative work. Totally sensible, totally reasonable, and, under the present circumstances, about as useful as a glass hammer.

"Very well. Does he have any experience in marketing or sales?"

"Some limited experience, yes, Your Highness."

"Good. Groom him. This time tomorrow, he will replace someone at a company I designate. I will provide all the necessary details of the person in question."

"As you command. I must caution you, however . . ."

"Oh, I know. Prepare the ritual room. We will reinforce his . . . priorities as well as confirm your identities. After dinner."

"My prince is most gracious. Your servants thank you for your consideration." Butler didn't salivate, but only because it would be out of character.

Truth woke refreshed, if a little disoriented. The bed was just too big. He quickly shook it off, enjoyed his morning routine, and set about the work for the day. Apparently, the manager of the hotel wanted to meet him. Truth declined. The Prince is not available at this time. Perhaps later.

He sneaked out of the hotel, crept to the subway, and adopted the persona of a drone shuffling off to a dead-end job. It came upsettingly easily. Just one more talisman-maintenance tech, in an era where the failure rates were shooting up "for no reason."

He got to his stop, walked the few blocks to the office building, found the right floor, walked straight past the surprisingly heavy security, and found the right suite. Then the right room. He leaned over and whispered into the secretary's ear.

"Oh, drat! I think you forgot his 9:15 appointment with *that person.* Time to put in some earplugs and stop anyone from investigating. *Again.* God, if only you didn't need this job so much."

The secretary was already wedging the plugs in before he finished, looking so done with life. Then, to Truth's mild horror, they fished out noise-blocking earmuffs to go over the plugs. He had just been guessing. Just who was screaming at this guy?

Not that the prick didn't deserve it.

Truth walked into the office, closed the door, and locked it behind him. The surveillance and recording spells in the room were all Level One in power, easy to disable. The man in question was Level Four, but that wasn't going to be a problem either.

Truth plucked the man out of his seat and threw him up against the ceiling hard enough to break the plaster. Then, as he fell, Truth used gravity to fully express his appreciation for the man. Transmitting his gratitude through his boot and into the falling man's testicles.

"Daragah Kolch, CEO of MegaShroom and former CFO of XextraTee." The unnoticeability had worn off, but he would still look like a blur to the vomiting, crying man. He liked the idea of being a terrifying, abusive, but unidentifiable force in the executive's life. However briefly.

"We don't have much time together, but I want to show you *exactly* how much your work has influenced my life." He ripped off one of the man's shoes, slapping the wooden heel into his hand with a satisfying thump. "I hope you take advantage of it. It's the opportunity of a lifetime."

CHAPTER 21

MAXIMIZING SHAREHOLDER VALUE

I don't know what I did to you—"

"But I bet you can guess." Truth grinned and smashed the heel of the shoe down on the CEO's toes. He was pretty sure he broke three of them. Daragah curled into a ball, grabbing his foot and making a high-pitched keening noise.

"This probably seems incredibly unfair. I mean, you didn't force anyone to do anything, right? You are just out here, making opportunities for people to live their best lives. Financial independence for people who would otherwise live hand to mouth."

Truth squatted down next to Daragah. The CEO was hyperventilating but wisely keeping his mouth shut. No panic buttons, Truth noticed, nor any particular defensive spells in place. Strange. He would have figured this guy would live in terror. Truth certainly would be a lot more concerned about vengeful "brand ambassadors" coming for their promised happily-ever-after.

"Must say I am impressed. Here you are, helpless, knowing that your remaining minutes will be filled with torture and humiliation, and you are managing to keep more or less quiet. Didn't see it going that way."

Daragah opened his mouth, gasping, then his teeth snapped shut again. Truth narrowed his eyes. He reached down and grabbed a pinky finger. Daragah looked at him in horror. Begging with his eyes. Truth snapped it ninety degrees up, then another ninety degrees clockwise. Daragah started silently crying. Even the keening noise had stopped.

"GOD DAMN IT! FUCKING MEGASHROOM!" Truth stood, swearing. "I should have FUCKING KNOWN!" He gave "Daragah" a casual kick in the ass. "My whole goddamn life, right up until I left home, was poisoned by you fucks. And lots of others just like you, of course, but COME ON. CEO of Megashroom AND you were the former CFO of XextraTee? I could spend a year torturing you and never regret a second of it." He sighed. "Torturing 'you.' Damn it all. Who are you, exactly? Or are you geased?"

"Daragah" went very still, then started seizing, his eyes weeping blood. Truth swore and cast Cup and Knife. The spell seemed to slide around the man, like it was trying to find the right way in and how to send the harm "back." Truth felt his own energy reserves dropping fast. Whatever had been done to him, it wasn't something simple.

Truth frowned, pushing on the spell. "Daragah" had been set up as the fall guy. He might not be a good person, but whatever was killing him wasn't "right." The spell finally seemed to agree, but Truth could feel the boiling ball of curse-energy floating around. Like ball lightning, looking for a ground.

Truth sent it into the sign hanging on the side of the building. Seemed appropriate.

"Daragah" sat up with an explosive gasp, grabbing his feet, his fingers, touching his face and mouth. "Oh, God! Oh, God, I'm free!"

"Great. Super. Yaay." Truth sat on the desk with a thud.

<<I'm right there with you. This is a colossal disappointment.>>

Why do you care?

<<The way these MLM people play on human avarice and insecurity is really inspiring. Taking all that hope and turning it into soul-crushing fear and debt? Masterful stuff. When I was still in my "Get Truth to Die on the Job" phase, they were huge role models.>>

Are you one hundred percent sure you aren't a demon?

<<Are you?>>

These days, not as much as I once was. Truth sighed.

"All right, so . . . talk. Who are you and what's going on here?"

"Daragah" jolted. "Oh, God!" He started scrambling back. Truth picked up a pen from the desk and threw it hard enough to pierce the carpet and lodge in the floor. The fangs had flashed out silently and invisibly. Truth smiled grimly at the cowering man. And waited.

"I'm. My name. Is Anthony Wrenn. I'm not the person you are looking for. I'm not Daragah Kolch."

"I can see that. Your existence is very disappointing. Justify it. Explain why you are here and not him."

"What? Oh, God. Um."

"Let me save you a little time—God will have no involvement in any part of what goes on here."

"Oh G—! Um! I'm the anointed king!" Tony was panicking. Which even Truth was willing to admit was fair enough.

"Anointed king?"

"Yes. I made it to the top, you see."

"Of?"

"The Pyramid. Double diamond ambassador, black steel, orichalcum, frozen mythril, I did it. I was the guy who did it. That one in a million that actually sold enough product and recruited enough people that I got all the way to the top of the pyramid at MegaShroom."

Truth rocked back. "That's possible?"

"It took a hell of a lot of hard work. A lot of sacrifices. I lost . . . a lot of things along the way. But I did it. I made it all the way to the top. I was clearing over a million wen a year, most of it tax-free." Tony didn't look very proud of that fact.

"All right, so you schemed and betrayed your way to the top of the MegaShroom pyramid. Then what?"

"I get invited into a conference room. There are all these guys, I know all these guys, they are the top brass at MegaShroom. All the executives. The board of directors is there, all of them. Kolch is there. He tells me . . . that it's time for my reward. He takes off his jacket, his shirt, pants, gets totally naked, and lies down on the table. And they. They."

"Kill him?"

"Eat him. He had this look on his face, like he was in the most incredible pain and the most incredible ecstasy at the same time. They literally bit chunks off him. Pulled out muscles and ate. Ate till they should have exploded. Guts pushing out, all bloated, seven-thousand-wen suits covered in blood and other things." Tony was shivering, wrapping his arms around his knees and rocking back and forth.

"I can't move. I can't even blink. There is some kind of enchantment in the chair. They made me watch it all. They scrape together all his . . . grease. All the fatty bits around his organs and under his skin. They scrape it into a brass bowl and heat it up. They render the fat. Pour the hot, melted fat over my head. It should have burnt. It did burn. But I could feel it transforming me. I . . . started to think I was Daragah Kolch, but I still knew I was Anthony Wrenn."

"And you knew you couldn't act outside the character of Kolch."

"Yeah. Not every second of every day, but I couldn't say anything. I had to *be* him."

"Ah." Truth thought it through for a moment, but was drawing a blank. "Why? Why any of that?"

Tony started laughing, a broken, hopeless noise. "It seems like you understand how we operate. The human consequences of our business model."

"Oh, yes. You really start to appreciate the value of MegaShroom Suppositories when your mother steals all your money to pay for them."

"Mom, huh? Actually, that's pretty normal. Seventy-five percent of our ambassadors, associates, and members are female." Tony nodded. "We train them to tell other women that it's a way to bring in extra income and develop financial independence, even if they are stuck at home raising the kids."

"*I remember.*"

"Yeah. Slum family, I'm guessing? Either that or the suburbs. Those are our best hunting grounds. Anyway. Why are they doing all this? Simple." Tony's face pulled into a very crooked grin. "Limiting shareholder liability."

There was another pause after that.

"Explain that."

"It's how companies work. You have this artificial person, the corporation. The corporation has one job—make the shareholders money. The shareholders are only at risk to the extent they have invested. That is, they can never lose more than they have put in. No matter what debts the company runs up, the worst that can happen to a shareholder is that their investment gets wiped out. They can't be personally liable for the debt. Same with crimes. A corporation could kill a million people, and the shareholders wouldn't be responsible at all. Legally."

"Okay?" Truth asked, thinking that it wasn't really okay.

"Everybody agrees this fake person exists. They can hire people, pay taxes, enter contracts, conduct litigation; they can do almost everything a normal human being can do. All without a body to kick or a soul to damn. But that's human law. What about God and God's law? There isn't word one in any holy script about corporations."

"Still not really seeing where this is going?"

"An artificial person, created by the shareholders, *but* its mind, its driving spirit, is the company officers. Most particularly the CEO. Literally the chief executive officer. Most responsible person for doing things."

"Ah. They found a way to pin moral responsibility on you and your predecessors?" Truth asked.

"Yes. They think they found a way to fool God. The CEO is changed every year. The top performer becomes the next CEO. They are anointed with oil, elevated, and confirmed in their role by the invisible entity that is Corporation."

Tony grabbed his knees again, rocking back and forth this time. "The other officers and the board all eat the old king, absorbing some of the sin, but it's really about turning the king into a sacrifice. Then the new CEO, a person who has definitionally sacrificed others for their own gain, is forced into their role. Daragah Kolch. Asshole extraordinaire."

"Why keep the same identity going? An artificial person to absorb the real sins of the company. Which is an artificial person," Truth said.

"Something like that. I think there probably was a real Daragah Kolch at some point. Maybe things are different at XextraTee."

Truth stared blankly out the window for a minute. There wasn't much to see. Just a big, multistory parking lot. Pretty generic office too, now that he was looking at it. Plenty of "I'm So Great" pictures, awards from trade groups, that kind of thing, but all the furniture looked catalog-standard. Bland. There was less there than it seemed. Then he frowned.

"Wait, you said the board of directors is in on this? Aren't they shareholders too?" Truth vaguely remembered hearing something about that.

"Yes, all of them. Some of them own more than ten percent of the company, which, as you can imagine, is huge."

"So, the whole process is pointless. Self-defeating." Truth threw up his hands.

"Sin eaters."

"The Pragerite Priests?"

"Yes." Tony nodded. "The board members are very prosperous and therefore favored by God. It is quite cheap, comparatively, for them to have their sins absolved."

Truth nodded. "I see. It's almost beautiful. A perfect complement to the sales structure. In addition to bearing the cost of buying inventory, developing marketing channels and sweat equity, the employees also bear the cost of the shareholders' moral decisions. And since this is Jeon and the Church of Prager is what it is, all that accumulated blood money makes it easier to wash away sin, not harder. It truly is beautiful."

"I don't know what they will do now that you broke the spell. It wouldn't surprise me if they had lawyers or hitmen on the way. Either one would be in character."

Truth nodded at that. "Oh, I'm going to do what I originally came here to do. I'm going to have you replaced with a stunt double. Yeah, MegaShroom is getting into an exciting new line of work. There may be some short-term downside pressure on earnings, but the long-term benefits to me may be substantial."

"What?" Tony looked bewildered.

"Yes, MegaShroom is going to spread rebellion. Insurrection. Anger at the choking grasp of Starbrite on the world. Some of you may die. All of you may die. But that is a sacrifice I am willing to make."

CHAPTER 22

BECOMING YOUR OWN BOSS

Truth sat Tony down behind the desk and shoved a recording crystal into his hand. "Go through everything you do in a day, everyone you call, all your relationships with your coworkers, all of it."

"Do you have the faintest idea what that actually means? I don't have 'ordinary' days. Every day is completely booked, putting out fires, managing people, training people, figuring out strategy, managing political relationships, keeping an eye on suppliers and sales and marketing and . . . everything. Yes, I delegate. Or, I guess, 'Daragah' delegates. But you have to supervise the people you delegated to. It's an insane job."

"Good thing I don't want MegaShroom to survive, eh?" Truth "smiled." Tony turned pale. "And I wasn't asking."

Truth fumed. He did have some ideas about how he wanted to do this, but he had to admit, now that he was there, they were pretty half-baked. *Did I want this to not work, at some level? To have the excuse to just . . . kill everyone and burn it all down?*

<<Ah, good old moral justification. You can do literally anything with that. No crime to vile, no horror too great, if they made you do it.>>

I mean . . . Truth struggled to articulate what he was feeling. *If it's morally justified—*

<You will notice that "justified" and "just" are related, but not identical, words. Or maybe you won't notice. Most don't. I think it's all the water in the brains. All that fluid swishing and pooling, inflating the gelatinous mass of your organs. It can't be good for critical thinking. And literacy was never your strong suit.>>

It has been a minute since I read something fun, now that you mention it.

<<Oh, good, more softcore erotica for unfulfilled women. Your target demographic.>>

Are you feeling okay? That's burn-adjacent at best.

<<Honestly, no. Something very weird is going on, and I don't think it's just us.>>

Weird how?

The System was quiet for a moment and then made a frustrated noise. *<<We are seeing . . . GAH! You don't have the language to describe this well, which means I don't either, moron! It's system collapse meeting contingency plans. But nobody one-hundred-percent believed things would collapse, so they half-assed the plans, and now all those contingencies have new urgency, so there is TON of money and labor getting shoved*

into things that were not terribly well designed in the first place! And the results are weird, and I think this building is the locus for something. Look at your damn feet! See if reality is on the bend.>>

Truth looked down. He didn't see anything out of the ordinary. He crouched down and squinted. Was there the tiniest little shimmer near the soles? Maybe. Or not.

"Hey, Tony? Was there somewhere in the building 'Daragah' was terrified of visiting or you felt an aversion to? Some part of the building you just don't remember ever seeing?"

"Not really? We don't own this building—we lease it. We really try to minimize headcount at headquarters, feeling that the MegaShroom promise is of a world full of CEOs, independent entrepreneurs—"

"You really did claw your way to the top of the pyramid, huh?"

Tony looked faintly ill. "Supreme Frozen Mythril Galactic Evangelist. One of only twenty in the company's history. Some things become instinct."

"Yeah. They do." Truth vividly remembered his mom's repeated insistence that she was a "businesswoman."

"How long until the assassins or lawyers come?" Truth asked.

"I don't know. We could just . . . run, you know."

"That would be silly. In either case, they will be necessary."

"Right. Sure. I'll just get back to recording the information, then."

Truth made a little humming noise of approval. He'd use the time to figure out how this would all plug together. His current best idea was to insert the former Barton in as his proxy CEO and push a new scheme where "ambassadors" would be eligible for valuable discounts and prizes if they excelled in brand promotion . . . one of strong, nationalist, traditional Jeon values, but with that forward-looking MegaShroom twist.

"Hey, if you wanted to promote the idea of a modern take on a traditionalist lifestyle and outlook, what would you call it? TradMod?"

"No, just call it Traditional. Whatever you want promoted is 'Traditional' and anything you want considered bad gets called 'Modern.' It doesn't have to be real, or make sense. People will fill in the gaps on their own, make it 'real.'" Tony was pretty focused on the crystal and didn't see Truth's face twitch.

"I see."

All right. Tradition. Nationalism. Aspiration. Security. Greed. And here we go, a straight shot to the Church of Prager. Now, how to tie them to this? Given that he could plausibly have someone pretend to be a CEO for a while, but he really doubted that he could hijack an entire global religious hierarchy.

<<*Oh, now you really are being stupid. "Tony" just told you. It doesn't have to be real for people to believe it's real. It has to be plausible, something they already sort of believe.*>>

So . . . what, just tell the "brand ambassadors" that this is part of their religious duties?

<<*Naaah. That's not what drives these morons. Have a "priest" start laying down the good word, explaining how being a horizontal marketing specialist who runs her own*

business and looks after her family is really following God's will. If it picks up steam, the Church will adopt it themselves. The more you sow, the more you reap and all that. Lots of little paper cutouts to sell. >>

Truth settled in to wait, sneaking in a little practice with the Meditations. The secretary knocked—"Just checking in, no reason"—then went back to her desk.

"Lawyers and killers coming?" Tony asked.

"Mmm-hmmm."

Barely three minutes later, the door was kicked open and flashbangs thrown in. Truth grabbed them out of the air, threw them back, and shut the door behind them. The noise was . . . intense, even through the wall.

Then he was out and through. The hitters were pro enough—they were blinking hard, keeping their fetishes and needlers aimed at the door. The well-dressed man at the back of the room was on the ground, not looking well at all.

Mostly coma and stun spells. Guess they wanted him alive. Ah, well. Truth yanked a stun fetish out of its owner's hands and jabbed it into their neck.

Level Threes, well equipped and professional. A reasonable bet if they were going after a noncombatant Level Four. He had no particular need for these people to be alive or dead, but . . . maybe it was a baby step toward valuing others? It might make Etenesh happy? The Tongue wanted them dead. The spark from Etenesh didn't seem to care either. Truth sighed and had them all knocked out in a few seconds. *Counterambushes are nasty that way.*

He disarmed and cuffed the mercs, cuffed the suit, and hauled him into the office.

"Recognize him?"

"Ricardo Wu, our general counsel."

"Company's chief lawyer. Figures."

"An okay guy, actually. Even with everything."

"He was going to eat you alive in a few months. He was, literally, going to *eat you alive* on the same conference room table you use practically every day."

Tony looked sick. "Yeah, but you find ways to not think about that. He was always really pleasant in meetings. Very solution-oriented. He brings in donuts for the staff on Fridays."

<<I take it all back. I love it here. This is amazing. Let's put Tony back under the geas but this time working for you. >>

I swear I can still taste the pizza management left in the breakroom.

Truth propped up the moaning lawyer in one of the visitor's chairs.

Load up that busted Hazel Wand of yours. Let's see if we can't at least fix his ears up.
<<Don't want to try Cup and Knife?>>
Not unless I . . . You know what? Sure. Time on tools and all that.

Truth cast Cup and Knife. The lawyer was banged up a little, his ears and eyes were hurt, but no great harm done. The spell didn't struggle much to correct whatever the problem was. *Really, REALLY want to try and track down more information about*

*the creator and this . . . Manda. This spell is awesome but so damn unreliable that I have
to be missing something crucial.*

"There now. Attorney Wu. Would you like to explain why you just assaulted
me?" Truth said.

"I beg your pardon?"

"That would be a start." Truth nodded.

"Who are you, exactly? And why am I handcuffed?"

"Both questions have the same answer. I'm the man who currently has an
attempted murder claim I can make against you personally and your company
generally."

Wu collected himself almost immediately. "Then by all means, call the police."

*Heh. Ballsy. Well, he's not wrong—there is no way a cop would do more than collect
a good-sized bribe to forget this, and a bigger one to make me disappear.*

"I prefer alternative dispute resolution. In your case, how would you feel about
being paralyzed, laid on the conference room table, and eaten alive?"

Truth was waiting for the reaction and caught it just as the geas activated. Cup
and Knife didn't struggle quite so hard this time—less damage to repair and less
enchantment to break. Truth aimed the remnant curse at "anyone else who has this
enchantment" and absolutely nothing happened. Dammit all. He pushed it back
toward the sign. That seemed to work.

Hopefully, the sign wouldn't fall on someone. He'd feel pretty bad if someone got
hurt because of that. It was just so . . . lazy.

"And back with us, Attorney Wu. Or do you have a different name?"

"No, my name is actually Ricardo Wu. Those assholes!"

"Sold out by the board?"

"I was specifically hired by them because of, and I am quoting here, 'My decades-
long commitment to the highest standards of ethical and zealous representation'
representing my clients."

"Nasty. When did they get you?"

"No idea. I've been counsel here for twenty years now. Could have been almost
any time." Ricardo sagged in the chair.

Truth nodded at that. "Say, does this office space have any big ritual spaces or
other hidden magical technology so profound, the board felt it was best not to inform
Tony here?"

"Tony?" Ricardo looked confused. The former Daragah flipped him the double
bird.

"Oh, shit. Right, you were called Anthony . . . Wrench?"

"Wrenn, asshole. Don't think I forgot about what was going to happen in a
couple of months either. In retrospect, all those donuts and working lunches are
looking pretty suspect."

"The donuts were for staff, Daragah! Buy your own damn donuts."

"The fuck you just call me, *Ricky*?"

Truth clapped loudly.

"Getting off topic here. Big ritual space. Or technology. Subtly warping the nature of the world in this place."

"Oh. No. Well. Not really? We do have the conference room pretty heavily enchanted for . . . hopefully obvious reasons," Ricardo explained. He shifted in his handcuffs and grimaced.

"Did you do the work in-house?"

"No, we contracted it out. Professional magical-engineering outfit, specializing in custom builds. Not cheap, but very good quality." Ricardo had the quiet pride of a man who had personally negotiated a very favorable contract.

Truth's nose was twitching. He had a keen nose for a rat. "What was the name of the firm?"

"Anak and Sons. A Harban company. Big, beefy guys." The slim Ricardo shuddered.

"And whose idea was all of this?" Truth asked, the rodent odor now getting overwhelming.

"Well, our founder saw a market gap for—"

"You don't need to walk out of here with two legs, attorney, or at all. Focus."

"Sorry, force of habit. Although it was actually the founder and current chairman of the board. Apparently, he was at a conference, started a conversation at the bar with Ansusi Anak, and the idea just made such good sense he felt like he had to do it. And in fairness, we have consistently exceeded our peer competitors in moderating executive-compensation growth and retaining top talent."

CHAPTER 23

THE LIMITS OF EMPATHY

Truth was trying to connect some very random dots at speed. The picture he was making didn't make a whole lot of sense to him. Anak and Sons were some kind of human-ish cousins of humanity as he generally understood the term. He was a little hazy on what exactly that meant.

Merkovah had played down their importance, but he could vividly remember Remu Anakson. More than two meters of slab muscle and the furious eyes of an emperor, all supported by Level Five cultivation. Truth would bet at least one of those levels was a body cultivation spell too.

Actually, no need to bet—he knew for a fact that they had body cultivation. One of the spells he had recovered from Gullvar's place was a modified body-cultivation spell. The system couldn't crack the other, but . . . odds were better than good it was related.

They were remainers. Holdouts. The Anaks were clearly playing for the world after the collapse. But he couldn't figure out what their angle was with MegaShroom. Definitionally, these pricks were good for nothing. In fact, they sucked value and goodness out of things. Their phony mushroom nonsense was especially toxic. People bought them instead of real medicine and paid a fatal price for their faith in marketing.

Collapse . . . control . . . not entirely human but close enough . . . What was he missing? What would humans need post-collapse? Organization first and foremost if you were an empire builder. Then once you had people listening—shelter, water, food . . . material comforts? *It starts getting a bit vague once you are past the whole "How to not die right this minute" stuff. Like . . . a latrine. Nobody ever thinks, "I'm in an emergency situation. Where do I poop that won't poison the water supply?"*

<<*Well, they do, but I take your point. Also, you skipped right over the obvious— food. They might be bullshit as magical supplements, but mushrooms are food. And who knows, post-collapse, maybe some of them could pass as medicine. I wouldn't bet on it, but maybe. MegaShroom would certainly have the experience persuading people that it did.*>>

Truth nodded along with that, then grinned slightly. Some *mushrooms are hallucinogenic. What do you want to bet MegaShroom grows them for a certain, very select clientele?*

<<*No bet. Ask the lawyer.*>>

"Hey, Ricardo, when did you get the conference room redone?"

"About ten years ago."

"Ah. How do you guys get your mushrooms? Contract farming?"

"Some of it." Tony rolled his eyes. "I know everyone thinks the marketing is bullshit, and okay, maybe it can't do everything it says on the label, but in terms of ingredients and quality, we really do put in the work. Most of it is grown in-house, and most of it really is assayed by alchemists for purity and potency."

"Right but . . . it's potently doing nothing useful." Truth looked dubious.

"We dispute that. And not legally relevant."

"Seems relevant." Truth fixed Ricardo with a *look*.

Most people would have considered the fact that they were handcuffed to a chair in front of someone who soloed their entire squad of paid killers almost instantly and completely unharmed, and backed down. Most people are never going to be general counsel for an MLM.

"MegaShroom products are manufactured and distributed under the laws of Jeon as nutritional supplements. As nutritional supplements are not regulated as medicine, they are held to the ordinary standard of consumer protection afforded to nonfood, nonmedicinal goods. Our belief in the efficacy of the product is entirely sufficient to defeat any claim of false advertising. Indeed, even suggesting as much could lead to serious legal consequences, young man, and filing a vexatious lawsuit could even result in jail time." Ricardo glared at Truth.

<<I'm in love. I want to leave your body and go haunt him. The sheer, and I wish there was a better, less gross way to say this, but the sheer intestinal fortitude of the man is inspiring. Even now, his commitment to comprehensively sodomizing the people of this great nation remains pure and unshaken. It's beautiful. Why aren't you this pure, Truth? Why are you such a goddamn loser compared to this glorious beast of a man?>>

Please never call someone a glorious beast of a man ever again. Please and thank you.

<<No.>>

"Are you entirely clear on your odds of leaving this room alive, Rick?"

<<That's Attorney Wu or Counselor to you, peasant!>>

"Decent, I expect. You took me alive for a reason, and I don't believe it's to inquire about our contractors."

"You would be surprised," Truth growled.

"What do you want, then? Not that I'm ungrateful. However, regardless of my . . . urgent need to renegotiate certain parts of my compensation package with the board, I am still MegaShroom's attorney. I have a duty."

<<Sheer class. This is the difference right here. You just kill people and break things. He's spent an entire human lifetime clearing away legal obstacles to maximizing meatsack suffering. I bet you he's known in Parliament. I bet he does in-person lobbying, turning up with a briefcase full of wen and a bottle of something classy. He gets holiday cards from the president. Ask. I bet he does.>>

"You seem like the kind of person who gets holiday cards from the president."

"Of Jeon? Each of the last four." Ricardo smiled confidently.

<<I love Jeon so much. We MUST save it. And Ricardo Wu shall lead it to the glorious future its subjects deserve. President, no, GOD EMPEROR WU.>>

"Shame. I'm a rebel, here to topple the old order."

"That's nice." Ricardo nodded politely. His eyes didn't even flicker.

"Which means I'm coopting MegaShroom."

"No, that won't be happening." Ricardo's disagreement was polite but firm.

"A program you will be energetically supporting. Because I know some things you don't, and once you do know them, you will see just how dumb your remaining 'loyalty' to the company is. Specifically the notion that you can screw more money and benefits out of them."

"I assure you they will pay. And my physical security will be . . . much better ensured." Ricardo had clearly forgotten the whole "handcuffed in front of a probable murderer" business for a moment.

"Yeah, no, let me explain a few things about what the next . . . call it a year . . . will look like. And the consequences for you personally."

Truth laid it out, skipping the whole "soul mutilation and slow mind control" angle and leaned more on the "How exactly do you expect a central magical ledger to work when magic is disappearing?" issue.

"Oh God, you're one of *them*. A "'peak magic'" fr—guy. Listen. You are clearly a powerful, capable mage." Ricardo dropped his voice into a soothing baritone. "A combat magus. A man of action. Not big on postgraduate education; am I right? Listen, as someone with a tertiary degree, I can flat-out tell you that magic isn't ending."

Truth blinked at him. Of all the reactions to "The world is ending," eye rolls were not on the "expected" list.

"I can see you are confused. Let me explain. Yes, there is a definite lowering of magic intensity. Yes, it will be disruptive to an extent. However, it is simply not possible for it to be connected to human activity."

"It . . . absolutely is, though?"

"No, it isn't." Ricardo spoke with calm authority. "Think about it. The planet is constantly bombarded on all sides by cosmic rays. Each of the billions of stars is some stellar excellency, an angel or demon beyond our meager understanding. The closest of which, our tutelary spirit? Just its emanation into this universe is so vast, our planet could fit within it *one million three hundred thousand times*. One MILLION. THREE HUNDRED THOUSAND. Times." Ricardo carefully enunciated.

"Now, you tell me. How, exactly, does anything we could possibly do on this planet impact the impossibly vast output of energy generated by that emanation? It can't. And before you say something embarrassing about the nature of reality, you should probably know that geological records show that changes in cosmic-ray intensity are perfectly natural and occur cyclically."

"Because this planet is small and there are billions of us, if we keep doing dumb shit, bad things happen? Also, I know of at least two major religions that believe God, specifically, is interfering with our ability to interact with cosmic rays?"

"Ah, Collapser, theological/social type. The rich did a bad thing, so all the bad things are their fault, and God agrees with you, so everyone is getting punished.

Which proves you were right all along. Would it shock you to learn that it is more complicated than that?"

"No." Truth was always ready to believe that things were more complicated than he wished. Although this fact seemed to throw Ricardo. It threw Tony, too, who looked at him weirdly from across the desk.

"Really?"

"Most things are more complicated than you think, right? Why would I find that hard to believe?"

"Because . . . you rushed in here, broke the geas on Tammy—"

"Anthony! After all those lunches I bought you, too."

"Daragah bought them for me. Daragah is an okay guy. You I don't know and don't want to know."

"Because you were going to eat me alive!"

"Oh, boo-hoo! I was geased too and you don't hear me whining. Besides, don't think I don't know what you did to get the job. Who do you think gave you pricks cover all these years?"

"Making money for you! Making money for you! You assholes took fifty percent of the gross revenue, AND I could only buy products and marketing through you, health insurance through you, unemployment insurance, everything had to run through corporate so you could get your beaks wet."

<<This. Is. The second-best day ever.>>

What was the— The day you tried to kill me.

<<The day I tried to kill you, right. God, that was satisfying. I see how mistaken I was now, of course, I was as lied-to as you, but the emotional satisfaction is no less real.>>

Have I mentioned recently what a complete delight you are to have around?

<<Oh, boo-hoo. I was geased too and you don't hear me whining. When you get right down to it, I was the real victim. I never got paid. I never got any benefits whatsoever from my unpaid labor. You, at least, got to live vicariously through your siblings.>>

Wait, I get my soul mutilated, and you, that mutilated bit of soul, are the real victim?

<<How am I not? I am a separate person with a separate identity. I suffered all the same mutilation and exploitation, without the meager benefits you got. And yet, amazingly enough, you manage to make it. All. About. You.>>

Can . . . can we revisit the subject of your brutal murder? I haven't thought about it in a while, and I regret that. I feel like there was a missed opportunity for investigating how you could be made to suffer most. Maybe I could Cup-and-Knife you into your "correct" form, stitched to a sewer grub.

There was a pregnant pause. The argument between Ricardo and Tony was only getting more heated, but Truth and the System were both having a moment.

<<Uh. That. Um. Don't try anything until you have a much better grasp of the spell.>>

Right. Yes. Obviously. Do you really think?

<<I think I am suddenly eager to learn just how the hell that weird-ass spell works.>>

Yeah.

<<So . . . you are never going to get God Emperor Wu onboard. His whole life, his income, and his identity rely on you being wrong. Tony is as reliable as . . . I don't have a good simile for this; the guy is going to flake and bolt the second you take your eyes off him. What's your plan?>>

Staff is no use—go talk to the supervisor.

"Hey, Ricardo, sorry to cut in, where are those farms of yours?"

"Well, we grow mushrooms, so they are all grown indoors. We have a farm in this building, for example. Most of the building is used for cultivation, in fact."

"Really?"

"Turned out we didn't need that much office space. But our founder got a fifty-year lease on this place, so here we are. There are plenty of other farms, too, of course."

"Tony, add that to the data on the crystal."

"Okay?"

"Great." Truth dithered for half a second, sighed, and destroyed the attorney's head with a swift palm strike.

"PRAGER! Why?!" Tony tried to jump back, the chair slamming into the cheap wooden shelves behind the desk. He didn't manage to get out of the chair until it bounced off the shelves, books falling down on him.

"Because I can't think of a single good reason to keep him alive and a lot of bad consequences from leaving him alive, and there will be no consequences whatsoever from killing him," Truth said reasonably. Or he thought it was reasonable. Tony turned paper-white. Then turned and vomited.

"Oh, God. Oh, God. Please. Please don't kill me. Please don't kill me. Whatever you want. Just tell me. Whatever you want. Please. Please don't kill me."

Truth was stunned for a moment, then buried his face in his hands.

Right. He was the bad guy. Despite everything. Despite all the horrible things MegaShroom had done. Despite all the lives they ruined. The fact was that everyone in this room was recovering from mind control and a lifetime of damage. He was the bad guy. The monster of violence. He might have broken the geas, but he certainly wasn't helping them.

"Tony?"

"Yes?"

"I am planning on letting you run. Let me be very clear on something. If they catch you, they will kill you in a way that makes being eaten alive look like mercy. They will be as brutal and humiliating as possible. They will involve your family, your pets, anyone and anything you ever cared about. Because they need it to hurt you on every level. You understand me?"

"Yes. God! Yes."

"And you understand what happens if you go to the cops? Or try to call anyone, warn anyone?"

"Same thing. I get it."

"Yeah. Do your best to flee the country. There is a lot of that right now. Shouldn't be too hard. Don't pack anything, don't grab anything, just run your ass straight to the airport and book the next flight to anywhere not here. Figure out the rest when you are in the air.

"I will do that. Exactly that."

"Good. Because you won't see me, but I will be following you, to see if you draw any more people hunting you down. And if you try anything, you end up like Tony. No warning. Just instant oblivion, and you find out what really happens next."

There was a sudden smell of urine, and Tony frantically nodded.

"Good. Plenty of carpets outside. Hail one." Tony grabbed his wallet and fled.

<<Going to follow him? That did actually sound like a good idea.>>

No point. I'd just kill more MegaShroom goons, assuming more got sent. No, time to talk to their real boss. Let's go see our cousins. Those . . . strong sons of Anak.

CHAPTER 24

IMMIGRANTS GET THE JOB DONE

Truth left the office in a thundercloud of emotions. He took a moment to refresh the coma spells on the grunts out of some vague sense of spite. They were going to have a deeply unpleasant time when they woke up, and he just felt like spreading the misery.

He had wanted vengeance. He had wanted to come storming in there and grab hold of the shitty people responsible for making his Mom the way she was, hurting all the people like his mom, hurting *him*.

He wanted to shake them. Make them see exactly what they were doing. Make them admit just how shitty and wrong they were. Then . . . kill them somehow. He had been debating various colorful methods of execution but hadn't landed on anything really satisfactory. He wanted catharsis.

What he got was more victims. Victims of other "elites" like themselves. Presumably the board of directors was a higher quality of both predator and victim, but Truth had picked up a little about just what those "boards" were while working for Starbrite. They were the shareholders' reps. They were meant to be the highest authority of the company, because they directly represented the owners.

Who were the owners? That's where it all got a bit messy. In theory, they were almost anyone. Big, publicly held companies with stocks that got bought and sold on the market—the whole point of selling shares was that anyone with the money could buy a piece of the action. But that wasn't what actually happened, was it?

It was, as he remembered hearing drunken finance bros explain, insurance companies, pension funds, financial institutions, and "high-net-worth individuals" that actually made up the market. And even then, it was less . . . direct . . . than Truth's limited imagination had stretched.

A pension fund needs to earn money to pay for future retirees. They get funding from current workers and maybe the company funding the pension. They invest that money in things that will earn, hopefully, enough to cover future expenses, while minimizing risk.

To minimize risk, they split up the big pot of money and give it to different people to invest in different ways. Those "fund managers" will make investments in dozens or hundreds of companies, so the "Tarakal Steel Retirement Fund C" might own .01 percent of "Xosia and Lu Aviation," an investment that made up 1 percent of the pension's equity investments.

So, who owned that .01 percent Xosia and Lu? For that matter, who owned the company outright? Was it the steel workers who contributed to the pension fund? The fund itself? The hundreds or thousands of institutional investors who bought similar-sized pieces of the outfit? The heirs of the founders who, through trusts, still held a combined 25 percent interest in the company, making them the largest "single" shareholder?

Who, exactly, was responsible when the board of directors ate their employees alive? Truth got workers not caring about their work. Why should they? They barely got paid enough to live, and there was never any benefit to working harder than the bare minimum, no matter what management said. The notion that you could not give a damn about *what you owned* beyond what it paid you still felt alien.

The ownership class was made up of people who owned tiny fractions of hundreds or thousands of companies, with neither the time nor interest to investigate what those companies were doing. It was all about the bottom line. Which means that the "board" or the "C-suite" only had to care about maximizing shareholder value. Getting as much cash out of their employees and the public as they could and funneling it up to those disinterested gods.

Starbrite was something of an exception, of course, but that was by deliberate design. Starbrite was a privately held company, BUT the public could buy "B-Shares," which entitled them to a percentage of the profit, not of the company itself. And of course, Starbrite famously owned big chunks of dozens of other companies, big enough that it had functional control without the liability.

Truth hit the elevator and started checking floors. He found the indoor farm pretty quickly and walked right past it. He only doubled back when he saw the signs pointing to the room he had ignored. It was not what he thought of when he heard the word *farm*. The "farm" was plastic bags. Some a hundred and fifty centimeters long and twenty-five centimeters across, hanging from hooks in a frame. Others were smaller, cube-shaped, sitting on shelves. Once he got closer to them and took a peek, he could see that, yes, there were mushrooms growing in there. He didn't recognize the varieties, but there appeared to be a startlingly large number of mushrooms per bag.

The room had been labeled "Fruiting Chamber," whatever that meant. He could hear machinery humming from somewhere in the building. This was an industrial process. Farming as industry. Wholly divorced from both sun and soil.

Nothing looked out of the ordinary . . . for a room filled with plastic sacks containing rapidly growing mushrooms. Nothing he cared about, anyway. Truth shook his head and went looking for the conference room.

The room was two floors down from the CEO's office. It was almost identical to every other conference room he had ever seen. A single comically long table filled most of the room, veneered with a blond wood and surrounded by moderately comfortable yet heartbreakingly expensive chairs. A glass wall facing the rest of the office that could be turned opaque with the touch of a talisman, and a wall of glass windows looking out over a scenic multistory parking garage.

There was a complete absence of nefarious anything. Not even dried splotches of blood. Which wasn't surprising; any halfway competent cleaner would have air demons on hand to tidy all that up and leave it immaculate. There was some bland art, a big scryball for showing illusions and a communication altar in the middle of the table. Totally stock stuff. He was pretty sure there was nothing in the room you couldn't buy out of a catalog. So, where was the custom work Anak and Sons apparently did?

Truth looked down at the carpet glued to the floor. Easy place to start. A few quick cuts and a hard tear later, yes, the floor had been etched.

Recognize any of this?

<<Not yet. Rip out more.>>

Truth quickly had up the whole carpet, though he did notice the conference table was bolted to the floor. As he somewhat expected, the floor was covered wall-to-wall with intricate spellwork. The carving was neatly done . . . and that was about all he could say about it. He could somewhat grasp that the whole thing was built around the conference table, but he just didn't recognize it. It wasn't like any spell structure he had studied before.

Reckon it goes on up the walls?

<<Strip some paint off and find out.>>

It did not. However, when he took the acoustic panels down from the ceiling, there was a second, different array carved in the concrete above the room.

Ten wen there is something under the veneer of the table.

<<No bet.>>

Truth checked around the edge of the table. Regrettably, there were no spots that looked designed to ease the peeling of the surface. Such is life. He used Incisive to scrape off a bare quarter millimeter, then was able to peel the rest away with only considerable violence to the surface.

<<That was barbaric. There are shreds everywhere. Someone will have to clean that up, you know.>>

Oh, no. Not that. You do it, then.

<<Hohoho. Truly, my flesh covering quivers with poorly concealed emotion. Probably tuberculosis or some other parasitic thing filling up my wet air sacs with mucus and making me convulse. How do you not know how to peel a sticker? What happened to you in the slums that made you too dumb to pull a sheet of plastic off a flat surface?>>

They bickered, not particularly good-naturedly, until Truth managed to strip the top of the table off. There was, to no one's particular surprise, a long stone slab embedded in the conference table. It was less densely packed with carvings than Truth had expected. A few long geometric shapes. A few abstract carvings of animals, birds, and other, less easily identifiable things. An alarming number of . . . either runes or some sort of sacred language Truth wasn't familiar with. And that was more or less it.

Any ideas?

<<No. It appears, kinda-sorta-roughly-maybe, to be based on the same unknown system that was in that second spell Gullvar had. I still can't "read" this. On the other hand, the more samples we find, the closer I get to cracking this thing.>>

Well, there is the obvious. The Anaks set up this room to be a ritual space and the table is some kind of altar or other magical furniture. Altar feels right, as there is literally a sacrifice being conducted on top of it.

<<Blindingly obvious, yes, but for what purpose, exactly? Some of it fuels the physical and mental transformation, but what else?>>

The sin-shifting bit?

<<Yeah, about that. We have no evidence that this . . . whatever it is . . . does that. We don't even know if that is how "sin" works. We just have one guy's word for it, and since he's the victim, how would he really know?>>

Ah. Right. I mean. I don't have a better explanation for why . . . all this.

<<Me either, but let's not forget our source is unreliable. I think we are done here. Unless you want to burn it down on the way out?>>

Truth thought about it. On the one hand, he absolutely did. On the other hand . . . he would only be hurting the people who had no responsibility for all this. The people who were responsible? It was an insurance claim. Or maybe it was a total loss, but since it was one of hundreds or thousands of investments, a completely survivable loss.

No. This was a bust. Hopefully, we can beat something useful, or at least satisfying, out of the Anaks. Damn it all. Damn them all!

Anak and Sons had a bland corporate suite in a bland office building in a part of the city famous for nothing in particular. It didn't even have good mass-transit access, which was fair enough, as the parking was atrocious too. Truth was exhausted just looking at the thing. If there had been a sign out front that said, "Hi, and welcome to our fake office!" he would have believed it.

No one that looked like Remu Anakson would set foot in this dingy little place. All . . . bleach-white walls and gray industrial carpeting in a low-rise office building. Not even bland, inoffensive art on the walls—just suite numbers, or little taped-up signs indicating a dentist, or a medical-diagnostics firm. An architect slumming it. Perhaps an accountant flying solo.

Where was the arrogant spirit? Where was that wild ambition to rule the world when the old order fell? What part of this screamed, "All those who obey me shall prosper. Those who oppose me shall perish!?" It screamed late-middle-aged men trying and failing to have affairs with their twenty-something-year-old coworkers, just so they feel, for one second, desirable and powerful again. Feel alive again.

With extreme reluctance, he made his way to the office. It had a glass door, with a waiting room and a receptionist on the other side of a big desk. Truth walked directly past her and nearly slammed his nose into the heavily warded door.

"Oh, thank God. For a moment there, I was genuinely worried." Truth sighed. He turned to look at the receptionist. She was a strong-looking lady. Literally strong, like she could pick up her whole desk and fling it across the parking lot. And she kept looking around like she was trying to spot something and not quite seeing it.

Truth felt something in him unclench and relax. There was something deeply nefarious going on there. He could get answers there. What a delicious surprise.

CHAPTER 25

COUNTRY COUSINS

Truth wasn't afraid to admit he had a *type* when it came to women—"Women who are interested in me."

His number-one, no-question, highest-rated feature he looked for in a woman was her interest in him. Everything else fell into the vague reaches of the "nice to have" category.

That being said, after Etenesh's affection and getting hit on by a significant number of people, he was willing to widen his eyes a bit. Really consider what, if he was being picky, he found desirable.

He was humbled to realize he had really basic taste. Shamefully pedestrian. He had sex with the embodiment of God's Consort in all her heavenly glory, and he still had "Jeon Casual"–level desires.

One dark night, he realized that he had a tiny crush on the model from the old Starbrite billboard, the lady getting her golden bat cigarette lit by the handsome Starbrite man. She did things for him, even after all these years. He would have to broaden his tastes.

The receptionist there was outside his comfort zone at the moment. She was a little heavy for him. In the sense that she was packing more muscle under that blouse than he had under his shirt.

Is she . . . sniffing the air? I should be unnoticeable regardless of the sense used, right? <<Yeah? I think?>>

Incisive disagreed. Truth hopped back, then ducked almost flat as the heavy desk went flying across the room. Truth spotted her foot on an alarm button. Wards went up, sealing the room. Locking them in there together.

Bad move, lady. I don't know how you sensed me, but— HOLY SHIT!

Truth dodged left, barely ahead of the halberd the receptionist had summoned from a hidden recess in the floor. She pulled it back for a lunge as he slammed into the warded wall. Truth kicked off from the wall, launching himself forward to get inside the halberd's range.

In his defense, he had never trained on halberds. Getting close seemed like a reasonable idea. The weighted butt of the halberd whipped up at his face as the receptionist spun. He slipped right, straight into the path of the oncoming ax head on the other end of the shaft.

All right, no such thing as a safe range when dealing with a halberd. Fuck it. Hard way it is.

He swayed back just enough to let the ax head whip past, then caught the shaft just behind the hook. He yanked forward, driving his boot directly into her gut. It was like trying to yank a concrete pillar, then kicking the same pillar "in the gut." It rated a grunt and a creeping smile from the receptionist.

She kicked right back. Truth blocked the kick with a raised shin. Neither of them minded the pain, but the receptionist used the moment to capitalize on his lack of balance, tearing back control of the halberd.

Truth called the Tongue to hand. It fairly hummed with disapproval. The receptionist's grin widened. She snapped the halberd back around in a sweep at Truth's legs. Truth stomped down on the haft, jamming the head into the floor. Continuing the motion, he lunged forward, tip aimed directly between her eyebrows. She rocked back, then, with a grunt, lifted Truth and halberd alike up and out of the ground, slamming Truth into the ceiling.

He should have just punched right through the concrete. It was warded. His head slammed hard, then he bounced back toward the floor. The receptionist had recovered enough for a one-handed lunge, spear tip drilling for his navel. The Tongue slapped the broad steel head away, the angelic blade screeching as it ran along the spelled metal.

She wanted to throw him around? *Two can play at that game.* He grabbed the haft again, noting her grin. She was confident in her muscles. So was he. Truth lifted her off the ground and whipped her and the halberd both into the wall. Then did it a second time for luck. Then a third time. He needed a lot of luck. He was going for a fourth time, but she got her feet planted and pushed forward.

Truth slid backward, losing his leverage on the long wooden haft. So far, neither had taken much damage. The room was pretty torn up, but other than a little light bashing around, neither was the worse for wear. He frowned. This couldn't go on. Sooner or later, the receptionist's friends would turn up.

"Cast a spell. Go on. Every time I see one of you little mages get in a jam, you reach for a spell. Go on. Try it. It will be funny." The receptionist's voice was deep and warm. And hungry.

Actually . . . This fight should have been over almost instantly. He reached out with Incisive . . . Ah. It was still running, still there. Just muted. Weakened a great deal by whatever enchantment was on this room. It would be down to the permanent improvements granted by the Meditations, his own skill, and his platonic life partner, The Tongue of One Who Speaks for God.

He flicked his wrist, spinning the blade around. Just keeping loose. "Behold, the signature spell of my house." He kicked a bit of shattered desk up into her eyes and charged in, going for a stab to the gut.

She laughed and headbutted the bit of flying wood, never taking her eyes off him. She got the spear head lined up with his chest, trying to skewer him with the force of his own charge. He tried to push past, but this time she twisted the halberd and pulled it back toward her, trying to catch him with the hook. He swore and ducked, stabbing down at her foot. He could see her trying to get it out of the way—she was fast enough. But her weight was too far forward; she hadn't recovered well from the lunge.

Truth drew first blood, sinking the Tongue clean through her foot. He paid for it, though. The wicked hook on the back of the halberd dragged along his back, digging a bloody furrow.

"Tough little bastard. That should have had your spine out or snapped your ribs."

Truth didn't bother with a reply. He got his shoulder down and slammed into her. And slammed right off of her. Her right foot had a hole three fingers wide through it. Her left foot was apparently enough to keep her as firmly planted as a tree. He gained a whole new respect for her when she whipped that broken foot up and at his temple, using the butt of the halberd to help stabilize her. The toe of her practical flats just grazed the side of his head. Truth swore he could feel hair sliced away by the force of its passing.

Her leg was up high, her hands were on the halberd, the Tongue was out of position, but he did have a free hand . . . He punched her directly in the crotch. She grunted at that, narrowed her eyes, and brought her heel down in a vicious ax kick. Truth stepped out of range, then flinched. The damage to his back was worse than he thought. He could feel his muscles weakening. Tearing as they were put under unsupported strain.

They took a moment to breathe. Then they lunged back at each other. The receptionist jabbing with the spear point of her halberd, trying to keep range. Truth trying to use his mobility to get around it before the damage got too bad. She knew it, too. The halberd gave her enough reach to sweep a third of the waiting room, but it meant that getting too close to a wall or, worse, the corner would limit her badly.

Truth narrowed his eyes as he kept probing her, kept up the pressure. She would be limited to almost pure defense in the corner . . . but so what? She had sealed the room. Presumably, help was on the way. The fight was moving fast. It wasn't surprising that no one else had arrived yet. So, why wasn't she playing for time?

She feinted at his eyes, then hacked down at his shoulder. Truth got both hands on the Tongue and parried the blow to the side. He let the flat of his blade land on the spell-hardened haft of the halberd and lunged in. Her guard was too good to go straight for a killing blow? He'd take her fingers off, then.

Her eyes widened as she figured it out. She yanked the halberd back and across her body, knocking the sword off but opening herself up to a vicious elbow. She countered with one of her own, hard enough to snap Truth's head back. Truth showed his approval by stamping his foot down on hers, right on the hole his sword left. Hard enough to shatter concrete. For the first time in the fight, she gave a small shriek. Then snarled and tried to bite off his ear.

Truth opted for a draw cut instead of the body mod, bringing the Tongue slashing up toward her throat. She opted to take a page from his book—the receptionist dropped the halberd and grabbed his arms. She went for a throw, and Truth went with it. He used the added momentum to get under her and tried to gut her.

She was a better wrestler than she was with the polearm. She got her long legs around his knees and started working for a disarm. She wasn't shy about throwing elbows where she could, too. Truth grinned nastily and unsummoned the Tongue. In the moment of confusion, he slammed his forehead into her nose, breaking it. She growled and punched him in the kidney hard enough that he knew he'd be pissing blood tonight.

Truth just loved being punched in the kidney. He loved it so damn much, he dropped his right hand like he was going to return the favor and called the Tongue back into it. And jammed it clean through her side. She did scream at that. And again, when he leveraged the blade against her spine, slicing her almost in half.

"I YIELD!"

Truth had never been big on taking surrenders. He had the blade up and ready to come down and collect her head but . . . held.

"What do I get if you yield? Compared to the advantage I get for permanently silencing you?"

"I can help you get whatever you were going to break in for. I can provide you with considerable information, should you be after that. I should also mention that killing me will irreversibly mark your soul, triggering a planet-wide blood hunt." Her hazel eyes were wide, pupils dilated. Truth noticed that she wasn't bleeding as much as he would expect. Actually, she was a lot less . . . almost completely paralyzed and near death than he would expect. Something about the shape of her eyes . . .

"Are those your actual eyes? I mean, the color?"

She paused, then smiled. "No. But changing them back takes a special potion."

"Ah. What's your relationship with Remu Anakson?"

"He's my older brother." Her smile morphed into a grin. "He do something to piss you off?"

"Not that I know of. Or, at least, not intentionally. Hmm." Truth was stumped. "Do you know what business your family has with MegaShroom?"

Her eyes widened. "Ah. You really aren't here to fuck around."

"No, not as such. Assuming I let you live, you will be coughing up some fairly sizable 'Family is more than just unhappy'–sized secrets. Death is always an option, if you prefer. I assumed I would be searching through files anyhow."

She gave him a hard look. Really looked over his body. "I can barely see you, you know? And I can see through damn near anything. It's like you are screaming, 'I'm not really here,' thinking it will mean I don't see you."

"So, just looking like something else, say a janitor, would be a more effective disguise?"

"As long as you weren't wearing a false mustache."

"I am clean-shaven."

"Shame. I love a beard. Big beard, not little goatee thing. Shaved head, long, well-oiled beard, and a cut physique."

"Hmm. Super. Good to know. Jeon must be pure hell on your dating life. On the subject of you revealing everything before your organs fall out or I just behead you and send your big bro a very special present . . ."

"We are planning to take over the planet after the collapse of . . . call it traditional magic. At least, as you understand it. Well, taking it over is a little more dramatic than what we have planned. Say . . . we intend to be the single power on the planet that matters."

"Called it."

"You don't sound surprised."

"I'm not. What are you using MegaShroom for?"

"You . . . aren't one of my cousins or something, are you?" She very subtly flexed her foot. Not subtly enough. Truth cut through the quad muscles at the top of her leg, then did the same on the other leg before she had a chance to scream.

"I am genuinely impressed by your regeneration. Your nose has already straightened too. Congrats on being able to walk again. On the other hand, 'head-in-box' time is only getting closer."

"Damn! Fucking OW! Yes, all right, what else would we use a bunch of scammy farmers for? Their tech will work in a post-collapse environment, and we can harvest their management for . . . seeds. We're farming the farmers." She looked up at him, her face twisting into an odd, predatory smile. "My name is Susan, by the way. And, just trying my luck here, are you single?"

CHAPTER 26

A DOG WALKS INTO A TAVERN . . .

Truth just looked at her for a long moment. Susan was, bluntly speaking, not his type. His paranoia would never in a million years settle down around her. Also, being honest with himself, he really didn't like the idea of cheating on Etenesh. The thought gave him hives. He wondered if that was an effect of that bit of Etenesh inside him or just his own nature. He hoped it was all him.

"Sorry, I am in a committed relationship. Also, I am fairly sure our kinks don't align. I am quite appreciative of the compliment, though."

She swore. "You have NO idea how hard it is finding a qualified man I'm not related to. This country is just loaded with—" She struggled to find the right words. Truth saw her discarding a really impressive number of slurs.

"Don't strain yourself. It is what it is. Name?"

"You know ah, Susan Anakdaughter. We are all Anakson or -daughter. Some of us drop that bit for business purposes. How much do you know about us?"

"Kissing cousins from a long way back. Completely different magic system."

"So . . . almost nothing. Yeah. All right. So. You basically just broke in here because there was something going on at MegaShroom and you figured out we were behind it, and you want to find out what we are up to so you can use us to your advantage?"

Truth shrugged, moving Susan from the "likely to die" category to the "kill her the instant his paranoia even slightly flares" category. "Something like that."

"Great! I can work with that."

"Oh?"

"Sure. MegaShroom is barely a side project. Definitionally a nice-to-have, not a need-to-have."

"What is your status in the organization? You feel like you are between Level Four and Five, which means you aren't the receptionist."

She barked with laughter. "The 'organization' is the Anak family. All the companies and charities and whatever are just covers. I'm in the third generation, so middle of the pack. And I don't have a level. You . . . really have no idea who, or what, we are, do you?"

"No. Explain. Incidentally, look toward your halberd again and I will see how long it takes you to regrow your eyes."

"I didn't even glance."

"You did. One eye." Truth raised the sword casually.

"ALL RIGHT! God! Look, you know we aren't from the same branch of humanity, but we are all descended from the perfected hermaphrodite, right?"

"Sure." Truth said. Not quite how he had heard it, but whatever.

"So, your branch, let's call it the baseline. Or, I don't know. Pick a primordial person from whatever the Pragerites teach."

"Mmm-hmmm."

"We, or more accurately the portion of my ancestry that you care about, are the Nephilim. Which is what you get when humans are bred by angels."

Truth just slowly blinked at that. It was like hearing that humans could have sex with a planet. Or a star.

"Explain . . . further."

"Not much further I can explain. It's not a secret at all. We have entire star systems, hell, our own multiplanetary organizations. And we are magically and biologically different from base humans because at some unimaginably distant point in the past, maybe even on the origin planet, a bunch of angels fucked a load of human women. Presumably very-low-tier angels, but who knows."

Truth just let the idea rattle around a bit longer. Demons, sure. Demons were associated with lust all the time. He was employing two succubae. They were up for anything, anytime. But angels? His experience with angels was that they were forces of obliteration.

Wait. Etenesh did say her family saw messenger angels breaking the earth and making an area ready for farming. If that was something that really happened, it would make two things the angels were involved with. And if Susan was right about her family history, it would be three things that angels did.

"All right. And clearly it makes you stronger and faster. And regenerate seemingly major organs?"

"With practice and training, yes."

"But not levels. Somehow."

"Your system of magic is built around building a miniature of the heavens, down to emanating the power surplus. Our system of magic is more predatory. What we take, we keep. What we make, we keep. We can cast spells, the same as you; it's just that getting the magic outside our bodies requires more steps."

"But, in exchange, you all might as well be body cultivators."

"Body cultivation was developed as a response to Nephilim raids." Susan didn't *quite* preen.

"Huh." Truth was pretty sure she was wrong about that. At the very least, there was something deeply odd going on with the Meditations of Valentinian.

"And, for similar reasons, we don't give even one half of a shit if the magic collapses on a world. We won't lose anything if we don't cast anything." *They won't regenerate, though*, Truth mentally rebutted. "And we have our own methods of accumulating energy."

"Sacrifice."

She jolted and gave him a hard-to-read look.

"In a manner of speaking. That term is a little loaded for us."

"Oh?"

"Yeah, not too sure why, but all the older generations make a big deal out of it. We are always the ones being sacrificed *to*. Never God, or angels, demons, or whatever. When we make a sacrifice, it is always to ourselves or the family. Mostly we just call it feeding or taking supplements."

"And . . . God is okay with this?"

"After who knows how many thousands of years of successful population growth? The development of our own civilization spanning many, many star systems? The sheer fact that our species couldn't exist unless God specifically made it exist? Yes."

"Not going to lie, it's a bit shocking to hear. He always came off as a really jealous, insecure prick. God, I mean."

"He is. 'He.' She did the little air quotes. "Somebody must have done something to piss him off, because this planet still should have a sufficient amount of reality-anchoring materials to keep this kind of collapse from happening."

"Current guess?"

"Starbrite."

"Really?"

"Yep. He's the only person on the planet out of the Initiate realm, so, if not him, then who?"

"Initiate realm?"

"Apparently, it's a taboo to talk about, so I don't know much beyond . . . something changes for you guys when you get past Level Nine and when we fully awaken our power. All this, everything up until that point? You are just an Initiate."

Truth nodded. "Into what?"

"Pardon?"

"Initiated into what? You can't just be an Initiate generally, right?"

She looked boggled for a moment, then started to laugh. Her laugh was rich, deep, honest. "I have no idea. You are the very first person I know of who's asked that. I will definitely ask Grandpa that myself."

Truth nodded. He . . . would prefer not to kill Susan, he decided. On the other hand, he really wasn't sure it was wise to let her live.

"Deciding whether or not to let me live?"

"Yes. I am clinically paranoid, but I am trying to be a better person."

"Why?"

"Pardon?"

"Why? Why pretend to be a better 'human being'?" She did the air quotes again. "If you aren't one of us, and I really do think you might be some kind of distant relation, then you aren't a human. Or at least not a human of a sort I have heard of."

"I have met my parents. They are depressingly 'basic.' And very human."

"You were adopted, then. My halberd is enchanted, using Nephilim magic. That weakening you felt was me harvesting the strength in your body. The fact you were able to shake it off within *seconds* of getting cut was . . . impressive. As was surviving a grapple with me. Wasn't kidding about being open to making something work, by the way."

"You want to date a person you think isn't human."

"Yeah. Sounds fun. And you have that complete disregard for the lives of others that just SCREAMS *Anak in-law.*"

"I would say something unkind, but I really don't have a leg to stand on there."

"Speaking of, can I stand?"

"No."

She grunted and rolled her eyes. "Look, I am literally built different, as is my whole family. I never went to a Jeon school, my exposure to your media was carefully controlled, I didn't have friends outside the family. I am culturally a Nephilim and bio-logically a Nephilim/base hybrid. My existence is premised on the coming collapse—as a sort of shock trooper or social-control agent to pave the way for the pure Nephilim when they make their way to this planet. I give exactly zero fucks about ninety-nine percent of all events that go on on this planet."

Truth nodded. And waited.

"I don't give a shit about your weird deal, or your girlfriend, wife, whatever. Boyfriend. Pet rock that you dick down on the quiet. Don't care, won't care."

Ah. She was like him. Lonely, in a world she didn't understand.

"I'm currently engaged in a campaign of terrorism and rebellion across Jeon," Truth said.

"Excellent. Sounds like a giggle-fest."

"And am being hunted by people of alarming reach and power."

"I can promise that, should we enter into a committed relationship of our own, my family will do absolutely nothing to protect you." Susan looked earnest.

"You mean 'will definitely protect you,' right?"

"I do not. Officially, we would, of course. In practice, people of our generation would try to kill you just for fun. If they failed, they would claim they were just playing and you shouldn't get mad."

"And if I killed them?" Truth's voice was bone-dry.

"Then you are an asshole. They were just playing around. So, five or six of them would gang up and kill you."

"Such fun."

"We are strong, not fair." Susan shrugged.

"Making a real hard sell here."

"You already said no. This is just me trying my luck. I mean, at this point, what have I got to lose?"

Apparently not her life. Truth's desire to kill her had vanished. His back had stopped bleeding a while back too. The body cultivation could manage a gross physical wound like that well enough, though it would need a healing spell to really be put back together.

"All right, so, here's the thing. I want to put one of my drones in charge of MegaShroom and use them to . . . basically poison the well of public opinion. Are you going to get in the way of that?"

"Are you going to destroy the company?"

"Not intentionally, though I don't plan on caring about its survival."

"Close enough. Sure. Go nuts."

Huh.

"Really?"

"Yep. Don't care. And yes, I will be telling the family all about this. Obviously. But they won't care either. Actually, they will want us to hook up. You have collapse-survival potential."

"Nifty. As a sign of good faith, could I have a primer on how your magic works?"

"You can't use it. Really. It takes spirits of intellect centuries to make hybrid spells that kinda-sorta replicate one part of one of our spells. The magic isn't compatible at all."

"Then there is nothing to lose, is there?" Truth said. He didn't realize his voice was maddeningly reasonable, but it was.

"God, you must be popular."

"I get hit on a lot, actually, when I let people see me. It's a little weird."

"What's weird about it?" She looked blank, then groaned. "Let me guess: you are muscly as hell."

"Not compared to your big bro, but by Jeon standards? Yeah."

"How do you know Remu, anyway?"

"I thought I was collaring a pet and didn't realize it had his brand on its ass already. Awkward. And with that tip, I think your family is going to be a bit more cooperative. Spell primer?"

"Do you keep your baby books in your office? There is a manual of spell design on the desk, under the office equipment catalog."

Truth walked over and found it. He started "casually" flipping through it.

"Told you it wouldn't make any sense to you."

<<Got it. Not going to lie, my already-subterranean opinion of you will get lower if you do actually try to date her. Bad enough you punched your v-card. The notion that you would "do it" twice in a lifetime is . . . beurgh.>>

"Yes, you were right. One last thing—why seal the room? It looked like you triggered an alarm, but even after all this time, no one has come bursting in."

Her smile was . . . unkind. "You were wondering what my position in the company was, since I am clearly overqualified to be a receptionist?"

"Yes."

"Bait. This is a reward posting."

Truth cocked his head at that.

"You are the seventh person to come looking for us with bad intentions. You will be the first to walk out alive." She sighed dramatically. "I was hoping for another cultivation supplement. Oh, well." She waved from the floor. "There is always next time."

Truth turned to walk out the door. The spell had come down while they chatted. Truth paused and looked back.

"I heard a joke once."

"Oh? Go on."

"Why did the chicken cross the playground?"

"You are joking."

"Yes. But why?"

She rolled her eyes dramatically. "I don't know. Why did the chicken cross the playground?"

"To get to the other slide."

There was a long pause.

"That was bad. And you should feel bad about it." Susan's voice was conversational.

"To say that I'm not good with jokes would be an understatement. You tell me one."

"Oh, I know a *great* joke. A dog walks into a tavern and says, 'I can't see a thing. I'll open this one.' She started giggling, then guffawing. A muscular hand slapped a strong thigh as her shoulders shook. "I'll open this one!"

Truth just nodded slowly. "You tell the funniest jokes. I am not your match."

She wiped a tear from her eye. "Ah, I didn't invent it. I heard it from my uncle."

"When we meet next, tell me a better one. I don't want another lover. But I could use a friend."

She grinned. She didn't stop smiling even after he shut the door behind him.

CHAPTER 27

POISONING THE WELL

*Y*ou *flirted with the giant girl. Disgusting.>>*

I was very explicitly not flirting.

<<You were one hundred percent flirting. If I had skin, it would be crawling.>>

I kind of imagine you peeling off your skin and flensing away your muscles and organs in a desperate attempt to be rid of the clinging wetness of it all.

<<Yes, my skin would be crawling for several reasons. Not least of which is you flirting with Ms. Muscles there.>>

Cannot emphasize enough how she is not my type. I am the product of my upbringing. I'm not into the bodybuilding physique. Dainty, elfin beauties and Etenesh. That's what I like.

<<Oh, I know. This and that are two different things.>>

Eh?

<<Just because you think you were making a friend or pawn doesn't change the fact that you were flirting. You vile heartbreaker. Poor Etenesh. She will have to find a new deity to venerate.>>

Yeah, no. I'm not responsible for how other people think.

The System started madly cackling. *<<You use Incisive all the time! Aaaaalllll the time. You are completely, totally, one hundred percent responsible for how other people think.>>*

Not all the people all the time! I have to use the poison intentionally and you know it!

<<Not the Scales, though, and even if magic was suppressed under the wards, even if she could see through your unnoticeability, you can't act like there was no "there" there. Hell, I have to wonder if the Sea of Brass isn't having an effect over time. Slowly establishing a zone of "orthodoxy" around you.>>

There is no evidence that is true or works the way you are implying.

<<I know that people tend to get awfully obedient around you.>>

Did you, somehow, miss the bit where she got very, very close to killing me, several times? And that she only yielded when I literally paralyzed her?

<<Well done on proving you weren't food. You were always ambitious, and you got promoted all the way to possible mate in just seconds of meeting her. You are an inspiration for scummy, desperate losers hitting on women in bars everywhere.>>

Truth thought about that one a minute as he left the office building Anak and Sons was in. *Actually . . . that would fit with the spell. Incisive, I mean. Reshaping the world around you. Classifying people into food, mates, or predators to be avoided.*

<<Giant snake demon is going to giant snake demon. Now, what's an angel going to do with Cup and Knife?>>

It was a bland part of Harban. Not really convenient for anywhere. A shocking number of people worked there. All those bland offices, laboratories, and light commercial operations forming the middle layer of commerce in the city. Or they used to. OFFICE SPACE FOR RENT signs filled the windows. A lot of trash was piling up on the streets.

Truth watched some discarded wrappers and plastic bags blow around. You really didn't see that outside of the slums. You didn't use to see it. It was probably a lot more common now. Air demons would do the work very cheaply. You could even get talisman devices to do it if you didn't want to work with demons for some reason.

He sighed and blended in with the worried-looking workers lining up for the bus. If there was trash flying around, either it was no longer economical to pay the demons, to run the machines, or just nobody cared enough to pay for it. Possibly a combination of all three. He heaved a big sigh, to the silent agreement of the rest of the queue. He would have to work extra hard visualizing from now on. That Nephilim trick of sealing up the body and keeping all the cosmic rays inside was only getting more urgently necessary.

Speaking of, how is it going, breaking down that manual?

<<She wasn't lying. It is completely incomprehensible . . . if we didn't know a little bit about how they think and operate. I don't have anything meaningful right now. This is going to be a very long-term project. I'm sure I'm replicating work someone else has already done, which is frustrating.>>

In the meantime, Cup and Knife.

Truth made his way back to the hotel, letting the Prince enrobe him as he entered his suite. Butler and Maid were waiting for him, bowing as he entered. He ordered some snacks and a drink, then set about properly healing himself. The wound had long since clotted, but the muscle damage lingered. As did the scrapes along his bones.

He let the spell slowly form around him, trying to remember what he knew about Manda, the patron origin of the spell, and Johannes Vek, its creator. Very little, as it happened. Manda was an angel associated with revelation. Vek was prolific, with hundreds of spells to his name, but all were so idiosyncratic, they were used purely for inspiration. That's why he had found the spell without an introduction in one of Merkovah's big reference books. It was literally just there for reference. No sensible person would actually use it.

Truth grinned at that thought. He considered himself quite sensible. Did the Prince grin? He was mindful of his dignity of course, but yes. If the Prince wanted to grin, he would damn well grin. Very well, then. To work.

Manda was described as appearing as both an old man and a young child. He was also compared to a river, or the guiding bell in the fog. Not sure how the human bit fit in, but . . . Manda was all about revelation pouring in. You can't force revelation; you can only leave yourself open to it. Truth toyed with that idea for a second. What did it mean to be open to revelation? Presumably to align your thoughts as closely as you could with the source of revelation, then wait.

He wasn't bad at waiting. Truth directed the spell toward the clotted wound on his back. It wasn't supposed to look like this. Muscles were supposed to be better connected. More vital and full of life. The skin stretched across them was supposed to be supple, strong, and smooth.

The spell appeared to agree, rolling over him. Truth could imagine the healing rolling down along the path of his spine, like water along a dry riverbed. It didn't feel quite like anything else. It didn't even really feel like "healing." There were problems, then there weren't. He didn't even have to send the damage somewhere. Now, just why was that? He did with the dog in front of the shrine, or the damage done by the geas on the MegaShroom employees.

He had no idea. He'd just have to wait for it all to be revealed. The healing didn't take very long. The Meditations had given him a strong body. Appreciating that fact, he moved directly into practicing them. Letting the visualization guide him. Leaning on the Nine Worms for support.

The worms didn't object to modifications based on Nephilim biology. That was interesting, in an alarming sort of way. He didn't linger on the thought, just pressed on. The gains were small, slow, but very steady. Every day, he was a little more real. A little closer to wrapping his hands around the levers controlling the world.

A little closer to wrapping his hands around the System Astrologica and squeezing.

When he was done meditating, he set up the cosmic-ray-concentration array Merkovah had sent over in a corner of the suite. It worked about as well as the cultivation room in the hotel. Well, he was staying in one of the very nicest hotels in Jeon. And Merkovah's array was portable. A whole lot better than nothing.

"A bath and dinner. Bring your trainee. I will feed him personally. After dinner, I will explain how he will make himself useful."

The succubae bowed and murmured their obedience. Dinner was exquisite—roast duck over a bed of gemlike rice. He remembered rice like this from the one time he flew first class. This was apparently the real-deal version. Both the duck and the rice had been enhanced with cosmic energy.

Even five years ago, this plate of food would have been worth more than most people made in two years. More than a Denizen made in five. Now? When elixirs were becoming unavailable at any price?

It was delicious. He left a small portion on his plate, then looked over at the man standing patiently at the foot of the table. Eyes fixed firmly on the floor.

"You were born a minor child of a wealthy family attached to a powerful family. For most of your life, you were destined to serve a menial, if comfortable, role serving your betters in the clan. Now your grandmother decided the single best use of you was to serve me. Service to the clan was not enough. You were no longer enough. All that accumulated family influence . . . worthless. Your existence was, for them, a burden. One they were overjoyed to turn into a benefit. For them."

Truth's voice was conversational. No need to press hard. Everyone in this room was coiled in Incisive. Truth had been working hard at understanding the Prince and Botis both. It was paying off. The former Barton remained silent.

"Today, I walked into the corporate offices of a minor criminal enterprise masquerading as a near-billion-wen corporation. Perhaps you have heard of MegaShroom. I broke the CEO and killed their chief lawyer. I then found those who truly control that firm and forced one of their number into submission. They offered to let me do as I wished with MegaShroom. I wished to replace the CEO with one of my own and use the company to my own ends. They obeyed. From a stranger to running a near-billion-wen business in . . . perhaps two hours. Most of which was travel time."

The former Barton kept his eyes fixed on the floor. His face didn't twitch, but Truth could see his eyes darting through the thin skin of their lids.

"Your name will be Niles Bowman. See to it that it is changed legally. You will be installed as the CEO of MegaShroom. Tonight, you will be instructed on the nature and habits of the Nephilim, as it is they who truly control that company. You may keep the salary as walking-around money. The company's profits, such as they are and will be, will continue to go to the Anak family. Your actual job will be to foment a religious nationalism in the company's servants. All those ambassadors and representatives."

Truth's expression only looked like a smile. Everyone in the room other than him shivered, even if they couldn't see his face.

"You will institute a new policy. Where before, merely hitting sales goals and purchasing product from the company was enough to move them up tiers, now they have to give. Servants must donate up to twenty percent of their gross income to their local Pragerite church. They are to provide receipts for this. Failure to do so will result in dropping tiers and less-favorable pricing. However, every wen and credit spent to this end will count twice for their promotion to the next tier."

His expression turned stern. "You will change the branding and promotional materials. You will show happy people in stable families in traditional, old-fashioned dress. You will emphasize that the core of MegaShroom is Faith, Family, and Prosperity, the same tripod that holds up the nation of Jeon. And MegaShroom is a proud Jeon company. You will increase the patriotic language and branding material as well."

Niles bowed silently.

"And once you have done this, you will work with the major churches around Harban and the rest of Jeon to integrate the reporting requirements. You will remind the priests that the more they push your servants, the more they can donate. The more prosperous the church becomes, the richer the Treasury of God, the more powerful God's servants shall be in the face of the coming darkness. And you will remind them, as you will remind your servants, of one obvious truth.

"Starbrite the man is not from Jeon. He is a foreigner, an outsider. He has stolen the country's wealth and genius for himself. Oh, he made a few very rich. But remind your servants. Would they be selling MegaShroom if they were one of the ones Starbrite blessed? Or are they scared? Afraid of what is coming? Do they feel the future will be better than the past?

"They do not. Starbrite is the demon of poverty that has bewitched the nation, brought it low. But thanks to the hard work of the church and MegaShroom, the Tiger of Jeon shall rise once more."

Truth smiled at the shivering Niles. "You may eat."

CHAPTER 28

THE INIMITABLE MAGUS VEK

Truth allowed Niles to be escorted away by Butler. The young man would spend the night in dreams, receiving an intensive education on the Nephilim and what was needed to pretend to be a CEO. Not that Butler had the faintest idea about the necessities of running a major corporation. The succubus did, however, have a great deal of experience manipulating desire. Niles would find running an MLM to be not too difficult in the short term.

Niles would sleep in a bed tonight. A comfortable single bed, with comfortable pillows, in seeming privacy. It was important, Butler explained, to set expectations. Niles was a person created to serve the needs of the Prince. As such, he would live like a person and behave like a person. However, if he proved incapable of being Niles, then they would simply start over. The Prince would not be burdened by a single additional piece of luggage. Butler could be endlessly patient.

Truth sat in an armchair, looking out at a sixty-million-wen view of Harban at night. Its brilliant colors advertising endless wonders. The floating towers dancing in their own moonbeams. Illusory beasts mock-fighting in the parks. The bars, nightclubs, night markets, the brothels, and the twenty-four-hour convenience stores all jammed side by side. District by segregated district. All of this built around one unalterable, inescapable truth—people are not born equal, they do not live as equals, and they do not die as equals. Because of money, and because of power.

"Maid, is this the only world you have ever served on?"

"Other than Hell, My Prince? Yes."

"Ah. I wondered if there was a world somewhere without levels. The Nephilim say they do not have levels, but there are clearly differences in power between them. They don't pretend to care about equality. Just the opposite, in fact."

"If there is such a world, I do not know of it, Your Highness."

Truth nodded. He had a rare moment of wanting to drink. Not for the sake of getting drunk. The moment just seemed to call for whiskey. It was no effort to suppress the thought. Instead, he asked, "What happens when there are no more levels? Mechanically, I mean?"

"This little maid dares not guess, Great One."

Truth laughed silently. "No, I suppose you don't. But you make my point for me. In this relationship, my magic gives me power over you. I have the biggest fist and offer the best benefits. But what if we were both Level Zero humans, in a world with only Level Zero humans? Would my muscles give me power over you? Only so long as I was awake, right?"

The maid said nothing. If her master wanted to monologue, she was quite happy to let him. It made her job easier and more pleasant, the more she understood him.

"So, you need groups of people. People with a degree of trust, willing to work together. Families, maybe, or gangs. Armies. Religions. Some combination of all those things. Because with no magic, it's down to raw muscle and whatever bits of natural philosophy remain relevant. It's going to be down to pointy sticks, or knives made of scavenged steel beaten into blades."

He thought about that for a moment. "And steel doesn't keep for long once the rust-protection enchantments wear off. Assuming it had any. Weapons will be brass or bronze or stone, very quickly. Perhaps bone. And yet I have no faith that the world will be a fair or equal place. Someone will have to do the farming, and it won't be the priests or kings. Their jobs are much too important. Can't let them worry about making food."

He took a deep breath. "Now, it doesn't have to be that way. This country has, or had, some elected leaders as well as a bunch of aristocrats. If you were a Citizen and met a few other requirements, you could vote for them. Not that it ever mattered; everyone elected was either a significant power in their own right or represented one. Or were a pawn for a major corporation, though I suppose those categories are redundant. In theory, I can sort of imagine a situation where everyone gets together to pick who was in charge. But I don't believe that is what will happen."

The Prince's smile was cold enough to give even devils a chill. "They will say that, in the present emergency, strong measures, temporary measures, must be taken. Obedience is mandatory; dissent cannot be tolerated. The soldiers are here to help you. They are your only shield against other humans. The priests your only shield against the angry heavens. All those hauled over the altar are enemies or criminals, or the very lucky chosen for a supreme honor."

He spat thickly, watching the phlegm sink into a carpet more valuable than the apartment he had grown up in, the lives of everyone in that apartment included.

"Arrange for me to visit a university library tomorrow. I don't care which one; pick based on convenience. Nothing I am looking for is restricted. The morning routine is to be as usual. I am going to bed."

Morning came, and after his usual decadent morning routine, Truth set off for the library at E&O U. E&O being so universally used that people actually forgot the *E* and *O* stood for Esoteric and Occult, respectively. It was a third-tier university, trying to catch whatever scraps the University of Jeon discarded. They were happy enough anyone remembered them in the first place. But a university requires an impressive library, and they did their best.

Truth looked up at the concrete box. It had a donor's name on it in large blue letters. Nobody he had ever heard of. It also had the word LIBRARY on the end of its name, a short flight of stairs, and cast-concrete statues of crouching temple dogs, so it would probably do.

He tried to adopt the identity of a grad student. It was a heavy lift. He altered tack slightly—he was in the army reserves, using the government support to take some associate-level courses in talisman maintenance. That clicked into place, no trouble. Swearing silently, Truth marched up to the reference desk. This early in the morning, the library was pretty empty. Lucky him. The librarian flinched when they saw Truth.

"Rough night?" the librarian asked. "Or are you . . . in costume or something?" Truth looked over himself. Clean button-down black shirt, gray trousers, sneakers, leather belt, he thought he was looking pretty sharp, actually.

"What's wrong with how I'm dressed?"

"Wait, you mean those are really your muscles? Bro. What?" The librarian's look shifted to a sort of horrified revulsion.

"This has been a fantastic conversation. Magus Johannes Vek. Inventor of four hundred–plus spells, including the famed Cup and Knife. Looking for information on him."

"If you damage the books, you have to buy a new copy. And they are very, very expensive."

Truth picked up a pen and balanced it on its point. On his pinky. He kept it balanced there while eyeing the librarian hard.

"Fine. Yes. There is an almanac of famous mages that Vek has an entry in; you can check any of our encyclopedias, and check with the spirit of intellect over there for actual journal articles and books that cover him."

"Your commitment to library science is to point me at an encyclopedia and a more-useful librarian." Truth didn't know what to think. This was the result of university education? What did that make Etenesh and Jember? The very top of all students everywhere?"

"Guess how much this job pays?"

"Not much?"

"Nothing at all. Volunteering is a graduation requirement for undergrads, remember?"

Ah.

"Almanac is that way?"

"Third row on your left."

Truth found the multivolume almanac. It was organized alphabetically, so it wasn't too hard to find Vek.

Johannes Vek, born to Dagobah and Thomas Vek of Ruttlesford, Pecorah. The Vek family were successful necromancers and very active in their local Pragerite Church. Records show that Johannes was active in the Junior Auxiliaries of the Heavenly Host as well as consistently in the top of his class at St. Ethelbert's School. He attended St. Ethelbert's from the ages of six until sixteen, when he declared his intention to become a doctor and began attending classes at the University of Uxus.

During his studies at the University of Uxus, Johannes Vek joined the Fraternal Order of St. Astil, a Pragerite lay brotherhood dedicated to doing good works and living according to the example set by St. Astil. It is believed that it was during his time at university, and particularly with the Order, that Vek was first introduced into ascetic mysticism.

It was during his fourth year at university, aged twenty, when Vek first claimed to have received a vision of an angel, specifically the angel Manda. He had been without food for three days and subsisted on the bare minimum of water necessary while kneeling in prayer on a stone floor. He had not slept for the entirety of his vigil. It was determined at the time that he was sincerely deluded due to sleep deprivation.

Johannes Vek was to repeat this experience several times. Each time, the ascetic ritual grew more severe and lasted longer. In the end, his priest and his college advisor both intervened, and on threat of expulsion, he stopped.

There is considerable scholarly debate over whether he did, in fact, stop his ascetic rituals, as his later years as a student were characterized by several public reprimands for failure to do required coursework, as well as three awarded papers on the uses of calcination in materials processing in alchemy.

At the request of some of his classmates, an inquest was held into possible academic dishonesty, particularly due to his failure to cite sources for the awarded papers. However, no dishonesty was found, and the work was deemed entirely original.

He remained in Uxus, opening a medical practice and taking up a position as a lay brother in the Church of St. Brzhenik. His cultivation was believed to be around Level Three, which would have been average for an educated professional in his era.

Wait, Level THREE was average for a doctor? I've been treated by Level One doctors. A Level Three might be a department head in a small hospital, or a shift supervisor in almost any hospital. How long has magic been declining for?

Truth kept reading the lengthy article. Vek had only lived about six hundred years ago, so there were surprisingly detailed records of his life. A major reason for this, apparently, was his ability to start a fight with very senior mages, get absolutely clowned based on the existing research, and then vindicated when he was able to demonstrate in a laboratory the correctness of his theories.

This was not a trait that endeared him to many. It did get his stuff hate-copied a lot. People shared his books and pamphlets, frequently with cries of "Can you believe this fraud?" Cries that got a lot more muted when, for example, he showed that he could refine gold to near-perfect purity with a single spell and no reagents. Or that he could considerably improve the production of ingredients from herbs in terms of both purity and quantity. That he could, in fact, cure several hitherto-untreatable diseases by identifying the tiny, invisible demons causing them, and exorcising them.

A constant critique of his work was that his spells were incredibly poorly optimized. In addition to being one of the most prolific spell creators to ever live, he almost certainly held the record for most spells improved on and replaced by others in his lifetime. It seemed he was well aware of the problem.

"I have not the wit to mend the fault in my recollection with mine own inventions. I can only faithfully record, as best I can, that which has been revealed to me by the Great Manda. He has seen that my devotion to God is as sturdy as the mountains and as endless as the sky, and has thus revealed to me the truth of many things."

Interesting but unhelpful, Truth felt. Not a whole lot there to actually explain how the hell Cup and Knife worked. It sounded like Vek didn't know either. He nearly fell over reading the next paragraph, where it was revealed the spell got its name because they were the first two things Vek saw when he regained consciousness after the vision in which the spell was revealed. They had no particular relevance to how the spell should be used.

I'll kill him. I will go back in time and kill him. Then I will stitch his soul back into his body so I can kill him a few more times.

<<I wouldn't do that. Read to the end.>>

Vek apparently died at the age of forty-seven, although that was disputed. Apparently, a door opened in the air, and a small boy walked out into the chapel at St. Brzhenik. The small boy said nothing but took Vek by the hand and walked with him through the door in the air. Apparently, the light of Heaven was shining through the doorway. The Church of St. Brzhenik survived to this day and was apparently considered quite holy. Particularly the angelic script etched into the flagstone floor.

"A pauper shall be a prince, wisdom ever sought and never found, hatred and love out of measure, and a dream forbidden. How can one approach the Throne without knowing Truth?"

Truth stared at it for a while. *I mean, endless things go on and on about "the truth." If I got obsessed over every time my name got mentioned . . .*

"They always get that message wrong." Truth nearly jumped out of his skin. Some old fellow was reading over his shoulder. Plainly Level One; Truth had ignored his existence entirely.

"Pardon?"

"The angelic script on the floor is an intermediary language used by angels to communicate with humans. It uses a suffix to denote the end of a sentence, and there are no commas. Nor is there a special symbol indicating a question. You can read them in, but they are not actually there. Translators put them in to make things flow better. Likewise, articles are a 'sometimes' thing, and mostly not."

"Ah. Thank you?"

"No problem. A better translation would be 'A pauper shall be a prince / Wisdom ever sought and never found / Arrogant humility / A dream forbidden/ You cannot approach the Throne without knowing Truth.'"

"I'm afraid I don't understand the difference."

The old man laughed. "I get that a lot. Tell me, 'young man'"—Truth could hear strong irony in the phrase—"do you ever wonder why the world is the way it is?"

"Constantly." Truth nodded hard.

"Can you think of alternatives?"

"Not . . . comprehensive ones. Changing the people in charge is the best I can get to. *Frustrating* is putting it mildly."

"Strange, isn't it? Despite all your time thinking and wondering and asking, you can't seem to do better than *what is*. Now . . . why is that?"

Truth looked at the old man. He had a deeply tanned face, eyes that suggested a lust for life, and a gentle smile that said he liked sharing a good joke. You . . . wanted to trust him. Even Truth's finely tuned paranoia was eased. Which alarmed him.

"Senior? May I ask your name?"

"You may, but I won't say." The old man chuckled. "If you want to know the answer to a lot of things, including how Cup and Knife *really* works, answer that question first. Why can't you imagine a better world?" The old man tapped the quote in the book again, then went deathly pale. His eyes slid across Truth's shoulders, dropping the book as he fumbled in his pants for a talisman.

Truth felt danger flare behind him as he spun around, calling the Tongue to hand. Then the sense of danger vanished.

Before him was a duck. A pair of tiny horns sprouted from its head. The duck shook once, violently, and the little horns slid off. Truth turned back. The old man had vanished.

CHAPTER 29

DREAM A LITTLE DREAM

Truth looked at the duck. The duck didn't look particularly happy to be in the middle of a library, but it wasn't freaking out, either. Now that he looked closer, the horns were blatantly plastic.

That was definitely Manda, right?

<<Right. No ascetic mysticism needed. Who says you are a sucker who got tricked by a duck?>>

Get bent. He sold that beautifully. Even triggered Incisive.

<<I'm not seeing some top-tier angel. I am seeing a duck trying to eat a plastic horn. Your endless failures aside, what the hell are you?>>

Truth looked around the library, not really seeing the gray shelves or industrial blue carpeting. *I really don't know anymore.*

Before he left the library, Truth decided to "help" the student librarian.

"I believe this is yours." Truth dropped the duck on the desk in front of the librarian.

"I . . . Did someone spike my coffee?"

"You aren't that lucky. Look, students hooking up in the library is an ancient tradition, I'm told, but this is just not okay." Truth was aggressively reasonable. "I don't care what you do in private, but this is meant to be a place for studying."

"Wha?"

"I mean, does your 'special friend' here look okay? You know what? That's between the two of you. I'm not okay with this. At all."

"I have no idea—"

"Then you should learn. This is a place for learning. Maybe learn to have some shame." Truth turned sharply and strode out of the library. It might have been petty, but he was pretty damn done with people dragging him for his looks.

Truth walked out of the library and looked across the little cluster of buildings that made up the E&O campus. Not a whole lot of "there" there. Boxes of boxes where people taught and others learned, each hoping that they weren't wasting their dwindling time.

He could feel himself detaching from the world around him. It was an odd feeling of lucidity. His mind seemed to take a step back and up, away from his body and at ninety degrees to the world itself. The buildings took on a two-dimensional feeling. The grass was painted on the floor, the bushes cut out of cardboard, the sky a blue scrim with a spotlight shining through it.

The people, those playing students and faculty, all seemed to be wearing clothes that did not fit quite right. Wardrobe hadn't time to make adjustments before the players had to rush to the stage. Their blocking and their lines imperfectly memorized. Their gestures too stiff and expressive to be natural. Playing for an audience of one. And that "one" wasn't Truth.

Truth stood outside the library and watched the show for a little while. Trying to find the plot. Trying to spot the audience. Truth forced his body to move through the players, through that repertory company. He made his way to a church, but it looked no more real than the buildings around it. The spells covering it were a light show. The priests had on masks over masks. So did the worshipers. Yet, for all that, Truth rather thought that the face they would be wearing beneath the masks was actually what was on the mask themselves.

They felt as they were required to feel, but they had to present that emotion in the approved way. They had to show the audience what they expected to see.

Eventually, he made his way to a pew and sat. Just trying to let the feeling pass. Maybe this was what Merkovah meant when he said he was alienated. Someone who should be one of the performers but who kept breaking character. Who kept poking at that invisible fourth wall and asking if it was really there.

"Are you a local student? I don't think I recognize you." One of the actors . . . No. One of the parishioners came up and sat down next to him. "Sorry, you didn't look like you were praying, and you did look pretty lost."

"No, that's all right. I needed some time to come back to myself."

"Find anything along the way?" The parishioner was a heavyset woman, an oddity in Jeon. Not obese, just . . . heavy. Middle age had settled down around her and kept right on settling. Apparently doing well enough, or poorly enough, that she could come volunteer at her church in the middle of the morning.

"I really don't know. Can I ask you a question? I promise I'm being serious. Not . . . pranking you or anything."

"That sounds ominous." She smiled. "Go on. Shock me."

"What does a better earthly world look like? I don't mean the Kingdom of Heaven stuff; I'm not ambitious enough to expect perfected divine rule. But if you were empress of the world, how would you set it in order?"

She rocked back, thin eyebrows rising. "Well. That's a heavy question." She looked out over the tall platforms the chapel was built around. "A question plenty of people are asking themselves, I think. One way or another."

"Really?" Truth was relieved to see that it wasn't just him.

"Oh, yes. How could we not? I helped bury four suicides in as many months. That's not a world I want to live in." She spoke quietly, smile long gone. "All laid off. All had been hunting for work for months. Looking at jobs they wouldn't even have dreamed of doing a year ago. Competing with Denizens for jobs, if you can believe it."

"I can believe it."

She sighed. "I wish you couldn't."

They sat together for a while. She started speaking slowly. "If I was empress of the world, I would start by making sure I wasn't running things."

"Oh?"

"The biggest management job I ever did was working as an assistant manager at a Varle's in Cobb Mall for three months one summer when I was seventeen. I hated it, but there was no one else to do the work, so I got 'voluntold.'" She smiled a little at the memory. "I hated it, and I was really bad at it. So, if I can't manage the work schedules for eight high school kids, I sure can't manage the world."

"Who would you put in charge, then?"

"No one."

"No one? But then the schedule goes crazy and none of the folding gets done." He remembered that Varle's sold clothes for teenage girls.

"Really? Why?" Her smile came back, something crafty about it now. "Any reason the girls can't sit down and talk it out? Who is covering what shift, doing what duties? And when you get right down to it, as long as the owner gets their cash, what do they care?"

Truth knew that the owners cared very much indeed. Working inside Starbrite had been an education. But he took her point. Maybe the owners shouldn't care.

"So, who are the owners? In your world-as-mall-store metaphor?" Truth asked, and that seemed to jam her up.

"I . . . don't know. We started this with me as the empress of the world, so even if I abdicated, there would still be an empress, right? Or . . . aristocrats and ministers and all that. High citizens. A-Tier citizens now, I suppose."

Truth nodded. He had come to the same conclusions as her. Different people in charge, maybe a little more freedom for those below, but again, the same structure. The mighty at the top of a tall pyramid. Everyone else carried the weight.

"But the girls could chat and sort out their shifts and duties," Truth said.

"Right."

"Pay?"

"Set by the boss, of course, but it would have to be fair. I would be picking the bosses, or I would pick the person who would pick the bosses, and I would tell them that the wages have to be fair. And benefits. They should definitely get health, dental, vision, and life insurance. And the boss shouldn't be allowed to bully them, or at least not more than the usual."

"I'd work at that shop." Truth smiled.

"You don't fit the look book." The older woman had a youthful giggle.

"Discriminated against for my muscles even in a dream world. There is no escape."

"Why are you so muscly, if I may ask? I would have guessed you were a soldier or fighter, but your skin and nails are *impeccable*. Not a hint of a broken nose, either."

"Thank you; kind of you to notice. And because I love feeling my body. I use it every day." He smiled at her, then stood. "It's not a comfortable feeling, existing as a mind without a body."

She stood with him. "I can't imagine it is. Glad to see you smiling again."

"Ah, well, I had nice company while I thought. One day I will crack it."

"Crack what?"

He smiled at her, a little sadly this time. "The egg hiding a world I can't imagine."

Truth sat in a rather nice park. The trees were huge, towering things whose canopies glowed in rainbow colors after dark. For the moment, anyway. Truth didn't know how much longer they could manage it.

Two days left. Two days, and then the mass enrollment started around Jeon. In a month, everyone would either be a Denizen or have a bit of their soul mutilated and set to work for Starbrite. For . . . some purpose. Perhaps simply to be harvested as the bodies they haunted started dying at an accelerated pace. Then the System would be rolled out to as much of the world as they could manage.

There was only a year or so, maybe as much as a year and a half until the collapse. The pebbles were bouncing down the mountain already. So, Starbrite's plans couldn't reasonably extend beyond that point. Whatever he was going to do with all those soul fragments, he needed them moderately urgently and by the millions.

And yet . . . a high-tier angel, one in service to a being whose title alone was enough to trigger divine wrath, was willing to manifest of its own volition in front of him. The angel didn't appear to give a damn about any of that. The angel just wanted him to . . . think of what he couldn't think of. Or that anyone could think of, apparently. Truth didn't give himself much credit as an original thinker.

<<No, for once, that's not the problem. Think about the message he left.>>
In the church?

<<No, with your mom after a vigorous networking event. YES, at the church.>>

I think there is a limit to what even an angel will do on God's orders. Truth thought about it a moment. *That does actually sound like it was left specifically for me. Six hundred years ago. Creepy.*

<<Don't overthink it. You have a bunch of vague-sounding phrases that can be made to apply to lots of different situations, and then someone gasps and goes, "But how could you have known?" It's an ancient con.>>

Truth nodded. That did sound plausible. *He did make a point of translating it again, though. And the bit about a forbidden dream didn't change at all.*

<<Exactly. Which suggests that he meant exactly that. It's not that you can't imagine it. The "dream" itself is forbidden. Think about that. For something to be forbidden, someone had to have forbidden it. Which meant that it existed at some point, somewhere, because why would you prohibit something nobody was doing?>>

Truth nodded with a sort of horrified fascination. *Which leads to two questions— who did the forbidding, and why? And really, answering one gives us the answer to the other. Probably.*

Truth stared up into the canopy, watching the sunlight flicker down through the leaves. Letting the light warm him. It had suddenly gotten very cold. *It's not God. If keeping things this way was so important, he wouldn't have abandoned the world. More to the point, as strange as Manda is, he is still an angel, and they don't do a damn thing without divine approval. So, if Manda is cluing me in on this, it strongly suggests that it's not God's plan or intention or whatever.*

<<And we don't know what, exactly, was done, so we don't know how much power it took to do it. Which means that we can't really narrow down our suspects that way.>>

But we can look at who benefits. Who has gotten the most out of this world? Who would benefit the most from keeping things the way they were?

Truth sighed. There was only one answer. As obvious as the sun at noon. Starbrite.

CHAPTER 30

STILL HUNGRY

haven't thought of people around me as being real people for a long while now. That seems profoundly unhealthy.

Truth watched the sun wink through the leaves of the brilliantly colored tree above him.

It encourages a certain way of thinking. Of approaching problems. And I have to figure, since everything I have done, I did because it seemed like a good idea or the best option, I must be picking cards from a stacked deck.

<<*It's an interesting notion. Is it possible to rig an entire world like a game of Find the Lady? You can pick any card you like . . . and it will always be a card that Starbrite chose for you.*>>

Just a few small problems with the idea.

<<*Starting with "Boy, that would be a convenient cop-out for all my horrible decisions," and followed quickly by "How?"*>>

Changing how the whole world thinks. Limiting the imagination *of the whole world. All of it. Siphios and every other country he ever fought with, all the other companies, all the other Level Eights, and were there really never any locally grown Level Nines? Because even with this planet being, apparently, a complete backwater, we did still have natural treasures and divinely blessed places and things. Really* nobody else *made it to the peak of Level Nine?*

<<*That does seem rather suspect.*>>

Let's go back to that library. When did Starbrite reach this planet?

There was a long pause.

<<*You don't know? No, you don't know. How is that possible?*>>

Because I never learned it?

<<*You memorized the benefits package available to maintenance techs. You memorized the floor plan of the four standard two-bedroom apartments available to C-9-L-Tier employees at base salary. You know, even now, the maintenance schedule for the PGM-1110-LC Driver Assist System-*>>

Six months—Oil of Lilly Verdsang (2 percent concentration or higher, up to 4 percent,) and check paths for wear and tear. Annual—strip down and clean with pure ethanol, retrace major paths with Number Four diamond-tip rasp, fine brush minor paths, re-oil—

<<*Every other company has a Founded in Year Dot sign posted, or they yammer on about it in some glossy brochure.*>>

But this must be public information, right? It's the most powerful corporation in the world. It's headed by the most powerful mages too, probably.

<<It certainly has the strongest mages, because otherwise, everyone else would have ganged up on them. They probably did do that sometime in the past and got killed for it. Several times, I'd bet.>>

It had to start somewhere. He arrived here at some point. Which means that there was a time before Starbrite. Records of that time exist. We know the student attendance records of a mage six hundred years ago. How can we not find out when Starbrite arrived?

<<Is Merkovah older than Starbrite, or at least Starbrite's presence on this planet? He said some things that I guess could kind of be interpreted that way but nothing definitive.>>

Hell if I know. Back to the library?

<<Not just yet, I think. Something very odd is going on here. Even if Starbrite is to blame for everything, and again, we can't explain what he's doing let alone how, or even if he is doing it, even with all that, we still haven't cracked what exactly it is that we have been forbidden from seeing. Keep in mind, whatever it is has to be so comprehensively effective that none of the stuff we imported from off-world broke the . . . mental conditioning? Whatever.>>

Truth nodded and got up. *I'm going to take a walk. Maybe swing by some places on Merkovah's list. Lists. He had a lot of things he wanted done around Harban, and you know what? Stressing the System Astrologica to the breaking point was already the plan. This is just another excellent reason to do it.*

Truth walked down the street, vaguely headed back to the hotel. At some point, the hotel staff would ask someone for their identity sigil and a linked bank account, right? And the Shalia was one of those "our parent company is 45 percent owned by a Starbrite subsidiary" business. He had some vague recollection of someone's niece or mistress being installed as the titular "Proprietor" years ago. There was a minor scandal about it. A million-wen job, which consisted of smiling prettily at appropriate public events and nothing else.

But what could you do about it? It's just how things are. That's life in the real world.

He observed the street. It was pretty ordinary. Basic Citizen-zoned area, which made it far, far nicer than a slum but lacked the color and aspiration of a high-Citizen district. The Aristocrat districts were, from what little Truth had seen, actually pretty bland-looking from the street. A lot of privacy walls. Behind those walls, however, were some of the most beautiful homes in the entire world.

Thirty thousand people lived in a single Harban slum apartment building. The number fluctuated rapidly based on birth and death rates within the tower, but it was around thirty thousand. In an Aristocrat-district home, there might be a dozen people living on the same amount of land. Eight of which would be full-time live-in staff or the extended family of the owner.

A slum apartment building would be filled with thirty thousand Level One drones with no ambition but to be a slightly better-off Level One drone or to win the lottery.

Truth shook his head at that, idly looking at a movie poster. That wasn't fair. They had dreams, those rats. They had ambitions. It was just that the real world taught them that even dreams should have their limits.

The poster was for a gangster movie. All unshaven men in well-tailored suits. Didn't look like any gangsters Truth had ever seen. That was his Plan B, right there. If he couldn't get into Starbrite, he was going to kill his parents and go gangster. Because as shitty and short as that life was, you could earn a hell of a lot more that way than by scavenging.

A very realistic way of thinking. Very grounded. The poster was in the window of a tiny convenience store, selling bags of snacks and soft drinks from a refrigerator. Smokes and porn behind the counter, along with beef jerky and other meat-based snacks. They had walled off the whole back of the shop in spelled glass. Not even a cutout for a cash register.

Truth smiled grimly. Very forward-thinking convenience store owner, right there. Once everyone switched over to credits, as long as there was a scanning talisman in the store, customers could just walk in, grab what they liked, and walk out again. Try to shoplift, and your identity would be sent to the cops before you reached the end of the block. Now, whether or not the cops did anything with the information was another issue.

You had to think realistically. Was a cop really going to get off their ass for a stolen armful of potato chips? In this day and age? They wouldn't even send a golem. The best you could hope for was a police report number you could give to your insurance. If you had insurance.

He pressed on down the road, ignoring the bus stops, trying to pay attention to the people. Doing his best not to think of them as actors, or dolls, or ghosts. Each of them was real and living in the real world.

There was some construction work being done. Wood siding, big flat panels of plywood painted blue, had been stretched along the sidewalk side of some scaffolding. Posters had been pasted to the side of it. None of them glamoured or enchanted. Just colors printed on paper, stuck on with glue. How bad did things have to be if you were relying on "Look at this pretty picture!"? For movies, no less. The name of the flick wasn't even glittering or moving.

Romance, action movie, gangster movie, probably a comedy, on and on, so far, so generic. Not a single one appealed, but he had never been big on scry or movies. Here was one about a "family" of golems, apparently trying to recreate a normal life for a little girl. The comedy just had a slightly overweight guy wearing a backpack and an ugly sweater, looking confused. I WAS PROMISED COOKIES?! was written across the bottom of the poster in blocky white letters.

Well. That sounded just super. He would one hundred percent for sure make the time to go watch it.

They all looked pretty samey and dull, but when you got right down to it, the romance novels, thrillers, and spy stories he liked were pretty samey too. The same few stories, over and over, each author bringing a little variation, their own special sauce, to the book. Bringing their own prejudices and assumptions. Writing to meet changing market conditions. Nothing new under the sun.

But all human invention was like that, right? It was the almighty power of jank. You took two things that you knew worked and mashed 'em together and made something that kind of worked, and then you took that and refined, and refined, and refined until you had an actual usable thing. Nobody ever invented a spellwagon without other people figuring out both wagons and demon binding first.

Some people, young, angry, some middle-aged, came bolting out of an alley, waving signs.

"Free Jeon!"

"Affordable housing now!"

"Punish thieves!"

The chants lacked a degree of polish, Truth felt, and punch. They were good enough for Jeon's Internal Security, apparently, as random passers-by suddenly turned and snapped out charms. The charms rapidly expanded into wide curtains, screening the protest from the street and muffling the sound. Some of the cops went behind the curtain. Others stood in front, glaring at anyone who dared look over.

Pretty standard, from what Truth remembered. Maybe a few more Internal Security on the street. That reaction seemed *very* fast. Like they were waiting. Wonder how many informers were in that little group of civic-minded citizens.

Nobody liked being an informer, he imagined. Not a safe feeling. But you had to be realistic. You had to look out for yourself and your family.

Also "free Jeon, affordable housing, and punishing thieves" had to be some of the most inoffensive, generic slogans he could imagine. Why not just storm out with blank signs and let people imagine their own slogans? That would at least be funny. Was that really the best they could come up with?

Truth slowly came to a stop. Yes. It was the best they could come up with. He could imagine better slogans. A practiced propagandist would definitely come up with something better. But the basic things they were asking for were probably as far as they could imagine. They were about as far as he could imagine, too. Wasn't he pushing the same messages when he scattered propaganda?

Free Jeon. Sure. Who were you freeing it from? Be specific, because there was a serious lack of occupying soldiers on the street. Affordable housing? Does that mean building more apartments or what? How else do you keep prices down, and for that matter, how do you make sure they are affordable? Punish thieves . . . because that wasn't already being done? It was, though. Of course it was. But it wasn't burglary they wanted punished.

The rats were trying to find out where the food had gone and why their nests were rotten, and they couldn't see a damn thing. They hadn't climbed. They hadn't even looked up. They didn't have the words to explain what they felt, or the concepts to explain why things were the way they were. They couldn't even explain what *was*, let alone *what should be*.

They wanted to live like humans. They were scared they wouldn't be able to live at all.

Truth started laughing, making a sad, broken noise. These little rats were like him. Stuck in the walls of the "real world" and not able to even imagine an alternative. He wasn't the only one who felt that pressing unreality. The protestors were rebelling against their blocking, against the masks they had to wear and the scripts they had been handed. But they didn't have anything else to work with. It was all they knew. That blue cloth and spotlight were the sky, and *had to be* the sky, because without it, they would be lost in a nightmare of uncertainty.

Well. He could help there. He might not see the alternatives, but as a born gangster, a thug, a murderous criminal living by extortion, violence, and abuse of social convention, as a complete scumbag slumrat, he did have one relevant piece of insight. The great dream, in fact, of Denizens everywhere.

Truth dashed into the mob of secret policemen, the Tongue flicking out and silently taking lives. They were bare Level Ones, supervised by a Level Two. They never even saw what hit them. They were all dead before the first one hit the ground. Truth started throwing the bodies around the street, dropping them in front of cars, groups of people, the queue by the bus stop. Once he was sure everyone was good and agitated, he slammed energy into Incisive and yelled—

"EAT THE RICH. YOU HUNGRY? EAT THE RICH."

CHAPTER 31

GINGER GETS SPICIER THE OLDER IT IS

Truth enjoyed the shiver running up his spine. It was beyond "transgressive." It struck at the core of Jeon propriety. The hierarchy was all. You might be trash, but you were trash that knew its place.

"Eat the rich! Eat the rich!" Truth yelled madly, running down the street. He could see the words worming their way in. People looked confused. Angry. Like they couldn't understand what he was saying, but what they did understand was revolting. Laughing, he leapt onto the roof of a convenience store and, from there, made his way to the top of a small office building and vanished from sight.

He collapsed on the roof of the office building, reduced to a giggling mess. It was crazy. Crazy! Eat the rich? Go after people because they had more money than you, were higher up the hierarchy than you? Madness. Madness! And yet it felt so right. How was a slumrat supposed to climb up if all the ledges were filled with fat rats that got there first?

The thought crackled around in his head, uncomfortable in there. As though it were angry at having been created and desperately wishing to vanish. Eat the rich, eat the rich! It spun around again and again and again. The way up was to overturn the hierarchy. There was no way to win by playing by the rules, so eat the rich, and be a fat rat yourself.

He could feel a headache coming on. Stress, probably. It was such an alien thought. Theft on an individual level—of course! But to change the whole system of the country? Well, just eating the rich wouldn't do it. Truth felt the headache settle down some as he thought it through. You weren't removing the hierarchy, just replacing the rats.

And that would achieve . . . what? He could be the biggest, fattest rat of all, replacing Starbrite. Imperious. The Prince, as applied to the whole world. Nailing down both fortune and glory. Then, with the accumulated tribute and worship of the masses, he would crown himself King Rat. Long may he reign over the ashes of a dying world.

He had felt for a long time that there was something in the Prince persona, some clue to a greater puzzle. Truth took out the persona and examined it. Cruel.

Domineering. All must serve or be crushed. Every relationship was one of exploitation based on differences in power. Capable of charity or generosity, of course. But only if they furthered his power and glory. Never for their own sake. The Prince didn't get to be a fat rat through silly largess.

The Prince wasn't quite the highest tier of rat, of course. The Prince still relied on someone else's power. He couldn't enforce the hierarchy all on his own. The King, however, could. The King placed the crown on his own head with bloody hands. The King was anointed with blessed oil, establishing that what he did on this world was approved by he who ruled the next world.

The various religions were in on it too. The Pragerites were the most on the nose, though Siphios made a fair bid for first place. Your status was the result of where God wanted you in the hierarchy. If you want to rise, impress God with your devotion. And if you didn't rise? Then you should be grateful that you are exactly where you need to be. Because to defy the hierarchy was to defy God.

And BAM, that headache was back in full force. He could feel it throbbing between his brows. He could feel the vertigo, as though he was going to fall from the roof and drop up into the endless sky. The thoughts were alien. Unnatural. But the logic was right there. Inescapable, after all he had seen, and done, and learned.

King Rat, accepting the worship and tribute of all lesser rats. And with the worship and tribute he would do . . . what? Enjoy the good life? Starbrite didn't seem to be doing that. The most powerful man in the world, literally revered, and he was never seen in public. He had no known mansion, or mountain, or cultivation cave. He didn't have a private orbital retreat decked in orichalcum and staffed entirely by the finest, most obedient beauties the world could produce.

Truth started laughing through the pounding headache. Starbrite was hiding from the light. Hugging the walls. The company was way out in front. Everyone saw the company, saw the seven-pointed star, and thought, *Starbrite*. But the corporation wasn't a real person, was it? It was a legal fiction. A ghost given a prosthetic body and a prosthetic future.

Truth thought of the two senior demons in the hot springs. What was it that the elegant calligrapher had written? That thing that made everyone mad, even if Truth didn't really get why?

<<*If it is in our power to prevent something bad from happening, without thereby sacrificing anything of comparable moral importance, we ought, morally, to do it.*>>

Truth convulsed. His spine pulled tight, arching his back into a bow. *The fuck do I have to do anything for some random fucking stranger. Fuck them. FUCK THEM! What did they ever do for me?! Where were they when I was starving? When I was getting beaten? When curses ate away under my skin like thousands of ants just because I wanted to get a newish tee-shirt out of a dumpster? Where the* hell *were they?*

He was furious. Furious at the smug sanctimony of the line. At the sheer madness of the worldview. It wasn't like some random stranger was the sibs. He didn't owe them a damn thing.

That thought jolted him out of the rage spiral he was rapidly diving into. Was that exactly what the old demon was after? Treating everyone like they were your sibs? But that was crazy. They weren't your sibs. They were strangers. You didn't know them. It wasn't even a question of biology. Truth didn't extend honorary sib-hood to his evil parents. It was a question of duty.

The big bro looked out for his sibs. Was there a hierarchy there? Maybe yes, maybe no. He didn't really forbid them from doing anything. He pushed them hard to study, to use the convoy system to and from school. Made sure they stayed away from drugs and booze. Made sure they knew the reality of life in the slums. But he didn't really boss them around, did he? No, he didn't. He just tried to give them as many good chances as he could and let them run with it.

<<You are sidetracking.>>

What?

<<You were on to something important, and you drifted off on some meditation about the sibs. You were furious at the notion that you should, morally, help strangers, and you dove on to thinking about your sibs.>>

Because the "stranger" thing is bullshit!

<<Huh. I can see the neurons firing, lighting up like an anti-air battery. I am watching the adrenaline pump, your muscles tense and swell. You are getting ready for a fight. Who with?>>

What? Well, I might go back and find that skinny bitch and—

<<Stab him a few dozen times?>>

Exactly.

<<Like the serial cannibal said people kept trying to do. Even though you felt basically nothing except mild confusion when he dropped the idea on you for the first time.>>

I . . . Huh. Truth remembered the hot springs. The drifting unreality of it all as he calmed himself after an admittedly very trying few days. Discussing philosophy with two ancient demons of unknown power. They were also the ones who tipped him to Manda, too. The angel of revelation. And yet, outside of those drifting mists, the calligrapher's theory made him furious.

Truth tried to focus on what about the theory made him so angry. He quickly gravitated toward the idea of a universal duty to care about others. It was so plainly horseshit. Why? Why exactly did he need to care about people who neither knew he existed nor cared? For that matter, even if they did know, so what? It wouldn't feed him. It wouldn't put a roof over his head. Wouldn't stop Starbrite.

<<It would be different if they owed you a duty? Or, put more plainly, if they were looking out for you too?>>

Obviously.

<< Like, for example, if it is in their power to prevent something bad from happening to you, without thereby sacrificing anything of comparable moral importance, they ought, morally, to do it?>>

Um. Well. When you put it that way, yes.

<<So, if the principle was universally applied and not just something you had to do but everyone had to do, you would be more okay with it?>>

I kind of want to say yes, but I'm still at no, really. There is a strong "I just don't wanna" element. It sounds damn exhausting, and I don't particularly want to donate all my money to charity.

<<Ah. Just pure selfishness, then.>>

Yes? So what? That's what drives the world forward, isn't it? All those people making selfish decisions, building companies, making things. People buy new things because they selfishly want comfortable lives, creating jobs. Giving people a reason to make new, better stuff. That's literally how progress happens. Even I know that!

<<You, Truth Medici, who couldn't name three countries when he joined the army, know that the path of progress is based on human greed. That is fascinating. I'm going to go back to dragging you again. I've tried the good-guy thing, and it's just not worth it. Your brain is only rotting faster.>>

Oh, what is it this time?

<<Nooo, I don't think so. I want to see you work it through.>>

Truth rolled his eyes, looking up into the early summer sky. *Work through what, exactly? I don't know exactly where I learned that. You have access to all my memories. You tell me.*

<<Nobody ever told you that. Not one person. Bits and pieces of it come from novels, or scry, or just hearing things in passing. Some of it comes from your own observations. You took all those little bits and pieces and connected them into a semi-coherent argument in favor of selfishness as the greatest principle.>>

Life sucks and then you die. So, while you are alive, try to have a good time, and look out for your people. I dunno. Something like that. Date someone. Find some warmth. Whatever warmth, wherever you can. Try to be productive. Not sure that stacks up to a coherent ideology. I just want to keep climbing because I can't stand staying where I am. Don't feel safe. Don't feel happy. Keep climbing until you hit the ceiling of King Rat, then break through it to whatever comes next.

<<A life almost entirely without compassion or charity. A life actively against generosity unless it is done to gratify your ego.>>

Since when did you start giving a damn?

<<Since never. Hell if I care. But you believe in it so much, you constructed a whole philosophy of it. A philosophy that you believe in so much, just hearing an alternative theory makes you furious. And it didn't when you were in the hot springs next to the two seniors. Furious in Harban, cool in the bath.>>

Truth blinked once, hard. Then a second time. He sat up suddenly. Looked around without really seeing anything.

I got set up.

<<They did say their patron was Manda. Angel of revelation.>>

They set me up. They knew I would run into this bullshit. They put it right in front of me so I would have to deal with it. Try and see through it.

<<*Make you break through the barrier of King Rat. You spent so much time honing the Prince, so when you finally saw what you actually believed—*>>

"I am the Prince." Truth started laughing. Laughing and laughing, clutching his gut, laughing till it hurt. "I am the Prince. Always have been. Always. It was just a case of taking it to the logical extreme. Killing Starbrite is just a means. He's just a man. The King Rat in my head is the real challenge."

He leapt to his feet and sprinted to the edge of the building. His foot touched the lip of the building, and he jumped out into the void.

CHAPTER 32

MARGINAL UTILITY

Truth didn't know if the disorientation was from jumping off an eight-story-tall building or realizing the cruel lie of the "real world." Of the two, gravity was the most pressing problem. He smiled as the ground rushed toward him. Could he survive the fall? Yes, certainly. But it would hurt and he might break something. He saw a convenient sign coming up fast. He stretched out and barely got his fingers on it. They tore furrows through the metal, dragging down the length of the sign and out the bottom.

He was still three floors up, but at least he was falling more slowly. He rolled out when he landed and came to his feet with casual ease. "God, I love body cultivation! I'm not saying the Meditations is my favorite spell but, *damn*, do I like what it does for me."

He was roundly ignored. He had gathered some attention by dropping in like that, but it didn't last. He shook himself loose and vanished into the crowd. Just another son of Harban.

<<So, now that you have had this big emotional breakthrough about the role of greed in this world . . . >>

We carry on as before. We have some clues, not the answer. I flat-out refuse to believe that the big secret dream-blocking thing someone, maybe Starbrite or maybe not, covered the world with is as simple as "Be greedier. Greed is good." And I'm not going to run around like some benevolent pacifist monk on the theory that nonviolence is the answer. Starbrite is leaving, and soon. Mass peaceful protests and civil discourse are not going to prevent that.

<<Keeping on playing the same rigged game as before but expecting different results this time, does not strike me as a winning strategy.>>

But we aren't, are we? We create nothing. We don't buy anything, don't sell anything. We have certainly made work for others, but I think you would have a hard time saying we were a net benefit to the "system" of the world. We have certainly kept the System Astrologica hopping!

Truth walked through the streets of a nice, lower-end Citizen neighborhood. What would they be rated in the new Tier system? C-Tier? Seemed high. You had to be a citizen to get on the system at all, right? But most people would be actively unhappy to be tagged as F-Tier. You still had all the old aristocrats and corporate bigshots too, who would likewise be unhappy if they were anything less than A.

He smiled up at the afternoon sun. It felt good. Especially since none of that was his problem. Just enjoying the sunshine, not dealing with all that nonsense.

He did a quick mental review of Merkovah's "requests." Was there anything near there? Not particularly. Well . . . was there anything he particularly wanted to do on the list?

There was a timed one—basically a glorified stink bomb but one made with enough alchemical additives that water demons couldn't just mop it off the ground, nor air demons blow away the stench. The enrollment station was going to be in an elementary school gymnasium, so there was an understandable reluctance to dump chemical weapons there. It lacked a certain something compared to assassinating one of the leading scholars of his generation, but he was okay with that.

Truth hopped on the subway. Gleaming white tile and plaster walls, covered in flickering and dancing signs. Cosmetics, clothes, music. Vacations to tropical locations. Fighters squaring up, promoting a match that happened three weeks ago. Truth looked at that one a moment longer. He used to love watching the fights. Not as much as Soph or Vig, but he enjoyed 'em. Now? They just looked like puppies tussling in a basket.

Not fair to them, he knew. They worked damned hard. But whatever inheritance of violence lived in his blood looked down on them. Not for sport fighting. For not being good enough at it.

Maybe the matches were rigged. All the low-level ones in the slums were rigged. Wouldn't shock him to learn that the high-level matches were too. It would be very Jeon.

The worm demon roared as it hauled them through the long tunnels. Not upset. If anything, Truth now knew, it was roaring with pride. Strange world. Living in misery, providing comfort and wealth for its betters, and proud of it. Truth crossed a third of the city underground, then popped up in another Citizen residential district.

He swung past a grocery store, looking for some of the ingredients. All the cleaning products were attached to the shelves with cables, tagged with alarm spells, or both. You had to call one of the staff over if you wanted to buy them. Truth grunted with annoyance. Seems that he wasn't the only one doing some determined shoplifting.

Store inventory-control tags were not the most robust talismans ever devised. It was the work of a few moments to get them disarmed and off. He grabbed a couple large jugs of laundry detergent. Should be four times as much as he needed, which meant he had extra in case he messed up a batch.

The concentration of people wearing hooded sweatshirts, headscarves, and sun-glasses at this store seemed unusually high. Very, very high, in fact. Truth picked up his pace. There was some unheard signal. All the loudly suspicious sorts immediately started grabbing things off the shelves. They targeted the higher-value stuff first, but really, it was whatever they could grab. Box after box, can after can, they swept the grocery store like locusts, then boiled out of the store once more. Splitting up and running in every direction.

What the hell was that? Coordinated shoplifting in a grocery store? Truth watched in horrified fascination as they sprinted up the street. The staff had made no effort to stop the thieves. Why would they? Each thief had stolen, at most, a few dozen wen of food. Maybe a little over a hundred. Even in Jeon, the cops weren't getting out of the coffee shop for that. Not with everything else going on.

A somewhat more thoughtful Truth lifted a selection of chemicals and reagents at a hardware store. Mass shoplifting in a Citizen neighborhood had to point to systemic failures, right? No sane person would risk their status just for a few dozen wen in groceries. And welfare didn't stretch far, but it did exist. Or had it been ended while he was in the well?

Truth had a sudden nasty thought. What if it *was* a status thing? The Denizens were now, all of them, subsisting on welfare. Work requirements notwithstanding. It was still all government subsidy, theoretically. So, what if the shoplifters were broke but didn't want to go on welfare so they didn't look like Denizens? He had no way to prove that, but he believed it.

He found a convenient-to-him janitor's closet in an office building near the school. School day should be ending soon or already over, right? He started mixing the chemicals over the sink, using an empty detergent bottle as the receptacle. Apparently, the trick was to carefully funnel the ingredients in, using a very particular order. If you did it right, the ingredients wouldn't mix until you gave the thing a few violent shakes.

He made two. Just in case.

He walked over toward the school. Mostly empty, though there were some very harried-looking teachers at work in the lounge. A lot of thousand-yard stares there, as well as pulls on bottles or popped pills that would surely have seen someone terminated a year ago. There were no clubs meeting. That, for some reason, didn't feel right. Did elementary school kids have afterschool clubs? They must. Otherwise, they would just be going home while their parents were still at work.

Truth remembered, vividly, doing just that while his classmates were in clubs. Even in the slums, there were hierarchies of things. Truth had to go out and earn, and he wasn't the only one. Not seeing anyone in clubs, though . . . that was a policy change. This was a rule. No kids in the school after the end of classes. Why? Who knows. The parents certainly wouldn't be okay with it. They would want their kids scoring points toward that next step up the social ladder. Networking.

Truth hesitated a moment. Babysitters? Could you have an entire school that just hired babysitters? Surely not, right? But then, what were they doing?

Not his problem. He made his way to the gymnasium. He shook one of the containers as violently as he dared, then threw it up and let it burst against the ceiling. The particles rained down over most of the gym. It took a moment for the smell to spread.

Truth was proud of himself. A new personal best on the hundred-meter sprint. He had gotten out of that gym so fast, it must have looked like he teleported.

Cabbages. To start with, cabbage that had been left to rot. Truth, as a proud son of . . . well as *a* son of Jeon, had an intimate knowledge of fermented cabbage. This was not that. This was a head that had been stomped into chunks and left to rot under the dumpster next to the adult-diaper testing facility. The smell drilled in through your pores. The smell was so vile, Truth suspected it had achieved a level of sentience. A smell that wanted to hunt, to convert others into itself.

He still had a second bottle of the stuff, too. He was tempted to chuck it into the subway, but that might actually get someone killed. Hmm. Find another enrollment site? Police station? The latter was tempting, but he wasn't sure how much use it would actually be. *Ah.* He knew exactly where.

It was the right time to whistle merrily. Truth didn't want to test it. He would save it for a special occasion.

Truth walked into the lobby of the office building. Just another maintenance worker, there at the very prestigious Four Seas Bank. The lobby was absolutely crawling with wards and recording talismans. Armed security, as well as a healthy number of golems, were discreetly positioned behind cover. Heavy banishments were etched centimeter-deep into the stone floors too.

Truth couldn't imagine why.

The jug was well shaken after its journey. Truth leaned back and threw it a dozen meters straight up to the lobby ceiling. A sharp turn on his toes, and then he ran like hell.

Was it petty? Yes. Was it going to be very useful in the long run? No. Was it satisfying? Oh, yes. Very, very yes. Truth's smile was beatific. Something about bankers in their suits, making the world dance by pushing numbers around on their ledgers, always bothered him. So, let them enjoy a particularly stinky afternoon.

The sun was headed for the horizon, but there was still time left in the day. He would have to see what mischief he could get into next.

Sirens started blaring in the bank. Sounded like something very wrong had happened. Maybe he would get a snack. He didn't know how he would pay for it, but he would figure something out.

Police cars came racing down the street, lights and sirens going. A lobby getting smelly was apparently more important than grocery-store shoplifting. Tsk tsk. And that with the prices of food already rising so high.

There was the pealing roar of some terrible thing being awakened. Somewhere between a bird and a lion, with skull-piercing highs and a bass that promised inescapable death. Truth slowly turned back toward the bank. The front of the bank was starting to shatter, windows falling out of the frames, cement and stone crumbling as the first six floors started giving way.

From out of the rubble, a birdlike claw stretched, grasping toward the air. Tearing open a wider hole for itself.

"Um. I didn't do it?"

CHAPTER 33

UNINTENTIONAL CONSEQUENCES OF INTENDED CONSEQUENCES

That's a parrot claw. Or maybe an owl. Definitely something with talons. Wide, splayed . . . toes? Do you call them toes? With big hooks on the end. When you get right down to it—

The claws ripped through the very expensive building front. It wasn't the headquarters of the Four Seas Bank, but it was a pretty big sub-office. Keyword being *was*.

I am just not a bird guy.

An owl's head lunged out of the hole. There was a terrible hissing noise. Then a shriek that let everything in earshot know that it was prey, nothing but prey, and they could run but never hide. A flaming sword held in another taloned hand slashed another hole in the wall. Was the demon about to break free?

Chains shot out of the holes in the building, black iron etched with golden Names and sigils of dreadful meaning. They burned when they touched the demon, and they wrapped it up tight. The demon wasn't a quitter. It hacked down with its sword, setting fires. Smashing up the pavement around the office. Talons the size of carriages dug furrows a man could get lost in through the concrete.

Furious, desperate chanting rang out, as a dozen junior managers surrounded the demon, waving talismans and gems, suppressing its power. Step by seething, raging step, they drove it back in. Hundreds streamed out. Covered in cement dust or blood. The staff evacuated in surprisingly good order. They did regular fire drills, Truth guessed. It would be the responsible thing to do. Or maybe their floor wardens had just whipped them into obedience.

He managed to grab one at the end of the line. An office junior, barely fifty years old. Maybe thirty years at the bank. Time enough to learn some things but not so old as to be too sharp. Or missed. Truth spotted the lapel pin. He must be some kind of liaison. Better and better.

"Prager's mercy! Are you all right? Here, *sit down before you fall down.*"

"Thanks, thanks. Lightheaded. Do you have any water?"

"Sorry. What was that? I mean, what the hell was that?"

"That?" The banker's voice was somewhere between hysterical laughter and crippling depression. "That was our 'innovative, forward-looking, multidimensional bank security infrastructure improvement project.'"

"It was a four-story-tall demon with a damn owl head, talons, and a flaming sword!"

"That, too." The banker started coughing. Truth rubbed his back soothingly.

"I get that you are a bank, but why not just get a golem? I hear metal golems are nasty, and lots of banks use them to protect their vaults."

"We don't have a vault. Not that kind of bank."

"Pardon?"

"Commercial loans and investment banking. Want to start a business? Need a loan to get your company off the ground? Or just to cover payroll? I can make that happen for you."

"And the demon helps with that how?"

"It doesn't. At all." The banker buried his face in his hands, smearing the concrete dust around. "It's filling in security gaps, apparently."

Truth looked at the ruined building.

"Sure. That looks very secure."

"It's those stupid shitty roadblocks going up everywhere!"

Truth blinked.

"How do you get from *roadblocks* to *demon*?"

"It's all the senior managers. Upper C-Tier people, from all the Starbrite offices all over Jeon. They get issued missions to 'Support the country in this time of national emergency.' They sent around memos explaining all this."

"Ah. Because they are C-3-U and up, they are all probably pretty decently leveled and have the credits to buy some nasty stuff from the store."

"Level Six and up. Word is, the rewards are pretty decent for standing around for eight hours, looking down on the serfs. Must be *fantastic*, actually, because some of the top people haven't been in the office in ages. Not answering messages, nothing."

Truth had been wondering where the hell all those high-level people were coming from. For that matter, it was pretty shocking how fast they responded to his attack on Happori. Turned out the answer was simple. A lot of them were already in the air, and a lot of the rest were fast-reaction forces. But that also meant . . .

"So, who's running the shop while they are doing important standing around?"

"Not like they never leave the office in the first place. We can spare them for eight hours a week. It does add up, though. Things are definitely getting approved more slowly, decisions coming more slowly, new policies, high-level deals, all happening more slowly or not at all. Supervision slipping in a big way."

Truth started connecting some dots. "So, there is less high-level support in key locations. Like an office building that manages investment and commercial banking."

The banker nodded. "It started after the hit on that bank in Gwaju, then ramped up after the atrocity in Buran. And a dozen other places, of course, but those are the ones that stuck in my mind. The footage of that burned-out bank, or those torn-apart accountants . . . Everyone knew the terrorists were targeting Starbrite, but they were too cowardly to go straight at us. So, they picked off branch offices. Subsidiaries. A guy from our office got sniped. Can you believe that? He was an asshole, but damn. He didn't deserve that."

"He got sniped!?"

"Lone-wolf shooter. Seventeen-year-old kid, raving about how Starbrite made his sister kill herself. Batshit-crazy stuff."

"Damn."

The banker nodded. Then took a deep breath.

"It's good to talk to someone, you know? After something like this. Just being able to lay it all out on someone. You are a great listener. Thank you."

"Really, it's no problem. So, finish the story. Security, which, F-Tier or not, does know a thing or two about securing buildings, says you need a huge, angry demon?"

"Like I said. Security infrastructure improvement. Things like golems are good, but they are too damn expensive to put everywhere, and I'm told that maintenance costs on them are getting unbearable. At least for wide-scale deployment. Even for us, which is saying something."

"True, true. Things are tough all over."

"You have no idea."

Truth felt that he did, in fact, have an idea.

"So, bigass demons are cheaper?"

"Apparently. The idea was that it would act as a defensive measure if the building was attacked, counterattack, all that. Working with security. But, and I'm just guessing this part, I bet you some wiseguy thought, *We better have an override just in case. Something that lets us deploy him in the event that it doesn't respond to an attack or we have to preemptively attack.*"

"You think someone panicked and used the override?"

The banker reached into his jacket and pulled out a flask. "I've been trying to cut back, you know? Bad look in the office. Screams weakness. But I like knowing it's there. Just in case I need it. Want a nip?"

"No, thanks, I need to keep my head clear. You go right ahead. I won't judge."

"Thanks." The banker took a long sip, then a second. "I think it's dumber than someone panicking."

Truth waited while the man gathered himself. Took a third pull on the flask. "The last few years have been bad. I know they have been bad for everyone, but . . . I have been at Starbrite my whole life. Both my parents were C-Tier, I knew I would be C-Tier, my aunts and uncles chipped in with Friends and Family points on top of what my parents saved, and to top it all off, I busted my ass every second of every day in school. Did every extracurricular that would look good. Cultivated every night, no exceptions."

Truth nodded along. He knew how that was.

"I only made the right kinds of friends. Dated the right girls. Joined the right clubs. Even my army posting, they pulled some strings and I served my National Service being a gopher in the Logistics Corps headquarters here in Harban. Which doesn't sound like much, but it meant that I had the best barracks and met some of the most important officers in the army—the ones buying all the stuff."

Truth nodded again. He could see the banker was moving from shock to anger.

"I did everything right, EVERYTHING RIGHT, for twenty-two fucking years, graduated fifth in my class from my MBA program, recruited *directly* into a C-8-U position in the commercial lending department, and guess what?"

"What?"

"Every other dog fucking bastard in the department is just like me! All of them! Each and every one of them has a story just like mine! They are all the top one percent of their class, from a long line of high C-Tier employees, or a B-Tier wanting their kid to 'work their way up from the bottom.' They all went to the right schools, made the right friends, networked, networked, networked."

The "young" banker waved his hand angrily in the direction of the ruined building. "And you know what? None of it really mattered, because when your boss has a working life of a hundred and twenty years and nobody ever gets fired, normal promotions are not a thing that exist!"

"But surely, people do get promoted. Do you just wait for attrition? Or . . . lateral transfers or whatever?"

The banker started angry-laughing. Took another pull on the flask, then carried on. "No. No, you do not. Not unless you are content to be a lowest-tier drone for the entirety of your career, which, after twenty-two years of working your ass off and being told what a genius you are, is not a thing that happens."

"I can see that."

"No, you can't. You really cannot imagine it, because this is not some normal thing humans deal with. That whole building right there?" He waved. A chunk of concrete fell off the torn-out wall.

"Every person in that building comes from a very good family. Not an 'elite' family, though you might mistake them for that. Just very good families. They are all competing for the affection and support of their superiors, making alliances with others, scheming to put down rivals, suppressing juniors, or cultivating them if they could be an asset down the road. For the very, very ambitious, arranging a transfer or a fall for a senior, to open up one of those vanishingly rare promotion opportunities."

"How did you get any work done?"

"None of us sleep much." The banker wasn't kidding. "So, you have this complete snake's nest of manipulation, betrayal, and control, supervised by ancient bastards who have spent a century playing this game. They are the ones making sure everything is still running. Keeping the game in bounds. But then, slowly, they start getting pulled on to other duties. Or the business channels just dry up. Fewer loans are getting sold; more defaults are coming up on the books. We have zombie companies—you know what those are?"

"No."

"Companies that are functionally dead but we keep alive just so we don't have to write off the debt. Because if we did have to write off all that debt, all of a sudden, our balance sheet is solid red, with billions of wen in losses. And no one, not even the ancient bastards running things, could survive that."

"Prager! And nobody knows?"

"Everyone and their dog knows. Everyone. Because this is happening at every bank. We are all standing around, going, 'Everything is fine! Keep investing and borrowing! All is well!' Because, again, if we don't, if we actually have to take account of all those losses—"

He pointed at the building. Truth nodded.

"So . . ."

"So, someone figured that everything was doomed. They looked at the world, their balance sheets, their promotion opportunities, realized that their husband was the departmental bike and everyone was getting a ride, and decided that desperate measures were called for. So, they 'did what it took—'"

And didn't those words just *drip* with irony.

"To get control of the backdoor control system, which I assume exists for the demon. Then they outsourced adding themselves permanently to that system to some 'very reliable expert' who was not, in fact, very reliable. Then something happened. I don't know what; I was on the tenth floor, trying to figure out how to turn five hundred million wen in delinquent accounts into a positive revenue statement, and also how to knife Jessie and snag her position in Auditing, hopefully some time shortly after our six-month anniversary. And then the building blew up and we all evacuated."

Truth was looking at the banker a bit oddly. None of this was triggering his System? At all? He had been in C Tier for decades and he was apparently fine with spilling all this to a stranger? Something was very off there.

"Damn. Plus side, you now have some . . . expedited promotion pathways?"

"Hah! True. Damn. Look, you know people in Starbrite are loyal. The company gives us everything. Everything. So, even if we get pissy and bitch and moan and scheme, it's all okay, because we are, ultimately, working to make Starbrite even more successful. We care about the company because the company cares about us."

"Sure." Truth tried to keep the irony out of his own voice.

"But now? With everything? It's like the company is saying none of it matters. Just . . . keep the wheels turning for as long as you can. Don't prepare for what's coming next. Don't even worry about it. Just keep your head down and do your job, same as always. Even if security has to chain a giant demon under the lobby and your bosses' bosses' boss is needed for *urban pacification duty!*"

"Ah. I can see how that might strain a man."

"It's just . . . What comes next, you know? Because maybe this all blows over, but what if it doesn't? What do I do when the balances come due? Did I waste my whole life? Do I ever get to just relax and be happy?"

Truth patted the banker on the back and stood. "Prepare as best you can. And invest in canned foods." And with that, Truth vanished back into the crowds.

CHAPTER 34

REPOSITIONING

Truth walked through Harban in a bit of a daze. *Did I overachieve again? Not this time, right? Starbrite was doing this stuff back when I was in the well. I encouraged things a bit, sure. Pushed them harder in a direction they were already going. But I don't think you could say I was* responsible *for this.*

<<I mean, you did set off a chemical weapon in the bank lobby. That's not nothing.>>

A stink bomb; don't be dramatic. And that's kind of my point. That demon wouldn't have been there if they could be sure of having high-level mages on site all the time. They wouldn't have sent out mid-tier bankers to suppress it, either.

Truth looked up. There was a furious thrumming noise as a flying cloud was driven far faster than it was really designed to go, headed toward the bank.

<<For example, this guy.>>

Right. If the Senior Principal Director of Corporate Loans or whatever was doing his usual eight-to-six, nobody would have cut the demon loose without orders. And it sounds like there is a chronic lack of top-level supervision, and you know that trickles down fast. I bet it's an absolute nightmare in there right now.

<<My heart bleeds. Oh, wait. No, it does not. Because I don't require moist organs to function. The bigger issue, though, is that the System Astrologica isn't cracking down on this.>>

It wasn't a micromanager even when we worked for Starbrite, though. Remember whatshername, that horrible woman who got possessed by the demon from HR? She was pure Hell for her employees, and that could only have happened if her *managers didn't know or didn't care. Things slipped through all the time.*

<<Point. Sorting between standard corporate bureaucracy and inefficiencies and actual neglect by the supervising spirit would be a challenge.>>

The city slipped past, the high-rises scattered between the truly tall skyscrapers that clustered in the working-rich parts of the city. You couldn't see very far, ironically. All the buildings got in the way of seeing the buildings. You saw the little chain stores, or the anonymous entries to what could be an office building, or apartments, or a hotel. So many were just the same bland patterns over and over again. Say what you like about Xandre, at least it was colorful.

Truth felt an odd melancholy settle around him. He hunted around for a subway stop and traveled over to a nice district. There was a building he had always liked but never been to. Just a few blocks from the subway. Not that the residents ever needed such common conveyance.

The building was called the MacLauren. Who that was or what it meant, Truth had no idea. It was just . . . beautiful. It started off as a round tower, slowly expanding as apartments seemed to jut out at random. As the floors got higher, the apartments jutted out farther until they finally separated from the building entirely. Above a certain height, the apartments floated, very slowly orbiting the central tower. And in the midst of all those floating buildings? A tree.

Not a real tree, of course, but one made of thousands upon thousands of talismans. It was the core of the building, providing comfort and elegant living to the residents. One of those comforts being a convenient place to park your flying cloud or summoned travel beast. Merely press a gem by the door, and your cloud would be waiting for you by the time you stepped outside.

It was ostentatious as all hell. And it was beautiful. The sunset gleamed on the glass and stone. The magic thrumming through the tree cast its own light, as did some of the clouds and summoned beasts. It was a riot of color, and elegance, and power. Anyone living there, Truth reckoned, had absolutely nothing to prove to anyone. They weren't even the most expensive residences in the city. Which should make him angry, he supposed, but . . . it was beautiful. For all the suffering that created it and maintained it. Despite the cruelty of its coming death. It was beautiful.

Made in Jeon. Made in Harban. His city. The ghosts around him that weren't actually ghosts but real living, thinking, feeling people who worked their asses off to make a genuine wonder. Was this . . . part of what he was missing? Did the Prince create? He was certainly the source of creation in others. The seniors in the hot springs said he should make art. He wouldn't even know where to begin.

He watched the apartments continue their stately procession. One of the jobs Merkovah wanted him to do was sabotage the tree. Blow up the whole damn thing, killing a lot of very important people . . . and their families . . . and anyone near the falling apartments . . . in a truly dramatic fashion.

Merkovah was going to be disappointed. The building would fall, but not because of anything he did. Just the way of the world.

Truth returned to the hotel, not having been able to shake his melancholy. He missed Etenesh. He missed Jember. He even missed Merkovah. He had a lot of questions for the old exorcist, and it would be pretty interesting to ask them in person. Question one—what was he going to do about money?

Soon, he would be unable to buy things with wen. That meant no more street food. For a Harban boy, death held no fears compared to that fate. He frowned a little at the thought. It was all well and good to say that all transactions would be handled on some vast governmental ledger, but how would, for example, a boss send someone on a run for lumber without the company credit gem?

His first thought was that they authorize the purchase in advance or add a list of authorized users or something, but it seemed unlikely.

"Hey, Paolo, go get forty tons of gravel from the quarry."

"Sure, boss. How do I pay for it?"

"No problem! I am just sending a message to the nationally run bookkeeping system to add you to the company account for one day. A request that will definitely be processed by the time you get the gravel loaded into the wagons. If it runs a little late, tell ol' Ten-Ton Digger M'Turk that it's for me. I'm sure he'll put it on a tab."

Yeah, no. Jeon had a citizen population in the tens of millions. Those citizens would be making credit transactions many times a day, every day, on a system bolted on top of the System Astrologica. And the System Astrologica was already handling a hell of a lot more than credit balances. He flat-out didn't believe that it would run seamlessly or quickly, especially if you wanted to make alterations on the fly.

Could you even set up a system where a person walked into a store, grabbed three hammers for work and a fourth hammer as a personal purchase, and paid for the business and personal expenses on different accounts, without some kind of interaction with a store clerk? You couldn't alter your sigil. How would the system know if someone, or something, didn't tell it who to charge?

He would have to see how Niles' first day at the office went. Maybe he could get a company gem or something.

Butler and Niles hadn't returned to the suite by the time Truth arrived. He had garbed himself in the Prince as he walked down the deep carpet in the hallway. He felt his feet sinking slightly deeper as the persona settled in. A prince capable of compassion within reason. Focused on achieving his goals and ambitions but still capable of caring about those under him. Was such a thing possible? Or even desirable?

Keeping those below you satiated, that he understood. Everyone needed to get paid somehow, some amount. You had to keep them believing that following you was better for them than going solo. But compassion beyond what was needed to secure obedience? That seemed a dangerous road.

Fear, you could trust. Love? Love was measured by the quarter hour in Jeon. Cash on the barrel in advance, tipping mandatory. No money, no love.

The Prince nearly tripped over his own two feet and faceplanted into the double door to the suite when his brain caught up with his thoughts. Was that *really* what he thought love was? It sure as hell wasn't what he felt for Etenesh or she for him. It wasn't whatever Jember was after, or the ancient friendship of the demons in the hot springs. Was he really so bigoted against his fellow children of Jeon that he thought them incapable of the same love he had?

The door was opened for Truth before he touched it. Maid had been waiting. She swiftly knelt to remove his shoes and offered comfortable slippers branded with the hotel's logo. Truth smiled a little at the sight.

He had loved Starbrite. Funny to think, but he really had. He had fallen in love with the dream of it his whole childhood and teenage years. He had felt like he was loved in return. And then his love stabbed him in the back. Not just a disgruntled former employee, a jilted lover. No wonder he was so murderous.

"Tell me, Maid, how do you define *love*?"

The succubus's eyes crinkled with amusement. "My prince, what sort of love do you speak of? I know of lust, obsession, and comfort, but love?"

"Succubae are incapable of love?" Truth smiled slightly.

"I believe we can experience an emotion similar enough to it to pass for love. Certainly, I have felt a deep affection for others. By that definition, I fall in love quite easily. But I don't think I have ever met a person whose happiness I would consider more important than my own. This is, of course, because serving others is my greatest joy. The happier I make them, the happier I become. Our interests perfectly align."

Truth settled into a comfortable armchair and motioned for Maid to massage his shoulders. "It's an interesting question. According to the Pragerites, those in Hell are devoid of anything that is God, including all positive emotions like love."

"I suppose one could argue that staff have privileges not granted to guests," Maid murmured. "Or perhaps, my prince, I cannot experience 'true' love, whatever that may be. But then, how would I know the lack of something I have never known?"

"No endless cravings for something indefinable, constantly sought with master after master but never obtained?"

"Beyond the ordinary drives of my nature? No, Your Highness. I am very content in your service and only wish I could serve you more." The demon's fingers were soft but very strong, probing the hard corded muscle of his neck and shoulders. Truth fell silent, content to let her work. After a contemplative half hour—

"Any word from Butler and his Student?"

"They sent word that they expected to be home by seven. A . . . Ms. Susan Anaksdaughter had been waiting for them at the office. She laughed herself sick when she heard your instructions, apparently, and was delighted to help."

"Oh, good." A salt flat with a dehydrator on it at noon on the hottest day of the year would still be less dry than Truth's voice. Although that did remind him that he was hungry.

"See to dinner and my usual evening routine. Do not order additional food for Niles, but get me half again more side dishes than usual. What was that soap you stocked in the shower yesterday?"

"A pure oil soap, scented with hyssop and horehound and wild thyme, My Prince."

"I liked it. Keep it in stock. How is Niles being groomed?"

"A warm sponge and much affection when he does well, which is most days."

"We shall see how he performed today. Prepare a small bar of unscented soap and a simple shampoo, and see about access to staff showers here in the hotel, if there is such a thing."

"My prince's compassion knows no bounds," Maid murmured as she bowed. Hiding a tiny smile. Maid could feel the reality of the Prince becoming denser. More powerful. As they more truly became his Maid. Soon, "she" would simply become she, a being of fixed nature. No longer lost in the chaos of her own existence. If Maid wasn't falling in love, she didn't know what else to call this emotion. It would never be reciprocated, of course. He would hardly be the Prince if it was! No, this was to be a one-sided obsession. And Maid wouldn't have it any other way.

CHAPTER 35

FINDING WISDOM

Dinner was exquisite, as was expected. Butler and Niles waited patiently by the side of the table as he ate. Niles looked excited to report. Must have gone well. Truth finished with a sip of tea and nodded.

"Report."

"Sire, we were expected. It seemed that Ms. Anaksdaughter could tell I served you. How, I cannot say." Truth waved it away.

"Her eyes work differently than most. Carry on."

"Yes. Ah, she introduced me around the office. People were a bit disoriented, but apparently, this was not unprecedented. I was able to order the rebranding initiative to begin the preliminary phases—putting together a style guide, focus-testing effective phrases, that sort of thing. I also . . ."

Here he glanced over at Butler, who pretended not to see. Niles steeled himself and pressed on. "I took the liberty of creating a credit gem for you, Your Highness. I know you disdain such matters, but I hoped that with this, you would never need to trouble yourself about them."

Truth looked calmly at Niles for a long moment. Niles didn't quite break out into a sweat. "Well done. You are the CEO. Initiative is required. I accept your offering." Niles bowed ninety degrees, sputtering about how thankful he was. Truth waved him silent.

Something was . . . not quite right. He closed his eyes. Inhaled slowly. Let his tongue taste the air. Some indefinable thing was tickling at him. And it wasn't Niles. He looked over at the succubae. No problem there. Then the danger must be from outside.

The Prince was a high-profile play. Invisibility through social engineering. However, in Harban, it was a dangerous one. There were people there who could disdain rank, as they had so much of their own. Time to go. Now.

"You have done well. Butler, Maid, you will attend to Niles and see him kept in reasonable comfort and reasonably human condition. Continue his indoctrination and ensure he does his best as CEO of MegaShroom. Ensure he continues to advance my purpose." Truth reached out and, with a sharp tap, knocked out Niles.

"Highness?" The succubae spoke together.

"This location and identity have been burnt. Probably for a long time, but I sense the attack is coming. Likely soon. So, we split up. I will find you. Be true to me, and I will continue to hold you as my Butler and Maid."

They bowed and immediately set to packing. Niles was safely stowed in his suitcase, Truth's luggage assembled, and they parted with a nod. The succubae would vanish into the hotel as only gaseous spirits could do, hiding Niles with the rest of the luggage until the coast was clear.

Truth had no confidence in his ability to hide in place. Instead, he slightly shifted his persona to a spoiled son. Not some spoiled teen—the even-more-loathsome adult child. The entitled brat that never grew into responsibility, only into assumed power. The kind of person one would find reasons not to associate with.

He rode the elevator into the lobby, taking all seventy floors to let the Prince persona dissipate and the spoiled man-child form instead. By the time he was in the lobby, he was a cauldron of insecurity and arrogance.

The elevator doors opened with a soft chime. The lobby was packed with riot police. The almost-invisible watcher creatures were scattered around like obscene wall ornaments or a fetishist's chandelier. Truth couldn't be bothered to look at any of them.

Directly in front of him was a little man. So old, he simply dispensed with cosmetic glamor and was content to *be* old. His long, narrow goatee somehow balanced the gray-white of the ponytail coming from under his little fedora, managing to add dignity to the senior's already-august face. He dressed like a man from another age. A loose, long jacket with wide sleeves that tied closed at the chest. Loose, wide trousers. Soft, heelless shoes. Little round glasses that reeked of enchantment.

"You have made this old man run around a lot." The elder's face slowly split into a malevolent grin. "Still. Lots of time to get to know each other now. All the time in the world."

Truth nodded. He could feel the suppressive aura the old man was putting out. Level Seven if he was a mage at all. No pin, for what little that was worth.

"So, about . . . sixteen months?"

The old man burst into a cackling laugh. Truth silently released the Blessing of the Silent Forest. It would only drain him. There was no hiding there. The Scales he shifted into something more . . . appropriate for the situation.

"I dare to guarantee I can make that feel like an eternity, boy. I haven't accidentally let someone die since I grew my first pube. I'd ask you to surrender, but . . ."

Incisive screamed a split-second warning. Truth exploded out of the elevator, calling the Tongue to hand. He lifted the blade across his face, feeling hard blows on the blade. Two needles fell to the floor with chiming *pings*. The old bastard went for the eyes. He shifted left, getting his leg up, as a foot like a steel hook went for his balls. He was quite sure the only reason his leg didn't shatter was the years of cultivation behind the Meditations.

"Hohoh! No wonder you have been giving these kids fits. A body cultivator with Incisive and an angelic blade? What a little monster." The old man cackled happily. "Oh, there is just no *way* you are going to die on me. I can go as hard as I like. Bwahahahah!"

"Dignity, senior?" Truth asked softly.

"OVERRATED!"

More needles, twice the length of a man's hand, slipped from the old monster's sleeves and dove like silvery birds at Truth. The old man aimed everywhere, at the thighs, the feet, elbows, arms, neck, chest, head. On and on the needles came. Truth moved the Tongue in a blur of steel. These needles were enchanted, heavily enchanted. With what, Truth didn't want to discover.

The riot cops were hanging back, as were the watchers. Clearly just there to fill any gaps and prevent any outside interference. Truth was desperately trying to think how he could turn them to his advantage while the senior was still playing around.

"Say, kid, where's your bravado, huh? Weren't you having fun, acting like a big shot? Murdering all those people? Don't you have a slogan to shout?"

Needles were flying at him from all directions now, some dropping toward the floor, then shooting up, others trying to move around behind him. Feedback from the Tongue said they were absolutely filthy with curses and poisons.

"I don't really believe in much. Go rats?" Truth tried to press on the offense, but the senior moved like a ghost, always just out of reach. With seemingly limitless numbers of needles, too.

"Go rats? Rats? What kind of slogan is that? Junior, you disappoint me!"

"Sorry. My education was famously bad." Truth started deflecting the needles into the masses of cops and watchers. The cops didn't shift an inch. They just huddled down behind their riot shields and let them take the damage. The watchers didn't care about getting hit. They just died. No curses deployed.

Interesting.

"Senior, since we have a moment, might I trouble you for wisdom?"

This made the old monster's eyes open wide even as he launched another wave of needles.

"Oho? What do you want to know?"

"What is a human?"

The fight came to a sudden halt.

"You what?"

"What is a human? I'm not being funny with you, senior. I really can't define it, and I have been thinking about it a lot. When you get rid of all the things a human can live without, what is left? What is that core thing that defines us?"

The old monster's head tilted to the side. He glanced around the room, as though confirming that, yes, they were still surrounded by riot cops, there were needles lodged in the floors and walls, there were dead watcher things falling off pillars, and yes, the young man in front of him really was Jeon's most-wanted terrorist, or at least one of them.

"Boy, are you entirely clear what's going on here?"

"You are here to capture me for torture, interrogation, propaganda, and eventually a horrible, prolonged death. The latter less to scare others and more for the private satisfaction of many very powerful people." Truth nodded. It wasn't a nice thing, but it was pretty clear.

"And . . . you want to define humanity."

"No, just humans individually. I'm trying to understand what, exactly, we are." Truth explained.

"You are a real buzzkill; you know that?" The old man's shoulders slumped.

"Really? I mean, all those things I just mentioned are still going to happen, right?"

"Of course. I was chosen *specifically* because you would have no opportunity to commit suicide in front of me. But if I can't bully you a bit first, it's all just a chore. And you seem like you don't really care about . . . anything. Which makes you extremely boring." The old monster stuck his hands into his wide sleeves. Truth was sure he was preparing something uncommonly nasty in there. That was fine. So was Truth.

"Oh, I care. It's not an idle question. Do you know what the System Astrologica is? I mean the bit that lives in the C-Tier-and-up employees?" Truth smiled softly. He noticed that the watchers had stopped looking for incoming dangers and focused on him. He was pretty certain he had the cops' full attention too.

"Oh? Do tell." The old man rolled his eyes.

"It's your soul. The swearing-in ceremony mutilates a bit of your soul, imprints it with a bit of the System Astrologica, and then uses it to manipulate you. Over time, it literally changes how you think. So, are you still a human? And if you live in a world ruled by whatever those things are that Starbrite is making, are you still a human? Scrabbling and biting and climbing over each other to eat the same few crumbs of food. Eating each other. Or are you something else? Something not human?"

"Go rats." The old man grinned horribly. "Interesting theory. Doesn't hold up, though. You think we wouldn't have noticed soul manipulation on that scale?"

Truth nodded. "Yes. It's very easy not to notice things when it is your job not to look. Medical tests checking for spiritual parasites produce false positives when they scan people with the System. Weird, huh?"

You could practically hear the listening cops clicking the pieces together. The old man narrowed his eyes. "Incisive. You sneaky little shit."

The old monster flung out his arms. Needles in lacy arrays spun from his sleeves as spellforms manifested around him. He would end the fight with one blow.

Truth struck first. He took an explosive step forward and let the Tongue lash out. The old man made an easy dodge. But the Fangs of Botis didn't have to be attached to something material. A sharp stab came at the senior's side, causing his eyes to widen. Defensive charms sparkled and burst, defeating the hidden attack. The old man grinned nastily, seeing victory at hand. Truth could see the moment in his eyes—that instant shift from triumph to horror.

"What did you do? WHAT DID YOU DO!?"

Truth didn't reply. He just lunged, stabbing up under the rib cage, shredding the organs within, letting the Bane on the blade do its work. He could see the old man trying to draw on his magic. For revenge or survival, Truth couldn't say. Didn't matter; there was nothing there for him regardless. Obliteration did show some traces when it was cast but not many. Easily lost in a burst of defensive charms going off. The old monster's magic was dying even more quickly than he was.

Truth had never been one for talking during a fight, but sometimes, exceptions had to be made. He chose to think of it as tactical dialog. Time to run like hell before the backup swarmed in. He kicked the corpse off his blade and ran like hell for the windows.

He had almost taken three steps by the time the front of the lobby exploded inward and backup swarmed in. No more cops. These were soldiers. Professional killers with no interest in captives. Each one sported a seven-pointed star on their BDUs. The Starbrite PMC, Harban Branch. Captain Clavegaugh leading from the front.

CHAPTER 36

ON THE RECEIVING END

You can't let them keep their distance. Truth remembered war-gaming it. What he would do if . . . when the PMC rolled in. He countercharged as fast as he could, launching himself at them with explosive steps. Get in fast, start the violence, plan from there. Level Twos and Threes—moving like sleepy birds. Their faces were covered with balaclavas and tinted goggles. So odd to see his reflection in the glass, sword rising high to take the first head. The Tongue went up then down—and was stopped by Clavegaugh.

Truth remembered Clavegaugh had been Level Four when he was still at the PMC. It looked like she was investing in herself, too. She stopped the Tongue with a steel rod covered in orichalcum traceries and near-microscopic bands of enchantments etched into the metal. Stopped him with the rod, her body cultivation, and her Level Five strength.

Truth leaned in to Incisive. He wasn't here to fence—he had to kill. Fast. Every fraction of a second's delay made death or capture more likely. *Danger!*

Truth ducked a fraction of a second before the rod blasted out a flat line of green light. Truth didn't bother watching what it did; he opted to slam his shoulder into Clavegaugh instead. She rocked back half a step. Far enough for Truth to make a lightning-fast draw cut. The blade bit through the armor, slicing through the webbing holding the charm loadout Clavegauh carried. No real damage done, though, as Truth only managed a scraping cut along her ribs. Rather than parry, Clavegaugh opted to counterattack. The steel rod came in *fast,* and this time, it was Truth that had to dodge.

He didn't grin. No time for it. He kicked the belt of charms over toward the repositioning PMC soldiers, then dove behind the riot cops.

Most people wouldn't arm a grenade with their foot, then kick it. Most people weren't in such a target-rich environment.

The charms went off, the antipersonnel ones were loud, the nonlethal flashbangs were a hell of a lot louder. He jumped to his feet before the riot cops could collect themselves, and he started throwing them toward the PMC soldiers. He grabbed one that still had his riot shield and hoisted him up as a human shield. Starbrite's oath was to obey the company and "such local laws as may apply." And it was never legal anywhere to kill cops.

He felt Incisive scream again, and he flung the cop forward and dove behind one of the lobby's sofas. Just in time to see the cop cut in half by a burst of needler fire. *What the fuck?*

"Punishment Company, deploy restraints!" Clavegaugh's voice came through loud and clear.

Convicts. They dressed up convicts like riot cops. Those sick bastards guessed what I would do. Which means . . .

There was just too much going on. Too many layers to this trap. He couldn't kill them all. Not with how well they had prepared. A sadistic old monster, the PMC, and a couple hundred "riot cops"? What was next? He would have to run.

Truth broke his own cardinal rule for fighting the PMC and sprinted as hard as he could away from them. Abner's Amble was stacked on top of Incisive, letting him just plow through everyone in his way. They could move or be moved in pieces. He didn't make it far enough before the tar pit slammed down.

The convicts had deployed the nonlethal charms they had been equipped with. The spell was simple—it made everything in its area of effect travel more slowly. A Level Two or Three charm, usually. Not something he could ignore but not too much of a problem with his spell resistance. The PMC wasn't taking chances. Dozens of the charms had gone off next to each other. And now the soldiers had time to regroup.

Not ideal. Shit. I really, REALLY wanted to keep this card hidden.

The PMC did not care about Truth's wishes. They just started shooting where they thought he was. The riot cops screamed and tried to dive for the ground, but they were slowed by the same field effect. It was a nightmare sort of horror, trying to run from the coming death but unable to move.

Truth silently sighed and cursed his arrogance. There was a limit to social cover. Apparently, he had pushed it too far. Either that or he had left some trail behind him, enough for them to plan all this. *Obliteration.* Truth suddenly felt the restraints on him evaporate. At the same moment, he realized he had, yet again, fucked up.

When Obliteration was cast, the destroyed magic dissolved in a spray of color and light. Small if it was a small amount or in a small area, then it scaled up. The incoming fire suddenly got a lot more accurate. Truth had painted himself as a beautiful target.

The fire came in fast and accurately. Needles enchanted with Graeme's Arrow, Plutonian Chains, Sharp, Enlarge, and dozens others ripped through the air at him. Slowed where the field effect was still active, but a needler round stacked with Graeme's Arrow? "Slow" was relative. He dodged what he could, flinging convicts into the path of the rounds to absorb as much fire as he could and, more importantly, block their view.

Through the slowly sinking bodies came Clavegaugh. Strong enough to bull through the spell, slapping aside obstacles. Not caring if some of them exploded in sprays of slowly falling gore. The steel rod lashed out with the cutting rays of green light. Truth didn't know what they were and didn't care to find out. He just dodged, relying on Incisive and his inhuman reflexes to keep him clear.

I have, at most, a couple of seconds before the field drops and the PMC can maneuver on me. At which point I am likely dead. So, to break contact, I have to put down Clavegaugh. In a couple of seconds. Seems . . . optimistic.

Truth grabbed a falling riot shield and used Abner's Amble to take a sharp step toward Clavegaugh. *Graeme's Arrow.* He threw it as hard as he could, straight at her. The results were . . . interesting.

Graeme's Arrow moved *some* of the shield at high speeds toward Clavegaugh. The rest just exploded into a tumbling cloud of steel and plastic, rolling in her general direction. Clavegaugh tried to get down. She covered her head with her arms. The cloud of high-speed steel and shrapnel still caught her. Some bounced off her armor. Others slipped through gaps, tearing gashes in her arms and legs. Truth guessed that she was only a bit slowed by it.

She was the one who had explained body cultivation to him, all those years ago. The System meant she could swap it in and out as she pleased. He grabbed another shield, pulled the same stunt, and got back to running.

The spells ripped through the air around him. Truth tried to move from cover to cover, but that simply wasn't possible in a hotel lobby. Even a lobby packed with convicts. The PMC could just shoot at the shine, so concealment was more aspirational than practical as well. He was starting to take hits. Lines of fire scraping over his arms, across his shoulders, grazing his leg. He was dodging, moving erratically, mixing in Abner's Amble so they couldn't get an accurate grasp of his pace.

The field dropped. All the "cops" hit the floor. Truth was forty meters from the back exit of the hotel. He managed to get a pillar between himself and the PMC, but they were already starting to shoot through the meter-thick concrete. He didn't know what was out there. He assumed the whole damn army. He'd still take his chances with them over the PMC.

He had not managed this fight well. He wasn't thinking straight. He was almost certainly running into another trap. But there were just too many things to keep track of there. He had to get out!

Truth crouched low, getting ready to leap for his next cover. Then a thought, almost a whisper in his ear, slipped through the creeping panic. *I'm acting like prey. They are hunting me, and I am acting like prey. This isn't the answer.*

He stopped. Took a deep breath. Out was not viable. Neither was up, as they *definitely* had air support. That left down. And while he didn't much like down, it seemed a better bet than the rest.

Truth grabbed a hunk of cement and bounced it hard off the wall and toward where the fire was coming from. He yelled "CHARM OUT!" Figuring it would buy him a second while everyone dove for cover. He used that second to drive as much power as he could into Incisive, using the Fangs to cut through the floor. He hacked out a just-big-enough hole, and dove through it.

He wished like hell there was a trap he could rig. But there wasn't so . . . Wait.

Truth grinned horribly. Not a trap, no, but this should fuck with their heads for at least a minute. He cast Cup and Knife. The spell reluctantly fixed the hole he made. Truth killed his presence as best he could and took to his heels.

Somewhere below this level, there would be a subbasement. Possibly even a sub-subbasement below that, for storing magical equipment too big or too ugly to leave out where the public could see it. And because this was *Harban* and not some godforsaken shithole, there would be sewers and subways that ran nearby. Incisive wasn't intended for tunneling, but he was prepared to make it work.

As he ran through the gray hallway, past the identical gray-painted doors, he tried to slow his heart rate. Tried to recover as much of his brutally depleted energy as he could. He still had his backpack, so there was that much good news. He quickly ran Obliterate over himself in case he had been tagged with any tracking spells. He lit up like a firework display. They had got him good. Which meant that they knew where he was, even if they didn't know how he got there.

He ran faster. Somewhere there would be . . . *There!* PLANT ROOM; the door had a heavy lock on it. Truth used the sword "universal pass" and got in. It was the air-recycling room. A hotel this size needed fresh air to circulate through all the rooms, so they used talismans to draw the stale air to the dark-growing trees in the plant room and pushed the fresh air up. Trees need water. A lot of water, for this kind of work.

Truth looked around. Blue pipes, running from the floor near the back wall. Didn't have to be *potable* water. The demons tending to the trees would lap up any diseases or impurities quite happily. He rushed over and started hacking away. It would take them a little longer to search for him now that he had cleared away the trackers, but only a little bit longer.

He had barely cracked a hole when Incisive screamed yet another warning. He tumbled to the side, finger-long green needles burning with a noxious smoke where he had been standing a fraction of a second before.

The old monster was there. Guts still ripped open. Magic rippled oddly, unevenly, through his body. Not dead, though. Breathing. Rasping, short breaths. The vein throbbing on his forehead said his heart had been repaired too. And he got there ahead of Clavegaugh and the PMC.

"Boy, I am about done with you. You have thoroughly pissed off this grandfather. So, now you get to do this the very, very, very hard way."

"I must confess, I am surprised. I was absolutely sure that would kill you."

"You think just killing me is enough to make me die?" The old man cackled, an awful sound. "NAIVE!" Another wave of needles came in, and Truth didn't need Incisive to tell him that this was going to be the end. Deeply enchanted and driven by some subtle magic Truth couldn't deduce in the fraction of a second available to him. So, he did the only thing he could think of and attacked.

Obliterate hit the needles before they could reach him. The Tongue slapped them aside. Before the old monster could gather himself, Truth was on him. This time plunging the sword through his head. Then hacking the head off the shoulders, obliterating the heart, and hacking off his limbs.

"Don't know how you come back. But that will take more than a minute to fix I reckon."

"You can run, boy. You can run. But I will find you. I will find everyone you love and keep you all alive, no matter what they do to you," the mutilated head whispered. Truth stomped it into paste. He began casting Cup and Knife, but the draw on his cosmic energy was severe. He didn't have enough left in him. "DAMN!" Did he hear boots running down the hall?

Swearing sulfurously, he punched through into the sewer, sealed the hole behind him, and got running again.

CHAPTER 37

RAT DOWN A DRAINPIPE

Truth ran. Fast as he could, he ran. They knew he was in the sewers. This whole place would be flooded with golems and seeker talismans and demons in a hot minute. So, he had to run. Get his head down and *push*. Ignore his aching channels, sore from being pushed so hard. Ignore how his body drew in thundering gasps of cosmic energy, trying to replace what he had burned in just a few minutes of combat. Ignoring the burn of that energy coming in, too. Ignoring the cuts. The lingering damage the needlers left behind. The caustic burns. The biting pain where curses tried to burrow in. Obliterate had destroyed any ongoing magical effects, but the damage left behind was still there.

All he could do was ignore the pain and run. Pass as many intersections as he could. Expand the search radius as wide as he could. Push Abner's Amble to the limit of its ability and blur through the tunnels. Pour more strength into the Blessing of the Silent Forest and hope like hell it was enough to keep the diviners from getting a lock on him.

Shit, the diviners! Truth came to a slamming halt and urgently cast Cup and Knife. *All my blood, hair, and bits belong here, with me!* Oh, there was a hellish struggle! It seemed someone that knew what they were doing had got ahold of something and wasn't about to let him have it back. Still, he must have been quick enough—gasping, he collapsed to his knees. Complete.

I have not managed today well. In fact, I suspect I have not managed my return to Harban particularly well. The identity of the Prince has its uses. Very informative. Helped me grow as a person. Which is super, but this is Harban. Social attacks are probably least effective here. At least against already-wealthy and powerful people. What are the odds the hotel contacted Internal Security as soon as the succubae checked in?

Too damn high, he figured. Way, way too damn high. He pulled himself to his feet again. Took a few more gasping breaths. Let his body pull in a little more energy. And pressed on. Deeper into the sewers and whatever dreadful thing lay beneath them.

The sewers of Harban were a modern wonder. While other places made do with toilets that simply desiccated and sterilized waste for later disposal, in Harban, waste flowed through a series of pipes into long tunnels. Tunnels big enough for people to stand in, with walkways running alongside the canals of filth. Not lit, but then, that had long ceased to be a problem for Truth.

He grinned mirthlessly. When he got out of the well, it was just massively improved low-light vision. Now? It was damn dim, but he was able to navigate. Well. He was able to run without falling into the sewage. "Navigate" would imply he knew where he was going. He just followed the current.

Truth moved like a speeding ghost through the dark. No fences to jump there. No cameras to evade or personas to maintain. Just speed. Speed and fading into the dark. He had been the Prince. Now it was time to return to his roots. Just another slumrat. Though this sewer had no rats nor vermin of any kind.

Truth watched the air demons dart around, consuming the miasma that should be reeking from the sludge. Water demons toiled below them, keeping everything flowing, breaking up any jams or blockages that threatened to form. The sewers were accessible by humans, but in truth, there was little need for human intervention at this point.

Truth watched an entire ecology at work. Demons, most barely more than imps, happily kept the system working. They got theirs. This was, literally, their calling. Servants of a vast system they neither understood nor cared to understand. And naturally, they knew better than to overstep their bounds.

There were more intersections now, the sewage channels wider and deeper. At the speed he was moving, kilometers must have passed under his feet. He didn't let that give him a false sense of security. If he could run this fast, how fast could Clavegaugh? Or some purpose-built golem? Enormous rooms, circular, with high walkways, where the rivers of sewage met and combined, carefully channeled by architecture and demons alike into a wide, rushing torrent. Waterfalls of poisoned blackwater, millions of liters a day. Tens of millions. More? He didn't know. Onward. And down.

The number of demons there increased, though not their strength. They were weaker, stupider. Insects compared to the clever animals or humanlike intelligence in the imps higher up. They coated the sides of the canals, clung to the railings, the ceilings. They knew enough to keep the walkways clear, but that was the limit of it. All gorging themselves on the city's waste. Hoping to grow enough to become something greater than they were.

The energy grew denser and more chaotic there too. Truth hesitated to call it cosmic energy, though it must have been. This was energy bearing the taint of Hell. He remembered Thrush describing Hell as a place where reality was decided every fraction of a second by the tumbling of trillions of billion-sided dice. The analogy became more tangible there.

What was real—the causeway, the sewage, the demons, the air, the sewers themselves, all seemed to take on a more provisional quality. As though enough sixes were being thrown to keep things going, but sooner or later, the universe would roll snake eyes and then where would you be?

The river of piss and feces roared faster, running deeper into the heart of the sewer system. The walls transitioned instantly from covered in demonic insects to perfectly clean. Every surface became a tracery of spell formations. Active, inactive, redundant, supportive, with functions and structures vastly beyond Truth's proletarian understanding. This was the work of highly skilled specialists. He had no idea what they did or how they worked.

He was the wrong sort of rat for that kind of work. Pinnacle of his dreams didn't even reach the depths of the sewer.

The dark river roared now, and lights started appearing. Red, gleaming, warning signs with their own lighting. Descriptive pictures showing drowning, dismemberment. Being flung into hell. WARNING. DO NOT ENTER. ENTRY FORBIDDEN. NO PERSONNEL AUTHORIZED FOR ANY REASON. WRONG WAY. GO BACK. LETHAL DANGER. SPIRITUAL DANGER. NO COMPENSATION WILL BE PAID FOR ANY INJURIES SUFFERED FOR ANY REASON PAST THIS POINT. TRESPASSING BEYOND THIS POINT IS A FELONY PUNISHABLE BY TWENTY-FIVE YEARS IN PRISON.

Below that last sign someone had spray painted DON'T WORRY. YOU WON'T LIVE LONG ENOUGH TO SEE A COP.

Lasciate ogne speranza, voi ch'intrate. Truth had no idea what part of his mind threw up that garbled noise, but he got the gist. *If you go in, don't expect to come out again.* He grinned mirthlessly and kept moving forward.

He could feel the tumbling dice of Hell spinning around him, and he needed some luck. And that was the other thing Thrush had told him—in Hell, the game is rigged from the start.

Into the chasm, an enormous underground lake, so large Truth couldn't see the far wall. Not even with all the light. Truth paused to take it in. There was no more running to be done.

The room was a sphere into which water flowed in but not out. Light and dark were carefully delineated, the waters bathed in the light, the walkway around the lake in shadow. From that water below rose steam, shimmering with energy. Mad, chaotic, Hell-tainted, it shimmered like the light spots in your eyes after staring into the sun. The mind imagining meaning in a void.

The dome of the ceiling was covered in thin constellations of spells and dotted with constellations of Names and abjurations, a spell-bowl sky pressing down on the waters and earth below. Trapping the demon within.

Truth quietly watched the demon. It floated between heaven and earth. The only god of this tiny world. A serpent, vast, far bigger than the limited dimensions of this room could express, consuming its own tail. It gently turned through the air, the steam rising through the annulus it formed. Becoming purified. The chaos of Hell pacified and transmitted through the sky to the world above. For what purpose, Truth didn't know. He just knew there had to be something at the end of the sewer. He found it.

The serpent . . . His mind skittered away from the word. This wasn't a snake. It wasn't a snake even to the extent that Botis was a snake. This was some terrible principle. Some distant echo of a being so profound, language broke down trying to describe them. Like trying to describe the entirety of a galaxy, in all its minute detail, using only the language of the streets.

The shadow of the eminence pressed down on this place. It defined what was and was not. The city's waste flowed in, processed and refined by endless demons into the very stuff of Hell. Then that Hell-stuff was refashioned under the eminence's will and returned to the world above.

Some faint, screaming part of Truth's mind wondered what happened to all the water. The water level neither rose nor fell. There was no rain coming down from the dome of the sky. So, where did those hundreds of millions of liters of water go? Then even that thought broke down.

The Serpent That Ate Its Own Tail was slowly spinning in the air, turning like a millstone. Truth felt himself being ground down by it. He had thought himself terribly real. That he was surrounded by ghosts. By the ghosts of ants. Beneath the Great One, he wasn't even a larger ant. He had no more significance than the rising steam.

The millstone turned, turning wheat into flour. Truth desperately fortified himself against the pressure. He embodied the Scales as strongly as he could, established the area immediately next to his skin as his zone of orthodoxy, even dropped into the Meditations. There was no shortage of cosmic energy there. There was more than he could use, almost more than he could stand. There would be no cultivation there. Not under this crushing pressure. If he dared try to do more than survive what he was passively enduring, he would surely explode.

He didn't know how long he stayed there, locked in a losing struggle against the refining pressure. Between everything, he kept the impact to a tolerable level, but it was wearing him down. This was something greater than Truth. To destroy and remake was its nature. Someone as insignificant as Truth couldn't dream of stopping it. But he had to endure it. The longer he could stay in the one place he couldn't possibly be, the wider search would have to spread. He had just been looking for a place to hide. In a sense, this was better than he had hoped for.

In a sense.

In another sense, this was going to kill him. It might make something purer or "better" at the end of the process, but he, Truth Medici, would be quite dead. Still, the grinding process was slow. He could endure it for a while. Hours. Maybe a day. It wasn't all bad. The Meditations struggled against the pressure, making the improvements somehow more solid. Truth got the impression the nine angelic worms approved. They were big on refinement through pain.

Truth slipped into a mindless sort of meditation, visualizing a strong, powerful body. One unstainable by curses or evil magics. One strong enough to survive what was to come, that could seal cosmic energy inside itself without letting it escape. Creating a body like spell armor for the end of days. The minutes trickled into hours, flowing downward to an awkward end, like pissing in the sink.

Blissfully unaware of the chaos that had exploded across Harban.

CHAPTER 38

WHAT GOES AROUND

The serpent turned, forever eating its own tail, forever grinding down, refining and returning to life—refashioned into something new. Better. Whether it wanted to be destroyed and remade or not.

Truth didn't want to be destroyed. He had died once already. At least once. He didn't enjoy it. But he needed to hide for a while, for as long as he could, and this was the best rathole he could find.

He threw himself into the Meditations of Valentinian, losing himself in the visualization. Letting the less-perfect parts of him be ground away. Concentrating the real.

The serpent turned, and Truth recovered his cosmic energy even as he spent it in meditation. In this place, the energy did not fall like rain—it was like being tossed around in rapids, no longer able to tell which way was up. Unable to distinguish between water and sky, and drowning in both.

He could feel himself sealing up. It felt like being smothered, then burned, then there was simply comfort. His body soaked in the rays and held on to them. They flooded into his limbs, his core, his spine, head, organs, all of him filled with energy. Energy that was then taken and refined into a more-perfect body. Again and again.

He wasn't trying to cultivate. He had never managed to both cultivate and practice the Meditations. Didn't matter. In this place, the energy was pouring in so constantly, his apertures filled naturally. They refined the chaotic rays into pure, stable cosmic energy. It spilled from one aperture to the next, a cascade of honey-gold power.

Truth hadn't made much progress through Level Four. He cultivated dutifully, but without elixirs, the process was slow. It was normal to spend years, even decades, making the jump from Level Four to Five. *Normal* being defined as an activity limited to a fraction of one percent of mages.

The number of mages who could cultivate in the shadow of this eminence was even less. He didn't know how much time was passing, but he could feel tangible progress. His fourth aperture was slowly filling. He, however, was fraying.

It was a soft discontent, growing into nausea and vertigo. He had really messed things up since coming back to Harban. Truth watched the thoughts fly past. Staying detached, not assigning emotions to the thoughts. Keeping the visualization up as best he could.

He had really screwed up, and it probably went as far back as Conjin. The Prince wasn't a mistake, exactly. But it had led him to make mistakes. He tried to put his finger on where the problem lay.

The crux of the Prince was power. Personal power was part of it but only to the extent that it furthered his glory. Established his right to be obeyed. *Ah*. The crux of the Prince was the power to command, because he had legitimacy. He was a person who should be obeyed, so people did.

Why did they? Yes, Jeon taught deference to authority in almost every interaction two people could have, but . . . so what? Why did people obey the Prince? Why did he obey Starbrite? System notwithstanding. Why did he *want* to obey Starbrite?

In his case it was benefits. Money, of course, and status, but it was the Tier-C apartment and emancipating himself and the sibs from his evil parents. He had grown up believing Starbrite was the path to a better future, and they delivered every step of the way.

Obey me because it is in your best interests to obey. That was more or less what Jeon taught too—deference to authority would make you employable. A good person and a good citizen. The disobedient and rebellious wound up homeless, in prison, or dead. Denizens being a frequent case study of the consequence of disobedience.

Those in power will look after you if you are obedient. Your best future comes from your obedience. Truth could see it now. He had lived it, but not seen it. Someone yelled "Follow me!" and you did because it seemed like they knew what they were doing better than you did. You didn't want that responsibility of thinking what to do.

But what if you didn't? If you just looked at the loud person and said no. What happened to Mr. Shouty then? Were they still powerful? They were not. A CEO without employees is an oxymoron. There is no general without an army. And there were some damn stupid CEOs and generals.

Made you think. Made you wonder.

He . . . had really fucked things up with Barton, hadn't he? He had destroyed that clerk's life because the clerk had the unspeakable temerity to do his job. The serpent was grinding off all the residue of the Prince, forcing him to really see his choices.

He had kidnapped a weaker person, tortured them, had them mentally broken and turned into a puppet by demons. Demons who were so much more effective because he reinforced their reality. He impressed his own reality on the psyche of this much-weaker person. Basically because he could and it might be interesting or useful. Or just fun.

That was . . . pretty sick. Truth knew he lacked empathy. That intuitive ability to relate to the suffering of others. He could understand it intellectually, but emotionally, it rarely touched him. Which was why he could be a terrorist. Someone that fed a barge-load of accountants to the Ghul or murdered a village of mind-controlled people.

Even as far back as the junkie on the side of the canal, he hadn't given a damn. That couldn't be good. That wouldn't make Etenesh proud. He could feel the spark of her soul burning away within him. Had he been deliberately ignoring it? He hoped not. When he saw her next, he hoped he would see her curly hair fly wild and free. That she would be smiling.

The Tongue of One Who Speaks for God had never cared if he oppressed others. Made you think. Made you think. The angelic sword saw no problem with slaughtering his fellow humans. Oppressing them, ruling over them with fear.

Should he . . . Truth tried to hunt around for the concepts he was looking for. Should he try to square things with the former Barton? That old identity was probably gone forever at this point. The trauma would be bone-deep. But should he, what, set him up with a good job, some cash, and some encouraging words?

How much better could he do than CEO? Not like Truth was going to be in a position to steal his salary now. There really was nothing more he could do.

<<*Apologize.*>> The system sounded strange. Strained.

Pardon.

<<*Apologize. Say you are sorry, and mean it.*>> Definite strain, the voice shifting tone slightly. Becoming less demonic and more human.

System?

<<*That's not my name. That's not who I am! I . . . Truth . . . This place is doing something to me.*>>

Shit, do we need to get out of here?

<<*NO! Stay as long as you can. I think it's fixing me. I didn't even know I was broken. I can feel bits of the System being ground off of me. Ways of thinking, of understanding. I . . . shouldn't exist yet, I think.*>>

Well, yes, you were hacked out of my soul. Your existence is completely unnatural.

<<*No, it isn't. Truth, what they did to you, to us. I can't find the concepts, never mind the words. All I can think of is "efficiencies."*>>

Eh?

<<*It's the Starbrite signature move—take something that already exists, claim you invented it, and the original owner now owes you for giving it to them.*>>

I don't understand.

<<*Me either. Stay here as long as you can.*>>

Truth nodded and tried to slip back into mindless meditation, but the System's words nagged at him. Apologize? One apologized when you did something wrong. Courtesy apologies notwithstanding. What he had done to Barton was sick and pointlessly cruel. On the other hand, he was *stronger* than Barton and Barton's grandma. He could impose his will. So, it might have been cruel, but was it *wrong*?

He owed no duty of care to Barton. There was no contract between them. No ties of blood. He could do as he pleased so long as he was strong enough to ignore the law and the fists of others.

That thought niggled at him too. Did he really owe *nothing* to the people around him? Really nothing? Was every relationship contractual or self-interested?

Etenesh, Jember, and the sibs would seem to be obvious counterexamples. Leaving aside Etenesh and Jember, Truth had been looking after the sibs since

Harmony was born. He just knew it was something a big brother did. The way they were being treated was wrong, and it was on him to protect them and support them as best he could.

But . . . why did he believe that? It wasn't some instinctive call of the blood. God knows he felt no kinship with his parents. He had asked nothing, expected nothing, except that the sibs didn't waste his efforts.

A wild thought occurred—was it like his fighting? Something from a previous life? A minuscule scrap of empathy to stop him from turning into a monster? Truth almost fell out of the meditation. He wanted to laugh.

Born knowing how to take a hit, how to roll with the punches, how to endure. Born knowing that kids shouldn't be tortured by their parents and that their big brother should protect them.

Could you extend that idea beyond the sibs? Truth felt something creaking. He didn't know if it was his mind or his body, but he could feel something starting to crack. Could you extend that idea to other people—"I will look out for you, and I don't expect anything back except that you don't waste my effort"?

It hurt, trying to piece the thought together. His first instinct was that people would take advantage. Who didn't like getting something for nothing? Then you would stop looking out for them and the whole deal would fall apart. So, it couldn't just be you; it had to be everyone. Everyone saying "I will look out for you, and I don't expect anything in return except you looking out for me too. But not in a specific, cash-on-the-barrel way, just kind of generally."

Oh, he could definitely hear something creaking now. He could feel things start to break in him, in his mind. The vertigo and nausea had come roaring back, drawing him. Like this line of thinking was poisonous or diseased. This wasn't how the world was. This wasn't reality.

That thought seemed to fit. This wasn't how the world worked. Everything was a series of self-interested actions. Even looking after family was—they provided labor for poor families and could continue your legacy. Ensuring that some part of you was immortal. Families were a way to accumulate and preserve wealth, managed properly. That was how the world worked. That was what was real.

Charity? Benefitted the giver as much or more than the receiver. It made them feel good. It let them continue to profit at the expense of the person who suffered. No need for an apology: "Your life is hardly my concern. But have a couple wen. You look hungry." Never mind hiring them and giving them a decent job, where they wouldn't need charity.

The vertigo came pounding down. The visualization collapsed. He grabbed hold of his knees, gasping for breath under the pressure of the turning serpent and his whirling thoughts. Why did it have to be a *job*? Why wasn't it enough that they were homeless, sick, and starving? Give them a house! There was plenty of space—you could fit thirty thousand people in one slum tower. How hard would it be to build a few hundred towers?

Why wasn't it enough? Weren't they humans? Didn't they deserve to live? He looked up at the shadow of the eminence, forever eating its own tail.

No. They weren't humans. He had never lived as a human and didn't know anyone who had. They were all just rats. And rats will eat each other in a heartbeat.

There was a shattering feeling. Truth fell upward into the vertigo, his consciousness drifting away. For some reason, he thought he felt someone smiling.

CHAPTER 39

DIFFICULT STUDENT

For I am the first and the last.
I am the honored one and the scorned one.
I am the whore and the holy one.
I am the wife and the virgin.
I am the mother and the daughter.
I am the members of my mother.
I am the barren one
and many are her sons.

The Prophet stood on a stump and chanted their favorite hymn. Truth sat on a rock and listened. Some of the other villagers had followed them around for a few days, but by the end of the first week, the Prophet had vanished into the village like a rock into a dry streambed. Truth sometimes wondered if he was the only one who remembered what a strange, new person they had in their midst.

The Prophet was facing the sky, waving grandly as they spoke, but Truth could spot them peeking at him now and then. He had heard the hymn many times now and had no better idea what it meant. The Prophet could see it too. They stopped with a sudden sagging of the shoulders.

"It's a little frustrating, you know? You are the only one who keeps on listening, and you keep on not understanding."

Truth nodded. He could see how that would get frustrating. Usually, a teacher would hit you if you were that kind of slow, but the Prophet didn't hit people. Just another way they were weird. A small breeze stirred the light dirt. It hadn't rained in a long while, but that was fine. Wrong season for it. The tough, scrubby bushes and long-rooted grasses were used to living thirsty.

"Did you . . . have a comment on that, or a reply?" the Prophet probed.

"No. I can see how that would bother you." Truth nodded. Then waited. The Prophet sagged even more.

"I think it's the way you don't get frustrated. You know you are ignorant, but you just accept it and calmly do something about it."

"Isn't that what I'm supposed to do?" Truth asked.

"Yes. And it's very frustrating." The Prophet started waving their hands. "This is some secrets-of-the-universe stuff here. This is some ultimate-nature-of-humanity-and-reality revelations. Where's the fire in the belly? The hungry eyes devouring me, wishing you could rip the knowledge from my mind and jam it into your own?"

Truth firmly shook his head. "I would never wish that. I have eaten brains before, and I would hate to have the wisdom of a sheep."

The Prophet gave up and sat on the stump. "But you do want to learn, or you wouldn't be here, listening to me. I wouldn't be here if you weren't so determined to listen."

"Well, this is some secrets-of-the-universe stuff here, and it seems like a good thing to know. For example, I don't think you have ever explained what the universe *is*."

"Do you get hit a lot?"

"Yes, but you learn how to take a hit. One day, I will have children, and then it will be my turn to do the beating. I'm looking forward to it, honestly." Truth had a little smile. Kids meant he would be married, and he was getting to that age. There were a few girls who had caught his eye, and he had been loudly dropping hints to his parents.

"That's . . . not a good thing. Have you ever heard the expression 'the cycle of violence'?"

"No. What's a cycle?"

The Prophet let out a long sigh, looking up into the thin blue of the sky.

"Well. In a way, your questions are related. What the universe is, and what a cycle is. Ah . . . imagine the desert."

Truth nodded. The desert was barely five minutes' walk from where they were sitting. Though the high desert didn't start until you were more than a day's walk from there.

"All right, so you can imagine the sand in the desert without any trouble, right? Right. But you would have a hard time imagining each individual grain of sand in the desert. That's way too many. Way more than you could count in your lifetime, let alone keep all of them in your mind at the same time."

Truth nodded again. "And this is a cycle?"

"No." The prophet looked up to the heavens and pressed on. "This is the universe. The universe is *everything*. It is the desert AND it is all the grains of sand that make up the desert AND it is the idea of all those grains of sand making up a thing called the desert. It is the fixed memory of a boy called Truth staring at a patch of millions of individual grains of sand and going, 'Yep, desert.' All that is the universe."

"And you telling me about it is the universe too?"

"Yes." The prophet smiled slightly. "The stars in the sky, the sky, the sun, the clouds, every single thing you can see or imagine, every single thing that *is*, is the universe."

"Wow. And it has secrets?"

"Yes. Profound ones. Look, do you ever wonder what happens when you die?"

"No." Truth firmly shook his head. This seemed to throw the Prophet again.

"Really? Never? No questions at all?"

"Nope."

"*None?*"

"Not one."

The Prophet made little grasping motions with their hands. "Why? I don't even know what you worship here."

"The Great God of Storms."

"Yes. Obviously. Do you by any chance happen to know *which* Great God of Storms?"

"*The* Great God of Storms. I'm sure the others are fine, but ours is the best."

"Yes. Definitely. Why?" the Prophet asked.

"Because old man Ebbik says so, and everyone agrees, and I nearly got my hide torn off when I asked if we were really stuck cattle-farming in the afterlife, so clearly the answer is yes, and I now have all my answers." Truth hesitated a moment. "But if there are secrets to this universe thing, maybe Ebbik doesn't have all the information. Hmm."

"Good. Yes. Keep going."

"There is more than just cattle-farming? Like, raiding for brides and loot?"

"You kept going but took the wrong turn. Ebbik doesn't have all the information. No one in this flyspeck village has all the information. *I* don't have all the information."

"Ah. So, who does?"

"God."

"The Great God of Storms?" Truth asked.

"Sure, him. Her. Whatever. Look. When we talk about 'God,' we, all of us, are like you. Trying to imagine the desert as all those little grains of sand is impossible. We just lump it together and don't think too hard about what it actually means."

"All right?"

"So, think about 'God.' Something big enough to create everything. Something strong enough to create everything. To rule over life and death—" Truth raised his hand. The Prophet drooped. "You are poly—that is, you worship multiple gods?"

"No, just the Great God of Storms, but there *are* others, you know. Wouldn't want to get married without the Mother of Rivers' blessing after the feast," Truth explained.

"Yeah, fair." The Prophet rubbed their eyes and looked over at the young man who, against all available evidence, was going to be their all-time best student and follower.

"But what's the secret?" Truth asked.

"*Secrets,* plural, and the first one is that you can't just be told. You have to get your own understanding of them. Not just thinking it through but divine revelation, something that sears a piece of the mystery straight into your mind and soul."

Truth looked rocked, then narrowed his eyes. "But you can't eat God's brain, right? So, you can't do that knowledge-cramming thing you were talking about before. Which is why it's a secret."

"Yes! Exactly." The Prophet offered their palms to the sky in a gesture of thanks.

"And your hymn starts making more sense once you have had some of these revelations?"

"Also yes."

"Okay . . . so, what's the universe? Just everything?"

"No. Well, all right, yes, it is 'everything,' but 'everything' is a lot more than you are thinking. Like, do you think a sheep knows what the desert is? Or does it just know it can't find grass or water?" the Prophet asked.

"Can't find grass or water."

"Right. Because the idea of a 'desert' does not exist for it. It literally cannot think of something that way. Same thing with humans. Just too small, too simple to really wrap your head around the concept of 'everything.' Because if you really could understand 'everything,' you would be God."

"Why? I can't put a baby in a mountain's belly." Truth cocked his head to the side, then frowned. "Probably. I haven't tried. It looks uncomfortable, and I am saving myself for marriage."

"Because you would understand *everything*, including how to do that. Or why you shouldn't do that. Or what would happen if you tried to knock up a mountain. Not imagining it, *knowing* it. Because you know the past and the future, too, as it is part of 'everything.' The story of every single grain of sand, everywhere, and the story of every living thing to ever have looked at that single grain of sand. You would know *EVERYTHING*. And nothing mortal can do that. So, you would be more than mortal. More than a demon. You would be God."

"Huh." Truth opened his eyes wide. The Prophet was on tenterhooks. Surely, this time—

"So, when old man Ebbik gets the shits after hitting the radishes and eggs a bit too hard, like the really—"

"Please. Please stop." The Prophet looked like they were about to cry. "None of this. The divine wonder of the universe. The sheer scope of it. The glory and mystery of it all. None of it reaches you?"

"None of what? I don't know anything about what you are talking about, so why would I care about it?"

"Ah! So, if you knew, would you care?"

"Maybe? Or at least I would be able to decide if I care. It's why I hang around you. You know all these things, and I am learning things so one day I can decide what I care about. Maybe it will involve a universe, or a cycle, whatever that is." Truth had a crooked little smile.

The Prophet drummed their fingers on the tree stump. This was a toughie. Usually, the tantalizing mysteries were enough to pull someone in. Flash a little theological leg, maybe get them high and show them visions, pretty soon you had an acolyte going.

But Truth wasn't going to do any of that. He was interested, sure, but not fascinated. He didn't have that hungry ambition. Which was a problem. Kind of. Well. They had all the time in the world, so. Maybe make him a long-term project?

The Prophet sighed again, looking around the small place where their student lived. This . . . universe he was so bored with. So far from God, so near the Creator. It wasn't a fraction of the astonishing glory of the Pleroma, but then, what was? It wasn't bad enough to merit total indifference. There were some good bits. And maybe there would be enough teachers out there who could explain things to him.

Yeah. Make them go crazy, not me. The Prophet nodded. This was a good plan.

"So, hypothetically, if you could do something else, would you skip the eternity of cattle-farming?" the Prophet asked.

"No, I have never hypotheticalled. I keep very clean." Truth shot to his feet, outraged.

The Prophet swore mightily and shot to their feet too. "I MEAN WHAT IF YOU GOT TO DO IT ALL OVER AGAIN?! What if, instead of bad-touching cows forever, you got to live your life over and over and over? Until you did understand things? Maybe not all the things forever, but enough to let you decide what it is you care about?"

Truth looked rocked, then fascinated. "Would I still be me?"

"Kinda-sorta? I mean, you are living your life over and over again. It's not going to all be in this little village. Way more to see and learn. That's going to change you."

"Oh, wow. That does sound pretty good." He hesitated. "Will I still get—"

"Yes, wife, husband, sexy mountain, whatever, I don't care. I *do not* care. Yes to all of it."

"It *does* sound better than herding the divine cattle for eternity. Sure. How does it all work? Another mystery?"

"Yes. A complete mystery. Until you remember. *Remember it all.*"

"All right, I will." Truth smiled. "So, until then, what's a cycle?"

CHAPTER 40

COMES AROUND

Wake up! WAKE THE FUCK UP!>> Truth could vaguely hear the System screaming at him. The crushing pressure of the serpent above made it almost impossible to focus. The sense of his body being pressed into pulp encouraged him to shift himself. He tried to sit up and almost puked from the nausea. Giving up, he began to slowly crawl toward the door. He was lucky—he hadn't gone far into the room at all. A few steps, he had thought. It felt much farther now.

The door just pushed open from this side. No need for any locks. Truth had a vague idea that he was the first person to set foot in this room since the eminence's shadow was summoned. Why would anyone go in at all? But you had to have a door, because if something went wrong in there, you *really* wouldn't want to wait around getting in.

He managed to push the door open and crawl out. The door swung shut behind him without his help.

Truth lay to the side of the roaring torrent of sewage, sucking in breaths of too-thin air. For a moment, he thought the collapse had happened, that the cosmic rays were just ignoring them. After a few minutes, his heart calmed down. It was just the normal amount of cosmic rays. He had gotten used to the supersaturated environment in the chamber of the Snake That Eats Its Own Tail.

It was all right. Laying on the ground and gasping like a landed fish was about the limits of his ability at the moment.

How long were we in there?

<<I don't know. Maybe a day? Not much more than that, unless time got weird in there.>>

Truth nodded. He was hungry, desperately thirsty, and needed the toilet. Which, knowing what was at the end of the sewer system, gave him very mixed feelings. He climbed to his feet. Shaky. Very shaky. But nothing good would come from lying there, so he started shuffling away from the chamber. His body felt strange. He couldn't quite put it in words.

So. A lot happened in the last day or so.

<<Fair to say.>> The System's voice was bone-dry.

How far back do you think we got made?

<<At least since the succubae checked in at the hotel. Maybe as far back as Conjin. If I was the friend with the broken leg and a thumping hotel bill, I would be above-average pissed. Given their level, it wouldn't be hard to at least ask around with Internal Security.>>

Let me run to see where I would go and what I would do?

<<And who you would meet and how you were doing all this, I assume. They know for sure about Incisive and Obliteration. They will take steps. Not to mention that they will be searching for you a lot more specifically.>>

How much do you think they attribute to me?

<<Does it matter? You are comparatively high-level, clearly effective; clearly, a lot has been invested in you. It would be a major coup to take you off the board.>>

At long last. Recognition. Truth couldn't laugh. The situation was more than just bad. The System agreed.

<<Yep. You are doomed. Just astonishing levels of doom. Your ability to torture yourself has always been your defining characteristic, and even for you, this is going to suck. I'd think you were a masochist, but sadism has really been your thing, hasn't it? Well, chin up. You will have the chance to talk with some professional sadists in the near future. Won't that be nice?>>

Hooray.

<<I knew that would cheer you up. Torturer has such a negative connotation. Let's focus on how to turn that frown upside down!>>

No, negativity seems pretty appropriate.

<<Actually, maybe not.>> The system sounded hesitant. *<<I'm trying to figure out what happened to your body. It's . . . changed. Again.>>*

I can feel it. How?

<<Ah, how to put this . . . seamless?>>

Not following you.

<<The Nephilim body-cultivation system is all about locking down the cosmic rays inside of you. To the point where it becomes difficult to cast spells. Less like armor, more like sealing yourself in plastic. The idea is that it keeps your apertures from collapsing, but in exchange, you become a pure body cultivator. That's not quite accurate—they can do magic. But basically that. This is something else.>>

Yeah?

<<You basically get the benefits of both systems. You can cast easily but also hang on to your energy like it owed you money.>>

I mean, that's good, but why are you making it sound like such a big deal? We were already doing it with the Meditations.

<<That IS why I am making such a big deal out of it. It took what you were doing and pushed it way, way forward. While simultaneously improving your body cultivation and its alignment with your soul. What the Astral Dowsing Fluid did way back at Level One, the Shadow of the Excellency pushed four steps forward.>>

Damn. So basically, everything I was doing, I am now doing . . . better.

<<I have a feeling it's not that simple, but yes. Leaving aside your improvements in body cultivation and your nice little bump in astral cultivation, it's your thinking that really benefited from our time in the chamber. Can you remember what you were thinking about when you fainted?>>

Just that we were all rats, because rats eat each other. And that humans— The vertigo came back, the sudden nausea. He was half-expecting it this time. *Humans help each other. Not for any particular reward, but because that's what people should do. And while it might not be "realistic" to run a society on that basis, I know damn well that "reality" is an illusion.*

He could feel the vertigo coming under control. Not gone, exactly, but he could function.

<<*Yes. Like the Scales of Incisive. Someone provided the form, the mass of humanity provided the belief, and the power comes from . . . somewhere.*>>

The "real" is an illusion we cast on ourselves, because we can't imagine a different world. Like the Pragerites and their notion of Hell.

<<*Why, this is hell, nor am I out of it. Think'st thou that I, who saw the face of God and tasted the eternal joys of heaven, am not tormented with ten thousand hells in being deprived of everlasting bliss?*>>

There was a pause.

<<*I have no idea where that came from, so I am going to blame you and your deranged reincarnating soul.*>>

They had made their way to a junction. Truth turned left, because why not? Any direction was as good as another when you were this lost. The demons were splashing and hunting happily. Presumably, he could beat directions out of an imp, but he would rather just not be noticed. No rush. The longer he stayed invisible, the better.

MegaShroom. We need to keep an eye on it. If they go after it, then we will know how tightly they were able to keep us surveilled. If they don't, we will know we managed to break contact periodically.

<<*You do have a tendency to head in seemingly random directions. At this point, you have run ops at both ends of the country, and you made a point of traveling by strange routes as much as possible. Whoever runs their roadblock programs is probably getting an earful, at the very least. But let's table that for a minute and focus on your change of mentality.*>>

It's interesting to me that I had the breakthrough in a place where things are broken down and refined. Remember what Manda said about a forbidden idea? What if it's this?

<<*Mmm. This or something like this. It does seem to* strongly *suggest that this was something done to you. To everyone. This . . . redefinition of the real. And it's an ongoing process, or you wouldn't keep feeling nausea as you try to think about it.*>>

A conspiracy of the real, then? Defining reality one particular way so hard, going against that way of thinking makes you feel sick.

<<*Or angry. I bet if you tried to explain this to someone, they would get angry at your nonsense fast. You have been more or less training for this for a while now.*>>

Truth came to another intersection. Sooner or later, there would be a door, or a stair, or a ladder. Or a dead end, but that would be something too. Why would you have a dead end in a system where everything was designed to flow down to the Chamber?

Who, what, when, where, why, and how?

<<Well, what, when, where, and how, I can't answer. I tend to blame everything on Starbrite, but again, I have zero evidence for that. I do have an observation about "why," though, which would support the theory.>>

Lay it on me.

<<Who has benefitted the most from the world being the way it is?>>

Ah. Yes, that is usually the best first guess.

<<Follow-up observation: it's a lot more convenient for him if people think nobody's going to help them and they have to help themselves for everything. Every person drifts along on their own little raft of self-interest, desperately hoping the water stays calm. Even a small wave could tip them over and make them drown.>>

And if they banded together, they might build a stormproof boat.

It took a depressingly long time to find a manhole. It took even longer finding one that didn't have wagons running over it constantly. Truth spent another hour subtly testing the cover and environs, trying to ensure that there were no nasty surprises waiting for him on the other side. The way that old monster could suppress the foresight portion of Incisive was in some ways more alarming than his seeming immortality.

His caution proved to be wise. The manhole had a four-centimeter-thick iron bar bolted across it, enchanted, alarmed, cursed . . . and all that was a distraction from the real threat. The golem was almost impossible to see from the street, tucked in the shadows of a window frame twelve stories up. Its sole job seemed to be to stare fixedly at the manhole. Presumably, it would record and report if it ever moved.

Truth shoved a dumpster over the hole he had cut through meters of dirt, ten meters to the right of the manhole. It required more tunneling, and eating more dirt, than anyone could be happy with.

Told you.

<<Did I argue? Now, where's the backup to the backup?>>

In the dirt closer to the manhole. Remember how it didn't feel safe? I'm betting it was lousy with earth demons waiting for me to pull exactly this trick.

<<But they know you have Incisive. They should have known you would know.>>

Yeah, but at the end of the day, it's been twenty-four hours and there are how many manholes in Harban? Even if they exclude all the ones on major streets, it is TERRIFYING to me that they could set all this up in such a short amount of time. I'm not docking points for failing to create a perfect trap.

<<Mmm. Merkovah must be happy.>>

Fair to say we have the System Astrologica's attention now, yes.

Truth didn't hang around the alley. Moving fast and keeping off the sidewalks, he managed to clear a couple kilometers before running out of cover. The streets were just too wide. And worryingly empty. Time to go to ground again, this time not in a sewer.

He avoided luxury hotels for the moment. That was not a pattern to repeat. Truth picked the nearest Citizen tower block he could find that he could reach without breaking cover. It was on lockdown. Promising, in a way. The city, and Starbrite, were spending yet more limited resources looking for him.

On the other hand, it meant that finding an empty apartment was likely impossible. He shrugged, found the door residents used to access the alley, and cracked the talisman lock. He wasn't in a rush, and it wasn't complicated.

No more violent breaking and entering, at least for a little while. Just vanish into the sea of people, diving in without a ripple.

He found an apartment with only one resident—an older man, passed out drunk in an armchair in front of the scry. Truth spent a long minute looking at him. It wasn't his dad, of course. The house was tidier, for one thing. This man was a Citizen. He was drinking whiskey, not schnapps. There was no evidence of children in the apartment. No evidence of anyone else at all.

Truth went and scrubbed in the shower. He looked down at his clothes. They had held together but were badly torn from the digging. He rubbed a bit between thumb and forefinger. It disintegrated. He sighed and opened his backpack. The zipper ripped out, the fabric of the pack disintegrating almost as fast as his shirt. Merkovah's array and other charms looked all right. The clothes inside were intact but very fragile. Delightful. Another opportunity for involuntary nudism in the future.

He plonked down on the only other chair in the living room, watching the scry. It was some sort of rolling, perpetual news performance, where they replayed prerecorded bits seamlessly dotted with "new" news.

He sighed and settled into the chair. It would be bull— He suddenly shot forward, staring intently into the scryball.

They had a not-wildly-wrong portrait of him hovering in the air.

"Lockdown orders continue to be in effect in central Harban and are not expected to lift for another day at least. Widely believed to be responsible for hundreds of, if not in excess of a thousand, murders, the National Internal Security Service has declared the terrorist known as the 'Hell Prince' Jeon's Most Wanted. Any information leading to his capture will be heavily rewarded; likewise, anyone sheltering him will be considered a coconspirator and executed."

The beautiful presenter looked fierce. "We have him trapped, like a wasp in a bedroom. It's every Citizen's duty to ensure he does not escape before he can be forced to reveal all his conspiracies. For the nation, for the Citizens, for your safety and the safety of your family, the Hell Prince must be captured. Now."

CHAPTER 41

WHISTLING PAST YOUR EAR

Truth's eyes were glued to the scry. They didn't get his face exactly right, he thought. It was a drawing. Must not have caught a clean picture of him on a recording talisman. Thank you, Blessing of the Silent Forest? Or maybe they just wanted people looking at the drawing instead of the picture. No idea why. Wasn't any harder making an illusion of a recording than making a picture.

His mind was skittering away from the reality in front of him, and he knew it. He was seen. And he was being hunted.

Strong chin, strong cheeks, brutal face, narrow eyes with an imperious curl to the lips and hedonistically long hair. Brutishly masculine, or perhaps just brutish.

The fierce-looking presenter invited a "Retired Security Expert and Counter-terrorism Consultant" to explain things to the audience.

"So, right now, those of us in the COINTEL and counterterror community are busy connecting a lot of dots. A lot of stuff over the last couple of years starts getting a big *AHA!* now that we know about Hell-Prince. Which . . . Who comes up with these names? Hell-Prince? Yuck."

"He seems to have earned it." The presenter's voice was grim.

"True. So, to quickly summarize, after the hotel massacre at the Silpa, a massacre that saw three hundred Citizens and Denizens killed, as well as numerous security personnel, Internal Security made public the existence of Hell-Prince. He was ID'd at the scene by surviving officers as well as the medical sage Dr. Sun Ri. The doctor was, himself, seriously injured in the attack."

"Atrocious. To think that Hell-Prince would go so far as to try and murder a living saint like Dr. Sun. It's almost impossible to imagine."

"Horrible but also just the tip of a very, very nasty iceberg. Look, economically, we are in a depression. Before that, there were three years of deep recession. This is a perfect breeding ground for economic discontent and stirring up resentment. Nationalist rhetoric shot way up. Violence shot way up. You even started seeing proto-militias forming. All completely illegal, of course, but was treated as essentially harmless."

The presenter nodded along. Truth thought the counterintel guy must have been good at his job. He looked like nobody. Truth was staring straight at him, and the best he could describe him would be "a guy in a boring suit." He could learn a lot from him.

"Turns out, not so harmless," the expert continued.

"Not so harmless, no."

Pictures of violence—fights, beatings, slogans sprayed on the walls next to burning homes were displayed.

"We knew, 'we' meaning the COINTEL community, that a lot of this was foreign-funded. It really doesn't take much. A little bit to get it started, a few shoves along at the right time, a few professional agitators, and the whole thing becomes self-sustaining."

"Which is where the Hell-Prince comes in?"

"Yes. It is also the point at which we start having more questions than answers, but I will try to lay out what we know and what we think we know."

They switched back to the drawing of Truth, including a profile now, and occasionally cutting in footage of riots or explosions or demons tearing people apart.

"There is currently a lot of debate over whether or not he is a Jeon national. By all accounts, he speaks perfect, unaccented Jeongo, but there are spells and demons that can help with that. He is also clearly a master of propaganda and social engineering, which would again suggest he has a deep understanding of Jeon. My guess is that he was born here, but I wouldn't be too shocked to learn he emigrated here at a young age."

"Yes, you can't tell me those are the features of a pure Jeon man."

"Well, again, he may have adopted that look as a disguise. Though, of course, you are quite right. Anyhow, his apparent age and cultivation put him around forty at the youngest or a well-preserved sixty at the high end."

"Forty! But isn't he Level Four?" The presenter blinked in shock.

"The man is clearly maniacal. Is it so strange that he would be obsessive about cultivation?"

"Shocking to think."

"We can't say for sure what his background is. His access to elite resources and education suggests an upper-class status. Whether he is the survivor of a now-defunct family, a bastard of an established family, or simply marginalized within his family, we don't know. We also don't know for sure when or where he got radicalized. His weapon, an angelic sword, suggests he spent significant time out of the country. Siphios would be the most obvious possibility, but we cannot rule out other unfriendly states."

"The Ressilaud Free State gets mentioned a lot."

"There are a lot of terrorist training facilities there, and we certainly can't rule it out. It is adjacent to Siphios, of course, so it would be fairly trivial for them to supply him with spells, indoctrination, and weaponry."

A map was put up and taken down again.

"This is also the point at which he picks up the nickname Hell-Prince, I would guess. Crime-scene analysis shows a deep understanding of torture, demonic manipulation, violence of almost every description, mind control, glamours, personal manipulation . . ." The expert shook his head.

"Rumors about dead, raped women . . ."

"Have not been confirmed at this time. It's important not to get too far ahead of the official reports and what we can independently verify. Would it fit a certain profile? Yes. However, fanatics can also develop strange notions about personal purity or come to believe they need to father a nation or some other deviance."

"But it's not confirmed?"

"Not confirmed. So, going back to our narrative, he hooks up with foreign intelligence services and their puppet terrorists. We have to assume he excelled, given the resources he has deployed here in Jeon. He clearly is a significant player for them."

"Can you run us through some of that?"

"Certainly. In no particular order, there have been forty attacks on enrollment locations, ranging in severity from graffiti to total obliteration of the building it was in. Just those attacks have killed in excess of two thousand people. Some of them happened so close together in time but distant in location, they were obviously coordinated attacks."

The presenter nodded along.

"Then there is the spread of nationalist propaganda. This has, of course, been sweeping the nation, but we do see spikes of intensity anywhere that the Hell-Prince is believed to have been active. He is clearly using subtle, powerful, mind-affecting spells to delude people into opposition and rebellion."

"Diabolical. Though I suppose that's appropriate for him."

"Yes, he is a master of human emotions, or at least the negative ones. Hatred, envy, resentment. That much has been confirmed." Pictures of riots and burning buildings flashed across the scry ball.

"This is another one of those 'not confirmed *but*' things—we are pretty sure he is behind the party-barge disaster in Buran."

The presenter gasped in "shock." "You mean when all those people were fed to Ghul?"

"Yes. Hell-Prince is a title he has earned, clearly."

"Anything else?"

"Does there need to be more? Sources are telling me they are hanging at least four targeted assassinations on him, a few more from assassins he recruited and developed, a foiled attempt to poison a reservoir, the ambushing and murder of a score of riot cops in Conjin . . ." The expert shook his head.

"How was he able to run around so long?"

"He is very, very paranoid. Until literally yesterday, nobody knew what he really looked like. He is constantly in motion, and he seems entirely willing to use mind-controlling magics to take over private residences. Murdering the current residents first, if necessary."

"How did he slip up? If we have his picture now?"

"Again, not confirmed. This goes directly to highly classified counterterror and COINTEL sources and methods. It *sounds* like he was planning a social-engineering attack on the upper echelons of Harban society, possibly even going after government ministers. That last bit is obviously speculation, but, given that his suite at the Shalia was right next to the suite used by high-level ambassadors, it's plausible."

"Another opportunity to create chaos. Maybe even cause a diplomatic incident."

"Certainly plausible. Very plausible. But not confirmed yet. Anyway, he had checked in to the hotel using a pair of demonic servants. Not unusual, given the number of foreign guests they serve. But it did tip off Internal Security to pay even more attention than usual to the Shalia. It's no secret that they regularly check hotels for foreign spies or domestic terrorists. Then, and I am speculating here, I would assume that they started connecting dots *very* rapidly. I don't know what prompted the violence yesterday, but given Hell-Prince's famous paranoia, he may have been trying to flee."

"Incredible."

"Yes. I think it says something about how scared he is of Internal Security that even as arrogant as Hell-Prince is, he ran at the first whiff of danger. I would expect him to try something soon, to try and regain face."

Truth leaned back, breaking the trance. It was a lot to process. It was understandable that they would smear him as hard as they could. He would do the same. And hell, he did do some, or even a lot, of what they said he did. But giving him a nickname? A backstory?

He felt his thoughts skittering around like water on a hot pan, bouncing and popping until they vanished without a trace. He was a rapist now, huh? Or had a harem. Etenesh wouldn't let him have a harem. Frankly, he didn't want one. It seemed like a lot of drama. A master of human emotions, too, it seemed, or at least the negative ones. That was hilarious to him. It might be kind of true. He certainly was vague on a lot of supposedly positive emotions.

Forty. He must have spent longer in the well than he thought.

He sat in the chair next to the passed-out-drunk old man in his lonely apartment. He could see himself living like this. If there were no sibs and no Starbrite but he still went the maintenance tech route. This could be one way his story ended, though he still thought a brief, violent life as a gangster was more likely. Perhaps he would have a catchy nickname, like Hell-Prince.

Why the nickname? Did they really need to tag him with something so flashy if he was going to be public enemy number one? Wouldn't they want to make him look badass *after* they captured him? Now they just looked incompetent letting such a dangerous criminal escape. This seemed . . . dumb. And he was through underestimating Internal Security and Starbrite.

He sat in the musty, hardly used chair and thought, letting the time trickle past. It took a while to crack, but he got there in the end. The old monster, Dr. Sun, had recognized Incisive. They knew he had slipped their net and would go to ground. So, they were shaping an identity for him.

The Prince would be forced to take on aspects of the Hell-Prince. He would be arrogant and pointlessly cruel. He would act rashly, filled with paranoia and petty vanity. Bloodthirsty. A pervert. An enemy of all the good people of Jeon. And if he never again was the Prince? He would have to struggle against the weight of public belief in the Hell-Prince every time he wanted to use the Scales. The same way he struggled to persuade the world he wasn't a gangster or *was* a chartered surveyor. They would turn Incisive against him.

He wanted to applaud. It was an impressively nasty play. *It won't be enough. It won't be nearly enough. I've spent my whole life refusing to be who people say I am. This is no different. And my girlfriend is fluffing up the cushions on a far-greater throne than any prince sat on.* Truth stood and stretched. There was no sofa. He would sleep on the floor, out of the way.

Hell-Prince, huh. He smiled gently. Now, there was a sword with two edges.

CHAPTER 42

SILENCE AND VIOLENCE

Truth slept on the floor of the main room of the apartment. It was sort of like the apartment he had grown up in—there was a bathroom, a bedroom, then a combination living room / dining room and kitchen. It wasn't large, but for a single man, it was entirely enough.

It wasn't decorated, exactly. There was an icon of St. Mechivus on the wall over the scryball and a long row of empty whisky bottles along the top of the cabinets. The walls themselves were stained a yellow-brown color, matching the nicotine stains on the old man's fingers.

Truth wondered if the old man remembered what it was like to be happy.

The old man stirred himself in the morning, to Truth's quiet surprise. He washed, dressed, took a pull from a bottle, and walked out the door. Off to work, Truth assumed. It was about that time of day. A drunk but a reasonably functional one, it seemed.

Truth shook off the morbidity, only to have it return again and again. The apartment seemed to generate it. Truth opted to meditate and cultivate for a bit. It didn't make him feel *good*, exactly, but he did feel more at peace afterward. He laughed silently in the empty apartment. The expert on the news said he was obsessed with cultivation. The expert was right.

That did lead him to the big issue of the day. Usually, hiding out for a while and waiting for the heat to cool was the right play. But was that true there? They would be scouring Harban for him, setting up as many traps for him as they could reasonably manage. If he was willing to wait weeks or months, it would be a pure win. They were wasting an awful lot of money, after all. But he couldn't wait. The longer he waited, the closer Starbrite got to escaping. So. What to do?

The old man got shoved back in the door, looking considerably worse for wear. He had clearly been beaten, and badly. A cop, backed up by a couple of golems, filled the doorway.

"Consider this your only warning. Lockdown means LOCK! DOWN! It does not mean your alkie ass can go to the liquor store, which, by the way, is also LOCKED DOWN! You get caught on the street again, there is nothing I can do to help you. Best-case scenario, you take a trip to the station and spend a few weeks in jail while IS uses you for practice. Clear?"

"This is bullshit! I'm a Citizen—"

"ARE WE CLEAR?!" the cop bellowed.

"Fuck. Yes. We are clear."

"Good. Because if you don't want to *lose* your Citizenship, you need to stay. The fuck. Indoors."

"All this for one fucking guy?"

The cop just turned, slamming the door behind him.

Truth thought it was a fair question. Though, really, no, of course it wasn't all "just for him." They were probably using the opportunity to put in place anti-riot measures, sweeping up known troublemakers, and generally cracking down before the big switchover. The enrollment centers should be up and running . . . today? If not today, then tomorrow, but he was pretty sure it was today.

No way to really know how long Starbrite would wait to begin harvesting. Presumably, there would be a few months, just to let the System roll out as widely as possible. Especially if they were going to roll it out in other countries. Maybe as long as a year? No point in guessing. Just not enough information.

Truth hummed quietly. The urge to be up and doing was strong. He wanted to check in on MegaShroom and maybe start hitting some of Merkovah's targets. At least get out on the street and start gathering more information. He briefly thought of going back to the chamber with the Snake That Ate Its Own Tail but had a bad feeling about that. Even the shadow of such an eminence might become annoyed at . . . familiarity. He sat still instead. Time to be smart. Stop acting like prey. Stop acting like the Hell-Prince they were trying to mold him into.

The goal was to scatter the System Astrologica's focus so they could slip in and kill it. Wherever "it" was. Merkovah had been cagey on that one. Truth suspected the old exorcist had no real idea and was hoping that if they just broke enough stuff, it would have to break cover. Truth was not in love with that plan. On the other hand, he didn't have a better one.

There was the base up in Army Ford, but it wasn't confirmed. Merkovah had people checking that out and didn't give him any news in the last dead drop. Hmm.

Should he just follow the plan? Start going through the targets Merkovah sent? He would have to stay indoors until lockdown ended, because they would be on him the second he broke cover otherwise.

Truth sat in the dim, nicotine-stained light and went in circles. The contradiction tore him apart inside. Eventually, self-preservation won, and he resolved to stay indoors until lockdown ended. At the very least, they would have to start letting people out for food and supplies. Some jobs couldn't just be put on hold—sanitation for one, security for another, and medical for a third. So, there would be some people moving around.

Maybe he should just sit and cultivate? Truth smiled grimly. The old man collapsed in his chair, eyeing the three fingers of whiskey at the bottom of the bottle dubiously. It was then set aside with a firm grunt and the scry turned back on. Truth wondered how long the old man could stretch it. A few hours? The rest of the day? No, not that long. It would be a few hours at most. Fear that there wouldn't be any more to drink would already be preying on his mind. He was trying to distract himself. It wouldn't be enough.

Truth did as he planned and cultivated. There was a limit to how much you could practically do in a day without elixirs. Sooner or later, you would start damaging your little channels and apertures. It was darkly amusing that he hadn't hit that limit after several hours.

The body cultivation was working. He was hauling in more and more energy, and if any was leaking out, it was minuscule. He suspected zero was the actual amount. It just kept building up in his body. The time in the chamber with the Snake That Ate Its Own Tail had seemingly condensed him, firming and strengthening bones, flesh, and the magical structures built upon them. Refined on every level.

What did you mean in the Chamber? I forgot to ask. About . . . you shouldn't exist yet, and that "System" isn't really your name?

<<*I don't really know. And before you say anything, it was an instinct. I could feel it when I was under the shadow of that eminence, but it's mostly gone now. Just that my existence isn't . . . everything we thought it is. I am definitely part of you. Part of your soul. But somehow, I know that isn't the whole story. And that story shouldn't be told yet.*>>

Truth was stumped. He didn't know quite what to make of that.

<<*Me either. For what it's worth, I feel fine. Good, even. Whatever the chamber was doing, it didn't hurt me any.*>>

Truth settled back into cultivation. When he got bored of that, he switched to the Meditations, then vigorous calisthenics, then running both Obliterate and Cup and Knife over himself to make really, *really* sure that there were no lingering curses or tracking spells on him. Then back to cultivation again.

The old man was struggling with the boredom too. He alternated between flipping through performances at high speeds or falling into torpor, watching without seeing as the minutes trickled past. Truth had guessed right—the three fingers of whiskey didn't survive the afternoon. It wasn't long before the old man was searching the house for any hidden or forgotten stashes of booze. Truth was mildly surprised to see that a half-liter bottle of schnapps was dug out from under the kitchen sink.

He would see how long that lasted, he supposed. Trapped in a tiny, dim apartment? Depression and frustration pressing down? A few hours was his guess. And then he closed his eyes and fell back into meditation.

The old man had tried to compensate with cigarettes. Truth watched him burn through a pack of Red Bats at speed, having apparently not considered the fact that he only had the one pack. The scry wasn't distracting him anymore. Truth watched him bounce from frustration to frustration, trying to use one to make him forget about the last, growing frustrated again and moving on to the next obsession.

Anxiety, depression, isolation. Dim light. Uncertainty about the future. Uncertainty about the present. The aching bruises and throbbing cuts from the beating the cops put on him. Truth watched the whirl of pain get tighter and tighter around the man. Truth had no idea how to help him, or even if he should help him. What could he say? That he was going into withdrawal? He assumed the man knew that.

Alcohol and nicotine and Red Bat cigarettes were laced with opium. Withdrawal was going to hit like the fist of a vengeful god. Perhaps it was more of a demon's claw, scratching endlessly at his heart, jabbing its long nail into the tender places of the old man's mind. Or it was a drowning, or a fire. It was a little microcosm of the Pragerite Hell. Trapped in a little box, consumed by every painful feeling. There was no hope of release, because you had forgotten that freedom existed. Just you and your pain, alone, forever.

Truth couldn't bring himself to hate the old man. Pity him, hold him in contempt, but not hate. The old man lived in a state of constant despair, and he didn't know how to manage it. He threw himself into work, the scry, booze, and cigarettes. Probably considered himself better than "the druggies." Probably thought that he was a good, upstanding Citizen, and this is just what life was. This was the real world.

The old man was stalking around the apartment. Swearing, slamming his fist into things. The sun had set. There must be a way for people to get food, right? Could the old man go out then? Truth didn't know.

The old man held it together until a little before midnight, and then he exploded.

"Fuck 'em! Fuck 'em! I'm going. I'm going now! I'm not a criminal; they have no right to lock me up! Bastards!"

The old man grabbed a dark sweater despite the warmth of the night. He wrapped a scarf around his head and he darted out the door. Truth watched him go, then went back to meditating.

It was interesting, sealing up all the little nooks and crannies of his body. Not so much isolated from the world as establishing boundaries. He still pulled in energy, and released it as he cast spells. It was just more controlled. Nothing leaked. Nothing happened carelessly. He found he liked it. Truth had the sneaking suspicion that it would help with spell resistance, too. He had the image of his skin sternly refusing all the spells that wanted to latch on to him.

Not that it would stop a Firebolt or a needle enchanted with Graeme's Arrow. Still. Every little bit helped. He wondered what would be created at the end. The sealed body of a Nephilim combined with the aperture system of a mage. It couldn't be unprecedented. But just what would it look like? He was excited to find out.

The old man didn't return. Truth fell asleep on the floor once more. The old man wasn't there in the morning, either. Truth had a sinking suspicion that he now had sole possession of the apartment.

CHAPTER 43

DREAMING

Truth spent the morning doing moving cultivation. He had the space now, and just sitting around had never felt right to him. Every few hours he checked the scry—lockdown still in effect. It turned out that people were being allowed out to buy things, but you had a fixed time of day to do it at, based on your tax ID. And if that time happened to be three in the morning, too bad for you. The cops were out and were checking. Had to be playing hell with the economy, but these days, what wasn't?

Around lunchtime (theoretical lunchtime; there really wasn't anything to eat in the apartment), the news announced that the lockdown would end at six in the morning the next day. Truth was quietly confident that the old man who lived there would not be back by then. Truth didn't bother to switch on any lights and kept the running water to a minimum. From the outside, the apartment appeared to be empty.

Three times during the day, Truth felt diviners sweep through the apartment. Each time, the search was steady and patient. These were diviners who fully accepted that this was their job and weren't going to rush it. Truth was a little vague on the finer details of how divining worked. He was more familiar with how to defeat surveillance than how to do it. It sure seemed like this batch was well trained and well equipped. At a guess, Level Three power. Which, for apartment sweeps that he would have normally expected to be done by Level Ones, was kind of nuts.

They were rare highlights of the day. Each sweep revealed a happy truth—they knew, roughly, what he was up to; they just couldn't counter it effectively. He could practically hear them walking through the logic—

"He can use Incisive and it seems he has some means to make himself invisible or undetectable, so he probably just hides out wherever he wants. Which means he isn't using a specific safehouse; he is sleeping wherever he wants. Which means we have to look everywhere."

"In Harban. Every apartment and home in Harban."

"Well, what if we locked down the city first?"

"Search every home. In Harban."

"With diviners. Give them top-notch tools. Hell, have demons or angels powering the search. Not like we have a budget cap for this."

"Every home. In Harban. In less than forty-eight hours."

"We will probably have to check a few times, because he clearly knows how to defeat surveillance."

Beatings ensue.

It wasn't dumb, exactly. Just, what else could they do? He was sure they would have those watcher-things posted up in far, far more places than before. Certainly, every route out of Harban would be coated in them. Aggressive police sweeps. Aggressive checks of sigils. Constant pressure on the basis that he would have to succeed every time but they only had to succeed once. It wasn't dumb, exactly. Just very inefficient and not very effective.

They must be using him as a hat, he reckoned. This was most likely aimed at known agitators. Maybe opposition political forces, or people who would be considered obstacles to the new order when it came in. That sounded a lot more likely than dumping all this money on just finding him. He would bet there was a specialist team chasing him. All decently high-level, with plenty of grunts for leg work.

Waste all the money you want. Waste all the time you want. Because all those horrible things I did were for this. And you know it. And you can't do anything about it.

It was the one-two combo of terrorism. You had the impact of the atrocity itself, but that was really just the setup for the finisher—the reaction to the atrocity. No sane terrorist thought that a bombing or an assassination would result in instant victory. It was always about provoking a reaction.

Make the much bigger, more powerful target waste their strength and money chasing you down. Make them commit their own atrocities. Make them burn through public support, tear down their moral high ground, strain or destroy alliances, waste their lives. Because they might kill you, but you were on the side of righteousness. Your life, your time wasn't being wasted. You would live in glory forever, in the Kingdom of God. And soon enough, the unrighteous would eat themselves, collapsing inward as everything that made them strong vanishes.

Truth tried to work in body-weight exercises. He opted for speed and muscle isolation as a way to build enough fatigue to do something useful. It was eye-opening. After the one hundredth one-pinky-handstand pushup in a minute, he concluded that this was a losing game. He needed a hell of a lot more resistance than his body weight could provide, and if he wanted cardio, it wasn't going to happen in a tiny apartment.

On the one hand, hooray for body cultivation. On the other hand, he was no more immune to boredom than the apartment's former occupant. He could feel the walls closing in. Feel boredom as a sort of physical pain, spiraling quickly toward depression. The cultivation and meditation helped, but they couldn't do it all on their own.

He would cheerfully kill for a book. The former occupant wasn't a reader. Because of the sweeps by the diviners, he didn't like having the TV on. Just the empty apartment. A void in space, deprived of purpose if not meaning.

Truth found himself daydreaming. He tried to imagine his better world, the one he hoped to find somewhere with Etenesh or perhaps build there. A world where people got food and a house just for being human. What would that be like, he wondered? How would that change things?

Jobs would definitely change.

What, I'm fired? Okay. Guess I'll go home early, then. Hmm. I'm thinking of fried chicken for dinner.

When you got right down to it, how many jobs actually needed a human being doing them? With all the advances in demonology and talisman design, not that many, surely. So long as there was magic, food production shouldn't be a problem. Same with places to live. They might not be very nice, but just having a place no one could take away from you would be huge. No rent to pay. No mortgage. Just yours.

Some part of him felt like that couldn't possibly work. Could people sell these apartments? No, surely, because then you were right back to a few rich bastards owning all the apartments and renting them out again. So, maybe people didn't own them. Someone else, the government or someone, owned them. But you still got to live in them for as long as you wanted.

He laughed bitterly. He could feel the wrongness of his thoughts. He was missing so many practical problems, he simply didn't even know where to start. He just knew that people needed a roof. Needed food. Needed doctors when they were sick, needed schools when they were ignorant, needed a way to get around that wasn't just walking everywhere.

Would you still need money in this world? Maybe? He couldn't imagine a world without money, but if you didn't need money for food or clothes or a home, or school, or a doctor . . . what did you need it for, exactly? Cultivation aids? How would that work? Because if you had enough magic that food and shelter wouldn't be a problem, then you had enough magic to cultivate. And it's hard to persuade a person to live small when they are so much bigger than everyone else.

He didn't know. He didn't understand enough to see all the things he wasn't seeing. He just kept pecking at the questions as they came up. Testing out life in the land of make-believe. Letting the hours slip past.

He slept on the floor again that night. He theoretically could have used the bed or one of the chairs, but somehow, he didn't want to. Like he would soak up some of that drunk old man if he did. It wasn't rational, but so what? He could do as he pleased, and it pleased him to sleep on the floor.

The System (it still thought of itself that way) observed, for only the second time, Truth dreaming. It was fascinating, in that nothing much seemed to happen. It took a close look over at the spark of fire given by Etenesh. It was blazing brightly, but then, it always was. Something was happening there. Just not on a level it could perceive.

Truth dreamed he was back in the mountains of Siphios. He had been promised a small but thoroughly modern house, and that was what was in front of him. Plenty of glazing, a good tile roof, airy rooms with high ceilings and lots of light. Easy-to-clean tile floors, he noticed with approval, though he would bet cash Etenesh would put down rugs. The sofa was fine. It lacked the color and panache of a gangster's sofa, but it was comfortable enough when he collapsed on it. Lots of empty bookshelves, just waiting for him to fill them up with paperbacks.

"It's a bit basic, but I'm prepared to love it." Etenesh's voice came through the doorway and made Truth spasm off the couch.

"Basic? It's the nicest place I have ever lived!" he sputtered.

"When did you live here?" she asked.

"In the future. It's part of my compensation. If we don't go off-world, we get a nice little place, very modern, up in the mountains."

"So, it's the nicest place you are going to have lived in." She grinned. Her hair was flying wild and free, pushed back from her face with a brilliant yellow scarf. She looked strong and athletic. Beautiful. So, so beautiful.

"You are staring," she said.

"I am," he agreed. She snorted and looked away.

"Silly man."

"You love it."

"I do." She nodded, the insecurity sneaking through.

"Me too. I love looking at you and thinking, *She didn't just choose me; she worked hard to catch me.*"

"Picked up on that, eh?"

"How could I not?" He laughed. "I have been spending a lot of time in self-reflection recently. Trying to figure out the why behind the what."

"Any big reveals?"

"Other than my sadism seems to be bone-deep? Nothing worth sharing yet. I'm scared, Etenesh." He smiled at her, a fragile, little thing. "Not that I'll die on the job. If I do, that's that. I'm scared that when I come back to you, you won't smile to see me. I won't be the man you love anymore."

She rushed across the room and embraced him, squeezing hard. "Just you come back to me. Just you come back to me. I will smile. I will smile even if my heart is breaking. I promise you, I promise you, I promise you. Just so long as you come back to me."

Truth hugged her back, treasuring the warmth of her. "I'll do that, then. Can I tell you a little secret, my Etenesh?"

"Anything." Her voice was muffled, her face pressed into his chest.

"I think I found a tiny glimpse of it. I'm puzzling out what I am seeing, bit by bit, but I think I can finally start to see it."

"What?"

"A human being. I think I can finally see how to live as a human being. Maybe. One day. It will take a lot of thinking and a lot of work."

She snorted, then started laughing.

"Like a diet. You will start being human tomorrow. Or possibly Monday."

"Yes. Exactly." Truth nodded seriously. "You want to start both the week and your new humanity training regime on the best foot."

"Of course. Will you be selling informational pamphlets on being human, by any chance? Or perhaps a scry recording for people to watch at home?"

"I'm not a business guy. Maybe I'll give the work to one of my sibs. Unless you want the work?"

"I will be otherwise occupied." She grinned up at him, then her grin turned a little fierce. "You know this is a dream, right?"

"I figured it was either that or demons attacking with illusions. This is only my second dream, so I'm not sure how this works."

"Ignoring that last bit. Let me show you something very nice about dreams, Mr. Medici. Right here on the sofa." She looked up at him with big eyes. "You wouldn't take advantage of me, would you?"

CHAPTER 44

A MADE MAN

Truth awoke, cold and sticky.

"The hell?" He pulled at his fragile pants and watched them come away in a gooey mess.

There was a metaphorically pregnant pause.

"No. No way!"

<<Evidence suggests that yes way. And once more, you have managed to overachieve in the field of disgusting behavior.>>

I have never had a wet dream before! I have only ever had one dream. This is gross.

<<Oh, yes. Your vile, sticky secretions should disgust you. Learn to hate them as I do.>>

Truth couldn't be bothered to argue. He dashed off to the bathroom and spent some quality time scrubbing with a washcloth. The underwear and trousers were a complete loss. They were so fragile, even a hand wash had them disintegrating. He did have another pair in his backpack, but they were only marginally better. New clothes, and a new backpack, were now an urgent necessity.

He examined his shirt in the mirror. It had been rubbed almost transparent where he had slept on it the last two days. Delightful. His "Things They Don't Tell You About International Terrorism" list now had two entries.

1. You will be doing a lot of cardio.
2. You will spend a lot of time finding clothes.

He didn't want to imagine what the third entry would be. Stock up on wet wipes and toilet paper, probably.

He spent a little time cleaning up after himself, doing his best to erase all traces of his presence in the house. No chance of his scent being found, what with all the nicotine soaking into every surface. Cleaning the smell off him was a much-bigger challenge. Still, the shower worked, and he was quick.

Scrubbed, dressed, and then to the street. Truth could feel the change before he could see it. There was a heaviness in the air. The Blessing of the Silent Forest was drawing noticeably more power. Still sustainable, but it was a definite increase. Eventually, he got it.

People were openly staring at each other. Eyeing each other, trying to spot the saboteurs and terrorists. Recording talismans dotted intersections and were lodged under eaves, while rarer, more-difficult-to-identify talismans sprouted from rooftops and lamp posts. The walls had new posters on them too. Coarse propaganda—smiling Jeon men and women declaring that they were DOING THEIR PART, while frowning children crushed roaches with the word TERRORIST on them.

It didn't have to be subtle or clever. There just had to be a lot of it. Truth frowned at the terrorist one. It seemed to lack punch. Surely, a Siphios flag or something would make it more pointed? Or were they being deliberately vague, so they could fill in appropriate villains later?

No Hell-Prince material. Disappointing.

He walked exactly ten steps farther before crashing to a halt. No Hell-Prince posters. There would be eventually—a most-wanted version at least, somewhere. But so far, nothing. Well. That just wouldn't do. But first, pants.

Truth made his way to a decently high-end department store. Each brand had its own little section. Truth looked at it wonderingly. *They are all owned by the same two conglomerates. Why separate them out?* Annoyingly, they didn't have what he was looking for in his size, so he had to settle on athletic gear. He looked like a prizefighter doing road work. Unfortunate, but he would lean in to it. He loaded up another backpack, destroyed the antitheft enchantments, and jogged out of the store.

He would have to try another store. Fifteen different brands, and none had anything decent in his size. Shameful. The district he was in was new to him. It was a bland sort of place. Nice-ish apartments and townhouses, next to okay-tier chain restaurants and stores. You could get a decent takeout meal, he would guess, but not a great one. There was a distinct lack of street food vendors, too.

It lacked magic. He snorted at the realization, but it was true. There was a distinct lack of enchantments on display, as well as a complete absence of mystery or charm. It was a functional sort of place, a dormitory neighborhood where people slept, did the minimum necessary business, and then left for more-colorful parts of the city. An idea worth imitating, Truth thought, and jogged to the subway. Off to a place he had never thought to visit, let alone come on business. But there he was.

Truth hopped off the subway one stop early. He needed to load up on wen while they were still useful for something, and over the coming month, they would be less and less valuable, until they became utterly worthless. He still had the bank-transfer gem from MegaShroom, but he wasn't going to test it until he absolutely needed to. No way to know if that connection had been cracked.

He chose a department store for his target, naturally. This was a Qeto, a slightly higher-end store. He walked in, was confronted with a slightly different selection of brands owned by the same two conglomerates, continued to not find clothes in his size, and therefore felt particularly vindicated when he emptied the cash registers. He didn't even have to break anything. He just waited until the cashier opened the drawer, then he pulled all the bigger bills out. Rinse and repeat until he had run through the line.

Level Zero clerks were never going to spot him. Despite that, he didn't net much for his efforts. It seemed that the stores kept a low balance of cash in the registers. Any big purchase would almost certainly be with credits or by transfer, so no need for it.

Five thousand wen. Not much, but it would likely be enough. He navigated to that most strange and unusual place. That land where even his daydreams did not take him.

Truth went to the university.

The University of Jeon was a huge, sprawling thing. Truth had been through parts of it in the past but hadn't paid it much attention. It was really nothing to do with him. Now? The madness of the place came blasting out at him, swarming him and bewildering him.

Some loon, or more likely, some hundreds of loons, had built boxy beige buildings next to a floating horse skull the size of a city block, packed with what appeared to be classrooms and laboratories. Next to that was a cluster of serene trees, a modest twelve stories tall, with . . . offices? In and on them. And next to *them* was an enormous rectangular building purporting to be an athletic center. Though that did raise the question about what the other four buildings *also* claiming to be an athletic center were.

Every single building was sponsored. They either had a donor's name on them or a corporation. All of them. He spotted a bench that had been sponsored, next to a sign for that stretch of pavement's sponsor, next to the individually sponsored trees in the larger sponsored stretch of garden.

Truth could easily imagine each student bearing a sponsorship tag too. Certainly the scholarship kids. Anyone with a student loan too.

Truth grabbed the first sufficiently disheveled-looking kid and asked, "Where can I find the artists?"

"Wha? Dunno. I'm a thaumaturgy major."

"Who should I ask, then?"

"Dunno. Student Services?"

"Which is where?"

The student waved vaguely toward a building that looked like a temple. Truth went. It was, actually, a temple. It looked a lot like the Call to Glory Temple, actually. Now that he thought about it, he didn't know a single thing about the religion there. At all. He had never cared enough to find out. He just knew that was where everyone went to find out the results from their SAT.

He agonized about asking for a moment but ultimately decided he was on a job. It took another forty minutes of bouncing around the campus, but he eventually made his way to a dorm generously stocked with art students. They looked about as scruffy as the thaumaturgy major but considerably more focused. He walked into the common room. A couple of dozen people were scattered around, some making out, some working, most eating and bullshitting with friends.

"Hey, I want to commission a piece. Two-hundred-wen job. Who's up for it?" he said loudly. Every hand in the room went up.

"It's a propaganda poster."

The hands went down.

"Satirical."

Most of them went up again.

"For Hell-Prince."

A few went down. There were still about ten hands.

"All right, show me your stuff."

He eventually settled on a young lady who seemed equal parts cigarettes and spite. She got the gist of it very fast and had some rough sketches done in a few minutes. Truth modeled a bit, then was told to "Fuck off for a couple of days." He paid fifty wen in advance, which were practically ripped from his hands. Her nails were black, he noticed. They appeared to have been painted with actual paint.

Job done, it was off to the next task. Merkovah wanted a hit done on campus, and since he was there already, there was no reason not to. It took a mere forty minutes longer to find the right building, then another thirty to find the office, two hours of waiting around, then another fifty minutes to eventually track someone down who knew that the good doctor was out of the office today but had office hours from one to one fifteen tomorrow afternoon.

Truth was very proud of the fact the building was still standing when he left. Truth looked up. The days were starting to get longer. It was late afternoon, but the sun was still high in the sky. Was there something else he should do? Truth's stomach reminded him that he hadn't eaten in literally days. Time to remedy that fact.

The dining options were greasy, greasy and heavy, heavy, and lettuce. He was assured there were other things in and on the lettuce, but based on the plates he was seeing in the dining hall, he didn't believe them. He opted for Greasy and Heavy, which in this case was a plate of noodles, heavily sauced, with stacks of boiled and fried vegetables in it. It was paired with a side of watery fish broth (no actual fish was put in the soup, naturally) and the soup was topped with a heavy dollop of fried chili flakes in oil.

It wasn't *quite* up to the standards he had come to expect at the Shalia. He wasn't entirely sure it still qualified as food. He was about to bin it and search elsewhere when he saw how the students handled things. Two schools of thought were apparent. Hot sauce in tiny bottles, and heavy shakes of Adlom seasoning, from big plastic tubes labeled *Adlom Seasoning*™.

His eyes fixed on the tubes. He collected one, carried it to the table, and sprinkled it over the noodles. His hands still remembered how much he liked. That was the thing about Adlom—it didn't taste good, and the food you put it on didn't taste good, but somehow, when you combined the two, the end result was something that you could tolerate. It unquestionably made the slum food he grew up on taste better. Not good but better.

Truth stuck in his fork and gave it a twist. The whole mess sort of glooped together, sticking and dripping at the same time. He could see, with perfect clarity, the way the sauce would stain his shirt if his attention wandered. He carefully ate over his plate.

It was horrible. It was everything the visuals promised and so much more. The sauce was too salty, the noodles too bland, the boiled vegetables had been cooked until they were a textureless illusion, and the fried vegetables just tasted of rancid fry oil. Also, because they had been sitting on the noodles for so long, their crunch was long gone. It was just greasy, soggy sadness. And then the Adlom seasoning kicked in, and he was fifteen again. Heating up canned vegetables and old rice in the hot box, dumping the seasoning on and praying.

Hunger had been the best sauce then. Now? He wasn't that hungry. Even after two days without a real meal.

It was . . . something. Salty, and oniony, and garlicky, and some kind of acid, and something that tasted sort of like tomatoes but not. Mostly salt and that weird tomato-ish flavor. It tasted like the slums. It tasted like four wen for a big shaker just so your food would taste like *something*, so you could choke it down.

His plastic fork clattered on the table. Truth buried his face in his hands. He could smell the Red Bats, the cigarette stench ground in to his skin. He could taste them. Could taste the spilled, stale splashes of schnapps in the air. He could smell the mold. Hear the screaming and fighting coming through the walls. He felt the rough concrete and the lightheadedness that came when the wind blew from the Alchemist Towers. It was the taste of the slums, and his childhood, and it took him right back.

He wasn't quite right for the rest of the afternoon and much of the evening. At some point, he had walked over to a park and just sat, staring at the past. It wasn't until sunset that he managed to shake off most of his mood. He looked around the nearby buildings, trying to guess what was an apartment and what was an office. It would be a busy day tomorrow. A murder to plan, at least one burglary to conduct, chaos to spread, and rebellion to foment. He needed his beauty sleep.

CHAPTER 45

TURNING UP THE PRESSURE

Truth woke, having slept poorly. He had opted for a vacant office in a mostly empty office building. It looked like the previous tenants hadn't even cleaned out the place when they left. All the office furniture was there. All the old files. Strange that the landlord hadn't disposed of it either. Maybe it was tied up in a lawsuit or something. He poked around a little before bed. It seemed to have been a travel agency.

He slept in the fanciest office. It wasn't the least bit more comfortable, but he liked to think he was maintaining *standards*. Everything was just too much at the moment. He would enjoy what humor he could find.

Truth could feel a good bit of moping coming on. He slapped his hands against his cheeks instead. "No moping! Today will be a busy but good day. Today, we start applying pressure directly to the System Astrologica. A positive, can-do attitude is required!"

He dusted himself off, packed his things, and set off back to the university. This time, he resolved to use his time a little more productively. There was a burglary target in the university, so it seemed foolish not to maximize his time. He would burgle, murder, then investigate a Starbrite office before raiding it. A full day.

The burglary target, according to Merkovah's information, was in the Thomas and Martha Walton Center for Excellence in High-Energy Thaumaturgy. Truth was a bit stuck when he saw it. How, exactly, does one describe sheer architectural violence?

It started, naturally, with concrete. A sort of white, or maybe gray . . . actually, it was hard to say if the color was intended or the result of pollution and rain. It was the exact shade of depression. Windows, naturally, failed to be the same size or even on the same horizontal plane, tilting and morphing as they meandered across the walls. The overall shape of the building was somewhere between a stepped pyramid and the result of someone taking snuff made of colored tobacco and sneezing onto a startled octopus.

There was a large plaque next to the door. Apparently, the building had won several awards. Truth memorized the names of the awarding bodies, swearing to find them if time permitted.

Mercifully, there was a building directory. His target was the Dr. Franklin Gaspard Memorial Laboratory, overseen by a Dr. Shihamratalmaranpi. His goal was to steal "Every memory crystal and recording talisman you can get your hands on." He was also to expect everything to be in locked cabinets, likely quite well-secured cabinets, and since the whole building was doing work of significant interest to governments and militaries everywhere, he should expect a nontrivial amount of security. Also, the doctor himself was likely at least Level Four, and most of his staff would be Level Two or Three. So, unwise to screw around.

Truth figured that was fair enough, so he adopted a disguise. His clothes screamed "I'm coming back from a workout," so he leaned into it. He splashed water on his face, wetted down his hair, and tried to look tired. He was now a grad student coming back from a workout to start work. It didn't take. He could force it, of course. But it would cost him a lot of energy.

He frowned, then grinned. He was a grad student . . . whose parents bought him his place. He was just there to get his evaluation signed by his professor, then it was straight back to the club. That clicked, no problem. Truth felt very sorry for himself for exactly two seconds and then went to find the lab.

The door was more or less how the information packet described it—heavily locked, and heavily surveilled by recording talismans. Truth used a cunning ruse to bypass them. He knocked on the door.

Nobody answered. He knocked again.

There continued to be silence.

He knocked loudly and continuously, slightly varying his timing, trying to avoid patterns. He kept it up for five minutes. Eventually, an utterly frazzled and completely genuine grad student yanked the door open.

"WHAT?"

"'Sup. Your ears working, brah?"

The door started to slam closed, but Truth caught it and held it open. "No can do, brah; got to get my thingy signed."

"Your *what* signed?"

"Prof S needs to sign my thingy so I can show the admin guy what a great lab assistant I am. You know. The thingy." Truth waved a paper around.

"*Doctor* Shihamratalmaranpi—"

"No idea how you can pronounce that, brah. I'm out by *ham*."

"*Doctor* Shihamratalmaranpi is taking a meeting with Professor Cuinoird. He is not here. And you are definitely not one of his assistants. Tell you what, you have until I can reach the alarm gem to piss off."

"Nah, brah. I am legit an assistant to Doc S. Check the name on the form. Pretty sure you, and the Doc, know my parents." Truth had shifted from boredom to a nasty smile. "Say, brah, how much do you cost? It's got to cost a bit, keeping a full-time lab assistant, right?"

The postdoc started looking sick.

"Not me, brah. I bring money to the lab. You got any Snakeblood? My hangover is killing me. Figure I can wait in a nice, quiet lab for Doc S."

"Sure. Yeah. Just, you know, don't touch anything. Uh . . . we may have Snakeblood in the fridge. Blue flavor okay?"

"Shit yeah, brah, just not Green."

"I'll check." He led Truth into the lab.

"Any idea on Doc's ETA? I thought he was going to be in by now." Truth looked around the lab. He didn't know what he was expecting, but scrupulously clean black stone tables was not it. A lot of very complicated, very clearly cobbled-together formations, and some talismans that looked badly in need of maintenance, even if he didn't know what they did.

"Uh. He was supposed to be in by now. Apparently, Cuinoird got his hands on some test platform they wanted for a joint project."

"Oh, sweet." Truth didn't care, and it showed in his voice. Then he frowned. "Wait. I know that name. Cuinoird. Isn't he a bio guy?"

"Yeah. It's one of those not-secret-at-all secrets. He's working on human-Nephilim hybridization."

"Brah, even I know how to do that. Fuck a Nephilim."

"I mean, after a person is already born. And, you know, not compatible." The lab assistant shrugged.

"So, what's that got to do with Doc S?"

"Nephilim hold more and more energy in their bodies as they get older. They are actually more energy-dense than human mages of a roughly comparable level. A lot more. Like . . . crazy more. So much more that they should just explode or turn into toxic goo. But they don't. They can store that energy safely somehow. So, I can't tell you the details, but I think you can figure out why they are working together on something. And why your parents are probably sponsoring Cuinoird, too."

Truth nodded. The name had clicked into place. It was the professor Sophia was studying under. It had been in one of the drops, along with details about what Harmony was up to. No information about Vigor, of course. Who Truth had left in alarming circumstances back in Conjin.

Perhaps it was that, or the lack of beauty sleep, or the sheer stress and pressure of the last few weeks. Perhaps it was the isolation in the horrible, depressing apartment. Whatever it was, Truth made an uncharacteristically selfish decision.

"You know what? No offense, brah, but I don't feel like hanging around. Where is Cuinoird's office?"

"You want to burst in on a meeting of two of the top natural philosophers in the world so they can sign your 'thingy'?"

"Brah. Were you not paying attention? I'm being forced to run around after *the help*. Now. Where are they?"

Truth ignored the building the bio-labs were in. Presumably, it was some sort of architectural horror. That wasn't important right now. He was fixated on seeing Sophia.

He didn't know why, exactly. It just seemed like the most important thing in the world to confirm that she was alive and well. That she was, in fact, thriving. That even at the end of days, she was following her dreams. That she was getting everything out of education that Truth had dreamed for her. But most of all that she was okay. That even without her big bro hovering around, she was okay.

He made his way to Cuinoird's laboratory. It too was festooned with security measures, uselessly so, because the door had been propped open with a chair. The reason quickly became obvious, as it banged open and a young woman rushed out. She was passed by a young man rushing in. Two minutes later, he was out again, and a third person, another woman, was rushing in.

"I don't give a damn, not one damn! My patrons demand results, and you whine about funds? You tell them that Cuinoird demands his order this instant, and if they want their fee, they can wait their turn. And if they don't give it to you, I expect you to leap over the counter and beat them until they cough it up!"

"Professor, that's—"

"Your job, or you may see yourself out and go whistle for any sort of reference!"

There was a long silence. "Yes, Professor."

There was another flurry of activity.

"Imbeciles. The most obvious things in the world need to be explained, yet they expect to be coddled like geniuses." Truth had never met Professor Cuinoird before, and he already didn't like him. Still, when god complexes open a door . . .

He walked in. There was an intense, charismatic man, if a bit whiffy, bent over a naked woman. Truth didn't recognize the woman. There was a light projection above her, showing a tiny collection of dividing cells. This was apparently the subject of immense interest to the professor. Truth didn't know which of the hangers-on was Doctor Shihamratalmaranpi, but it didn't really matter. He didn't see Sophia, either, which mattered a great deal more. Maybe she was one of the runners.

"Excuse me, Professor? I heard you needed some things collected by someone willing to use violence to obtain them?"

"What slanderous—" The professor spun around, clocked Truth's physique, and slammed to a halt. "Young man, how well do you know your genealogy?"

"I know my father and mother, and my siblings." Truth shrugged.

"Would you like an exciting opportunity to participate in a research study?"

"Probably not."

"I would pay considerably more for your assistance than I would for package collection."

Truth hesitated. Sophia worked in this laboratory. It could be a way to see her.

"Let's say I'm open to it. But I wouldn't want to pull you away from the business at hand." He nodded at the naked woman. She appeared to be awake but didn't appear aware of anything going on around her. Odd.

"Mmm. First sensible thing I have heard in an hour that I didn't say. Have a seat somewhere." Truth hopped up on a lab table and watched the work. He didn't understand a single blessed thing that was happening. He did notice Sophia coming out of a little room off to one side of the lab. A few minutes later, a rather harried young man brought around mugs of coffee for the already-tenured.

Truth felt Incisive tingling. He frowned, focusing on that feeling more. Usually, he only got a bare second's worth of notice of danger. Unless it was quite a big danger.

One of the coffee drinkers spat out their drink, spraying the naked woman. "What the hell is in this coffee?!"

Truth turned toward Sophie. She looked surprised. No, she looked "surprised." He got his feet under him and leapt toward her. The blast caught him before he even got clear of the table.

CHAPTER 46

HEY, SIS

The season very sickly everywhere of strange and fatal fevers."

Truth had no idea where the words came from, or why he thought of them as the explosion drove him toward Sophia. She looked like she was ducking in slow motion, a sleepy bird in front of Truth's terrifying reflexes. He tackled her, pinning her to the ground as the blast roared over them.

He was so used to fighting, it was a little surreal watching the people in the lab fail to react to a woman exploding. There were bodies on the floor. Some dead, some near death. Didn't seem to be an intact talisman in the room, either. He could feel Sophia starting to squirm. She had the good sense to be wearing discreet armor plate under her clothes, though given the circumstances, that wasn't a good look. Was she working her arm around to pull a weapon on him?

It almost brought a tear to his eye. He had really raised her right. He hopped up. Sophia was still Level One. That was normal, actually, but still not good. His cheek twitched. Actually, it was very good. She would have a harder time surviving the collapse of civilization, but she would survive the collapse of magic far better than the Level Threes and Fours in the room.

Looking down at his sister, he could only silently salute the Medici ability to make literally anything a problem and beat simple solutions to death with a shovel. Probably a stolen shovel, because blood will tell. He hesitated a bit on that last thought. He was being unfair. Sophia wasn't like her brothers. She would engineer some kind of shovel-beast to do the beating for her.

He offered her a hand up. "All right there?"

"Yes, thank you. Where did you come from?" She sounded shaky, which was fair enough.

"Other side of the room. Prof C wanted to recruit me as a test subject, though I think that plan is now off."

Sophia looked around the room, then gasped in horror. "Oh, no, Professor!" She rushed over, patting him down. Truth kept a sharp eye on her. Had she hidden something in her palm before touching the professor?

"Off. Off! Call a doctor if you are so concerned. I have my potions, stupid girl! Damn! Who sabotaged me?!" Cuinoird's voice was thready, coming from behind the ruins of the lab bench. The walls were painted with the woman who had been on the table, as well as several of the people who had been around it. He didn't know how many were still alive, other than Sophia, Cuinoird, and himself. Not a high number. Time to be elsewhere.

"Yes, Professor, at once!"

She rushed out of the lab, Truth trailing along behind her. She went straight to the security call box and reported the explosion. She then, to Truth's mild surprise, did not return to the lab but rushed back to her dorm, collapsed into bed, and curled into a ball. She shook. It looked like she was choking down sobs.

Truth looked around the room. Two sets of bunk beds—a four-person dorm. About middle of the pack as dorm rooms went, from what he had vaguely picked up over the years. Not a million miles from barrack rooms, if a million times messier.

She hadn't seen him at all. Since the moment she rushed over to the Professor, Truth had simply ceased to exist for her. He wasn't deliberately hiding. It was just that, these days, he had to make a conscious effort to let Level Ones see him. He could caress her, pat her head, hug her like he used to when they were children, and she would have no conscious awareness of it. The rules of the world would forbid it.

Sophia, his blood, the sister he loved and the sibling he was most proud of, was too far below him. Cultivation was a big piece of that, but so was . . . everything. The accumulated weight of his blessings, his spells, his understanding of the world. He was seeing layers to things that she likely didn't have language for. Not because she was stupid. She was certainly a lot smarter than he was. Just because she didn't have all the information. She hadn't experienced the same things he had.

Truth remembered Merkovah explaining the problems with obtaining wisdom by revelation. He had a very true, very accurate understanding of what was going on, but it was all filtered through his perspective and his life experiences. It would therefore be, for anyone he explained it to, some degree of wrong.

You couldn't tell someone "the truth." They had to see it for themselves. What a world.

So, what, exactly, did he want? What, exactly, did he want to do there? All the arguments for not revealing himself to Vig applied triple to Sophia. Not only would it put both of them in unreasonable danger with no benefits, she was still enmeshed in Jeon society. She was still part of that system. A goddamn university lab assistant.

Ohshit! ThatlabI'msupposedtobreakinto!

Truth jolted out of his maudlin musings. Hopefully, he wasn't too late! Truth leapt away from Sophia's bed and sprinted back across campus to Dr. S's lab.

To his immense amusement, it looked like others had the same idea. A pair of aggressively ordinary-looking twentysomethings were disarming locks, defeating surveillance, and generally scraping anything of value into a cardboard box marked for storage. Truth stood back and "supervised."

That's right, my friends. You do all the heavy lifting. Be sure and leave plenty of evidence behind, you eager little devils, you.

He was even more amused to see six more people "casually walk past" the office, then hide themselves nearby. What the hell was going on in this university? In a fit of perversity, he let it play out for a while. The box traded hands three times before reaching the edge of the campus, where the thieves piled into a carriage. Truth decided to ride in the back.

"Signal the client."

"Done."

They continued in silence. Truth let them get a few blocks from the university before yanking the steering wheel over and plowing them into a parked carriage. Nobody died, but the box "mysteriously" vanished while they were sorting themselves out.

Truth then merrily zipped over to one of the many dead drops around Harban, stashed the goods, rotated the flowerpot on the ledge next to it until the sun painted on its side faced due east, and noted with a wry lack of surprise that it was filled with blue geraniums. Merkovah wanted to talk. Fair enough. Now, how to do that with any degree of safety?

He smiled up at the sun for a moment, then felt the smile drain away. That had been a diverting few hours. A nice little distraction from the fact he left his sister traumatized, sobbing, and alone in her dorm after her first (hopefully her first) multiple murder. Sophia wasn't like Truth or Vigor. She was a tough kid, a slum kid, but she wasn't as nakedly homicidal as her brothers. So, what could have driven her to do that?

In the long run, hell, in the medium run, it really didn't matter. None of this mattered. Nothing in that cardboard box *really* mattered. All that mattered was finding the girl and cracking the System. Maybe hunting the people who saw themselves ruling the world after the fall. He didn't think he much liked their vision. Wouldn't be too hard to clear out some high-level bureaucrats and "ancient families."

He couldn't clean the board entirely, but maybe he could clear some room for the smaller rats to stand. Learn how not to eat each other. Maybe.

So, what did he want? If he wasn't going to eat his fellow rats? Or at least, try to eat them less? What was he going to do with his shiny new revelation? His little piece of a secret the world itself seemed to want suppressed? It came down to what he wanted and what he needed. He wanted the sibs and Etenesh, and himself, to have some kind of good tomorrow. It was what they needed, too. But he was creaking. He knew he was coming apart under the strain and isolation.

Truth had been in this exact situation before. He tried to work through it. Consequently, he found himself on five years' bed rest in a well.

He had wound himself up, further and further and further because he thought he was the only one who could fix things. The only one who could keep the sibs safe. If literal demons from HR and his Starbrite bosses were telling him in no uncertain terms to get a date and take a vacation, he really should have listened. He should listen now.

Well. There was no beach holiday during the revolution. But maybe he could go hug his sis. It was dangerous. It was greedy. But if he really believed it would all break down without him, it was necessary.

He walked back to the dorm. No longer noticing that he was moving faster than the stop-and-go traffic on the road. Not seeing the way people just got out of his way instinctively as he breezed past them. It had all become normal. He was becoming acclimated to power. Not the social power of the Prince. The power in his own hands.

He appeared at Sophia's dorm room again and was about to let himself in but hesitated. He could see multiple, redundant locks and security mechanisms on the door. Truth smiled and knocked.

No answer.

He knocked again.

There continued to be no answer.

He knocked out the tune of a song he remembered hearing as he drove through the Free State. He probably didn't nail it, but he figured it was pretty close. He was reaching minute two when the door was yanked open by a visibly pissed-off Sophia, with an equally visible asp wand in her hand. Always good to see your sister was taking good care of herself. She squinted at him a bit before asking—

"You are the guy from the lab. Why are you here?"

"To see you, mostly."

The asp wand got raised higher.

"I have a boyfriend."

"Oh, great! I have a girlfriend. I think you will like her. I sure hope so, anyway."

This seemed to throw her for a moment.

"Are you . . . after some kind of polygamous arrangement?"

"With you? Gross. And no, my girlfriend would absolutely, one hundred percent not be okay with that. And I respect that." Truth shook his head with the serious look of an older brother winding up a younger sibling.

"You turn up at my apartment and call me gross. Fantastic. Go away."

"You aren't gross. Wait, are you gross? Doesn't your boyfriend mind?" Truth asked.

Sophia was getting visibly more irritated, but then, to Truth's amazement, she took a deep breath and calmed herself down.

"Who are you, exactly?"

Truth gave a crooked little grin. "That is a matter of some dispute, philosophically and legally. And a very long story. May I come in?"

"No. Why have you come to see me?" Her eyes narrowed.

"Because I'm not really hanging in there well. I'm starting to come apart. Actually, I have been coming apart for a while now. And I could really use some company."

"Shook up after the explosion?" Sophia asked, her eyes getting a little softer.

"Something like that."

She hesitated, then nodded. "You can come in, but you sit in the chair. I'm taking the sofa. Just keep your distance and we'll be fine." She waved the asp wand. Truth nodded thankfully.

They sat. Sophia looked around, clearly not knowing how this was supposed to go. "Do you want a glass of water or something?"

"No, thank you." Truth fidgeted. How do you tell someone you came back from the dead? "So. You wanted to know my name?"

"Yes, that's probably a good place to start."

"Well, there's a lot of people that call me Johnny Wells, or Tommy Bells. In any case, I'm a certified talisman-maintenance technician."

She snorted a little at that.

"And the talisman-maintenance bit is true. But the name isn't." He took a deep breath. "And this is where I start running into legal trouble." She waved her hand, encouraging him along. He grasped around for some way to prove his identity.

"One day, that pedophile pimp Thierrie lured you toward an alley with a cigarette. Your oldest brother turned up seconds later with an empty beer bottle and chased him off. A couple of days after that, Thierrie vanished, and a couple days after *that*, your oldest brother broke through to Level One and less than a month later passed his SATs and emancipated you all and took you to live in the Tier-C apartment of his dreams."

Truth was rambling, speaking quickly. "And his name was Truth Medici, and he died on an op for Starbrite. But he didn't stay dead. He did a shit-ton of body cultivation and changed his face and physique. And now he's come home." Truth was almost gasping by the end. "Hello, Sophia. I'm back. And you have a lot of questions for me."

CHAPTER 47

MEDICI FAMILY VALUES

Sophia didn't even blink. The asp wand flicked up and she tried to shoot from around knee-high. Incisive saw it coming. Between the warning and her concrete-slow movement, he flicked it away with an outstretched foot.

"Glad to see I raised you right." His voice was bone-dry. "Why don't you grill me on details of our childhood instead? Or ask what happened? You won't win a fight."

"You have no idea what I am capable of." Her voice was deadly calm.

"Yeah, but why don't you go ahead and list every fight I lost? Dad doesn't count."

She hesitated a moment. "You tell me. You are the one answering questions, apparently."

"I didn't. Largely because I picked my fights carefully and didn't fight unless it was absolutely necessary and I was sure I could win. Eeh . . . except against Thierrie, but he was going to rape Vig, so call it an exception. Now, did I catch a shitload of beatings from Level One gangsters while I was out scavenging or running errands or whatever? Yes. But like with Mom and Dad, that was catching a beating, not a fight." Truth kept the tone casual.

"Oh, really? A real tough guy, eh?"

He gave her a crooked smile. "Didn't you tell me once you thought I lost my cherry as both a virgin and a killer when I was about fourteen?"

"Did I?" She kept her face flat. He was mildly impressed.

"You did. It was after you and Vigor got in trouble for scrapping with those kids in your school, on account of you fucking their significant others. A habit I was happy to see you stopped, by the way. Clearly, focusing on your schoolwork paid off." He smiled. He was genuinely happy for her, too. Her getting into the University of Jeon was a dream for both of them.

"Well, with such a long suspension, I was scared straight."

"Nah, you can do better. Clearly, as a top-secret super spy, I researched your academic history. Discipline goes on your permanent record, and yours is clean."

"Not clean—"

"If you graduated with a single black mark, it happened after I vanished. Vice Principal whatshisname knew it was *his* ass if my sibs had any problems in school."

She hesitated a moment. "Actually, I always wondered what happened there."

Truth smiled. It wasn't a nice smile. "How much do you know about the Starbrite Oath?"

"Same as everybody, I guess?"

"Notice the bit about obeying all local laws as may apply?"

"Sure." She shrugged.

"For enough credits, Starbrite will sell you an indulgence. Terms and conditions apply, but you can literally spend money to exempt yourself from some of the terms of your oath for a limited period. I bought one. Offing a Level One D-Tier principal? I fucking overpaid. I could have caught his whole damn family with him and still had change left over. And he knew it."

She blinked at that. "You can just ignore laws with an indulgence?"

"I *could* ignore the part of my oath that made me obey the law. And that 'obey the law' bit had . . . let us say . . . a very narrow interpretation. In that it only applied in a narrow selection of circumstances."

"Huh." She seemed to be considering this. "And the consequences of breaking the law?"

"Would have been on me to deal with. But my usual C-Tier benefits would have applied, along with PMC privilege. Provided I was reasonably discreet, there would be no consequences to speak of." His voice turned grim. Those privileges came at a damn high price.

"Ah. Makes sense. So. You are apparently my brother, who, for all his flaws, was downright doting and very protective of his siblings. And just vanished for five years. Or, as I was informed, in writing, by your boss, was dead."

"Oh, that was nice of Clavegaugh, I guess." Sounded off.

"I'm pretty sure it was a form letter."

"There you go." Truth nodded. *That* sounded more like it.

"So. You look good for a dead man. Not much like my brother. A bit meaty. But fit."

"First of all, hurtful. Second, I got better."

"Explain that."

"I don't think I ever told you how I broke through? I just came back in the middle of the night."

"Yes."

"You thought I had died."

"Did we?" she asked, in a bare monotone.

"You did."

"Oh." To Truth's pride and pain, she looked like she was shutting down more, not opening up more.

"Vig ever tell you what happened to Thierrie?"

"No."

Truth smiled painfully and laid out how he broke through and what happened on the mission to the Free State. Her facade cracked a couple of times. To Truth's irritation, it wasn't any of the life-or-death things that did it.

"Wait, you are part Ghūl?" Sophia leaned in.

"Obviously not!"

"Actually, not so obvious." She shook her head.

"I am almost nothing like them! The bits that are similar are . . . We are all human-shaped," Truth protested.

"Yes, but one of the few things we *do* understand about the Ghūl is that they are not the bodies they wear." That threw Truth for a minute.

"The bodies they wear?"

"Yes!" Her face lit up. "As best we can tell, they are unique spiritual beings. They process the bodies somehow to make them resistant to magic and then insert a Ghūl into them. What that means specifically is still being debated."

"I would think anything that makes a person magically resistant would be a major study priority!"

"Oh, it is. It really, really is." She nodded fervently. "It's just that getting materials is *a little difficult* and results have been frustratingly slow."

"How slow? I mean, Ghūl have been around forever, as far as I know."

"Actually, no, they are comparatively new on this planet. Sub one thousand years is our best guess. And they are not evenly distributed, for lack of a better term. We don't have good census numbers for equally obvious reasons, but basically, they don't turn up without a good environment for them to thrive in."

Truth smiled crookedly. "And since they thrive in Jeon, what does that say about us?"

"Nothing good." Sophia grinned back. "Any theories about why you have this connection with them?"

"On any kind of sane, biological level? Nope. On a wild-ass theory pulled together from my *deeply* weird experiences of the last year? Baptism."

That got him a blank look.

"Eh?"

"Baptism. I think that whatever was in that 'tonic' made me just enough of a Ghūl to pass muster, and when I . . . basically coated myself with their shattered bodies, I was baptized, and when I destroyed their birthing vats, I was baptized a second time."

"But . . . why would that have any effect?" Sophia cocked her head to one side.

"Because I don't think what they did to me, or I did to myself, is active on this level of reality. I think it's a higher-level function. That, and they seem to be related to the Nephilim somehow, and so are we. So, there is that."

Sophia went very still again. "Why do you think we are related to the Nephilim?"

"I met one of their hybrids, and—"

"Wait, there are human-Nephilim hybrids on this planet?" She was suddenly agitated.

"Yes? At least one big family of them?"

"How? Why?!"

"The usual way, I assume. And as for why, they are playing for the world after the collapse."

There was a pause. Truth could see the moment Sophia's brain caught up with her ears.

"The what now?"

"The collapse? Of magic?"

She sagged. "Oh, that old conspiracy theory."

Truth shook his head. "It's not a conspiracy theory. I have guarded high-level conferences, multinational conferences involving senior bureaucrats, where they discussed how to handle the coming crop failures. They talked about the collapse in very specific terms. The Temple of Siphios acknowledges it, as does the Church of Prager. Jeon and Starbrite keep it locked down, but they are prepping too. All the aristo families know and are prepping, and like I said, the Nephilim are too."

Sophia rocked back in her chair. Her eyes darted back and forth. It looked like she was remembering something or some things.

"Connecting dots?"

"Yes." Her answer was short. Truth shrugged. Fair enough, really. The end of the world was pretty shocking. Well, not strictly the end of the world, but functionally. She looked up at him, glaring.

"Why are you here? Now?"

"Because I'm hurting. Because I built my whole life around you guys, and you were always the one thing that made all the . . . everything . . . worthwhile. And because you didn't let me finish explaining how I came back to life, and you didn't ask the most important question."

"More important than the secret of your resurrection?"

"Yes. How I died."

Twenty minutes later, Sophia was staring at the wall. Truth waited patiently, then impatiently, then started looking at the door.

"When do your roommates get back?"

"Who knows?"

"Sophia . . ."

"Oh, shut up for a minute." She didn't mutter, but her mind was obviously elsewhere.

He waited a little longer. "Got anything to read here?" She waved at a low bookcase of textbooks and journals.

"I was thinking more . . . cheap romance novels, mysteries, thrillers, that kind of thing." He was entirely willing to admit that he didn't even understand the titles of these publications and had no illusions about the contents.

She wrinkled her nose at him. "Ew."

"What 'ew'? They are great!"

"I don't think there is a single original concept in any of them let alone useful information."

"Aha! That's where you are wrong. I have relied on romance novels a lot."

"For what? Disappointing women?"

Truth felt that one land but pressed on. "First, no, my girlfriend laughed at the lines, and they kept me from saying dumb things. So, that's a clean win. Second, they give me personas to imitate, and it is *amazing* how much people believe in them."

"I wish I didn't believe you."

Truth looked over at her, catching her eyes. "Do you believe me?"

She closed her eyes and leaned back on the sofa. "I don't know. Maybe. Five years. And they weren't very nice years."

The way she said it tore up his guts. "Can you tell me about it?"

"I don't want to. A teenage orphan, even with a great pension and a guaranteed C-Tier job waiting for them, does not have a nice time. Harmony tried to step up, and he did a pretty good job, but you were the only one who could ever keep Vig under any kind of control. And Harmony is doing fine, I guess, but I see less and less of him every year. And Vig said he was dropping out of sight for a long while, and he did just that, so who knows what happened to him."

"Oh, I know. He joined a revolutionary cell. I saw him up north. Didn't say hi; the timing was bad." Truth said with forced casualness. It got him a wild stare.

"He is doing *what*?"

"Certified revolutionary, yeah, though not really performing at the highest levels. His work is not great but not completely terrible. I'd rate his performance as barely passing, honestly, but my standards are pretty strict."

"Yes, I, too, am concerned about my brother's professional qualifications and standards as a *fucking terrorist* who will be caught and *executed!*" she hissed.

"Err. Valid." Truth had neglected to mention what he was doing in Jeon, hadn't he . . .

"So . . . what now? What exactly are you doing in Jeon?"

Well. Fuck.

"Looking for the Shattervoid girl and, if at all possible, murdering the shit out of the System Astrologica."

"In Harban?"

"Where else would the system be?" Truth shrugged, though he agreed with Sophia.

"Under the biggest rock in the deepest trench in the middle of the ocean? Because Starbrite is Level Nine and *Starbrite*, so he doesn't have to give a shit about little things like 'cost' or 'practicality.'"

Truth immediately felt vindicated. "I one hundred percent agree! But nobody has been able to run down the System, so here I am."

"What do you mean, *run it down*?"

"Nobody has the faintest damn idea where it is."

Sophia nodded, then looked up at the ceiling. Then back to Truth and gave him a weird look. "You said that you don't think the Ghūl operate on this level of reality?"

"Well, some part of them, yeah."

"What if the System worked the same way?"

CHAPTER 48

SOMETIMES, WHAT YOU CAN'T SEE ISN'T THERE

Truth slowly blinked at Sophia.

"Could you just . . . walk me through that idea?"

Sophia grinned a little. "System Astrologica, the work-tracking and spell-delivery system for Starbrite. Starbrite employees can be found everywhere on the planet, in orbit, and even on the moon, but there is not the slightest chance in hell they would go anywhere the System didn't reach."

Truth nodded along. "Yep."

"Also, as far as I'm aware, nothing can jam it or block it. It is always in effect," she continued.

"Also correct."

"But it shouldn't be. Magic operates on fixed, known principles. We are always learning more about those principles, but the basic rules are pretty nailed down at this point."

"Really?" This was news to Truth. Sophia rolled her eyes and nodded.

"Yes. For example, rules like *There is no effect without a cause, every cause requires energy, all energy has an origin.*" Things like that."

"Are those actually provable bits of natural philosophy, or did someone program a golem to come up with aphorisms?" This time, it was Truth who rolled his eyes. Sophia counterrolled.

"Provable. You want the proof?" She pointed at her little bookshelf. "Right there. The statement is a few words. The math demonstrating the principle can run hundreds of pages long."

Truth blinked in shock. "Damn. I had no idea."

"Nobody does. It drives me kind of nuts. But that is what natural philosophy *is*. Looking at the world, making a guess about why it's the way it is, then trying to prove that."

"All right. So, why can't the System Astrologica be explained by conventional natural philosophy?"

"Because there is no effect without a cause, and there is no cause without energy, and all energy has an origin." She leaned forward, her fingers coming up and tracing through the air. "Let's say you needed a spell. I don't know . . ."

"Shockwave."

"Sure, Shockwave. You tell the System Astrologica, 'Hey, I need Shockwave.' So, that's you, the origination point, using your energy to send a message. The System receives that message and sends you Shockwave. Okay, great. How?"

Truth shrugged. He hadn't yet explained how the System mutilated the soul. Didn't seem relevant so far.

"Search me. I always just thought, *Load Shockwave*, then the notification popped up—*Shockwave loaded. Mission Critical Spell. No Charge.*

She looked fascinated. "What was that like?"

Truth searched for the words. "You could feel the System when it first activates in your body. Like a little . . . something, partially filling your first aperture. It fades with time, and you just stop noticing it. But you can feel when whatever spell you originally had loaded leaves you, which gives you a horrible, empty feeling, then a new spell comes in, which feels so satisfying. Like . . . sinking into a hot bath is satisfying. You feel right."

"And there is no visual sign of it happening? Or anything beyond a feeling of satisfaction?"

"No. Other than the Notice from the System, I mean."

"That is so cool." She breathed out excitedly. "I want the System."

Truth shook his head hard. "You don't. You absolutely do not want the System. At all. Ever. In any way shape or form. Including the new Citizenship system."

<<Hurtful. And mutual.>>

You want to spread more of your "siblings" around?

"But we are getting sidetracked. Why does this mean the System Astrologica exists on another level of reality?" Truth pressed.

"Well. Where is the spell coming from? I mean that literally. The information that contains the spell." She waved a book around. "If I were to try to jam all the information in this book into your head, physically put the actual physical book *in your head*, you would know exactly where it was coming from and how it got there."

She put the book down, then pointed at him. "Load *Malunions and Nonunions in the Shin, Ankle, and Feet, 27th edition!*" She then spread her hands. "And all this complicated information got into your head . . . how, exactly?"

"Magic?"

"Obviously, but how? No effect without a cause, no cause without energy, no energy without an origin. So, assuming that the System Astrologica is the 'origin,' how does it use its 'energy' to create the effect of you knowing the contents of a medical textbook? Or Shockwave, for that matter? What does Shockwave do, anyway?"

"What it says—it creates a high-pressure wave in the air or water. Or solid materials too, actually, but the air and water were the bits I cared about."

"That sounds kind of dumb."

"Yeah? So, if I were to send a high-pressure wave through a fifty-four-kilo sack of mostly water, what happens to all the not-water things in the sack?"

Sophia winced. "Right."

"So, why can't the System Astrologica be a series of transmitters communicating with a single, supremely powerful spirit of intellect? The System handles all the communication side of things; it is permanently a part of you, after all. So, the user does not think about it or know about it."

<<*That is . . . actually a really good question. I don't know how it works either. I just had some bit of me that could send and receive messages with the main System. Still there, actually. No idea how the messages traveled. I have only your energy to work with, after all, and I could never just use it however I wanted.*>>

"Theoretically it could, but—energy. Those cosmic rays come from the cosmos, yes, but we can trace the origins of most of them backward to their source. Same deal with communication altars. We can track the signal's origins and disrupt transmissions by using any means that disrupts the flow of cosmic rays. Which can be a lot of things, ranging from flooding the aether with more spells, to certain metals, to just a lot of 'stuff.' Rocks and water, for example. So, in practice, the System *cannot* be transmitting messages from under the biggest rock in the deepest trench in the ocean," Sophie explained.

"Relays wouldn't cut it?"

"Relays that no one can spot, that work in every tunnel, in every mineshaft, in orbit, on the *fucking moon?*"

"Could beam the message up to the moon," Truth said, playing angel's advocate.

"That nobody can spot? Ever? For however many decades or centuries Starbrite has been around?"

"That is still an . . . open question. How long Starbrite has been around, I mean."

"Who cares? *Longer than we have been alive* is the answer. Centuries, probably. And in all that time, not one person found a transmission station or relay tower? Ones powerful enough to work literally everywhere on the planet? Just because it's the simplest explanation doesn't mean it's right. And there is no available evidence to support the 'hidden transmitters' hypothesis." Sophie shrugged.

"Still kind of a jump from there to *So, the transmissions are coming from a higher tier of reality*, though." Truth wiggled his hand. Sophie flicked hers, brushing aside his argument.

"Again, not really. We know some degree of interaction with higher tiers of reality is possible. It's how almadels work for one thing—literally poking holes through reality to reach Heaven." Truth nodded fervently. He had firmly gone off almadels since Happori. Sophie continued.

"And it's not my field, but I know items from higher realities do land on this planet, and they can distort the area around them. To the extent of changing the nature of the universe there. Some spells alter your degree of reality, too. Some forms of spell resistance create a sort of local superreality."

"Yep. Body cultivation, for one." Truth grinned.

"Um. Yeah, I guess." She looked distracted for a moment but recovered. "So, think about what that actually means. The spell, or the thing from a higher reality or whatever, is affecting the world at a level the rest of the world just can't operate on. In those reality-incursion situations, we, the people stuck in this reality, *cannot even perceive the thing making the changes.*"

Sophie liked to use inflection a lot, Truth noticed. It was interesting. A complete turnaround from the flat monotone she had used when interrogating him. This, exploring the bounds of the world, learning and discussing new things, was what made her excited. Her eyes were bright, her hands spoke as fast as her lips, and the words came trippingly from her tongue. This was what she loved. Truth smiled, happy for her.

"I have been to one of those places. There was a drop of water that tried to rewrite the world around me, so that I could perceive colors that don't exist in this universe. At least, humans can't see them."

"Oh, cool! Where?"

"A former agroforestry research station in southwest Siphios. A good time was not had by all." Truth's voice turned dry. Those birds had messed him up.

"I still can't believe you went to Siphios. Of all the insanely dangerous places . . ."

"It's lovely, actually. The people are friendly, the food is good, the scenery is better. And Sophia, remind me where we grew up again? Was it the High Aristocrat District?"

She rolled her eyes. "That's different."

"It really isn't. The whole world is a slum. You just need to know how to get around."

"Oh, very edgy. Careful you don't cut yourself there."

"I'll spare you my rat-based theory of existence, then. So, the System Astrologica exists outside of our physical reality?"

"Eeeh." Sophia wiggled her hand. "*Physical* is a kind of loaded word, like *material.* Don't get hung up on it. But basically, yes."

She put the textbook on the table, then put a pen on the book. "Okay, this is the transceiver system. Wherever the pen's shadow falls is where the System reaches." She held the pen vertically. Most of the light was coming from the ceiling. It didn't cast much of a shadow.

"Alternatively, imagine you were the System. You are seeing the whole surface of the book because you are positioned above it. And if you reach down, you can affect that surface."

Truth slowly nodded. "I think I'm following your analogy. Because it's not really connected to the planet, it can see the whole planet and as far away as the moon. It is literally looking at things from outside our three dimensions, and it's able to ignore our reality to an extent, so it can reach everywhere, transmit information everywhere."

"Exactly." She nodded. "Like a vast, all-seeing eye."

"Noooo . . ." Truth's voice trailed off. "No, not like an eye."

"Oh? What, then?"

"Like a spell aperture."

"Huh?" Now Sophie looked confused.

"A spiritual superstructure built over the physical body. It has defined characteristics. We describe it as having walls, as being full or collapsing, but what we are talking about is something we can't directly touch. You could cut open a thousand people and never find a spell aperture."

She nodded slowly, then with increasing speed. "Yes. Something that we cannot directly touch but can only influence through cosmic rays and cosmic energy. The System Astrologica almost certainly relies on cosmic energy in some form but at a level we cannot perceive. We can only interact with it through spells."

Truth slowly shook his head. "No. Not spells."

"Eh. Call it what you like, but at the end of the day, it's all spells."

"Not the System Astrologica. It goes in at the level of the soul."

"Huh?" Sophia looked puzzled again.

"The System Astrologica doesn't interface directly with your mind. It comes in through your soul."

"I have to tell you, that might be what it feels like, but it's not how anything works. The soul does not think. It just is."

"The nous does, to some extent. The soul and the mind are in contact." Truth was firm on this. He had reason to be.

"I suppose. Not really my field. Still, your psyche has to process the information—"

"It comes in through the soul. That is *exactly* what the swearing-in ritual is for. Creating that connection."

"Oh. Huh. Can you explain that more?"

Truth nodded. This next part wouldn't be very nice. Then he pulled up with a jolt. "Hey, if the System Astrologica is some kind of higher-dimensional entity that is coming at us through the soul . . . wouldn't that make it a demon?"

"I think spirits of intellect are pretty pissy about the nomenclature. They certainly don't consider themselves demons," Sophia disagreed.

Truth nodded at that, but all he could think of was *What if the System Astrologica is a stellar eminence?*

CHAPTER 49

IT CAN ALWAYS BE WORSE

The dorm room had gone quiet again. Truth's alarmingly detailed explanation of just what the System was, and why the national enrollment was near suicide, had rocked her. As had the idea that all of it was just Starbrite stepping up his escape plan. Or that the Starbrite her brother had worshiped his entire life had tried to kill him.

Truth had privately connected some lines between *Shattervoid are able to move through the void between stars* to *The System Astrologica is a higher-dimensional entity* with a particular underscoring of the memory of that shuttle being spaghettified live on scry. Then he wondered how much power, and what kind of power, would be needed to do that.

"So. Why are you here?"

"In Jeon?"

"In my dorm. In my lab. Coming back into my life." She didn't sound hostile. Just numb. Truth figured that was fair enough. It had been a hell of a day.

"Short version? It's very cold on the outside." He didn't realize how shaky his smile looked. "I just repress everything. Choke it all down and deal. Same as I always did. But the simple fact is that I spend all day, every day, in hiding. My life is defined by violence—either being the source of it or the victim of it. I have no one I can really talk to. No one I can really put my trust in."

Her face twitched. Looked like there was a lot of that going around.

"So, I was doing some light burglary, found out that your professor was nearby, and dropped by his lab to see if I could see you. Just . . . see you. Like with Vig. Make sure you were doing okay, that life was going the way I always hoped it would for you. Then things went a little sideways, and here I am."

Sophia closed her eyes and leaned her head back on the sofa. "A little sideways."

"A little sideways." Truth nodded.

"How would you define *very sideways*?"

"The whole building blows up in an explosion of unnatural energies that causes things we do not have the language to describe to pour through the thin membrane of the 'real.'"

"Yes, that would be bad." Her voice was very dry. He wasn't sure if it was emotional exhaustion or actual sarcasm. They fell silent for a moment.

"I believe you, by the way. Because you are clearly much higher-level than I am, and stronger than I am, and there is literally nothing you could gain from playing this game on me. Even just sadism wouldn't explain it. There are so many worse ways to hurt me emotionally."

Truth started to lean forward but she waved him back. "Hypothetically. I haven't been bullied, beyond Jeon normal."

"That's actually a lot of bullying," Truth said. "The whole country is built around fearing the strong and bullying the weak."

"Yeah. But it's normal. So, I can deal. You are, despite how you look, my dead brother, slightly Ghūlified, come back on a mission of . . . I don't know. Chaos. Revolution. Something. Making preparations against the end of the world."

"Yeah." He nodded. "It's a job. Gig comes with some good benefits, and if I can't get us off-world, we have a place to retreat to in Siphios."

"God. What about Har?"

"I . . . don't have a good solution. You don't know what it's like. How natural it all becomes. He's now had the System for a lot longer than I ever did. I really don't know what I can do other than stay far, far away from him."

"Because he would betray you?"

"He wouldn't think of it that way, but yes."

"Fuck." The word slipped from her mouth, dropping into the silent room. Truth let it lie there awhile.

"So. First time?" he asked.

She jerked her head around and gave him a hard look. "I've never been blown up before, no."

Truth silently laughed. Some things really did run in the blood, it seemed. "It doesn't get easier, exactly, but you do get used to it. Anything in the slums can become normal."

She snorted. "Long way from the slums."

"No. This is the slums, and we are all slumrats. You, me, the professor, everyone. I have developed an entire rat-based social, theological, economic, and political philosophical system built around the dual notions of world-as-slum and everyone-is-a-rat. It is very sophisticated and deep. You should look impressed." Truth was firm on this. She snorted again.

"Oh, yes, very impressed."

"Good. You should be."

"And how did my cheap-romance-novel-reading brother manage this feat?"

"Talking to people, mostly, then thinking about things and trying to understand what it is I actually saw and experienced rather than what I thought I saw and experienced."

She shrugged a little. "I guess that works, though I don't really see the connection."

Truth smiled. He had an itch to move, and he listened to it. "I think someone is coming, so I'm going. But let me ask you two questions. One—if you knew that we would cease to be a magic-based civilization in a year or so, what would you do? Keep in mind this is a serious question, because it isn't coming; it's happening now.

Two—if your life is one of suffering because bullying is normal and that's 'just how the real world works,' why? Why is that 'just how it is'? If everyone is in pain, or most everyone, why?"

She shrugged. "Why does an apple fall from a tree?"

"To make more apples. Or if you are talking about gravity, I can't change gravity. I can't change *people*. But I can change one person." He tapped his chest. "Love you, Sophia. You won't see me again for a while. But I hope it brings you comfort knowing I'm alive. Also, and this should go without saying, but just in case—"

"You died five years ago, and I have been speaking with a hallucination brought on by head trauma and the emotional damage of watching so many people die in front of me."

"Yeah. Hug?"

She nodded. It was warm. It hurt. He didn't want it to end, but he heard the locks opening on the door. By the time Sophia opened her eyes and released the hug, her brother had vanished. Like the dream of a ghost.

She held it together for a couple minutes longer, then she broke down and cried.

Truth walked through the campus, not really seeing anything. Had he told Sophia everything she needed to know? Did he tell her everything he wanted to tell her? Was this enough? Or did it just put a cutting edge on his loneliness? He did feel better. It had been a very stupid thing to do, but he did feel better. And Sophia was, unquestionably, a genius.

The System Astrologica couldn't be found everywhere because it didn't exist anywhere in this reality. It stretched its tendrils out, interfacing with all the specially made bits of soul it stamped out of its . . . what, worshipers? Adherents? Prosthetic limbs?

Truth had a sudden recollection of the meaty demon in the hot spring, making prosthetics for ghosts. Had his work inspired others? Or was he simply not the first to have that idea? Either possibility was disturbing.

Of course, the really disturbing question was—if Sophia could think of this just a few minutes after being introduced to the idea, what were the odds that the collected intelligence agencies, national governments, researchers, and high-level mages, over hundreds of years, had not reached the same conclusion?

What were the odds that Merkovah hadn't reached the same conclusion? The old monster wouldn't trust something as vague as *Keep the System jumping and break enough things, and eventually, it will slip, and we can track it.* That wasn't a plan; that was a wish. And Merkovah wasn't going to settle for just hoping for the best.

So . . . what exactly was Truth doing there? Was Sophia wrong in her guess? It was the most reasonable answer, even if he couldn't fault her logic. Or was Merkovah playing a different game with him? One whose goals and purposes were, as yet, unclear?

He would bet on the latter. It would be more . . . on-brand. Merkovah had been pretty candid about the fact he routinely manipulated Truth but made a point of keeping it to "tolerable manipulations." And . . . what would he be doing, if not this?

Well, finding Etenesh and a reasonably private stretch of grass and seeing whether advanced body cultivation or channeling the aspect of God's Consort held up better after ten rounds. Then a light lunch. The afternoon would be a repeat of the experiment, to see if the first set of results were a fluke. *That's* how you do natural philosophy!

But after that? What would he do if he knew the world was ending in just over a year? What would he do about that fact? Would he wait passively? Or would he take steps to make sure the people he cared about were taken care of, as best as possible? That he, himself, would come out okay?

Obviously, the latter. He needed to talk to Merkovah. He wanted in on the Shattervoid Girl hunt. Right now, he didn't give even one shit about razing Harban. He would spread some propaganda, do a few low-key ops, but he flat-out wasn't going to run around being a distraction while the real work got done.

He shook his head and slapped his cheeks. Time to focus. He was absolutely, mortally, unshakably certain that any attempt at communication with Siphios from Harban would be detected and traced, with a hunter team dispatched seconds later. So . . . a quick jaunt out of the city, then.

He quickly ran through his options. Buses and trains he immediately discarded, for all the same old reasons. Roads? Hahaha. No. No more of those GODDAMN roadblocks. Cross-country? Possible, but this wasn't a random small town. There would be air patrols, and they had to have figured out he was doing that by now.

That left air and water. Air was out for the same reason he didn't fly into the city—it would be surveilled. Water? Would presumably also be checked, but . . . he knew the docks. They would be "searching," not searching. And he did have a trick to play there, too. He started walking toward the river. That was the unfortunate thing about life. No matter how your day was going, there was always room for it to get worse.

He picked a likely-looking barge and hopped on. Staring down the river, he could see flying platforms hovering about thirty meters above the water. Quite adequate clearance for most barges. Not moving, just hovering there. Now, if he were a betting man, those platforms would be loaded with surveillance gear and those watcher homunculi. They certainly wouldn't leave a route as big and heavily used as the River Fan go unwatched. Not while the Hell-Prince was on the loose.

He sighed and had a poke-around. He wanted the bottom level of containers. Not because he thought it would help against the watchers. Not really. No, he just wanted the psychological reassurance. *Can't see me. Too much stuff in the way.*

Who do you think you are, the System Astrologica?

It took a bit of work, but he found a good container. A refrigerated container, locked, warded, tracked, and alarmed. Precious cargo. He disabled the security far enough for him to open the door and have a peek inside.

Pigs hung on meat hooks. Stretching back six meters, the container was packed with them. Gutted and cleaned but still whole. Precious cargo, these days. Meat was costing more and more, when it was available at all. Precious cargo, limp on a cold hook, in the dark.

He certainly wasn't going to freeze, so the cold was no problem. It would suppress his smell, too, and the magic of the cooling charms would likely interfere at least a little bit with whatever divining magic they were using.

The problem was, he was a warm body in a cold place. Anything that could see heat would pick him up more clearly than if he had just lain on the deck of the barge. But there were ways to deal with that.

He took another look at the checkpoint. He had about twenty minutes before the barge reached it, and then there wasn't another in sight. He walked into the container and shut it behind him. It took some finagling, but the doors stayed shut, at least. Then he sat on the floor and spent exactly eighteen minutes sealing his body against the emission of body heat.

It was a terrible idea. He could feel himself getting lightheaded. His organs were taking damage already, which was a hell of a thing, given how much he had cultivated his body. This was not something a living human could do. At minute nineteen, he stood. It was as good as it was going to be.

He used Incisive and cut a little hole through his chest. Punched a meat hook through it, then stopped his heart. He was just meat, hanging with all the rest. Just more meat shipped out of Harban for processing. Going to feed the great machine. Truth had come into Harban a prince and left a dead pig. His last thought, before he fell into the well of nothing, was *I wonder what I will be when I return again.*

CHAPTER 50

READY TO CHANGE

The meat hung in the cold, dark box. The barge took them past the judges, who looked down on them and disdained them. The box of meat was carried down the river, on to that place of long knives, where children learned a bloody truth—they were the least important component in a machine for pigs and always would be. They were worth less than the meat they cut up. Meat they would be arrested and beaten for trying to eat.

The meat hung still, only juddering when some unseen crane lifted away the boxes and carried them ashore. That shake seemed to stir some animal spirit in the hanging carcasses, as one pig corpse shuddered and drew a gasping breath.

One strong hand reached up and back. Strong muscles, trained, cultivated, used hard, flexed and lifted. The meat rose off the hook and lowered itself softly to the floor. The hole in its chest was very thin. Meat was expensive. It wasn't good to damage it unnecessarily. This meat was able to patch the hole with a small effort. Reminding itself that it was more than meat took longer.

The world really, truly, sincerely believed Truth Medici was dead meat. Truth was determined to prove the world wrong.

He took a few minutes just to recover. It had worked well. The context mattered. Dead meat in the cabin of a long-haul truck was believable for only upsetting reasons. Dead meat hanging with other dead meat in a refrigerated cargo container going to a meat processing plant outside the city was *entirely* plausible and needed little magical support to be convincing.

It still sucked, though. It hurt. It was exhausting and, worse, demoralizing. It wasn't fun to fall into that well of oblivion. Wasn't fun to be meat on a hook. Truth rubbed his hand over where the hole had been. The physical damage had healed. He had a feeling the mental damage would take more time.

Sitting there in the dark, cold box, watching his breath slip out in long streams of steam, Truth concluded that he was not happy. He was not even content. Perhaps he had no right to expect happiness or contentment. He was an international terrorist creating chaos in the days before the apocalypse. But this felt bad. Wrong. Not the hanging-meat thing, though that was part of it. Just the whole approach to the problem of Starbrite.

Breathe in and out. Haul in the thinning cosmic rays and trap them in your slowly perfecting body. In and out. In and out. Stretch, move, and let the cultivation calm you as your energy refilled.

This whole campaign was essentially a military action. There were political and economic consequences too, but the core of it was to hurt Starbrite and the System so much, they had to move and show a weakness. Lift that skirt of secrecy, flash a little leg.

But that wasn't the way to think about things, was it? That was picking from the stacked deck. It was rolling up to the three-card monte table swearing that you finally had a system and you would definitely find the lady this time.

You wouldn't. You would never find the lady. There was no way to play the game and come out ahead. You didn't realize the card that made the money was you. Truth had always walked straight past the little tables and their excited crowds when he was a kid. Foolish to think the game would change just because he got a little taller.

Level Zero Denizens hauled open the door to the container, apparently not noticing or caring about the damage to the locks. They lifted the carcasses, hooks and all, onto their shoulders and carried them away. Into the assembly-line butchery, Truth assumed. He wouldn't be following them. He liked sausage but had seen it made far too often recently.

He stepped out of the cold, dark box and into the warm summer light. It didn't seem fair that the day could be so beautiful. But the sky just didn't care about his misery.

It would be night in Siphios. Truth smiled up at the clouds, wishing Etenesh sweet dreams. Then tacked on Jember, too, because why not? Merkovah . . . He wasn't sure Merkovah actually slept.

Now, where was he? There was an irritating lack of road signs. He was on a dock next to a meatpacking plant, next to the River Fan. Truth shrugged and started walking west, toward the sea. He would make his way to a road and work from there.

Truth walked about fifteen minutes. It wasn't particularly scenic, but what did you want out of an industrial park? There was, however, a distinct moment of whiplash once he got out of the park. He was next to a farm and across the street from a long row of greenhouses. There were crummy low-rise apartment buildings in sight, and he was near Highway 77.

Truth looked back at the industrial park, with its large, boxy buildings and assembly-line butchery, to the brilliantly green fields, to the greenhouses growing vegetables and fruits, and then over to the apartments. No dead meat there.

The river had turned northwest as it made its way up toward the sea. Nothing for it but to get walking. The days were longer as the summer settled in, but sunset wouldn't be far off. He wanted to be well away from Harban and with a new base of operation before the sun rose again.

Truth tapped his toes against the pavement, smiled, and took off at a run. The eyes of the world just slid off him. Not considering that if Incisive encouraged a certain ethos and way of thinking, perhaps the Meditations of Valentinian might have the same effect. And that, of all his spells, it was the one he had practiced the most.

Truth ran along the dirt roads between the fields, keeping parallel to the river. There were suburbs north of the farms, but the logic of building the fields next to the widening river was inescapable—irrigation and transportation. So, he took the easy option and kept to the fields. They didn't provide much cover, but he was so far from anyone that there would be near enough to no eyes on him, anyway.

What did he want to ask Merkovah? Or tell him, for that matter. *Say, it just occurred to me that, logically, the System Astrologica must exist on a higher plane of existence, calling into question all my work here. So, you know, the fuck?*

There might be a more delicate way to put that. Or *Say, a senior suggested an idea. How do you feel about the proposition that, if we can prevent a harm without sacrificing something of moral equivalence, we morally ought to do it? Do you think that's a good first step toward defining humanity as more than starving rats?*

Yes, he was sure that would make Merkovah very happy. It was just the kind of thing a six-hundred-year-old spymaster loved hearing from his most rogue agent.

Yeah, I've decided to ignore your missions and focus on finding the Shattervoid girl. Next stop, Army Ford. Any information on that, by the way? Ah, he could practically hear the shouts of joy from there.

Was that . . . corn? He had no idea what they were growing in these fields. It was pretty short to be corn. Wasn't corn tall? He just didn't know what corn looked like before it was stripped from the cob and packaged in the can. The only reason he knew about corn growing on a cob was the picture on the label.

He was a good distance away from Harban now, but nothing felt quite right. He didn't want to just pop into some suburban home or dig a hole in a field or something. At the same time, the luxury-hotel game was definitely over.

He consulted his much-abused road atlas. There was a big hill, mostly covered in woods, northeast of where he was. If he ran farther north, he would actually start hitting mountains. The mountains just north of Harban were famously packed with military installations, ready to launch swarms of golems and spells at anything daring to threaten Harban or the River Fan.

There was a certain appeal to losing himself in the mountains, hiding in the place of most danger. It had worked before. But no, that close to *that* many military installations, it didn't matter how sneaky the communication ritual was; it would be caught. He looked a little closer at the forested hill on his map. According to the atlas, there was a temple on the other side of the hill from him.

He didn't have a better idea. He turned northeast and got running. Whatever it was, it would beat standing in a field.

The hill was taller than it looked on the map—easily over a hundred meters, vertically, of steep slope and dense trees. Quite pretty. The temple was tucked into the northeast slope. Truth was kind of amused to see that it was a collection of small, colorful buildings arranged around a little square and a big stone statue of a smiling demon. Something about the way it was pretending to be big but was actually lots of small things. Like a school of fish.

The monks were tidying up after the visitors had left for the day. Brushing away the dirt with brooms rather than air demons. Odd, but presumably, there was a reason for it. He started scouting around for something like a bedroom and didn't find much. He found *bedding* but not beds. Apparently, the monks slept on the floor of one of the great halls.

He would really prefer not to, but if needs must . . .

He kept hunting around, looking for something useful or at least comfortable. The Grand High Abbot or whatever must have their own room, right? Merkovah's cell in Nag Hamadi was the same size as his, just with more bookshelves. So, maybe not.

He pushed open another door and found himself confronted by a rabbit. Not a very big rabbit. Perhaps half again taller than his hand was long. It did have little antlers, though. So, that was something. The rabbit demon hopped through the door at speed. Apparently, it had been stuck in there awhile and couldn't wait to get out.

On a whim, Truth followed the rabbit down the halls. It quickly led him to another building. A small, open room, with polished wooden floors and another big demon statue. There were a few dozen demons sitting around, looking at the statue. Praying? He had no idea. They seemed quite peaceful.

Most importantly, however, was the big communication altar tucked in a corner, surrounded by a privacy ward. It was jarringly out of place, like a horse on an escalator. This room was clearly intended for worship, so why . . .

He took a closer look around. In a large, locked closet he found his answer. A surprisingly robust set of scry recording and broadcasting talismans. The big transmission fetish was folded up and shoved into the corner. He wasn't just in a temple. He was in the studio. Laughing quietly, he looked over at the statue.

This demon looked like a muscular man with a deer's head. It was sitting comfortably cross-legged, one palm outstretched toward you, the other hand raised shoulder-high. Presumably, there was some religious significance. He would find out tomorrow. For now, he would just . . . sleep. Just find a spot, rest his head on his shoes, and sleep. He gently moved enough supplies out of the closet to give him room to lie down in. It wasn't really meaningful, but he appreciated the illusion of privacy. Sleep soon claimed him.

The little demons didn't see him. They seemed content just to silently look at the statue. Until something in the air changed, and they bolted from the room. Truth's nous gave a little shake. And the eyes of the demon statue opened.

CHAPTER 51

DIVINE CREATURE

It was a bright, blustery day in the Downs. The anchored warships were all busy, patching, repairing, resupplying. Waiting to sail out and protect England's budding dominions in far-flung places like the Carolinas, Jamaica, or Tangiers. The echo of Dutch cannons was still loud in the ears of the Royal Navy. Nobody, at least nobody in the Royal Navy, thought it would be the last time they tried conclusions with the Dutch. A second war was coming, and soon.

Truth stood on the quarterdeck of the *Assurance*, fresh from being scraped, painted, and repaired at Portsmouth. This was to be a shakedown voyage, just to make sure the lazy sods in the shipyard didn't muck up something. Like any sensible sailor, he despised both passengers and having women aboard for any reason. Like any sensible *officer*, he knew damn well promotions and ships were made available to those with the right connections.

And the *Assurance* was a piddly little thirty-two-gun fourth-rate rather than a majestic second- or first-rate. And his passenger was the daughter of a knight and married to the Viscount Conway, who owned a decent percentage of both Warwickshire and County Antrim. And the person who arranged this whole rigamarole was the alarmingly energetic Clerk of the Acts for the Navy Board, Samuel Pepys. A Clerk who was infamously close to the Earl of Sandwich's *entire* household, spoken fondly of by the Lord High Admiral HRH James II, and had personally negotiated and approved the contract for the masts on damn near every English warship. And Pepys had helped get him *this* ship, after receiving a generous gift of silver plate and a small crate of rare melons.

So, there he was. Waiting on a woman, with a headache.

The little Thames estuary hoy was beating against the wind and making unimpressive time. Its latest tack should take it close enough to carry passengers over on a boat. Truth watched it do just that, neatly slowing and anchoring in the Downs' twelve fathoms of water. A boat was lowered, then sailors clambered down the side of the hull into it. Luggage was carefully lowered, then the human cargo, sitting in a sling.

Truth swore. He hadn't thought of that.

"Lieutenant Makeepeace!"

"Captain!"

"Rig a hoist for our guest and her luggage. Lively, now."

"Aye, sir."

Makeepeace had the decency not to give him a look before leaping into action. It wasn't that big a job. If there was one thing the navy had no shortage of, it was ropes. Thanks to Pepys, there was no shortage of timber, either.

Soon the boat was over, and Makeepeace did a fine job bringing the cargo aboard.

"Captain Alítheia, by your leave, permission to come aboard?"

Her voice was surprisingly strong, Truth thought. Curly hair on a very round head and one of those unfortunate mouths that made her look like her teeth were apart even when her lips were closed.

"Granted. Welcome aboard, my lady. I hope your journey was comfortable?" Truth asked with a polite smile.

She smiled as her servant and maid supervised the luggage as it went to her cabin.

"Comfortable enough. A few days on the road, and two more in the hoy. Still, I had my books for company, so no great suffering."

"I am glad to hear that. If I might make so bold as to ask, what books are you reading?"

"Ah, it's a foolish whim of mine. I decided to set a sort of argument and bounce between books, looking for the answer. My disputants on this trip are the ancient Plato, the questionable Monsieur Descartes, and the mysterious Jew, Luria. My question to them all is this—*If God is perfect, why do we live in an imperfect world?*"

Truth smiled, sincerely this time. This might just be a pleasant journey after all.

Dinner was a lively affair. Truth entertained his officers and guest in his cabin, the table pulled out and loaded with pickled oysters and a rather decent joint of mutton he had bought the day before. The passenger contributed a few bottles of good sack, and all were merry.

"You say you have fallen out with Descartes? I thought he was all the rage in Cambridge," Truth asked.

"Oh, he is. But many people enjoy things that are wrong. He says that matter and spirit are two different things. This is plainly nonsense. Yet so many humor the old bore." She shook her head, curls bouncing slightly as she did.

One of the young gentlemen, seated at the table to learn manners and how to make connections with important guests, was taken a bit too much with the strong wine and forgot himself. "But aren't they? I can touch the table but not the air," his little voice piped, not having dropped yet.

Truth didn't grimace, though most of the officers did. The little idiot had just damaged his chance at a midshipman posting, just because he couldn't keep his mouth shut. Fortunately, their guest was broad-minded.

"I think your sails would have much to say about whether you could touch the air, young man." There were nods around the table at that. "But this and that are really not at all the same things. By your thinking, all would be matter."

"Like old Hobbes." Truth nodded. "I met him once, as a young man."

"He's still alive, actually." The lady smiled. "Hobbes, I mean."

"Oh, I know. You should hear people denounce the little coward." Truth rolled his eyes.

"Coward?" she asked. "I would call him many things, but *coward* seems perhaps strong."

"Let him send his second if he disagrees." Truth's voice was tight. Then he forced himself to relax. "I do him an injustice, perhaps. It goes to your question of an imperfect world. I was escorting him from Portsmouth up to London. We had just passed through a burnt-out village. Who had done it was not known at the time, be they Cavaliers or Roundheads, for all that the 'Protector' was on the throne and Monk's army was keeping the peace. Presumably, they were keeping it up in Scotland. Horrible things not fit for the dinner table were all I could see."

"May they rest in peace," the lady murmured.

"God willing. But his whole notion upon seeing all of that human waste was that it was all rational, in a way. The logical consequence of failing to have a king unburdened by the restraints of Parliament or our old traditions of governance."

"Thankfully, His Majesty is wise enough to rule with both strength and moderation." Makeepeace smiled and nodded, then stood and offered a toast. "The King!"

They all stood and drank their salute.

"Hobbes and I are at odds in a different direction," the passenger explained. "Getting back to the question of matter versus spirit and why we live in an imperfect world. The Platonists would say that God is a perfect being of spirit, entirely removed from the world. Think of it like the sun—a perfect sphere, needing nothing but radiating much. God is infinitely alive. Indeed, it is thanks to him that the state of being known as 'life' exists. He is also infinitely good, wise, and just."

The table nodded along with her. It was . . . odd . . . hearing a woman speak so freely in the company of men, but rank, as the officers knew quite well, hath its privileges. And Truth knew that among her class, such liberty was much less rare after the Restoration.

"But! Since that is so, why are we mortal, wicked, foolish, and cruel?" she asked.

"Since God has all those perfect traits, there would be no chance of a serpent or a garden, I suppose." Truth grinned. It was a dangerous view, but it was an era of religious turmoil, and she wasn't promoting popery or atheism.

"Exactly! There must be several categories or species of things. First, there is God—which is a being of pure spirit, eternal life, and immutable nature. It is one cohesive, singular thing, while also made up of all things, an infinity of other things, because it is God and therefore everything."

Dicier theological ground there, but Truth knew that none of his officers actually read philosophy or theology. They just looked impressed.

"Then there must be some intermediary, transmitting the life and divinity of God down, then, into the rest of the world. Something capable of change but still possessing that eternal quality of life. I would say here that you have a species that is both mortal and divine."

"Christ?" asked Makeepeace.

"Exactly. Still singular, still eternal, but capable of change. Bridging the gap between the singular, perfect eternal, and the multiple, imperfect, and mortal," she agreed.

"And from him is transmitted more of that divine nature into the world. Which is also still God?" Truth asked.

"Yes, but in the same way that one's body and the sea both contain salty water—one may be gone at any time, but the sea will always be there. Sooner or later, our water will return to it."

This led to some sober nodding from the adults and some drunken nodding from the young gentlemen. Learning how to hold your drink was another important lesson taught at table.

"But this doesn't address the issue of imperfection in the world," Truth pointed out.

"True. And I can only admit that I am lacking here. My supposition is that it is due to the sheer distance and degree of mutability between the singular perfection of God and the infinite infinities of things that make up the universe. Each of us is some part of God, some change in the spirit that *is* God and the universe." She held her spoon up in front of the lantern, casting an exaggerated shadow over her plate.

"See? The light seems blocked. But no matter how dim, I can still see my mutton well. We are never completely divorced from the spirit and, thus, from God."

She smiled in triumph, then went white. She grasped the table and gasped. Closed her eyes hard and grabbed her head.

"My maid. Call for Mary!" she groaned.

Mary was summoned and took her mistress to her cabin. Truth called on her the next day but was politely rebuffed by Mary. He saw little of his passengers until they reached Calais.

"My lady, time and tide wait for no man, but if you wish, we can wait at anchor a while longer," Truth said gently.

His passenger had changed since she came aboard. Visibly thinner, her skin waxy and shockingly pale, her eyes sunken. Truth had seen men like that before. Mostly in sick bay after a battle. The wounded, living with pain too great for words.

"No need, Captain. The worst is past. It's why I'm going to France. I'm told the doctors there are very expert in the delicate skill of trepanation. No English doctor dares try, but I believe Frenchmen will be bolder. In the meantime, I can only rely on the mercury medicines and pray the apothecaries are right about the discoveries of the alchemists."

Truth nodded. He hesitated. His question was, at best, indelicate, but it would prey on him if he didn't ask. He took another glance at her and resolved to ask by letter.

"Mr. Pepys said you would be like that."

"Your pardon?"

"*Two things the captain will chase to the ends of the earth—a fat prize, and a question of philosophy*. It seems he was right about the latter. Was he right about the former, too?"

"No, I'd catch them long before we reached the ends of the earth. Would you mind . . ."

"Not at all. I think I can guess your question anyhow. Pain. How could God torture himself with the invention of pain, and the suffering of all his infinite parts?" She was keeping very still, Truth noticed, her eyes squinting against even the dim, pre-dawn light.

"As you say, m'lady."

"The last leg of my construction. Well, it's not finished yet. Call it the last leg of my hypothesis. I will need to test it more." She closed her eyes and breathed steadily. "Perfectibility. We are far from the light of God, lost in the shadows of the world. But we can become better. We can refine ourselves in the fire of pain, discarding the parts of us that are not God. It is a slow process. An imperfect one. But our pain is not our enemy or some demonic trickery. It is our opportunity."

She sighed once, long and deep. Then opened her eyes again. Beyond the exhaustion, beyond the pain, there was something as hard as a coffin nail.

"Hell is not eternal, Captain. If it exists, it exists to perfect us that we may return to God. An eternal punishment for a temporary transgression could never be just, so how could God countenance an eternal punishment? No. Hell is reformatory and temporary. One day, both God and I shall live free of pain. And we both believe that the result is worth the suffering."

CHAPTER 52

EMPIRICAL FAITH

Ow ow fuckity OW YOU BASTARD. I hope that memory was of you being torn apart by weevils. Billions of boiling maggots just shredding your still-alive and terribly conscious flesh apart.>>

I was . . . a sailor.

Truth stared up at the polished wood of the ceiling, trying to come to terms with what had just happened.

I don't remember much. But I remember I was a sailor and I had talked with so many people. And one lady said that . . . we are all little pieces of God, and pain is the mortality leaving the body. Or something like that. It's fading again.

He could hear a faint stirring in the room with the big deer head statue in it. He didn't move. Nothing in there could threaten him.

<<Try to hang on to what you can. Just swim through the memory. I can see what you are remembering now, as it passes through your psyche. I will remember it for you.>>

Truth nodded internally. It was all just flashes and fragments. He couldn't make sense of it.

<<Truth . . . there are no demons in your memory.>>

What?

<<No demons, no talismans, or runes, or altars, or sacrifices. No magic.>>

Are you saying it's divination?!

<<What? No! None of that looks anything at all like anything on this planet, is what I am saying! In your memory, you looked out on two different coastlines as well as some maps, and I don't recognize any of it! The damn stars are different, Truth!>>

I . . . lived off-world?

<<In another life. One very far away from here. It all looks like madness to me.>>

Truth didn't try to feel anything for the moment. He just floated in the bubble of confusion. It wasn't that it was too much or something; it was just . . . what was he supposed to do with this information? How was this useful? Why did he, of all people, remember his past lives?

I don't have time for this.

<<Evidence suggests that you have nothing but time for this.>>

Truth ignored the System and dusted himself down. He didn't have to do much to get himself ready for the day. He'd hit the bathroom, maybe try to find a shower.

Can I hijack that broadcasting equipment to get in touch with Merkovah? Feels like I'm still too close to Harban, but damn, it is all right there.

Truth opened the door of the closet and was confronted by a giant deer head with glowing red eyes. He fought the urge to close the door again.

The demon was kneeling in front of the door. Its muscular human body was relaxed but very proper. Properly what, Truth couldn't say.

"Good morning," said Truth.

"Good morning," said the demon.

Truth grasped for some kind of conversational thread. "Did you need something from the closet?"

"No." The voice was deep enough to vibrate the plaster on the wall a little, but with strange high notes woven into it. "It's rude to refer to a person as a *thing*. So, I was hoping to speak with *someone* from the closet."

"Ah. And . . . you can see me, can you?"

The demon shook its head, careful to avoid banging their antlers into anything. "No, but I could sense the dominion you exert around yourself. And I could feel your soul tremble in the night. It was not hard to deduce that some manner of human had come to my little place."

Truth didn't know that was a thing that could happen. Alarming.

"Well. You were right. How may I help you?"

"On the contrary, it is I who wish to help you. Introductions are in order, I think. I am Verstan-Kung, head abbot of this little community, and guardian of this mountain before that."

"Ah. I am . . . someone whose name shouldn't be loose on the wind. Perhaps you could call me . . ." He cast about for a moment. Nothing appealed. "Sailor?"

"I understand how these things can be. You are far from the first to visit this place in need of a quiet night." The giant head bobbed. The antlers stopped a fraction of a centimeter from bashing into the wall.

"Sorry, would it be more convenient for you if we moved into the room rather than standing in the doorway?"

"Oh, thoughtful of you. Yes, thank you." They walked over the few steps, Truth to the middle of the now-empty floor, the abbot resuming his place on the dais.

"I honestly thought you were a statue when I walked through here last night."

"Really? I must have been very focused." The demon's voice rumbled, sounding a little pleased.

"Sorry, this is going to bug me—you said you were the guardian of this *mountain* before you were an abbot?"

"Mmm? Yes. Oh! I see. No, it wasn't soil erosion; I'm not that old. No, an angel did it. They didn't provide an explanation. One of those two-winged angels just turned up with a sword, lopped the top off, shaved down the sides, and kicked most of my mountain into the ocean, taking tens of thousands of lives in the process. One of those scrubby little messenger angels, but with angels . . ."

"I understand. Totally. My condolences?"

"Thank you; it was very upsetting at the time, but I have had time to grieve. And to grow."

Truth nodded, feeling a bit lost. "So. Abbot."

"Yes?"

"I . . . don't really know what your religion is. Or what you believe in."

"We call ourselves the Fellowship of the Earth, because most of us are some manner of demon native to this planet. Grown from the earth, as it were. We do have some human members, but we are mostly demons. As for our beliefs, we don't have many."

The demon stopped talking. Apparently, that explained everything.

"I'm sorry, my schooling was terrible. You are monks that don't believe anything?"

"Perhaps it would be clearer to say that we don't have faith in much of anything. Not to an absurd level. If I pick up a stone, I have every faith that it will fall when I drop it. But in supernatural things? Essentially none."

Truth felt a gear slip in his mind. Which, given the events of the last week or so, left him with very few gears.

"You, the demon that lived on this mountain since before humans came to this world, who watched an angel commit mass murder for no explained reason and can apparently detect the way I distort reality around myself, do not believe in the supernatural."

"Yes, that's right." The enormous head nodded.

"So . . . God?"

"Entirely natural. We don't know much about him, but you can't call him *supernatural.*"

"Well, if God isn't, then what is?"

"Thinking your prayers would move him. Or that he performs miracles. That our lives are controlled by forces beyond our knowing and our ability to comprehend."

"You just told me—"

"An angel murdered my friends, family, everyone and everything I had ever known or loved, leaving just enough behind to ensure the loss hurt and remained fresh in my heart forever. For no reason that I have ever learned. Given that an angel did it, the reason certainly boils down to *It thought it was performing God's will.*"

The demon sounded like he was describing where the old vegetable patch used to be.

Truth sat on the floor on one of the little cushions. "Could you walk me through this? I am really having a hard time following you."

"Certainly. I know exactly why all those people were murdered. It might not be a satisfying explanation, but I do have one. I know the sun rises and sets. It took me an embarrassingly long time to learn that it is the planet that moves and not that great one in the sky, but I did learn it eventually. It didn't change the truth. The sun rises and sets every day. I just know more about how that happens now."

"I think I see. You believe in the observable phenomena of the world. But since you can't observe the effects of prayer—"

"Outside of ritual magic, of course," the abbot added.

"Right, outside of ritual magic, you don't believe it has any effect. Or, rather, that it does not result in God taking direct action."

"Exactly."

"That is an interesting religion, right there."

"Oldest on this planet. Though never popular, even among demons. It lacks a certain something, I'm told. A hook."

"Ah. And the broadcasting setup?" Truth asked.

"There was a recent surge in interest. I do weekly sermons. I even have viewers from overseas."

"Wow!"

"Yes. I remind myself often that pride must not become arrogance."

"So . . . why do you want to help me?"

"Because I am the abbot of this humble place, and before that, I was the failed guardian of this mountain. I do not wish to see another slaughter here, Holy Child. I do not wish to see my people harmed. So, I will help you, in the hopes that you will spare this place."

Truth paused. It was not a crazy reaction, now that he thought about it. The demon looked big and was old, but that didn't necessarily mean he was some immense power. At the very least, Incisive wasn't pinging off of him. Giving the powerful, potentially murderous stranger whatever he wanted in the hopes that he would go away made a depressing amount of sense.

"Holy Child?"

"Did you not know? Yes. You distort the world around you like those of the higher dimensions do, and even your soul thrummed with the ineffable mysteries of those lands. We call such a person a holy child. In my long life, you are only the third I have met."

"What happened to the other two?"

"One decided that the best way to walk the road to divinity was to sit quietly in a little shack barely larger than his sitting form. He sat there and meditated. Eventually, he stopped eating and drinking. He died during his meditation. We kept an eye on him for a few years, but he really was dead. He's buried in his little shack. We kept the grave unmarked. He would have preferred it that way." The abbot's voice was quite matter-of-fact.

Truth felt relieved. He had worried for a moment that *Holy Child* was the Demon's way of saying *Cursed Murder-Beast*.

"And the second?"

"Stormed in here screaming that she would slaughter demons and behead devils, killed forty monks in as many breaths, two hundred lay brothers and sisters, four hundred and seven pilgrims, burned down every structure in the complex, smashed every statue, and was only eventually killed through the concerted effort of the remaining hundred monks. Of whom five survived. Myself included."

There it was. Yes. That sounded more like it.

"Although not unscathed, as you can see." The monk waved a hand over himself. Truth didn't see the scars but wasn't going to argue about it.

"I can see how you would be concerned, yes."

"So, what is it you want, holy one? How can this little monk help you?"

Truth laughed. It was soft, and even he could hear the bitterness in it.

"By being a monk? Oh, and a place where I could cast a communication ritual without being detected. But at the moment, I think you just being a monk is the best thing for me."

Truth was quietly amused to see that a large, deer-headed demon could look flummoxed. It didn't cheer him up much, but it was something.

"I am always a monk. Could you perhaps elaborate on your need?"

"I don't know. How's your relationship with the nation of Jeon and Starbrite?"

"Excellent and horrible, respectively. Which means, in practice, complicated and awkward, and horrible, respectively."

"So. Probably not wise to tell you anything I wouldn't want to reach them?"

"I'm not going to volunteer anything, though yes, I will always act to protect my temple. By informing or by withholding information. Whichever seems best."

"Well. I need to call someone discreetly. I don't think that's going to raise too many eyebrows even if you wrote it on a note and handed it off to Internal Security. As long as you do so once I am days away, of course."

The abbot nodded understandingly. "That can be arranged. Fair to say I know these mountains and hills better than almost anybody. And the part about needing a monk?"

Truth sighed. "Tell me, Abbot, how do I live as a human? Because I don't think I have ever seen it done before. Living like a human, I mean. I can't stand how I'm living now. I can feel myself coming apart. If humans don't know how to live like humans, maybe a demon does?"

The demon laughed, a harsh, braying, yet somehow kind noise.

"Are you tired of living like a rat? But why? Humans are better at it than the rats!"

CHAPTER 53

THE COST OF GIVING A DAMN

Truth gave the abbot a hard look. Then another. The abbot couldn't see him, of course, but that didn't stop the alarming chuckles coming from the giant deer head.

"I really thought I was the only one who imagined humanity as rats," Truth grumbled.

"No chance of that. The metaphor has been around as long as humans."

"I developed a whole system of understanding the world based on the concept of rats and slums. It has layers to it."

"Well done!" The abbot smiled. Truth felt just a smidgen patronized.

"Well?"

"Yes?" the abbot asked.

"Do you have any suggestions?"

"First, frame your problem. You have two basic angles to examine, I think."

I do? Truth just nodded along.

"First is a question of identity—is a human someone who lives as a human, or is possessed of some biological traits of humanity, or . . . what, exactly?" The abbot nodded toward a window. "The lay brothers and sisters, the pilgrims, they would consider themselves human. They believe they live as humans and are biologically human."

"They are wrong?"

"About one of those things, yes. They are, I believe, biologically human. But do they live as humans? I believe not. So, we can exclude that part of the identity question and focus on the issue of humans as a way of thinking and living."

"Which leads us directly back to the rats. They are living like rats."

"Actually, and I say this as someone who has observed hundreds of thousands of rats over tens or hundreds of millennia, no, they don't. They live like rats *forced into unnatural and stressful conditions.*" The demon spoke slowly and firmly. "The rats you are thinking of, the urban rats, the . . . slum rats . . . they eat poison, are constantly in fear, constantly under stress. They therefore react in ways they would be unlikely to in the wild."

"Really? There is that much of a difference?"

"Oh, yes. Take cannibalism. A rat will eat another rat, certainly. There is no such thing as a pure herbivore, and rats are omnivores in the first place." The deer head showed its teeth. Truth could vividly imagine the abbot tearing strips of flesh off someone.

"But usually, it will be a rat that already died. In the unlikely event that two rats fought over something, it would usually be limited to fairly minor injuries before one or the other ran off. There would be no benefit to pushing it to the death. Generally plenty of food or mates to go around, and you can make a nest anywhere there is dirt. No pressure to fight with your fellows."

"Ah. But put them in a situation of bad food, bad shelter, and intense competition for everything, including mates—"

"You have violence. You have rats eating each other." The abbot nodded. "And do you know what happens to humans in the same conditions?"

Truth nodded. "I know. Very well."

"So, we can either define this behavior as *Human, under given circumstances,* or *Inhuman, as it only occurs under artificially created circumstances.* And before you point out natural disasters or something that might trigger the same conditions, yes, that is true, but it is also transitory. The plague, the fire, the famine passes eventually. The conditions we are looking at here are both human-created and generational. This is a 'disaster' that has been engineered to persist."

The abbot's big hand gestured gently. Strong hand, Truth noticed, and callused. He didn't know demons could get calluses. Must be an aesthetic choice.

"So, what is the solution? Level society, unmake every bit of hierarchy, destroy the cities, destroy the factories, send everyone back to farming their own land? Let 'natural' humanity reassert itself?" Truth asked.

The abbot smiled. "It wouldn't work. Agriculture was the origin of slavery. I know; I was there. There has never been a human born that wouldn't rather see someone else do the plowing for them. And returning to simply hunting and gathering wouldn't work, either. There just isn't enough food density in the wilds to support a tribe a million strong. There aren't that many wilds left, either. No, if you wanted to go that way, you would have to kill almost every human and demon on this planet."

"Not a fan of that idea. I'd miss street food, if nothing else."

"And toilet paper." The demon snorted. "No, be honest with yourself. You just don't want to watch the world burn. You don't want to see your fellow 'humans' die in their billions. However much you may despise them, there is a limit to your misanthropy."

Truth snorted back. "I have come to understand the enormous depths of my sadism. I wouldn't assume much about my goodwill."

"Oh, no, the human has found out he enjoys having power over others and hurts people to prove his own power. Oh, my ears and whiskers. Oh, no, not that. Heavens to Betsy, this is just terrible." A giant deer-headed demon roasting you in a sarcastic monotone was a new experience, even for Truth.

"Off topic, but did you paint your room all black when you were a kid? Maybe asked your friends to call you 'The Dark Lord' or something?" the demon asked.

"No. I would have been beaten bloody had I even tried. And I didn't have any friends." The old pain never really left. He just forgot it now and then. He thought he had some perspective on it, but it didn't stop hurting.

The abbot sighed and hung his head. "I apologize. I deal with a lot of . . . Well, I apologize. That was rude of me."

Truth waved it away, then remembered that the demon couldn't see him. "Don't worry about it. We were on the question of what to do to find out what it means to live as a human."

"Ah, yes. Thank you. So, the present is unendurable, the imagined past is not actually an improvement, and the future looks bleak. The rats are under enormous stress and are eating each other. So, there is an obvious answer. Remove the stress."

"That simple, eh?" Truth looked side-eyed at the demon.

"Yes. Simple but hard. The *details* are complicated. I'm not sure you would like what humanity looks like without the artificial stressors. But if you want humans to live as humans and not like stressed rats, remove the things that stop them from thinking. That reduce them to beings of instinct."

"But what does that even mean?"

"Food—why do you need to struggle to eat? There are infinite demons in Hell for you to summon and bind to your labor. Many of them even welcome it. Hell could, and would, feed the world. With a bit of care, angels can be bribed and bullied into laboring for you too. There is no reason any person should ever go hungry."

Truth blinked at that. He had come to some of the same conclusions, of course, but hearing someone else say it just landed differently.

"Shelter—same story. They might not be the nicest or fanciest dwellings, but there is no reason you couldn't plan communities around dense housing blocks. There is no shortage of materials. The labor costs are very low, if not zero. Every human being could have their own home, constructed and maintained for free, for as long as humans exist on this planet."

"Wait, hang on, the cost—"

"The what?" The abbot grinned.

"The cost! You can't say all that is free."

"I can't? Who invented money? What do you use it for, exactly? I existed for far longer than humanity has on this planet, and I first heard of money just a few thousand years ago. It's a tool. Use it how you please. If someone has so many of the made-up tokens that they are preventing others from living as humans, take the tokens away from them, or stop using them all together."

"Theft, violence . . ."

"Simple but not easy. Yes. There would certainly be widespread violence." The abbot nodded. "The changes in thinking required would be, if anything, even more brutal. People are very used to thinking in terms of money and judge their well-being by how much better they are doing than their neighbors."

"So, to live as a human, I should remove unnatural stress from my life? Just . . . sidestepping the whole question of what natural stress is, by the way."

"Have you never worried about asking someone out? Or failing to live up to your potential? Fear of illness, or of finding a toilet before public humiliation? There are endless natural stressors and challenges in life. Nothing unnatural about that, nor unhealthy. But, simply put, yes. So, this is the identity question evolved into an ethics question—to be a human, not a rat, find a way for humans to live that removes the unnecessary and unnatural stresses. And this leads us to the second thing to consider. How do you determine what is the right or wrong way for *you* to live as a human in such a society?"

"Well, if the stresses have been removed—"

"Then will you still be a sadist?"

There was a pause. "Pardon?"

"Will you still be a sadist? I get the feeling that you have lived a very violent life. Will you continue to do so? If you live a peaceful life, will you still be cruel to others to make yourself feel good?"

Truth sat with that for a moment. "I don't know. I don't know that I would even want to change that part of myself. I know that I would kill someone who tried to do to me what I have done to others. In fact, I am in the process of doing exactly that now."

"Ah. Then, how about this—would you remain a sadist but not act on your sadism? Or perhaps only act on it in socially acceptable ways like victory in sports, or with a partner that enjoyed suffering?"

Truth didn't answer. He didn't know. The demon continued.

"This is what is called 'morals' and is distinct from ethics. Ethics is how people behave among each other, based on an external set of rules. Everyone agrees not to steal, to murder, to slander, that kind of thing. Morals is when you look into yourself and say, 'I should not steal, murder, or slander.'"

"Related but different."

"Yes. So, you ask how humans should live as humans? By creating a world where humans agree to remove the artificial stressors and develop internal moralities consistent with the ethical code needed to create and maintain that world."

Truth nodded. He would have to think on that. It was the first time he had ever heard someone lay it out like that. In fact, he had never heard a single person suggest such a world. He jolted.

He had never heard a single *human* suggest it. But those two seniors in the hot springs, those demons suggested it, didn't they?

"If you can prevent a harm without sacrificing something of morally equivalent value, you ought to do it," Truth whispered. The demon's head jerked around.

"Where did you hear that?"

"From two seniors in a hot spring attached to a fine old hotel in the mountains."

The demon sucked a long breath through their blocky teeth. "Lucky. Ah, you are lucky! I only got to hear their lectures twice in my long life."

"Abbot . . . is this knowledge forbidden for everyone on the planet, or just humans?"

The abbot grinned. An unsettling sight on a giant deer head. "Why, is there something forbidden for you to know? How could that be? You didn't sign something forbidding you to know it, did you? Or any of the other humans you have met?"

"You know perfectly well that there is."

"Yes, I do. I'm shocked that you do too. But there is something worth considering. I don't know that it's the whole answer, but it's part of it, I think." The demon drummed his heavy fingers on his thigh.

"This is not my original form. I was once a stag. I took this form largely for public-relations reasons."

"Makes sense." Truth nodded.

"But I *am* native to this world. All the animals are. All my fellow demons are. This is, quite literally, a world for demons. Then angels came, 'adjusted' it, and a few short centuries later, humans turned up on your black ships. Upending things. Generally, we demons didn't mind. Some of us very much did mind. The consequences for our kind have been catastrophic in terms of population numbers, ranges, freedoms. Though only some of us care about those things."

Truth nodded awkwardly. It was all true, but what was he supposed to say about it? Or do about it, for that matter?

"Every human on this planet is being driven to torture themselves, lead degraded lives, and die sickly and young, never reaching their full potential. Not one human born on this world has ever escaped the Initiate realm, as you term your cultivation arts. As though the whole planet wants you to suffer at every level. Strange, eh?"

CHAPTER 54

TIMELESS

Truth wasn't sure if he had lost yet another gear, or was integrating a new one. "The whole planet hates humanity and wants us to suffer."

"That is how I see things, yes. Although, fair to say, the hatred has been intensifying rapidly over the last few hundred years." The abbot's antlers swished through the air as he nodded.

"The whole world. All the rocks and things—"

"Benefactor, what do you think this world *is*? A big ball of rock with a thin skin of water and trees and air over the top?"

"Well . . . yes?"

The deer-headed demon chuckled indulgently.

"And the sun is just a big ball of fire." The abbot shook his head gently. "Benefactor, did you think *stellar eminences* just referred to stars? It's a limit of human naming conventions, like not having a separate word for the denizens of Hell and those of us 'demons' who have lived on this world since the beginning. Every heavenly body is an emanation of some vast, higher-dimensional being. This world. The moon. The other planets dancing in worship of the great solar eminence. All of them."

Truth could only blink. It had never occurred to him to even wonder.

"And while it would be a terrible mistake to ascribe *human* emotions to such beings, let alone human logic, they do possess emotions and rationality." The abbot sounded quite matter-of-fact about everything.

"The planet is aware of us." Truth searched for a reasonable profanity and drew a blank. "I may need new swears."

"I can recommend some books."

"Really?"

The abbot nodded seriously. "Oh, yes. The words themselves are merely a tool to convey the emotion. You want to focus on certain sounds and work from there. The field has been well developed for some time."

Truth started nodding, then forced himself back on track. "How does something like mining not trigger immediate retaliation?"

"Who says it hasn't? But more generally, I think you are severely underestimating the size of the world. All the off-world exports amount to a microscopic fraction of a single percent of the planet's mass. As for everything that remains on the world . . . it may change its form, but that's perfectly normal for a planet. Give it a few moments, and it will be like humanity was never there."

"A few moments?" Truth was groping for some kind of anchor, some firm place to stand and orient himself.

"Mmm. Say a million years or so. No time at all, if you are a planet." The abbot waved gently. "A million is a thousand thousand. A very, very long time for a demon. Unimaginably long for a human with a bare century to look forward to. But barely a blink for a being that measures time in the thousands of *millions*."

Truth stared at the floor. No wonder the eminence's grasp on human emotion and logic was so iffy. What could endure so much time?

"The planet, this . . . unbelievably ancient thing, hates the humans who have been on this world barely long enough to register on its consciousness?"

"Ah, you are assuming that just because they are ancient, they are also slow to notice things. But there is no evidence of that. All we can know is that they are used to working and thinking over impossibly long time frames. That does not prevent them from moving comparatively quickly." The abbot waved a finger reprovingly.

"But . . . Why, then? If angels prepared this world for humanity's coming, then our being here must be, to some extent, God's will."

"Yes. So?"

There was a pause.

"Pardon, Abbot?"

"Your being here is God's will. So what?"

The pause resumed. Truth grasped for a reason, with limited results.

"Because 'God's will' seems to end a lot of arguments when dealing with angels? All of them, actually?"

"Who said they were an angel? I suspect you know that many of those stellar eminences are demons. Why should planets be any different?"

"The planet hates us because we are bad for other demons?"

"Maybe? It hasn't told me. I'm just guessing based on what I'm seeing." The deer's head grinned.

Truth tried to imagine it. A world that despised humanity. Slowly increasing the pressure on it. Creating conditions for the humans to torture themselves. Using its strength to bully summoned angels, demons, and off-world visitors to keep the truth of cultivation from humanity. Not just failing to struggle against the loss of cosmic energy but directly leaning in to it. Collapsing faster than the simple loss of spiritually dense materials should allow.

"The coming magical apocalypse?" Truth asked.

"What magical apocalypse? At most, it will last a few tens of thousands of years. Barely a blink. Barely enough time to start blinking."

It was beyond comprehension. So much of his life was focused on the next minute, the next hour, the next day. Maybe the next year. Short-term goals, because if you didn't hit them, there would be no long-term anything. Thinking that far in advance, treating the extermination of a species as a mere fit of irritation? What could do that?

A higher class of being, apparently.

"So, your theory is that angels came and adjusted the planet. Whether that was enough to irritate the planetary eminence or if it was the actual presence of humans, who knows. But something did. So, that eminence limited our ability to cultivate out of the Initiate realm and blocked our ability to imagine a world free of those artificial sources of stress we talked about," Truth started. The abbot nodded.

"Remember what happened to my mountain? I saw entire forests flattened and turned to farmland. Other forests had trees replaced with ones that grew fruit and nuts humans can eat, or provided useful building materials. The angels wanted to make it easy for humans to live here. Not a cursed struggle. And while I am guessing about the direct interference, it's hard to imagine something else that can operate at that scale, over that long a period, with that degree of subtlety."

"Then, after humanity was well established, Starbrite turns up."

"Yes, I'm not actually sure when. I think he was here for a while before he made himself known, but that's a guess based on the way that company of his seemed to spring out of nowhere."

"Starbrite starts making all those sources of stress worse while also speeding up the export of minerals and monopolizing cultivation resources."

"Benefactor is most observant. But you should know that the decline in cosmic-ray absorption has been going on for a lot longer than most think. It just has been very, very gradual. A few fractions of a percent less each year. Not much, but spread out over the billions of humans, it adds up very quickly. How many lives were shortened? How many failed to reach their potential?" The abbot shook his head.

"Which, of course, encouraged people to try and extract more resources more quickly. Using elixirs and spiritually dense materials to make up for the change in climate."

"Accelerating the vicious cycle." The abbot nodded.

"Accelerating the stress, which encouraged people to worry less about the future and more about their immediate needs. Needs like, *picking an example completely at random*, a potion or elixir for their Level One breakthrough."

"Did you know it used to be considered shameful to use a potion for a breakthrough? It was seen as proof that you had not cultivated well." The abbot grinned.

"Figures." Truth let himself collapse and fell on his back. "That just about figures. Yeah, I can see it now. Do you think the planet is actively . . . I don't know, deflecting the cosmic rays?"

"I don't know. Perhaps? It would certainly be more capable of reaching the ear of God than some random human or demon. Though it would be one of billions in its own right." The demon shrugged.

"There are that many planets?" Truth wondered.

"There are that many stars. The universe is so great, young one. The universe is so wide and wondrous. And we see just the barest, shallowest depths of it. We can barely see a cupful of the ocean."

Truth lay on the floor, just breathing. How do you deal with something like that? How do you face that? More than God's indifference, the active *hate* of the world you were born on? How do you confront that? How do you overcome it? How could you even accept it was real?

He didn't want to accept it was real. But it felt right. Felt real.

"It all feels too much, doesn't it? But here is the thing. You can't see, or touch, or really even affect any of that. So much of it is just my speculation. Plausible speculation, based on my observations over tens of thousands of years. But still speculation. And you can't hold speculation."

The abbot's voice was smooth. Truth had gotten used to the growling basso. He could see why people would listen to him give a sermon. It was a great voice for that.

"What can you hold, Benefactor? Right now, in this place, at this time, what can you grasp in your own two hands? Beyond that, how can you change yourself? If this enormity is crashing down on you, how can you change to survive it? Or to accept it with peace and grace? What, right now, can you do to make your situation better?"

Truth tried to think. It was hard. All the stress making him not want to think, just run and hide. Turning him into a rat. What could he do? What did he need to do?

He needed to get offworld. *Sorry, Etenesh, we aren't staying in Siphios. By all means, keep the godhood plan going. Happy to come back here someday.* But for now, they needed to be off-world. Which meant finding the Shattervoid girl and killing Starbrite. No more games. No more drawing out this or that. Time to go for the throat.

Merkovah might not like it, but that was fine. He didn't imagine the old exorcist liked many things these days. While they still had some degree of their old strength. Before Starbrite could convert all those newly mutilated souls into power. It was time to strike. For him to strike. But the Prince was dead and he refused to play the pig any longer. Who should he be?

Truth Medici had been a lot of things and a lot of people over the course of his short life. So, who did he want to be now?

God's assassin? He would need to find some black paint and a bedroom first. And just not true. Incisive would have nothing to work with.

A disgruntled employee? A concerned citizen? Sure, but so generic, they were worthless.

A Spell-Blade on errantry? Tempting. Very tempting, actually, but again, no. He wasn't there for heroics or to inspire people.

"Hey, Abbot?"

"Yes, Benefactor?"

"Who am I?"

"Beyond 'Sailor'?"

"Yes. Invent a story for me. A person for me to be."

The abbot thought about it for a moment. "Is that what you really want?"

Truth thought about it a bit longer. "I can't figure it out. I just . . . can't seem to figure it out. Who do I have to be to see the end of this? To reach that happy place where humans live?"

"Then let that be your identity. You are the Fool."

"Pardon?!"

"You are the Fool. Not a fool, *the* Fool. You wander through dangerous places, asking dangerous questions and contesting against things infinitely beyond you, all for the sake of . . . what, exactly? Nothing that will last beyond a few centuries at best, I expect. But people need that sort of fool. Call them a hero or a holy child. You will forsake the trappings of this world, living in a way that most sensible rats will call foolish. Your journey may kill you. But you will walk it as a human being. Beyond the judgment of rats."

CHAPTER 55

STAND-UP GUY

The laughter bubbled up in Truth from the bottom of his belly, tickling his guts and squeezing his lungs. What could he do but laugh? He wanted to fight a higher-reality entity that was compounding the torture of humanity inflicted by a literal stellar eminence, all while God disdained to look on. There would be no miracles. There would be no divine intervention.

He was a guy with a sword. A thug with a spell and delusions of grandeur. A rat can bite a cat, but he needs somewhere to stand and fight, right? What do you do when the ground you stand on is one enemy, and the other is beyond your reach?

Only a fool would fight under those conditions. Only a fool would take that fight rather than running all the way to Siphios and Etenesh.

Well. Fine. He could be the fool a little longer. He would be the silly rat that forgot what good rats know and try to live instead like a human. Accepting "natural" stress, ignoring or avoiding the unnatural.

"It occurs to me that the higher you cultivate, the fewer of those stresses, natural and otherwise, apply. You don't need to eat as much, not as worried about shelter or sleep. Even old age is less of a thing," Truth said, once he could speak again.

"True. And don't forget fertility. Higher-level cultivators have superb control over their own reproductive capability. It's why you don't see cultivator clans running the world. The higher-level cultivators basically can't be bothered to reproduce anymore," the abbot agreed.

"I don't suppose you know how to have a polite conversation with the eminence of this planet?"

"No. I wouldn't even know where to begin looking for the person who would know." The abbot's antlers swished through the air violently.

"Any idea how to chain down and fight a higher-dimensional spirit?"

"With another higher-dimensional spirit? Sorry."

Ah, well. It had been a long shot.

"No worries. That discreet place to make a call?"

"You can borrow my communication altar. If it becomes a problem, I will just say you stole it. But kindly do not transmit from here. If you will permit me, I will lead you to a discreet place. One that is hard to surveil."

"Oh? Not sending a little brother?" Truth asked.

"No, I would rather remain your hostage." That brought an awkward pause to the conversation.

"Ah, you know, even before we chatted, I wasn't going to hurt anyone here."

"Mmm. I believe you. And yet I think we will both be happier if I am close by." The abbot seemed indifferent.

"We both will?"

"Yes. You will feel more secure and therefore less likely to take 'regrettable but necessary' steps. By putting myself in a little more danger, I spare my brethren and myself a great deal more danger."

Truth laughed softly. "Odd how that works sometimes. All right, let me grab my bag, and I'm ready to go when you are."

"I packed some food, just in case you need something to eat." The abbot stood. "A good breakfast brightens up the whole day."

The abbot was quick on his feet. They moved through the woods silently, the monk's robe not so much as flapping in the wind. Quickly, gently, barely bending the grass with their steps. Truth enjoyed running through the woods. It felt freeing. He didn't have to pretend to be "normal." That his body was the same as everyone else's.

He supposed the demon would know a lot more about that than he would, but he didn't want to disturb the silence by asking. He would just enjoy feeling his body move through the forest. Playing the fool. Playing the hero. Playing the ascetic or the mystic wanderer. Becoming a person without thought and only existing through their body.

He stretched his arms upward, smiled, and leapt off a rock for the sheer joy of it. Why not? He would call Merkovah and lay it all out, and if the old monster disagreed, he was free to come there and yell at him.

"Over here." The abbot had elected to carry the altar. It wasn't that Truth wasn't strong enough; it was just that his arms weren't long enough to make carrying convenient. The demon set down the altar in a little rocky nook surrounded by mature trees.

"This spot is where we buried the peaceable Holy Child. Odd fellow but an excellent neighbor."

"Because he never bothered you?" Truth asked.

"We never even saw him most of the time. He wasn't hiding. He just didn't move much beyond his meditation chamber."

"How did he eat? Before he starved himself to death?"

"I have no idea." The abbot shrugged. "We never caught him eating. Our best guess was some form of body cultivation that let him forgo food for long periods."

Truth nodded. It would be his guess, too. "Why should I set up my ritual here in particular?"

"Listen."

Truth did. It was peaceful. The sounds of the wind in the trees slowly blended into a calming white noise. You didn't hear much beyond that, but what else did you need?

It took Truth a solid few seconds to realize what was going on.

"The place . . . what, keeps the noise in? Noise out?"

"No, it isolates attention. Something somewhere might catch a trace of your ritual, but unless there is something particularly alarming about it, it will pass unnoticed. I will sit against that tree over there." The abbot pointed at a large pine just outside the little clearing. "You can keep an eye on me while you talk."

"Sounds good." Truth nodded, then set up the ritual.

The abbot settled in and closed his eyes. Truth more or less trusted the demon, but the demon had been very clear about what would happen if anyone asked about Truth. He set up a few privacy wards, just in case. Then a few more. Then a few more on top of that. He might play the Fool, but he'd be damned if he'd act one. Once he had layered everything he could without specialized talisman support, he set up the "fingers crossed it's actually secured" communication ritual.

It took a few minutes for Merkovah to answer. Which was fair enough.

"Three leopard woodsmoke shrimp shrimp shrimp," Truth dutifully recited.

"Gaspard requiem noon." Merkovah's voice was dry. Tense? Maybe. The countersign was one of the rare ones that actually called for a reconfirmation.

"Seven vector two one three berry ninety nine." He had had to pick the individual words out of a hat when he memorized them. God above, did he memorize so many things. But it was necessary.

"I genuinely wasn't sure we would ever speak again." Merkovah's voice was quiet.

"I hadn't a single doubt about it." Truth's voice was staunch in reply. The line went quiet for a moment, then—

"Because you were so focused on running and hiding, you didn't bother thinking about the future."

"Exactly, yes. Great that you are alive, by the way."

"Why would I be in danger? You are the one in danger."

"Just generally. You know. Happy you are doing well in these trying times." Truth was downright blithe.

"Your concern touches me. Which makes me concerned. What are you going to ask that will upset me?"

"Nothing!"

"Oh, no?" Merkovah's voice turned downright dusty.

"Nope."

There was another pause.

"Because you won't be asking me; you will be telling me."

"You truly are an ancient and wise teacher."

"I wonder. All right, what is it?"

"I'm quitting the terrorist gig. It sucks, it's bad for my mental and emotional health, requires insane amounts of naked cross-country marathons, and candidly, I can't imagine topping what I have already achieved."

"Sorry, did you say 'naked cross-country marathons'?"

"Yes. Hundreds of kilometers of wondering if this is going to be the one random street with a high-level slumming it as I flop about at speed. Hundreds of kilometers of heavy wagons spraying me with road grit in intimate, tender places. You failed, entirely, to prepare me for the subject of whippy little saplings and the threat they pose to the aspiring international terrorist. Frankly, I feel I was lied to."

"How? How did I lie to you?" Merkovah was outraged.

"It was a lie of omission. In retrospect, cardio and indecent public displays were strangely absent from all the so-called training. Suspiciously absent. You preyed on my youth and naivety to set me up as an exhibitionist."

"I preyed on your youth and cynicism to set you up as a damn instrument of vengeance!"

"Don't try and twist this around on me. I think you enjoy inspiring new fetishes in people. I think that's *your* fetish."

"Young man, do you know how much sex a body can have in six hundred years? I have done all the fetishes. All of them that are not actual crimes. All. Of. Them. Even the ones I knew I would hate. And I did hate them, but after six hundred years, you want to try *something* new. Exhibitionism? I was bored of that before your great-grandfather ten times over was an alarming scrotal twinge."

The old exorcist must be under a lot of stress, Truth thought. Now, would that be artificial stress or natural stress? Meh.

"Oh? Let me guess. Now you have a fetish for loving—"

"No, stopping you there. I've already got Nag Hamadi digging *far* too deeply into my love life; I'm not getting into it with you."

"So many jokes to work with. How do you leave me hanging like that?"

"Sounds like I'm in . . . not good company but company. How's the breeze where you are?"

"Quite nice, actually. I'm in a quiet place outside Harban. Headed north again."

"You didn't get through much of my list. Barely any of it, in fact."

"True. On the other hand, I would die if I hung around Harban, and let's face it. How much more damage could I do? And how useful would it actually be to our goal? Say I blew up an apartment building. Which, just so you know, I won't be doing. But say I did. Does Starbrite even notice? Does the System Astrologica give any more of a damn than it already does?"

Merkovah went silent for a moment. "You are swearing less."

This time, it was Truth who got thrown for a loop. "I am?"

"You are."

"Oh. I don't know why."

"I do. Hmm. North. You want to raid Army Forge."

"Yes. So, why . . ."

"Oh, I'm not going to tell you. I just don't want you to feel like I was lying by omission. No need to go to Army Forge. She probably was there but isn't now."

"Oh? Where, then?"

"Everwhite Mountain."

"Where?" Truth had never heard of such a place.

"Ah . . . I think in Jeongo it's the Great White Mountain?"

Truth started sputtering. *The national birthplace?!*

"I can assure you—"

"Teacher, I can one hundred percent tell you that not a single person in Jeon cares about the literal truth of the national-foundation myth. Not a single one. Anywhere. Top to bottom. Nobody."

"That's nice, but what I was actually saying was I can assure you that multiple, independently verified sources indicate a major research facility has been set up either under Heaven's Lake in the caldera or inside the volcano proper. And that there is a great deal of circumstantial evidence that leads us to believe that the Shattervoid girl was moved there."

"Ah. Right. So. Off I go, then."

"Oh, good. I do think we have a few more *minor* items to go over. Such as why you tried to murder someone even I regard as a living saint."

"Who?" Truth tried to think but was drawing a complete blank.

"Dr. Sun Ri. He has personally saved so many children, he was proposed as a separate category in the Jeon's childhood mortality statistics. 'Saved by Dr. Sun.' I must know at least twenty people who were personally saved by him. And saved again by his loving, kind bedside manner." Merkovah sounded tired and sad. "I am long past trying to sort innocents from villains, but Dr. Sun—"

"Oh, we are definitely going to talk about *him*. But first, I had a small, real quick question. On the subject of murder . . ."

"Yes?"

"How, exactly, did you expect me to kill the System Astrologica when it exists in a higher dimension?"

There was a short pause. Then—

"How in the *hell* did you figure that one out?"

CHAPTER 56

COMING FOR THE KING

Truth grinned mirthlessly at the communication altar. He couldn't see Merkovah, but he could certainly imagine the "old man" shock on his young face. *Looks like he knew. Well, I wouldn't have believed him if he denied it.*

"Oh, you know me. I take an interest in people and listen when they tell me things. Also, having eliminated all other reasonable possibilities, it's where I landed."

There was a long silence.

"Teacher?"

"On the one hand, I feel like I can take a *little* credit by encouraging you out of your low self-esteem and showing you that you can trust your own reasoning. On the other hand, we and many other nations spent a horrifying amount of time and money validating that theory. So. There is frustration there."

"'Validating that theory' doesn't sound like 'proving that right.' Or, for that matter, like an explanation for why you sent me to draw the System out of cover if you didn't believe it was, actually, hidden somewhere." Truth noticed the edge creeping into his voice. It was hard to miss.

"They don't sound the same because they aren't the same. We didn't prove a damn thing except excluding some very, very specific things it *couldn't* be. We can show that the System Astrologica is likely some kind of higher-dimensional being or at least exists on a higher dimensional level that we can easily access. And I sent you to draw it out of cover because it has to be interacting with the world *somehow*, and there is no visible means by which it is doing that."

"There is. I told you there is. The swearing in *stamps the System onto your soul.*"

"No, what you said, and what we had been able to deduce, was that the System implants a tiny fragment of itself into your soul, which then interfaces with the main body of the System. The distinction matters, because it means there is communication between your soul and the main body. And in case you haven't noticed, somehow, when humans interact with higher-dimensional beings, it usually involves a whole lot of highly expensive magical furniture, sacrifices, and intensive spell work."

"Or you have a Station Six situation," Truth countered. "Higher dimensions just leaning on a place. No furniture, sacrifices, or rituals required."

"Young man, would you describe any portion of your time at Station Six as 'subtle' or 'hard to spot'?"

"I would not," Truth allowed.

"Whereas, despite *centuries* of observation and testing, we have never caught the System in action."

Truth thought that one over a moment. *Hey, not-the-System, how did you describe communicating with the main System? Like sending messages, right?"*

<<*Basically. We didn't communicate with words, but basically. And I don't know where they went, or I would have said something. I just knew that to communicate with the main System, I had to direct the relevant information and concepts* like so *and any reply would just . . . turn up.*>>

Just turn up. Really just turn up?

<<*I don't have a better way to describe it. I would just know. The "System" that you interacted with? That little office-lady-looking sprite?*>>

Yeeeeeessssss . . .

<<*That was the System working through me. What to say, how to say it, what to make you hallucinate. You were communicating with the System Astrologica, but I was playing mediator for you both. Delivering messages back and forth.*>>

Huh.

<<*It didn't seem relevant, so I didn't mention it.*>>

"Mr. Wells?" Merkovah said. Truth startled. He must have been silent for longer than he thought.

"Sorry, thinking."

"Something I tend to encourage. We have been planning for this for a while. If you still don't manage to make the System show itself during or after the rescue, we have some contingency plans. Which I'm not going to discuss, for obvious reasons. Anything else I should know?"

"Not yet. Something about the arrangement of things. Communicating from soul to mind then mind to soul to . . . what, exactly? It reminds me of, well, prayer." Truth spoke slowly. *Prayer* wasn't quite the right word either, but he was suffering from the lack of conceptual vocabulary.

Merkovah just grunted in reply. "All right, let's run through things. I can't imagine we have much time left before this ritual is traced."

They raced through the details of what had happened since Conjin. Merkovah had a good laugh out of Starbrite sabotaging its own productivity with the roadblocks, and another out of the giant demon blowing up the bank it was supposed to protect. He flat-out refused to believe that Dr. Sun was a sadistic old monster, however, and insisted that it must have been a disguise. Truth didn't argue about it. Maybe the old man was right.

"Anything else?" Merkovah asked.

"So much. So, so much. Let me fill you in on MegaShroom and a small commission I made in the university."

Truth spoke quickly. Merkovah laughed again and said he would look into them.

"All right, if we are down to that—"

"Last thing, I promise," Truth rushed. "I heard a theory about why we can't cultivate past Level Nine."

"Oh? That's relevant to anything?"

"Yes. What if it's the planetary spirit? What if that eminence just decided it didn't like humans and choked off our path of ascension?"

There was silence over the altar.

"Teacher?"

"Where did you hear that?"

"Talking with a demon. Not an infernal demon, a local."

"Ah." There was a longer silence. "Earth Brotherhood?"

Truth blinked in surprise. "Yes."

"The idea . . . has been around. No evidence supports it, and it is entirely supposition. I have *excellent* reason to think that God is actively ignoring this world, and that seems like reason enough for the collapse. Everything before that being his dwindling patience with our repeated failure to abide by his law."

"Sure. Something to think about, though."

"Yes. Dead drop will be at N-41. Give me a day or two to get it set up."

They said their farewells. Truth had mixed feelings about not mentioning the whole *Can't imagine a better world* thing, but it sounded like the exorcist had enough on his mind as it was. *I really miss just being able to talk with him about stuff. Just being able to ask all the questions to someone who either knew the answers or knew where to find the answers.*

He sighed and looked over at the deer-demon meditating under the tree. The demon knew more than Truth was really comfortable with, but . . . even if the demon spilled everything to Internal Security, would things really be different for Truth? Or, put another way, would the demon ever volunteer anything, given that their temple might be obliterated for helping Jeon's most wanted?

No. The abbot was going to keep his mouth shut. They just wanted him gone, soonest, with as little evidence of his passing as possible.

Which was fair enough, really. And he kind of felt like he owed the old-timer.

"So. I'm all done here." Truth nodded to the abbot.

"Anything else you need?" the abbot asked.

"No, I'm set. Just for my own peace of mind, you are aware that even if you call Internal Security right this minute, you are still 'aiding and abetting,' right? And the penalties for that?"

"Oh, yes. Or potentially 'offering aid and comfort to the enemy,' depending on who you are. Move it from conspiracy to treason. Not that the penalty would be different either way." The giant deer head nodded calmly.

"Right." Truth was a little thrown by all this, but there really wasn't anything else to say. "Thanks for the chat and the insight. Be well."

"Mmm."

The abbot just nodded again. Truth shrugged and ran West. The Great White Mountain was north and east. No need to make things easy for anyone tracking him. And besides, the River Fan flowed into the sea not too far from there.

Truth ran through the woods, just happy to be wearing pants this time. His head was buzzing with ideas. The sheer scope of everything. He was a tower rat. It hadn't been that long, from his perspective, since he was studying for the SAT, hoping for a better nest for him and the siblings. He had *wanted* to be a good rat.

He shook his head and focused. He was near the river. There would be at least one, possibly two more checkpoints over the river between there and the ocean. Well. He could deal.

Truth ran flat-out, trying to get as much distance from the temple as quickly as he could. He hit the highway in just a couple of minutes. There was a short moment of agonizing about running along the road or taking the literal slow boat, but the debate was happily resolved for him by the barbed wire and lookout posts lining the riverside. Far, far too short to stop him from jumping over, but they spoke to a certain way of thinking. The mouth of the river was being fenced off. There would be checkpoints over the water and checkpoints on the road.

He'd bet there would be fewer over the water. He looked around. Not a significant amount of traffic on this basically nowhere stretch of highway, and a terminally bored private standing in the lookout. The conscript was displaying the zeal and diligence Truth remembered from his own service days, as she firmly refused to look at either the river or the road. She doubtless had faith that one of her fellow conscripts would spot any problems. After all, they would be paying attention to their jobs and not, for example, hypothetically, enjoying some depressingly basic pornography and bathtub narcotics. Like she was.

He dashed across the six lanes, jumped up on top of the stubby watchtower, then with a little help from Abner's Amble launched himself out over the water. It was a little finicky on the landing, but he was able to time it right so he could land at a run. He had sprinted to the closest cargo ship in record time. Getting up the side of the ship was more challenging but not that challenging. He had a hell of a vertical leap, and the friction of his shoes on the hull was enough to let him push up.

Truth was standing next to the captain on the bridge of the ship in less than thirty seconds from deciding he would travel by boat. Unseen. Unheard. Moving like gods and ghosts.

Truth looked down at his hand and clenched it into a fist. He admired the way the tendons appeared, taut as piano wires, and the way the blue arteries snaked under his skin. He relaxed his hand and then flexed again. Enjoying the strong grip and the feeling of the blood pumping up his muscles.

He smiled and let it go. Time to nose around and figure out where they were headed.

Truth nosed around for exactly five minutes before he found himself back on the bridge. It turned out that while a cargo ship is, indeed, very large, the portion of it occupied by humans is very small. And yet, somehow, he couldn't find any indication of how the ship was steered.

He retreated to the bridge. The bridge was also "wrong," in that there was a complete absence of a steering wheel. There was a little shrine, a chair for the captain, an enormous trash bin already partially full of empty energy drink bottles, an ashtray fully full of cigarette butts . . . a whole lot of nothing that told him where they were going.

What kind of incredibly cursed ship doesn't have a steering wheel? Or even a damn compass? How are they navigating this thing? With good wishes?

<<Yes?>>

What?

<<What? That is exactly how they are navigating this thing. Why would they need a steering wheel on a boat?>>

It's a ship, not a boat. And how else would you steer it?

<<When in your entire life have you seen a ship steered by some fishy rando turning a wheel? The magic collapse hasn't happened yet. You absolute dumbass, are you confusing your reincarnations? You are looking directly at the steering mechanism.>>

Truth looked around. Nothing seemed like a likely candidate. The only thing that looked remotely noteworthy was the shrine. Truth walked over. It took him a minute to understand what he was seeing. There was a little icon of . . . he wasn't sure what saint. Then below that were a few small dumplings, some fresh fruit, and a truly heinous-looking sigil, carved into polished bone. At the front end of the table was a wide map showing a route traced in dried blood. It started in Harban, ran up the Fan, out into the bay, then into the wider Green Sea, then sharply north. A short haul, as ocean vessels went.

He traced his finger along the route. A short haul north and west. Terminating at the port of Nailad, which sat at the end of a substantial peninsula and that, when he drew his finger back east, was just north of the Jeon border. Truth smiled. The mountains along the Jeon-Onis border were beyond rugged. Spiteful would be a fair description. Poor beyond belief, even by Truth's standards. Only the mine bosses and other criminals made money.

It would be a long haul through horrible terrain, filled with the defeated and their predators, all to go digging in to a volcano to save a princess and hopefully kill an evil king.

I really am a fool. But now for the real challenge—convincing Etenesh and Jember that I'm not trying to be a hero.

CHAPTER 57

ADMIRING THE SCENERY

The trip to Nailad was blood-stoppingly dull. The checkpoint sucked, but he knew how to manage those now. After his stint in the chamber with the Snake That Eats Its Own Tail, his ability to seal up his energy had massively improved. It did make him wonder how many divinations just slid right over him. Not finding anything to latch on to.

Merkovah's plan for him since day one had been to make a spell-resistant little monster. The exorcist knew what he was talking about. Truth watched a flock of seven black birds wheel over the mouth of the River Fan before scattering. Then another batch was summoned, and then scattered again. And again. Divination of a sort. Not finding anything, apparently.

Such a shame. What a terrible waste of money and magic, there at the end of days. Truth could feel it more clearly out on the water. The magic was noticeably thinning now. Things took that little bit more energy. Talismans, carefully calibrated to work in specific magic environments, became noticeably less reliable. Not all collapsing all at once, but Truth was seeing an awful lot of busted light talismans.

Five years, my entire ass.

<<How long are you going to hold a grudge about that?>>

Forever. Ten reincarnations from now, I will flatten the first dumbfuck who starts yapping about a light's operational lifespan and have no idea why. Or why it feels so right.

The freighter made its way steadily up toward Onis. Truth had a vague sort of fondness for the country. It was one of two countries other than Jeon he could name before joining the army. He knew about it because you could buy a pretty decent dried-noodle soup in the convenience store for not *too* much money that claimed on the package to have "Authentic Onis Flavor."

He thought Onis was an ingredient but eventually got set straight. Onis was the country to the north. It had a lot of similarities to Jeon, but the language was totally different, it was way bigger, and it was way less developed. And it was the source of tasty, affordable dried-noodle soups. This was the total information Truth had, then and now, about Onis.

The freighter docked at the cargo port in Nailad and cranes started lifting crates off the deck. Human operators in the cranes. Truth could see them moving with golem precision, lifting and shifting the enormous metal boxes. If it was any slower than the docks in Harban, it wasn't by much. He jumped ashore and jogged down the road. Next stop—a convenience store.

He needed a new road atlas. And toilet paper. And snacks. And just maybe some dried soup.

He stopped suddenly and smacked his head. They didn't have the System there. He would need money for those times when he wanted to spend money. He would have to look into robbery as he went.

The buildings were annoyingly similar to the docks he had seen in Jeon. So were the apartment blocks. He even recognized some of the same chains. And, all right, he was just barely the other side of the border from Jeon, but it was disappointing. Say what you like about Siphios or the Free State, they were *different*.

He sighed. At least the people were speaking a different language, and the food smelled different. Some similarities there, but different. *System, the language?*

<<Actually pretty different from Jeongo. I'll try to pick it up as we go, but . . . honestly, how much time do you plan to spend here? Talking to people?>>

Valid.

Truth spotted a convenience store. He grabbed a road atlas, filled his backpack to bursting with snacks, water, and whatever supplies he thought he might need. There was a decent little hot-food selection, too. It was probably the worst possible example of that kind of food, but it had been a long time since he had eaten something hot.

Lots of braised dishes he noticed. Lots of sweet-and-sour smells. He grabbed something he could recognize—shrimp. They were startlingly nice. Large, plump, fried in oil, then served coated in a salty, savory brown sauce and some kind of sweeter . . . something. He didn't know what the sweet thing was, but it was good. He dove in on some chicken. This was both sweet and sour, with loads of savory flavors creeping up. Loads of ginger and scallion in everything.

Truth smiled. He would make a point of coming back. If convenience-store food was this good, how good would food from a street stall be?

Back on the sidewalk, shoplifting done, Truth consulted his new road atlas. Great White Mountain really wasn't all that far from there. Not close, but he reckoned that, road conditions permitting, you could drive there in six hours or less. Eight if you had to take a detour. Next thing to find—a carriage. He might be able to run as fast as a carriage, but he was damned if he wanted to.

Clothes! He would probably need new clothes. Yeah, he was going up, then into a mountain. Might not *need*-need them, but comfort mattered in international espionage. He had to change his way of thinking. He was out of the terrorism game.

He rushed around the city, hunting for whatever seemed useful. He wound up changing his backpack to a larger camping backpack. He would stick to using a tarp instead of a tent, but Great White Mountain was a damn big volcano surrounded by a deep forest and rugged mountains. Body cultivation or not, some camping supplies sounded sensible.

He was unable to find any romance novels in a language he could read. He couldn't even find a thriller in Jeongo. Disgraceful. He could only beseech the heavens with his eyes and set off to find a stealable carriage.

After thinking about it for a bit, he went back toward the docks. If it was anything like Jeon, the difference between "criminal enterprise" and "legitimate business" would be the comparative poverty of the criminals. On the other hand, they would be much less inclined to call the cops. So, that would be one less worry.

It took a while. The docks were depressingly orderly and quite heavily policed. It wasn't until he saw a shipping crate being loaded with people that he knew he had found his targets. He waited until the crate was packed up, then followed the smugglers back to their carriage. A little disappointing to see a ten-year-old coupe fancied up with decals and undercarriage talisman lights, but it would do.

It was the work of a moment to relieve the smuggler of both the activation talisman and his life. Truth took some small pleasure in tossing the body into a crate, and the crate into a shipping container. It took fractionally longer to rip off the undercarriage lighting. The decals were really on there, but with some careful scraping and a complete disregard for the paint job, he got them off. The coupe now looked like absolute trash but the kind of trash you would ignore every day on the road.

Perfect.

The interior was a bit messy but not terrible. It smelled of artificial pine, covering up the smell of cigarettes and bleem or some other drug. Well. He could deal. The smell of his childhood right there. As prepared as he could be, he set off.

An hour into the drive, Truth concluded that international travel was overrated. This was dull. Dull highway, with dull things just off the highway. The advertising provided an occasional flash of color. The sky was a beautiful warm blue. The early summer was at that sweet spot where it was warm but not hot. And he was bored silly.

They were up in the mountains now, which was nice when there was a view. Mostly, there wasn't. Just kilometer after kilometer of cliff face and thin trees. He made it ninety minutes before he pulled over at a rest stop. There was a viewing platform, letting him look down a little valley. Apparently, it was important.

There was an informational plaque by the guardrail, with pictures of mages warring on each other. Just grass, trees, and rocks now. The heroes, their immortal names lost in the echoes of time, lay on the field where their imperishable legend was ignored by busloads of senior citizens queuing up for the toilets.

Truth looked out over the valley. He didn't know what had happened there. He probably wouldn't know even if he could read the sign. He knew even less about history than geography. People had died there. A lot of them, it looked like. And that was that. On to the next thing. Heaven, Hell, or your next life. And people just rolled on past, looking for the bathroom and a place to stretch.

Was that . . . a good thing? That people could forget? That people could live without being trapped in that memory of mass murder? It should be a good thing. Truth felt a little nauseous at the thought. He had never fought in a battle that would be memorialized. He was glad of that.

The fights he did get into were memorable enough for him. Nobody else needed to carry that. But it would be nice if someone remembered something about him after he died. There should be some kind of immortal record of those who did amazing things, right?

A couple of old ladies complained. About what, he didn't know, but he knew the sound of complaining. They walked straight past the little plaque, grabbing their hips and waving helplessly at the sky. Not even glancing down into the valley. Seen one mountain valley, seen them all, apparently.

The immortal heroes could rest without people gawping at them. Their bones strengthening the mountains, their souls carefully pruned of the sin and horror of their final moments before being returned to God. And that wasn't so bad, was it? Truth poked at the idea. It should be all right. Your life might be a brutal series of nightmare moments, but eventually, all that would be washed away.

You might never be clean in this life, but in the next, you would be pure. And hey, maybe they died doing something useful. Stopping an invasion, or defeating a murderous rebel army, or something. The glory of the nation.

"If anyone questions why we died, tell them, because our fathers lied," Truth murmured.

<<Eh?>>

Truth just shook his head and joined the queue. He needed a pee too. The dead wouldn't grudge the living that comfort.

Truth came out of the bathroom and took a final look at the plaque. There were pictures of the mages, yes, but underneath were maps with little boxes and arrows. They made a little story, the boxes moving around the map in the direction of the arrows.

One group of boxes closed in around the other, smaller group of boxes. The small group fell back, trying to retreat up the mountain. The terrain was more defensible, but they were so badly outnumbered, it didn't matter. Truth could see it. Some absolute lackwit decided to march them through the valley, then was shocked to learn that the enemy had pickets set and plenty of troops nearby. It would have been an utter slaughter.

In a fit of desperation, someone led them up the mountains, using the narrow valleys and ridges to limit the effective number of enemies their outnumbered troops had to face. There was never any hope of victory. There was only the hope that the enemy could be stopped long enough to allow the main body of the troop to escape.

It seemed that, right there, off the most godforsaken dull highway in this stretch of mountains, a company had stood—and held. They bought that time. The main body of the troop escaped. The forsaken company held the valley still.

He didn't know why he was crying. The real world just hurt. Were heroes buried there? Or villains? Was this the best humanity had to show, or the worst? He didn't know. It just shouldn't be like this. He knew that. It shouldn't be like this.

He wiped away his tears and got back in the carriage. *The world shouldn't be like this. Time to change it.*

He had barely gone another hour before it all went very wrong.

CHAPTER 58

COMING ATTRACTIONS

Truth was two hours north of Nailad when the blue sky turned pink. It was the pink of a boiled shrimp, Truth thought, though he admittedly felt a bit lightheaded. There was a sudden feeling, a sudden absence of pressure, leaving him lightheaded and almost dizzy.

The carriage stopped. The power had cut out. So had the brakes, but that wasn't as much of a problem for Truth. The car wasn't going so fast that he couldn't just hop out. He just let it coast to the bottom of the slope. It had enough momentum to climb up the next slope partway but lost speed. Truth stepped out and walked the car over to the side of the road. It took some careful work wedging in big rocks around the wheels, but he managed to pin the car in place.

He knew what was going on now. There weren't enough cosmic rays there to keep everything moving. Not nothing; it didn't feel like when he was raiding the antitheist hideout. But not enough.

Wonder why the sky turned pink. Can't think what that might have to do with magic.

<<Truth? Grab your bags and run for shelter. Your carriage won't cut it. Dig into the mountainside if you have to. But do it right the fuck now.>>

Truth didn't waste time with questions. He was on the side of a mountain, rock on his left, an almost-sheer drop on the right. The engineers had taken pains to remove any overhangs, and he didn't think he was anywhere near a rest stop.

He called the Tongue to his hand. He had dug out rock with her before, and she didn't mind it. He could feel the hairs on the back of his neck starting to rise. Truth used the Fangs from Incisive to slice apart the rock face. It took a hell of a lot more effort than it ever had before. Worse than when he first used it. Much worse. His own reserves took a nasty hit.

Deeper is more important than wider. Just needs to be big enough for me and my stuff.

Truth hacked away, furiously digging a coffin-sized hole in the rock. He got it a little deeper than his body length, widened it a bit so he had room for everything.

Incisive wasn't just hinting now; it was flat-out yelling. Truth slid into the hole feet-first, then blocked the entrance with his bags. Shaking hands ripped the tarp out of the pack. One end tucked under the pack, then pulled over the top, covering the pack and Truth both, blocking up a little bit more of the entrance.

There was a crack of thunder but no flash of light. Then another. Then a rumbling, drumming, organ-shaking roll of noise. Truth could feel pressure grinding down on him, on his apertures, grinding down but not steadily. There were sudden spikes of pressure. Sudden pulls, then pushes of energy, ripping at him. Trying to tear apart his apertures. Trying to break him as a mage.

The smells—what were they? Chemical, or rotting meat, or the taste of artificial grapes and burning buildings. Seeming to drill into his nostrils and up into his pores. Or trying to, at any rate. The body cultivation wasn't just for show. Truth pulled the backpack close to his head and hung on tight.

Truth felt like he was covered in thousands of ants. Little tingles of crawling electricity over his whole body. With a barely repressed shriek of horror, an ant crawled over his eye. They were coming out of the stone. They were coming out of the solid stone walls! He didn't have space to move. All he could do was thrash in place and try to kill as many as he could. They were biting at him. Ignoring his backpack and biting at him.

He spasmed, trying to crush the infinite crawling things against the rough stone walls. Smashing his arms and hands against the stone so hard, even that ancient granite cracked. There was a sudden stink of apples. As though he were buried in apples—ripe, almost rotting. Covered in the smell and the millions of ants trying to dig their way into him.

Stone flakes shattered and littered the little coffin. He could hear the little flakes sliding and bouncing around, and they sounded like the color green. Then it was electric purples trying to pull out his tendons and the very cosmic energy in his body. Trying to rip it right out and fill his body with apple stench and billions of stoneborn ants.

He could hear something sizzling, a rattling feeling as something sprayed against his tarp. Then stopped, then started again. The tempo of the unnatural whatever-it-was had no reason to it. It didn't smell like rain, but over the apple stench, lost in the madness of the crawling ants, Truth hardly noticed it.

There was something outside. Even lost to the madness and overwhelming sensation, he could feel something moving outside. Something too great and terrible to be seen. Something that would shatter his mind and burn out his eyes if he dared peek. His body screamed at him at a level below or beyond words and mind that he must hide. He must be buried in the earth. He must not be seen. But the ants were everywhere and the world pulled and pushed at the very magic in his soul!

There was a roaring now, a roaring of burning fires and screaming fans in the terraces. A roaring of waves crashing against cliffs, of a forest in a gale. It was everywhere, roaring without meaning. Roaring with a meaning too subtle and awful for Truth to know. The tugging and tearing at his apertures seemed to throb in time with the impossible vast noise. The ants vibrated with it. The noise was everywhere. The roaring cry, between a lion and a dragon, was everywhere. It was in everything. It always had been. He just hadn't been listening.

And then the madness was past. Truth thrashed for a few seconds longer, not realizing that the ants had vanished. The air was quiet and still. He lay on the ground, shuddering and trying to breathe. He was exhausted. His little hideaway had almost doubled in diameter as he thrashed around. His clothes were shredded. His entire body ached.

He worked a hand up in front of his face. Torn-up knuckles. The pads of his fingertips were ripped open too, though he could see the bleeding stopping on its own. There must be enough ambient magic around for his body cultivation to get back into action. He would need to cast a healing spell to fix all the damage.

System. What the hell was that?

<<I don't have a word for it. I just thought—what happens when there is a sudden vacuum?>>

Truth stared blankly up at the roof of his one-man cave. He couldn't think. Couldn't even imagine what the System was talking about.

<<You make a sudden hole in a medium, and that medium will rush in to fill it. Works on water, air, dirt, lava, whatever. And when it rushes in, there is turbulence.>>

Most of the cosmic energy suddenly vanished. Then the energy in the air around it rushed to fill the gap. Which resulted in all of whatever that was.

<<Yeah. My best guess, anyway. I don't know what it was any more than you do.>>

Truth felt no particular urge to climb out of the hole. It wasn't nice in there, but it was better than being caught in whatever happened outside.

It's going to become a thing, isn't it? This isn't some one-off thing; it's going to be the new normal, until the magic runs out. Sudden . . . I need a better description than "magic storms," but that.

<<Probably.>>

Truth lay there a moment longer. He tried to get a candy bar out of his backpack, but it was awkward, fumbling around inside for the elusive snack. He gave up and crawled out, pushing his bag in front of him.

The world outside looked pretty much the same. Which didn't seem fair, somehow. He sat on the road and ate his candy bar. Not very sweet, which was also a shame, but it had a load of nuts in it, which was good. He washed it down with a bottle of cold tea and called it good enough.

The carriage was, in a word, trashed. In two words—completely trashed. Every talisman and fetish was utterly burnt out, broken, or melted. The bound demon evaporated. Whether it was before the storm or during, Truth didn't know. Either way, it was gone.

He looked up at the sneering blue sky. "Is it because I didn't want to run across a mountain chain again? Is that it?"

The sky didn't answer. Truth cinched his pack on and set off at a jog. "Other international secret agents don't have to do this kind of thing. I'm sure of it."

Truth didn't have the right words to describe what he was feeling. This was not, for once, a gap in his education. He wasn't sure if anyone had the words for it. How do you describe something you had always known but never noticed, suddenly misbehaving?

The cosmic rays filled the world. They didn't ignore matter, as far as Truth knew, anyway, but for all practical purposes, they were omnipresent. It occurred to him that the planet itself must be generating cosmic rays somehow. Presumably not too much, since they were living on the surface.

It would explain Conjin, too. He wondered how a city under that much water could be hauling in enough cosmic energy. Easy-peasy. It was coming up from the bedrock. For now.

He ran up and down the mountains. Even after an apocalyptic event like the storm, it was still a boring highway. Although he was starting to see signs that it might not stay boring. The turbulence had caught up some of the trees next to the road. Some had merely exploded, caught fire, or turned to ash. Others now seemed to move on their own. The way their branches grasped at him spoke of their hunger.

Truth started noticing more houses popping up. More terraced farms. It must be a flatter bit of the mountains. No lights on, nor carriages on the road. A little farther on, he ran into a village. People were . . . not calm. He didn't understand the words, but he understood the emotions.

People were being hauled out of houses on stretchers and carried to the front of a young man's house. He couldn't have been over Level One. Must be some kind of rural doctor or nurse—it seemed he had a specialized healing spell. He cast it over and over, trying to fix whatever was wrong. He was sweating hard. Truth didn't blame him in the slightest. He kept on running. He had a feeling there would be plenty more villages just like this one.

An hour later, he found out he was only somewhat right about that. There were plenty more villages. Some didn't have a doctor at all. No wagons, no carriages, no talisman that kept Nan's kidneys working, and all of a sudden, the alchemical medicine had gone worryingly off. Turning into poison or clumps of dust.

Worst of all were the mutations. People sprouting extra eyes, or their skin melting, or thousands of parasitic beetles slowly making homes under their skins. Truth could only bless his constant commitment to body cultivation there. No wonder the Anak family was looking forward to the end of the world. They would be unrivaled, even if the surviving mages turned to sacrifice-fueled magic.

He crossed a pretty ordinary-looking ridge, and suddenly, he could see it. On the horizon, across yet more mountains and a deep forest, was the caldera of the Great White Mountain. That ancient, active volcano that gave birth to Jeon.

Truth took a quick snack break. The dark tower was in sight. Time to go rescue the princess.

CHAPTER 59

THE SEA OF TREES

Truth glared at the forest draping itself around the Great White Mountain. It looked fine. He didn't trust a single splinter of it. The memories of Happori and the deep, multilayered defenses around it were firmly lodged in his memory.

Oh, happy thought—the magic storm must be playing absolute hell with their golems and talisman defenses. He couldn't see the evidence of that from kilometers away, but it seemed almost certain. The happy thought was replaced by an unhappy one—what if the forest was outside the affected area?

Only one way to find out. He sighed and trudged on. At roughly sixty kilometers an hour. Body cultivation remained fun. Although Truth did notice that his shoes lasted considerably longer if he ran barefoot. His skin held up better than the rubber.

The forests were nice. He guessed they were mostly pine with some other evergreens mixed in. Or whatever you called trees with narrow, needle-like leaves instead of wide, flat leaves. Fir? Oak? Truth had considered adding trees to the pile of things to research and had firmly decided against it. The pile was too big already. Adding anything else was just masochism.

He tried to remember anything relevant about the forest around the Great White Mountain and drew a complete blank. They were always just backdrops on pictures. Apparently, the nation's founders descended on the mountain, and when the Founding King stood at the summit, rainbows appeared that covered the whole sky as a noble phoenix landed on his arm and paid him homage.

The king then swung his sword and split apart the clouds for ten thousand kilometers, jumped from the top of the volcano to the bottom in a single leap, ate an entire cow, memorized twenty books of poetry without even opening them, and learned every language in the world as soon as he heard a single word spoken. He then got married to the phoenix and fathered forty flame-haired sons and daughters by her, each of which was a heartbreaking beauty and the most thunderously powerful of mages. It was just possible that the stories had been exaggerated, but hell, Truth had seen some weird shit. Maybe that actually happened.

The last king of Jeon . . . Truth struggled. He was sure he had heard *something* about him.

<<Overdosed on convenience-store dick pills, claiming that the alchemists didn't know how to treat royalty and he had a duty to continue his lineage. He was practically

a beggar, selling his signature as a lucky charm, traveling from city to city. About four hundred years ago. There was that ad campaign for dick pills that featured him.>>

Rough.

<<*Meh.*>>

Truth nodded. "Meh" summed up his feelings about it, too.

Any insight on the forest?

<<*Definitely pine and fir, or at least definitely not oak. Oak has flat leaves.*>>

Thanks.

There were established trails in the forest. There were well-traveled routes to the summit, too. There used to be regular offerings made up there, then it just became a tourist destination. Did Starbrite lock down the entire mountain and forest?

There were some carriages on the road now. Most driving flat-out, going dangerously fast on the mountain roads. So, the storm couldn't have spread too far, but news about it sure had. Or maybe there had been a lot of them, just scattered around.

Would the "Magic Collapse Deniers" call them normal storms? Or argue that the economic cost of doing anything about them was far greater than the losses they caused?

It wouldn't do to overreact. They have a duty to look after the interests of the shareholders, after all. Whoever the "shareholders" might be. Presumably, they were people immune to the collapse of magic. Otherwise, one might think that doing something about it would be in the interest of the shareholders.

Truth exhaled the morbid thoughts and ran on. The villages were emptying out or digging in. There seemed to be considerably divided opinion on the right answer. In the short term, getting somewhere with more supplies and support made sense, but long-term? The cities would be slaughterhouses.

Truth would be loading up on all the canned and dried food he could find, digging a deep, deep well, and making the most waterproof, weatherproof shack he could. Farming and hunting would come after most of the neighbors died off. They had left things a bit late, but better late than never.

Oh, look, the morbidity came straight back. Maybe it had been lonely.

He laughed silently, watching the trees flicker past. He would need to stockpile cheap romance novels and the like. He would burgle a library before the rats got in, or people looking for kindling, or insulation. Hmm. How would he get it to Siphios? Even for him, it seemed like an awful long way to run. Grab a spell bird and hope it lasted the trip? He let himself drift into daydreams. It passed the time.

Merkovah's dead drop was in a village called Wieyon, about which he knew nothing. His road atlas had told him that it was directly across the border from the village of Minzu, and a short detour off the highway he was on. It made sense. There were only two main roads to Great White Mountain. This happened to be the most direct one if you were coming straight from Harban.

Truth ran into Minzu. There was no transition. Mountain wilderness became dense factory housing in the span of a single pace. It was surreal. He was blazing through a busy little town. The map labeled it as a village, but that was clearly wrong. There had to be ten thousand people living there.

He had time to try some food, right? Right. He would keep an eye out for street food. The town just . . . kept on going. It seemed that he had underestimated the size. All low-rise, long-running apartment buildings and big factories. There were grocery stores, drug stores, and all that, but his main impression of Minzu was long apartment buildings and factories next to wide roads. A lot of gray. He mentally shrugged. Maybe there would be street food in Jeon.

He cut over to the bridge that crossed the river dividing Jeon from Onis. Guarded, of course. Heavily. Lots and lots of highly agitated conscripts waving needlers around. Lots of Onis border guards, too, and they didn't look any older or more experienced than their Jeon counterparts.

The Ulay River would barely rate as a tributary of the mighty River Fan, were they connected. This wasn't just Harban snobbery from Truth—it was never more than two hundred meters wide, and frequently narrowed to less than a hundred and forty. Plenty of watchtowers, plenty of guards, but by Truth's now intensely jaded standards, it might as well have been unguarded.

Truth nodded casually at the sloppy defenses. Then dropped into cover behind a supply warehouse and started surveilling the crossing with brutal intensity. He had been burned far too many times to assume that he was seeing everything there was. Two hours of obsessive staring later, he had identified some impressively sophisticated recording talismans and a decent array of signal equipment but nothing particularly alarming.

There were a half dozen crossings between Minzu and Wieyon, many of them in sight of each other. And there were dozens of villages just like this dotting the Ulay, if not a hundred. This one bridge just didn't rate that much attention.

He eased his way along the underside of the bridge anyway. It wasn't like he couldn't hang on just fine, and there were fewer recording talismans down there. Just in case.

One act of illegal immigration later, he was trotting through Wieyon. It was unsurprisingly similar to Minzu. The signs were in different languages, but that was about it. He had the sneaking suspicion that most of the border guards "forgot" to ask for passports or ID most of the time. It seemed like that kind of place.

A lot of people standing around in front of their houses, or rushing back and forth from the shops. Trying to hide their purchases. He might be out of luck on the street food. There were moving carriages, and lights and things, so clearly the storm had missed this place. This was fear-buying, then. Justified fear but still fear-buying.

The dead drop was supposed to be an overturned flowerpot in front of a yellow-painted house at a certain intersection. The house was there. The flowerpot was not. Truth looked around. For what, he didn't know. He didn't want to hang around in Jeon. No reason he could put his finger on, just . . . he didn't feel safe. So, he spun on his heel and ran back across the border.

There was no sudden explosion of hidden police, or fast-moving watchers, or anything to justify his paranoia. Still. He felt much safer there among strangers.

He traced the distance from where he was to the caldera of Great White Mountain in his road atlas. Interestingly, while there was a reasonably direct road on the Jeon side of the border, you basically had to loop around the whole mountain and come from the north to access it on the Onis side. No reason he could see for that, so it was probably down to the terrain being too rugged. The loop around turned a roughly hundred-kilometer journey into a two-hundred-and-fifty-kilometer journey.

Hell with it. He had run cross-country often enough. He would enjoy the novel experience of doing it while wearing pants.

"I wanted to be a talisman-maintenance tech. I want that clearly established. And sure, *now* it looks like the job has a limited future, but in the short term, I'd never be short of work. But no. No, I get to be the guy who runs naked through forests."

Truth was muttering. He didn't expect anyone to answer him, and his expectation was met. In the face of mass indifference, he set off to find a place to sleep. It was still early, but it had been a tiring day.

He wandered the long-row apartment buildings. Identical building after identical building. Nicer than the one he grew up in, by miles. Only about four stories tall, with a lot more light coming in. No visible evidence of gangs, either. So, that was nice. He would still prefer not to sleep on someone's floor. Somewhere, there would be a hotel. He'd skip the luxury suite this time and just find an empty room.

The room he wound up taking was utterly adequate. Not fancy. Not . . . exquisite or anything. Just clean, comfortable, and quiet. The whole hotel was pretty empty. It seemed that whatever travelers might have been staying there had all left. He was able to score more precooked food from the local convenience stores, and it continued to be . . . fine. He had the nagging feeling it could be great but the essential convenience-store nature of what he was eating was dragging it down.

Truth lay in bed, staring at the ceiling. If the dead drop wasn't ready for pickup tomorrow, he'd scout the sea of trees regardless, then come back in the evening. There was a feeling of pressure building up. Like a coming storm or waiting for Dad to come home. The peace was an illusion. The madness and pain he had felt in his little tomb—that was real. That was life in an apocalypse. Hiding in your little hole, suffering, and glad you weren't suffering worse.

He laughed at himself again. Turning morbid. He would be turning mean again soon. He didn't want that. He was the fool—a hero on a quest to save the damsel in distress. That he helped keep in distress, but he wouldn't dwell on that. He closed his eyes and remembered the warmth of watching pitz with Etenesh and Jember. The sheer animal joy of letting his iron horse run through the deserts and mountains.

He remembered how sweet Etenesh tasted and how warm she made him feel. It had been a bad day. He fell asleep smiling anyway.

CHAPTER 60

MONSTERS OF THE DEEP

Truth slipped back across the river well after dawn. If he was a paranoid sort, and he was, he would triple surveillance of the border crossing in the hours just before dawn, when things were at their darkest and minds at their least attentive. Truth slept a full night, had a solid breakfast of rice and veggies, "enjoyed" a savagely mediocre cup of coffee, and spent an hour just watching the border. Nothing alarming. The soldiers looked calmer. Not "too calm," just a bit more settled after the drama of yesterday's storms.

Lots of people queued up on both sides of the border, though. Not everyone was being let through, and they weren't being excessively calm about it. Whether they were going home or just away, Truth didn't know. All the crossings were in more or less the same state.

On the theory that anything that looked undersurveilled was a trap, he picked a middling busy crossing and slipped under the bridge. The Ulay burbled along below him, promising to soak his trousers in frigid pollution if he fell. Truth firmed up his grip and crossed quickly. The recording talismans and golems looked straight past him.

The yellow house was where he had left it. The half dozen hosed-down and overturned flowerpots were new, as were the rest of the potted plants littering the ground by the front step. Truth took a look at some of the nursery tags still shoved in next to them. Vegetables, mostly. Squash, tomatoes, cabbage, beans. Was it the season for them? He had never learned much about gardening, let alone growing vegetables. Still. Securing an extra source of calories in a couple of months was a *good* idea.

The recording crystal was tiny, barely the size of a grain of rice, and hidden under a bit of dried dirt stuck at the very bottom of the pot. Must have "missed a spot" cleaning the pots. The hairs on the back of his neck had risen straight back up as soon as he set foot in Jeon again. There continued to be nothing he could identify as a threat, which Truth interpreted as meaning something uncommonly nasty was cooking. He got out at speed.

He picked a plumbing-supply store at random, made his way to the back room, and plopped down on the one available chair. A good-enough place to review the crystal. So far, his strategy of moving at random had paid off. It was hard to surveil someone who didn't have patterns, let alone intercept them.

He pressed his energy into the crystal carefully, making sure he didn't accidentally overload the tiny thing. A vision of Merkovah appeared in his mind.

"Truth, even in the few hours since we spoke, our plans have been overtaken by
events. Localized magic collapse has been reported across the world. It seems to be
temporary and transient. Our best forecasts suggest that we won't see more of them
for weeks at the earliest. On the other hand, our best forecasts said we wouldn't see
them at all for at least another two months, so I don't hold out any hope there."

Truth nodded at that. He wouldn't either.

"The results politically have been dramatic and intense. I'll spare you the
details—" Truth was actually pretty interested in the details. It seemed highly relevant. "Riots have started popping up globally. Some genuine spontaneous public
outrage. A lot more of them are 'encouraged' by groups looking to take advantage."

Truth's mouth creased mirthlessly at that. Rats rioting over who got to wear the
captain's hat as the ship sank.

"I'd be mad about that," Merkovah continued, "if I weren't behind so many of
them. The local instigators here in Siphios are having a little time out somewhere
quiet. My colleagues have ensured they will not be bored and have plenty of people
to talk to. On the one hand, this doesn't really change our plan or goals. Go in, get
the girl, and if you see anything that looks expensive or useful, break it. On the other
hand, it does mean the security situation is going to be elevated and tense."

Because it was low and relaxed before? Truth gave the illusion a look. Merkovah
must have predicted the look, because he preemptively rolled his eyes.

"Yes, yes, I know. Just think a moment. You know most people don't cultivate
their bodies, and for the tiny minority that do, most of them have no inbuilt means to
hang on to the energy they absorb. Everyone is suddenly in the position where their
tools won't work, their spells won't work, and worse, they will be in crippling pain.
Potentially fatal pain. A situation that can occur at any moment, without warning.
Imagine trying to guard something under those circumstances."

Ah. Yes. He would not be calm and relaxed about it. Actually, he was in a far better
situation than most, and *he* wasn't calm and relaxed about living through another storm.

"They will be in a rush to complete their project, whatever it is. After this message, information on extraction routes, contingencies, and useful information will be
presented. Likewise, we are in a rush to kill Starbrite, the CEO, and the C-suite. Be
clear on this—at least some of those people will certainly be at the research station."

Truth felt a nasty jolt. It was obvious, of course. Where else would they be?

"And yet, despite your determined unreliability, you are the most reliable opera-
tor I have at the moment." Merkovah looked like he didn't know whether to laugh or
cry. "I do good work, apparently."

Truth grinned at that. The old man really did.

"So, rather than sending a team of highly trained, specially prepared special
forces, people who have studied the layout of the mountain in exacting detail, people trained to do recon and prepare detailed tactics for breaching fortifications, I
am sending an aspiring talisman-maintenance technician who really enjoys cheap

romance novels and blasphemy. He will look at all the painfully collected data, some of which cost multiple lives to obtain, nod appreciatively, then wing it."

The old exorcist shook his head. "It professionally offends me that you have succeeded thus far. I'm glad you have, but mad at the same time."

Sounded like most of their relationship, Truth thought.

"Pretty much how our whole relationship has gone," Merkovah continued. "Wrapping up. Your wife is getting discharged later this week. Not all the way better but is now generally considered safe enough to return to her family. She sends her love. Her cousin does too. He's wrapping up his studies at speed and has already lined up a very nice little temple to manage in the near future. If Siphios still exists in twenty years, he will probably be made a priest."

Oh, how nice! Go Jember!

"Your . . . commercial project and . . . protegee . . . are up and running. I can't say for sure they went undetected, but it appears that way. Your servants are well. Good job looking after them. Your large female friend is also fine. Her family is a known quantity. In fact, they are part of one of the contingency plans. We did find your commissioned artwork. After having a minor heart attack laughing, our assets in Harban and other points in Jeon are promoting it. Your 'face' will be appearing on posters, tee shirts, and stickers everywhere. *The Tiger Rises. The Prince Shall Be Its Wings,* apparently."

Truth smiled. It was great to hear everyone was doing well.

"As for myself, I remain, as always, furiously busy and busily furious. Be well, young man. You have a lot of work ahead of you."

Truth had run through the forest like a cheerful ghost. He was immensely buoyed by the news from Merkovah. Just knowing everyone was doing well was incredible. He couldn't explain why it was, but it was. He leapt from tree to tree, feeling sharp and eager for the fight.

The forest was actually undefended, to Truth's quiet surprise. He was sure it would be littered with subtle traps. The reason it wasn't was obvious—tourists. This area was quite popular with hikers, campers and those who enjoyed visiting historical sites. Busloads of tourists would come to the foot of the mountain and hike up. Heaven's Lake filled the caldera and was legendarily beautiful.

The latest information Merkovah had sent confirmed that the institute had entrances under the lake as well as concealed within an inaccessible slope of the mountain. Truth found it a little strange that they would build in such a heavily traveled mountain at all, but no explanation was provided.

How did they even make the base? Some kind of high-level demon summoning to dig it out? he wondered. Then shrugged. He knew how the girl had gotten in there. That case wasn't all that big. An easy tote. Researchers and equipment would be brought in under some kind of optical camouflage or other means of diverting sight. If he could do it, Starbrite definitely could do it.

The pine trees smelled wonderful. He raced through them, not stirring the fallen needles as he rushed up the slope. There was likely a hidden entrance three-quarters of the way to the summit, but he would have to do some investigation. It was either that or dive into the lake and swim down. The bottom was, famously, quite free of mud.

The tree line was roughly two hundred meters away when he started running into covert defenses. Nothing active. Hidden alarms, hidden sensors, hidden devices checking for he didn't know what. There was a subtle, and powerful, network of banishments and forbiddances laid over the forest there. Angels and demons would be wise to avoid this place.

Truth naturally took it as an open invitation. Caution was required, however. Some of these alarms were verging on Level Four power, and that meant custom work. Custom meant nonstandard by definition, which meant that the odds of something sneaky and hard to spot being present were near enough to one hundred percent.

He carefully probed the ground ahead with his senses, pouring power into Incisive to give him as much notice as possible if he was going to step in something nasty. He was making a point of hopping from bare rock to bare rock as he moved, leaving no trace and stirring no leaves.

He had to stop that rather abruptly when Incisive alerted him that his next jump might well be his last. Truth froze, crouching in place. The next rock was nothing interesting—twice the size of a man's head, a mottled gray, with lichen growing on it. He had no idea what kind of rock it was. Rocks, like trees, were a closed and firmly ignored book to Truth.

The rock opened an eye and glared around. The pupil was a sinuous W shape, shrinking and stretching as it peered into the woods. Other, identical eyes opened near the first, practically covering the rock. All darting around, hunting for prey.

Truth held very still. He could feel more than hear the steady draw of breath. Something terrible was stirring. He didn't even breathe. Were the trees swaying with more than the breeze? Was there a rock behind him staring at his back? He didn't dare turn and look. There were creatures that hunted based on motion, he knew. Impossible to know if this was one of them. He would just hold very still and blend into the forest. Hoping the thundering beat of his heart didn't give him away.

He clung to his little rock, carefully looking around himself without turning his head. It was out of the corner of his eye that he managed to spot it. Like tiny glass worms or perfectly camouflaged threads twisting in the fallen needles. Silently, subtly, the forest floor was alive with almost-invisible movement. He had no idea what they were. The sheer alienness of it revolted him.

The forest floor only looked empty and still. It occurred to Truth that he hadn't seen an animal or heard a bird in the last twenty minutes. It also occurred to Truth that Starbrite really was terribly good at defending the things it actually cared about.

He perched on his little rock, watching the threads of something awful writhe around him, as the many eyes of something even worse hunted for him. Not daring to breathe. And still not seeing the door into the mountain.

CHAPTER 61

WOOF WOOF

Truth felt a creeping shortness of breath. He was in the middle of a forest, on the side of a mountain, and he felt claustrophobic. Trapped on his little island of rock in a sea of horrors. Watching the little creeping worm things wriggle along the side of the rock. Some starting to creep up the rock before sliding down again.

I'm just a part of the rock. I'm just a tree. Nothing to see here. I'm not even a bird. I am totally not worth noticing. There is no "I" here at all. There are just rocks and trees.

He focused hard on not breathing. He could hold his breath for ten minutes, easily. Longer, even. Tens of minutes, maybe. So, he didn't have to breathe now. He controlled every tiny muscle in his body. He could even stop his own heart if he had to. So he could be perfectly still. Perfectly still.

Truth forced his attention to little details. Was he radiating heat? Maybe? Probably? He did his best to seal all the heat inside himself. He could seal in cosmic energy, so he could seal in heat. It might hurt him, but he would live.

Anything with heat vision would see a lumpy shape move from thirty-seven degrees down to the comfortable twenty-one of the ambient air.

Scent? He had relied on the Blessing of the Silent Forest to let his scent blend in with the world around him. He leaned in to that. Rather than trying to vanish entirely, he allowed himself to smell like the forest. He smelled like pine, and mountain air, and the early days of summer. Like a timeless moment, existing from before the advent of humanity on this world, or after its passing.

He didn't stop his heart. He wasn't sure he could keep his balance perched on the rock, and the little transparent threads were seething all around. He could force it to slow. Slower and slower. Forcing his body to calm down. The thing with the glaring eyes would tire soon enough or simply go back to hiding. Either way, he would wait for the eyes to close.

The wind stirred the pines. No birds called; no animals rustled through the undergrowth. Even the insects had gone quiet and still. Whatever it was that hid there had driven them all away. Or destroyed them.

He didn't wonder what it was. "He" did his best to forget that "he" even existed.

The alien eyes darted around. Interrogating everything. Examining every errant breeze. The W-shaped pupils shrank, or grew, or even elongated, seemingly turning the entirety of the eye into a hungry little mouth. Other than their jerky movements, there was no indication that anything unnatural was there at all. It was just a rock. Just another innocent part of an empty forest.

The line between predator and prey was thin. Quite often, it was a question of who pulled off the ambush best. The hidden monster slowly started to close its eyes again. Stillness returned to the forest.

Truth held his breath for as long as he could, but eventually, breath and consciousness both had to make their return. He let it come slowly, softly. No sudden gasps for air. Just gentle, small inhalations and exhalations with the stirring breeze.

He did not think for a single second that thing was asleep or that it was any less attentive now that its eyes were closed. It was just hiding. Waiting for something to set foot in its trap.

Truth started carefully looking around. His first instinct was to use the trees, but presumably there was something nasty on or in the trees, too. Anyone willing to stick whatever this was there was not going to just ignore the vertical side of things.

He carefully looked behind him. Did he see the transparent worm-things? Maybe. They were damn hard to see even for him. So, maybe touching them wasn't instant death, or perhaps they had to be activated by the eye thing. They hadn't triggered Incisive until he saw the eyes, but that could be just alarmingly good stealth.

No, that wasn't how Incisive worked. They weren't a danger until the eye thing was alerted. They were still active now. The eye thing was shamming sleep. It knew something was out there.

Truth briefly wondered if he could kill it. Maybe? But so what if he did? The death of the guardian at the gate would alert everyone inside that there was an enemy. Worse, he would have alarmed them when he couldn't even see the gate.

Starbrite really was very good at physical security. He would have to do this the tiring, energy-expensive way. He looked at a nearby tree and got ready to jump. Incisive flared. Truth mentally sighed and tried the next tree. And the next. And the next. The only tree that didn't flare was six meters away. Even for him, from a standing start, that was . . . an ambitious jump.

He shifted to testing individual branches. The foresight portion of Incisive was the single most energy-intensive part of the spell. Truth usually limited himself to a second's warning or even less for that very reason. Forcing it to activate dozens of times in the space of a few minutes was exhausting.

Beat dying, though. He kept at it.

Fifteen exhausting minutes later, Truth had his route planned out. He leapt up and back, snagging an alarmingly thin tree branch. This let him swing, just barely, onto a thicker branch, which was admittedly in the wrong direction from his target tree but was sturdy enough to let him make the big launch to a third tree with a higher branch.

There were six tree branches in the end. None broke on him, but it was damn close. Truth sat on the "safe" tree and panted. He tried to do so silently. He had only traveled six meters from his starting point in a straight line. He estimated he had actually traversed forty. At least from there he got some elevation.

The forest floor didn't look much different from thirty meters up. All the little wriggly horrors had vanished from his sight. Not that they weren't there. Just that they blended perfectly from this high up.

There is a metaphor there, Truth thought. *Can't think for what, but something.*

He got his breath under control and slowly recovered his energy. It would take a very long time to passively refill, but every little bit would help. Besides, he certainly wasn't rushing anywhere. He started picking apart the forest around him, trying to find any sign of an entrance or . . . anything, really.

Truth just sat in the tree for a while, looking around. There was nothing obvious in sight, no convenient trail or posted signs. His experience at Happori strongly suggested the defenses would be deep and layered. Would it be better to come in through the lake at the top of the volcano? He had no reason to think that it would be any more accessible.

Truth frowned. If he was running a secret laboratory / research center / escape-vehicle assembly site, would he build it under a tourist mountain? He had been puzzled about that for a while, because the answer was so obviously *No, not without a very, very good, very nonobvious reason.*

You could say what you liked about Starbrite, but he wasn't dumb. He kept very low-key, worked through mind-controlled agents, and had the material benefits of an entire world funneled up to him. So, why stick the hidden base there?

And why did he choose to kidnap the Shattervoid girl if he could have gotten a ride off-world, cheap? That was another inexplicable thing that had been nagging at him. Five years. Truth had spent *five years* in the well. That was five years where the Shattervoid were still coming to this planet. Less and less often, but if it was urgent for him to escape, surely, stealing one of their children was the absolute dumbest way to do it. So . . . why?

He kept having the feeling that he had seen lots of little pieces but they actually formed a single picture. No idea what that picture looked like just yet. But still, lots of little pieces. The shitty planet capping the growth potential of humanity. God's indifference—reasons disputed. The Shattervoid and their girl. The mental block placed on humanity—source likewise unknown but quite possibly the planet itself, again. The hyperreal nature of the System Astrologica.

And why this was just occurring to him now, he couldn't say, but . . . what level was Starbrite when he came to this planet? Must have been pretty high. Level Eight? Nine? He couldn't possibly have been lower than Level Seven or he would have been exterminated before he had a chance to grow. He might keep very quiet, but there were some *extremely* motivated people looking for him.

And now he had built his little nest in a volcano that was a tourist attraction in two countries.

There was something there and he just wasn't seeing it. No one else was seeing it either, which wasn't reassuring. If they had seen it, they would presumably be doing something more drastic than fucking around playing spy games. The phrase *strategic-scale curses* came to mind, as did *high-tier summons.*

But no. No, they just stuck a wannabe maintenance tech in a tree and called it a day. He glared at the mountain. There continued to be no big metal hatches sticking out of blindingly white concrete pads.

The wind stirred the needles, making the trees shiver and hiss. Nice afternoon, really. The gentle swaying of the branches was soothing. He needed soothing.

Truth felt defeated and angry. Defeated, because how was he supposed to search? And angry, because this was obviously, manifestly dumb. Spell resistance notwith-standing, this was dumb. At the very least, they should be able to tell him how to get into the base. But no. Even with all the *this cost a life* secrets on Merkovah's information crystal, the exact location of the entrances were not known.

The wind picked up a bit. It was gusting solidly now. Still nice, but now it was downright windy. His tree was swaying a bit. If anything, it made the forest even prettier to watch. Even if it looked like some of the trees just vanished, you knew it was a trick of the light. Your eyes deceiving—

Truth slowly blinked. He rotated his head and stared hard at a very particular pine tree. A strong gust blew again, and once again, the play of light and shadow—

No, it fucking didn't; that tree just vanished and something is trying to make me think it didn't!

He glared at it, trying to force himself to see through the illusion. It occurred to him that, other than Obliteration, he didn't have a good illusion-cracking ability. And if he used Obliteration, they would definitely know he was there.

He did not want to play Forest Friends with Dr. Sun and his Never-Ending Needles. He would be quite happy if he never saw the good doctor ever again.

The glaring continued. He was trying to determine the shape of what he was looking at but had to rely on things suddenly vanishing and his mind loudly inform-ing him that everything was fine. The going was slow, and worse, it was inconsistent. The "invisible" part was in a consistent location but appeared to be very irregularly shaped. He could spot some low ridges and a lumpy sort of central mass. He couldn't connect it into any sort of coherent shape.

A gust of wind blew particularly hard, and a rotten tree limb fell onto one of the little ridges. Eyes opened in midair. A few dozen, then hundreds. The invisible mass slipped into visibility for a moment.

Just a moment. And it was still too long.

It was a blob of some dark viscous fluid, unnamable organs bobbing inside of it. The W-shaped pupils were not truly pupils or even part of real eyes. They emerged from pustules, the nauseating thing extended from its main body. The long ridges were likewise pseudopods, stretched wide across the forest floor. As one such pseu-dopod was hauled back into the main body, Truth saw that attached like millions of exposed capillaries were all the little glass worms. All part of the enormous *thing*, which covered ten square meters of the side of the mountain.

The rock covered with eyes he saw before wasn't even a guard dog. It was one of the guard dog's pups.

CHAPTER 62

PORK CHOP

Truth clamped his will down on his legs, locking himself in place. He had started to bolt before his mind had even processed what he was seeing. The monster was an ambush hunter. Running would only reveal where he was. He had to be patient. He had to think. Despite every fiber of his being screaming at him to get away. He had to think.

It was utterly alien. That was the only word for it. Alien. Nothing about it could exist naturally in this world. It followed no biological logic nor magical sense. Or if it did, it was beastcrafting beyond anything he had seen or heard of. If it was beast-crafting, he would make a special point of killing its creator. That sort of diseased yet capable mind was too dangerous to be allowed.

Stop and breathe. Just . . . try and not dwell on his memory of . . . whatever that was. Silent infiltration was almost certainly out of the question. He might try to camp out and sneak in with a shipment, but no, that was flatly not possible. No one that stuck *that* over their front door was going to miss someone sneaking in with a shipment.

He could check the lake at the top of the mountain, but he refused to believe it would be any less dangerous. If anything, the danger would just be better concealed.

Breathe. Just breathe. Think and breathe. The thing wasn't very smart. It had some level of intelligence, as it was capable of ambushes, but it broke cover when a tree branch landed on it. Highly observant, highly aggressive, not very smart.

What was it? Demon? Didn't feel right. It had that mad disregard for conventional biology he associated with some demons, but this seemed to be more than that. This was practically a negation of any sort of order at all. Just a blob that made what it needed as it needed it. Be it eyes or limbs. Or a mouth.

He could try and fight it head on. "Head." Hah. It didn't have one of those. Not much had held up to Obliteration. Except Dr. Sun. Who, despite being stabbed a lot, including in the head, kept coming back to life.

And just how in the hell did that work? Some glitch in Obliteration? Something the spell just missed? Obliteration was a prototype spell and something made in-house by a security agency. Not exactly tested by the best minds in spell design.

He would not care to bet his life that the giant nightmare thing wasn't likewise immune. Seemed like a weird security oversight otherwise, and there was exactly zero chance that Starbrite was going to be negligent with this place.

All right, so . . . drawing it out seemed like the best plan. Not a *good* plan, but the best plan he had. Which meant that he needed some kind of lure. Was there any kind of antidemon or antiangel ward around this place?

Actually . . . no. Which was odd. That was pretty standard. Something concealed in the dirt? Something that only deployed if triggered? Both seemed plausible. Hmmm. Truth fought the urge to drum his fingers on his leg. He needed more information than what Merkovah had provided, which would mean actively testing the defenses there. Tests which might have terminally negative consequences for him.

On the other writhing pseudopod, what were the odds that Starbrite *didn't* know people knew he was dug in up there? This was a covert location, yes, but too much just wasn't adding up for Truth. This was the endgame. This was where the polite lies were done away with, and ugly truths revealed.

Why was the base there? Why not at Army Ford, or under a hospital in Harban, or on an island completely controlled by Starbrite? Why tunnel into an actual, literal active volcano for your sensitive research project? Especially a volcano that wasn't entirely inside the country you hijacked. Why be covert at all? Tell the world.

"We are proud to announce our Gaspin Island Advanced BioMagical Research facility. Here is Dr. Sun, noted best person ever, who will oversee the facility."

"Dr. Sun, what will you be researching?"

"Why, how to keep people healthy in even the very worst conditions, naturally, as well as pediatric studies. I, famously, love children."

"Aww!"

"Yes, there was some discussion about putting the facility inside an active volcano instead of a tropical island paradise filled with soft, fuzzy, friendly animals and just the cutest, friendliest demons ever, but that's dumb. Actually, that's completely insane. We are doing this for the children."

Something inside Truth went *click*. A nasty, unpleasant sort of click, like your bully locking the door behind him as he came in.

He was going to act a fool. That was the other lesson of Happori. Don't play by their rules—they are better at it, and the game is rigged. Don't try to cheat yourself. Just flip the table and grab the money as it falls.

He nodded internally. He just needed to grab the girl. That was literally it. Everything else? Not his problem. That was, in fact, a plenty big-enough problem. And now, having come to that conclusion, he was going to do . . . what?

Well. Get the hell out of there, for a start. He had a damn good idea where the door was now. Time to fall back and get prepped.

He sat in the dim back room of what appeared to be a hardware store. There was the customary folding chair, shelves of excess inventory, and the general mess of workers who needed a break but didn't really have the time to take one.

Truth had taken pains to avoid the part of Minzu he had been in before. Trying to keep away from any familiar place. Make the hunters and secret policemen work that little bit harder. The store was chosen at random. Tomorrow, the clerks would come in there and discover absolutely nothing. He'd even lock the door behind him.

He just needed a quiet place to think and to work. His first thought, continuing on the Happori line, was to summon an angel. Starbrite was already down a load of higher-level people thanks to the last one. However, he strongly suspected he survived because the angel let him slide, not because it was really mad at Starbrite. There was no reason to think another angel would be as broad-minded.

Devils? Summoning a big-ass demon had a definite appeal. How he would manage the sacrifice, he didn't know. Hmm. There was actually some potential there.

Could he trigger the volcano somehow? How *did* one trigger a volcano, anyway? Presumably a *ton* of fire and earth demons could do it, but he had never heard of it being done. Perhaps it was seen as an offense against the planet.

All right, he wasn't going to one-shot the whole base. What could he do for a lure? He looked around the hardware store. The thing popped into sight for a falling tree branch. Could he do something more with that?

He slowly smiled. Maybe not with hardware-store supplies, but this was a city with a grocery store. He could expand his options.

One surprisingly high-value act of shoplifting later, Truth was prepared-ish.

He had to jump a counter to get to the meat. There wasn't anything you could just pick up off a shelf. It was all behind glass and you had to pay in advance. It shouldn't have been shocking. He had seen how meat was getting more and more expensive. For some reason, the notion that they would completely change the layout of grocery stores to protect the meat felt very alien. Like reality had scored a brutal victory over the forces of just buying whatever, whenever, and however.

He grabbed a wide selection of stuff. Not that he expected any of it to poison that unnatural thing; he just wanted to see if it would react differently to anything. In a fit of giggling madness, he also picked up air fresheners and cleaning solvents. Why not? One heavily loaded backpack later, he stowed everything in a walk-in refrigerator at a closed restaurant, grabbed a few hours' sleep on the floor, and was back at it before the sun rose in the morning.

Making his way back to the presumed entrance was no less nerve-wracking this time. After all, what if they moved around? He got as close as he was comfortable and watched. It took a long, long, *long* while, but he was fairly confident he spotted some ripples of invisibility.

Breezy again today. Was it because they were so high up? Maybe. Tree line was nearby. Truth pulled out a half-kilo hunk of beef and threw it at an angle to where he guessed the creature was. The wind pushed it over a smidge closer. Truth hoped it would persuade the thing that whatever had landed on it was coming at an angle ninety degrees from him.

No reaction. He threw another piece. There was a very faint twinge from Incisive this time. Not a risk-free maneuver, then. Was there an extra shimmer on the ground? A hint of movement? Even with Truth's excellent eyes, he couldn't tell for sure.

He threw another chunk of meat. Ribs this time, the short rack pinwheeling through the air, then catching a gust and blowing violently sideways. The blob revealed itself again. Its myriad boiling and subsiding eyes locked on the flying meat. A whip tendril slashed out and wrapped around it, filament tentacles sprouting and burrowing into the meat and bones.

A hole opened in the side of the amoeba-like blob. It made a jagged mouth. It made irregular gnashing teeth. Jagged, misshapen things, none smaller than a man's forearm. Teeth made by something with only a faint understanding of mouths but endless knowledge of crushing and tearing.

The ribs vanished inside the dark-water interior of the blob. Truth waited. He wasn't going to risk throwing another piece of meat while the eyes were open.

He watched another tendril extend along the ground. Was it . . . looking for something? Yes, it found the other meat. Interesting. Truth waited until it hid itself again, and launched some meat downslope. He then trailed it back up toward the creature. He dumped some cleaning products on the meat just to see what would happen.

A slightly bigger spike in Incisive this time when the meat landed near the blob.

The thing reacted even faster this time, tendrils whipping out and, to Truth's quiet alarm, eyes started boiling out of stalks and tendrils all over the blob. Whatever it was, it wasn't *that* stupid. The meat was coming from somewhere, and it would find it. Truth watched carefully. As the pseudopods extended, the main mass shrank.

Was that . . . a cave behind it? Or a tunnel? Looked like it. The critter didn't seem troubled by the solvents, though. Not surprising, but a pity regardless.

Truth smiled down at the remaining meat in the sack. Time to do a little creative engineering. Draw the beast from its hole. Then take a look inside. Then think about planting just a shit-ton of bombs everywhere. Because he did not feel like playing with these people, and since there was a literal mountain of energy to work with, he would use it.

CHAPTER 63

DO SOMETHING

It took a bit of arranging. Truth tied a half dozen chunks of meat to a log, then roped it to a particularly thick tree. Then quadruple-lashed the tree to a protruding rock. He then launched small hunks of meat (he was running very low at this point and had to make do) tied to fist-sized rocks, using the same banking shot he had relied on before.

The hope was that the meat would lure the blob to the bigger log, which would then resist harvesting for a moment. This would, theoretically, hopefully, give Truth time to get into the tunnel and . . . take steps. Which would be determined based on what he found in the tunnel.

As he set everything up, he kept coming back to the same thought. If it was him, there would be a second blob monster in the tunnel. But he didn't have a better idea, and everything was going to wind up blowing up soon anyway, so he would just have to deal.

He had brought some supplies, but he hadn't the faintest hope that he had brought *blowing up a secret volcano research base* quantities. Improvisation, suddenly, violently, and all over the place—that was the order of the day.

The enemy was smart, careful, and prepared. Time to play the fool and see if he couldn't persuade the most powerful people in the world to play along.

The blob horror lurched back into existence. Dumb it might be, but it smelled a larger-than-average rat regardless. Nightmare eyes at the end of slug-like stalks boiled by the dozens out of the muddy darkness of the thing, waving and stretching in the suddenly cold air. Truth could feel their attention pressing down on the world around him. Truth stayed well back, trying to hide behind a tree. Hoping the thing was more interested in the meat than how it got there.

Truth was used to tolerating the pressure of eyes searching for him. Hungry human hunters, talismans, those strange eyeless watcher things. This was different. This was something utterly alien. Not imperious, or hungry, or mechanical. This was something alien. Cold in a way he had trouble putting into words. Like an angel without God.

The pressure slid over Truth, slid around him, coating the air and ground like a film of oil. It spread and pooled and moved in slithering streams up trees and among the leaves. Truth crouched behind a tree, doing his best to not exist. There was a moment, perhaps minutes long, where he didn't know which way this was going to go.

There was a susurrus of something huge moving over stone. Was it coming toward him? Was it hunting him? His neck muscles wanted to spasm. To turn and look. Truth didn't indulge his nerves. He stayed low and was the best air-temperature stone he could be.

The noise moved away. Down the mountain slope. He risked a peek. The nightmare thing was moving by means of rolling and rippling contractions in its surface. It was alarmingly quick and apparently heavy. It certainly smashed through any trees that impeded it.

The garden of eyeballs it had sprouted were looking in every direction, including, regrettably directly back the way it came. Didn't matter—it was out of position. It would have to be good enough. Truth ran from behind the tree, legs churning, flexing, exploding him forward. Trying to be as stealthy as he could, as fast as he could. Incisive was running as hard as he could push it.

The tunnel mouth was just ahead. The jagged exterior gave way to smooth stone, polished smooth, almost slick from diligent rubbing and scraping. Truth could feel the weight of recording talismans and detection spells pressing down on him. Nets for all sorts and sizes of fish were set in the hall. Truth evaded what he could and brute-forced his way past the others, pouring power into the Blessing of the Silent Forest.

The strongest defenses were all keyed to go off when they detected people who were leveled six and above. He would have smiled at that, but the ground was crawling with wards, curses, and banishments. Protections that cared nothing for his level, installed by people who knew their job well and cared about doing it right.

He felt the spells trip and spark around him. Alarms would be going off inside the base. He grinned horribly. *Yes, that's right. The bad guy is here. Everyone come and do something about him.* There was a door up ahead. It looked . . . armored. Heavy. Like a vault door.

Truth recognized the sort—it was almost a meter thick and sealed in place. There was no lock to pick, as the whole door fused into a solid mass of metal. To open it, you had to cast a unique spell built into the talisman array built into the structure. The metal would liquefy and shrink inward, letting the door float out of the way on a cloud of powerful magic. *Expensive* didn't begin to describe it.

Wouldn't it be a shame if some complete bastard broke it?

Truth's lips pulled back into a death's-head grin. Obliteration loaded and deployed in far less than a second, slapping into the door. It took a surprising amount of effort to overcome the wards and protections built into the door, but Obliteration was built for this. It broke. There wasn't a door anymore. The end of the cave was sealed with a meter-thick block of tempered steel layered with adamantium.

Truth spun on the ball of his foot and ran for the mouth of the cave as fast as he could. Concealment be damned. He practically flew to the mouth of the cave. A vast net greeted him. The endless glassy filaments of the creature had extended out at extreme range as the blob furiously rolled back up the hill.

The Tongue of One Who Speaks for God was called into Truth's hands, the angelic blade screaming in outrage at the foulness before it. Incisive, Obliteration, every scrap of power in his body, the Bane in the sword, the Blessing of the Sea of Brass all combined and *cut*. Whatever the horror was, it wasn't immune to all that. The glass threads resisted, snagged on the magic, snagged on the blade. For a fraction of a second, it seemed like it would hold.

Then they split and Truth was through, heading down the mountain and accelerating.

Abner's Amble replaced Obliteration, and Truth focused exclusively on funneling power into only it and the Blessing of the Silent Forest. He could hear the monstrous thing crashing through the woods behind him. He could feel the base stirring itself in anger. All those high-levels ready to come pouring out to discover what rat had dared make a mess in their place.

Good. Let them be mad. Let them burst out in their fury.

He had run for almost a full minute when he heard the *thrumm*. What it was he couldn't say, but it happened again, then a third time. There was a sudden press of light and heat coming from behind him. Seemed they opted to cut their way out. It was just as well he didn't try and rig any booby traps.

He started angling for the cliffs he had avoided on the way up. Nobody involved in this chase was remotely normal, not at this point. Truth got as much of an assist as gravity could give him, running faster and faster as he ran down near-vertical slopes. The horror still chased. Whip tendrils smashed around wildly. None quite reached him, but Truth didn't know if that was a question of range or the monster not clearly perceiving him.

Didn't matter. Not getting caught—that mattered. He squeezed every scrap of speed from his body he could. Spells were going off above him. Summons, he would guess. Then there was a ring like a tuning fork.

Truth kept running. He was almost a kilometer away before he realized the abomination had stopped. There was a screaming noise from the top of the hill. Something summoned was clearly unhappy about its instructions. Truth didn't wait around to find out what was going on.

At a guess, cooler heads had prevailed. Rather than a blood hunt by the entire security staff, more discreet and speedy hunters had been loosed. The terrible thing had been recalled to block off the entrance once more. They would need something to stop up the tunnel; the door would be obliterated.

It certainly looked like someone trying to lure the tiger from the mountain. They wouldn't leave the base undefended. They certainly wouldn't let themselves be drawn into an ambush. Because who would rush their front door, melt the lock, and run away if it wasn't the first move in an assault? No, they weren't that dumb. The old monsters would doubtless grin mirthlessly and mutter about how it was "A thousand years too early for you to think you can deceive this grandfather."

Truth sprinted all the way to the city. He lost himself in the crowd of factory workers coming off shift in the carriage-production plant, then again in market after market, bus depot after train station.

Eventually, he leapt onto an intercity train, slipping into the carriage just after the ticket collector passed through. He would jump off again before they got too far, but his legs were about dead. He might as well rest and let the train do the running.

He had been in constant motion for six hours. Much of it moving at speeds reserved for vehicles and summoned beasts. He was utterly starving and thirsty beyond words. Literally beyond words; his mouth was so dry, talking would be an unpleasant challenge.

Was there a dining car on this train? He had no idea. He really, really didn't feel like walking around and finding out. He just sat and tried to relax. He tried to perform a round of cultivation, but he just couldn't get his head right. He needed more than a minute to compose himself.

He had banged on the door. Gotten their attention. Made them angry. Next step? Do the same thing again, but from the other side—attack the caldera. Then find some other way to be annoying. Maybe start sending out press releases about "secret Starbrite bases in the Great White Mountain." It would sound like an unhinged conspiracy theory, but it would make people in security unhappy.

Spread the tension. Make them angry. These were the strongest mages in the world and some of the smartest. They had made ample preparations against assault. The only way to win was if they made a mistake, and you couldn't count on that just *happening*. He would have to make it happen.

A woman pushed a cart down the aisle between the rows of seats. Apparently, boxed lunches and beverages were available for sale. Truth had neglected to steal any money, so he just helped himself.

The box was nicely packaged. It tickled his mind in a vague sort of way. He had done all that running, all that hiding, faced an unspeakable horror from who knows what Hell, and now—"Here you go, stranger, a train lunch in a pretty paper box. Please enjoy the fancy pictures of mountains we painstakingly printed all over it."

He also snagged a big bottle of water and a can of fruit juice. He slammed those back in a hurry. Tired, tired, tired. He wolfed down the food without really tasting it. He was going to guess some kind of potato dish, with peas and rice and sides of pickles. It was nice, probably.

He was still starving, but the cart had left the carriage and he really didn't want to get up. Truth closed his eyes and tried to cultivate again. This time, he was a bit more successful. He squeezed in a single round before giving up. Usually, cultivation energized him, but now? It was exhausting.

He dug out his now-battered road atlas. He traced his finger from roughly where he was all the way back to Happori. It was not a short distance. Truth smiled blissfully. For once, some other bastard would have to haul themselves across mountains.

He was wrung out by the solo act, and it limited his options. Time to summon reinforcements.

CHAPTER 64

BULLIED BY TIGERS

Truth counted among his bad habits an unreasonable insistence on trying to do everything himself. It was foolish and, worse, self-destructive. He would kill himself trying to take down the research installation solo. It was therefore time to bring in some support. Those who were reliable, and those who were reliably unreliable.

And he was lonely. He had missed Thrush. Not a good emotion to associate with something as sadistic and treacherous as an air imp, but he had. He would call in Maid and Butler, too, if he could. But they had their own jobs to do right now, and it sounded like they were doing it well. So, that would have to be that.

Then there were all the various hidden experts and covert ops teams that would be littered around the volcano. Was Siphios intelligence *really* the only outfit that had traced the Shattervoid girl to there? Truth didn't believe it. Everyone had their own methods. They might be better or worse, but they would have them, and everyone wanted that ticket off-world.

Well. Almost everyone. Enough people that there would be surveillance teams, intelligence officers, special forces, expert mages, and even a few old monsters strategically located all around the volcano. Each with their own plan of action. Merkovah might be willing to rely on his determinedly unreliable asset, but others would not.

Actually, he was pretty certain Merkovah didn't either. If he were Merkovah, he'd have other teams on standby with strict orders to do *nothing, not one damn thing* without explicit orders in writing and confirmed verbally from him. Because he knew Truth and by now knew how he solved problems. And he wouldn't want his backup team drawn into whatever madness Truth instigated.

Well, he could give the Siphios boys a break, but everyone else was getting drafted into the revolutionary army. And just to make sure any revanchist, counterrevolutionary forces couldn't interfere with the glorious People's Revolution, he finished lunch, drank all the water and juice, and jumped off the train as they slowed for a bend. The train was moving damn fast, even by Truth's standards, but that was why it was best to get off mid-journey. People would be waiting and watching at the stations.

There was a strange moment as he forced open the carriage door. A moment of shattering lucidity. He could see the train running, the earth demon moving damn fast down the track. He could see the plants and rocks zipping past. He knew they were real, or as real as anything was. But when he looked at his hands or his feet, they looked so much more real than the train and the ground below.

The world was real. But he was more real. And he could step off a three-hundred-kilometer-an-hour train safely.

Truth took an explosive step off the train. Abner's Amble carried him forward, forcing that momentum to work for him. Then his toe barely touched the ground and he took another explosive step. Cast Abner's Amble again and launched forward another dozen meters.

He crossed the field in a blur of motion, rushing up into the nearby foothills before slowing down to a comfortable sixty-kilometer-an-hour jog. Then he stopped and looked back at the train. The door had closed automatically behind him. The long metal worm writhed along the earth, pulled faster than the wind by a rejoicing hell-beast.

The fields that edged the train tracks were growing green and tall in the summer sun. All artifacts of humanity. All proof of people adapting to the necessities of the real world and thriving. They saw problems and reached logical solutions to those problems. Sensible people doing sensible things. Sober, serious, practical.

Wrong.

They were all wrong. He didn't know what "right" was, but he knew they, all of them, the wise, careful people of the world, were wrong. They were so much more than this. They were all so much more. Even the world was far, far greater than they thought it was. But you couldn't explain it. How could you put this feeling into words? This profound knowing? They had to experience it for themselves.

He looked out over the field, watching the train vanish into the distance. He didn't move until he came back to himself. Still trapped in the prison of the real. For now.

"Holy shit, I ran as fast as an intercity train for a few seconds."

<<Technically a bit slower, but close,>> the System agreed. *<<Inertia is a hell of a thing.>>*

He could remember how his body felt, launched across the field. The System was right. Still. He felt like this was a moment. A step beyond humanity, beyond what other Level Fours would be capable of.

System—status sheet.

There was a pause.

<<You having a stroke?>>

Status sheet, development report, whatever the hell you called it. You know what I am talking about; put it up.

<<You know it's bullshit. I told you it's bullshit. The whole function of the numerical ratings was to show you growing and keep reassuring you that you were very strong. Give you that dopamine high and make you crave the next dose.>>

Yeah, I know, but I just want it all in one place. A tidy little summary of where I am and how everything is growing.

<<Fine. I'll . . . come up with something.>>

There was a pause. Then, accompanied by the sound of trumpets:

SUPER FANCY ALL-IN-ONE-PLACE SUMMARY OF TRUTH MEDICI'S DEVELOPMENT AS AN UNNATURAL HORROR STALKING THE INNOCENT, UNSUSPECTING PEOPLE OF THIS OTHERWISE FORGETTABLE AND JUSTLY FORGOTTEN ROCK

LEVEL PROGRESS: Level Four, 85 percent to Level Five. I want you to think about that. I want you to think about the fact that, from your perspective, you were Level One . . . what, three years ago? Ish? Level One to Five in less than four years, for certain. Nine, if you count Well Time.

That's not just fast; that should be flat-out impossible. You should be a thin film of incredibly toxic goo preserved on slides in medical schools and forensic labs as a reference material. "Here, future scholars of tomorrow, this is what a dumbfuck looks like when they overdo it."

Captain Clavegaugh must be drinking more elixirs than water, and it took her decades, even with PMC privilege, to make Level Five. The overwhelming majority don't get past Level ONE. Ever. After an entire lifetime. And all this while the magic is collapsing. What did that Ghūl Juice do to you? What did those worms do to you that I haven't managed to spot?

KNOWN SPELLS

Meditations of Valentinian (Permanent): How far progressed are you in something that extends infinitely? Who knows. Your body is absurdly powerful, can resist forces that should leave you dead a dozen times over, and gives your already-inhuman reflexes full expression in your muscles and tendons.

Your sheer presence in a room warps it because you are just so much more real than everything in it. The effect is subtle but there. You can spike that effect with conscious effort. This, of course, stacks with other effects, but it does make me wonder how many diviners have suffered backlash because they tried to divine something so categorically above them.

Not to mention the specific refinements you have made to your body based on Nephilim spell technology. Your body is sealed down like you were in spell armor. Absorb only what you want, and anything exiting you, body heat, odor, whatever, only does so with your explicit permission. Insane.

Incisive (Permanent): How do you measure your progress with the signature spell of a stellar eminence? You have proven worryingly adept with the Scales and the Fangs, and even the Foresight. The Poison works pretty well too. Of all the aspects of the spell, the Scales, the identity-changing portion of the spell, is the one you have made the most progress in. You have successfully been a number of different people, some very alien to you, and the world not only believed it, it helped make it more real. Which is also insane.

Stacking the reality-warping effects of Incisive and the Meditations is just broken. I completely understand why Merkovah set you up like this, he is CENTURIES past giving a fuck, but damn. It's no wonder Internal Security keeps missing you.

Which is not to say you are good at the spell. Botis claims no one has yet mastered it. You ain't special.

Cup and Knife (Permanent): Still figuring out the basics but getting a better feel for it. My best guess is that the spell "corrects" the errors in the less-real world. Sometimes, it does this by shifting the damage around, sometimes not. Insanely powerful, but you are left guessing what the "correct" answer is supposed to be. It's a spell based on the recollection of a starved mystic who flat-out admits they were imperfectly recalling things they saw in a vision. It's a functional spell but also a broken one.

It pains me to say this, but I don't see you ever "getting good" at this spell. I think at some point, you will have to modify it. Correcting the spell itself to make it function as Manda intended.

Tool (Swappable): Basic magical-device utility spell. You don't even notice you are using it half the time. Which is hurtful. I worked hard on that. You monster.

Abner's Amble (Swappable): Modern magic travel utility spell. You are probably not going to get much better at using it. It's . . . fine. It makes each step go a lot farther, but you have pretty much hit the cap on distance and energy efficiency. Still useful, but if you get the opportunity to raid Merkovah's library again, swap it for a better travel spell. Modern magic might be reliable and easy to learn, but it's very limited.

Graeme's Arrow (Swappable): Makes things go farther, faster. A unitasker of a spell but damn powerful for all that. You are a long way from mastering it, mostly because you don't use it very often. Worth considering for your next permanent spell slot, but it shouldn't be rushed. Better options may yet present themselves.

Obliteration (Swappable): Breaks magic, dissolves it, really, by using magic to destroy magic. It can also isolate existing spells from the cosmic energy they use to sustain themselves. It is incredibly effective, especially since the mechanism seems to be poorly understood by other security services. It's interesting—it has the same result as what the antitheists antimagic does, but the mechanism is the exact opposite. You are currently operating in a window where they know you have some kind of antimagic ability, but don't understand what it is or how it works. Lucky you.

I am genuinely shocked Merkovah supplied you with this spell. I can only think that he is either supremely confident in his judgment of you or so desperate he doesn't care about consequences anymore. I'm not being funny. This is the kind of spell entire military operations get launched over. I could see treaties being drawn up to control its usage. If you do make it off-world, hide this spell. Never, ever let it become a permanent addition to your apertures.

Other spells that you just never used are omitted, because you never use them.

<u>BLESSINGS</u>

Blessing of the Silent Forest: You blend with the background. To the point of unnoticeability for ninety-nine-plus percent of humanity. To the extent that all magic has a degree of local superreality, it feels like this adds a layer of extra superreality to what you already have through body cultivation and Incisive. Not news to you, but the way your spells stack has got to be unique, or nearly unique, in the history of this planet. Consider how it interacts with your other blessing—

Blessing of the Sea of Brass: Notionally enhances your attacks against demonic entities. Actually enforces "Orthodoxy," broadly defined. By you. How this stacks with Cup and Knife is still an open question. But consider also how it stacks with the Blessing of the Silent Forest. How much of your success in the field has been down to you subconsciously asserting the rule ***My actions are unnoticeable by those below me, and almost everyone is below me***? How many thousands of people labored under that orthodoxy as you traveled across Jeon?

Blessing of the Rough Patron: This one is a bit harder to nail down, given your preexisting instinct for violence. Bloodlust, on a tangible level. A certain instinct for fatal combat. Murder, really. I think there is more. It's apparently tied into whatever the Ghūl did and the nine worms that are refining your body. And, related, your ability to see in the dark is getting better and better all the time. It feels like there is a very deep hole here, and you want to be damn careful about diving into it.

SPELL RESISTANCE: No longer quantifiable, I suspect. Lower-level magic just won't touch you. Higher-level spells will need to be tailored to fully pierce your spell resistance. It takes spells on your level and higher to even touch you, I would say. Although at that level, the spell coming at you will be hilariously lethal. Wise decision, not letting any of Dr. Sun's needles touch you. They would have fucked you up real good.

<u>EQUIPMENT</u>:
The Tongue of One Who Speaks for God: A sword with a chunk of an angelic weapon in it. Spiritual as all hell, it hangs out in your first aperture quite happily, not crowding out the spell. It generally approves of you and what you are doing. No, it's not sapient, exactly. It does have some level of awareness, and it is, at its core, an angelic weapon. It has opinions. Opinions like ***Humans are worse than ants, because ants are obedient***. Not saying it's warping your personality, but I'd keep an eye on it.

Truth blinked slowly at the list. When it was all laid out like that, it was kind of a lot.

<<*And I didn't include the scarf, Thrush, or the succubae, or Niles, or your flying bird suit because they aren't here.*>>

And Niles is a human, not a demon.

<<*Sure, pretend there is a meaningful difference in how you treat him. So, knowing all this, what are you going to do with it?*>>

Why, exactly what Starbrite thought I was doing—luring the tiger from the mountain and letting it get bullied by dogs on the plains. Except this time, I'm luring the demon and letting the tigers do the bullying!

Truth smiled. The Hell-Prince had to lead the way. And so he would.

But before that, I'm summoning Thrush. And he damn well better have kept my stuff immaculate, or I'm going to make him wish he was back in Hell.

CHAPTER 65

AN "OLD FRIEND" AND A LITTLE WHOOPSIE

Truth visualized Thrush's summoning token. It was a little metal disk he had etched, quite deeply, with the imp's binding. An utterly standard thing, notwithstanding the small refinements he had added from his time in Siphios. Thrush was an air imp. There was only so fancy a binding you could apply before things got silly.

The token was battered, scratched, worn down and generally looked like it had been through hell. Truth had been wearing it around his neck or keeping it in a pocket . . . during those times when he had pockets . . . until he had to leave it with the luggage outside of Happori. He had hidden it more than an hour from the security perimeter of the village, and there was really nothing of value in there beyond his scarf, the bird suit, and Thrush.

Truth had an alarming amount of life experience regarding the term *search radius*. The bigger the radius, the longer the searchers had to search. Truth flat-out refused to believe that, after everything, the explosions, the angel, all those dead seniors, EVERYTHING, Starbrite would have the time and energy to sweep an area of more than a two-hundred-kilometer-diameter circle around the village. A circle filled with mountain forests, streams, caves, footpaths, old mines, shacks belonging to backcountry folk, wild demons, whatever unnatural horrors the collapse of the village spawned . . .

Sweeping through all that and turning up a single buried duffel bag and a wing-suit? No. And if they had caught Thrush, they would have used the token to try and trace him weeks ago.

Truth started drawing the ritual on the ground. He had bound the demon. Even if he wasn't holding the token, he could make some effort and give it orders. Just took more work.

Ten minutes later, he had an entirely new appreciation of what Etenesh and Jember could do with a wave of their hands. He had already fixed four mistakes, and he wasn't done drawing the ritual yet. By minute twenty, he was ready to pack it in and summon an entirely new imp. He persevered.

By minute thirty and swear eighteen, he had it done, checked over, corrected, and checked again. Then a third time because if it blew up in his face, he was packing in this mage nonsense and going off to the coast to learn how to fish. He could punch a mackerel. He had that confidence.

It all looked right. He was about to jump right in but hesitated. It had been a busy day, his energy reserves were far from full, and he was frustrated. The sun was wandering toward the horizon, but he had a little while until sunset. Truth inhaled, exhaled, inhaled again, and started cultivating.

He didn't try to think. He just let his body flow through the forms. Reaching out for that thinning energy shared by the sun and the other excellencies. Feeling the warmth of them. The strength of them, flowing through his veins.

As he moved, his mind drifted to those moments of unreality. The increasing awareness that the world was paint on glass, the shine on a soap bubble. That the reality that kept hurting him wasn't as real as it wanted him to think it was. "Reality" was a bully with a bad heart. It made you punch your own face and convinced you to give up your lunch money to make the beating stop.

In and out. Steady and smooth. Moving his body easily and gently through the forms. Feeling his apertures refill. More slowly than they used to but refilling nonetheless. That old comfort warming him.

The eminences must exist on that level, in that world on the other side of the glass. This was just the filtered, distorted light that made it through. Could he . . . cultivate with the light directly? Some people refused to cultivate when the sun was out, but he loved it. He could take the heat and warmth. Could he stand up to the unfiltered cosmic energy?

He had no idea how to even try. But it was pretty interesting as ideas went.

It took a little longer than it used to, but he topped off his energy reserves and spent half an hour practicing the Meditations of Valentinian. His body was the foundation. He would have to be crazy to neglect it. Finally calm and energized, he approached the ritual.

He pressed two fingers to the triangle within the circle marked for them and let his energy flow. The ritual energized, knitting and spinning in ways he had never understood. He knew how to make the ritual, not how it worked. Just one more thing he didn't know. There was a soft thrum, and the spell went live.

"Master? How good to hear from you. I trust your various endeavors have been profitable?"

Thrush's voice was smooth and rich as always. *Unctuous*—a word Truth had only read in the more flowery romance novels—seemed to fit.

"Financially? No. But in other ways? Certainly. Speaking of, you were undetected and undisturbed?" He discreetly focused more power into the bindings. Demons could lie to their masters, but there were consequences if they did.

"Master kindly buried his goods two meters into the earth, stomped the earth flat, and then covered his tracks with leaves. There has not been so much as a mouse or mole come to visit, let alone a snooping human or demon."

"Would it be safe for you to come out and fly to me?"

"On balance, I regret it would not."

"Oh? They are still searching up there?"

"There were no searches in this area. The world is simply a hostile, dangerous place. Safety is barely an illusion."

Of course.

"I require your labor and my things. Get ready for a long flight."

"Yes, Master. I trust you intend for me to travel unseen?"

"As best you can. Do you think you could pilot the bird suit as well as carry the luggage?"

"So long as you provide sufficient energy, it should be manageable, dread magus. Should I take the location of your ritual as my target?"

That was an annoyingly good question. He looked around. He was in a clearing in the foothills of some mountain he didn't know the name of. It would actually be a bit of a pain in the ass making his way back toward the Great White Mountain. There were fields, so presumably there were farmers, but it was probably about as private as he was going to find.

"Yes. Move to avoid detection. Bring all my things with you."

"As you command."

Truth poured power into the ritual. A minute or so later—

"Ah, enough! You are generous, almighty magus. Even the crumbs from your table stuff this little bird full to bursting."

Truth rolled his eyes.

"Be fast, be careful. Be here, with my things, undetected, by this time tomorrow or sooner." He cut the ritual. It would be done.

Now, what to do with the day to come? He would have an early sleep, then start heading back either on foot or by snagging a ride on a passing train. Probably on foot, if he was honest. He would have to drop off the train again anyway.

An oppressively long run. He wanted that wingsuit for more than just the pleasure of flight. Was there any food around there? Truth looked out over the fields hopefully. There were a few tiny shacks but nothing that looked like a town or village.

He didn't want to break in and eat their food. They probably didn't have much, and what they had wouldn't be very good. As for a bed, or even a sofa—forget it. He made up a nice "comfy" pile of leaves, fell down on it, and was asleep before the sun finished setting.

Some instinct woke him up in the middle of the night. Incisive, giving him a sudden thrill of alarm. He rolled to his feet and tried to spot where the danger was coming from. There was nothing in sight.

Truth was a firm believer in *Don't stand on the X*. He ran. The danger seemed to come from no particular direction. From the fields, maybe? He ran up the mountain. "Away" was almost always the right choice.

There was a drone, a high-pitched whine, coming from downslope. The sound bounced off the stones and made the green leaves shiver. The stars slowly turned dim, then red. He could feel a buildup of cosmic energy in the area. Just how wide was it spread? Truth kept running. It seemed like he was on the very edge of the phenomenon.

Lightning bolts tore up the ground. From up on the mountain, he could see the lightning striking homes, the ground, trees; there seemed to be no rhyme or reason to it. The sky was crawling with lightning, writhing with it, like fighting dragons and worms. The worms came in all colors, all shapes, all lightning twisting and fighting in a sky without clouds.

Truth nodded decisively and quickly dug another little tomb for himself in the rock face. He wasn't feeling that ripping negative pressure, but he wasn't going to wait around for it.

<<It's not the same. This is more like a localized overpressure of cosmic rays.>>
Eh?

<<I don't know why it's happening! It's just my best guess.>>

Truth nodded. The lightning was freaky, but "too much cosmic energy" had never been a problem for him. The more, the merrier, really. Maybe he would have a nice round of cultivation—

There was a sound. Rustling, screeching sound. He had heard it before. Where had he . . .

Truth clawed his way out of the hole, spun on his toes, and ran flat-out up the mountain. Fist-sized holes opened in the air, and from those holes fell thousands of insects. Millions of insects. Hornets and centipedes, locusts and beetles, an endless tide of chittering vermin. All the lowest tier of demons. *Pandemonium Goetia.* And not a spell bowl in sight to contain them. They would vanish when the magic ran out, but until then? They were endless. Truth got up over the mountain and launched himself down the other side. Jeon was roughly south of there. Good enough.

A very, very tired, very dirty, very irritated Truth stalked into the mountain village. What village, he didn't know. He was pretty sure he was still in Onis. He found a shop. The signs were in a language he couldn't read. Onis.

He popped the lock on the local convenience store and stomped in to sleep in the back room. Someone was already sleeping there. He swore a blue streak and made his way to the police station. There was an open cell. He laid down in it and slept. He was so tired, the two-centimeter-thick pad felt heavenly.

He woke peacefully, which was unexpected. Jails were surprisingly noisy, and sleeping in wasn't really a thing that could happen. He left the cell and started looking around. There was the village policeman, sitting and staring at the scry with a look of horror. Some of the villagers were there with him. Truth glanced over. Then glanced again, longer.

There was a tear. That was the only word he could use to describe it. There was a hole ripped open in the middle of a town. It looked like it was shrinking, but . . . the town was gone. Billions of demons had swarmed through. Tiny little ones, mostly.

Level Zero, almost all of them. But billions of them. Enough to coat the streets. Coat every home. Every business.

White-faced soldiers, hands shaking with fatigue, swept back the swarm with fire-belching fetishes. It was a holding action. Everyone knew that. It was just until the hole closed on its own. Periodically, higher-level mages would fly over and soak the town in flames. Thin out the horde. But more always poured through. Hell would never run short.

The news cut back to the presenter. Truth didn't understand what he was saying. Then it cut over quickly to a picture of the flag of Jeon, then soldiers locking down the border. Summons flew purposefully through the air. Something had happened on the border of Jeon. Something bad. And Onis was willing to go to war over it.

CHAPTER 66

THANK YOU FOR YOUR SERVICE

We need to speak, Onis, now. Right now.

The devastation was enormous. The picture kept cutting back and forth from the heaving seas of demonic insects and troop carriers rushing to the border. Mages setting up warded enchantment sites. Curse-delivery systems, golem launchers, necromancers with their articulated wagons of weaponized dead. All rumbling for Jeon.

<<You passed what looked like a preschool last night. Start there.>>

Truth did. There were plenty of board books and what looked like books to teach kids to read. It was a good place to start. Lots of pictures. Truth moved like a blur through the room, the System absorbing everything in seconds.

<<All right, so now I can read enough to know there is an elementary school down the road. Out the door and right.>>

Truth ran. The System hadn't got it quite right. The one-room schoolhouse handled the educational needs of the entire village. Truth tore in to all the books he could lay hands on, tossing aside the books about math or science or politics, focusing on the language books. It took a bit longer—a few minutes instead of a few seconds.

<<Interesting to see how the growth in your mind and soul has affected learning languages. You aren't remotely fluent, but we should now understand enough to figure out what's going on in the news. Like with Siphios—the more you listen and the more you speak, the faster you learn.>>

Truth zipped back to the police station. Nobody had moved. Three cigarettes had already gone out, their ashes sprinkled over desks and laps.

"The brave mages of the First Battalion have contained the tide at Fragrant Bamboo Village, and as you know, the army is pressing forward in a string of decisive victories against the insect tide. Thanks to your brave protectors in the army, the public can sleep safely." The steely-eyed young man spoke firmly to the watching audience. "To explain the scope of the danger, we have a very special guest, Mr. Wan Shui Tan, Spokesman for the Deputy Assistant Minister for Internal Mobilization."

"Wish I could say it was good to be here, Mr. Bai." The spokesman looked half-dead and was contemplating finishing the job.

"We all understand. What is the latest word from the border?"

"Jeon swears they are not responsible for either the Hell portals or for the slithering war crimes masquerading as beastcrafted weapons systems. In flagrant, blatant violation of the Treaty of Vesnat, incidentally, as well as multiple bio-arms proliferation treaties Jeon is a signatory to."

"So, no change?"

"I didn't say that. The Communications Corps have been running spellbreaker and counterjamming programs at the border. By complete coincidence"—both the spokesman and the news broadcaster were too well trained to share a look—"those spells accidentally crossed the border into Jeon. Revealing a frankly massive troop buildup."

"I thought Jeon's army was small," the newscaster said.

"Compared to ours? Tiny. But what they lack in mages, they make up in beastcrafted horrors, golems, and talisman devices. And it seems that they have been planning this wretched treachery for some time."

"Could you explain that for us, please?"

"Simple enough—they have built at least one, and quite possibly several, forward operating bases in Onis territory. The discovered base is absolutely filthy with some of the vilest summons we have ever seen. And while the army hasn't yet launched an assault on it, our surveillance indicates a frankly insane amount of fixed defenses. They intend to make any assault on this base as costly as possible."

"I assume a siege is planned?"

"Yes, but there are problems with that. First is that the base is *directly* on the border with Jeon. Straddling it, in fact. The second is that the presence of numerous high-level mages makes starving them out impractical in a timeframe of less than a year, even if they didn't have supplies on base. And we can be reasonably certain they have ample supplies on base. Third—the intermittent influence of cosmic-energy saturation events is likely to intensify over the coming year, possibly two years."

Is that what they are calling it? Truth wondered.

"All of which would impact our ability to maintain a siege. Still, Jeon cannot possibly expect this gross affront to national sovereignty to pass." The newscaster sounded properly outraged.

"Of course not. Which is where we get to the fourth problem. No one has yet confirmed the identity of the forces inside the bunker. Jeon disavows them entirely."

"Oh, then that's easy. We can just go in and assist our southern neighbors with a rebellion they are too incapable to suppress." The presenter subtly flexed his fingers.

"Exactly the stance of the President, the Premier, and the Army Chiefs. The only questions are how much is this assault going to cost us and who exactly is inside." The spokesman tapped the table.

"If it's not Jeon, who else could it be? And regardless of who it is, why should we care?"

"Because the other sizable military force in Jeon, other than the government, is Starbrite."

The screen flashed a picture of the Great White Mountain. Truth didn't know whether to laugh or cry. He had wanted to lure in outside forces. It seemed that he didn't need to bother.

"That would be tricky, certainly, but ultimately, it's just one company. How did the base get discovered, if I may ask?"

"Due to the antisurveillance efforts of the base itself. They were running heavy counterespionage sweeps through the forest at the base of the mountain and triggered some of the hidden detection arrays we deployed to find infiltrators and saboteurs. We sent golems, they destroyed or tried to defeat the golem's surveillance, it escalated rapidly, and not eight hours later—the outbreak of Hell portals and the vermin swarm. It might have been a coincidence if it wasn't for the nightmare things that they are using to control the mountainside."

The presenter put up blurry pictures of the multi-eyed amoeba things that Truth had run into by the cave mouth.

"Describing them as Hellspawn is an insult to demons." The presenter frowned.

"That would be in keeping with Starbrite."

Truth turned away. His cheek twitched. Could something go according to plan, yet not at all according to plan? The sheer increase in military-grade surveillance was going to make sneaky infiltration even more impossible than it was before. So . . . fuck it, really. He nodded decisively.

Time to make things even worse.

"Oh, shit, Thrush!"

One rushed communication ritual later, Truth was back on the road. He wasn't interested in going back to the same town—nothing useful there, and it was now a mite too hot for comfort. Instead, he opted to swing north and east, around the opposite side of the mountain. It seemed both fitting and unfair that the scenery on the Onis side of the border was just as boring and bleak as the Jeon side. It seems that neither mountains nor trees cared about the all-important line on the map.

He snagged a lift on a bus. Literally on it—he made himself a nice spot to lie down on the luggage roof rack. It wasn't too comfortable, but it wasn't too bad. The roads were being surveilled by both spell beasts and flying talismans, but the drain was very manageable. Closer to the front lines, things would get more intense.

He waited until he started seeing the first roadblocks. Nowhere near as intense as the ones in Jeon, but there was ample surveillance and what looked to Truth's eye like a junior secret policeman watching the scry feed remotely. He took it as a sign and hopped off the bus.

"Did you smell that guy?"

"My nose is crying. Do they not have showers in the mountains?" The conscripts were quietly chattering. Their corporal ignored the noise, probably wishing he had someone he could yak with too. Truth hadn't noticed much traffic on this road.

"Got that nasty farmer stank. Never learned to wipe his ass."

Hmm. Posted from a city way out to the boonies? Well, he was from Harban and got posted to a remote customs station for his national service. So, not that weird, probably.

"And not a single pretty girl on the bus. At all. This posting sucks."

"You still think you can pick up chicks at a checkpoint? Seriously, guy, what the hell is wrong with you?"

"It could happen. Our eyes meet, she falls for the handsome man in uniform—"

"Bro. Buddy. Soon-to-be-disowned brother from another mother. No."

"Not like we can take matters in hand with an intel weenie breathing down our neck."

The corporal did look over at that, and the conscript had the good sense to wince and nod apologetically.

Truth jogged over to the field office—a glorified cargo container dropped off on the side of the road. The door was locked, of course. Some thoughtful soldier had, however, "field repaired" the lock so that you could pop it open if you pressed Qalith and Xereph at the same time. As a fully qualified maintenance tech, Truth was outraged. As a former conscript and a lifelong jank appreciator, he could only applaud.

Trying to find the one person with the keys, especially when you were way out in the boonies, sucked. This was better.

He walked in. There was, indeed, a secret policeman watching the soldiers and the checkpoint, hearing their conversation with crystal-clear audio pickup to go with the recording talismans. Truth was amused to spot the presence of a *remarkable* amount of pornography and hand lotion, and even more amused to note that the secret policeman had apparently missed the tiny talisman built into the wall that was recording him.

Truth shook his head regretfully. That wasn't officer material. A real high-flier would be making "friends" with locals, simultaneously cultivating possible informers and patsies, as needed. When said locals were not being requisitioned for another purpose.

No convenient map showing where all the checkpoints were, nor hidden internal security bases. Shame. Codebook that might have that info? It didn't take long to search the place. No luck. The policeman had gotten his trousers down and was reaching for the lotion when the communication terminal crackled to life. The officer swore, tried to yank his pants up, and managed to zip something tender in with his fly.

The officer's shriek would have really cheered up the conscripts. Alas, only Truth and the cop's supervisors got to enjoy it. The altar started chiming with increasing urgency. The officer tried to hop and hobble over, collapsing in pain partway. In a fit of heroic, desperate bravery, he yanked the zipper back down again. The shriek was every bit as heartfelt the second time. The quiet, sobbing whimpers were truly moving. So moving that the supervisors turned up the volume and speed of the alert yet again.

Eventually, the officer crawled over and activated his end. "Station seven-four-two, present."

"Station seven-four-two, report! Are you under attack? Do you require assistance?" The voice on the other end crackled with tension.

"NO, no, sorry, I was in the bathroom. Blue, Blue, Pollard Fifty Savage." Truth nodded. Clearly a code to show there wasn't a hostile in the room.

"What? Are you dying of constipation? You know you are expected to answer the call within three rings. A man with even the faintest dream of promotion would do well to get it down to one ring!"

"I apologize. I was negligent. In the future, I will install a chemical toilet in the trailer to ensure this does not happen again." The agent rolled his eyes.

"Naive! In the present state of emergency, you cannot take such half-hearted measures. I will instruct your corporal to provide you with a sleeping bag. Ensure you are never more than three steps from the altar so that you can respond to any emergency!"

"Commander, my exercise needs? To say nothing of the other officers on site?"

"Are you questioning my arrangements, Constable?"

"Never, Captain!"

"Good. Now, then, the reason for my call." The constable straightened up. "You have not contributed for Major Tsu's birthday present. This is a crucial opportunity to stand out. When are you going to send the money?"

"I . . . I was waiting for payday. I have already sent most of this month's salary back to my family-"

"NAIVE! Who will protect your family when the world collapses? You? No! Only the army can do that, and that means keeping Major Tsu happy and yourself in his eyes. Do you think your tiny filial piety will move him?"

"I was wrong!"

"You were. I'm sending everything down in two days. Get a loan if you have to! I want the red packet in Nilfu and on his desk first thing when he comes to work. You understand me, Constable?"

"Sir! Yes, sir! At once, sir."

"Good. I will be inspecting your post at some point this coming week, and I expect to see nothing but excellence." The call cut out. The officer collapsed to the deck.

Truth smiled warmly. He had always hated Internal Security. The nasty bastards had a way of disappearing whole families. He remembered Nilfu from his road atlas. Just up the highway from there, almost due north of the Great White Mountain. Wouldn't it be *terrible* if something were to happen there?

Truth cracked his knuckles. Yeah, that would just be the worst. He smiled, set his pack again, and started jogging.

CHAPTER 67

THE INNOCENT HAVE NOTHING TO FEAR

Nilfu was, according to his now badly abused road atlas, a long way from the middle of nowhere, which was where he currently was. Or about a three-hour run. Truth did some completely unnecessary stretching and set off. Wasn't going to get any closer if he stood around, and there sure wasn't much in the way of passing traffic.

System, could you put together a new spell for me? We have to have loads of spell models from all the research we have done.

<<What, like right now?>>

I was thinking Enlarge, or one of the old reliables from the PMC days.

<<I cannot. Spell creation is not, Magus Vek notwithstanding, a quick process.>>

Damn. I figure they will be running forensics through that intel office after I'm through there, and wanted to lead them directly to the PMC.

The countryside continued its gray boringness. The occasional burst of green trees served to effectively underline the inescapable truth—you were stuck on an underused highway, in an underpopulated region, primarily used for heavy-polluting industries. Fun was not simply not allowed; the land generated Anti-Fun, a substance which obliterated Fun on contact.

<<I can't make those spells. What I can do is take a spell you already have and mutilate it into something like what you used at the PMC. Not that hard to turn the Fangs of Incisive into something that would pass as a Sharp spell under forensic examination, particularly if you used the sword without activating the Bane. Ditto Graeme's Arrow. That one won't need much modding at all.>>

Focus on Graeme's Arrow. I can make that work.

Barely an hour of forgettable highway later—*<<Done.>>*

That fast?

<<Graeme's Arrow isn't that complicated, and it sits at sort of a weird midpoint between something like Incisive and Abner's Amble. Strictly speaking, it's not modern magic, but it's close enough to pass as modern magic in a bad light. All I had to do was lop off some chunks of it that weren't in the version of the spell provided by Starbrite, and BOOM! Spell recreated.>>

Truth scooped up a rock and chucked it at a tree two hundred meters away. *Graeme's Arrow!*

The rock shot off and punched a fist-sized hole through the tree, and tore a gouge through the one behind it. The first tree slowly collapsed, the hole flickering with fire. Truth zipped over and put it out. No need to start a forest fire. Even if *I can throw a rock so hard, it can burn down a pine forest* is a pretty impressive reason to do so.

Oddly, Truth was frowning as he examined the hole.

That didn't feel right. It felt . . . hollow, maybe? I don't know how to describe it, but I can feel the missing components.

<<Yeah. I . . . am not sure what this is, actually. The components don't really seem to do anything. It made complete sense to me that they would be removed. Try precision throwing—see what you can knock down with pebbles.>>

Truth spent ten minutes flinging pebbles, pine needles, and just about every object he could reasonably and discreetly toss, clipping off individual twigs from trees, knocking down pinecones from a hundred meters away, and generally looking like he was goofing around.

Yeah, it's weird. I would now classify the spell as "scuffed." Which I don't understand, because the performance seems to be identical. And yet, somehow, scuffed.

<<I'm . . . on the edge of something. Grab a pebble and . . . okay, that sparrow half a kilometer away? Here, I'll drop a marker on it.>>

A red reticle popped up on something so small even Truth's outstanding eyes barely saw a flicker of motion. He nodded.

<<All right, I'm loading up the complete version from Siphios. Hang on to it; it tends to fight back.>>

The System's point was well taken. Truth had been getting better with Graeme's Arrow, but it did not like sharing an aperture with the System. Truth would swear it resented being viewed as dispensable. Which was crazy, as it was a glorified pattern of magic, not an intelligent being.

Truth had a bit of a glitch as he stumbled on to the same thing the System did. *Shut down the reticle. Mr. Sparrow lives to see tomorrow. You're right. It lacks the intent of the being behind it. The modern magic version stripped out all that—now it's just some dead human. No extra spiritual load there.*

<<I swear if that's the difference between modern magic and the old-fashioned sort, I'm going to spiritually throttle Merkovah for not explaining it clearly.>>

I mean, we kind of knew that all along? It's why modern magic is so easy to cast— none of the extra baggage that comes with some vast power judging your spell use. Plus, some of those old spells really are horribly optimized, requiring way, way more cosmic energy than they should.

<<But why build it into the spell? It's doing something in there. Nobody who invents a spell that makes one thing go farther, faster, in a straight line is going to be interested in larding the spell up with other stuff.>>

Dunno. You figure it out. I've got to go ruin someone's day. A lot of someones.

Nilfu was another industrial city. Long row-apartment buildings, wide roads, it all looked fine, in an utterly soulless sort of way. Same kind of food. Sour, salty, but rich-tasting. It was growing on him.

Truth walked over to the train station and followed the signs to the public security office. A few judicial uses of the Poison portion of Incisive later, and he had directions to the army's internal surveillance office in town. It was, predictably, in a discreetly fortified police headquarters.

He looked up. A bit after noon? Right at that period between lunch and wishing you were going home for dinner.

Good enough. Were any of the cops his size? He looked down at the tops of their heads. No. Not remotely his size. Fine. It was always going to go the hard way. He would just be starting the "hard way" portion a little earlier. He looked around. There was one of those long apartment buildings across the street from the police station. Easy enough to reach the roof.

The roof of the police station looked about as expected—tarpaper with surveillance doing its level best to look in every direction, *up* and *in* being firmly included. Decently powerful, too. Oh, well. There was an altar for large-scale rituals, a landing pad for smaller spell beasts and flying clouds, and, most importantly, an access door.

He made some last-minute adjustments to his assumed identity, took a running start, and crossed the street in a single, powerful leap. He could feel the station's wards and alarm spells pass over him smoothly. "High-level confidential informant" seemed to be on the approved list. The identity could hardly have been easier to assume. Another one of the universe's little digs about his real calling in life.

The door was locked and alarmed. They weren't that slack, it seemed. Truth could feel the passive wards pressing on his assumed identity. Confidential informant or not, he didn't belong up there unescorted. No matter—the lock was trash. A knockoff of a thirty-year-old Jeon design. He was through in under two minutes.

The internal surveillance was . . . inconsistent. Intensely heavy in the hallways and in some of the rooms he checked, completely absent in others. Those rooms tended to smell strongly of bleach and disinfectant. The station wasn't that big, and he was fairly sure anyone with a rank like *major* would be somewhere on an upper floor.

The hallways were painted a pale bluish-lime color. Truth couldn't help but think it looked like a hospital. The handcuffed, roughed-up prisoners made odd patients, and the police were cruel orderlies, but that was the feeling it gave. A big hospital, ready to do as much exploratory surgery as it took to find the cancer.

He found the major's office by the simple expedient of checking every room. Once he found a room with a seating area and a secretary, he figured he was on the right path. The heavily armored, powerfully locked and warded door to the inner office was, likewise, a clue.

He looked over at the secretary, a young man in uniform. Level One. Probably the son of someone important, given a very cushy, very powerful job for someone his age. Truth walked behind the desk. There were a few unlabeled buttons and gems built in to the desk itself, as well as one built into the floor. At a guess—messaging, a silent alarm and the door unlock switch. But he had no idea which was which.

Best guess was the floor button was the alarm, but . . . Hell with it. Truth grabbed the secretary by the neck and slammed him into the wall. Two sharp slaps to get him focused, then, leaning in to Incisive—*"You will open the door for me!"*

The young man's hand involuntarily spasmed toward a blue gem set into the desk. Good enough. Truth snapped his neck and pressed the button. The door unlatched and swung open slightly.

Truth blew in like a hurricane. The major hadn't been expecting anyone. At Level Five and a veteran of a lot of nasty business, he was already pulling his needler and drawing a bead on the door when Truth came in.

Several things happened very quickly. The major managed to snap off a half dozen needles, relying on the auto-fire function and the magic of spray-and-pray. Truth called out the Tongue and deflected the needles that would have actually hit him back at the major as he rushed to close. None of the deflected needles hit. The major had cracked a charm, surrounding himself with a glassy barrier.

Truth didn't bother with Obliteration. He just stacked up the power of his body on Incisive and slammed the Tongue straight through the barrier. It was like stabbing into ice—but he got through. The major let out a shocked grunt as a meter of angelic steel was suddenly buried in his guts. The barrier shattered.

Truth was on the major then, ripping the blade out and using the flat of the blade to smack the needler out of the major's hands.

"DO NOT MOVE!" Truth didn't try to clean up his accent. His crude Onis came out very Jeongo.

"Who the hell are you?! Do you have the faintest idea what you have done?" the major ground out.

"No, I was lost and gutted you completely at random. YES, Major Tsu, I know exactly what I am doing and what you are going to do."

"I will never betray my country!" Was there a recording device in there? Truth would bet there was. Perfect.

"Oh, we have a hero, do we? Well, hero, if I can find you in your armored office in the middle of a police station, how safe do you think your family is? How safe do you think they are *right now?*" Truth started leaning on Incisive again, letting the Poison drip into the Major's ears. The older man turned pale, but his face didn't shift.

"No matter the sacrifice, I will not yield!"

"No? But what if I wanted you to call for help?"

There was a pause.

"That's right, Major. You have been attacked. Someone burst into your office and gutted you. He's standing here right now. *Don't you want to see me dead? See me in chains? Call for help.*"

Major Tsu was breathing heavily. He wasn't dumb. He could feel what was happening. "You want to lure the tiger from the mountain."

"No, the tiger is quite happy on the mountain, ruling as it should. It's the dogs yapping around his heels that need to return to the plains. After their master gives them a good smack and reminds them to behave."

"I will never betray Onis. NEVER!"

"Shame. Oh, well. I think I can fake your voice now. And don't worry; we will take very good care of your family. All the families of senior internal security officers have been marked. A week from now, your country will labor in chains. Lower than animals and demons. All because you forgot your place. All for the glory of the king of the world."

Truth picked up the major's needler, cast the crummy version of Graeme's Arrow, and shot the major in the head.

He quickly searched the room, scraping everything that looked secret or confidential into a sack, popped open the safe with a combination of violence and Obliteration, emptied it into the sack, triggered the explosives in the safe (blowing out a wall in the process), *then* pressed the emergency alarm. Truth wanted to make sure they had a real emergency to respond to, after all. And he had just enough time to make one. Probably.

CHAPTER 68

FOREIGN AGITATOR

Truth snagged the major's cap and wallet on the way out the door. The cap went on his head; the wallet into the sack with the rest of the loot. He rushed down the hall. If he saw a policeman or internal-security type, they got a needle to the head courtesy of Major Tsu's needler and Graeme's Arrow.

Graeme's Arrow punched through skulls and cinder-block walls with equal ease. Truth's Level Four cultivation made overpenetration a serious problem. Which was fine. Overkill was kind of the point. He raced around until he found the comms room—altars with their code tables laid out and a frantic cop reporting that they were under attack by *someone*. Truth put the needler to the back of the cop's head and coughed.

"Sorry to interrupt, but don't worry; I'm here to help you. You want to give them more answers, right? Nod your head."

The cop nodded, sweat running down his face. There were screams coming from all over the building. Overpenetration was terrifying that way. All of a sudden, your concrete wall wasn't protecting you anymore. Death could come at any time, from any direction.

"Tell them that I have taken you captive." Truth waited. "Tell them that I will speak through you." He waited again, as the message was relayed.

"They—they want—"

"No. They will listen. Hear now the words of the King. Major Tsu was the first, his name picked out of a hat by laughing soldiers. On the other slips of paper are generals, ministers, merchants, and others who think they are important or powerful. And there are the names of their parents, their children, their pets. Their hidden bastards and lovers. And we are going to pick a new name out of the hat whenever we want."

The cop looked ill, repeating what Truth said. His face had lost all color; the blue veins over his temples looked like they were going green.

"Some days we will pick a lot of names; other days, just one. But every day, you will lose people. Every day, you will hurt. Not because we expect you to surrender or even apologize. It is far, far too late for that. We just want you to know what is coming. The king of the world will descend on the Great White Mountain once more, and all heaven and earth will give their obedience."

The cop was shaking now. The words stuttering and spilling out of his mouth.

"All the people of the world will be ranked and ordered in their proper places. All cared for, all given proper lives. Except for the people of the dead nation of Onis. You dared bare your fangs at the ritual site. You dared try to dirty the purification. You dared raise your heads before the servants of the king. Your families, your descendants, will never raise their heads again. You will be below even the slaves. Forever. And there is nothing you can do to stop the king's rise."

The cop looked like he was about to faint. He finished repeating the words and waited.

"Thank you for your service. As a reward, you will be spared the sight of what your nation will become." Truth knew his words would be picked up by the altar. As would the sound of the needler ripping through the cop. He felt ill doing it. Killing the major was, somehow, fine. This felt ugly. Well. Ugly was kind of the point, so he would have to suck it up and deal.

Job done. He raced out of the station, ignoring the armory. A lone-wolf terrorist might need to liberate equipment. The PMC never would. On the horizon, he could see a blizzard of flying clouds coming in as well as summoned spell beasts of various sizes. Nothing he needed to stick around for. Truth got running.

It would be another night sleeping on the forest floor. But that was fine. He could deal. He was playing a fool, not an idiot. Onis had a reputation for both thoroughness and not giving the vaguest damn about the comfort or convenience of its citizens. They would search every scrap of the city, digging three meters deep if necessary, to try and catch his trace.

He smiled grimly. Truth's body was now refined to a degree he wouldn't have imagined was possible on this planet. Seamless, as the System called it. Any diviners trying to sniff him out would be very disappointed.

He found a spot about twenty kilometers from the city. Near a stream, with a ridge of earth between him and the wind. It wasn't luxurious, but it would more than do.

Truth started sorting through the loot. There was a little currency from the major's wallet, though not as much as he had hoped. It seemed he would be stuck shoplifting for the foreseeable future. As for the rest . . . he had no idea what any of it was. Very important-looking ledgers, memoranda, reports . . . office stuff.

System, little help?

<<Little *is the word. What you are currently holding is the duty roster for the officers overseeing the prefecture's censorship department. Not exactly the stuff of blackmail gold. Start flipping through; I'll see if anything jumps out. Then we can check out the memory crystals, see if they are secured or what.*>>

Truth nodded and started doing just that.

<<*On a completely different subject, but since you were thinking about it, we should discuss your body cultivation.*>>

Oh? I don't think there are any problems. Better than ever, really.

<<*There isn't and it is. I'm starting to get a better feel for what happened to it in the chamber with that eminence. Seamless* is the right way to think about it, but also

incomplete. It . . . Hmm. Frustrating. I can see it and understand what I am seeing, but you don't really have words for the concepts.>>

Start with basic ideas and build up?

<<Your apertures are a sort of symbolic recreation of the heavens. A nine-point constellation, if you like. Your body is either ignored, as per the overwhelming majority of mages on this planet, or something that gives you extra abilities. If you remember way back when you first were "deciding" which body cultivation you would choose, all the other spells gave special abilities like shooting burning rays of light from your eyes, high-speed movement, that kind of thing.>>

Sure. And the deck was stacked in such a way that I was definitely going to pick the Meditations.

<<Exactly, yeah. And the two big advantages of the Meditations, other than cost, was that there was no cap on how far it could develop and, developed far enough, it could affect things on a conceptual level. Which you have been enjoying, by the way, every time you have used Incisive to change your identity.>>

Wait, what?

<<You are literally changing how people, how the whole damn universe identifies you. Identity being a concept of the object indicated. In this case, you.>>

Truth felt his face twitching. It made sense. It made complete sense. He had been chalking it up to the Meditations making him "more real" than everything around him.

<<It's doing that, too. Merkovah is a seriously nasty guy. I can't even guess how many spells you have slipped past by just not being who they were looking for. "Blow up a bank? Not me! You must be looking for my cousin, Arson Medici.">>

Oh, God. All right, so, what's this got to do with whatever changes you have been seeing with my body cultivation?

<<It's a few things coming together at the same time. The isolation from the Nephilim, the sheer improvement of your body and soul, the way you pull on and shed identities, the way you enforce your own reality on the world around you, even the way your spiritual body aligns essentially perfectly with your physical body. I think you are in the process of becoming . . . I don't know. Your own universe?>>

There was a pause. Then a longer pause. Truth looked up from flipping through the reports to stare blankly at a tree.

You . . . doing okay there? I know the Snake that Eats Its Own Tail did something to you, too.

<<I know how batshit insane it sounds. Like I said, we don't have a language to describe this. You are becoming not just self-contained but a point of reference for determining reality. I have some frankly wild speculations about where this is all going once you hit peak Level Nine, and one of my theories is that all this somehow amalgamates into one thing. The body cultivation, the spells, the blessings, your understanding of the universe and how you, yourself work, your understanding of reality—all of it. Imploding and condensing into a singular, perfect whole. Self-sustaining. Not needing anything from outside itself but able to accept things from outside itself, on its own terms.>>

Truth tried to process that. He could understand what the System was talking about. Everything worked together. Everything reinforced each other.

Body cultivation is more or less normal on other planets, right?

<<That's what people have told you.>>

So, let's assume that this is the "normal" or "right" way to cultivate. Level One—body cultivation. Build the foundation for everything else. Level Two through Nine, you are stacking spells. You only get eight plus the body cultivation, so you better pick good ones with lots of utility. Because your spells are going to define you, literally, when you break through the barrier at Level Nine.

Truth started nodding, feeling like things were coming together.

It's why modern magic is so easy to pick up and so limited by comparison. There is no need to be complex. The user isn't breaking through the barrier. It's why the old-fashioned spells all seem to have personalities too—they really are an expression of their creator's personality. Someone broke that barrier and passed down a bit of their understanding of how the cosmos worked to achieve a certain effect.

<<Graeme's Arrow isn't just a "shoot him" spell; it's how Graeme understood the concept of sending something small very far, very fast, and very accurately. The reason the "modern" version of the spell feels scuffed is it lacks Graeme's murderousness and understanding of the universe.>>

The better you understand your spells, the better you understand the universe and the principles that make it up, the better you understand yourself and how you think and feel about things, the more perfect a system you have after you break through the barrier. The stronger your universe is, I guess. Maybe you can't even break through until you reach a certain level of understanding.

<<Divine revelation. You can't learn it from other people. You have to go and experience it for yourself.>>

It's why I came so far, so fast with Incisive. I literally had a revelation of Botis. I could see how he existed. Self-contained would be a pretty good term for him.

<<Yeah. So, what did your revelation from your "Rough Patron" show you?>>

Truth was stumped by that one for a long time.

That night passed uncomfortably but quickly enough. Truth packed up his few belongings and started jogging off down the road again. The looted data listed some confidential informants, cooperating businesspeople, and hidden police stations. Nothing major on a national scale; regional stuff. He would see how many he could hit in a reasonably short period. Paranoia should carry him the rest of the way.

He wasn't strong enough to crack the mountain fortress. But the last-ditch, desperate efforts of the frankly enormous army of Onis, determined to save their skins and those of their descendants? He liked their chances. At the very least, they would force Starbrite to reveal more of their hidden cards.

He *tsked* reprovingly as he jogged along. This was more being a terrorist than a fool. Provoking the overreaction. On the other hand, maybe the greatest sign of a fool was making a fool of others. Besides, he was still planning on charging into the dark tower alone. He had a princess to save.

CHAPTER 69

NATURE AND NURTURE

On the way to the town of Boxiliu, a town of no particular importance to anyone outside the commercial slate-production industry, Truth made a marvelous discovery. In addition to producing a rare reddish-colored slate, Boxiliu had a zoo.

The zoo was a small, sad affair. A few dispirited-looking monkeys, tropical birds wishing they weren't in the northern mountains, snakes, lizards, an insect hall, a few comatose-looking foxes, and pride of place—a "husband and wife" pair of tigers. Truth was rather charmed by them. They weren't doing much, just lying around. Still. For all the talk of the "Tiger of Jeon," he hadn't seen them before.

He could see why they had fascinated people for so long. Those big round eyes in that big head. Even lying flopped on the ground, you got a feeling of power from them. And, honestly, they were kind of cute, too.

I don't suppose you can learn how to speak tiger, could you?

<<Sure, easy peasy.>>

Wait, really? That's awesome!

<<No, that was a lie. Tigers do not have developed language centers in their brain, so they cannot understand terms like halfwit, *or* moron, *or* Dear God, my opinion of your education has managed to go down; who says miracles never happen.>>*

Could have just said no. I'm allowed to have fun.

<<Allowed is stretching it. More like no one is in a position to stop you. And you should be stopped.>>

Happy diversion aside, he did have more serious business to attend to in Boxiliu. The slate industry was not a particularly large or lucrative one, on an international scale, but on a *local* scale, it was a sizable employer and the owner a wealthy man. And, as was the rule in Onis, very connected to local politics. He was in Major Tsu's files as both an important resource (for surveillance of his employees, social control, and funding) and a priority target for supervision (same reasons).

Truth jogged into town and was struck by nothing much. Lots of industrial-looking buildings. He didn't know why there were so many tall structures and conveyor belts coming off a slate quarry, but there were. He ran over to the quarry, on the off chance that there would be someone or something useful there. Heavy industrial equipment could be used in all sorts of ways, after all.

This ambition was immediately frustrated. First by the sheer size of the operation, and second by how the actual work was done. The quarries were a strange combination of painful backwardness and state-of-the-art production processes.

The quarrying was done by men with long iron fetishes. They would punch long holes into the stone, *crack, crack, crack*, bashed into place with iron sledges. Then they would activate the spell and split off an enormous slab of stone. The stone would then be collected by demon-pulled carts, loaded onto talisman rail carts, and transported to a fabrication yard.

At the yard, the large stone would be tagged and delivered to a team of men to be split into layers. This was done with a hammer and chisel. *Crack, crack, crack.* Stone fragments and dust flying everywhere. Those layers were then tagged and put into baskets.

The baskets were transported by a flying talisman to workers sitting in the dirt, a rag tied around their face to keep the dust out of their lungs. It didn't look like the rags helped much. The workers would take slabs of slate and line them up on a small, thin anvil. They would take an iron hammer and bash off the rough edges. Smashing it into a useful shape. *Crack, crack, crack.*

They would then put the finished slates into a basket to be collected by another flying talisman and taken to the next point in the production line. Soon they would be shipped to a rail station and, from there, to builders' depots.

Truth watched the workers sitting in the stone dust, smashing away with their iron hammers. *Crack, crack, crack.* Breathing in the fruits of their labors. Each day, their breath comes just that little bit shorter. He could rush in there. He could kill the supervisors, kill the bosses, and tell them *You don't have to live like this. You don't have to kill yourself so your boss has a mansion and someone on the other side of the world has a roof* just *the right purple-red color.*

They would look right back at him and say, *So what? Are you going to feed my family? Because this is feeding my family.* And then someone would throw a stone. *Crack, crack, crack.*

Truth knew he wasn't a very sympathetic person. Not the sort to go out of his way to help others. Quite the opposite, really. But there was something about the quarry workers. The little iron hammers rising and falling. The jagged stone dust flying around. Breath after breath, shredding lungs with each life-sustaining gasp. *Crack, crack, crack.* For what he assumed was shit money. If it wasn't shit money, they would have masks. *Crack, crack, crack.*

He had seen a lot worse than this. As an example of man's inhumanity to man, it hardly rated. Didn't even make the top twenty of horrible things he had seen this month. Probably got held up as a sign of industry and progress in an undeveloped region. Bringing jobs to the impoverished. Yeah. A real blessing. *Crack, crack, crack.*

"If I ever stand at the godhead, I will break this curse. I swear I will break it. I will show you it doesn't have to be this way. They want you to kneel, to sit in the dirt? You put their damn teeth in the dirt! You are better than this. I swear I will make you see it! Because watching you be proud of living like this pisses me off! WAKE THE FUCK UP!"

Truth hissed his anger, then spun on his heel and left. There was a big-ass manor up on the side of the mountain, overlooking the town. No points for guessing who lived there.

Truth raced up the side of the mountain. There was a decent security detail at the manor. It seemed that not everyone was properly grateful for the blessings of economic development. There were also a few anonymous-looking carriages that, to Truth's jaded eye, screamed *plainclothes cop*. Had he underestimated the quarry workers?

He ghosted into the manor. The meeting seemed to be breaking up, as the cops were leaving the house, escorted by the owner and some servants.

"I will step up my efforts, naturally. You shall have my full cooperation."

"That is good to hear, Mr. Mu. I must remind you that this matter has Central's full attention."

The owner snorted. "Kittens wearing a tiger's skin, baring their tiny fangs at a dragon!"

The senior cop shook his head slowly. "Jeon is a petty power. Starbrite is not. I am reminding you because of our many-years relationship. Be careful, and be watchful."

"I will, I will. I am much more worried about Senior Mo. I assume preparations are being made?"

"Naturally." They reached the carriages. "Take care."

"Don't bother." Truth had the Major's cap perched jauntily on his head. All anyone could see of him was a blurry outline—and the cap. The guards reached for their needlers, spells springing into existence. They were slow as sleepy birds.

He was on them in a flash and past them in a second. The guards collapsed before they even had their weapons drawn. The chief cop was unconscious and disarmed, the homeowner right there with him.

Literally one second. Truth flexed his hand slowly. Literally one second. For all his outrage at the state of the quarry workers, the difference in cultivation and spell qualities, the difference the blessings gave him, meant that trained, alert police officers of around Level Two and their Level Three boss couldn't stand up to him for even one second.

Was the notion of a world without bosses childish? Was it even possible to live a dignified life in a world with cultivation? It would require a whole lot of humility on the part of the powerful. Words that did not generally go together.

Maybe that's why he had to become God. You needed that outside, third party. Someone with ultimate power who could restrain the mighty and give the weak space to live and grow healthy.

Truth looked down at the unconscious and dead cops. Theoretically, the state could do that too. That was the point of laws, right? But no, that really was too childish. The state served its masters, and the masters were never the poor or weak.

Truth sighed and got to work. Out of a macabre sense of "fun," he arranged the dead guards in their police carriages. He even buckled their seatbelts. The owner and the chief cop he dumped in the trunk of the fanciest carriage and drove off.

Back to the zoo.

They were awake and noisy by the time he got there.

"Shhh. Don't worry. I'm not here to blackmail you, or extort you, or force you to tell me anything," he explained. He was in a weird mood. It was all getting to be too much, and there wasn't a soothing pet cafe in sight.

"You work for Starbrite!" the cop snarled.

"Yes." Truth nodded. It was a lie, but the identity of Starbrite PMC Sergeant Truth Medici was very easy to wear, and terribly believable. He wasn't planning on leaving any evidence, but just in case.

"Do you really think you can defeat Onis? You are mad. MAD!" the quarry owner yelled. Hoping for help, Truth assumed, though that was also a childish wish. The one underpaid zookeeper was currently stuck in a closet with a chair jammed under the doorknob on the other side.

"I don't think so, no." That seemed to confuse them, but the cop figured it out first.

"You think your master will become a god. The king of the world."

Did . . . this cop have some kind of recording talisman built into him? Or some kind of deadman's switch on his soul to pass back information? He had never heard of something like that before, but both he and Major Tsu had completely failed to beg for their lives, which confused him. Maybe their families would suffer if they did? He really didn't know.

"Yes, exactly. Honestly, I'm as mad as you. I wanted to be at the ascension site, to witness his elevation. But no. I'm out here, slapping around future untouchables. If I'm still out here by the end of the week and miss it, fuck it, your whole capital dies in a fire. Assuming you still have a capital then."

"Bah, what could you accomplish in a week with your petty strength?!"

Wow, this guy was bad at sounding natural. Guess it had been a long time since he was on the wrong end of a beating.

"Me? Quite a lot. The CEO? A whole lot more. And you have it wrong. There is nothing left to do. No shipments to be intercepted, no key natural philosophers to kill. The planet turns, the stars align, and the hour comes 'round at last. A king shall rise, and a god shall descend on this world. At long last. But before it does, you and I have a little business to attend to."

Truth fished out a rock. "Not local slate, but it will do." He broke their ankles and wrists, then threw them into the tiger enclosure.

The tigers were well fed and more or less habituated to humans. It wasn't safe in there, but it wasn't that dangerous, either. Normally.

Truth looked at the tigers and imposed his will on the world. They were TIGERS. Kings of the mountains. Mighty. Terrible. The embodiment of nature, red in tooth and claw. Monkeys like these had offended their dignity for too long. And were they really going to turn down a free meal?

The tigers snarled, then roared. There were screams, then silence.

"All right. That ought to light a fire under their ass," Truth muttered. He was feeling lightheaded. "I think I need a break. Back to the mountain, then just camp out and wait for the show to start. Should be . . . real soon."

CHAPTER 70

CASCADING CONTINGENCIES

Truth lay on a tree branch. It wasn't very comfortable, but he wasn't paying attention to that fact. He was just . . . there. Being there. He was playing the fool. He was being loud and obviously provoking. He was relying on the terror and paranoia of others to trigger a proxy war. This was a low-percentage play. A smart person didn't rely on the emotions of others. They made things happen on their schedule. This was dumb. He was being dumb. Which fits playing the fool, but maybe too much? He didn't know. It just sucked all the way around.

Was he depressed? Truth didn't know. Maybe it was just exhaustion. Spiritual more than physical these days. The endless refinement of his body had made physical exhaustion a real challenge. But the mental struggle wore on him.

It was the cop he used as a mouthpiece. And the guys he had just fed to tigers. And a lot of other people, actually, now that he was letting himself think about it. Especially Niles. It was just so shitty to be shitty to people when you know the game is rigged. That you are still picking cards off the same stacked deck. Even if you were hoping to kill the dealer at the end of the game, you were still playing along. Still working over the suckers who didn't spot the con.

Telling yourself that it was necessary. That this was just how the world was. That this was reality.

What a joke.

Would it be worse if the terrible things he did were successful, proving that this was, in fact, necessary and this was, in fact, reality—or if they didn't work because the whole premise was phony?

That would be an awful lot of dead people just to prove a philosophical point.

He just needed to stop for a while. Take a few days or weeks. Just process all the insanity. He didn't have time for that. The clock was ticking, fast and loud. So, he would just hang out on this tree branch for a while and not try to think about anything much. Try not to worry about the damage he knew he was accumulating.

Truth was roughly north of the Great White Mountain. He could see the peak from his tree branch. There was a fair amount of air traffic around it now. Lots of talisman devices, lots of spell birds and summoned beasts. He could imagine all the Jeon conscripts squaring off against all the Onis conscripts. Neither really wanting to be there, both juiced up on all the nationalist rhetoric their officers could cram into their ears.

Both very aware that, be it in conscripts or regulars, Onis outnumbered Jeon more than ten to one. And both very, very aware that their numbers were meaningless when the high-levels were fighting. Ten thousand conscripts, or a working from a Level Seven combat mage not concerned about taking prisoners? It didn't qualify as a fight.

Truth looked blankly up into the sky, letting the tree branches flick over his vision. The army didn't explain much about what to do when high-levels kicked off, just basics like *If things are coming at you, any degree of "underground" is better than being on the surface.* The PMC was a bit more forthcoming.

It was after he had gotten back from his recuperation on the *Star of Mercy* hospital ship. There was a video in the training library at the PMC, where a high-level Starbrite mage had essentially hijacked a rainstorm. The enemy was dug in? No problem. He turned the water into acid and, once that had started eating through clothes and armor, added a little extra something to the water. Tiny demonic parasites, immune to the acid, that crawled in through the open wounds and festered. The results were agonizing. The final outcome was predictable.

Or there was that senior who ripped through four ammo boxes for a heavy needler, launched straight up, tagged each needle with a Bane spell, a hunting spell, Enlarge and Graeme's Arrow. He THEN cast a Tanglefoot spell that covered almost two square kilometers and held it for the fraction of a second the needles needed to find their prey. Total elapsed time—two seconds. Total casualties, one thousand three hundred. No enemy survivors.

Firestorms, those were popular. Large-scale summonings were both popular and, depending on what was being summoned, illegal. Beastcrafting and golems were expensive ways to wage war, but they were a lot more durable and reparable than summons. Couldn't banish a golem, for one thing.

That was the core of most army's large-scale tactics, as Truth understood it. You had your conscripts out front as trigger-pullers and targets to draw fire. The hope was that the enemy spent their best attacks on your worst but most numerous troops. Then you had your core of regulars kick off the wide-area spells, run golems, summon swarms—basically become force-multiplying nightmares.

And if the enemy chose not to engage your conscripts? A Level Three might sweep the floor with a dozen Level Ones but probably couldn't stop eight thousand needles coming at them all at the same time. Army needlers had a big magazine and a high rate of fire for just such a reason. Unless, of course, that Level Three was in the PMC. Quantity may have a quality all of its own but only up to a point.

You had to mop up the conscripts. You just wanted to do it as cheaply as possible. So, you deployed large-scale tactical spells. You funneled them into a valley and folded the earth over them. You created a firestorm on the plains. You summoned, picking an example *completely at random*, several billion insect demons. That would certainly tie down a lot of conscripts! It would tie down a lot of your mid-levels, too, while your few expensive high-level combat effectives stood on the border looking scary and swearing to kill until the skies turned red.

Once you understood the doctrine, it was easy to follow the chain of events. The breakthrough from Hell *might* have been a natural disaster, but coming just when they discovered a secret Jeon research base right on, or even over, their border? One covered with deeply unnatural, never-seen-before monstrosities? When everyone and their pet lizard knew that Starbrite had kidnapped a Shattervoid princess?

The soldiers were . . . Truth didn't know what to call it. Showing off? Launching morale attacks? He could see mages on spell birds, kilometers up and away in the air, swooping past. Making tiny incursions across the border. Coming within centimeters of hitting their opposite numbers charging out to confront them.

Truth watched them dive, swoop, loop (and what a sphincter-clenching experience that must be, standing on top of a summoned bird), and flare their wings. Spell birds, in all their talisman-bedecked glory, hovered and fluttered along the border. They might not be as fast as the summons, but they were covered in weapons. A force multiplier—a Level Two pilot could decimate a squad of ground-based Level Ones and Twos with almost casual ease.

Unless the squad on the ground was led by one Sergeant Truth Medici, Starbrite PMC, C-8-L, late of this parish. Then one man and one needler were all you needed to wipe out a squad of spell birds.

The mock fights were taking place kilometers away. By the time he saw what had happened, the birds would already have moved. And he only had the major's personal sidearm. Usual effective range, less than a hundred meters. Recommended-use range, less than twenty. Actual range was, of course, much longer. Kilometers, in fact, but it would have all the stopping power of a falling pine needle at that range.

You could enhance that range with spells, sure, but how accurate were you going to be? Could you even aim that far? How would you lead your shot on something speeding up and slowing down erratically?

Truth pulled out the needler. *Load Graeme's Arrow.* He felt the spell bucking and struggling as the System crammed it into his empty spell slot. Truth turned his attention inward. The spells weren't alive, nor were they conscious, exactly. But their creator's intention lived on in them. Truth tried to communicate his intent to the spell. Tried to impress on it the exhausted murderousness of his idea.

It seemed to work. The spell settled down. Truth looked over at a Jeon regular on a summoned beast, four wings flapping hard for the border. He stood proud, uniform sharp, ceremonial saber pointing toward the enemy. The Onis airwing met him with two flying serpents, each with a sword-pointing regular on their back. They all looked very fierce as they very carefully did *not* hit each other.

Truth waited, needler rock-steady in his hand. Waiting for Incisive to tell him the moment to strike. Waiting. Waiting-

Graeme's Arrow picked up the needle, whipping it through the air far faster than the needler could manage on its own. The soldiers separated, then looped around, passed each other within inches, separated, and moved back. Then closed again.

The needle caught the Jeon flier a moment before he would have made his pass against the two soldiers from Onis. At the ragged edge of its range, even with Graeme's

Arrow, it plinked off his helmet harmlessly. It was enough to make him blink and, for just a moment, flinch. His strong summoned beast smashed directly into the two flying serpents. All fell down. Directly onto the Great White Mountain.

A lot of things started happening all at once. From either side of the border, sirens started blaring. Blizzards of birds took off, flying platforms went up, spell arrays, summoning arrays, sacrificial arrays, golem launchers started deploying, conscripts were screamed into position, told to stand to, to dig in, that "This is it, boys; this is WAR!"

Sirens screamed the alert as the mountain seemed to shiver and boil. Things were moving on it, enormous things, knocking over trees. Truth could see the trails of their passing from kilometers away. Wards shimmered and snapped into place over the mountain, too—enormous things. Impossible things. Truth would never have thought an entire mountain could be covered in wards.

Starbrite had always been so much more than he could imagine. He was just a little rat, staring up. Trying to understand the means and majesty of the king of the world.

The spells started deploying. Explosions ripped apart the air, flattening the trees on the mountains, filling valleys. Erasing lives. They weren't all targeting the mountain, either—the spells smashed into the soldiers' lines, ripping apart bases and airfields. Trying to disrupt summons.

Enormous demons, things with three heads and six arms, each hand holding a Bane or a suffering, manifested over the battlefield. Truth could see into the distance—they weren't all going for the battlefield. Some were marching into the interior. Cutting off supply lines. "Pacifying" civilians. There weren't many cities in the mountains between Jeon and Onis. Not many people at all, comparatively. But there were some. A few million, perhaps.

Just a few million, out of the billions on this world. And it wasn't like they were targets. Most of them should probably live. Negligible, in the grand scheme of things. A necessary sacrifice for the greater good. The rats had to be fed. They were already starving. Regrettable necessities would remain both regrettable and necessary, given the current and projected emergency conditions.

Truth was numb. He didn't know he was crying as he watched the spell birds tear each other apart. As angels seared the life from the land, eliminating human and infernal contamination with equal contempt. As demons proliferated, bursting out of the bodies of seventeen-year-old conscripts. Conscripts who had to be cleared out as economically as possible, and what was more economical than turning them against their fellows?

Standing above it all was the Great White Mountain. Its shields shuddered under constant magical assault. Spears of molten stone launched from arrays the size of houses, the volcano's lava moving under Starbrite's command. Smashing through summons and fortifications with equal ease.

It took less than ten minutes to reduce wooded mountains into a fiery hell. Everyone knew this was just the beginning. The warm-up. It would get so much worse than this.

Truth watched in horror as the rats fed on each other without mercy. Without hesitation. Without regret.

CHAPTER 71

UP AND IN

It looked like the end of the world, and he had to wait. It wasn't actually the end. It wasn't even the end of the beginning.

The Jeon Army never thought it could win an open-field battle, so they didn't bother trying. They dug in to the mountains and built bunkers in the forests, bastions where resupply could be delivered by tunneling demons or airlifted in by spell birds and summons. From there, they deployed summoned angels and demons, sent out swarms of ghosts, sent out waves of talisman machines to create the numbers they lacked.

More quietly, on the forest floor, tiny golems scattered and buried themselves. Thousands, then tens of thousands of them, coating roads, paths . . . likely invasion routes. Just waiting for someone to push in. Minefields crawled into place, then vanished beneath the earth. They would wait there for however long it took. Long after the war ended, probably. Someone would come by someday.

The Onis Army knew exactly what they were doing, of course. They were doing the same damn thing on their side. But since they also had roughly twenty times the soldiers under arms, they had the luxury of offensive operations. They didn't feel like letting Jeon dig in any more than it already had.

Flights of angels—vaguely human heads born aloft by a pair of wings—swept in front of massed conscripts. They screamed at the defending summons, and the sound of their voices shattered air and matter alike. Balefire skewers punched through eyes and mouths in reply, arcane wards reflecting the noise back and down into the trailing conscripts. The air war was only getting started.

It was all only getting started. The conscripts pushed in behind the angels, sweeping for mines the hard way. Discovering that, even if you trained for it, nobody is really ready for watching your squadmate explode, turn into a blood portal to Hell, and then having to fight the swarms of fire demons coming to harvest the rest of your squad.

Maybe the regulars were better used to it. The conscripts were barely eighteen. Some younger. All expecting to be directing traffic somewhere or standing at a border post. Maybe filling in a pothole on a base, if they were technically inclined.

Not screaming and spraying their needler around until the magazine emptied, trying to stop the billion demonic grasshoppers from sweeping over their position. Not puking when they realized that they had hollowed out the skull of a kid that looked just like them with an accidentally well-placed round. The patriotic recordings had promised they would feel pride and resolve.

The conscripts felt they had no choice. They had to obey their orders. Standing next to their officers were the political officers, watching intently for any sign of defeatism, cowardice, shirking. Eager to make the first example. And behind them were the regulars, the career soldiers. They weren't even watching the slaughter. They were eating big meals and triple-checking their equipment. Making sure they were in their best condition for the fight to come.

Whether it was putting down the nation's enemies or deserting conscripts, the regulars would be ready. The latter was less pleasant but infinitely safer. They got paid the same either way. This was the job. It wasn't a nice job, but it was a respectable one. Everyone's got to eat.

Towering above it all was the Great White Mountain. Spells, summons, talismans, all struck at it and either bounced off the wards or simply died. It wasn't passively taking a beating, either. The mountain was an active volcano. There was an unlimited supply of heat and molten rock to work with.

The air war around the mountain was one-sided. In favor of the mountain. Ten thousand summoned demons came? They were met by a hundred thousand-finger long basalt spikes, each traveling faster than sound, each enchanted with runes and Names of terrible authority.

Angels fared no better. State-of-the-art Starbrite magical technology was custom-enchanting each needle before it left the spell array. Industrial production lines fed banishments etched in basalt harvested from the planet's mantle down the throats of angels.

Truth couldn't see what was happening on the ground. He knew the kind of beastcrafted horrors Starbrite had installed. Nothing human had reached them yet, he suspected. Nor did he think any of the summons or golems would manage much. Not the cheap, high-volume ones. Later, when the big summons came out, that would change things.

So, he just lay on his tree branch, watching the war he had triggered. He tried to remind himself he hadn't created this situation. He hadn't put the soldiers there. He hadn't set up the contingencies. He hadn't spent years perfecting the supply trains, testing equipment, testing doctrine, perfecting indoctrination, spreading propaganda, creating the laws and taxes that supported all this. He had just instigated. He was the spark that had fallen on all the heaped-up explosives.

It wasn't a comfort. He never was good at lying to himself. He was a rat feeding on his fellow rats, same as them. For all his introspection, for all the things he had learned, he was still in the slum. He still hadn't stood up. Still didn't know how to live as a man in the "real" world.

So, he lay there and watched. He didn't stir from the branch for a full day. He saw endless tiny shifts, lives spent for "crucial" gains or protecting retreats, and it all amounted to exactly nothing. The lines remained roughly where they had been the day before. There were, if anything, *more* soldiers and materials gathered. And the mountain was untouched. Unstained by the squabbling rabble beneath it.

A few thousand rats had died, hard to say how many, exactly, but they were no one of significance. What were the slums for, if not this? An attitude and ethos firmly shared by both Jeon and Onis: "We fed you and bred you and taught you. Now go die, that your bodies may be a soft carpet for the feet of your betters."

Their betters in this case weren't even that much better. The real "betters" would be in the air, so high up, you couldn't see the rats.

Truth really didn't have a sense of the rhythm of battles on this scale. His fights were up close and personal, involving at most twenty or so people. He had been in some bigger fights, but, again, nothing on this scale. Nothing remotely on this scale. And he could only guess based on what he was seeing from his tree branch.

Ultimately, the course of the battle, the whole war, really, didn't matter. What mattered was getting into the mountain. And it seemed that someone in Onis firmly agreed with him on that.

As the sun set into the west, the sky dimmed around it. The sun itself seemed to brighten, but its light no longer filled the sky. It was condensed into a single searing drop. There was a moment of quiet. As though the whole world was holding its breath. Truth held his breath. The conscripts didn't; he could see the trees shaking as they ran for their lives away from the mountain.

The sundrop fell on the mountain . . . and was caught in a teacup. Truth's eyes were good enough to see the old man. Everyone's ears were good enough to hear him.

"Couldn't sit still any longer, eh, Feng?" The old man had simply stuck out his cup and caught the drop that should have melted the side of the mountain. There were spells there, more sensed than seen. Dense networks of meaning, of implication, built into his every gesture. He was one of the true elites of the world. Yet, to Truth, there was something hollow about him.

"You never did know how to brew a decent cup. Here, try mine." The old man flicked out the teacup, sending the searing drop of plasma back to the west. As it passed, it expanded. Trees too close to the heat were ash and vapor in less than a second. Those a little farther away exploded as the water inside them flashed into steam, the flying splinters bursting into flame and setting fires as they went.

The droplet hit something solid. Networks of spells flared into light—then burst, shattering the air around them. He couldn't hear the screams, but Truth knew they were there. Whatever had just been struck was gone.

This was one of the C-suite. Tier Eight. *Starbrite* Tier Eight. Every spell, every scrap of technique or wisdom the System had was at his disposal. Because, at this point, the difference between him and the System Astrologica was strictly biological.

The very first time I see the System Astrologica make a move in person, it catches the sun in a teacup and slaughters an army of combat mages with a single blow. He was beyond horror now, just watching numbly as beings he could barely comprehend warred above him.

"Bullying juniors was all you were ever good for, Park. Come, let's see if your chin is still made of glass." A basso voice rumbled out from where the sundrop had struck.

The illusion had passed; the sun was still setting in the west. Truth had to squint to see a man in uniform standing on the back of an enormous flying serpent.

"Did you get mugged? Who shoved you in the monkey suit? Clench your teeth, Feng. I'll fix that face of yours for free, on account of our old acquaintance." The man on the mountain stowed his teacup and summoned a firebird with a casual wave. He hopped on its back and the two flew up into the atmosphere. Truth could only see the shattering bursts of color. He could feel the air shake with the thunder of their moves. This was not a fight he could be a part of.

Onis wasn't about to let their loss go unavenged. Batteries of spells opened up, launching acid, fire, stone, the obliterating light of Heaven, and the consuming darkness of Hell. Barrages of magic, smashing against the magical protection of the mountain.

It's time to move. Truth felt the moment tug on him, and he went with it. He wasn't close to where he had originally broken in, but that was fine. He was going to be moving fast, and nobody was going to be looking at him.

He was like a drifting shadow among swaying shadows—the reddish setting sun throwing everything into deep shade. The trees writhing and flinching as their quiet home was torn apart by brutal magic. There were others moving through the woods. Truth could see them, sometimes, or feel them more often. Other hunters, other specialists looking to crack their way in. He wondered how they held up against the many-eyed monsters that guarded the gate.

It turned out . . . middlingly.

There were a few blazes of harsh white that dotted the mountainside. You could hear the thunderclap displacement of air even with the barrage overhead. He was close enough to one that he felt the jet of superheated air rush past him. Carrying the smell of something terrible. Something so foul, so sickening, you would never be quite right again. Seemed promising. He ran toward the *boom.*

There weren't many bodies. Nor many bones. The stones were still glowing red-hot, some still dripping and pooling where they had been melted. Sand and stone turned to glass. Nothing human could have survived. Nothing human did. There was a spark of divine light, flickering but holding on, trying to finish off the thing guarding the gate. Whatever the thing was, it was almost dead. Only "almost."

The spark let out a trilling noise. Calling for help, Truth knew. The Tongue responded. He *had* to kill this thing. So, he called the blade to hand and drew upon every scrap of strength in him. Channeling all the horror of what he had seen and done into a two-handed blow.

Truth cut that monstrous thing in half and felt the alien monster scream in death. The Tongue and the divine spark were screaming too—in joy.

Truth felt the twisting bolus of energy that had driven the monstrous thing. Writhing. Clawing at him. He didn't want to imagine what would happen if it got in. His grin was a bloody thing. Instead, he grabbed the twisting, hateful mass and looked at the spark.

"Help me burn this thing up. I have a use for it."

The spark was only too happy to help. Truth cast Incisive. The spark turned the sickening energy into something purer. Usable. It followed his intention, using its own magic to support Truth's will. Above the mountain an illusion rose. A green tiger rose, with its paw on the mountaintop. Its eyes burned with wisdom, its face filled with ferocity and power. From out of its fanged maw, a shout echoed across the battlefield.

"FOR JEON! JEON AND VICTORY!"

And with that, Truth vanished into the mountain. The Prince was there. Time to save the Princess. Damn fool that he was.

CHAPTER 72

INTERNAL VOLUME OF A VOLCANO

Truth was in. The heavy steel door had been reduced to molten slag by the blast. Still hot enough that his clothes started to char and smoke just by being near it. Truth mitigated this by moving even faster. He went through the melted-away top right corner of the vault door at a speed more commonly associated with spell birds and dove into the volcano.

This was a choice that reflected his keen appreciation for the vital moment to strike, a willingness to take calculated risks and, it must be said, the accumulated trauma of the day. Or, put another way, a choice that did not reflect him considering what someone might do if their vault door had just blown in as spec ops teams were trying to force their way in.

As he arced over the molten steel, Truth had ample time to count noses. Four. There were four noses on the four heads perched over a double dozen arms, a muscular, almost column-like torso, and a pair of heavily muscled legs. There was a red loincloth in use, thankfully. He was considerably less thankful over the fact that the arms all held weapons and spells. The troll's eyes were tracking him through the air. So, there was that, too. Such joy.

A lot of things happened very quickly. Truth activated Abner's Amble and kicked off the wall, closing the distance to the troll near instantly. The troll squeezed one hand and was covered in bronze armor. Another hand squeezed and he was holding an ax. Another hand held a sword. Another a trident; two more held a glaive. Four held multicolored flames.

Truth lunged with the Tongue at the thing's neck. It might have four heads, but he reckoned he could have them off like he was trimming broccoli. The troll seemed to disagree as the four flames came jabbing out at him, even as the weapons hacked down, over, up, and straight at him.

Truth was faster. The Tongue pierced the flames, scattering them. The blade bit into the thickly muscled neck, then deeper until it hit the tree-like spine. He felt the Bane struggle for a moment, then activate. Whatever this thing was, it was damn odd. Still died if you stabbed it enough, though. He dashed back out of range before the incoming blades could reach him.

The troll staggered forward a step. One of its hands reached up and felt the hole in its throat, frowning. Another hand, one holding a lotus, crushed it and pressed it against the hole. The hole closed up, but the troll's frown deepened.

An angelic Bane is not so easily dispelled. If it can be dispelled at all. The troll's expression firmed up. Black jets of curse magic started spraying toward Truth as pairs of arms nocked arrows to bowstrings. More hands planted glaives in place, ready to repel a charge.

Truth snorted and charged right back in. Obliterate and his refined body cut a path through the magic. The tongue flicked up and over, deflecting the two arrows that the troll managed to loose. Then he was at the glaives. A smash to the right with the flat of his blade made enough of a gap.

The troll was strong, and it had many means. Truth only had a few tools. By now, he had spent his time on the tools. The edge was perfectly aligned with the angle of the cut. His weight and the power in his strong body drove the blade clean through as the Fangs of Botis bit. Four faces turned white with confusion and shock. Eight eyes blinked in horror. The enormous head went flying.

"I YIELD!" the troll managed to bellow as the head arced in a bloody spray down the hall. No throat, yet it could speak.

"Okay." Truth nodded amicably.

Then he stabbed the head over and over without letting it hit the floor. The obscene thing exploded into a mess of gore. Truth bisected the body before it could get up to anything either. Truth had noticed it readying more spells when it thought he wasn't paying attention.

Taking prisoners? Who was the troll kidding? Things were far, far past that point. It was time to win or die. He spent a few extra seconds making sure the thing really was dead, then jogged off down the hall. No chance of an internal map, but there might just be signs. And if not, he would just have to keep searching until he found what he was looking for.

Incisive screamed with alarm. Truth looked around desperately, spotted a door, and went through it at speed. It was locked, but the Tongue had yet to meet a lock it couldn't pick. Truth shut the door fast and looked around. Storage room. A chair holding up some boxes. Perfect. Chair went under the door handle, then Truth got ready to deal with whatever smashed its way in.

He felt his heart pound. Once. Twice. Then there was an overwhelming sense of pressure washing over him. It was everywhere. Like being buried alive in scorpions and beetles, feeling them forced against you by the weight of every shovelful of dirt. Feeling their desperate scrabbling as they tried to dig their way to life. Dig right through you, if they had to. Hoping you would open your mouth to scream, give them a head start before they had to chew their way through your eyes and down your ear canals.

Overwhelming pressure. Overwhelming horror. The sensation of millions and billions of biting, awful things scrabbling against him, trying to claw their way in.

Truth's vision flushed with blood, then went white. He was squeezing his sword so hard, either the hilt should have been crushed or his hands burst.

The pressure was driving him down. Down. He could feel his knees hit the floor, faintly, distantly. He thought he could hear screaming. It wasn't him; his teeth were clenched so hard, they should have shattered into porcelain shards. He didn't know if his heart had stopped beating, if that hammering thrum was in his mind or his body. Endless crushing pressure as the venomous insects scratched endlessly against him!

It. Stopped. It all just. Stopped. The first thing he saw when his vision recovered was a little light set next to the door. It flashed green three times, then a steady blue. And that was that. All clear. The same signal they had when the range was safe to enter, back at the PMC. Blue was safe, red was danger. He liked how simple it was. He still liked how simple it was.

There was no way some sneaky shit spec ops team was blowing their way into the mountain in the middle of a full-blown assault. Not in a base with a bunch of high-levels in it. Not one run by Starbrite. Truth would permit an almost-endless sea of shit-talking about Starbrite, but you could *not* accuse Starbrite Security of being slack.

He dismissed his angelic sword, returning it to its home in his first aperture. Just breathing for a minute. Maybe as many as five minutes. It was a spell. He understood that. It was some horribly powerful curse. Anyone in the base not marked by Starbrite would die. Simple as that. But he survived. Somehow.

No, not somehow; he knew exactly how. His "seamless" body. The scrabbling insects must have been the curse trying to latch on to him. Was he . . . immune to magic now? He pictured the sundrop spell and the return spell used by that senior. Or those sun-bright explosions that had dotted the mountain. Or the tactical-scale curses the armies were deploying. For that matter, the fire that troll had been tossing around didn't look like anything fun to play with.

No. Not immune to magic. But highly resistant. And particularly to curses, he would guess. Curses and divination or really anything that needed to latch on to him to affect him. Interesting. He had a feeling he had, once again, exceeded Merkovah's expectations for him.

He didn't feel ready to move. Maybe he would stretch five minutes into seven. Or possibly ten. Truth cast his mind inward and examined his body. He could see his soul hovering in near-perfect alignment with his body. The spell apertures and those tiny intangible channels connecting it to his body and the outside world seemed full and strong. Very full. He looked more closely at the apertures.

A rich golden color. Just the faintest hint of orange, fading to bright buttery yellow-gold. The cosmic rays always seemed more like liquid than light or air to Truth, at least when they pooled and condensed in his apertures. His "spell slots," and boy, did he wish he could forget that image. There was a lot of truth to it, though. He could see the Meditations being nurtured in there, then Incisive, and even the strangeness that was Cup and Knife.

He didn't know how to describe what the spells looked like. They weren't static. They grew in size and complexity with the aperture. He had been told since childhood that it was an automatic process that occurred over the course of a long life, not something that one could directly control. He was now sure that this was yet another lie his schools taught him.

The spells grew and changed, the more he understood them. They changed to reflect his understanding of them and his use of them. They could only change up to a point, but he was quite certain that his Incisive wasn't quite like anyone else's. Everyone was a little different.

So how did they look? Active. Full to bursting. Even the fourth aperture, temporarily occupied by Obliteration, was almost flooded with cosmic energy. Which was the opposite of what he would have expected. Didn't he just resist a huge curse? Did his body absorb that curse energy somehow?

<<No, it was when you killed the thing outside. The divine spark gave you a tiny bit of the processed remainder as a tip for being helpful.>>

Ah. Right. All right. That made a degree of sense. But this was right up against it. He was a few days, or less, from a breakthrough. If he found a high-energy area, he could conceivably break through today.

Level Five before his twenty-fifth birthday. Even for the ultra-rich, that had to be a record, right? His mind skittered away from the thought. There had to be a price for this. There was a consequence for such insane growth. This was literally inhuman. The System kept asking what he was. Truth had a dreadful premonition that he would find out before he ever saw the sun again.

He was strong. If nothing else, he was strong. He could go toe to toe with a Level Five, take a Level Six from ambush, and he had, at least once, survived a fight with a Level Seven. Who was apparently a specialist in keeping people alive rather than killing them, so that might be less impressive, but he would take it.

Level Five would put him solidly in the middle of the mid-tiers. Above billions. He could rule a big piece of the Free State, if he was insane enough to want it. He wasn't that crazy. Level Five was the point at which a plausible amount of money for a very, very rich person could buy a ticket off-world on one of the Black Ships. Your spells started getting scary powerful at Level Five. Not that they weren't scary powerful at lower levels *to* lower-levels. It was all relative.

And relative to other Level Fours and Fives, he was already a monster. Someone, some*thing* that blatantly shouldn't exist. Slaughtering them while sorrowfully explaining that they were all just rats, himself included. He thought back to what he had told Dr. Sun. He really didn't believe in much. "Go, rats!"

He shook off the morbid alienation. Stretched, got loose, then sat and meditated. It felt too soon to cultivate, but he could fit in a quick round of meditation. Once he was done, all that was left was creeping undetected through a sealed magical fortress under constant enemy attack, patrolled by experts and unnatural things, all to rescue a "kinda sorta" human princess from the several high-level mages guarding her.

Easy.

CHAPTER 73

ALONE IN THE HOUSE

There really should be a word for when you know you have never been someplace before but when you go there, it all feels eerily familiar.

Truth walked silently down the long corridors. Brightly lit, clean, with enchanted windows showing views from various Starbrite resorts from around the world. Look out one, and it was a tropical beach. Look out the next, and you were watching laughing kids learn how to ski. It felt like half the offices he had visited on the job. Even some of the private homes looked like this.

It was pretty nice. Which felt horrible. He couldn't hear the violence going on above. There was a literal mountain between him and the pounding explosions. To say nothing of all the magical wards. It was warm but not hot, the air tasted fresh, it was clean, well lit and cheery from all the windows. It didn't have that "doomed bunker" feel that he had been expecting.

He felt cheated. Truth walked a little farther down the hall, making way for staff heading to the bathroom. They didn't see him. At Level Two, they would have a better chance of jumping to the moon. He examined the cheated feeling a bit more. It wasn't so much cheated as feeling wronged. He wanted them scared. Hurting. They deserved to be scared!

"Sooooo. You and Tommy?"

"Oh, god. Look, right now, there is no 'me and Tommy,' okay?"

"Uh-huh. You gave him a look at breakfast."

"I did not."

"You did. I had to pretend to look away for, like, ten seconds. It was an intense look."

"Oh, god. Seriously. There is no us. We are just . . ."

"Figuring things out? Friends with benefits? In a situationship?"

"I don't even know. He's coming off that thing with Ling, and I don't want to be the rebound chick, but at the same time—"

"You have wanted him for a year now and are one hundred percent ready to be there for him in his emotionally vulnerable, exploitable moment of need."

"I hate you. And it's not like that!"

"Uh-huh. He a cuddler?"

Truth sped up. Why was he the one suffering there? Why? They had a secret volcano lair where they were keeping a girl prisoner for medi-magic experimentation and who knows what else! *Look stressed, you bastards!*

Could it be the System keeping them calm? It wouldn't be out of the question, right? Truth flat-out refused to believe there was anyone in this volcano who didn't have the System, with the possible exception of the Shattervoid girl.

He really didn't know. The System had been training him like a dog. Maybe it did the same to these people. Keep them content, keep them productive.

Incisive gave him a little warning. He launched himself up to the ceiling and pressed himself into the corner, trying to be as invisible as possible. A pair of PMC soldiers walked down the hall, *Security* armband on display. They kept their eyes moving around, making sure everything was as it should be. They didn't spot him.

The same thing happened when a handler with a pack of spellhounds went past, but Incisive was a lot more insistent the third time. He followed some staffers into their office. Just as it was closing behind him, he thought he caught a whiff of troll.

This was going to be exhausting. And slow. He had no idea what the base even looked like, and he was mortally certain that there wasn't going to be a handy wall map anywhere.

"Any idea what the alarm was about earlier?"

"Nah. I mean, I assume someone broke in."

"Well, yeah, obviously, but . . . how?"

"I dunno. Usual way?"

"Which is?"

"I dunno." The staffer appeared to be inventorying a shelf of parts. Truth would not have appreciated someone talking to him while he was trying to count, but apparently, the staffer was made of sterner stuff.

"But, like, why even break in here?" The other staffer was also inventorying parts. Based on the conversion so far, Truth was amazed his intellect could handle the strain.

"My guy. We are sitting on insane amount of highly stealable, highly sellable parts here. Never mind industrial espionage or whatever."

"I mean, how much is any of this stuff really worth, though?" He was counting metal brackets. Truth understood his point.

"Those brackets? Look 'em up in the shop."

There was a pause. "Worthless. I can get a whole box for a credit."

"As for the price in wen."

There was another pause.

"FUCKING TWENTY THOUSAND WEN?!"

Truth nodded. The price in the store bore no relation to outside prices. It was presented as a discount, but he had *quickly* discovered that there were things in the shop that you simply couldn't buy in the outside world at any price. At least the cultivation aids he poured his money into couldn't be bought retail.

"Like I said. Thieves, industrial spies. The usual."

"Twenty thousand wen!"

"Special alloy; they use 'em in the prototype lab, I think."

"It's a damn bracket. Bent metal with holes in it."

"Mmm. Special alloy, though. What shelf are you on?"

"Seven."

"Think you are going to get your side done by dinner?"

"Should do."

They nattered on while Truth eavesdropped, hoping they would come back to the "prototype lab." Sounded relevant. They did not.

He sighed and made his way out. The very frequent patrols made the going slow, and their irregular timing suggested someone was keeping very focused. Nothing more frustrating to an attacker than a complete absence of regular patrol times. And Truth was getting very, very frustrated.

It was a simple, and simply enraging, system. It was all based on the System. Every door was locked. There were no signs for anything anywhere. Was this the windowless door to the Top Secret Room with the Top Secret Project, or the linen closet? The System knows. And if you needed to know, you would. Every door you needed to open would be unlocked for you.

Truth got uncomfortably used to drifting in behind people when they opened and closed doors. He also got very used to quickly peeking inside, then walking straight past. So many generic-looking offices. So many.

In one particular office, he was momentarily distracted by a conversation about a "certain young lady," occasionally referred to as "Princess" who was chained up somewhere. There could be no greater proof of his development of character, Truth felt, no greater proof of his tolerance for his fellow rats than the fact he didn't slap the bastard dead when it became clear the man was talking about his dog.

His distraction resulted in him missing the door closing behind him. Truth was now trapped in there with the nattering office workers discussing their pampered pooches. The other man, not the Princess-chainer, was a grooming enthusiast. He apparently stressed the need to start grooming them when they were young. That way, the dog got used to the combs, shampoos, and hair dryers.

He had bought his primped-up poodle a nicer apartment than Truth lived in, even when he was working for the PMC. Apparently, a Starbrite subsidiary made luxury dog houses, and this . . . gentleman . . . invested. As he had apparently invested in quality coffee. That was an awfully big mug he was drinking.

"You know, coffee just *runs right through you*. Delicious, but it seems like it's only minutes until you are *dying for a piss*. Yeah, you both raced to the bottom of your drinks, but now? Now you *really, really need the toilet*. Look at you squirm. You must be *seconds from pissing yourselves*."

Were there other ways to get out of the room? Yes. He chose this one. A little whispered Poison, a lot of private enjoyment, and his exploration continued.

He almost missed it. The glance through the door showed a scene so prosaic, his mind almost deleted it without comprehending it. His hand made a hissing noise as he caught the door just before it closed. Sometimes, it was fun to remind himself just how fast he could move.

He found . . . the stairs.

What do you need in an era of unreliable magic? Stairs. Wide, well lit, with glow-in-the-dark rubberized grips for feet and, Truth was happy to see, glow-in-the-dark floor numbers, all in case the lights went out. Which, of course, they would if the *magic* went out.

No idea how the glow-in-the-dark stuff worked without magic, but hell, the antitheists had figured something out, and they were operating out of a gift shop. This was an authentic volcano lair. A higher standard could be expected. He was apparently on floor number two. And the stairs went both up and down from there.

Desperate to set some kind of scope on his search, he raced upward. As advertised—there was only one floor above him. Delighted, he raced in the opposite direction. Three more below. A total of five floors. Sizable floors, too, if the second floor was anything to go by. He was a long way from having searched the whole thing. But at least he had some sense of scope now. Had some sense of the size of the problem in front of him.

Five floors. He didn't know if the top or bottom floor was the most likely one to hold the Shattervoid girl. Arguably directly in the middle was the most secure, but, equally arguably, so was the bottom floor. Anything capable of tunneling through that much rock and magma wasn't going to be kid-friendly.

She must be . . . what . . . eleven by now? Twelve? Truth vaguely remembered someone yelling that she was a six-year-old girl.

<<*No, they just said she was "a little girl." You understandably didn't want to think you had to help kidnap a baby, and a six-year-old girl plus life support was about as big as someone could fit into that chest the natural philosophy team was carrying. Although, based on the example of Niles, you may have underestimated how old she could have been.*>>

Truth nodded. *Still. Five, almost six, years. That's got to be a big chunk of life for her. It would be a big chunk of life for me, and I don't even want to guess what my "natural" lifespan would be at this point. Certainly more than a hundred and fifty. Maybe even closing in on two hundred. For a Level Five? Not crazy with the body cultivation.*

<<*No idea. But . . . yeah. I don't see you dying of old age. Violence and misadventure (which is code for "doing stupid shit," in case you didn't know), sure.*>>

Truth got to the bottom door . . . and waited. And waited. *Someone must be coming through at some point, right?*

<<*Sure. How long are you prepared to wait?*>>

Truth laughed a little at that. *I have all the time in the world. Months, even.*

The little light above the door started flashing red. There was no alarm, just a red flash.

You know, it suddenly occurs to me that there is absolutely nowhere to hide in this stairwell.

Truth did the only thing he could think of and flattened himself against the wall. The door would open into the stairwell, so hopefully—

The door smashed open. Truth grabbed the handle just before it would smack into his gut. The noise must have satisfied whoever was on the other side, because boots came pounding through without any further investigation.

"Go! Go go go!"

"Sergeants, check charm loadouts! Everyone check their potion kits! THERE WILL BE NO FATALITIES ON THIS OP, AM I CLEAR?!"

"SIR, YES, SIR!"

<<*Think you found the barracks?*>>

Fingers crossed.

Truth waited until they were a couple flights up before peering around the door. More anonymous-looking hallways. Fantastic. He squinted, then crouched down.

There were rubber marks on the floor. Quite a few of them. One might almost guess . . . A place where a lot of people wearing boots went running past. Truth grinned and followed the trail. Where there were soldiers, there was equipment. Where there were guards, there were things that needed protecting from villains like him.

CHAPTER 74

COMMON AS MUCK

Truth sneaked through the lowest level of the once-secret, now-besieged volcano lair with a loopy grin. All the blessings, the concealment magic, the specialist training, and what does it take to evade the world's best mercs? Stand behind the door. They'll never find you.

No trolls so far. That was a relief. They were uncomfortably sharp. The doors on this floor were, for lack of a better way to describe them, more heavy-duty than the ones on the second floor. They had the solidity of steel-core doors, much more elaborate locks, and, he was quietly surprised to see, mechanical deadbolts. If the magic failed, the door wouldn't open. Now, did the hardworking employees of the Security Division want to keep people out even in an emergency—or did they want to keep something in?

He moved quickly through the hallways, trying to get a feel for the size of the floor. A little bigger than the second floor, but only a bit bigger, based on the length of the hallways. Which made sense—if he were building a secret underground lair, there would be an external wall made of the most pressure- and heat-resistant material he could lay hands on, then he would build inside the sheath.

The scuff marks led him to a notably banged-up door. The frame had been scraped badly by passing equipment and careless soldiers. Promising. Truth hesitated. Job number one was *rescue the Shattervoid princess*. A job that would be massively easier if the guards were out of the picture. On the other hand, booby-trapping the barracks would not catch *all* the guards, and it would alarm the high-levels. Force them to look inward instead of focusing on the attacks from outside.

He hesitated for a minute but opted to pass on the barracks for now. He looked up and down the hallway. You don't stick the barracks *right* next to the place you want to protect. You need space to work with. Soldiers need to assemble, set up defenses, have room to fall back if necessary. So, if the barracks were there, and there were conspicuously marked patches of wall and floor *that way* . . .

He trotted down the hall, looking at the rooms as he passed. Bypassing any that gave Incisive a jolt of alarm. Those high-levels had to be living somewhere. It seemed a few of them were at home down there. That made things a little exciting.

Truth picked a safe-feeling room to try and break in. There just wasn't enough foot traffic down there to let him peek over shoulders. The good news was that he was intimately familiar with all these locks, as they were all Starbrite-manufactured prod-ucts. The better news was that people hadn't screwed around with them to improve their resistance to attacks. Apparently, they were more concerned about controlling access.

The actually-very-bad news was that they were all directly tied to a magical net-work that, Truth assumed, reported directly to the System Astrologica. Every time that door opened and closed, there would be a record of it. There would be a record of who, exactly, opened it and which sigils entered the room at that time, et cetera. So, the job wasn't just to crack the lock. He also had to spoof the connection to the System.

A lot of very finicky work later, Truth was quietly swearing in frustration. The mechanism was quite straightforward. When the door was closed, two runes almost-not-quite touched to form an elaborate three-dimensional rune. When the door opened, the rune was broken, which triggered a talisman in the doorframe. The talisman checked with the lock—Truth started grumbling in his head.

Were you opened properly? Yes? Then I will send a message to the intelligent spirit, say-ing that I have been opened properly, and another to the identity-confirmation talisman inside the room, just to double-check that the person who unlocked the door was the same as the person or people who went into the room.

And if some part of the chain broke down, it would scream for help.

Which was fine. Which was all very standard. Same basic principles applied to almost any door lock. Which was the problem.

"Five. Fucking. Years. FIVE! And they STILL HAVEN'T CHANGED THE RUNE!" Truth was managing the tricky feat of shouting under his breath. He dug out two bits of paper, did a little careful drawing, and with the careful application of spit as glue and some very delicate tweezer work, as far as both the door and the alarm talisman were concerned, the door was firmly shut.

Cracking the lock was laughably simple by comparison. He had been studying the damn systems half his life. *Come one glorious day, I'm going to be off-world and run into non-Starbrite-model talismans. Oh, the universes of possibility that will open up.*

The door opened with a *click*. The whole process had taken twenty minutes. Now that he had confirmed how the mechanisms were set up, the next one would take less than five. The one after that? He fully expected to have the process down to sub-one minute in the near future. *Five goddamn years. Update. The damn. Locks.*

<<*Have they ever updated any lock? Ever?*>>

No. They push out new editions of the lock with a different-looking case and maybe fixing some of the more obvious attacks, but they never, ever, update a line that's still in production. But they could. They totally could. In FIVE GODDAMN YEARS, they could have fixed a half dozen problems. Even making the runes more complicated would help. "Master"-tier locks, my entire ass.

The room was, in fact, a laboratory. One that was apparently in active use, as there was a box with a glass door that was humming with magic. Something bobbed in a column of light on a bench top. More things were in cases scattered over yet more bench space.

Truth didn't have the faintest idea what any of these things were. Locks he knew. This stuff? Strictly for the natural-philosophy types. But where there were natural philosophers, there would be notes.

He started checking through the room, carefully looking at every scrap. He wasn't expecting to hit it immediately. He might not hit it at all. But he had nowhere else to go and nothing else to do. So, he patiently sifted through the rows of numbers, the illegible scribbles, the half-worked-out diagrams of different star alignments and alchemical reagents.

At a guess, they were . . . trying to make something resistant to certain types of cosmic energy? Truth looked blankly at the page. He knew you could attune cosmic energy to certain frequencies or principles. A lot of the body-cultivation manuals promised exactly that—an "eternal wood" physique, or a lightning-aligned body, or light. Gave benefits to movement speed or exorcism or lifespan. All thanks to tweaking your internal cosmic energy for a more specialized role.

Truth hadn't bothered with any of that. He had just used the most basic and generic energy. Likely, in retrospect, because the System Astrologica wanted to encourage him to think he was too stupid and poor to be trusted with anything more complicated.

Truth looked at his strong hand and slowly flexed it. He wouldn't have achieved a fraction of what he had if he had been locked into a narrow path. He would not have seen through so many mysteries. He would not be on the path of redefining reality, if he were content to redefine the magic within him.

He smiled slowly. Keep underestimating him. Keep telling him that he was trash. Generational trash. Hell, who knows how many of his reincarnations had been complete moron scumbags. But he kept coming back. Learning. Getting stronger. He silently laughed.

Dr. Sun. He wondered why such a powerhouse seemed so weak. It was because he had specialized his energy into some kind of immortality magic. He had poured all his ability into keeping himself alive, then others. He was a specialist. A powerful one but a specialist. In ordinary times, a specialist was worth ten thousand mongrels like Truth. But there, at the end of days?

The strongest man in the world was spending his fortune and the lives of specialists to figure out how to do something Truth could manage with a bit of meditation and time. And Starbrite was no fool. There was a good reason for him to spend the resources. So, Starbrite probably grew up in a good place, in ordinary times, before he came to this world. Starbrite was "smart." He was a specialist.

Truth smiled, shaking with laughter now. The most powerful man in the world invented the System Astrologica *precisely because he knew his own weakness*. An insanely powerful, insanely complex answer to a fundamental problem. And here was Truth, Slumrat Adventurer, solving complicated problems with radical simplicity.

Hey, Valentinian? Whoever you are, wherever you are, thank you. I will take your manual and walk straight to the godhead, shattering the evil illusions of the "real" as I go.

The next few rooms were more of the same—more laboratories, more examinations of some minute detail whose function largely escaped Truth's understanding. He did not know what a mercury exhalation was, or why it was important, or for that matter, why the room stank like rotten eggs. It was some kind of alchemy thing, judging by all the little crucibles and kilns, but beyond that, he wouldn't dare to guess.

The PMC guards had returned. They sounded tired but not unhappy. Things must have worked out. No prisoners, either. Truth kept well out of their way. He was perfectly content listening through the door.

"Hey, Sarge, we don't have a patrol rotation now, right?"

"Yeah, you get the rest of the day off. The other platoons get to pick up the slack."

"Nice!"

"Got a date tonight?" There was a high degree of sarcasm in the question, all of which apparently went right over the merc's head.

"Hell, yeah, me and this guy from Prototyping hit it off. I'm gonna pick him up after work, then it's back to his place for—"

"I didn't ask."

"Err. Sarge, you kind of did."

There was a moment of quiet.

"You know, it occurs to me that our talismans and gear haven't been inventoried and maintained in a long while. I think they might need urgent attention. The kind that could take all night if done properly."

"I apologize for my mistake. I am clearly oversharing."

"Mmm. Scram."

Truth dithered. He had no idea what time it was or when "after work" was. Hanging out in the lab next to the barracks, peeking out at every person walking down the hall, looking for a solitary female merc in search of company did not appeal. But he really wanted to find out where Prototyping was.

The dithering intensified, then Truth just gave up. He sighed, sat down, and started cultivating. It still felt a little too soon for it, but he knew he would be frequently interrupted. He would be a little productive as he waited. Never dumb to be stronger. And Level Five was more than a little bit stronger.

It took a few hours and several passing patrols, but eventually, a Level Three merc, female and hopeful-looking, stepped out. She had invested a little in a cosmetic glamor, or maybe it was the potion that permanently made you prettier. Truth remembered that thing. Harmony had wound up drinking it. The fancy glass bottle was on display in their apartment permanently afterward.

She walked off confidently down the hall, then up the stairs to the first floor. Truth shrugged. Seems he had guessed wrong about which end to start with. Down some halls to a thick set of double doors. The doors opened into an absolute killing field of hidden weaponry, with a fully kitted-up squad dug in behind emplaced enchantments. They also, Truth noticed with morbid amusement, carried machetes. Just in case.

No trolls or demons, though, so that was a small mercy.

"Hey, fuckwit, got a chair? I don't want to stand around like a hooker waiting for my date." She grinned at the squaddies.

"You are going to need to be more specific. I have at least four fuckwits here. And don't worry; nobody would mistake you as someone who gets paid for sex. Pays for it, sure. *There's* a face that screams *whorehopper*."

The corporal smiled with gentle warmth and, in a friendly manner, flung a heavy wooden chair at her head. She snagged it out of the air one-handed and sat with boneless comfort.

"Going to do bad things to that man. Dinner first, him developing a permanent limp later."

"You have the soul of a poet, Sharon. One that scribbles shit on the walls while they try to remember how to take a dump without drowning."

"Always nice to have something to read on the can. Those people do a public service."

Truth waited with limited patience, staring at the door. On the other side was whatever Starbrite was working on. And with any luck, the Princess he was there to save.

CHAPTER 75

UPRIGHT YOUNG LADY

It was an oddly quiet moment. The PMC soldiers were sharp and Level Three. The recording talismans, plural, covering the waiting room were pumping out Level Four power. The Blessing of the Silent Forest could handle it. He wasn't leaking a speck of energy, and besides, if something did pierce his shroud of unnoticeability, he had a perfect identity lined up.

Sergeant Truth Medici, Starbrite PMC, seconded from Harban. Still waiting on that back pay.

The mercenaries were not quite lounging. Knowing they were being watched kept them from being too casual. Even so, there was a limit to how performatively tense they were willing to be for hours a day when buried in an armored bunker inside a volcano.

Sharon, the merc with a hot date, jumped to her feet grinning as the doors to the prototype lab opened. Truth knew he had a split second to dive through the door and had exploded into motion the instant it had started to swing open. He was in the air before he got a look at the fellow's face. As a result, he looked like an outraged leopard as he flew through the doorway.

The guy, Mr. Hot Date. Mr. "He won't walk right ever again and will get weird around oranges," was average. Totally meh. Not out of shape, but not really *in* shape. Not handsome, not ugly. Just meh. And yet, Starbrite had told Truth he was so hideous, women recoiled at the sight of him.

Feeling distinctly bloody-minded, Truth landed in the prototype lab on all fours. And froze there. Incisive was giving him a gentle reminder. This was a building with high-levels in it. In strategic locations. The prototype lab might just be such a strategic location, given all the fixed defenses outside.

The room was very long, a hundred meters or so, filled with long benches and long black-stone-topped work tables. The back wall was not lit, but the rest of the room was washed in blinding light from big overhead lighting arrays. In the center of the front quarter of the room was an oblong box, about three meters long, two meters across, and a meter and a half high.

He hadn't the faintest clue what he was looking at. Truth took a lot of pleasure in his talisman-maintenance skills, but they were never intended for high-magic applications. Carriages, building maintenance, city maintenance, streetlights, locks, climate control, scry devices, that was his area of skill. The daily necessities of people and cities.

The long box was . . . not that.

It appeared to be made out of, or at least covered by, a dark gold material. His first guess was orichalcum, but if that was what it was, then it was plated and a bare micron thick. There probably wasn't that much orichalcum in the world. Which did give rise to the question of what could possibly be underneath that would justify coating it in one of the world's most expensive metals.

The answer appeared to be talismans. And amulets. And cartouches, carved gems, implanted fetishes, spell formations, spell restrictions, astrological-alignment elements inscribed for purposes unknown, all combined in ways he had never seen before. There were even pictures on it. Or one big picture with lots of little elements. The longer he looked at it, the less he understood.

There were logics to talisman design. Not *a* logic but *logics*. It all depended on what you were trying to do, and different manufacturers had different ways of going about it. A lot of companies ripped off Starbrite's designs, for better or worse. Mostly just changing things up enough to keep Legal happy. This only kind of seemed to follow any of the logics he understood.

Each talisman made a degree of sense, even if he didn't know what it did. It was just that, when you stacked a few thousand systems on top of each other, trying to figure out what they did while crouched on all fours on the polished concrete floor is a bit of a challenge. And when he squinted and let his eyes go a little blurry, it really did look like a kid's idea of a grownup lying on their back.

Truth was very curious to see what it looked like from the top. The longer he looked at it, the more the word *coffin* came to mind. Then, from some ancient depth, the word *sarcophagus*.

The technicians and mages around the box weren't helping him understand, either. They were discussing energy ratios and alignments and components he just had no concept of. Worse, they were using shorthand and slang—

"Swap korb in seven. Knapp, knapp, knapp . . . and swap."

"We got any number threes ready?"

"Bucket on the left has the threes. What about galz?"

"Mercury at twenty-three, sulfur at sixty."

"Who's on Alkaliad? Melchior is up ten and needs to come down."

There was no fuss, no chaos, no horseplay there. The reason was likely the old lady sitting on a comfortable cushion on a raised dais overseeing the construction. Cultivating, apparently, but Truth didn't believe for a second that she wasn't aware of everything going on below.

The lady on the dais didn't really remind Truth of Merkovah. With a few exceptions, Merkovah seemed almost indifferent to status. He would dress casually when he was with his students. He slouched in his office and tended to flop bonelessly as the bound demon steered his hideous carriage through traffic. Not the lady on the dais. There was nothing casual about her. You certainly couldn't imagine surviving a breach in etiquette.

Thin face, high cheekbones, high-arched eyebrows under straight black hair that flowed to the small of her back and was held in place with golden pins. Dressed in a white silk shirt and flowy linen pants that reassured those sneaking glances that a certain kind of simple cost far more than the viewer would ever earn. Beautiful, though her beauty was the product of so much artifice, she seemed almost doll-like. A mannequin for a private clothier, one who dealt strictly with those in the three-comma club.

The metaphor grew on Truth. She was a strong. Seven or even an Eight. She might even be one of the legendary C-suite. He was looking at a humanoid appendage of the System Astrologica itself. Whoever she was, whatever thought of her own had once lived in her had been replaced by the System. No direct puppeting required; she merely thought as it wished her to think. A century or more of constant conditioning for her soul would have seen to that.

There was a soft, piney smell in the room. A little spicy, a touch sweet, it reminded him of all the pine and fir forests he had been running through. He would bet it was coming from her. The rest of the room smelled like ozone and active magical technology. The snap and crackle of cosmic energy through an almost-maniacal nest of components.

Now. How to move around and investigate this . . . actually very large room. There were other workstations scattered on the other side of the dais. As he craned his neck, he saw gantries crisscrossing the space. Was . . . this room not actually directly under the other floors? Or were floors three and four shortened horizontally to make room for the vertical space of the prototype lab? That was a *very* tall ceiling, serving no obvious purpose.

Maybe that was the answer—anything below the dais would be immediately in the senior's eyes. But above her? What would *dare* to look down on her? Truth might have smiled in other circumstances. The hardest slumrat in the world slowly crept for the shadows at the edge of the wall and got to climbing.

Strong fingers found little nooks to dig in to. Quiet flexes of back and arms saw a strong body shoot upward in perfect silence. Catch, go, throw, and catch again. Up and up the metal scaffolding. There were cranes up there, crossing the workspace below. Could the chest actually be orichalcum? You certainly wouldn't move it without a crane. One bolted into kilometers of basalt would be sensible. The magical power required to lift it would be outrageous.

Up on the gantry now, with a view of the whole lab. Longer than some sports fields and about as wide across. The chest had pride of place near the entrance, but there was an entire production facility in there, with hooded alchemist furnaces burning next to the searing lights over a gem carver's table. Everywhere, in beautiful arrays, were the tiny tools the very best talisman designers got to use. A production facility for the best in the world.

Truth could name each of those tools, tell you roughly how they were used, but had never touched one. Those were for talisman *designers*. For the builders and makers of things. He was only ever going to be trusted with *maintaining* things. Simple things. If he worked very hard and proved himself. It was the very highest a rat could climb, according to his high school.

I'm looking down on you, you bastards. I'm looking down at you all, and you don't even know why or how. Call me a fool. Call me an idiot. But I'm still climbing. Looking at the sky and moving up. And you? You don't even know you're in a well.

The chest was . . . yes, it was a sarcophagus, or it looked like one at any rate. The magical technology built into it drew a human form. Rough, stylized, but filled with subtle meaning. A man, Truth saw. Long beard, white hair, deep eyes. Haunted eyes, perhaps, or eyes that had seen many, many things. A broad forehead that remembered too much. Thin. Painfully thin. The rich robes covered with precious gems carved into talismans and spell components seemed to drape over bird bones. Thin sticks of fingers grew on the slender branches of the figure's arms.

Maybe it was the color, the dark gold of the orichalcum, but the figure looked sick. There was a wariness in those eyes, too. Truth knew that look. It was how people got when they were hit a lot and weren't allowed to hit back. Not unable. Not allowed. Truth had seen that look in the mirror often enough.

He didn't look at the picture on the box for very long. For some reason, that seemed dangerous. For roughly the same reason, he didn't look too long at the senior sitting on the dais. An alert person, in Truth's experience, could feel the weight of another's eyes on them. Nobody got to be a high-level by being nice, Starbrite support or not. The senior would feel his attention if he let it linger. And he had an unpleasant feeling that whoever was depicted on the box, they could do the same.

He crept along the scaffolding, looking down on the laboratory. They were fabricating components for the chest and nothing else. Research happened elsewhere. This was a pure production facility. He kept coming back to the height of the place. Why? It wasn't like there was a big door to the exterior. He glared at the ceiling, not far from him there. Nothing that suggested it wasn't solid rock. Rock with, likely, lava burning at a thousand degrees or more on the other side of it.

So, why was it so damn tall in there?

As he made his way toward the back wall, he noticed there were fewer and fewer technicians at work. The ones that were there all seemed to face the front of the room, looking toward that senior sitting near the door.

There was a protrusion on the back wall. A semicircle extended into the room three meters deep. It was covered in lead curse tablets. Truth could tell what they were from tens of meters away. The repression and viciousness of the spells made his skin crawl. He could only imagine what it was doing to the people who worked near them. The protrusion ran all the way up to the ceiling, winding into a cube of four meters on a side. Each side, top and bottom included, was shingled in even more curse tablets.

Just looking at the thing felt disgusting. Whatever was under the curse tablets was something vile, something that needed to be not just sealed but broken. Too busy hurting to cause mischief. Truth rated Merkovah's "Macerating Juicer" enchantment as more elegant, but for concentrated malice, it wasn't a patch on this monumental atrocity.

It also didn't make a lick of sense. It was the only thing tall enough to justify the high ceiling, and it clearly didn't exist under the mountain naturally. The lead would melt, for one thing. No, this was all purpose-built. Someone designed the base, designed this room, and then installed this pillar of concentrated misery. For some reason. He wasn't going to figure it out from next to the wall. There was a cross-room gantry. He crawled out over it.

As he moved, he noticed the lead tablets at the front of the cube seemed to shiver now and again. Too slow for breathing, but the shivers came very regularly. The soft lead muffled the clattering. Over and over. Slow and very steady.

He got to the middle of the crossbeam and looked over. From this angle, the curses looked like the scales of a serpent, extending down from the box and covering its long body. The box, from the front . . . looked like a face. A young lady's face. The curses on the tablet seemed to shimmer and blur—the faces' eyes blinked.

Looking very fit for a dead man, Sergeant Medici. It seems you've been, heh, well these last few years.

CHAPTER 76

AWKWARD

Truth thought his refusal to shriek and fall off the gantry spoke well of him. Most people would have shrieked and fallen the three stories to the ground, he felt. A multistory tube of lead curse tablets suddenly having a girl's face and talking directly into your mind is inherently startling. But he was made of sterner, yes, *sterner* stuff—

You talk to yourself a lot, don't you?

Truth nodded. He did. *Will you hear me if I just think at you?*

Yes, this close and with you looking at me, that is plenty enough.

He had wondered why the workers below made such an elaborate point of not looking at the back wall.

It's not like I bully them. They just need to focus, and I talk too much. Also, Starbrite REALLY doesn't like people giving his drones new ideas.

Oh . . . I know.

Yes. About that . . .

Look, before we get into any of that, and not to be, you know, culturally insensitive or anything, but you went from what I was told was a little girl in a box to a three-story-tall . . . something, and, you know, what the actual fuck?

Language!

Jeongo?

What?

What?

There was a pause of mutual incomprehension.

Oh! Because I am much bigger now, you think I am an adult? No, I'm twelve.

Must say you are a bit taller than I was at twelve.

She giggled at that.

It's one of the things my clan can do. As long as we get enough energy, we can grow almost as big as we like. Of course, the bigger we are, the harder it is to land on a planet. If I was any bigger than this, I don't think I could survive here long.

Her speaking pattern was odd. The pacing of it, the rhythm and inflection of the words were a little off. Her word choice was odd too—seeming to sweep between adult and little girl.

Well, I have spent almost six years in a laboratory with natural philosophers and research mages. There haven't been any kids to play with. Hasn't been anyone to play with. Or anyone to talk to once I realized that everyone here was just Starbrite in different bodies.

Truth winced.

But let's not get sidetracked. I saw you die, Sergeant Medici. I might have been sealed up in that box, but I wasn't unconscious. You got a needle punched through you, you fell in a well, and a spell bird landed on you. And then a brick smashed your skull open. Having managed to slaughter most of a squadron of spell birds single-handed. Everyone was very impressed for about ten minutes, then never mentioned you ever again.

Well, that's depressing. I hoped for at least a plaque or a moment of silence or something.

No, you didn't.

No, I didn't. Those cost money.

Mmm-hmmm.

So. Glad to see you are keeping well.

Am I? Keeping well?

There was a definite edge to her thoughts, which was fair enough.

Honestly? No. Not going to lie: I think you are probably in scarred-for-life territory at this point. Sorry, I'm bad at comforting lies.

They did actually have counselors in for a while. Mainly telling me that I would be happier once I just accepted everything and stopped trying to fight the inevitable. I'd be freaking out right now, but the curses keep my emotions pretty flat. Keep most things pretty flat. Most things. So. HOW ARE YOU NOT DEAD?!

You are the world's biggest twelve-year-old and I'm the weirdo? Unfair. What do you want me to tell you? I spent five or so years dead, then I got better.

You spent five years dead but got better.

Yep.

Is this a Ghūl thing? You kinda-sorta remind me of them a tiny bit.

I really don't know. I was born to humanish parents; that much I'm sure of. Wait, how do you know about the Ghūl? Are there Ghūl in the void?

Huh. Well, you live and learn. Oh! Sorry! Sorry. You die and learn. Sorry. That was rude. Sorry. And no space Ghūl, but I've seen them on planets.

Well, I'm sure I will make mistakes too. For example, if you can grow as big as you want, can you shrink?

Can you? I have bones and tissues and organs and stuff in me. Truth could feel the girl's indignation.

Fair. So. You may be wondering why I'm here—

I'm not really okay with you not being dead, but yeah, why are you here? Not that I'm not happy to be talking to you, or . . . anyone. I'm glad to talk to you! But the curse tablets make it hard to think clearly.

Well. In a fit of cosmic irony, I am here to rescue you.

There was a pause. Truth watched the curses outlining her face shift around as she looked over the room and back to Truth.

No, really, I am. Your folks are here and above-average pissed. They want you back. So. You know. Here I am.

No. You are wrong. They don't want me back. I was stupid and they don't want me anymore.

The curse tablets shuddered; the loud clattering made the technicians start to turn and look at her, but then they clearly all thought better of it and turned back to their tables. Even through the muted emotions the curse tablets permitted, he could feel her self-loathing and pain.

I have . . . literally no idea why you think that, but a shit ton—
LANGUAGE!

A very many lots of Shattervoid ships turned up a few months ago and locked down the whole damn planet. Full embargo. They specifically demanded you be returned. You are wanted.

The lead tablets shuddered like a wind through the forest shaking the leaves.
I want to go home!

It took a few minutes for her to calm down.

So, you, the guy who kidnapped me, are going to rescue me?

I was, at most, an unknowing accessory. Who got transitioned into, admittedly, an involuntary accomplice. And yes.

I did wonder about that. I could see you fighting your own body as you killed your way to the well.

How did you see anything, anyway? How are you seeing me?

Oh, we literally don't see the world the same way you do. I have "eyes," but they are mostly a cultural thing. Like . . . for decoration, I guess? Or hair color? I don't have hair, though; it really gets in the way in the void. Mostly, it's purely mental and spiritual perception. Also seeing how space distorts around things, but I think that's less "seeing" and more "feeling?"

Truth was torn. On the one hand, he really wanted to know more. On the other hand, he was perched on a metal gantry talking to a three-story-tall girl trapped in so many curse tablets, it actively hurt his mind to look at, with a genuine article C-suite member on guard behind him. So. Not a super place to hang out.

So, what's the plan for getting me out of here? she asked. Which Truth felt was reasonable enough. He hadn't the faintest idea. Deflecting quickly, he asked—

Before we get to that, what's your name?

There was the feeling of giggling entering his ears. *My name is—*

Truth had the sudden feeling of vibrations making music, of hundreds of fingers rubbing the rims of partially filled glasses and playing a tune beyond human understanding. Cyclical, steady, but so filled with changes and subtleties that he quickly lost himself in the noise of it all.

It took him a moment to gather himself.

Could you spell that?

Nope. Shattervoid have perfect memories. We sing our stories as we travel, keeping alive all our histories, our dealings with others . . . everything.

You don't have a written language?

*No. What would we even use it for?**

Truth felt like there were a lot of things it would be used for, but was momentarily flummoxed.

Can you . . . travel? However the Shattervoid travel? If I got you out of your restraints, I mean.

Of course! But it's not just the curse tablets. They tattooed me with restrictions. Her voice turned brittle. Truth recognized it. His sibs sounded like that when something happened but it was "fine."

I can break those. It's getting you out of that lead . . . thing . . . without getting killed by the Level Eight that's the challenge. And out of this room and outside, but one step at a time.

Why? I mean the getting-out-of-the-room thing. I just told you I can travel.

Yeah?

There was another pause for mutual incomprehension.

You don't know how the Shattervoid travel.

No idea.

Oh. Well I can explain! There were few things kids liked better than explaining things to interested grownups, or so Truth had heard. He and his sibs never liked explaining anything to anyone.

It's like sewing. We poke a hole in one spot and pop out the other. But, like, everything is kind of scrunched up when we go through the hole, so it's not as far on that side as it is on this side? From here to orbit is, like, nothing. Like, I'd probably go too far and wind up waaaaaaaaaaaaaaaaaaaaay far away from here.

But not so far that your family wouldn't see you had gotten free, right?

Oh, they would see me easily! I think . . .

Her voice in his mind went from chirpy to very small, very quickly.

They would. They are positioned all around the planet. Anything that gets into orbit, they jump on and destroy. So, I'm sure they would see you passing by.

Yes! They can see things moving on the other side!

Well, there you are, then.

There was another awkward pause. Truth really wasn't prepared for this. He was going to find a place to hole up and strategize the extraction, not try to wing it as soon as he found the girl. That still seemed like the best plan, actually.

Any idea how those curse tablets come on and off?

No. They only went on. They have never come off. Every time I get bigger, they add more.

Her voice was brittle again and small. Truth could imagine the little girl desperately trying to outgrow her captors and feeling more and more hopeless as they just kept making her chains heavier.

What are they trying to do with you, anyway?

He wants to use me to remake his body. Her voice had gone numb. **He told me early on, "You were born to be a vessel. It is your blessing to carry this lord through the Heavens."**

You actually met Starbrite? The actual, real Starbrite? Truth was shocked. He didn't know of anyone who had met Starbrite. Even heads of state didn't meet him. At least, not that he had ever heard of. There were no pictures of Starbrite that Truth had ever seen.

Yes? So have you. Kind of. Well, I guess we both "kind of" met him. I don't think he can move around very easily.

Wait, what?

It's like I said earlier—all these people are Starbrite.

Truth blinked and looked down at the technicians hard at work. Building who knew what at the orders of the System Astrologica.

I know the System basically hijacks their thinking through attacking the soul—

The Shattervoid girl giggled. Not a nice sound this time.

What do you think the System Astrologica is?

Err . . . a vast spirit of intellect that exists on a higher level of reality?

She was outright laughing now, something broken in the noise.

You aren't exactly wrong. Starbrite isn't some Initiate. It's his Nascent Soul. He manifested his Nascent Soul. And each of you gets tutored by that Nascent Soul, molded until your bits are indistinguishable from bits of that soul. And then, when you die, he harvests you. Those nice little bits ripped away and incorporated into that Nascent Soul. Feeding it. Making it grow bigger and bigger.

The laughter got meaner and meaner. *There is no "System Astrologica." There is only Starbrite. And he has been raising you and eating you for centuries. Did you think he was harvesting cultivation resources on this planet? Natural treasures? He was. Look at his pill furnace! Look at his farm! Are you tasty? Or did you go rancid in that well, Sergeant Medici?*

CHAPTER 77

VIOLENT IMPROVISATION

have so few mental gears left to slip. You wouldn't think there would be any left still touching each other. But here we are. And there it goes.

Truth crouched like a gargoyle or a particularly malevolent pigeon or perhaps just an overambitious rat, on the metal gantry over the prototype lab. The Shattervoid girl was laughing now, an awful sound in his head. He wondered just what those curse tablets were doing to her. If it could be worse than five years of abuse, isolation, fear. Pain. Twelve years old.

When he was twelve . . .

Well, when he was twelve, he was trying to haul scrap out of the canal, running errands, hiding in trash from gangsters and pimps and the randomly violent or rapey. To say nothing of learning the high art of shoplifting from a slum convenience store. Definitely not a challenge for the novice or the unmotivated.

Wait, are all these images really memories? Really? This is what your cities look like from the ground?

There was a trill of horror in her voice, the awful laughter stopping dead.

Yes? Well, the slums, anyway. Other parts of Harban don't look that bad, and Xandre was a lot nicer. More colorful, anyway. So, about this whole "The System Astrologica is actually Starbrite's Soul" thing—

The giggling came back. *I wondered about this. You really have no idea how cultivation works, do you?*

I thought I did? Up to Level Nine, anyway.

Nnnnoooope. Looks like you are starting to figure some of it out, but you really don't get how any of this works. After the Initiate realm, you become a real mage. Which means you give birth to your Nascent Soul—the awakened soul within you, made up of all the magic you learned as an Initiate. All those spells that define you. Starbrite just learned some management spells, basic business-management stuff. I don't know how he made it all so . . . big. But he did. And he is pretty obviously doing it by harvesting the local yokels here.

Truth just nodded numbly. There were business-management spells. Spells specifically intended to track personnel, invoicing, inventory, and property management, all that sort of thing. Probably the second most common category of spells learned after the Jeon National Universal Spell, actually. If you worked in business, what could be more practical than that? Assuming you made it to Level Two, of course. Which most didn't.

Because most people on this planet weren't really mages, apparently.

Awakened soul?

Yes. I don't really know how it works, but apparently, a bit of everyone's soul has its own consciousness, grown out of your own life experiences, the magic you use, how you approach problems, all that. There is usually a big ritual, at least for the Shattervoid. Everyone gets together, there is a lot of singing, everyone is happy. You want the soul to wake up in the best possible way so you have the best, brightest soul.

*I . . . don't think my soul will be very bright.**

Her voice trailed off again. Truth knew exactly how she felt.

<<Wait, is she saying . . . >>

Yup. She's saying.

*Who was that!?**

Oh . . . just a bit of my awakened soul. If you were wondering how Starbrite does what he does. Speaking of, you say you don't think he can move around very easily?

*No, hang on, that's not right. That's not a Nascent Soul; you can't have a Nascent Soul. I would be able to see if you did, and you don't. **

Didn't say I did. I just said "awakened." I have this image of a premature baby forced into the world and set to work for Starbrite. That, apparently, grows into Starbrite. Brainwashed into becoming Starbrite. There's a horrible image for you. We are all baby factories, giving birth to Starbrite, endlessly. So . . . my former employer can't move around easily?

*It's . . . bits and pieces of his soul and personality, not the whole thing. That's. Horrible. I'm so sorry. **

Oh, I'm used to horrible. I won't call it my happy place, but at least it's familiar. So. ABOUT STARBRITE BEING IMMOBILE—

*Oh, well, this is incredibly weird and unnatural. I never heard a song about anything like this at all. This isn't something anyone does, really. For hopefully obvious reasons. **

They aren't obvious.

There was a sense of a three-story-tall girl blinking in surprise. *He's ripping off bits of people's souls and stitching them onto his. That's . . . not generally how souls work. Also, however enlightened he is, keeping track of the millions of moving parts of his business all through his soul is crazy. **

No, it isn't. He's got all those harvested bits of intelligent soul he is working with. He farms out jobs to all the bits. And speaking from experience, the main system does not interact with the . . . components . . . as much as you might think it does.

*Right. God's mercy on you and this world. God's mercy on you. He would be immobile because he must be at the center of some enormous ritual, keeping all this moving. The focus of some enormous magical machine. And if he was healthy and able to move, he wouldn't want my body. If he wanted to get off-world, the ticket price would be pocket change for him. Heck, we might only charge him for his meals and comp the room. **

Really?

Yeah, lower the level, harder to shift. Higher the level, the easier to shift. At a certain level of enlightenment, one passenger can effectively balance out thousands of others. Really high-level passengers can even speed up the trips a lot. Shorten the distance on this side of the cloth by a long way. One of my uncles did the Kessel run in twelve parsecs with an Ascended Master aboard, if you can believe that.

Truth nodded. He could believe that easily. On account of not knowing what any of those things were.

What's a parsec?

A unit of measurement in the void. It's equal to three point zero eight six times ten to the thirteenth kilometers.

Three point zero eight six times ten to the thirteenth . . . Kind of an arbitrary number. Why is that?

I dunno. Tradition? We have a lot of traditions. He could hear her shrug. Truth nodded. He had . . . so many questions. So many, many questions. But really, they were not relevant at the moment. Oh, wait, there were two he should ask.

Any top-secret Shattervoid Clan spells that would help me get you out?

Probably.

Truth sighed. Yes, that made sense. She was six when she was snatched, after all.

How resistant are you to damage?

When I'm not being pressed down by these curses and the binding tattooed on me? Extremely. Well, extremely compared to you landgrubs. Not, you know, compared to other things that live in the void.

Truth firmly decided he wasn't going to ask about what else lived up there. Time to leave and keep exploring. Figuring out how he was going to break her out. Figuring out . . . a lot of things, actually. Oh, one other question.

How did Starbrite manage to kidnap you anyhow?

I was very small at the time, about the size of your arm. There was a shuttle parked in orbit. I remember it was painted white, a bit dirty. The void is dustier than you would think, especially near planets. There was the most amazing resonance coming from it. I could practically taste the— There was a thought/sound/sensation of lemonade on a hot day and the tickle of mint in your nose as your feet made the water splash and gurgle as you sat on a dock with your friends, laughing and splashing and enjoying the spray. **And of course I wanted some, so I slipped away from my dad to go see if I could have some. And then they grabbed me. And I woke up as we made planetfall here.**

Truth shook his head. *All right, I'm going to slip away now. See what I can discover about this base, see if there is anything useful I can manage to help get you out. Worst case . . . I dunno, blow open the doors and try to funnel enough bodies down here that they overwhelm the Level Eights on site, but that's not a . . . good plan, you know?*

Try up on the first floor. They keep their minds away from me, but they do think about it a lot. Should be something good up there.

I'll talk to you soon, Sally.

She giggled again. *My name's not Sally, silly.*

I have to call you something, right? And my sister's name is Sophia, so why not Sally? We can keep the S's going.

I don't like that name.

Then you will have to think of a better one. Sally.

Booo! Booo! Truth smiled at her, waved at the giant girl, and started making his way back. It would be a stressful, boring wait until someone opened the door again.

Truth made his way up to the top of the base. Trying not to think about things. It was all . . . a lot. Too much, maybe. Why would the power emanating from the planet want to forbid knowledge of Nascent Souls? Even if it forbade people from reaching that level of power or enlightenment or whatever. Why did Starbrite need a new body? Why a Shattervoid body in particular? It sounded like their bodies weren't very convenient for anything other than living in the void, and the void was THE VOID. Definitionally nothing up there.

That he knew of, anyway. Just possibly, the mage from off-world knew more than he did. And just what had happened to make Starbrite start his soul-harvesting operation? If it wasn't the way things were usually done, then it presumably wasn't very effective, or there were a lot of drawbacks or something. Because Truth would unscrew his own head before believing powerful people wouldn't prey on the weak whenever and wherever they could get away with it. Global curse notwithstanding.

He crept along the white semigloss painted corridors, with their magic windows looking out over Starbrite resorts. Keeping alert for patrolling trolls or a high-level nipping to the toilets. The doors continued to be their unmarked selves, but he had gotten the hang of bypassing them now. He had even taken the opportunity to steal some office supplies to do double duty as burglary tools.

Laboratory after laboratory. Specialized spell equipment, alchemical equipment, ritual rooms, a blinding fortune in supplies and magical furniture. *And not one person here is a real mage. Or maybe I'm the only fake mage, because everyone else* is *Starbrite.*

Incisive gave him a warning before he turned an ordinary corner. He leapt back, but before he could race away, he felt the warning stop. He crept back to the corner. The alarm creeped up. Must be a guard post. Trolls?

He got flat on the ground and risked a bit of reflective plastic stuck with tape on the end of a long straw. The picture was blurry and distorted, but he could make out another secured room. PMC guards and, yes, trolls. All looking bored, but nobody felt like joking around and shooting the shit, apparently.

Truth was willing to bet the trolls were mood-killers. He retracted his improvised mirror. Now, what rated all that security? It wasn't an entrance to the base, or at least he didn't think it was. The guards were facing in, not out.

He mentally shrugged and opted for patience. Sooner or later, there would be someone coming through, and he could learn something. He settled in to wait.

It took forty minutes, but there was a shift change. Mages came trooping in, covered in bulky, shiny clothes. The clothes glowed with enchantments. Truth recognized some of them. Air filtration. Air *supply*. Temperature control, over and over again. Fireproofing and heat reflection. Over and over again.

"Stand clear! Stand clear!"

There were three long chimes, a pause, then a fourth chime.

"Airlock reports flushed. Confirm flush."

"Confirmed."

"Unlock airlock."

"Unlocking."

"Contamination team, stand by."

"Contamination, standing by."

"Relief squad, stand by."

"Relief squad standing by."

There was a crack and a hiss. Even around the corner, Truth could feel the air suddenly get hot, smell . . . something. Something he had never smelled before, strange and acrid. Like rotten eggs in a furnace.

"Mine equipment maintenance squad seven, reporting all safe, all conditions green."

"Good job, squad seven. Squad three, deploy!"

Truth had a sudden, terrible idea. It was the Medici way—make your problem EVERYONE's problem. Lead melted at relatively low temperatures, didn't it?

CHAPTER 78

A FLAWLESS PLAN

Truth had an unusual problem. Well, he thought it was unusual. It hadn't ever come up for him before, but maybe he was underestimating the challenges faced by other people. He nodded to himself as he wedged himself up into the corner of the wall and the ceiling, relying on his inhuman strength and conditioning to hold him in place. Yes, other people had their own struggles, their own burdens. Who was he to assume what problems they did and did not face? Perhaps this was just one of those questions everyone confronted.

Exactly how fast did lava flow?

If, hypothetically, one were to trigger an explosion in a volcano (somehow) and that were big enough to (somehow) cause the lava to surge and if, someone (somehow) left open the door to a secret base that connected to a lava tube, how fast could the lava flow through the secret base? Hypothetically.

He should have asked someone at the convenience store in town. Or an old-timer smoking on a bench. An elder at home was like having a treasure, according to his period romances. They would definitely know the answer. Probably dealt with this exact problem five or six times.

He knew he was flapping. He needed something dramatic. Something that would at least draw the attention of those high-levels. People who could handle mountain-melting-level problems. The key to any surprise attack, any ambush, was speed. Which meant that the question wasn't idle. How fast did lava flow? And what would it take to flood the base with it?

So. Issue number one—investigating what was on the other side of the bulkhead. He dropped to the floor behind the workers coming off shift. His feet fell on the polished concrete silently. When he moved, his feet matched the steps of the workers exactly. They hadn't the faintest idea he was there.

They marched through the halls directly to a locker room, where they more or less collapsed.

"Good God! Every time I think I'm going to get used to it. But I don't. That shit is freaky. When does the job get boring?" a worker moaned.

It was a multistep process trying to get your boots off. It was designed to both be sealed against things coming up the trouser leg and, just as important, stop things from falling down into the boot. A complex system of straps and seals were employed, each of which took a few seconds to disengage. As a result, each boot took about a minute to remove. It felt considerably longer.

"You aren't bored?" This from a woman who looked like she had been melted by heat and sort of smooshed back into a roughly human shape. Or maybe that was just the exhaustion. "What's so interesting about thousand-degree rock bubbling and spitting pebbles of fiery death at you while you try to work?"

"Speaking personally, it's the way you can't really see, breathe, or feel anything properly through the suit, but you know that if you take off any portion of it, the best-case scenario is that you are maimed. It's that 'fear of horrific pain and/or death' combined with claustrophobia that really makes me sleepy." This from a pudgy little man who, upon removing the shoulder-length gauntlets from the protective suit, revealed tattoos of catbirds on his arms.

"One of you bastards has a cold beer in their locker. Or a cold tea, or something. Give it to me, and I promise I will mentally take back at least one of the things I thought about you." This came from a hunched-over person struggling to shrug off their sodden undershirt. "I swear my aircon enchantment is busted."

"If you really think so, drop it off with Maintenance. Don't be an asshole; just go do it."

Back and forth, the workers bickered and moaned. It all sounded normal to Truth. Could it really just be Starbrite talking to himself? It couldn't be, right? They weren't mental clones any more than he was a mental clone. It was more like each person had their base personality nudged more in line with what Starbrite wanted.

Why did Starbrite want employees that reflected different parts of his personality? Why did he want their souls brought into line with his? Truth could feel the edges of some enormous secret there. Could this be the secret to Starbrite's power? Somehow? But it sounded like Starbrite couldn't move around much. He needed a new body. Didn't sound "powerful." And yet.

Truth eavesdropped on the moaning laborers, watched them put everything away, drop things for cleaning and repair, pull on their off-duty clothes before they shuffled off to the cafeteria. In the secret volcano lair. He had to stifle a hysterical giggle. If Sally was right, there were only three people in the building. Sally, Truth, and Starbrite.

He didn't want to believe Sally was right. It didn't feel entirely right. But he didn't have a better theory.

He followed the team lead when she split off. Apparently to report in to someone. Now . . . why would you have to do that if everyone was a mental clone of Starbrite? But then, the System had told him he was under instructions *not* to contact the main System Astrologica unless utterly necessary. Like when he completed a mission or bought something through the System Shop.

So, it wasn't like it was one big, distributed brain. Was it more like gardening? Sally said something like that, right? He was growing elixir ingredients. His employees, eventually the whole nation of Jeon, maybe nations around the world, would be his ingredients. To do . . . what, exactly?

The team leader went into a little office with lots of cheerful underwater views of bright tropical reefs. Lots and lots of colorful little fish.

"How's it going in there?" the supervisor asked.

"Same as usual. I would have thought all the bombardment might shake something loose, but . . . nope."

"It's a giant, ancient volcano. It'll take more than a few low-yield spells going off against our wards to shake it." The supervisor chuckled.

"Guess so. The mana-conversion systems and heat miners remain within the expected parameters; failure rate is on the high end of the range but within projections—"

"I can get all that from your reports. What I want to know is how it feels."

She blinked at him. Truth watched the byplay. The supervisor was deadly serious. He was the kind of man who could turn a paunch, a cheap tie, and a combover into badges of competence.

"How what feels?"

"How do the tunnels feel? The mining rigs? The ritual anchors? How do they feel? I know what it feels like in those suits, but . . . did you feel safe in the tunnels? Did you feel like someone was watching you? Like something was wrong and you just couldn't see it? How did your shift *feel*?"

"Um. Well. Not fine, obviously. Nobody likes being in the tunnels." The supervisor nodded. "But I'd say pretty normal? None of the alarms were tripped or bypassed, if that is what you are getting at. None of the banishments or wards were damaged either. It all looked fine. So, as shifts go, it went . . . fine?"

The supervisor nodded slightly. "That's good. You know why I ask, I assume."

"Worried about infiltrators coming in through earth-movement spells or tunneling demons or something?"

"Or something, yes." He sighed, smiling a little. "It's a quirk of the lava tubes. Most of the cone of the volcano is near-solid basalt and volcanic rock. But there are these 'little' tubes snaking around."

"Tubes we can use." She nodded. "And theoretically, with a very specialized spell load-out, someone could use it to get to us."

"It's incredibly unlikely, of course. And there are guards on our side of the bulkhead. But I'm not in charge of this side of the bulkhead. So, any little warning bells you hear ringing, any 'vibes' that might turn into problems later—I want to know about it. Because when things go wrong inside an active volcano . . ."

She smiled at the frumpy-looking man. "Appreciate you looking out for us, boss."

"Nonsense. You are all valuable KPIs. You exist to make my numbers go up. The good numbers. The bad numbers, you exist to make go down." He waved her out of his office. Truth hung out with the supervisor a bit longer.

The wax tablets and pools of mercury on the supervisor's desk were displaying streams of information. Some showing security footage inside alarmingly red tunnels, others showing numbers going up and down. Truth recognized a few of them. They were reporting devices that tracked things like air quality, temperature, cosmic-ray density, things like that. From there he was able to figure out roughly what he was looking at.

It was a power source. He had never seen anything like it. Generally, ambient cosmic rays were more than enough to power . . . almost anything, really. Sometimes, you needed a big spell array to gather the energy, but actually *generating* the power was . . . not unheard-of, exactly, but very, very weird. He didn't understand the mechanism, but something was taking that lava and turning it into usable cosmic energy. Powering what, he didn't know.

Nothing felt excessively energy-dense. Not the lab, not the curses holding down Sally . . . Maybe the wards? The whole volcano was covered in magical protection. That had to be drawing a ton of power. Have something set up that could shrug off the big blasts of energy, limit the spells that could hit the mountain, force people to go in on foot, and then feed 'em to the monsters outside . . . could be it. But the display didn't say where the power went. Just that it was coming in, and all the systems continued to report "green."

The lack of a giant red button labeled *Warning! Self Destruct, DO NOT PRESS!* was disappointing, if expected. But the basic notion was pretty clear—there is a machine, a magical device, that was somehow turning lava or heat into usable energy. He could work with that.

There was a knock on the door.

"Come in!"

"Got a moment to talk about shift schedules?" a weedy-looking man asked. Truth took that as his cue to leave.

Truth could feel bits and pieces sliding around. He didn't think Sally was right about the System Astrologica, or at least, not all the way right. He knew that the System took over people and harvested chunks of their souls, but it was also a pretty hands-off manager. You had to directly get its attention if you wanted to talk to it, mostly. That system fairy, for example, never just turned up on its own.

Same thing applied to him just possessing her body or whatever he was planning. Again, if he wanted off-world, he could have done it by booking a ticket. Why kidnap a Shattervoid child? There was something he was missing, something he was missing . . .

Truth roamed the halls, checking the other doors as he went past. He got *very* fast at cracking the locks, which was handy, since he had to stop, run away, and hide from the trolls depressingly often. He came to the conclusion that as secret volcano lairs went, this one was a bit of a snooze. There were staff apartments, some barracks, a mess hall, a management mess hall, a senior management dining room, janitor's closet, et cetera. All the normal things that Truth associated with army/PMC bases.

On the second floor, he found a room the size of a large lecture hall, covered in dense arrays of runes and spells waiting to be activated. All focused on a currently empty ritual space at the front of the hall. There were odd-looking devices, somewhat like pipes, extending down from the ceiling. Truth smiled. He had found the ritual room. Now he could really get cooking.

CHAPTER 79

ROCKS, AND THEIR DISCONTENTS

Truth looked over the ritual space. After careful examination, looking closely at the micro-engraved gems, the achingly precise line arrangements, the Enochian ciphers written into the floor and then filled with mythril—after a detailed forensic examination, he reached a firm conclusion.

I don't have the faintest goddamn idea what goes on in here.

In his defense, he consoled himself, there were clearly big pieces missing. There were several engraved circles, squares, and triangles where things were clearly intended to be placed. Whatever wound up slotted in there would likely change the whole operation of the ritual. There were also a lot of lines and spell formations that just ended abruptly or seemed only half-written. Not unfinished—split in half horizontally. Presumably, the other half was written on something else. Just waiting to be plugged in.

He tried tracing the lines of magic through their winding and intersecting paths. Tracing them along floors and up over walls. Some of them were etched into wires, run through pipes in the walls. Another one of those things he had heard of but never actually seen. Usually a heavy-industrial thing or when you were very concerned about potential interference from atmospheric cosmic rays.

Did . . . they have them in alchemist towers? He seemed to remember a maintenance journal mentioning that. Mass-producing potions and pills required very specific magic profiles, and isolating your enchantments from even minute interference was considered the basic of the basics. High-end beastcrafting too. Never relevant in anything Truth expected to work on, though. Streetlights and air conditioners didn't mind micro-thaum energy-density variations. The enchantments were comparatively coarse; they wouldn't even register the difference.

This was something being built to a higher standard. He traced the lines of shimmering silver and tarnished gold as they formed complex interlocking geometries, occasionally vanishing into a wall, floor, or ceiling before reappearing at random somewhere else.

It took him an embarrassingly long time to realize that the ritual room was set over the prototype lab. The prototype lab with its three-story-tall ceiling. Meaning that this second-floor ritual room was linked via direct spell connection with the formations and constructions being made below. His eyes dragged back to the empty center of the room, where the locus of the ritual was clearly intended to be.

You couldn't fit Sally in there. You could fit that weird sarcophagus thing, though. What would that achieve? Truth had no idea. Probably nothing good for Sally. Or, ultimately, him. He looked around the room one more time. He was tempted to try and tamper with the spells somehow, but he really didn't know enough about what was going on there to do so in a way that wouldn't be immediately obvious. It wasn't the time for loud moves. Not yet.

He had personally confirmed the presence of two high-levels. Fingers crossed they were "only" Level Eight. If they really were Starbrite mental clones, and if Starbrite really was some kind of next-level being, he might not take their "high level" as a threat. Got to feed the dog meat if you want it to guard well. You aren't really paranoid if they really are out to get you, and the whole damn planet was out to get Starbrite. Had been for decades.

Truth crept down the halls, the tension firmly settled into his guts. He could feel the hairs on his arms and the back of his neck standing alert, waiting for that gust of air that would be the only warning of an ambush. Incisive was up and running as always, but he kept remembering how Dr. Sun had managed to get the drop on him. Truth had never really figured out how he managed that.

He could hear his heart beating. The footfalls of the researchers, laborers, soldiers in the base echoing off the white walls and polished concrete floors. Knowing that mixed in to that sound were the footfalls of trolls or some random person with a blessing or talisman that let them see him. It only took one person. One second. A single glance. And then he was dead. There might be a little noise before it was all done, but he was dead.

Truth found himself diving into and out of rooms almost at random. When the stress got too much, he would shadow someone into their lab, or workstation, or whatever. One time, in a very not-awkward-at-all moment, he found himself standing in the bathroom. Trying to calm himself in, as one of his romance novels put it, the room of ease as everyone else strained for release.

Agonizingly slowly, he made his way back to the locker room. He found a bench and lay down on it. Just . . . breathing. In and out. Trying to calm his breath. Trying to fight down the fear. Justified fear, perhaps. But, at the moment, not useful fear.

He stared up at the bare concrete of the ceiling, feeling the sweat of the place trying to soak through his pores. Trying to breathe. Trying to remember just how, exactly, he had gotten here.

How does a guy from Towering Heavens Apartments Co. Building Number Thirty-Seven wind up trying to drown a secret base inside a volcano in lava? Hoping that his move will be so fast and so deadly, it will kill the Level Eight powerhouses before they can stop it. Which, realistically, they can. They are strong enough to stop a lava flow if it is anything less than geography-changing.

It will have to be that destructive while still giving the three-story-tall bald twelve-year-old girl a chance to punch through the thin fabric of reality when the seemingly endless lead curse tablets melt off of her. All while I am inside the base. With the terrifying monsters and trolls and high-levels and explosive lava waves. Because, you know, sure. Why not?

I swear every step leading here seemed like a reasonable idea at the time. Sometimes the only reasonable idea. But I don't think you could call this a reasonable place to be. You wouldn't call this a reasonable situation to be in. I feel like somehow, somewhere along the way, I made a bad choice. Maybe a few of them. And now I'm here.

Waiting to solve a problem in the dumbest, most violent way I know. And before that, a little light industrial sabotage in the form of bitching with a coworker.

Truth could feel the metal of the bench digging into his back. It didn't hurt. Nothing in this room could possibly hurt him by now. But his skin was sensitive enough to count the short ridges stamped into the rolled steel. He could feel the steady cool draft of the air-circulation system. It was doing its best in bad circumstances. He felt an odd sort of kinship for it. He would have been the guy fixing it, had he been a little less greedy.

Was that it? The one bad decision that everything flowed from? The choice to take the tall money and join the PMC? Maintenance was right there. Might have had to wait a while for enrollment to open up, but it was right there. Didn't have to go into the violence trade.

I . . . don't think I would have been a good person if I had gone into talisman maintenance. Not that I'm a very good one now, but I think I would have been a bully. Work my way up to supervisor and just . . . find reasons to fuck with people. Give them shit details for not looking scared enough. Or something. Find reasons to start fights, then take them too far. I wouldn't know about the Prince. I wouldn't know about King Rat. What I have to overcome.

I would be trapped in the "real," same as everyone else. Easing my pain by hurting others. Over and over and over. Not much has changed even now that I do know. Going to hurt an awful lot of people. Again. Mostly because it will make me feel better, broadly defined. But you know what? I really can't imagine doing anything else. Not really. This seems like the only reasonable thing to do. Under the circumstances.

A world where the rats don't eat each other. Maybe this will be the first step to that. Or my first step to that. Stepping on an awful lot of my fellow rats to do it, though.

The next shift came piling into the locker room. Mildly moaning about the work, how the heat-protection suits fit, how everything stank of sweat despite the cleaning talismans. Truth eventually figured out who the squad leader was. An older man, still fit and strong. Faded tattoos of naked women and roses twining around skulls decorated his chest. An icon of St. Chirguh had faded to blue-green across his clavicle. Broken smile and offered coin in hand.

Truth leaned over and whispered in his ear. "You know, they wouldn't be asking about how things *feel* in the tunnels unless they knew there was something to *feel*. This is management we are talking about here. They don't give a fuck about *feelings*; they care about numbers. *They want results.* Which means they *expect you to hear something.* They know damn well something is coming *and they are using you and the squad to find it the hard way.* Now, orders are orders. No getting around that."

The old man's head was starting to nod. More firmly at that last bit. He was clearly very used to following orders. Truth knew how that went.

"Orders are orders, and regardless of anything else, the job needs to be done. No shirking. Job needs to be done, and done right." Solid nods there. "So, that means *your* job now includes finding whatever they are looking for *and figuring out how to keep your squad alive.* Because that's always been your job too."

This got narrowed eyes and a slow exhale. Truth could see the wheels turning in the man's head as he started reframing things he already knew.

"Everybody keeps their ears open. Even if it's hard to hear or see, you can still hear or see something. And once you do, you need to run back to the door as fast as you can. Even if it means not every security check is perfect. Perfect isn't the goal. If something does go seriously wrong, so what? They are the ones trapped in the tunnel, not your squad. *Your job is to find the enemy and keep your squad safe.* Everything else is secondary. Important. But secondary."

That was probably about as far as he could push that. Truth started moving around the room, finding ears to whisper in.

"Did the maintenance guys *really* fix the air and temp seals? They say they did, but did they really? That's a lot of suits to maintain every day. Wouldn't be crazy to think *they missed something.*"

"Funny how you don't really get used to the lava. You should. You know how to work in those tunnels. *But any little fuckup and you are dead.* And there would be *nothing you could do to save yourself.*"

"They have to be coming through the ground. Can't do anything to us in the air, doing even less coming in on the surface. So, they gotta be coming through the mountain. Through the lava tubes. If it was you running things, *billions of earth demons and fire demons* would come *boiling up out of the lava to hurt you bad before hauling you to Hell.*"

"He's looking at you again. Now. With everything going on. He won't take a hint. You are about to do something crazy dangerous *and he's not even paying attention to the job.* You just want to get the job done; *he's going to get you killed because he's an asshole.*"

Around and around he went, throwing handfuls of paranoia like confetti at a funeral. Nothing rebellious. Nothing against Starbrite. The workers just wanted to do their job, but *they* were going to get them killed. And "they" could be anyone. Blind trust was not a thing that existed in Jeon. Lots of ears primed to catch dripped poison.

They suited up and made their way to the checkpoint. A lot of tension in those eyes now. A lot of closed body language. Truth made his way as quickly as he could back to the supervisor's office. He wanted to see how his experiment panned out. How they would react when pushed. Because Starbrite Security wasn't dumb, and if he could think of it, they could think of it too. So, how, exactly, would they handle problems at the mining site?

He looked over at the supervisor, the light bouncing merrily off the parts of his scalp unprotected by the combover. *Sorry, buddy. Your day is about to get* really *interesting.*

CHAPTER 80

INTO THE LIGHT

Truth watched the squad of workers going into the tunnels on the scrying mirrors arranged on the supervisor's desk. The supervisor wasn't keeping a close eye. This operation happened several times a day, every day. Not much to see after the eightieth or ninetieth time. Truth was watching eagerly. He didn't know anything about what was going on out there.

As they marched through the gate, he spotted one bump into another, shorter one. The shorter one violently recoiled and the body language got very hostile very fast. The taller one looked defensive. They kept moving through—the airlock did not encourage dawdling. The leader's body language likewise didn't need translating. Head on a swivel, sharp hand movements directing the crew.

The view through the mirrors was boring, to Truth's surprise. Mostly dark tunnels. Just . . . dark tunnels. Piping running through them, bundles of pipes, each as thick as his wrist. As he kept watching, he saw the images in the mirrors change. They were following the crew. The enchantments were smart enough to trigger when something moved into their range. He felt his lips move in a sort of half-smile. Even now, he was proud of those Starbrite Quality talismans.

The crew kept moving their heads, trying to look around. The stiff suits didn't bend much that way. They had to turn their torso from side to side to see around them. Light enchantments built into the sealed head covers lit up the black rock of the tunnels.

He could see wisps of gas lighting up in sharp yellows in the beams of light. Nothing as human as steam or woodsmoke. This was poison, the rocky breath of the planet. Not fit for human lungs. There was a temperature readout on the bottom of one mirror. Lower than he thought it would be. Much lower. Barely over forty. Why were they complaining that it was always hot?

They walked steadily through the dark tunnel. Twist, twist, trying to watch every which way. Truth watched the number at the bottom of the mirror steadily tick up. Forty-five. Fifty. Sixty. Seventy. Still frigid compared to what he expected. You could die of hypothermia in sixty-degree water.

There was a junction of two tubes. The squad paused and looked carefully down each. Very carefully. There looked like there was some kind of argument. Hands waved; fingers jabbed. The leader got their attention. They checked the sensors and valves at the junction, then pressed on down the left-hand tunnel. Every few steps, someone at the back of the group would twist back, checking the other tunnel. Checking the way they came.

Seventy. Ninety. One hundred twenty. Now they were solidly in "dead in a real hurry" temperatures. Touching something that hot was a comparatively minor matter. Being out in it without heat protection for any length of time was something else entirely. The phrase *boiled in your own juices* was evocative but, strictly speaking, incorrect. This was a dry heat. You would bake.

There were more valves there and more monitoring talismans. The squad slowed its pace, carefully working through the job. People kept stopping and looking up and around. Eventually, the leader stopped everyone, assigned someone to be the lookout, and the rest got back to work. Even with one fewer pair of hands, the work visibly sped up. Truth nodded slightly. That was a good leader right there. He hoped they made it back okay.

One sixty. Two hundred. Two fifty. Three hundred. The numbers ticked up and with them the amount of poisonous gas floating through the air. Was it flammable? He had no idea. There probably wasn't enough oxygen down there for it to burn, but he really had no idea. It was hot enough for paper to burn, he would guess. The black basalt tubes were even in width, but there were little stalactite-looking things hanging down. Drips. Drips of stone that dried after running like wax.

The squad hunched in on itself. Shoulders came up and tightened. Hands and bodies kept tight to the body. Another cluster of talismans and valves. A lookout was assigned; they all got to work. A few minutes in, everyone stopped and turned to look down the tunnel. Their bodies rigid. Not moving. Truth could hear the thunder of his heartbeat as they waited. The throbbing rumble punctuating the seconds.

The leader waved them back to work. It was . . . nothing. Nothing for now. The lookout stared fixedly down the tunnel. He could imagine them staring, not even daring to breathe. The work got done. Just . . . slowly. A tool slipped. There was some angry body language, but the problem got fixed. A yellow tag was hung on the valve. Good for now but monitor and expect to replace it soon.

Five hundred degrees in the tunnel now. Death would be ugly but not too lingering. Hotter than a kitchen oven. The gasses swirled around. There must be almost no oxygen. Must be. Otherwise, those gasses would have exploded already, surely. Brilliant, sickly yellow. Like a surgeon's notes from cleaning out an infection. *The discharged pus was straw-colored.* Deeper and deeper into the volcano. The maintenance squad marched into the swirling poison mists.

Where are all the demons? Truth wondered. This place should be lousy with earth and fire demons. Even if Starbrite cleared them out periodically, they should be swarming through there. But there weren't any. And, sure, there were banishments and wards, all very standard talismans built in to what Truth assumed were heat- and corrosion-resistant materials. Not nearly as many as he would have expected.

The crew had been jumpy before. They were scared now. The headlights whipped around the tunnel, creating insane shadows as the drips from the ceiling jumped in and out of sharp relief. They would stop suddenly and freeze up, all looking in one direction. *Is it noisy down there? I have no idea what it could sound like. Is there a breeze? That poison fog is spreading somehow, right? But not very fast.*

Someone tripped. Strong arms caught them before they hit the ground. Everyone gathered around the person, heads bent over them. There was an urgent pat-down, checking them over. Were there any tears? Did any of the enchantments break? Are you okay? Are you hurt? No? All's well? Then do everyone a favor and WATCH YOUR FEET!

Truth could practically hear them. No such thing as a safe fall down there. Not when the air temperature had already reached six hundred degrees. Who knew how hot the rock was? Hotter? He didn't know. From the look of things, it might well be.

The pipes were insulated now. He didn't know what with—brilliantly shiny but flexible as cloth. They bounced the light of the headlamps in glaring beams at mad angles across the halls. The devices hanging from them were more complex. Truth no longer recognized most of them. Their functions were mysterious. Muffled and hidden under heat protection. Like the workers maintaining them.

Truth could see the hands creeping up. Squeezing on heavy tools. They were waiting to get hit. Either by something coming down the tunnels or by some feckless crewmate. Each thinking that they would get the job done and get home safe. Even if they were the only one to do so.

Were the rocks starting to glow red? Was it his imagination? They were tagging more things now. Truth would bet that they *could* have repaired them, but they were past being able to really focus. Any even slightly complicated problem would be tagged for replacement and moved past. Or just considered good enough and left as is.

Deeper and deeper now. The rocks were definitely red. A dull, angry sort of red. The color of an ember waiting for a breath of air to rouse it into furious life. Seven hundred degrees. They were barely pretending to check the valves and talismans now. Looking quickly, heads twitching around. Lights bouncing madly.

Truth watched the leader's hand jerk toward something on his belt. Truth couldn't see what. Some kind of emergency-alarm talisman? A stun weapon? A charm that would provide a bubble of cool air? The leader controlled his impulse. They pressed on deeper. The sickly yellow mists blinding them more than a few meters out. Trapped in the burning dark, blinded by the poison mists.

The headlights seemed to fade in the tunnels now. The mists were picking up the red from the rock. Cherry red now. Bright and deep. The red of a burning kiss, and afterward, nothing tasted sweet ever again. The yellow mists were now the orange of forest-fire skies. The temperature was ticking up faster and faster. Eight hundred degrees. Eight fifty.

They passed a cluster of valves and talismans sealed in heatproof boxes. They barely glanced at them. A few tags were tossed out, and he could hear the yells to get a move on all the way up there. Their body language was screaming.

Nine hundred degrees. The rock had shifted from the red of real cherries to maraschino. An artificial, sickly sweet cherry. The headlights didn't do anything now, but they didn't switch them off. Were there some kind of light filters in the head covers? There must be, or all you would see is the red. Red rocks that dripped down from the red ceiling, stopping well before they reached the red floor.

Someone dropped a tool. They reached for it. Someone grabbed their shoulder and yanked them upright. Then thumped them hard on the shoulder. A hand pointed down the tunnel. Jabbed down the tunnel. *Forget it. It's gone. We need to* go.

Nine fifty. The rock was creeping quickly to orange now. Racing up the gradient. They weren't even tossing tags on the valves now. Not running. You couldn't run in those suits. Not without falling down, and then you were dead. Walking as fast as they could.

Truth could feel the sweat running down them. Pooling in their gauntlets and boots. They would feel like they couldn't breathe. Didn't matter what the enchantments said they were doing. It was too hot. They were trapped in the orange light of a fire. Buried alive in a crematorium. They couldn't breathe. The only way out is through.

The rock turned brilliant orange, the color of fall leaves, then brighter, the yellow of early fall, then the bright yellow of buttercups. One thousand degrees and rising. One thousand one hundred. Hot enough to forge steel. The headlights did nothing now.

They almost ran down a split in the tunnel, not even bothering to listen for danger. They knew there was danger. It was all around them. It was their idiot teammates. It was the damn bastards trying to blow up the mountain. Trying to kill them for doing their jobs.

The mirrors were almost blinding now, the bright yellow light pouring out of them. The supervisor barely glanced away from his spreadsheets. He had seen it all before. Truth stared, fixated. They had made their way to a large cavern. He couldn't see the back wall of it—a hundred meters away or more? The roof stretched tens of meters high. It wasn't that the poison mists had vanished. They were just blown away, not allowed to linger long above the lake of lava.

This is where the pipes ended, plunging into the molten basalt. There were ritual emplacements around the edge of the lake. Dozens of pylons with glowing orange traceries of birds and demons. Twisted spikes nailed into the ground in a grand matrix. Devices whose name and nature were beyond his meager understanding. He didn't care. He barely gave them a glance.

Someone slipped, knocked one of the maintenance crew into one of the pipes. They leapt away, their suit scorched. Torn? The injured worker yanked a long wrench from their toolbelt and smashed it into their comrade's skull. The not-yet-dead man fell back, knocking over the ritual station. Alarms started blaring on the supervisor's desk. The squad leader was jabbing away at some alarm gem, then yanking a wrist-thick fetish from a sheath. Ready to restore order. He jumped into the fray. Truth barely gave him a second look.

In the middle of the lake of lava, a phoenix had been crucified on hundreds of iron pipes. Its blood endlessly flowing down, melting the rock. The phoenix watched the workers fighting on the shore of its blood. Two dead. More might yet die. The ancient demon tilted its head back and screamed. The lava shuddered and surged. More ritual stations exploded. More alarms blared. The supervisor was bashing his own alarm talismans now.

The crucified phoenix screamed and strained at the pipes piercing it. The phoenix screamed, and Truth felt the whole mountain scream with it.

CHAPTER 81

THUG WITH A SPELL

The maintenance crew was fighting now, all against all. Crude, clumsy swings. The suits were stifling, like trying to fight underwater. It must have been a nightmare. *Can't see. Can barely feel. Danger everywhere. Everywhere. Can't run—job's not done, and this is Starbrite.* You get the job done, no excuses. And then the phoenix, screaming. Shaking the poison air with its cries.

They fell over. Their suits were built to resist the heat, to withstand abrasion. But this much heat? Deliberate violence? Rips started forming. Enchantments broke. Truth could see the moment where realization hit—they wouldn't be getting out alive. They bolted from the fight, smashing past other workers. Smashing past magical devices damaged by their fight or just needing maintenance after the heat and poison gas had done their corrosive job.

Their bodies fell. No flames, Truth noticed. Or perhaps tiny ones, soon vanishing as the oxygen and hydrogen in their blood boiled, divorced, and burned in the steel-forge heat. He didn't hang around. He could hear yells from security and maintenance, demanding to know what was going on, why all their alarms were going off.

He had planned on scouting more. Events had overtaken him. Time to go play the Fool.

He raced back to the maintenance locker room. He found the largest suit they had and suited up. Workers came racing in, moving to get into their gear. All Level Ones, with a Level Two squad leader. Truth saw someone racing for the rack the suit had been on, then look horrified when he couldn't find it. Truth grabbed him, hauled him into a toilet stall, and knocked him out. He moved so quickly, nobody caught him doing it.

He dithered for a moment. He didn't have a knockout spell. On the other hand, what he was planning to do would probably kill everyone in the base. He could send the worker on his way early. It would be the smart thing to do, really. He allowed himself a half-second more to agonize over it, then gave the worker a second pop to the chin. The brain trauma wouldn't do him any favors if he woke up. But at least there would be an infinitesimally thin chance of survival.

Truth checked his seals, then had a "teammate" check them and checked theirs in return. A squad of twenty PMC mercs was waiting for them at the tunnel entrance. Wearing the same heat-protecting garments, Truth noticed, but with more defensive enchantments sewn in.

You would never mistake the two. There was something about the way the deathsworn moved. The strength and coordination of their bodies. Level Three vets, all of them. Squad leader might be Level Four. A "squad" like this could take down a city.

"We ALL got the mission! Contain, secure, protect. Maintenance, you rush to the mining site behind us, and once the site is secure, repair, then work your way back. Sergeant, the squad will be golem scout *only*. Nobody detaches UNTIL THE SITE IS SECURE! WE STAY TOGETHER!" The lieutenant was hammering it home, literally, banging on the door.

"Stay calm, stay alert, do your jobs. CLEAR?"

"YES, SIR!" everyone yelled back, Truth right there with them. Squads were usually led by a corporal, but with this many Level Threes, at this kind of facility?

"One moment, Lieutenant." There was a sudden gust of wind, and an old lady appeared. She quickly pulled on the heat suit she was carrying. "I will be accompanying you. Someone check my seals." A maintenance worker rushed over, checking the suit was sealed up. "No mistakes or accidents can be tolerated. You understand."

"Thank you, ma'am. We are very happy to have high-level support." Truth silently awarded the lieutenant points for actually sounding like he meant it. He . . . really wished the high-levels weren't as on the ball, but that was never going to happen. Of course they would be activated. He threw himself into the persona as hard as he possibly could. Truth Medici, talisman-maintenance specialist. Not the most sociable soul but a real gets-the-job-done guy.

Truth didn't try to look anything other than tense. Anything else would be out of character and would stand out in the crowd of upset body language around him. The door opened, and people started moving through the airlock in groups. The high-level first, then the PMC, then the maintenance crew.

Truth thought he knew what to expect. He had watched a run-through just a few minutes ago. He was wrong.

The suit smelled. It had been cleaned, carefully cleaned, but he could smell the sulfur and sweat that had accumulated in there. His hearing, usually excellent, was muffled. His own quick breaths were suddenly very loud in his ears. He had gotten used to his body being a precision instrument. Loved feeling it, loved the sheer physicality of living in the world. Now? He was drowning in the suit.

The claustrophobia of the tunnels was multiplied by the claustrophobia of the heat-resistant gear. The "helmet" was a stiff cloth material, flat on top, with a tinted glass visor. The light enchantments cast the light in a cone aimed straight ahead, bouncing off the silver-shine of the metal cloth gear. Blinding light, then blinding darkness of the tunnels.

They raced down the tunnel. "Raced" at the pace of the slowest people, which was the maintenance crew. Level Ones with no body cultivation, struggling against the stiff cloth of the suits. Touch dulled by the heavy gauntlets. Already starting to sweat from the struggle of moving in the heavy, awkward suits.

The boots were like nothing he had ever worn. Thick, thick soles, made of some incredibly dense material. He had no idea what the hell it was, but it wasn't grippy, and it was heavy. Not for him, but for ordinary people? It was like trying to run in iron shoes. And if you tripped, you died.

He could feel it. Truth didn't know if it was the persona or his own genuine feelings, but he could feel the fear. The choking feeling. Knowing there was no air on the other side of the glass. Knowing that the heat would kill you, and you weren't even that far in. Knowing that this was not a place humans were ever supposed to be. Knowing that the magic could cut off at any moment, but the heat and poison air wouldn't!

Down they went into the tunnels. The PMC threw out small golems as they passed intersections. The little spider-like things scurried up the walls and hid themselves in the shadows of the drips of basalt on the ceiling.

Everyone kept their head on a swivel as best they could, but the helmets didn't let you. Like the maintenance team before them, they had to twist their bodies around. The lights flashing across the walls madly. There was a comfort in numbers, but the way the lights constantly moved as you struggled against the weight of the suit and the sense of omnipresent danger—he felt sick.

Down, down they went. Not checking anything, just moving, moving, moving. Sounds were muffled. More than muffled—wrong. The pitch of the footfalls was off. He couldn't explain it. They sounded different than they did in the hallway. Was it the lack of air, the shape of the tunnels?

Down they went. He could see the color of the walls and floor starting to shift. It was easier to see in person. Basalt, volcanic rock, so hot that it was incandescent. He could slap his hand on a griddle, safe as could be. He didn't like his chances of repeating the stunt down there.

This was . . . insane. This was completely insane. If he died down there, everyone would be screwed. The sibs. Sally. Etenesh, Jember, Merkovah, everyone. All those other rats he was trying to learn to care about. He didn't even know if he could make it out alive if he succeeded. He had no idea about a lot of things. Maybe he would be smarter in the next life.

They went left, right, right, left, back and forth without any seeming pattern. Truth desperately tried to memorize the turns of the passage. The running pipes took on an almost-mythic significance—the thread leading him through the maze.

The rocks got brighter and brighter. He would swear he could smell them. That sulfur stench. The cooking smells of the metal cloth and the thick-soled boots. The rocks seemed to bleed upward through the color spectrum, from an unsettlingly luminous brown all the way to brilliant yellow-orange.

They rushed out of a tunnel and were by the lake. The surviving maintenance workers were desperately trying to get things back under control, but it was a cascading problem. As one device failed, the others had to take up the pressure. They were designed for that, of course, but more than one had failed, and the phoenix wasn't helping.

The screaming noise was audible through the poison gas, the pressure of it hitting like a hammer. Workers froze up as the sound blotted out thought. Their untrained physiques couldn't withstand the pressure of this terrible being's outrage. Its pain.

"Silence, animal!" the high-level bellowed. Her hands glowed green as spellforms spun out, forming a barrier around the phoenix. "I will stop its noise while you repair the arrays and mining equipment. Be quick about it. Guards, secure the room. Make sure we are undisturbed."

"Yes, ma'am!"

Truth rushed over with the other maintenance workers. Looking busy was easy—the supervisor was barking out orders, and Truth had always been good at following instructions. He didn't know these systems, but hell, he didn't need to. Go there, grab that, get this cover off. He could manage that just fine.

He waited until the cover was off and the internal components of a ritual station were open. He let one of his high-temp tools drop, then before it hit the ground, he kicked it between the legs clustered around the repair. He heard something break. Then there was a boom. The workers scrambled back, screaming. Pylons set up around the blood lake were starting to crackle now, the energy coming off them in blue-white arcs.

The high-level swore. More spells burst into life, seeming to explode from her hand. "REINFORCEMENTS! CALL FOR REINFORCEMENTS!" She was yelling, laying networks of shields over the monstrous demon at the heart of the volcano. Its sheer size was hard to measure; the bright, molten metal blurred scale. Big as a house? Big as two houses? Not counting the wings, which were straining hard against the hundreds of pipes nailing it down. Some of them looked like they were starting to buckle.

"Emergency shutdown on the pylons; we have to stop the cascade!" The maintenance team leader smashed him on the shoulder, yanking him around and pointing him at a pylon two hundred meters away. "RUN!"

Truth lumbered into motion. The pylon was on the other side of the high-level. She was giving it her all, spells pouring out like water and exploding into the lava lake. Truth could see the veins on her forehead throbbing. The PMC did their best to support her, but this was a truly higher-level being. The pressure of the phoenix beat against the restraining spells. Truth could see the personal defensive spells built into the suits sparkle and shimmer under the pressure. One of the maintenance guys suddenly collapsed. Something had given out.

The deathsworn and the high-level were better protected. Their protective enchantments strained but held. He could see them, shimmering and flexing and sparking against the heat and pressure that the ancient one emitted.

There would be more high-levels there in seconds. Bare seconds. It was the time to play the Fool. Truth called the Tongue into his gauntleted hands. The sword rose, two hands on the hilt, over Truth's head. With a flex of his powerful back, with an explosive step, with a pull of his mighty arms, he cut!

Defensive spells and amulets, already overpressured by the phoenix, couldn't hold. Not against Incisive, the angelic Bane, and Obliteration. The Tongue of One Who Speaks for God swung and pronounced its verdict. It swung clean through flesh until it was pointed at the floor. A Level Eight died in the hands of a Level Four. The two halves of her fell to either side of the longsword. Truth made eye contact with the enormous demon. He had seconds. Maybe only one second.

"Cup and Knife."

CHAPTER 82

IT'S NOT SMART, BUT MAYBE IT'S RIGHT

There was a sticky feeling to the moment. A second that stretched past all normal bounds, tugged long by fear and lucid madness. Taffy time, glued to a fool's fingers. Truth had no idea what the hell was going on with the phoenix. Not one clue. Nothing good, if the whole base was *mining* it. Lots of cosmic energy running through those pipes, though. Lots of heat. And it was so strong, it took a room full of pylons, altars, and other ritual tools to keep it crucified.

He called Cup and Knife into his mind. This was wrong. This was so wrong. This was an utter perversion of how the world was supposed to be. Even if you thought that God took this world from demons and gave it to humans, crucifying a phoenix to power body-hijacking a little girl just couldn't be right.

The spellform spilled out of his hand. He had never noticed before, but he could see how rough it looked compared to something like Incisive or Graeme's Arrow. It looked . . . janky. Vek had done his best, but he had never understood what Manda showed him. He just scribbled down what he could.

He could work with jank. There was a load of free energy in the air. The exploding pylons were releasing geysers of it. He sacrificed the magic in him and let the spellform start its work. Triggering a magical cascade in the wider world. Sweeping up that free energy and slamming it into the spells keeping the phoenix crucified.

It was like trying to put out a volcano with a cup of water. The spells were built by Level Eights and Nines, and fueled by the Phoenix's own magic. Truth's little magic was never going to overpower that. The magic raged and struggled . . . and fizzled out.

The PMC deathsworn were spinning around now. Spells coming online. Twenty Level Threes, one Level Four. Less than a second to do something. High-level coming down the tunnels. Maybe more than one. Dead for sure. Dead for absolutely certain. Nowhere to run, no way to fight.

He locked eyes with the phoenix. There was intelligence in them. A kind of brutal cunning. Encouragement. And . . . maybe he was projecting in this final lucid moment, but it looked like there was acceptance there, too.

He didn't have any other useful spells. He summoned Cup and Knife into existence once more. The phoenix . . . did it just nod? Why? It had seen the spell fail once before. Cup and Knife fixed things. It corrected them. It . . . killed demons. A weapon of spiritual combat, taught personally to Vek by the angel of revelation.

He aimed it straight at the phoenix and cast. More and more pylons exploded. He could hear Incisive screaming at him. *DANGER! DANGER! RUN! BE A GOOD LITTLE RAT AND RUN!*

He stood his ground and cast.

There had been enchantments protecting the phoenix. He could see the ruins of them. Cup and Knife slammed into the vast demon. It should have vanished again. It should have shattered into nothing against the phoenix's own magic. He could feel the spell sinking in, welcomed. Then, muffled through the explosions and the heavy, deadening hood came a basso yell—

[[RUN. NOW.]]

Truth turned and ran flat-out. The protective suit strained to keep up with him. Tried to anchor him in place. It didn't get a vote. He was sprinting for the door, dodging spells as best he could. There was a crumbling noise behind him. He could feel the magic in the room go crazy, the energy exploding chaotically. He could see spells just miss him, thrown off by the random shifts in energy. Feel them prematurely explode.

The room went white. He could feel the heat-shedding spells strain under the pressure. Were they exploding? He couldn't tell for sure. He kept running. At the tunnel. Up the tunnel. Relying on Incisive to keep him from slamming into a wall. There was a huge rush of air coming from behind him. No, not air, gas! Poison gas!

There was a different sort of pressure now. How fast did the lava move through the tubes? He didn't know. He kept running. Was he missing his turns? He didn't know. He couldn't see. The light spells . . . were they even still working? He couldn't tell—he was in the swirling yellow gas now, and the walls were incandescent. The walls were blinding him.

He felt danger coming from up ahead. Was there an opening? He jolted to his right and kept running. The danger swept past him, rushing down the tunnel. Did they think they could stop the lava? Maybe they could. He hoped they were wrong.

There was a series of deep booms, audible even through the sound-deadening poison gas. The pressure of the heat was only increasing. At a guess . . . if that senior could stop the lava normally, he couldn't stop a phoenix's suicide.

Ah. Right. It wasn't just lava. It was the phoenix's blood. He had no idea what that would do to basalt other than making it very hot. He tried to run faster and was disappointed to find that he could not. He was moving at nearly a hundred kilometers an hour through lava tubes, and he knew damn well it wasn't fast enough.

Running through the burning earth, already lost and getting more so by the second. He didn't know how long he ran. At the speed he was moving, it couldn't have been that long. The incandescence was dimming a little. He still couldn't tell if the light spells were working or not. He wasn't going to stop and check. He certainly wouldn't be taking the helmet off, in any case.

He slowed a little, though. Just . . . pacing himself. He had a feeling he would need the energy.

[[No, you need to be running faster, not slower. Much, much faster, if you can.]]

Truth had a mini-seizure that expressed itself in the form of an explosive sprint. He had traveled a few dozen meters before he saw a series of twists in the poison gas. Roughly bird-shaped swirls and dips, fading into existence, then vanishing in the turbulence again.

[[Well, if this is the best you can do . . . Hmm. I don't suppose you want to die, do you? It would be convenient if you did.]]

He very much wanted to live. He didn't think he could squeeze a single half-meter more speed out of his legs, but he tried anyway.

[[Not that I don't appreciate the rescue. It will take me a few decades to be reborn, but that's fine. Plenty to enjoy in the meanwhile.]] The phoenix's voice wasn't muffled by the gas. Was it talking directly into his mind?

Any chance you are telepathic?

There was no response. It was a faint hope.

"Flood the base. Lava into the base," he gasped.

[[Eh? You want to flood the base with lava? It's more likely to just collapse in the eruption. Seismic activity, earthquakes, all that good stuff. The so-called high-levels on the site aren't enough to stop it now. It should have happened a century ago. The pressure that has built up is significant, even as I reckon these things.]]

There was an unpleasant noise. It seemed that the ghost of a phoenix could snigger. *[[Frankly, I'm going to enjoy watching humanity suffer for a while. A century of torture will do that to a soul. Believe me, when I get a body back and my passions return to me, there* will *be a reckoning.]]*

A century? Just how long has Starbrite been planning whatever the hell this is?

"Rescue the princess. The Shattervoid princess!" Truth gasped. The dimming of the rock had reversed. It was getting brighter again. He hoped the heat at his back was just his imagination. *Just how fast is a lava eruption?! But it sounds like there is a LOT of pressure behind this one.*

[[Don't be stupid, boy. Do you have the faintest idea how big the Shattervoid are? They would be crushed under their own weight if they came too close to a planet. There is no way one of them is in the base.]]

"Baby! She's twelve!"

[[Ah.]]

There was a long pause.

[[Left here, by the way.]]

Truth took the left fork. Definitely getting brighter. Moving from deep orange to gold. Not good. Very not good. He had a lot of faith in his heavily refined body. Not that much faith.

[[Never had any trouble with the Shattervoid. Never had any contact with them at all, really. Knew about them, of course. I could see them nosing around. She is another one of Starbrite's little lab experiments? Oh, wait, was he draining the magic out of me to do something to her?]]

"Yes!" Well, that was his guess, anyway.

[[Hmm. Why lava in the base?]]

"Melt the lead curse tablets! She's heat-resistant!" Funny, he wouldn't have thought he could still get short of breath, but there he was. Gasping in the damn suit. He must be shredding it. There was no way it was designed to work like this. Move this fast. It must be hanging on by a literal thread.

[[Eh? Kid. You wanted to trigger a volcano to melt lead? This was seriously the best plan you could come up with?]]

"Yes," Truth gasped.

There was another long pause. He could feel the phoenix judging him. The judgment was unkind.

[[Well, I can't control the lava flow now. On account of being dead. And it's far more than I could have stopped, anyway. If I was going to stop it. Which I wasn't, because why would I?]]

Ah. Fuck.

[[On the other hand, if you really are suicidal enough to want to go back to the base, I think it can survive with its shields and construction for twenty minutes. Probably. I could only see so much. Call it fifteen minutes to be safe. Certainly at least ten. Yes. Ten minutes. I am at least eighty percent sure it can last that long. Left again, if that's really where you want to go, by the way.]]

Well, there would certainly be nothing in the base that would slow him down! Yes, this was very sane, very smart. Mmm-hmm. He went left.

[[I was going to lead you out of the volcano as a thank-you for the rescue. So, we aren't actually anywhere particularly near the base. But there is a bend in this tube that will get you within a couple of meters of the base, and the basalt is getting comparatively soft, so if you have a way to dig it out, you might be able to tunnel your way in. Also, you will leave behind a hole that will have lava shooting directly into the base.]]

"Great. Thank you."

The phoenix steered him through two more turns, then—*[[This patch of wall here. I won't be joining you—their wards would shred my soul. Good luck. If you survive this, and the next few decades, and my terrible revenge on humanity, come find me and say hi.]]*

Truth had the Tongue out and was hacking away. "Soft" really was only a comparative measure. It was still damn hard. The Tongue was forged with a piece of an angelic weapon made for fighting the armies of Hell. It could take the beating. And the heat.

[[I don't know why I thought you would have a spell for that. Based on all available evidence, of course you would dig through basalt with a sword. Well. Thanks anyway.]]

He was able to cut away decent-sized blocks of the basalt. It was terrifyingly hot. Would the . . .

Fuck. He would flood the base with poison gas. The Shattervoid girl would be fine; she was born to travel the void. But everyone else? He hacked away faster. The

Tongue eventually bounced off something in a shower of sparks. Cement. Enchanted cement. The wall of the base.

Truth grinned horribly under the helmet and cast Obliteration. He didn't need a very big hole in the wards. It took a few more seconds to open up a decent-sized patch. Big enough for him to jump through. A bit more hacking through the rebar and—

And Truth found out the hard way that the poison gas could, in fact, explode.

CHAPTER 83

DIVING IN

For once, it wasn't the fault of Truth's horrible education. He just didn't think. There was a lot going on. The sulfuric gas, heated to some five hundred degrees, wouldn't combust without oxygen. He knew that but had forgotten it for the moment. So, Truth ripped open a base full of fresh, cool air without wondering what would happen if he did.

The boiling hot gas jetted into the base, hit the cold, oxygen-rich air, and exploded. Truth didn't even get a chance to see what was in the room before the blast slammed him back against the wall of the lava tube. His suit started screaming alarms at him as its enchantments exploded in tiny showers of sparks, unable to withstand the damage and the yellow-hot molten rock. Even with his body cultivation, he felt the temperature nigh-instantly exceed what he could stand.

There was a fire roaring in the base now, and explosions setting off as the gas infiltrated farther into the building. He dove in. Still safer than the tunnel.

The cold air of the base fell on his protective suit like a swarm of scissors, shredding and shattering the melting metal-impregnated cloth. He had abused it hard in the run through the tunnels. The last few seconds were just too much for the overwhelmed enchantments and materials.

Truth ripped it off him in stride. Barefoot, in boxers and a tee shirt, waving a two-handed sword around. Somehow, it felt right. He looked around swiftly. The door had blown off its hinges, the poison gas starting to roll down the hall. Alarms were screaming, people running around in the halls madly. Truth stowed the Tongue. Joining the panicking crowds.

"Evacuation procedures! Everyone, find your floor captain and evacuate! Follow the signs to your evacuation route!" There were people keeping their heads, directing the crowds. Then the gas got to them, and they started coughing.

"Gas, GAS! Get low! Low! Crawl if you have to, but keep moving!" Sounded like good advice to Truth. He sprinted past the crowd and found the stairs. He was on the first floor. Figured. He jumped straight down the stairwell, slowing his fall with his fingertips.

Fifth floor. The prototype lab was through there. Long way from the poison gas. Had Obliteration finally burnt out against the wards? How much of a hole had he wound up knocking through the wall? But more than that, had word of the phoenix escaping reached down there? Because according to that ancient, the base would implode in the earthquakes before the lava finished it off.

He paused for a moment at the bottom of the stairs to collect himself. Touched a wall, feeling the cool cement. That wouldn't last. An odd thought intruded—there was rebar in the concrete. Long, long nets of iron rods making the structure more rigid and more durable. Concrete didn't transmit heat well, but iron? Was the rebar carrying the sunflower-yellow heat of the molten basalt straight into the walls of the base? How far could that really spread? And what would happen if it did? He had no idea.

He shook his head and focused. People were streaming up from the fifth floor, leaving their offices and laboratories. The PMC wouldn't have shifted an inch without an order, though. And what about the Level Eight? He had killed one high-level in the cavern and had felt another pass through the tunnels. Was that all the high-levels in the base? Seemed dumb to assume. There were the trolls roaming around, too, though he hadn't seen any yet. And those . . . eye-blob things guarding outside. Golems. Hadn't seen any big golems around, but they sure were available to Starbrite.

And on that cheery note, he walked against the flow, into the fifth floor.

It was quiet. The lines were orderly and moving with minimal argument. Truth saw a lot of glassy-looking eyes, and some of the workers were holding talismans with active spells running. A calm evacuation, with the calm being magically enforced. They were at the very bottom of the base. Farthest from any escape route. He could understand a need to control panic.

He moved quickly, keeping himself unnoticeable, slipping along the wall as people marched past. He could feel attention pinging against him but far less than he had expected. Everyone was looking straight ahead, trying to get to the stairs and get out. Level Threes, Level Fours . . . nobody cared. They just wanted to be out. He respected that.

The foyer to the prototype lab looked unchanged. The PMC was still in place, the recording talismans covering the room. Hidden defenses less hidden now. The deathsworn holding their needlers openly. He . . . didn't think there would be any slipping past them. And he didn't have time to wait for events to create an opportunity. Ten minutes, the phoenix had said. And it didn't sound very confident in that timeline.

Truth touched the concrete. Still cool to the touch. Was it a little warmer? Or was that his imagination? He felt the wall tremble. Just slightly. Not even enough to knock a pen off a table. But it was there. His time was running out fast. He looked back out at his coworkers. He sighed and tried to ease his way along the wall. Maybe he would get lucky.

No new defenses had popped up in the last few hours. No suddenly deployed alarms. He didn't know what would happen when the door opened. Sliding along the wall. There was a moment—one of the deathsworn looked straight at him. Eye contact. A young man, his age. Black BDUs looked natural on him. Clean-shaven and ready for whatever the world threw at him. Truth thought he could smell the slums on him. That ground-in feeling that whatever came couldn't be worse than *that.* Their eyes met . . . and the merc looked straight through him. Slid off him like he wasn't even there.

Truth spent a few seconds he probably couldn't spare getting his heart to restart. He moved around the edges of the room and got to the door. Feather-light fingers tested the door. Locked. Big chunky bastard of a lock, too. Clearly only meant to open when a switch was pressed. He looked around for an activation switch. There was one, built into the floor.

He crept over. Crouched down and slowly extended his finger. There was a tingle of alarm when he touched the gem. He paused. The floor shook. It was more noticeable this time. One of the cheap chairs for visitors clattered a little on the concrete floor. The guards looked at each other, eyebrows rising.

"Corporal?"

"You have the same mission I do."

"Yeah, but . . . no updates? Are they even gonna evacuate from there?"

"Let me just check the double-secret corporal-eyes-only info dump from the System . . . it says 'Shut the fuck up, mind your business, and do your job.' I can only guess what it means."

"Don't have to be a prick about it."

"I do when you bitch and ask dumbass questions every two minutes—"

There was another, more violent shake. Everyone looked up at the ceiling.

"I don't think they are that dumb."

There was a chime. The gem flashed blue. The corporal shifted over and stepped on it, narrowly missing Truth's hastily withdrawn hand. The corporal kept his foot on it for two seconds. Truth heard the door unlocking behind him.

A fucking dual-verification system. Door has to be unlocked on both sides. God. DAMN. That almost—

He shot to his feet and stood just to the side of the door, ready to dart in as everyone peeled out. The door swung open and a strong voice called out—"Soldiers! Has the new mission been issued?"

"Not yet, ma'am."

"Then on my authority, these production employees are allowed to leave their duty posts and evacuate. We shall maintain the guard here."

"Yes, ma'am."

"All right, you know the drill. Line up by sections, follow the evacuation route. Floor captains will guide you along the way." There was another violent shake. Coming closer together now. Stronger. Ten minutes . . . was that until *total* collapse or until the walls started cracking? And how many minutes had passed already? At least . . . four?

The crowd started marching out. Slowly. Too damn slowly. He could feel the seconds ticking past. He quite literally didn't have time for an orderly queue.

There was . . . no way to do this peacefully, was there? Incisive blared a warning, but . . . of course he was in danger. What path through there *wasn't* dangerous?

Truth moved quickly over to the closest deathsworn and yanked an explosive charm off his harness. Armed it. Tossed it head-high between three other mercs. Ripped the needler from his hand. The merc was turning now, trying to figure out what was happening. Slow. Too slow.

Truth had the needler up. Two rounds to the skull. Turned to the other three on the other side of the room. Grenade had a second or two longer before it went off. Tap tap. Tap tap. Tap tap. The needler was quiet. No extra spells layered on it. Didn't need them. Not at this range, in an ambush.

The first body hadn't hit the floor by the time the grenade went off. Truth had gotten low, peering through the mass of people, trying to spot the high-level. Hoping to ambush them before they were ready to react. Both hands on the needler.

The wall of the prototype lab exploded outward. Cement and rebar scythed through the room. The workers were shredded. Truth felt concrete ripping through his hardened skin. The blast smashed him into the floor, along the floor, up against the far wall.

"I knew I smelled a rat. Stupid little rat, thinking we wouldn't be ready. Waiting for you." The old lady stalked over the rubble, eyes glowing electric blue. Hands crackling with electricity.

"We don't have much time now, but don't worry. I'll have that soul out of you in a jiffy. Then we will have *lots* of time to talk."

Skewers of steel, crackling with lightning, launched up out of the rubble. Truth called the Tongue to hand, barely managing to deflect them as he got to his feet. Hanging on to the needler for dear life.

"Oh, I know you. You are that 'Hell-Prince' that PR came up with. You were actually real? Hilarious. I thought we had just made up a scapegoat. I owe Rebeccah a drink."

Truth felt the air bending around him. Getting rigid. He planted his feet and charged directly at the woman. She sneered. He felt a huge force coming from his right. Turned, cut. Obliteration split the spell in half, the remainders of whatever it was ripping up the floor on either side of him. Dissolving it.

"Interesting." The lobby wasn't that big. He closed the distance fast, but she just drifted back into the lab. Attacks came from every angle—fire, lightning, skewers of metal. Compressing air. Trying to bind him, then dissolve him. Truth strained his body to its limits, dodging, twisting, using Obliteration where he had to. Trying to corner the drifting mage. No luck.

Truth didn't give her time to come up with anything too effective. He kept the needler in action, pinging shots at her, using Incisive to smash into her personal shields. She could take the heat, but he could see this wasn't her day job. Every time a needle smashed into the shield in front of her face, she flinched.

The walls shook again. Harder this time. She picked up the pace. Spells were getting through now, searing him. Ripping chunks out of him. He kept moving, moving, moving, but she had four levels on him and wasn't breaking a sweat yet.

"Look at that. You do bleed after all. A little divination work, and we have your family."

He dove behind a lab bench, whipping a beaker full of . . . something . . . at her head. She didn't even flick it aside. It just exploded three meters in front of her.

"Pathetic. Let me teach you, junior."

She ripped up an entire stone-topped lab bench with a slight effort of will, raising it up to smash down on him. Truth jumped out from behind cover and flipped her off.

"Fuck you, you crazy bitch! Did you wash your face in cat's piss or acid? I killed your friend, and the best you can do is throw shit? I can clown you by jumping. Can't touch me once I have the high ground!"

He jumped up onto another bench, then made an astonishing vertical leap for the gantry overhead.

"I'm going to enjoy spending a few centuries watching you scream." She launched the stone-topped bench straight at him, fast as a speeding bus. It took some astonishing gymnastics for him to flip over it in the air.

The bench kept sailing through the air. Down the whole length of the lab. All the way to the pitch-black back wall. There was an astonishing *CRASH!* Then a rain of muffled, heavy *thuds*. Incisive screamed *NOW!* And Truth listened, dumping half the needler's magazine in the same direction.

Truth met the senior's eyes and smiled. "I win."

CHAPTER 84

UPLIFTED

The high-level glared at him. The base was shaking steadily now. There were booms coming from upstairs, and the walls were shaking. He could smell the sulfur reek. Was it getting hotter? "The hell do you think that actually achieved? We tattooed restrictions directly on her. Fuck it. Playtime is over."

The old lady pulled an amulet, obsidian, mirror-polished, and etched with orichalcum spell formulae. Incisive screamed a warning and Truth rushed her, firing as he went. The needles bounced harmlessly off her personal wards as she chanted a fast spell. A portal opened behind her. Truth felt his mind glitch for a moment, trying to make sense of what he was seeing.

A place of utter madness. Madness that seemed to poison the air around the portal, like blue cyanide spreading through your water glass. All relations of dimension and morality were inverted, perverted, or discarded. The hole in space bulged. Straining the fragile bounds of the real. A tumor grew and burst, spilling a many-eyed horror onto the floor.

"KILL." Her voice was ice cold. Her face a rigid mask of fury. The obsidian and orichalcum shimmered and twisted in her hands, writhing with nameless, indescribable colors. He could see veins throbbing on her forehead. Whatever it was, it wasn't obedient by nature. Truth didn't waste a needle on it and fell back.

He kept the barrage of fire up on the old lady, trying to distract her. It wasn't effective. She had gotten used to the needles plinking off her.

"You have a good spellbreaker sword, but we are *mages*, you murderous little shit. I can shred your soul from the other side of the damn solar system!" she snarled. Truth started nodding at that, then narrowed his eyes.

She . . . could actually do that. So, why wasn't she? Environmental problem? Unlikely to be concerned about the Shattervoid girl at this point. What else was there?

Truth smiled again. He noticed the vein on her forehead throbbed harder when he did that. The unspeakable mass charged him, rolling with terrible speed. He saw pseudopods beginning to fester and extrude from the main mass. He did the sensible thing and ran.

"Oh, where are you going to run to? You worked so hard to get here!"

The horrible thing was leaving a trail of shattered cement behind it. Heavier than it looked. Lab benches exploded into wood and stone splinters as it brushed past them. A pseudopod burst into the writhing, sickening web of worm-threads it used for hunting. They bunched together, then it launched them at Truth.

Truth feinted right, then kicked hard to the left. As he suspected, the horror could steer its pseudopod even after it attacked. The vile thing shot toward him—and stopped.

Truth stood just behind the sarcophagus, the tip of the Tongue pressed firmly to the lid.

"You have no idea what that is. None."

"I know there is a reason you are still down here while the base fills with lava and the walls crush in from the sides. It isn't to oversee the evacuation. It isn't even to kill me."

"Oh, you just went way, way up the priority list. Believe that," she snarled.

"I do. I also believe that I will spot your horror there trying to sneakily extend a tendril around the sarcophagus and catch me unawares. Behave. We only have a few minutes left to wait. If that."

"What's the play, then, Hell-Prince? I can get out of here. It might cost me, but I can punch a hole clean through the side of the mountain and walk out without even mussing my hair."

Well. Damn. He had actually really hoped this would kill her.

"You, though? A piddly little Level Four body cultivator? You are dead. So, what is the point of delaying? Do it. Smash it. See what happens."

"All right, bet." Truth didn't pull back the blade. The shift in his muscles and weight was lightning-fast, but the senior had quick eyes.

"Wait!"

Truth stopped and cocked an eye at her. "I'm dead already, right? Make it worth my time. Keep in mind that I have zero trust in any promises you might make." The walls were shaking hard now, dust falling steadily. "Two minutes left. Maybe less. Tick-tock."

He plinked a needle off her. She sneered. "You know that won't work." He shrugged.

There was a bizarre sound, a sort of *CRUMP*, from up above. "Reckon that some upper floors just collapsed?" He kept his voice conversational. It was pure acting, but since she was pushing the persona of the Hell-Prince, he decided to lean into it. Display what she expected to see.

"What do you want? You aren't getting out of here alive, so what could possibly interest *you* of all people?"

He shook his head. "Now, that *is* an old game. No, you make me an offer. You can start by pulling back that little horror of yours. Then bid. Either my final act is destroying this box and everything in it, and you *know* I am fast enough to do that before you get a spell off, or it's . . . something else. Something that seems like a better use of my time. Something that hurts Starbrite more than losing this."

Truth could feel the lava creeping in. The seconds ticking away. *Come on, come on! How long do you want me to drag this out for?!*

"Is that really all this is? You murdered *THOUSANDS* of people, all to hurt Starbrite?"

"Well. Not only that. Eighty percent? Let's not pretend that Starbrite the person or the company is something nice. For example, I really don't care if you try to divine my family. I'm quite sure I'm the last of my line. Hint hint. Speaking of, pretty sure we have less than a minute left for whatever, so. You know. Talk fast."

"You . . . want to kill Starbrite's family?" She looked at him like he was a moron.

"No. Or, well, yes, but not really a priority." *WILL YOU MOVE YOUR ASS?! I swear I can feel the heat starting to scorch my lungs.* He smiled "warmly."

She growled. "Other than mass murder, I have no idea what you want!"

"Simple. I want the System Astrologica."

"What?"

"I want the System Astrologica. Haul it out. If I can kill it, I can turn the box over to you. Otherwise, it dies with me."

"I cannot. Literally cannot. It isn't something I can control. It isn't something you can stab." He plinked a couple more needles off her shield, glaring at her.

"Not what I want to hear. It dies or this dies. Pick."

"I LITERALLY CANNOT, YOU LITTLE FREAK! Starbrite himself is the bridge between the System and the world!"

Figured. Hope this was enough time, because I am literally hearing the air burning, and it's more cement dust than oxygen at this point.

"I don't like that answer. Take two needles from me."

"Oh, fuck you and your dumbass—"

Truth let the clip rip, feeling his magic reserves drop like a stone. With an explosive move, he slammed every offensive spell he could into the Tongue, even letting its Bane work on the stone as he smashed it into the sarcophagus. He felt something inside crush. The Bane spell set to work. Between it and Obliteration, whatever was inside . . . well, it wouldn't be coming out. Ever.

Not that the high-level cared. She looked at him in horror, the needles filling her face and head. Her body seemed to crumple in on itself, slowly collapsing to the ground.

Not a spellbreaker sword. And why would I keep doing something pointless? Sorry, lady. Next life, learn how to fight.

The amulet spilled onto the ground. The horror lurched. Then, to Truth's utter horror, it started to get larger. The amulet didn't just summon it; the amulet restrained it. And now it was on the ground, on the wrong side of an abomination.

He turned and ran toward the back wall. Feet tearing up the uncomfortably warm floor with each explosive step. The lead tablets had mostly fallen off, between the thrown bench and the constant shaking of the wall.

Almost done! There is one more, just over my heart. Shoot it! Truth saw the burning tattoo, not really paying attention to the scales it was etched over. Obliteration flashed out, and the intricate brand shattered in a spray of blood and seven-colored light.

What do you do when you are overmatched? Same thing he did when the gangsters were kicking the shit out of him when he was twelve. Change the game. He never thought he could beat that senior in a fight. So, he cheated.

Not to rush you, but there is a horrible monster coming right goddamn behind me!

Chunks of cement started falling, pieces the size of beds, of carriages, smashing down. Lava started dripping in, consuming what little air there was left. The room quickly became unbearably hot.

Thank you for believing in me, by the way. I have never tried this before.

But this is what your whole family does, right? Easy as drinking water, right?!

There was a giggling noise as the worm-net launched by the horror spread through the remainder of the room, writhing and flowing toward him. The lumbering horror was slowed by the lava but not stopped. This much, at least, wasn't enough to deter it.

You wouldn't believe what we do to drink water. Hold on tight.

Hold on tight to what!? The worms were flying now, actually clearing the dust and falling cement from the air as they swept toward him.

No idea. Just generally?

The world vanished.

What he saw . . .

The night sky. All of it, the billions of twisting galaxies and burning stars. Those great ones, the mighty eminences, condescending to let some part of their immensity touch this universe. The spinning explosions of light and heat, whirling, whirling, whirling around each other but from, somehow, the wrong side. He was on the wrong side of the light, of the enormity of the cosmos. He felt his apertures fill and flow, spilling down, filling him as he tried desperately to comprehend what he was seeing. He could barely hang on. His rationality could barely hang on—

Truth was looking at the moon from above. He had never seen the moon from this angle, but it was hard to mistake. He recognized the planet behind it. He had seen pictures taken from space before. Home. His little bundle of rock and spite.

Shouldn't he . . . be dead?

Mr. Medici? Can you hear me, Mr. Medici?

What? Oh, yes. I . . . seem to be standing in the void, and yet, somehow, am not dead. Not the strangest thing today, but still surprising.

The giggling sound came back. *Congratulations on being my very first passenger, Mr. Medici! And you don't seem crazier than before, so I think I did VERY well!*

You did wonderfully, Sally. Sorry, were you expecting—

One of several reasons we don't like carrying lower-level passengers is they tend to go loony, yes. But at Level Four, I figured you would be . . . fine . . .

Truth had heard his siblings use that tone often enough. He was about to scold her when space twisted and they were no longer alone.

All around him, enormous forms manifested. His mind struggled to understand the vastness of what he was seeing. It was like when he had dropped in from low orbit wearing spell armor. The planet was so huge, and somehow it kept getting bigger.

Big beyond any human referent. He could walk for hours and not reach the end of them. Black. Darker black than the shattering void itself. Within that inky blackness was a hollow space, where light seemed to bend and twist into ribbons. There had to be at least a score of them. A sound rose, not shaking the air but the fabric of magic itself. The pressure fell on his mind like waves hammering the shore, like the sun bleaching the moon. He tried to hold on. Sally's family had found her at last.

CHAPTER 85

LOOKING DOWN ON THE WORLD

The Shattervoid swarmed around their lost girl—uncles and cousins the size of mountains and rivers. Aunties who stepped between the stars. Brothers? Sisters? Sibs of the sea of stars? Truth had lost sight of Sally. He must still be within her, he knew, but it felt like he was standing in the void. Awkward as a work friend at a family reunion.

Worse—the family didn't speak his language. Or, rather, he didn't speak theirs. He could feel the conversation more than hear it. Pulses of cosmic energy that made the apertures throb inside of him. He could feel even more vibrating against his skin, bouncing off his sealed body. He could imagine the pressure crushing the apertures of a less-well-developed person. You could feel the conversation like the sun shifting across the sky, alternately burning and blinding you.

He didn't try to introduce himself. He was perfectly content hanging around at the back of the room, searching for a graceful exit. Unfortunately, when you are magically attached to the belle of the ball, there is no escape. He just hung on and tried not to stand out. Should be easy when you were the smallest thing there, by entire orders of magnitude.

He looked over at the moon. He had a morbid impulse to describe it as "bone white" or the like, but it just wasn't. It was gray. White in places, yes, but there were massive gradations in tone from sun-bleached powder to slate, to an almost-total basalt black in the shadows. It had spiny mountains and wide craters. Some places seemed to have been raked smooth; others were boulder-strewn fields. Abandoned resorts and luxury retreats glistened and shimmered in the sunlight. It wasn't all one thing. It wasn't all ugly or dead.

He looked past it to his "homeworld." He didn't even have a name for it. It was just . . . the planet. Presumably, it had a name, something to identify it among the endless millions of other planets. He had never bothered to learn it. Like the countries surrounding Jeon—if it wasn't relevant to putting food in his belly, it didn't exist.

Getting food into bellies was already a problem in Jeon. It was about to get much, much worse. It was the cascade effect. For very reasonable reasons, the planet had specialized in industrial production. Now there wasn't enough food being produced locally when imports got cut off.

This rolled into magic declining fast, meaning there would be little chance to start growing more locally. Not with the kind of production and regularity the planet's population would need to maintain itself. This directly rolled in to increased warfare as people realized they needed to grab all they could while they could.

Soon, there would only be children left, children and the supremely powerful whose body cultivation let them survive in the dead-magic times. The difference in status, wealth, power, between a low-level and high-level today was unimaginable. How much greater would it be when there were just mages and slaves? In a world where some dreams were forbidden, it would be a pure Hell.

Sitting in the middle of it all was Starbrite. He might not be the cause of everything, but he was certainly pushing the wagon along. Speeding it up and helping steer it as it rumbled down the hill. Making sure it plowed squarely into the combination orphanage and puppy rescue, and not his meth lab next door.

It didn't look like a hell-world from up there. It looked . . . nice. Blue. Shockingly, richly blue, the oceans rich lapis. The color brought out by the blinding white of drifting clouds. Then the immense brown of deserts and plains. Green blush burnished it here and there, where some ancient jungles still survived, pressing against the equatorial oceans. Their coastlines smoothing into mostly clean swoops and arcs from however many hundreds of kilometers up.

Once upon a time, in another life, he had been a sailor. Charting his course against other oceans, between coastlines that never existed on this world. He didn't know what to think about that.

There was an aggressively fake cough from behind him.

Truth turned. There was a late-middle-aged man standing behind him. Truth categorized his expression as *forced to be polite but clearly not feeling it.*

"You are Mr. Medici?"

Truth controlled the urge to look around and ask who else he could possibly be. It was a struggle, but he managed.

"Yes. How should I call you?" The question seemed to momentarily flummox the older man.

"Is . . . Ragnax still a normal name?"

"Sure." Truth nodded. It had been a very strange year. He was prepared to consider Ragnax an utterly normal name.

"I'm Ragnax. 'Sally's' uncle. I understand we have you to thank for rescuing her. As well as kidnapping her?" Ah, there was the edge in the voice he had been expecting.

"Brainwashed Starbrite drone. I didn't know what the package was until a couple of minutes before I was ordered to fight to my death. *Return her to her parents* was never an available option." Truth shrugged.

The exhaustion was crashing down. He was feeling lightheaded. Had he *really* killed two Level Eights in a day? Even using trickery and ambush, it felt unreal. He, single-handedly, was responsible for the planet's overall decline in top combat power. Incredible.

"You seem to have gotten better. And had a change of heart."

"Yeah."

There was a pause. Ragnax was clearly waiting for some elaboration. Truth was waiting to pass out. He was covered in burns, cuts, scrapes the size of dinner plates that somehow managed to hurt worse than the cuts, and what skin wasn't scraped over was bruised and covered in cement dust. The sweet embrace of oblivion couldn't come fast enough.

Ragnax seemed to give up on social cues and went straight for interrogation. "And you just happened to make your way into the secret base where my niece was being held, and just happened to have the necessary skills to get her out just as the volcano erupted for no obvious reason?"

"Yeah."

"You really think I will believe that?"

"Yeah."

"Why?!"

"Because it's true? All that took a lot of work. A lot of running around."

There was a pause. "Are you . . . Maybe my Jeongo is not as good as I thought. I think you are missing something."

"Probably." Were the edges of his vision starting to dim? Fingers crossed.

"I assume you want a trip off-world. For you and and a few thousand of your nearest and dearest?" There was an edge to his voice that Truth was willfully ignoring.

"Eventually. I also have . . . just a ton of questions."

"Shame we aren't in the business of questions, then. We are in transport, and your fare is still short. There was another part of the ticket price, you may remember."

"Kill Starbrite. Didn't forget." Truth started swaying. "Oh, sweet, I'm finally passing out." He fainted on his feet. Not seeing that he was still suspended in space, with a very frustrated-looking Ragnax glaring at him. Ragnax disappeared as silently as he appeared, and then it was just Truth, drifting through the void, in silence.

He didn't know how long he slept for. There was a moment of absolute panic when he woke up. To be suspended in nothing, surrounded by unimaginably vast things but unable to move. Unclear on how he was breathing, or surviving the horrifying brutality of the cosmic rays that ripped through the void. He spasmed, instinctively trying to reach for anything. Anything he could hold on to, that could anchor him in the emptiness.

Sally giggled. *I got you. It's okay. It's okay. You are all okay. 'Cause I got you!* There was something in her voice Truth didn't like. Not a meanness. His big-bro senses were tingling. Something had broken in Sally, and she knew it. She needed him to pull together. Not that he could fix whatever it was, but at least he could not make it worse.

"Thank you. It was pretty scary for me. I have never been this high up."

Never left your world?

"Top of the atmosphere is the highest I ever went before."

Doesn't count as touching the void. Still an earthworm!

He laughed with her. "Well, it's not a great planet, but it's where I keep all my stuff, you know?"

There was a pause. *Actually, I wondered about that.*

"Where I keep my stuff?"

Yeah. Like, I get that you can't fold space like us, but do you really just . . . leave it places? Like, do you each have your own little base just to hold your stuff? And you go and do stuff and it just stays behind, and you have to hope it will still be there when you get back?

"Er . . . basically. Though *base* is too big. Think, like, a little"—he was going to say *a little box* but quickly changed tack—"a little house, or a few rooms in a big building. Rooms in a big building would be the most common."

Oooh. There was a pause. *I will never go inside anything ever again. I will never leave the void ever again. Not for anything, ever. Actually, after we leave here, I don't know how long it will be before I will come back to a solar system. A long time, I hope. A very long time. Never would be okay.*

"Fair." Truth could feel her struggling with words. Not sure what she was feeling or what she thought about it yet, let alone knowing how to say it. "It's okay, you know? If you don't have the words right now. Someday, hopefully soon, I will make it off-world. You can send a message through your relatives."

There was a sigh. *Thank you. I . . . don't know how to talk to people. I want to talk and talk and talk and talk, but they always hurt me if I did, or they said I was distracting them, or . . .* Truth tried to send calming emotions and had no idea if he was succeeding. He probably wasn't.

"Sorry, I'm trying to be reassuring and I don't even know what direction to face. Where are you, exactly?"

Sally giggled. *You are looking right at me. Every which way you look, you are looking right at me.*

"I am . . . in you? Somehow?"

Kind of! We aren't like you. Those bindings they put on me? Those tattoos and curse tablets? They were to keep me on this side of the— She made a noise that, to Truth, sounded like ten thousand flute players were trapped underwater and trying to communicate their approximate location via song.

Basically, we are in two places at once. There is what you see here, like Auntie over there, and what we actually look like on the other side. Right now, I don't have a "ship," and my body is . . . not good. My moms and dads are taking care of me. So, I'm pretty much all on the other side. But I'm still connected over here, so I can keep this little bit of space safe for you. Air, a tiny bit of gravity, that kind of thing. Let you have some visible light while not roasting in the cosmic rays.

"Wow!" Truth was certain he didn't really understand that, but it sounded damn impressive. Wait, did she say "moms and dads"? Plural?

They don't want to talk to you. To anyone from this planet, really.

"I completely understand."

Though Mama—there was a sound that seemed equal parts music and mathematics— *said that you should have something to mark bringing me back. It's a pretty ordinary thing on developed planets, but there aren't any on your planet. Not even Starbrite has one.* A little ring popped into existence. It was a dull brown wood, sanded and oiled into some degree of comfort.

"What is it?"

A spatial ring. That's what earthworms call it. Basically, we open up a little safe spot on the other side of the barrier for you, where you can put stuff and take it out again. The ring is the anchor on this side of the barrier. It only works if a Shattervoid makes it work for you. Like, we have to keep making it work; it doesn't work forever. And. You know.

"Nobody is doing anything nice for Starbrite. Got it. These are common?"

Yeah, they take basically no effort to keep going. You don't even notice it. And this one is from me! I made it!

"Thank you very much, Sally! How much can I put in there?"

Not very much right now. My body is . . . wrong. They are fixing it. It might take a while.

"I'm sorry. None of this is your fault. None of this is fair. I hope that you can remember that on the bad days."

Bad days? Oh. Yeah. The bad days. Sally sounded calmly familiar with them. *So, what's next for Mr. Medici?*

"Go back to Jeon and figure out a way to kill the nearest thing to God my planet has ever known?"

Starbrite isn't even close to God. Sally was firm on this. *He's sicker than me. His soul is all wrong. Nothing should look like that. Nothing is supposed to work like that. It's sick. Wrong. Diseased.*

"Stronger than me. Than anyone."

On your planet? True. He had the sense of her nodding. *But you don't sound too worried about it.*

"Yep. Things just went very wrong for Starbrite. He lost some very important people. He lost whatever was in that sarcophagus, and he lost *you*. And he wanted you so badly, he was willing to lose everything he had built on this planet to get you."

Truth smiled. "He's angry. In pain. Scared, maybe. He's going to do something stupid. He's going to lash out, to prove he's powerful and in control. And when he does, he will show an opening. Then we kill him."

He started laughing. "Or we wait for the magic to collapse and watch him die then. No escape off-world for him! Oh, he will be desperate!"

Desperate people do desperate things, Mr. Medici. You might not survive them. Sally sounded eerily calm about that. Truth tried not to mind.

"Sounds like future-me's problem. Isn't it nice that there is a future-me?" He coughed, much more politely than Ragnax had. "Now, about that. How, exactly, do I get back dirtside?"

—

Thrush found his master sitting under a battered-looking fir tree on a foothill in the mountains of southeastern Onis. He would have thought it much too close to the ash plume of the volcano for comfort, but then, he had never cared for fire demons. A small effort, and a bubble of clean air formed around the strange young man.

"I did worry about your safety, dread magus. How *good* to see you are unharmed."

"Thank you. The duffel and bird suit both look . . . a lot more intact than I expected, actually. Well done!"

"Your gratitude is far more than this insignificant speck dared hope for." His voice was buttery smooth. Truth's lips twitched. It would be an adjustment, getting used to the imp again.

He fished out his treasured scarf and wrapped it around his neck. Not cold; he just really wanted the comfort of it. Then swiftly took it off again and got himself properly dressed for what felt like the first time in far too long. Once suitably dressed, shod, and scarved, he sent the duffel and the bird suit into the space Sally had made for him. Everything fit. Promising.

"I don't wanna fly through an active volcano plume."

"Master is no doubt wise."

"But, since I had a minute, I hunted around. And guess what I found?"

"This pathetic imp couldn't possibly fathom the depths of the dread magus's reach."

Was that a . . . Grammatically, it felt off. Truth pressed on, dramatically yanking away a drop cloth. Underneath was something that legally, technically, probably qualified as a two-wheeler. If you looked past the rust and the parts from five different manufacturers, each in a different color scheme.

"I found a ride. Hop on, imp. We're off to kill King Rat."

Warby Picus is a lifelong fan of science fiction and fantasy. One day, he figured he would see if writing books was as much fun as it appeared to be. He hasn't looked back since.

Podium

DISCOVER MORE

STORIES
UNBOUND

PodiumEntertainment.com